PRAISE FOR THE MODERN LIBRARY
EDITION OF IN SEARCH OF LOST TIME

"Twice amended to bring it to documentary decorum and the kind of textual completion Proust himself could never achieve, the C. K. Scott Moncrieff translation of the *Search*, buffed, rebuffed, lightened, tightened, and in the abstergent sense, brightened, constitutes a monument which is also a medium—THE medium by which to gain access to the book, the books, even the apocrypha of modern scripture. A triumph of tone, of a single (and singular) vision, this ultimate revision of the primary version affords the surest sled over the ice fields as well as the most sinuous surfboard over the breakers of Proustian prose, an invaluable and inescapable text."

—RICHARD HOWARD

IN SEARCH OF
LOST TIME

MARCEL PROUST

IN SEARCH OF LOST TIME

VOLUME IV

SODOM AND GOMORRAH

Translated by
C. K. Scott Moncrieff and Terence Kilmartin

Revised by D. J. Enright

THE MODERN LIBRARY

NEW YORK

This edition was originally published in hardcover in Great Britain
by Chatto & Windus in 1992 and in the United States
by Modern Library in 1993.

This translation is a revised edition of the 1981 translation of
Cities of the Plain by C. K. Scott Moncrieff and Terence Kilmartin,
published in the United States by Random House, Inc., and in Great
Britain by Chatto & Windus. Revisions by D. J. Enright.

LIBRARY OF CONGRESS CATALOGING-IN-PUBLICATION DATA
Proust, Marcel, 1871–1922.
[Sodome et Gomorrhe, English]
Sodom and Gomorrah/Marcel Proust; translated by C. K. Scott
Moncrieff and Terence Kilmartin; revised by D. J. Enright.
p.   cm.—(In search of lost time; 4)
Includes bibliographical references.
ISBN 0-375-75310-9
I. Title. II. Series: Proust, Marcel, 1871–1922.
À la recherche du temps perdu. English; v. 4.
PQ2631.R63S6313   1993
843'.912—dc20   92-27272

Modern Library website address: www.modernlibrary.com

Printed in the United States of America

6 8 9 7

MARCEL PROUST

Marcel Proust was born in the Parisian suburb of Auteuil on July 10, 1871. His father, Adrien Proust, was a doctor celebrated for his work in epidemiology; his mother, Jeanne Weil, was a stockbroker's daughter of Jewish descent. He lived as a child in the family home on Boulevard Malesherbes in Paris, but spent vacations with his aunt and uncle in the town of Illiers near Chartres, where the Prousts had lived for generations and which became the model for the Combray of his great novel. (In recent years it was officially renamed Illiers-Combray.) Sickly from birth, Marcel was subject from the age of nine to violent attacks of asthma, and although he did a year of military service as a young man and studied law and political science, his invalidism disqualified him from an active professional life.

During the 1890s Proust contributed sketches to *Le Figaro* and to a short-lived magazine, *Le Banquet,* founded by some of his school friends in 1892. *Pleasures and Days,* a collection of his stories, essays, and poems, was published in 1896. In his youth Proust led an active social life, penetrating the highest circles of wealth and aristocracy. Artistically and intellectually, his influences included the aesthetic criticism of John Ruskin, the philosophy of Henri Bergson, the music of Wagner, and the fiction of Anatole France (on whom he modeled his character Bergotte). An affair begun in 1894 with the composer and pianist Reynaldo Hahn marked the beginning of Proust's often anguished acknowledgment of his homosexuality. Following the publication of Emile Zola's letter in defense of Colonel Dreyfus in 1898, Proust became "the first Dreyfusard," as he later phrased it. By the time Dreyfus was finally vindicated of charges of treason, Proust's social circles had been torn apart by the anti-Semitism and political hatreds stirred up by the affair.

Proust was very attached to his mother, and after her death in 1905 he spent some time in a sanatorium. His health worsened progressively, and he withdrew almost completely from society and devoted himself to writing. Proust's early work had done nothing to establish his reputation as a major writer. In an unfinished novel, *Jean Santeuil* (not published until 1952), he laid some of the groundwork for *In Search of Lost Time*, and in *Against Sainte-Beuve*, written in 1908–9, he stated as his aesthetic credo: "A book is the product of a different self from the one we manifest in our habits, in society, in our vices. If we mean to try to understand this self it is only in our inmost depths, by endeavoring to reconstruct it there, that the quest can be achieved." He appears to have begun work on his long masterpiece sometime around 1908, and the first volume, *Swann's Way*, was published in 1913. In 1919 the second volume, *Within a Budding Grove*, won the Goncourt Prize, bringing Proust great and instantaneous fame. Two subsequent sections—*The Guermantes Way* (1920–21) and *Sodom and Gomorrah* (1921)—appeared in his lifetime. (Of the depiction of homosexuality in the latter, his friend André Gide complained: "Will you never portray this form of Eros for us in the aspect of youth and beauty?") The remaining volumes were published following Proust's death on November 18, 1922: *The Captive* in 1923, *The Fugitive* in 1925, and *Time Regained* in 1927.

Contents

Numerals in the text refer the reader to explanatory notes while asterisks indicate the position of textual addenda. The notes and the addenda follow the text.

A Note on the Translation
(1981)

Terence Kilmartin

C. K. Scott Moncrieff's version of À *la recherche du temps perdu* has in the past fifty years earned a reputation as one of the great English translations, almost as a masterpiece in its own right. Why then should it need revision? Why tamper with a work that has been enjoyed and admired, not to say revered, by several generations of readers throughout the English-speaking world?

The answer is that the original French edition from which Scott Moncrieff worked (the "abominable" edition of the *Nouvelle Revue Française,* as Samuel Beckett described it in a marvellous short study of Proust which he published in 1931) was notoriously imperfect. This was not so much the fault of the publishers and printers as of Proust's methods of composition. Only the first volume (*Du côté de chez Swann*) of the novel as originally conceived—and indeed written—was published before the 1914–1918 war. The second volume was set up in type, but publication was delayed, and moreover by that time Proust had already begun to reconsider the scale of the novel; the remaining eight years of his life (1914–1922) were spent in expanding it from its original 500,000 words to more than a million and a quarter. The margins of proofs and typescripts were covered with scribbled corrections and insertions, often over-flowing on to additional sheets which were glued to the galleys or to one another to form interminable strips—what Françoise in the novel calls the narrator's *"paperoles."* The unravelling and deciphering of these copious additions cannot have been an enviable task for editors and printers.

Furthermore, the last three sections of the novel (*La prisonnière, La fugitive*—originally called *Albertine disparue*—and *Le temps retrouvé*) had not yet been published at the time of Proust's death in November 1922 (he was still correcting a typed copy of *La prisonnière* on his deathbed). Here the original editors had to take it upon themselves to prepare a coherent text from a manuscript littered with sometimes hasty corrections, revisions and afterthoughts and leaving a number of unresolved contradictions, obscurities and chronological inconsistencies. As a result of all this the original editions—even of the volumes published in Proust's lifetime—pullulate with errors, misreadings and omissions.

In 1954 a revised three-volume edition of *À la recherche* was published in Gallimard's Bibliothèque de la Pléiade. The editors, M. Pierre Clarac and M. André Ferré, had been charged by Proust's heirs with the task of "establishing a text of his novel as faithful as possible to his intentions." With infinite care and patience they examined all the relevant material—manuscripts, notebooks, typescripts, proofs, as well as the original edition—and produced what is generally agreed to be a virtually impeccable transcription of Proust's text. They scrupulously avoided the arbitrary emendations, the touchings-up, the wholesale reshufflings of paragraphs in which the original editors indulged, confining themselves to clarifying the text wherever necessary, correcting errors due to haste or inadvertence, eliminating careless repetitions and rationalising the punctuation (an area where Proust was notoriously casual). They justify and explain their editorial decisions in detailed critical notes, occupying some 200 pages over the three volumes, and print all the significant variants as well as a number of passages that Proust did not have time to work into his book.

The Pléiade text differs from that of the original edition, mostly in minor though none the less significant ways, throughout the novel. In the last three sections (the third Pléiade volume) the differences are sometimes considerable. In particular, MM. Clarac and Ferré have included a number of passages, sometimes of a paragraph or two, sometimes of several pages, which the original editors omitted for no good reason.

The present translation is a reworking, on the basis of the Pléiade edition, of Scott Moncrieff's version of the first six sections of À la recherche—or the first eleven volumes of the twelve-volume English edition. A post-Pléiade version of the final volume, Le temps retrouvé (originally translated by Stephen Hudson after Scott Moncrieff's death in 1930), was produced by the late Andreas Mayor and published in 1970; with some minor emendations, it is incorporated in this edition. There being no indication in Proust's manuscript as to where La fugitive should end and Le temps retrouvé begin, I have followed the Pléiade editors in introducing the break some pages earlier than in the previous editions, both French and English—at the beginning of the account of the Tansonville episode.

The need to revise the existing translation in the light of the Pléiade edition has also provided an opportunity of correcting mistakes and misinterpretations in Scott Moncrieff's version. Translation, almost by definition, is imperfect; there is always "room for improvement," and it is only too easy for the latecomer to assume the beau rôle. I have refrained from officious tinkering for its own sake, but a translator's loyalty is to the original author, and in trying to be faithful to Proust's meaning and tone of voice I have been obliged, here and there, to make extensive alterations.

A general criticism that might be levelled against Scott Moncrieff is that his prose tends to the purple and the precious—or that this is how he interpreted the tone of the original: whereas the truth is that, complicated, dense, over-loaded though it often is, Proust's style is essentially natural and unaffected, quite free of preciosity, archaism or self-conscious elegance. Another pervasive weakness of Scott Moncrieff's is perhaps the defect of a virtue. Contrary to a widely held view, he stuck very closely to the original (he is seldom guilty of short-cuts, omissions or loose para-phrases), and in his efforts to reproduce the structure of those elaborate sentences with their spiralling subordinate clauses, not only does he sometimes lose the thread but he wrenches his syntax into oddly unEnglish shapes: a whiff of Gallicism clings to some of the longer periods, obscuring the sense and falsifying the tone. A corollary to this is a ten-dency to translate French idioms and turns of phrase liter-ally, thus making them sound weirder, more outlandish, than they would to a French reader. In endeavouring to rectify these weaknesses, I hope I have preserved the un-doubted felicity of much of Scott Moncrieff while doing the fullest possible justice to Proust.

I should like to thank Professor J. G. Weightman for his generous help and advice and Mr D. J. Enright for his pa-tient and percipient editing.

A Note on the Revised Translation (1992)

D. J. Enright

Terence Kilmartin intended to make further changes to the translation as published in 1981 under the title *Remembrance of Things Past*. But, as Proust's narrator observed while reflecting on the work he had yet to do, when the fortress of the body is besieged on all sides the mind must at length succumb. "It was precisely when the thought of death had become a matter of indifference to me that I was beginning once more to fear death . . . as a threat not to myself but to my book."

C. K. Scott Moncrieff excelled in description, notably of landscape and architecture, but he was less adroit in translating dialogue of an informal, idiomatic nature. At ease with intellectual and artistic discourse and the finer feelings, and alert to sallies of humorous fantasy, he was not always comfortable with workaday matters and the less elevated aspects of human behaviour. It was left to Kilmartin to elucidate the significance of Albertine's incomplete but alarming outburst—". . . *me faire casser* . . ."—in *The Captive*, a passage Scott Moncrieff rendered totally incomprehensible, perhaps through squeamishness, perhaps through ignorance of low slang. Other misunderstandings of colloquialisms and failures to spot secondary meanings remained to be rectified. And some further intervention was prompted by Scott Moncrieff's tendency to spell out things for the benefit of the English reader: an admirable intention (shared by Arthur Waley in his *Tale of Genji*), though the effect could be to clog Proust's flow and make his drift harder to follow.

The present revision or re-revision has taken into account the second Pléiade edition of *À la recherche du temps perdu,* published in four volumes between 1987 and 1989 under the direction of Jean-Yves Tadié. This both adds, chiefly in the form of drafts and variants, and relocates material: not always helpfully from the viewpoint of the common (as distinct from specialist) reader, who may be surprised to encounter virtually the same passage in two different locations when there was doubt as to where Proust would finally have placed it. But the new edition clears up some long-standing misreadings: for example, in correcting Cambremer's admiring "niece" in *Time Regained* to his "mother," an identification which accords with a mention some thousand pages earlier in the novel.

Kilmartin notes that it is only too easy for the latecomer, tempted to make his mark by "officious tinkering," to "assume the *beau rôle.*" The caveat, so delicately worded, is one to take to heart. I am much indebted to my wife, Madeleine, without whose collaboration I would never have dared to assume a role that is melancholy rather than (in any sense) *beau.*

SODOM AND

GOMORRAH

PART ONE

*The women shall have Gomorrah and
the men shall have Sodom*
ALFRED DE VIGNY

The reader will remember that, well before going that
day (the day on which the Princesse de Guermantes's reception was to be held) to pay the Duke and Duchess the
visit I have just described, I had kept watch for their return and in the course of my vigil had made a discovery
which concerned M. de Charlus in particular but was in
itself so important that I have until now, until the moment when I could give it the prominence and treat it
with the fullness that it demanded, postponed giving an
account of it. I had, as I have said, left the marvellous
point of vantage, so snugly contrived at the top of the
house, commanding the hilly slopes which led up to the
Hôtel de Bréquigny, and which were gaily decorated in
the Italian manner by the rose-pink campanile of the
Marquis de Frécourt's coach-house. I had thought it more
practical, when I suspected that the Duke and Duchess
were on the point of returning, to post myself on the
staircase. I rather missed my Alpine eyrie. But at that
time of day, namely the hour immediately after lunch, I
had less cause for regret, for I should not then have seen,
as in the morning, the footmen of the Bréquigny household, converted by distance into minute figures in a picture, make their leisurely ascent of the steep hillside,

1

feather-brush in hand, behind the large, transparent flakes of mica which stood out so pleasingly upon its ruddy bastions. Failing the geologist's field of contemplation, I had at least that of the botanist, and was peering through the shutters of the staircase window at the Duchess's little shrub and at the precious plant, exposed in the courtyard with that assertiveness with which mothers "bring out" their marriageable offspring, and asking myself whether the unlikely insect would come, by a providential hazard, to visit the offered and neglected pistil. My curiosity emboldening me by degrees, I went down to the ground-floor window, which also stood open with its shutters ajar. I could distinctly hear Jupien getting ready to go out, but he could not detect me behind my blind, where I stood perfectly still until the moment when I drew quickly aside in order not to be seen by M. de Charlus, who, on his way to call upon Mme de Villeparisis, was slowly crossing the courtyard, corpulent, greying, aged by the strong light. Nothing short of an indisposition from which Mme de Villeparisis might be suffering (consequent on the illness of the Marquis de Fierbois, with whom he personally was at daggers drawn) could have made M. de Charlus pay a call, perhaps for the first time in his life, at that hour of the day. For with that eccentricity of the Guermantes, who, instead of conforming to the ways of society, tended to modify them to suit their own personal habits (habits not, they thought, social, and deserving in consequence the abasement before them of that worthless thing, society life—thus it was that Mme de Marsantes had no regular "day," but was at home to her friends every morning between ten o'clock and noon), the Baron, reserving those hours for reading, hunting for old curios and so forth, paid calls only between four and six in the evening. At six o'clock he went to the Jockey Club, or took a stroll in the Bois. A moment later, I again recoiled, in order not to be seen by Jupien. It was nearly time for him to set out for the office, from which he would return only for dinner, and not always even then during the last week since his niece and her apprentices had gone to the country to finish a dress for a customer. Then, realising that no one could see me, I decided not to let myself be disturbed again for fear of missing, should the miracle be fated to occur, the arrival, almost beyond the possibility of hope (across so many obstacles of distance, of adverse risks, of dangers), of the insect sent from so far away as ambassador to the virgin who had been waiting for so long. I knew that this expectancy was no more passive than in the male flower, whose stamens had spontaneously curved so that the insect might more easily receive their offering; similarly the female flower that stood here would coquettishly arch her "styles" if the insect came, and, to be more effectively penetrated by him, would imperceptibly advance, like a hypocritical but ardent damsel, to meet him half-way. The laws of the vegetable kingdom are themselves governed by increasingly higher laws. If the visit of an insect, that is to say the transportation of the seed from another flower, is generally necessary for the fertilisation of a flower, that is because self-fertilisation, the insemination of a flower by itself, would lead, like a succession of intermarriages in the same family, to degeneracy and sterility, whereas the crossing effected by insects gives to the subsequent generations of the same species a vigour unknown to their forebears. This invigoration may, however, prove excessive, and the species develop out of all proportion; then, as an antitoxin protects us against disease, as the thyroid gland regulates our adiposity, as defeat comes to punish pride, as fatigue follows indulgence, and as sleep in turn brings rest from fatigue, so an exceptional act of self-fertilisation comes at the crucial moment to apply its turn of the screw, its pull on the curb, brings back within the norm the flower that has exaggeratedly overstepped it. My reflexions had followed a trend which I shall describe in due course, and I had already drawn from the visible stratagems of flowers a conclusion that bore upon a whole unconscious element of literary production, when I saw M. de Charlus coming away from the Marquise's door. Only a few minutes had passed since his entry. Perhaps he had learned from his elderly relative herself, or merely from a servant, of a great improvement in her condition, or rather her complete recovery from what had been nothing more than a slight indisposition. At this moment, when he did not suspect that anyone was watching him, his eyelids lowered as a screen against the sun, M. de Charlus had relaxed that artificial tension, softened that artificial vigour in his face which were ordinarily sustained by the animation of his talk and the force of his will. Pale as a marble statue, his fine features with the prominent nose no longer received from an expression deliberately assumed a different meaning which altered the beauty of their contours; no more now than a Guermantes, he seemed already carved in stone, he, Palamède XV, in the chapel at Combray. These general features of a whole family took on, however, in the face of M. de Charlus a more spiritualised, above all a softer refinement. I regretted for his sake that he should habitually adulterate with so many violent outbursts, offensive eccentricities, calumnies, with such harshness, touchiness and arrogance, that he should conceal beneath a spurious brutality the amenity, the kindness which, as he emerged from Mme de Villeparisis's, I saw so innocently displayed upon his face. Blinking his eyes in the sunlight, he seemed almost to be smiling, and I found in his face seen thus in repose and as it were in its natural state something so affectionate, so defenceless, that I could not help thinking how angry M. de Charlus would have been could he have known that he was being watched; for what was suggested to me by the sight of this man who was so enamoured of, who so prided himself upon, his virility, to whom all other men seemed odiously effeminate, what he suddenly suggested to me, to such an extent had he momentarily assumed the features, the expression, the smile thereof, was a woman.

I was about to change my position again, so that he should not catch sight of me; I had neither the time nor the need to do so. For what did I see! Face to face, in that courtyard where they had certainly never met before (M. de Charlus coming to the Hôtel de Guermantes only in the afternoon, during the time when Jupien was at his office), the Baron, having suddenly opened wide his half-shut eyes, was gazing with extraordinary attentiveness at the ex-tailor poised on the threshold of his shop, while the latter, rooted suddenly to the spot in front of M. de Charlus, implanted there like a tree, contemplated with a look of wonderment the plump form of the ageing Baron. But, more astounding still, M. de Charlus's pose having altered, Jupien's, as though in obedience to the laws of an occult art, at once brought itself into harmony with it. The Baron, who now sought to disguise the impression

that had been made on him, and yet, in spite of his affectation of indifference, seemed unable to move away without regret, came and went, looked vaguely into the
distance in the way which he felt would most enhance the
beauty of his eyes, assumed a smug, nonchalant, fatuous
air. Meanwhile Jupien, shedding at once the humble,
kindly expression which I had always associated with him,
had—in perfect symmetry with the Baron—thrown back
his head, given a becoming tilt to his body, placed his
hand with grotesque effrontery on his hip, stuck out his
behind, struck poses with the coquetry that the orchid
might have adopted on the providential arrival of the bee.
I had not supposed that he could look so unappealing.
But I was equally unaware that he was capable of impro-
vising his part in this sort of dumb show which (although
he found himself for the first time in the presence of
M. de Charlus) seemed to have been long and carefully
rehearsed; one does not arrive spontaneously at that pitch
of perfection except when one meets abroad a compatriot
with whom an understanding then develops of itself, the
means of communication being the same, even without
having seen each other before.

   This scene was not, however, positively comic; it was
stamped with a strangeness, or if you like a naturalness,
the beauty of which steadily increased. Try as M. de
Charlus might to assume a detached air, to let his eyelids
nonchalantly droop, every now and then he raised them,
and at such moments turned on Jupien an attentive gaze.
But (doubtless because he felt that such a scene could not
be prolonged indefinitely in this place, whether for reasons which we shall understand later on, or possibly from
that feeling of the brevity of all things which makes us

determine that every blow must strike home, and renders
so moving the spectacle of every kind of love), each time
that M. de Charlus looked at Jupien, he took care that his
glance should be accompanied by a word, which made it
infinitely unlike the glances we usually direct at a person
whom we scarcely know or do not know at all; he stared
at Jupien with the peculiar fixity of the person who is
about to say to you: "Excuse my taking the liberty, but
you have a long white thread hanging down your back,"
or else: "Surely I can't be mistaken, you come from
Zurich too; I'm certain I must have seen you there often
at the antique dealer's." Thus, every other minute, the
same question seemed to be put to Jupien intently in
M. de Charlus's ogling, like those questioning phrases of
Beethoven's, indefinitely repeated at regular intervals and
intended—with an exaggerated lavishness of preparation—to introduce a new theme, a change of key, a "re-
entry." On the other hand, the beauty of the reciprocal
glances of M. de Charlus and Jupien arose precisely from
the fact that they did not, for the moment at least, seem
to be intended to lead to anything further. It was the first
time I had seen the manifestation of this beauty in the
Baron and Jupien. In the eyes of both of them, it was the
sky not of Zurich but of some oriental city, the name of
which I had not yet divined, that I saw reflected. Whatever the point might be that held M. de Charlus and the
ex-tailor thus arrested, their pact seemed concluded and
these superfluous glances to be but ritual preliminaries,
like the parties people give before a marriage which has
been definitely arranged. Nearer still to nature—and the
multiplicity of these analogies is itself all the more natural
in that the same man, if we examine him for a few min-

utes, appears in turn a man, a man-bird, a man-insect, and so forth—one might have thought of them as a pair of birds, the male and the female, the male seeking to advance, the female—Jupien—no longer giving any sign of response to this stratagem, but regarding her new friend without surprise, with an inattentive fixity of gaze, doubtless considered more disturbing and the sole practicality now that the male had taken the first steps, and contenting herself with preening her feathers. At length Jupien's indifference seemed to suffice him no longer; from the certainty of having conquered to getting himself pursued and desired was but a step, and Jupien, deciding to go off to his work, went out through the carriage gate. It was only, however, after turning his head two or three times that he disappeared into the street, towards which the Baron, trembling lest he should lose the trail (boldly humming a tune, and not forgetting to fling a "Good-day" to the porter, who, half-tipsy and engaged in treating a few friends in his back kitchen, did not even hear him), hurried briskly to catch up with him. At the same instant as M. de Charlus disappeared through the gate humming like a great bumble-bee, another, a real one this time, flew into the courtyard. For all I knew this might be the one so long awaited by the orchid, coming to bring it that rare pollen without which it must remain a virgin. But I was distracted from following the gyrations of the insect, for, a few minutes later, engaging my attention afresh, Jupien (perhaps to pick up a parcel which he did take away with him ultimately and which, in the emotion aroused in him by the appearance of M. de Charlus, he had forgotten, perhaps simply for a more natural reason) returned, followed by the Baron. The latter, deciding to precipitate

matters, asked the tailor for a light, but at once observed:
"I ask you for a light, but I see I've left my cigars at
home." The laws of hospitality prevailed over the rules of
coquetry. "Come inside, you shall have everything you
wish," said the tailor, on whose features disdain now gave
place to joy. The door of the shop closed behind them
and I could hear no more. I had lost sight of the bumble-
bee. I did not know whether he was the insect that the orchid required, but I had no longer any doubt, in the case
of a very rare insect and a captive flower, of the miracu-
lous possibility of their conjunction when I considered
that M. de Charlus (this is simply a comparison of providential chances, whatever they may be, without the slightest scientific claim to establish a relation between certain
botanical laws and what is sometimes, most ineptly,
termed homosexuality), who for years past had never
come to the house except at hours when Jupien was not
there, had, by the mere accident of Mme de Villeparisis's
indisposition, encountered the tailor and with him the
good fortune reserved for men of the Baron's kind by one
of those fellow-creatures who may even be, as we shall
see, infinitely younger than Jupien and better-looking, the
man predestined to exist in order that they may have their
share of sensual pleasure on this earth: the man who cares
only for elderly gentlemen.

All that I have just said, however, I was not to understand until several minutes had elapsed, to such an extent
is reality encumbered by those properties of invisibility
until a chance occurrence has divested it of them. At all
events, for the moment I was greatly annoyed at not being
able to hear any more of the conversation between the ex-
tailor and the Baron. Then I noticed the vacant shop,

which was separated from Jupien's only by an extremely
thin partition. In order to get to it, I had merely to go up
to our flat, pass through the kitchen, go down by the service stairs to the cellars, make my way through them
across the breadth of the courtyard above, and on arriving
at the place in the basement where a few months ago the
joiner had still been storing his timber and where Jupien
intended to keep his coal, climb the flight of steps which
led to the interior of the shop. Thus the whole of my
journey would be made under cover, and I should not be
seen by anyone. This was the most prudent method. It
was not the one that I adopted; instead, keeping close to
the walls, I edged my way round the courtyard in the
open, trying not to let myself be seen. If I was not, I owe
it more, I am sure, to chance than to my own sagacity.
And for the fact that I took so imprudent a course, when
the way through the cellar was so safe, I can see three
possible reasons, assuming that I had any reason at all.
First of all, my impatience. Secondly, perhaps, a dim
memory of the scene at Montjouvain, when I crouched
concealed outside Mlle Vinteuil's window. Certainly, the
affairs of this sort of which I have been a spectator have
always been, as far as their setting is concerned, of the
most imprudent and least probable character, as if such
revelations were to be the reward of an action full of risk,
though in part clandestine. I hardly dare confess to the
third and final reason, so childish does it seem, but I suspect that it was unconsciously decisive. Ever since, in
order to follow—and see controverted—the military principles enunciated by Saint-Loup, I had been following in
close detail the course of the Boer War, I had been led on
from that to re-read old accounts of travel and explo-

ration. These narratives had thrilled me, and I applied them to the events of my daily life to give myself courage. When attacks of illness had compelled me to remain for several days and nights on end not only without sleep but without lying down, without tasting food or drink, at the moment when my pain and exhaustion became so intense that I felt that I should never escape from them, I would think of some traveller cast up on a shore, poisoned by noxious herbs, shivering with fever in clothes drenched by the salt water, who nevertheless in a day or two felt stronger, rose and went blindly on his way, in search of possible inhabitants who might turn out to be cannibals. His example acted on me as a tonic, restored my hope, and I felt ashamed of my momentary discouragement. Thinking of the Boers who, with British armies facing them, were not afraid to expose themselves at the moment when they had to cross a tract of open country in order to reach cover, "It would be a fine thing," I thought to my-self, "if I were to show less courage when the theatre of operations is simply our own courtyard, and when the only steel that I have to fear, I who have just fought sev-eral duels unafraid on account of the Dreyfus case, is that of the eyes of the neighbours who have other things to do besides looking into the courtyard."

But when I was inside the shop, taking care not to let the wooden floor make the slightest creak, as I realised that the least sound in Jupien's shop could be heard from mine, I thought to myself how rash Jupien and M. de Charlus had been, and how luck had favoured them.

I did not dare move. The Guermantes groom, taking advantage no doubt of his master's absence, had, as it happened, transferred to the shop in which I now stood a ladder which hitherto had been kept in the coach-house, and if I had climbed this I could have opened the fanlight above and heard as well as if I had been in Jupien's shop itself. But I was afraid of making a noise. Besides, it was unnecessary. I had not even cause to regret my not having arrived in the shop until several minutes had elapsed. For from what I heard at first in Jupien's quarters, which was only a series of inarticulate sounds, I imagine that few words had been exchanged. It is true that these sounds were so violent that, if they had not always been taken up an octave higher by a parallel plaint, I might have thought that one person was slitting another's throat within a few feet of me, and that subsequently the murderer and his resuscitated victim were taking a bath to wash away the traces of the crime. I concluded from this later on that there is another thing as noisy as pain, namely pleasure, especially when there is added to it—in the absence of the fear of pregnancy which could not be the case here, despite the hardly convincing example in the *Golden Legend*—an immediate concern about cleanliness. Finally, after about half an hour (during which time I had stealthily hoisted myself up my ladder so as to peep through the fanlight which I did not open), the Baron emerged and a conversation began. Jupien refused with insistence the money that M. de Charlus was trying to press upon him.

Then M. de Charlus took one step outside the shop. "Why do you have your chin shaved like that," asked the other in a caressing tone. "It's so becoming, a nice beard." "Ugh! It's disgusting," the Baron replied.

Meanwhile he still lingered on the threshold and plied Jupien with questions about the neighbourhood. "You don't know anything about the man who sells chestnuts round the corner, not the one on the left, he's a horror, but on the other side, a big dark fellow? And the chemist opposite, he has a very nice cyclist who delivers his medicines." These questions must have ruffled Jupien, for, drawing himself up with the indignation of a courtesan who has been betrayed, he replied: "I can see you're a regular flirt." Uttered in a pained, frigid, affected tone, this reproach must have had its effect on M. de Charlus, who, to counteract the bad impression his curiosity had produced, addressed to Jupien, in too low a tone for me to be able to make out his words, a request the granting of which would doubtless necessitate their prolonging their sojourn in the shop, and which moved the tailor sufficiently to make him forget his annoyance, for he studied the Baron's face, plump and flushed beneath his grey hair, with the supremely blissful air of a person whose self-esteem has just been profoundly flattered, and, deciding to grant M. de Charlus the favour that he had just asked of him, after various remarks lacking in refinement such as "What a big bum you have!", said to the Baron with an air at once smiling, moved, superior and grateful: "All right, you big baby, come along!"

"If I hark back to the question of the tram conductor," M. de Charlus tenaciously pursued, "it is because, apart from anything else, it might provide some interest for my homeward journey. For it happens to me at times, like the Caliph who used to roam the streets of Baghdad in the guise of a common merchant, to condescend to follow some curious little person whose profile may have taken my fancy." At this point I was struck by the same observation as had occurred to me in the case of Bergotte.

If he should ever have to answer for himself before a court, he would employ not the sentences calculated to convince the judges, but such Bergottesque sentences as his peculiar literary temperament suggested to him and made him find pleasure in using. Similarly M. de Charlus, in conversing with the tailor, made use of the same language as he would have used in speaking to fashionable people of his own set, even exaggerating its eccentricities, whether because the shyness which he was striving to overcome drove him to an excess of pride or, by preventing him from mastering himself (for we are always less at our ease in the company of someone who is not of our milieu), forced him to unveil, to lay bare his true nature, which was indeed arrogant and a trifle mad, as Mme de Guermantes had remarked. "In order not to lose the trail," he went on, "I spring like a little usher, like a young and good-looking doctor, into the same tram-car as the little person herself, of whom we speak in the feminine gender only so as to conform with the rules of grammar (as one says in speaking of a prince, 'Is *Her* Highness enjoying *her* usual health').[1] If she changes trams, I take, with possibly the germs of the plague, that incredible thing called a 'transfer'—a number, and one which, although it is presented to *me*, is not always number one! I change 'carriages' in this way as many as three or four times, I end up sometimes at eleven o'clock at night at the Gare d'Orléans, and then have to come home. Still, if only it was just the Gare d'Orléans! Once, I must tell you, not having managed to engage in conversation sooner, I went all the way to Orléans itself, in one of those frightful compartments where all one has to rest one's eyes upon, between those triangular objects made of netting, are photographs of the principal architectural features of the line. There was only one vacant seat; I had in front of me, by way of historic monument, a 'view' of the Cathedral of Orléans, quite the ugliest in France, and as tiring a thing to have to stare at in that way against my will as if somebody had forced me to focus its towers in the lens of one of those optical penholders which give one ophthalmia. I got out of the train at Les Aubrais together with my young person, for whom alas his family (when I had imagined him to possess every defect except that of having a family) were waiting on the platform! My sole consolation, as I waited for a train to take me back to Paris, was the house of Diane de Poitiers. For all that she charmed one of my royal ancestors, I should have preferred a more living beauty. That is why, as an antidote to the boredom of returning home alone, I should rather like to make friends with a sleeping-car attendant or a bus conductor. Now, don't be shocked," the Baron wound up, "it is all a question of type. With what you might call 'young gentlemen,' for instance, I feel no desire for physical possession, but I am never satisfied until I have touched them, I don't mean physically, but touched a responsive chord. As soon as, instead of leaving my letters unanswered, a young man starts writing to me incessantly, when he is morally, as it were, at my disposal, I am assuaged, or at least I would be were I not immediately seized with an obsession for another. Rather curious, is it not?—Speaking of 'young gentlemen,' those that come to the house here, do you know any of them?" "No, my pet. Oh, yes, I do, a dark one, very tall, with an eyeglass, who keeps smiling and turning round." "I don't know who you mean." Jupien filled in the portrait, but M. de Char-

lus was unable to identify its subject, not knowing that
the ex-tailor was one of those persons, more common than
is generally supposed, who never remember the colour of
the hair of people they do not know well. But to me, who
was aware of this infirmity in Jupien and substituted
"fair" for "dark," the portrait appeared to be an exact description of the Duc de Châtellerault. "To return to
young men not of the lower orders," the Baron went on,
"at the present moment my head has been turned by a
strange little fellow, an intelligent little cit who shows
with regard to myself a prodigious want of civility. He
has absolutely no idea of the prodigious personage that I
am, and of the microscopic animalcule that he is in comparison. But what does it matter, the little donkey may
bray his head off before my august bishop's mantle."
"Bishop!" cried Jupien, who had understood nothing of
M. de Charlus's last remarks, but was completely taken
aback by the word bishop. "But that sort of thing doesn't
go with religion," he said. "I have three Popes in my family," replied M. de Charlus, "and enjoy the right to mantle in gules by virtue of a cardinalate title, the niece of the
Cardinal, my great-uncle, having brought to my grandfather the title of Duke which was substituted for it. I see,
though, that you are deaf to metaphor and indifferent to
French history. Besides," he added, less perhaps by way
of conclusion than as a warning, "this attraction that I feel
towards young people who avoid me, from fear of course,
for only their natural respect stops their mouths from crying out to me that they love me, requires in them a superior social position. Even then their feigned indifference
may produce nevertheless a directly opposite effect. Fatuously prolonged, it sickens me. To take an example from

a class with which you are more familiar, when they were doing up my house, so as not to create jealousies among all the duchesses who were vying with one another for the honour of being able to say that they had given me lodging, I went for a few days to a 'hotel,' as they say nowadays. One of the room waiters was known to me, and I pointed out to him an interesting little page who opened carriage doors and who remained recalcitrant to my proposals. Finally, in my exasperation, in order to prove to him that my intentions were pure, I made him an offer of a ridiculously high sum simply to come upstairs and talk to me for five minutes in my room. I waited for him in vain. I then took such a dislike to him that I used to go out by the service door so as not to see his villainous little mug at the other. I learned afterwards that he had never had any of my notes, which had been intercepted, the first by the room waiter who was jealous, the next by the day porter who was virtuous, the third by the night porter who was in love with the little page, and used to couch with him at the hour when Dian rose. But my disgust persisted none the less, and were they to bring me the page like a dish of venison on a silver platter, I should thrust him away with a retching stomach. There now, what a pity—we have spoken of serious matters and now it's all over between us as regards what I was hoping for. But you could be of great service to me, act as my agent . . . Why no, the mere thought of such a thing makes me quite frisky again, and I feel it isn't all over."

From the beginning of this scene my eyes had been opened by a transformation in M. de Charlus as complete and as immediate as if he had been touched by a magician's wand. Until then, because I had not understood, I had not seen. Each man's vice (we use the term for the sake of linguistic convenience) accompanies him after the manner of the tutelary spirit who was invisible to men so long as they were unaware of his presence. Kindness, treachery, name, social relations, they do not let themselves be laid bare, we carry them hidden. Ulysses himself did not recognise Athena at first. But the gods are immediately perceptible to one another, like as quickly to like, and so too had M. de Charlus been to Jupien. Until that moment, in the presence of M. de Charlus I had been in the position of an unobservant man who, standing before a pregnant woman whose distended waistline he has failed to remark, persists, while she smilingly reiterates "Yes, I'm a little tired just now," in asking her tactlessly: "Why, what's the matter with you?" But let someone say to him: "She is expecting a child," and suddenly he catches sight of her stomach and ceases to see anything else. It is the explanation that opens our eyes; the dispelling of an error gives us an additional sense.

People who do not care to refer, for examples of this law, to the Messieurs de Charlus of their acquaintance whom for long years they had never suspected until the day when, upon the smooth surface of an individual indistinguishable from everyone else, there suddenly appears, traced in an ink hitherto invisible, the characters that compose the word dear to the ancient Greeks, have only to remind themselves, in order to be persuaded that the world which surrounds them appears to them naked at first, stripped of a thousand ornaments which it offers to the eyes of others better informed, of the number of times in the course of their lives they have found themselves on the point of committing a gaffe. Nothing upon the blank,

undocumented face of this man or that could have led
them to suppose that he was precisely the brother, or the
fiancé, or the lover of a woman of whom they were about
to remark: "What a cow!" But then, fortunately, a word
whispered to them by someone standing near arrests the
fatal expression on their lips. At once there appear, like a
Mene, Tekel, Upharsin, the words: "he is engaged to," or
"he is the brother of," or "he is the lover of" the woman
whom it is inadvisable to describe in his hearing as a cow.
And this single new notion will bring about an entire re-
grouping, thrusting some back, others forward, of the
fractional notions, henceforward a complete whole, which
we possessed of the rest of the family. Although in the
person of M. de Charlus another creature was coupled, as
the horse in the centaur, which made him different from
other men, although this creature was one with the Baron,
I had never perceived it. Now the abstract had become
material, the creature at last discerned had lost its power
of remaining invisible, and the transformation of M. de
Charlus into a new person was so complete that not only
the contrasts of his face and of his voice, but, in retrospect, the very ups and downs of his relations with myself, everything that hitherto had seemed to my mind
incoherent, became intelligible, appeared self-evident, just
as a sentence which presents no meaning so long as it remains broken up in letters arranged at random expresses,
once these letters are rearranged in the proper order, a
thought which one can never afterwards forget.

I now understood, moreover, why earlier, when I had
seen him coming away from Mme de Villeparisis's, I had
managed to arrive at the conclusion that M. de Charlus
looked like a woman: he was one! He belonged to that

race of beings, less paradoxical than they appear, whose ideal is manly precisely because their temperament is feminine, and who in ordinary life resemble other men in appearance only; there where each of us carries, inscribed in those eyes through which he beholds everything in the universe, a human form engraved on the surface of the pupil, for them it is not that of a nymph but that of an ephebe. A race upon which a curse is laid and which must live in falsehood and perjury because it knows that its desire, that which constitutes life's dearest pleasure, is held to be punishable, shameful, an inadmissible thing; which must deny its God, since its members, even when Christians, when at the bar of justice they appear and are arraigned, must before Christ and in his name refute as a calumny what is their very life; sons without a mother, to whom they are obliged to lie even in the hour when they close her dying eyes; friends without friendships, despite all those which their frequently acknowledged charm inspires and their often generous hearts would gladly feel— but can we describe as friendships those relationships which flourish only by virtue of a lie and from which the first impulse of trust and sincerity to which they might be tempted to yield would cause them to be rejected with disgust, unless they are dealing with an impartial or perhaps even sympathetic spirit, who however in that case, misled with regard to them by a conventional psychology, will attribute to the vice confessed the very affection that is most alien to it, just as certain judges assume and are more inclined to pardon murder in inverts and treason in Jews for reasons derived from original sin and racial predestination? And lastly—according at least to the first theory which I sketched in outline at the time, which we shall see subjected to some modification in the sequel, and in which, had the paradox not been hidden from their eyes by the very illusion that made them see and live, this would have angered them above all else—lovers who are almost precluded from the possibility of that love the hope of which gives them the strength to endure so many risks and so much loneliness, since they are enamoured of precisely the type of man who has nothing feminine about him, who is not an invert and consequently cannot love them in return; with the result that their desire would be for ever unappeased did not their money procure for them real men, and their imagination end by making them take for real men the inverts to whom they have prostituted themselves. Their honour precarious, their liberty provisional, lasting only until the discovery of their crime; their position unstable, like that of the poet one day fêted in every drawing-room and applauded in every theatre in London, and the next driven from every lodging, unable to find a pillow upon which to lay his head, turning the mill like Samson and saying like him: "The two sexes shall die, each in a place apart!";[2] excluded even, except on the days of general misfortune when the majority rally round the victim as the Jews round Dreyfus, from the sympathy—at times from the society—of their fellows, in whom they inspire only disgust at seeing themselves as they are, portrayed in a mirror which, ceasing to flatter them, accentuates every blemish that they have refused to observe in themselves, and makes them understand that what they have been calling their love (and to which, playing upon the word, they have by association annexed all that poetry, painting, music, chivalry, asceticism have contrived to add to love) springs not from an ideal of beauty which they have chosen but from an incurable disease; like the Jews again (save some who will associate only with those of their race and have always on their lips the ritual words and the accepted pleasantries), shunning one another, seeking out those who are most directly their opposite, who do not want their company, forgiving their rebuffs, enraptured by their condescensions; but also brought into the company of their own kind by the ostracism to which they are subjected, the opprobrium into which they have fallen, having finally been invested, by a persecution similar to that of Israel, with the physical and moral characteristics of a race, sometimes beautiful, often hideous, finding (in spite of all the mockery with which one who, more closely integrated with, better assimilated to the opposing race, is in appearance relatively less inverted, heaps upon one who has remained more so) a relief in frequenting the society of their kind, and even some support in their existence, so much so that, while steadfastly denying that they are a race (the name of which is the vilest of insults), they readily unmask those who succeed in concealing the fact that they belong to it, with a view less to injuring them, though they have no scruple about that, than to excusing themselves, and seeking out (as a doctor seeks out cases of appendicitis) cases of inversion in history, taking pleasure in recalling that Socrates was one of themselves, as the Jews claim that Jesus was one of them, without reflecting that there were no abnormal people when homosexuality was the norm, no anti-Christians before Christ, that the opprobrium alone makes the crime because it has allowed to survive only those who remained obdurate to every warning, to every example, to every punishment, by virtue of an innate disposition so peculiar that it is more repugnant to other men (even though it may be accompanied by high moral qualities) than certain other vices which exclude those qualities, such as theft, cruelty, breach of faith, vices better understood and so more readily excused by the generality of men; forming a freemasonry far more extensive, more effective and less suspected than that of the Lodges, for it rests upon an identity of tastes, needs, habits, dangers, apprenticeship, knowledge, traffic, vocabulary, and one in which even members who do not wish to know one another recognise one another immediately by natural or conventional, involuntary or deliberate signs which indicate one of his kind to the beggar in the person of the nobleman whose carriage door he is shutting, to the father in the person of his daughter's suitor, to the man who has sought healing, absolution or legal defence in the doctor, the priest or the barrister to whom he has had recourse; all of them obliged to protect their own secret but sharing with the others a secret which the rest of humanity does not suspect and which means that to them the most wildly improbable tales of adventure seem true, for in this life of anachronistic fiction the ambassador is a bosom friend of the felon, the prince, with a certain insolent aplomb born of his aristocratic breeding which the timorous bourgeois lacks, on leaving the duchess's party goes off to confer in private with the ruffian; a reprobate section of the human collectivity, but an important one, suspected where it does not exist, flaunting itself, insolent and immune, where its existence is never guessed; numbering its adherents everywhere, among the people, in the army, in the church, in prison, on the throne; living, in short, at least to a great extent, in an affectionate and perilous intimacy with the men of the other race, provoking them, playing with them by speaking of its vice as of something alien to it—a game that is rendered easy by the blindness or duplicity of the others, a game that may be kept up for years until the day of the scandal when these lion-tamers are devoured; obliged until then to make a secret of their lives, to avert their eyes from the direction in which they would wish to stray, to fasten them on what they would naturally turn away from, to change the gender of many of the adjectives in their vocabulary, a social constraint that is slight in comparison with the inward constraint imposed upon them by their vice, or what is improperly so called, not so much in relation to others as to themselves, and in such a way that to themselves it does not appear a vice. But certain among them, more practical, busier men who have not the time to go and drive their bargains, or to dispense with the simplification of life and the saving of time which may result from co-operation, have formed two societies of which the second is composed exclusively of persons similar to themselves.

This is noticeable in those who are poor and have come up from the country, without friends, with nothing but their ambition to be some day a celebrated doctor or barrister, with a mind still barren of opinions, a person devoid of social graces which they intend as soon as possible to adorn, just as they might buy furniture for their little attic in the Latin Quarter, modelling themselves on what they observe among those who have already "arrived" in the useful and serious profession in which they also intend to establish themselves and to become famous; in these their special predisposition, unconsciously inherited like a proclivity for drawing, for music, a tendency towards blindness, is perhaps the only inveterate and overriding peculiarity—which on certain evenings compels them to miss some meeting, advantageous to their career, with people whose ways of speaking, thinking, dressing, parting their hair, they otherwise adopt. In their neighbourhood, where for the rest they mix only with brother students, teachers or some fellow-provincial who has graduated and can help them on, they have speedily discovered other young men who are drawn to them by the same special inclination, as in a small town the assistant schoolmaster and the solicitor are brought together by a common interest in chamber music or mediaeval ivories; applying to the object of their distraction the same utilitarian instinct, the same professional spirit which guides them in their career, they meet these young men at gatherings to which no outsider is admitted any more than to those that bring together collectors of old snuff-boxes, Japanese prints or rare flowers, and at which, what with the pleasure of gaining information, the practical value of making exchanges and the fear of competition, there prevail simultaneously, as in a stamp market, the close cooperation of specialists and the fierce rivalries of collectors. Moreover no one in the café where they have their table knows what the gathering is, whether it is that of an angling club, of an editorial staff, or of the "Sons of the Indre," so correct is their attire, so cold and reserved their manner, so modestly do they refrain from any but the most covert glance at the young men of fashion, the young "lions" who, a few feet away, are boasting about their mistresses, and among whom those who now admire them without venturing to raise their eyes will learn only

twenty years later, when some are on the eve of admission
to the Academy, and others middle-aged clubmen, that
the most attractive among them, now a stout and grizzled
Charlus, was in reality one of themselves, but elsewhere,
in another circle of society, beneath other external symbols, with different signs whose unfamiliarity misled
them. But these groups are at varying stages of evolution;
and, just as the "Union of the Left" differs from the "So-
cialist Federation" or some Mendelssohnian musical club
from the Schola Cantorum, on certain evenings, at another
table, there are extremists who allow a bracelet to slip
down from beneath a cuff, or sometimes a necklace to
gleam in the gap of a collar, who by their persistent
stares, their cooings, their laughter, their mutual caresses,
oblige a band of students to depart in hot haste, and are
served with a civility beneath which indignation smoul-
ders by a waiter who, as on the evenings when he has to
serve Dreyfusards, would have the greatest pleasure in
summoning the police did he not find profit in pocketing
their gratuities.

It is with these professional organisations that the
mind contrasts the taste of the solitaries, and in one sense
without too much contrivance, since it is doing no more
than imitate the solitaries themselves who imagine that
nothing differs more widely from organised vice than
what appears to them to be a misunderstood love, but
with some contrivance nevertheless, for these different
classes correspond, no less than to diverse physiological
types, to successive stages in a pathological or merely social evolution. And it is, in fact, very rarely that the solitaries do not eventually merge themselves in some such
organisation, sometimes from simple lassitude, or for con-

venience (just as the people who have been most strongly opposed to such innovations end by having the telephone installed, inviting the Iénas to their parties, or shopping at Potin's). They meet with none too friendly a reception as a rule, for, in their relatively pure lives, their want of experience, the saturation in day-dreams to which they have been reduced, have branded more strongly upon them those special marks of effeminacy which the professionals have sought to efface. And it must be admitted that, among certain of these newcomers, the woman is not only inwardly united to the man but hideously visible, convulsed as they are by a hysterical spasm, by a shrill laugh which sets their knees and hands trembling, looking no more like the common run of men than those apes with melancholy ringed eyes and prehensile feet who dress up in dinner-jackets and black ties; so that these new recruits are judged by others, themselves less chaste, to be compromising associates, and their admission is hedged with difficulties; they are accepted nevertheless, and they benefit then from those facilities by which commerce and big business have transformed the lives of individuals by bringing within their reach commodities hitherto too costly to acquire and indeed hard to find, which now submerge them beneath a plethora of what by themselves they had never succeeded in discovering amid the densest crowds.

But, even with these innumerable outlets, the burden of social constraint is still too heavy for some, recruited principally among those who have not practised mental constraint and who still take to be rarer than it actually is their way of love. Let us ignore for the moment those who, the exceptional character of their inclinations making them regard themselves as superior to the other sex, look down on women, regard homosexuality as the appurtenance of genius and the great periods of history, and, when they wish to share their taste with others, seek out not so much those who seem to them to be predisposed towards it, like drug-addicts with their morphine, as those who seem to them to be worthy of it, from apostolic zeal, just as others preach Zionism, conscientious objection, Saint-Simonianism, vegetarianism or anarchy. There are some who, should we intrude upon them in the morning, still in bed, will present to our gaze an admirable female head, so generalised and typical of the entire sex is the expression of the face; the hair itself affirms it, so feminine is its ripple; unbrushed, it falls so naturally in long curls over the cheek that one marvels how the young woman, the girl, the Galatea barely awakened to life in the unconscious mass of this male body in which she is imprisoned has contrived so ingeniously, by herself, without instruction from anyone else, to take advantage of the narrowest apertures in her prison wall to find what was necessary to her existence. No doubt the young man who sports this delicious head does not say: "I am a woman." Even if—for any of the countless possible reasons—he lives with a woman, he can deny to her that he is himself one, can swear to her that he has never had intercourse with men. But let her look at him as we have just revealed him, lying back in bed, in pyjamas, his arms bare, his throat and neck bare too beneath the dark tresses: the pyjama jacket becomes a woman's shift, the head that of a pretty Spanish girl. The mistress is appalled by these confidences offered to her gaze, truer than any spoken confidence could be, or indeed any action, which his actions indeed, if they have not already done so, cannot fail later on to confirm, for every individual follows the line of his own pleasure, and if he is not too depraved, seeks it in a sex complementary to his own. And for the invert vice begins, not when he enters into relations (for there are all sorts of reasons that may enjoin these), but when he takes his pleasure with women. The young man whom we have been attempting to portray was so evidently a woman that the women who looked upon him with desire were doomed (failing a special taste on their part) to the same disappointment as those who in Shakespeare's comedies are taken in by a girl disguised as a youth. The deception is mutual, the invert is himself aware of it, he guesses the disillusionment which the woman will experience once the mask is removed, and feels to what an extent this mistake as to sex is a source of poetical imaginings. Moreover it is in vain that he keeps back the admission "I am a woman" even from his demanding mistress (if she is not a denizen of Gomorrah) when all the time, with the cunning, the agility, the obstinacy of a climbing plant, the unconscious but visible woman in him seeks the masculine organ. We have only to look at that curly hair on the white pillow to understand that if, in the evening, this young man slips through his guardians' fingers in spite of them, in spite of himself, it will not be to go in pursuit of women. His mistress may castigate him, may lock him up, but next day the man-woman will have found some way of attaching himself to a man, as the convolvulus throws out its tendrils wherever it finds a pick or a rake up which to climb. Why, when we admire in the face of this man a delicacy that touches our hearts, a grace, a natural gentleness such as men do not possess, should we be dismayed to learn that this young man runs after boxers? They are different aspects of the same reality. And indeed, what repels us is the most touching thing of all, more touching than any refinement of delicacy, for it represents an admirable though unconscious effort on the part of nature: the recognition of sex by itself, in spite of the deceptions of sex, appears as an unavowed attempt to escape from itself towards what an initial error on the part of society has segregated it from. Some—those no doubt who have been most timid in childhood—are not greatly concerned with the kind of physical pleasure they receive, provided that they can associate it with a masculine face. Whereas others, whose sensuality is doubtless more violent, feel an imperious need to localise their physical pleasure. These latter, perhaps, would shock the average person with their avowals. They live perhaps less exclusively under the planet of Saturn, since for them women are not entirely excluded as they are for the former sort, in relation to whom women have no existence apart from conversation, flirtation, intellectual loves. But the second sort seek out those women who love other women, who can procure for them a young man, enhance the pleasure they experience in his company; better still, they can, in the same fashion, take with such women the same pleasure as with a man. Whence it arises that jealousy is kindled in those who love the first sort only by the pleasure which they may enjoy with a man, which alone seems to their lovers a betrayal, since they do not participate in the love of women, have practised it only out of habit and to preserve for themselves the possibility of eventual marriage, visualising so little the pleasure that it is capable of giving that they cannot be distressed by the thought that he whom they

love is enjoying that pleasure; whereas the other sort often
inspire jealousy by their love-affairs with women. For, in
their relations with women, they play, for the woman who
loves her own sex, the part of another woman, and she offers them at the same time more or less what they find in
other men, so that the jealous friend suffers from the feeling that the man he loves is riveted to the woman who is
to him almost a man, and at the same time feels his
beloved almost escape him because, to these women, he is
something which the lover himself cannot conceive, a sort
of woman. Nor need we pause here to consider those
young fools who out of childishness, to tease their friends
or to shock their families, obdurately choose clothes that
resemble women's dresses, redden their lips and blacken
their eyelashes; let us leave them aside, for it is they
whom we shall find later on, when they have suffered the
all too cruel penalty of their affectation, spending what remains of their lifetime in vain attempts to repair by a
sternly protestant demeanour the wrong that they did to
themselves when they were carried away by the same demon that urges young women of the Faubourg Saint-
Germain to live scandalous lives, to defy all the conven-
tions, to scoff at the entreaties of their families, until the day
when they set themselves with perseverance but without
success to reascend the slope down which they had found
it so amusing to slide or rather had not been able to stop
themselves from sliding. Let us, finally, leave until later
the men who have sealed a pact with Gomorrah. We shall
speak of them when M. de Charlus comes to know them.
Let us leave all those, of one sort or another, who will appear each in his turn, and, to conclude this first sketch of
the subject, let us simply say a word about those whom

we began to speak of just now, the solitaries. Supposing their vice to be more exceptional than it is, they have retired into solitude from the day on which they discovered it, after having carried it within themselves for a long time without knowing it, longer, that is, than certain others. For no one can tell at first that he is an invert, or a poet, or a snob, or a scoundrel. The boy who has been reading erotic poetry or looking at obscene pictures, if he then presses his body against a schoolfellow's, imagines himself only to be communing with him in an identical desire for a woman. How should he suppose that he is not like everybody else when he recognises the substance of what he feels in reading Mme de La Fayette, Racine, Baudelaire, Walter Scott, at a time when he is still too little capable of observing himself to take into account what he has added from his own store to the picture, and to realise that if the sentiment be the same the object differs, that what he desires is Rob Roy and not Diana Vernon? With many, by a defensive prudence on the part of the instinct that precedes the clearer vision of the intellect, the mirror and walls of their bedroom vanish beneath coloured prints of actresses, and they compose verses such as:

I love but Chloe in the world,
For Chloe is divine;
Her golden hair is sweetly curled,
For her my heart doth pine.

Must we on that account attribute to the opening phase of such lives a taste which we shall not find in them later on, like those flaxen ringlets on the heads of children which are destined to change to the darkest brown? Who can tell whether the photographs of women are not a first sign of hypocrisy, a first sign also of horror at other inverts? But the solitaries are precisely those to whom hypocrisy is painful. Possibly even the example of the Jews, of a different type of colony, is not strong enough to account for the frail hold that their upbringing has upon them, and for the skill and cunning with which they find their way back, not, perhaps, to anything so sheerly terrible as suicide (to which madmen return, whatever precautions one may take with them, and, having been pulled out of the river into which they have flung themselves, take poison, procure revolvers, and so forth), but to a life whose compulsive pleasures the men of the other race not only cannot understand, cannot imagine, abominate, but whose frequent danger and constant shame would horrify them. Perhaps, to form a picture of these, we ought to think, if not of the wild animals that never become domesticated, of the lion-cubs, allegedly tamed, which are still lions at heart, then at least of the negroes whom the comfortable existence of the white man drives to despair and who prefer the risks of life in the wild and its incomprehensible joys. When the day has dawned on which they have discovered themselves to be incapable at once of lying to others and of lying to themselves, they go away to live in the country, shunning the society of their own kind (whom they believe to be few in number) from horror of the monstrosity or fear of the temptation, and that of the rest of humanity from shame. Never having arrived at true maturity, plunged in a constant melancholy, from time to time, on a moonless Sunday evening, they go for a solitary walk as far as a crossroads where, although not a word has been said, there has come to meet them one of their boyhood friends who is living in a house in the neighbourhood. And they begin again the pastimes of long ago, on the grass, in the night, without exchanging a word. During the week, they meet in their respective houses, talk of this and that, without any allusion to what has occurred between them—exactly as though they had done nothing and would not do anything again—save, in their relations, a trace of coldness, of irony, of irritability and rancour, sometimes of hatred. Then the neighbour sets out on a strenuous expedition on horseback, scales mountain peaks, sleeps in the snow; his friend, who identifies his own vice with a weakness of constitution, a timid, stay-at-home life, assumes that vice can no longer exist in his emancipated friend, so many thousands of feet above sea-level. And, sure enough, the other takes a wife. Yet the forsaken one is not cured (although there are cases where, as we shall see, inversion is curable). He insists upon going down himself every morning to the kitchen to receive the milk from the hands of the dairyman's boy, and on the evening when desire is too strong for him will go out of his way to set a drunkard on the right road or to "adjust the dress" of a blind man. No doubt the life of certain inverts appears at times to change, their vice (as it is called) is no longer apparent in their habits; but nothing is ever lost: a missing jewel turns up again; when the quantity of a sick man's urine decreases, it is because he is perspiring more freely, but the excretion must invariably occur. One day this homosexual hears of the death of a young cousin, and from his inconsolable grief we learn that it was to this love, chaste possibly and aimed rather at retaining esteem than at obtaining possession, that his desires have turned by a sort of transfer as, in a budget, without any alteration in the total, certain expenditure is carried under another head. As is the case with invalids in whom a sudden attack of urticaria makes their chronic ailments temporarily disappear, this pure love for a young relative seems, in the invert, to have momentarily replaced, by metastasis, habits that will one day or another return to fill the place of the vicarious cured malady.

Meanwhile the married neighbour of our recluse has returned; and on the day when he is obliged to invite them to dinner, seeing the beauty of the young bride and the demonstrative affection of the husband, he feels ashamed of the past. Already in an interesting condition, she must return home early, leaving her husband behind; the latter, when the time has come for him to go home also, asks his host to accompany him for part of the way; at first, no suspicion enters his mind, but at the cross-roads he finds himself thrown down on to the grass without a word by the mountaineer who is shortly to become a father. And their meetings begin again, and continue until the day when there comes to live not far off a male cousin of the young wife's, with whom her husband is now constantly to be seen. And the latter, if the twice-abandoned friend calls round and endeavours to approach him, indignantly repulses him, furious that he has not had the tact to sense the disgust which he must henceforward inspire. Once, however, there appears a stranger, sent to him by his faithless friend; but being busy at the time, the abandoned one cannot see him, and only afterwards learns with what object his visitor had come.

Then the solitary languishes alone. He has no other diversion than to go to the neighbouring watering-place to ask for some information or other from a certain railway-man there. But the latter has obtained promotion, has been transferred to the other end of the country; the solitary will no longer be able to go and ask him the times of the trains or the price of a first-class ticket, and, before retiring to dream, Griselda-like, in his tower, loiters upon the beach, a strange Andromeda whom no Argonaut will come to free, a sterile jellyfish that must perish upon the sand, or else he stands idly on the platform until his train leaves, casting over the crowd of passengers a look that will seem indifferent, disdainful or abstracted to those of another race, but, like the luminous glow with which certain insects bedeck themselves in order to attract others of their species, or like the nectar which certain flowers offer to attract the insects that will fertilise them, would not deceive the connoisseur (barely possible to find) of a pleasure too singular, too hard to place, which is offered him, the confrère with whom our specialist could converse in the strange tongue—in which at best some ragamuffin on the platform will put up a show of interest, but for material gain alone, like those people who, at the Collège de France, in the room in which the Professor of Sanskrit lectures without an audience, attend his course only for the sake of keeping warm. Jellyfish! Orchid! When I followed my instinct only, the jellyfish used to revolt me at Balbec; but if I had the eyes to regard them, like Michelet, from the standpoint of natural history and aesthetics, I saw an exquisite blue girandole. Are they not, with the transparent velvet of their petals, as it were the mauve orchids of the sea? Like so many creatures of the animal and vegetable kingdoms, like the plant which would produce vanilla but, because in its structure the male organ is separated by a partition from the female, remains sterile unless humming-birds or certain tiny bees convey the pollen from one to the other, or man fertilises them by artificial means, M. de Charlus (and here the word fertilise must be understood in a moral sense, since in the physical sense the union of male with male is and must be sterile, but it is no small matter for a person to be able to encounter the sole pleasure which he is capable of enjoying, and that "every soul here below" can impart to some other "its music or its fragrance or its flame"), M. de Charlus was one of those men who may be called exceptional because, however many they may be, the satisfaction, so easy for others, of their sexual needs depends upon the coincidence of too many conditions, and of conditions too difficult to meet. For men like M. de Charlus (subject to the compromises which will appear little by little and which the reader may already have sensed, enforced by the need of pleasure which resigns itself to partial acceptations), mutual love, apart from the difficulties, so great as to be almost insurmountable, which it encounters in the ordinary run of mortals, entails others so exceptional that what is always extremely rare for everyone becomes in their case well-nigh impossible, and, if they should chance to have an encounter which is really fortunate, or which nature makes appear so to them, their happiness is somehow far more extraordinary, selective, profoundly necessary than that of the normal lover. The feud of the Capulets and Montagues was as nothing compared with the obstacles of every sort which have been surmounted, the special eliminations to which nature has had to subject the chances, already far from common, which bring about love, before a retired tailor, who was intending to set off soberly for his office, can stand quivering in ecstasy before a stoutish man of fifty; this Romeo

and this Juliet may believe with good reason that their
love is not a momentary whim but a true predestination,
determined by the harmonies of their temperaments, and
not only by their own personal temperaments but by
those of their ancestors, by their most distant strains of
heredity, so much so that the fellow-creature who is con-
joined with them has belonged to them from before their
birth, has attracted them by a force comparable to that
which governs the worlds on which we spent our former
lives. M. de Charlus had distracted me from looking to
see whether the bumble-bee was bringing to the orchid
the pollen it had so long been waiting to receive, and had
no chance of receiving save by an accident so unlikely that
one might call it a sort of miracle. But it was a miracle
also that I had just witnessed, almost of the same order
and no less marvellous. As soon as I considered the encounter from this point of view, everything about it
seemed to me instinct with beauty. The most extraordinary stratagems that nature has devised to compel insects
to ensure the fertilisation of flowers which without their
intervention could not be fertilised because the male
flower is too far away from the female—or the one which,
if it is the wind that must provide for the transportation
of the pollen, makes it so much more easily detachable
from the male, so much more easily snatched from the air
by the female flower, by eliminating the secretion of the
nectar, which is no longer of any use since there are no
insects to be attracted, and even the brilliance of the
corollas which attract them—and the device which, in order that the flower may be kept free for the right pollen,
which can fructify only in that particular flower, makes it
secrete a liquid which renders it immune to all other pol-

lens —seemed to me no more marvellous than the existence of the subvariety of inverts destined to guarantee
the pleasures of love to the invert who is growing old:
men who are attracted not by all other men, but—by a
phenomenon of correspondence and harmony similar to
those that govern the fertilisation of heterostyle trimor-
phous flowers like the *lythrum salicaria*—only by men
considerably older than themselves. Of this subvariety
Jupien had just furnished me with an example, one less
striking however than certain others which every human
herbalist, every moral botanist, will be able to observe in
spite of their rarity, and which will show them a frail
young man awaiting the advances of a robust and
paunchy quinquagenarian, and remaining as indifferent to
those of other young men as the hermaphrodite flowers of
the short-styled *primula veris* remain sterile so long as
they are fertilised only by other *primulae veris* of short
style also, whereas they welcome with joy the pollen of
the *primula veris* with the long style. As for M. de Charlus's part in the transaction, I noticed later on that there
were for him various kinds of conjunction, some of which,
by their multiplicity, their scarcely visible instantaneous-
ness, and above all the absence of contact between the
two actors, recalled still more forcibly those flowers that
in a garden are fertilised by the pollen of a neighbouring
flower which they may never touch. There were in fact
certain persons whom it was sufficient for him to invite to
his house, and to hold for an hour or two under the domination of his talk, for his desire, inflamed by some earlier
encounter, to be assuaged. By a simple use of words the
conjunction was effected, as simply as it can be among the
infusoria. Sometimes, as had doubtless been the case with

me on the evening on which I had been summoned by
him after the Guermantes dinner-party, the relief was effected by a violent diatribe which the Baron flung in his
visitor's face, just as certain flowers, by means of a hidden
spring, spray from a distance the disconcerted but unconsciously collaborating insect. M. de Charlus, the domi-
nated turned dominator, feeling purged of his agitation
and calmed, would send away the visitor who had at once
ceased to appear to him desirable. Finally, inasmuch as
inversion itself springs from the fact that the invert is too
closely akin to woman to be capable of having any effective relations with her, it relates to a higher law which ordains that so many hermaphrodite flowers shall remain
infertile, that is to say to the sterility of self-fertilisation.
It is true that inverts, in their search for a male, often
content themselves with other inverts as effeminate as
themselves. But it is enough that they do not belong to
the female sex, of which they have in them an embryo
which they can put to no useful purpose, as happens with
so many hermaphrodite flowers, and even with certain
hermaphrodite animals, such as the snail, which cannot be
fertilised by themselves, but can by other hermaphrodites.
In this respect the race of inverts, who readily link themselves with the ancient East or the golden age of Greece,
might be traced back further still, to those experimental
epochs in which there existed neither dioecious plants nor
monosexual animals, to that initial hermaphroditism of
which certain rudiments of male organs in the anatomy of
women and of female organs in that of men seem still to
preserve the trace. I found the pantomime, incomprehensible to me at first, of Jupien and M. de Charlus as curious as those seductive gestures addressed, Darwin tells us,

to insects by the flowers called composite which erect the
florets of their capitula so as to be seen from a greater distance, like certain heterostyled flowers which turn back
their stamens and bend them to open the way for the insect, or which offer him an ablution, and indeed quite
simply comparable to the nectar-fragrance and vivid hue
of the corollas that were at that moment attracting insects
into the courtyard. From this day onwards M. de Charlus
was to alter the time of his visits to Mme de Villeparisis,
not that he could not see Jupien elsewhere and with
greater convenience, but because to him just as much as
to me the afternoon sunshine and the blossoming plant
were no doubt linked with his memories. Moreover he did
not content himself with recommending the Jupiens to
Mme de Villeparisis, to the Duchesse de Guermantes, to
a whole brilliant clientele who were all the more assiduous
in their patronage of the young seamstress when they saw
that the few ladies who had resisted, or had merely delayed their submission, were subjected to the direst
reprisals by the Baron, whether in order that they might
serve as examples or because they had aroused his wrath
and had stood out against his attempted domination. He
made Jupien's position more and more lucrative, until he
finally engaged him as his secretary and established him
in the state in which we shall see him later on. "Ah, now!
There's a happy man, that Jupien," said Françoise, who
had a tendency to minimise or exaggerate people's generosity according as it was bestowed on herself or on others. Not that, in this instance, she had any need to
exaggerate, nor for that matter did she feel any jealousy,
being genuinely fond of Jupien. "Oh, he's such a good
man, the Baron," she went on, "so gentlemanly, so de-

vout, so proper! If I had a daughter to marry and was one
of the rich myself, I'd give her to the Baron with my eyes
shut." "But, Françoise," my mother observed gently,
"she'd be well supplied with husbands, that daughter of
yours. Don't forget you've already promised her to
Jupien." "Ah, yes!" replied Françoise, "there's another of
them that would make a woman very happy. It doesn't
matter whether you're rich or poor, it makes no difference
to your nature. The Baron and Jupien, they're just the
same sort of person."

However, I greatly exaggerated at the time, on the
strength of this first revelation, the elective character of so
carefully selected a combination. Admittedly, every man
of M. de Charlus's kind is an extraordinary creature since,
if he does not make concessions to the possibilities of life,
he seeks out essentially the love of a man of the other
race, that is to say a man who is a lover of women (and
incapable consequently of loving him); contrary to what I
had imagined in the courtyard, where I had seen Jupien
hovering round M. de Charlus like the orchid making
overtures to the bumble-bee, these exceptional creatures
with whom we commiserate are a vast crowd, as we shall
see in the course of this book, for a reason which will be
disclosed only at the end of it, and commiserate with
themselves for being too many rather than too few. For
the two angels who were posted at the gates of Sodom to
learn whether its inhabitants (according to Genesis) had
indeed done all the things the report of which had ascended to the Eternal Throne must have been, and of this
one can only be glad, exceedingly ill chosen by the Lord,
who ought to have entrusted the task only to a Sodomite.
Such a one would never have been persuaded by such ex-

cuses as "A father of six, I've got two mistresses," to lower his flaming sword benevolently and mitigate the punishment. He would have answered: "Yes, and your wife lives in a torment of jealousy. But even when you haven't chosen these women from Gomorrah, you spend your nights with a watcher of flocks from Hebron." And he would at once have made him retrace his steps to the city which the rain of fire and brimstone was to destroy. On the contrary, all the shameless Sodomites were allowed to escape, even if, on catching sight of a boy, they turned their heads like Lot's wife, though without being on that account changed like her into pillars of salt. With the result that they engendered a numerous progeny with whom this gesture has remained habitual, like that of the dissolute women who, while apparently studying a row of shoes displayed in a shop window, turn their heads to keep track of a passing student. These descendants of the Sodomites, so numerous that we may apply to them that other verse of Genesis: "If a man can number the dust of the earth, then shall thy seed also be numbered," have established themselves throughout the entire world; they have had access to every profession and are so readily admitted into the most exclusive clubs that, whenever a Sodomite fails to secure election, the black balls are for the most part cast by other Sodomites, who make a point of condemning sodomy, having inherited the mendacity that enabled their ancestors to escape from the accursed city. It is possible that they may return there one day. Certainly they form in every land an oriental colony, cultured, musical, malicious, which has charming qualities and intolerable defects. We shall study them with greater thoroughness in the course of the following pages; but I have thought it as well to utter here a provisional warning against the lamentable error of proposing (just as people have encouraged a Zionist movement) to create a Sodomist movement and to rebuild Sodom. For, no sooner had they arrived there than the Sodomites would leave the town so as not to have the appearance of belonging to it, would take wives, keep mistresses in other cities where they would find, incidentally, every diversion that appealed to them. They would repair to Sodom only on days of supreme necessity, when their own town was empty, at those seasons when hunger drives the wolf from the woods. In other words, everything would go on very much as it does today in London, Berlin, Rome, Petrograd or Paris.

At all events, on the day in question, before paying my call on the Duchess, I did not look so far ahead, and I was distressed to find that, by my engrossment in the Jupien-Charlus conjunction, I had missed perhaps an opportunity of witnessing the fertilisation of the blossom by the bumble-bee.

PART TWO

Chapter One

As I was in no hurry to arrive at the Guermantes reception to which I wasn't certain I had been invited, I hung about outside; but the summer day seemed to be in no greater haste to stir. Although it was after nine o'clock, it was still the daylight that was giving the Luxor obelisk on the Place de la Concorde the appearance of pink nougat. Then it diluted the tint and changed the surface to a metallic substance, so that the obelisk not only became more precious but seemed more slender and almost flexible. One felt that one might have been able to twist this jewel, that one had perhaps already slightly bent it. The moon was now in the sky like a segment of an orange delicately peeled although nibbled at. But a few hours later it was to be fashioned of the most enduring gold. Nestling alone behind it, a poor little star was to serve as sole companion to the lonely moon, while the latter, keeping its friend protected but striding ahead more boldly, would brandish like an irresistible weapon, like an oriental symbol, its broad, magnificent golden crescent.

Outside the mansion of the Princesse de Guermantes I ran into the Duc de Châtellerault. I no longer remembered that half an hour earlier I had still been tormented by the fear—which in fact was soon to grip me again— that I might be entering the house uninvited. We get anxious, and it is sometimes long after the hour of danger, which a subsequent distraction has made us forget, that we remember our anxiety. I greeted the young Duke and

made my way into the house. But here I must first of all
record a trifling incident, which will enable us to understand something that was presently to occur.

There was one person who, on that evening as on the
previous evenings, had been thinking a great deal about
the Duc de Châtellerault, without however suspecting
who he was: this was the Princesse de Guermantes's usher
(styled at that time the "barker"). M. de Châtellerault, so
far from being one of the Princess's intimate friends, although he was one of her cousins, had been invited to her
house for the first time. His parents, who had not been on
speaking terms with her for ten years, had made it up
with her within the last fortnight, and, obliged to be out
of Paris that evening, had requested their son to represent
them. Now, a few days earlier, the Princess's usher had
met in the Champs-Elysées a young man whom he had
found charming but whose identity he had been unable to
establish. Not that the young man had not shown himself
as obliging as he had been generous. All the favours that
the usher had supposed that he would have to bestow
upon so young a gentleman, he had on the contrary received. But M. de Châtellerault was as cowardly as he was
rash; he was all the more determined not to unveil his
incognito since he did not know with whom he was dealing; his fear would have been far greater, although ill-
founded, if he had known. He had confined himself to
posing as an Englishman, and to all the passionate questions with which he was plied by the usher, desirous to
meet again a person to whom he was indebted for so
much pleasure and largesse, the Duke had merely replied,
from one end of the Avenue Gabriel to the other: "I do
not speak French."

Although, in spite of everything—remembering his cousin Gilbert's maternal ancestry—the Duc de Guermantes affected to find a touch of Courvoisier in the drawing-room of the Princesse de Guermantes-Bavière, the general estimate of that lady's social initiative and intellectual superiority was based upon an innovation that was to be found nowhere else in these circles. After dinner, however important the party that was to follow, the chairs at the Princesse de Guermantes's were arranged in such a way as to form little groups whose backs were necessarily sometimes turned on one another. The Princess then displayed her social sense by going to sit down, as though by preference, in one of these. She did not however hesitate to pick out and draw into it a member of another group. If, for instance, she had remarked to M. Detaille, who had naturally agreed with her, on the beauty of Mme de Villemur's neck, of which that lady's position in another group made her present a back view, the Princess had no hesitation in raising her voice: "Madame de Villemur, M. Detaille, wonderful painter that he is, has just been admiring your neck." Mme de Villemur interpreted this as a direct invitation to join in the conversation; with the agility of a practised horsewoman, she would swivel round slowly in her chair through three quadrants of a circle, and, without in any way disturbing her neighbours, come to rest almost facing the Princess. "You don't know M. Detaille?" exclaimed their hostess, for whom her guest's skilful and discreet about-face was not enough. "I don't know him, but I know his work," Mme de Villemur would reply with a respectful and winning air and an aptness which many of the onlookers envied her, addressing the while an imperceptible bow to the celebrated painter whom this invocation had not been sufficient to introduce to her in a formal manner. "Come, Monsieur Detaille," said the Princess, "let me introduce you to Mme de Villemur." That lady thereupon showed as much ingenuity in making room for the creator of the *Dream* as she had shown a moment earlier in wheeling round to face him. And the Princess would draw forward a chair for herself, having in fact addressed Mme de Ville-mur only in order to have an excuse for leaving the first group, in which she had spent the statutory ten minutes, and bestow a similar allowance of her time upon the second. In three quarters of an hour, all the groups would have received a visit from her, which seemed to have been determined in each instance by impulse and predilection, but had the paramount object of making it apparent how naturally "a great lady knows how to entertain." But now the guests for the reception were beginning to arrive and the lady of the house was seated not far from the door— erect and proud in her quasi-regal majesty, her eyes ablaze with their own incandescence—between two unattractive highnesses and the Spanish Ambassadress.

I stood waiting behind a number of guests who had arrived before me. Facing me was the Princess, whose beauty is probably not the only thing, among so many other beauties, that reminds me of this party. But the face of my hostess was so perfect, stamped like so beautiful a medal, that it has retained a commemorative virtue in my mind. The Princess was in the habit of saying to her guests when she met them a day or two before one of her parties: "You will come, won't you?" as though she felt a great desire to talk to them. But since, on the contrary, she had nothing to talk to them about, when they entered her presence she contented herself, without rising, with breaking off for an instant her vapid conversation with the two highnesses and the Ambassadress and thanking them with: "How good of you to have come," not because she thought that the guest had shown goodness by coming, but to enhance her own; then, at once dropping him back into the stream, she would add: "You will find M. de Guermantes by the garden door," so that the guest proceeded on his way and ceased to bother her. To some indeed she said nothing, contenting herself with showing them her admirable onyx eyes, as though they had come solely to visit an exhibition of precious stones.

The person immediately in front of me was the Duc de Châtellerault.

Having to respond to all the smiles, all the greetings waved to him from inside the drawing-room, he had not noticed the usher. But from the first moment the usher had recognised him. In another instant he would know the identity of this stranger, which he had so ardently desired to learn. When he asked his "Englishman" of the other evening what name he was to announce, the usher was not merely stirred, he considered that he was being indiscreet, indelicate. He felt that he was about to reveal to the whole world (which would, however, suspect nothing) a secret which it was criminal of him to ferret out like this and to proclaim in public. Upon hearing the guest's reply: "Le Duc de Châtellerault," he was overcome with such pride that he remained for a moment speechless. The Duke looked at him, recognised him, saw himself ruined, while the servant, who had recovered his composure and was sufficiently versed in heraldry to complete for himself an appellation that was too modest,

roared with a professional vehemence softened with intimate tenderness: "Son Altesse Monseigneur le Duc de
Châtellerault!" But now it was my turn to be announced.
Absorbed in contemplation of my hostess, who had not
yet seen me, I had not thought of the function—terrible
to me, although not in the same sense as to M. de
Châtellerault—of this usher garbed in black like an execu-
tioner, surrounded by a group of lackeys in the most
cheerful livery, strapping fellows ready to seize hold of an
intruder and fling him out. The usher asked me my
name, and I gave it to him as mechanically as the condemned man allows himself to be strapped to the block.
At once he lifted his head majestically and, before I could
beg him to announce me in a lowered tone so as to spare
my own feelings if I were not invited and those of the
Princesse de Guermantes if I were, roared the disquieting
syllables with a force capable of bringing down the roof.

The famous Huxley (whose grandson occupies a leading position in the English literary world of today) relates
that one of his patients no longer dared go out socially because often, on the very chair that was offered to her with
a courteous gesture, she saw an old gentleman already
seated. She was quite certain that either the gesture of invitation or the old gentleman's presence was a hallucination, for no one would have offered her a chair that was
already occupied. And when Huxley, to cure her, forced
her to reappear in society, she had a moment of painful
hesitation wondering whether the friendly sign that was
being made to her was the real thing, or whether, in obedience to a non-existent vision, she was about to sit down
in public upon the knees of a gentleman of flesh and
blood. Her brief uncertainty was agonising. Less so per-

haps than mine. From the moment I had taken in the
sound of my name, like the rumble that warns us of a
possible cataclysm, I was obliged, in order at least to
plead my good faith, and as though I were not tormented
by any doubts, to advance towards the Princess with a
resolute air.

She caught sight of me when I was still a few feet
away and (leaving me in no further doubt that I had been
the victim of a plot), instead of remaining seated, as she
had done for/her other guests, rose and came towards me.
A moment later, I was able to heave the sigh of relief of
Huxley's patient when, having made up her mind to sit
down in the chair, she found it vacant and realised that it
was the old gentleman who was the hallucination. The
Princess had just held out her hand to me with a smile.
She remained standing for some moments with the kind
of charm enshrined in the verse of Malherbe which ends:

To do them honour all the angels rise.

She apologised because the Duchess had not yet arrived,
as though I must be bored there without her. In offering
me this greeting, she executed around me, holding me by
the hand, a graceful pirouette, by the whirl of which I felt
myself swept away. I almost expected her to offer me
next, like the leader of a cotillon, an ivory-headed cane or
a wrist-watch. She did not, however, give me anything of
the sort, and as though, instead of dancing the boston, she
had been listening to a sacrosanct Beethoven quartet the
sublime strains of which she was afraid of interrupting,
she cut short the conversation there and then, or rather
did not begin it, and, still radiant at having seen me come

in, merely informed me where the Prince was to be found.

I moved away from her and did not venture to approach her again, feeling that she had absolutely nothing to say to me and that, in her immense good will, this marvellously handsome and stately woman, noble as were so many great ladies who stepped so proudly on to the scaffold, could only, short of offering me a draught of honeydew, repeat what she had already said to me twice: "You will find the Prince in the garden." Now, to go in search of the Prince was to feel my doubts revive in a different form.

In any case I should have to find somebody to introduce me. Above all the din of conversation was to be heard the inexhaustible chattering of M. de Charlus, talking to H.E. the Duke of Sidonia, whose acquaintance he had just made. Members of the same profession recognise each other instinctively; so do those with the same vice. M. de Charlus and M. de Sidonia had each of them immediately detected the other's, which was in both cases that of being monologuists in society, to the extent of not being able to stand any interruption. Having decided at once that, in the words of a famous sonnet, there was "no help," they had made up their minds, not to remain silent, but each to go on talking without any regard to what the other might say. This had resulted in the sort of confused babble produced in Molière's comedies by a number of people saying different things simultaneously. The Baron, with his deafening voice, was moreover certain of keeping the upper hand, of drowning the feeble voice of M. de Sidonia—without however discouraging him, for, whenever M. de Charlus paused for a moment to draw breath, the gap was filled by the murmuring of the Spanish grandee who had imperturbably continued his discourse. I might well have asked M. de Charlus to introduce me to the Prince de Guermantes, but I feared (and with good reason) that he might be displeased with me. I had treated him in the most ungrateful fashion by letting his offers pass unheeded for the second time and by giving him no sign of life since the evening when he had so affectionately escorted me home. And yet I could not plead the excuse of having anticipated the scene which I had witnessed that very afternoon enacted by himself and Jupien. I suspected nothing of the sort. It is true that shortly before this, when my parents reproached me for my laziness and for not having taken the trouble to write a line to M. de Charlus, I had accused them of wanting me to accept a degrading proposal. But anger alone, and the desire to hit upon the expression that would be most offensive to them, had dictated this mendacious retort. In reality, I had imagined nothing sensual, nothing sentimental even, underlying the Baron's offers. I had said this to my parents out of pure fantasy. But sometimes the future is latent in us without our knowing it, and our supposedly lying words foreshadow an imminent reality.

M. de Charlus would doubtless have forgiven me my want of gratitude. But what made him furious was that my presence this evening at the Princesse de Guermantes's, as for some time past at her cousin's, seemed to flout his solemn declaration: "There is no admission to those houses save through me." I had not followed the hierarchical path—a grave fault, a perhaps inexpiable crime. M. de Charlus knew all too well that the thunderbolts which he hurled at those who did not comply with his orders, or to whom he had taken a dislike, were beginning to be regarded by many people, however furiously he might brandish them, as mere pasteboard, and had no longer the force to banish anybody from anywhere. But he believed perhaps that his diminished power, still consider- able, remained intact in the eyes of novices like myself. And so I did not consider it very advisable to ask a favour of him at a party where the mere fact of my presence seemed an ironical refutation of his pretensions.

I was buttonholed at that moment by a rather vulgar man, Professor E——. He had been surprised to see me at the Guermantes'. I was no less surprised to see him there, for nobody of his sort had ever been seen before or was ever to be seen again in the Princess's drawing-room. He had just cured the Prince, after the last sacraments had been administered, of infectious pneumonia, and the special gratitude that Mme de Guermantes felt towards him was the reason for her thus departing from custom and inviting him to her house. As he knew absolutely no- body there, and could not wander about indefinitely by himself like a minister of death, having recognised me he had discovered for the first time in his life that he had an infinite number of things to say to me, which enabled him to keep some sort of countenance. This was one of the reasons for his approaching me. There was also another. He attached great importance to never being mistaken in his diagnoses. Now his correspondence was so voluminous that he could not always remember, when he had seen a patient once only, whether the disease had really followed the course that he had traced for it. The reader may per- haps remember that, immediately after my grandmother's stroke, I had taken her to see him, on the afternoon when he was having all his decorations stitched to his coat. After so long an interval, he had forgotten the formal announcement which had been sent to him at the time. "Your grandmother *is* dead, isn't she?" he said to me in a voice in which a semi-certainty calmed a slight apprehension. "Ah! indeed! Well, from the moment I saw her my prognosis was extremely grave, I remember it quite well."

It was thus that Professor E—— learned or recalled the death of my grandmother, and (I must say this to his credit, and to the credit of the medical profession as a whole) without displaying, without perhaps feeling any satisfaction. The mistakes made by doctors are innumerable. They err habitually on the side of optimism as to treatment, of pessimism as to the outcome. "Wine? In moderation, it can do you no harm, it's always a tonic . . . Sexual enjoyment? After all it's a natural function. But you mustn't overdo it, you understand. Excess in anything is wrong." At once, what a temptation to the patient to renounce those two life-givers, water and chastity! If, on the other hand, he has trouble with his heart, an excess of albumin, or something of the sort, he has very little hope. Disorders that are grave but purely functional are at once ascribed to an imaginary cancer. Useless to continue visits which are powerless to check an ineluctable disease. Let the patient, left to his own devices, thereupon subject himself to an implacable regimen and in time recover, or at any rate survive, and the doctor, to whom he touches his hat in the Avenue de l'Opéra when he was supposed to have long been lying in Père-Lachaise, will interpret the gesture as an act of sardonic insolence. An innocent stroll taken beneath his nose and venerable beard would arouse no greater wrath in the Assize Judge who two years earlier had sentenced the stroller, now passing

him with apparent impunity, to death. Doctors (we do not
here include them all, of course, and make a mental reser-
vation of certain admirable exceptions) are in general more
displeased, more irritated by the invalidation of their ver-
dicts than pleased by their execution. This explains why
Professor E——, despite the intellectual satisfaction that
he doubtless felt at finding that he had not been mistaken,
was able to speak to me with due regret of the blow that
had fallen upon us. He was in no hurry to cut short the
conversation, which kept him in countenance and gave
him a reason for remaining. He spoke to me of the heat-
wave through which we were passing, but although he
was a well-read man and capable of expressing himself in
good French, he asked me: "You are none the worse for
this hyperthermia?" The fact is that medicine has made
some slight advance in knowledge since Molière's days,
but none in its vocabulary. My interlocutor went on:
"The great thing is to avoid the sudations that are caused
by weather like this, especially in overheated rooms. You
can remedy them, when you go home and feel thirsty, by
the application of heat" (by which he apparently meant
hot drinks).

Owing to the circumstances of my grandmother's
death, the subject interested me, and I had recently read
in a book by a great specialist that perspiration was injuri-
ous to the kidneys by discharging through the skin something whose proper outlet was elsewhere. I thought with
regret of those dog-days at the time of my grandmother's
death, and was inclined to blame them for it. I did not
mention this to Dr E——, but of his own accord he said
to me: "The advantage of this very hot weather in which

perspiration is abundant is that the kidney is correspond-
ingly relieved." Medicine is not an exact science.

Clinging on to me, Professor E—— asked only not to
be forced to leave me. But I had just seen the Marquis de
Vaugoubert, bowing and scraping this way and that to the
Princesse de Guermantes after first taking a step backwards. M. de Norpois had recently introduced me to him
and I hoped that I might find in him a person capable of
presenting me to our host. The proportions of this work
do not permit me to explain here in consequence of what
incidents in his youth M. de Vaugoubert was one of the
few men (possibly the only man) in society who happened
to be in what is called in Sodom the "confidence" of
M. de Charlus. But, if our minister to the court of King
Theodosius had some of the same defects as the Baron,
they were only very pale reflexions of them. It was only in
an infinitely diluted, sentimental and inane form that he
displayed those alternations of affection and hatred
through which the desire to charm, and then the fear—
equally imaginary—of being, if not scorned, at any rate
unmasked, made the Baron pass. These alternations—
made ridiculous by a chastity, a "platonicism," to which
as a man of keen ambition he had, from the moment of
passing his examination, sacrificed all pleasure, above all
by his intellectual nullity—M. de Vaugoubert did nevertheless display. But whereas M. de Charlus's immoderate
eulogies were proclaimed with a positively dazzling eloquence, and seasoned with the subtlest, the most mordant
banter which marked a man for ever, M. de Vaugoubert's
predilections were by contrast expressed with the banality
of a man of the lowest intelligence, a man of fashionable

society, and a functionary, and his grievances (made up
on the spur of the moment like the Baron's) with a malevolence that was as witless as it was remorseless, and was
all the more startling in that it was invariably a direct
contradiction of what the minister had said six months
earlier and might soon perhaps be saying again: a regular-
ity of change which gave an almost astronomic poetry to
the various phases of M. de Vaugoubert's life, albeit apart
from this nobody was ever less suggestive of a star.

His response to my greeting had nothing in common
with that which I should have received from M. de Charlus. He imparted to it, in addition to countless manner-
isms which he supposed to be typical of the social and
diplomatic worlds, a brisk, cavalier, smiling air calculated
to make him seem on the one hand delighted with his existence—at a time when he was inwardly brooding over
the mortifications of a career with no prospect of advancement and threatened with enforced retirement—and on
the other hand young, virile and charming, when he could
see and no longer dared to go and examine in the glass
the wrinkles gathering on a face which he would have
wished to remain infinitely seductive. Not that he hoped
for real conquests, the mere thought of which filled him
with terror on account of gossip, scandal, blackmail. Having gone from an almost infantile corruption to an absolute continence dating from the day on which his
thoughts had turned to the Quai d'Orsay and he had begun to plan a great career for himself, he had the air of a
caged animal, casting in every direction glances expressive
of fear, craving and stupidity. This last was so dense that
it did not occur to him that the street-arabs of his adolescence were boys no longer, and when a newsvendor

bawled in his face: "*La Presse!*" he shuddered with terror even more than with longing, imagining himself recognised and denounced.

But in default of the pleasures sacrificed to the ingratitude of the Quai d'Orsay, M. de Vaugoubert—and it was for this that he was still anxious to please—was liable to sudden stirrings of the heart. He would pester the Ministry with endless letters, would employ every personal ruse, would draw shamelessly on the considerable credit of Mme de Vaugoubert (who, on account of her corpulence, her high birth, her masculine air, and above all the mediocrity of her husband, was reputed to be endowed with eminent capacities and to be herself for all practical purposes the minister), to introduce for no valid reason a young man destitute of all merit on to the staff of the legation. It is true that a few months or a few years later, the insignificant attaché had only to appear, without the least trace of any hostile intention, to have shown signs of coldness towards his chief for the latter, supposing himself scorned or betrayed, to devote the same hysterical ardour to punishing as formerly to gratifying him. He would move heaven and earth to have him recalled and the head of the political section would receive a letter daily, saying: "Why don't you hurry up and rid me of the brute? Give him a dressing-down in his own interest. What he needs is a slice of humble pie." The post of attaché at the court of King Theodosius was for that reason far from enjoyable. But in all other respects, thanks to his perfect common sense as a man of the world, M. de Vaugoubert was one of the best representatives of the French Government abroad. When a man who was reckoned a superior person, a Jacobin with an expert knowledge of all subjects,

replaced him later on, it was not long before war broke
out between France and the country over which that
monarch reigned.

M. de Vaugoubert, like M. de Charlus, did not care
to be the first to greet one. Both of them preferred to "respond," being constantly afraid of the gossip which the
person to whom otherwise they would have offered their
hand might have heard about them since their last meeting. In my case, M. de Vaugoubert had no need to ask
himself this question, for I had gone up of my own accord
to greet him, if only because of the difference in our ages.
He replied with an air of wonder and delight, his eyes
continuing to stray as though there had been a patch of
forbidden clover to be grazed on either side of me. I felt
that it would be more seemly to ask him to introduce me
to Mme de Vaugoubert before effecting the introduction
to the Prince, which I decided not to mention to him until
afterwards. The idea of making me acquainted with his
wife seemed to fill him with joy, for his own sake as well
as for hers, and he led me with a resolute step towards the
Marquise. Arriving in front of her, and indicating me
with his hand and eyes, with every conceivable mark of
consideration, he nevertheless remained silent and withdrew after a few moments, with a wriggling, sidelong motion, leaving me alone with his wife. She had at once
given me her hand, but without knowing to whom this
gesture of affability was addressed, for I realised that
M. de Vaugoubert had forgotten my name, perhaps even
had failed to recognise me, and being reluctant, out of politeness, to confess his ignorance, had made the introduction consist in a mere dumb-show. And so I was no
further advanced; how was I to get myself introduced to

my host by a woman who did not know my name? Worse
still, I found myself obliged to remain for some moments
chatting to Mme de Vaugoubert. And this irked me for
two reasons. I had no wish to remain all night at this
party, having arranged with Albertine (I had given her a
box for *Phèdre*) that she was to pay me a visit shortly before midnight. I was not in the least in love with her; in
asking her to come this evening, I was yielding to a
purely sensual desire, although we were at that torrid period of the year when sensuality, released, is more readily
inclined to visit the organs of taste, and seeks coolness
above all. More than for the kiss of a girl, it thirsts for orangeade, for a bath, or even to gaze at that peeled and
juicy moon that was quenching the thirst of heaven. I
counted however upon ridding myself, in Albertine's
company—which moreover reminded me of the coolness
of the sea—of the regrets I was bound to feel for many a
charming face (for it was a party quite as much for young
girls as for married women that the Princess was giving).
On the other hand, the face of the imposing Mme de
Vaugoubert, Bourbonesque and morose, was in no way attractive.

It was said at the Ministry, without any suggestion of
malice, that in their household it was the husband who
wore the petticoats and the wife the trousers. Now there
was more truth in this than was supposed. Mme de Vaugoubert really was a man. Whether she had always been
one, or had grown to be as I now saw her, matters little,
for in either case we are faced with one of the most touching miracles of nature which, in the latter alternative especially, makes the human kingdom resemble the kingdom
of flowers. On the former hypothesis—if the future Mme

de Vaugoubert had always been so heavily mannish—nature, by a fiendish and beneficent ruse, bestows on the
girl the deceptive aspect of a man. And the youth who
has no love for women and is seeking to be cured greets
with joy this subterfuge of discovering a bride who reminds him of a market porter. In the alternative case, if
the woman has not at first these masculine characteristics,
she adopts them by degrees, to please her husband, and
even unconsciously, by that sort of mimicry which makes
certain flowers assume the appearance of the insects which
they seek to attract. Her regret at not being loved, at not
being a man, makes her mannish. Indeed, quite apart
from the case that we are now considering, who has not
remarked how often the most normal couples end by resembling each other, at times even by exchanging qualities? A former German Chancellor, Prince von Bülow,
married an Italian. In the course of time it was remarked
on the Pincio how much Italian delicacy the Teutonic
husband had absorbed, and how much German coarseness
the Italian princess. To go outside the confines of the
laws which we are now tracing, everyone knows an eminent French diplomat whose origins were suggested only
by his name, one of the most illustrious in the East. As
he matured, as he aged, the oriental whom no one had
even suspected in him emerged, and now when we see
him we regret the absence of the fez that would complete
the picture.[3]

To revert to habits completely unknown to the ambassador whose ancestrally thickened profile we have just
recalled, Mme de Vaugoubert personified the acquired or
predestined type, the immortal example of which is the
Princess Palatine, never out of a riding habit, who, having

borrowed from her husband more than his virility, embracing the defects of the men who do not care for women, reports in her gossipy letters the mutual relations of all the great noblemen of the court of Louis XIV. One of the reasons which enhance still further the masculine air of women like Mme de Vaugoubert is that the neglect which they receive from their husbands, and the shame that they feel at such neglect, gradually dry up everything that is womanly in them. They end by acquiring both the good and the bad qualities which their husbands lack. The more frivolous, effeminate, indiscreet their husbands are, the more they grow into the charmless effigies of the virtues which their husbands ought to practise.

Traces of opprobrium, boredom, indignation, tarnished the regular features of Mme de Vaugoubert. Alas, I felt that she was considering me with interest and curiosity as one of those young men who appealed to M. de Vaugoubert and whom she herself would so much have liked to be now that her ageing husband showed a preference for youth. She was gazing at me with the close attention shown by provincial ladies who from an illustrated catalogue copy the tailor-made dress so becoming to the charming person in the picture (actually the same person on every page, but deceptively multiplied into different creatures, thanks to the differences of pose and the variety of attire). The instinctive attraction which urged Mme de Vaugoubert towards me was so strong that she went as far as to seize me by the arm so that I might take her to get a glass of orangeade. But I extricated myself on the pretext that I must presently be going, and had not yet been introduced to our host.

The distance between me and the garden door where

he stood talking to a group of people was not very great. But it alarmed me more than if, in order to cross it, I had had to expose myself to a continuous hail of fire.

A number of women from whom I felt that I might be able to secure an introduction were in the garden, where, while feigning an ecstatic admiration, they were at a loss for something to do. Parties of this sort are as a rule premature. They have little reality until the following day, when they occupy the attention of the people who were not invited. A real writer, devoid of the foolish self-esteem of so many literary people, when he reads an article by a critic who has always expressed the greatest admiration for his works and sees the names of various inferior writers mentioned but not his own, has no time to stop and consider what might be to him a matter for astonishment; his books are calling him. But a society woman has nothing to do and, on seeing in the *Figaro*: "Last night the Prince and Princesse de Guermantes gave a large party," etc., exclaims: "What! Only three days ago I talked to Marie-Gilbert for an hour, and she never said a word about it!" and racks her brain to discover how she can have offended the Guermantes. It must be said that, so far as the Princess's parties were concerned, the astonishment was sometimes as great among those who were invited as among those who were not. For they would burst forth at the moment when one least expected them, and mobilised people whose existence Mme de Guermantes had forgotten for years. And almost all society people are so insignificant that others of their sort adopt, in judging them, only the measure of their social success, cherish them if they are invited, detest them if they are omitted. As to the latter, if it was the fact that the

Princess did not invite them even though they were her friends, that was often due to her ·fear of annoying "Palamède," who had excommunicated them. And so I might be certain that she had not spoken of me to M. de Charlus, for otherwise I should not have found myself there. He meanwhile was posted between the house and the garden, beside the German Ambassador, leaning upon the balustrade of the great staircase which led from the garden to the house, so that the other guests, in spite of the three or four female admirers who were grouped round the Baron and almost concealed him, were obliged to greet him as they passed. He responded by naming each of them in turn. And one heard successively: "Good evening, Monsieur du Hazay, good evening, Madame de La Tour du Pin-Verclause, good evening, Madame de La Tour du Pin-Gouvernet, good evening, Philibert, good evening, my dear Ambassadress," and so on. This created a continuous yapping interspersed with benevolent suggestions or inquiries (the answers to which he ignored), which M. de Charlus addressed to them in an artificially soft and benign tone of voice that betrayed his indifference: "Take care the child doesn't catch cold, it's always rather damp in the gardens. Good evening, Madame de Brantes. Good evening, Madame de Mecklembourg. Have you brought your daughter? Is she wearing that delicious pink frock? Good evening, Saint-Géran." True, there was an element of pride in this attitude. M. de Charlus was aware that he was a Guermantes, and that he occupied a predominant place at this festivity. But there was more in it than pride, and the very word festivity suggested, to the man with aesthetic gifts, the luxurious, rarefied sense that it might bear if it were being given not by people in contemporary society but in a painting by Carpaccio or Veronese. It is even more probable that the German prince M. de Charlus was must rather have been picturing to himself the reception that occurs in *Tannhäuser*, and himself as the Margrave, standing at the entrance to the Warburg with a kind word of condescension for each of the guests, while their procession into the castle or the park is greeted by the long phrase, a hundred times repeated, of the famous March.

Meanwhile I had to make up my mind. I recognised beneath the trees various women with whom I was on more or less friendly terms, but they seemed transformed because they were at the Princess's and not at her cousin's, and because I saw them seated not in front of Dresden china plates but beneath the boughs of a chestnut-tree. The elegance of the setting mattered nothing. Had it been infinitely less elegant than at "Oriane's," I should have felt the same uneasiness. If the electric light in our drawing-room fails, and we are obliged to replace it with oil lamps, everything seems altered. I was rescued from my uncertainty by Mme de Souvré. "Good evening," she said, coming towards me. "Have you seen the Duchesse de Guermantes lately?" She excelled in giving to remarks of this sort an intonation which proved that she was not uttering them from sheer silliness, like people who, not knowing what to talk about, come up to you again and again to mention some mutual acquaintance, often extremely vague. She had on the contrary a subtle way of intimating with her eyes: "Don't imagine for a moment that I haven't recognised you. You are the young man I met at the Duchesse de Guermantes's. I remember very well." Unfortunately, the patronage extended to me by this remark, stupid in appearance but delicate in intention, was extremely fragile, and vanished as soon as I tried to make use of it. Mme de Souvré had the art, if called upon to convey a request to some influential person, of appearing at once in the petitioner's eyes to be recommending him, and in those of the influential person not to be recommending the petitioner, so that this ambiguous gesture gave her a credit balance of gratitude with the latter without putting her in debit with the former. Encouraged by this lady's civilities to ask her to introduce me to M. de Guermantes, I found that she took advantage of a moment when our host was not looking in our direction, laid a motherly hand on my shoulder, and, smiling at the averted face of the Prince who could not see her, thrust me towards him with a would-be protective but deliberately ineffectual gesture which left me stranded almost where I had started. Such is the cowardice of society people.

That of a lady who came to greet me, addressing me by my name, was greater still. I tried to recall hers as I talked to her; I remembered quite well having met her at dinner, and could remember things that she had said. But my attention, concentrated upon the inward region in which these memories of her lingered, was unable to discover her name there. It was there none the less. My thoughts began playing a sort of game with it to grasp its outlines, its initial letter, and finally to bring the whole name to light. It was labour in vain; I could more or less sense its mass, its weight, but as for its forms, confronting them with the shadowy captive lurking in the interior darkness, I said to myself: "That's not it." Certainly my mind would have been capable of creating the most diffi-

cult names. Unfortunately, it was not called upon to create but to reproduce. Any mental activity is easy if it need
not be subjected to reality. Here I was forced to subject
myself to it. Finally, in a flash, the name came back to me
in its entirety: "Madame d'Arpajon." I am wrong in saying that it came, for it did not, I think, appear to me by a
spontaneous propulsion. Nor do I think that the many
faint memories associated with the lady, to which I did
not cease to appeal for help (by such exhortations as:
"Come now, it's the lady who is a friend of Mme de Souvré, who feels for Victor Hugo so artless an admiration
mingled with so much alarm and horror")—nor do I think
that all these memories, hovering between me and her
name, served in any way to bring it to light. That great
game of hide and seek which is played in our memory
when we seek to recapture a name does not entail a series
of gradual approximations. We see nothing, then suddenly the correct name appears and is very different from
what we thought we were guessing. It is not the name
that has come to us. No, I believe rather that, as we go on
living, we spend our time moving further away from the
zone in which a name is distinct, and it was by an exercise of my will and attention, which heightened the acuteness of my inward vision, that all of a sudden I had
pierced the semi-darkness and seen daylight. In any case,
if there are transitions between oblivion and memory,
then these transitions are unconscious. For the intermediate names through which we pass before finding the real
name are themselves false, and bring us nowhere nearer to
it. They are not even, strictly speaking, names at all, but
often mere consonants which are not to be found in the
recaptured name. And yet this labour of the mind strug-

gling from blankness to reality is so mysterious that it is possible after all that these false consonants are preliminary poles clumsily stretched out to help us hook ourselves to the correct name. "All this," the reader will remark, "tells us nothing as to the lady's failure to oblige; but since you have made so long a digression, allow me, dear author, to waste another moment of your time by telling you that it is a pity that, young as you were (or as your hero was, if he isn't you), you had already so feeble a memory that you could not remember the name of a lady whom you knew quite well." It is indeed a pity, dear reader. And sadder than you think when one feels that it heralds the time when names and words will vanish from the bright zone of consciousness and one must for ever cease to name to oneself the people whom one has known most intimately. It is indeed regrettable that one should require this effort, when still young, to remember names which one knows well. But if this infirmity occurred only in the case of names barely known and quite naturally forgotten, names one wouldn't want to take the trouble of remembering, the infirmity would not be without its advantages. "And what are they, may I ask?" Well, sir, infirmity alone makes us take notice and learn, and enables us to analyse mechanisms of which otherwise we should know nothing. A man who falls straight into bed night after night, and ceases to live until the moment when he wakes and rises, will surely never dream of making, I don't say great discoveries, but even minor observations about sleep. He scarcely knows that he is asleep. A little insomnia is not without its value in making us appreciate sleep, in throwing a ray of light upon that darkness. An unfailing memory is not a very powerful incentive to the

study of the phenomena of memory. "Well, did Mme
d'Arpajon introduce you to the Prince?" No, but be quiet
and let me go on with my story.

Mme d'Arpajon was even more cowardly than Mme
de Souvré, but there was more excuse for her cowardice.
She knew that she had always had very little influence in
society. This influence, such as it was, had been reduced
still further by her liaison with the Duc de Guermantes;
his desertion of her dealt it the final blow. The ill-humour
aroused in her by my request that she should introduce
me to the Prince produced a silence which she was ingenuous enough to imagine a convincing pretence of not having heard what I said. She was not even aware that her
anger made her frown. Perhaps, on the other hand, she
was aware of it, did not bother about the inconsistency,
and made use of it for the lesson in tact which she was
thus able to teach me without undue rudeness; I mean a
silent lesson, but none the less eloquent for that.

Apart from this, Mme d'Arpajon was extremely nettled, for many eyes were raised in the direction of a Re-
naissance balcony at the corner of which, instead of one of
those monumental statues which were so often used as ornaments at that period, there leaned, no less sculptural
than they, the magnificent Duchesse de Surgis-le-Duc,
who had recently succeeded Mme d'Arpajon in the affections of Basin de Guermantes. Beneath the flimsy white
tulle which protected her from the cool night air, one saw
the supple form of a winged victory.

I had no one else to turn to but M. de Charlus, who
had withdrawn to a room downstairs which opened on to
the garden. I had plenty of time (as he was pretending to
be absorbed in a fictitious game of whist which enabled

him to appear not to notice people) to admire the deliberate, artful simplicity of his evening coat which, by the merest trifles which only a tailor's eye could have picked out, had the air of a "Harmony in Black and White" by Whistler; black, white and red, rather, for M. de Charlus was wearing, suspended from a broad ribbon over his shirt-front, the cross, in white, black and red enamel, of a Knight of the religious Order of Malta. At that moment the Baron's game was interrupted by Mme de Gallardon, escorting her nephew, the Vicomte de Courvoisier, a young man with a pretty face and an impertinent air. "Cousin," said Mme de Gallardon, "allow me to introduce my nephew Adalbert. Adalbert, you remember the famous Uncle Palamède of whom you have heard so much." "Good evening, Madame de Gallardon," M. de Charlus replied. And he added, without so much as a glance at the young man: "Good evening, sir," with a truculent air and in a tone so violently discourteous that everyone was stunned. Perhaps M. de Charlus, knowing that Mme de Gallardon had her doubts as to his morals and had once been unable to resist the temptation to hint at them, was determined to nip in the bud any scandal that she might embroider upon a friendly reception of her nephew, and at the same time make a resounding profession of indifference with regard to young men in general; perhaps he did not consider that the said Adalbert had responded to his aunt's words with a sufficiently respectful air; perhaps, desirous of making his mark later with so attractive a cousin, he wished to give himself the advantage of a pre-emptive attack, like those sovereigns who, before engaging upon diplomatic action, reinforce it with an act of war.

It was not so difficult as I supposed to secure M. de Charlus's consent to my request that he should introduce me to the Prince de Guermantes. For one thing, in the course of the last twenty years this Don Quixote had tilted against so many windmills (often relatives who he claimed had behaved badly to him), he had so frequently banned people as being "impossible to have in the house" from being invited by various male or female Guermantes, that the latter were beginning to be afraid of quarrelling with all the people they liked, of depriving themselves throughout their lives of the society of certain newcomers they were curious about, by espousing the thunderous but unexplained grudges of a brother-in-law or cousin who expected them to abandon wife, brother, children for his sake. More intelligent than the other Guermantes, M. de Charlus realised that people were ceasing to pay attention to more than one in every two of his vetoes, and, with an eye to the future, fearing it might be he himself of whose society they deprived themselves, had begun to cut his losses, to lower, as the saying is, his sights. Furthermore, if he had the faculty of keeping up a feud with a detested person for months, for years on end—to such a one he would not have tolerated their sending an invitation, and would have fought like a street porter even against a queen, the status of the person who stood in his way ceasing to count for anything in his eyes—on the other hand, his explosions of rage were too frequent not to be somewhat fragmentary. "The imbecile, the scoundrel! We'll put him in his place, sweep him into the gutter, where unfortunately he won't be innocuous to the health of the town," he would scream, even when he was alone in his own room, on reading a letter that he

considered irreverent, or on recalling some remark that
had been repeated to him. But a fresh outburst against a
second imbecile cancelled the first, and the former victim
had only to show due deference for the fit of rage that he
had occasioned to be forgotten, it not having lasted long
enough to establish a foundation of hatred on which to
build. And so, perhaps—despite his bad temper towards
me—I might have been successful when I asked him to
introduce me to the Prince, had I not been so ill-inspired
as to add, from a scruple of conscience, and so that he
might not suppose me guilty of the indelicacy of entering
the house on the off chance, counting upon him to enable
me to remain there: "You are aware that I know them
quite well, the Princess was very nice to me." "Very well,
if you know them, why do you need me to introduce
you?" he replied in a waspish tone, and, turning his back,
resumed his make-believe game with the Nuncio, the
German Ambassador and another personage whom I
didn't know by sight.

Then, from the depths of those gardens where in days
past the Duc d'Aiguillon used to breed rare animals, there
came to my ears, through the great open doors, the sound
of a nose that was sniffing up all those refinements, determined to miss none of them. The sound approached, I
moved at a venture in its direction, with the result that
the words "Good evening" were murmured in my ear by
M. de Bréauté, not like the rusty metallic sound of a knife
being sharpened on a grindstone, even less like the cry of
the wild boar, devastator of tilled fields, but like the voice
of a possible saviour.

Less influential than Mme de Souvré, but less deeply
ingrained than she with unwillingness to oblige, far more

at his ease with the Prince than was Mme d'Arpajon, entertaining some illusions, perhaps, as to my position in the
Guermantes set, or perhaps knowing more about it than
myself, he was, however, for the first few moments difficult to pin down, for he was turning in every direction,
with quivering and distended nostrils, staring inquisitively
through his monocle as though confronted with five hundred masterpieces. But, having heard my request, he received it with satisfaction, led me towards the Prince and
presented me to him with a lip-smacking, ceremonious,
vulgar air, as though he had been handing him a plate of
cakes with a word of commendation. Whereas the Duc de
Guermantes's greeting was, when he chose, friendly, instinct with good fellowship, cordial and familiar, I found
that of the Prince stiff, solemn and haughty. He barely
smiled at me, addressed me gravely as "Sir." I had often
heard the Duke make fun of his cousin's hauteur. But
from the first words that he addressed to me, which by
their cold and serious tone formed the most complete contrast with Basin's comradely language, I realised at once
that the fundamentally disdainful man was the Duke, who
spoke to you at your first meeting with him as "man to
man," and that, of the two cousins, the one who was genuinely simple and natural was the Prince. I found in his
reserve a stronger feeling if not of equality, for that would
have been inconceivable to him, at least of the consideration which one may show for an inferior, such as may be
found in all strongly hierarchical societies, in the Law
Courts, for instance, or in a Faculty, where a public pros-
ecutor or a dean, conscious of their high charge, conceal
perhaps more genuine simplicity, and, when you come to
know them better, more kindness and cordiality, beneath

their traditional aloofness than the more modern brethren beneath their jocular affectation of camaraderie. "Do you intend to follow the career of your distinguished father?" he inquired with a distant but interested air. I answered the question briefly, realising that he had asked it only out of politeness, and moved away to allow him to welcome new arrivals.

I caught sight of Swann, and wanted to speak to him, but at that moment I saw that the Prince de Guermantes, instead of waiting where he was to receive the greeting of Odette's husband, had immediately carried him off, with the force of a suction pump, to the further end of the garden, in order, some people said, "to show him the door."

So bewildered in the midst of the glittering company that I did not learn until two days later, from the newspapers, that a Czech orchestra had been playing throughout the evening, and that fireworks had been going off in constant succession, I recovered some power of attention with the thought of going to look at the famous Hubert Robert fountain.

It could be seen from a distance, slender, motionless, rigid, set apart in a clearing surrounded by fine trees, several of which were as old as itself, only the lighter fall of its pale and quivering plume stirring in the breeze. The eighteenth century had refined the elegance of its lines, but, by fixing the style of the jet, seemed to have arrested its life; at this distance one had the impression of art rather than the sensation of water. Even the moist cloud that was perpetually gathering at its summit preserved the character of the period like those that assemble in the sky round the palaces of Versailles. But from a closer view one realised that, while it respected, like the stones of an ancient palace, the design traced for it beforehand, it was a constantly changing stream of water that, springing upwards and seeking to obey the architect's original orders, performed them to the letter only by seeming to infringe them, its thousand separate bursts succeeding only from afar in giving the impression of a single thrust. This was in reality as often interrupted as the scattering of the fall, whereas from a distance it had appeared to me dense, inflexible, unbroken in its continuity. From a little nearer, one saw that this continuity, apparently complete, was assured, at every point in the ascent of the jet where it must otherwise have been broken, by the entering into line, by the lateral incorporation, of a parallel jet which mounted higher than the first and was itself, at a greater altitude which was however already a strain upon its endurance, relieved by a third. From close to, exhausted drops could be seen falling back from the column of water, passing their sisters on the way up, and at times, torn and scattered, caught in an eddy of the night air, disturbed by this unremitting surge, floating awhile before being drowned in the basin. They teased with their hesitations, with their journey in the opposite direction, and blurred with their soft vapour the vertical tension of the shaft that bore aloft an oblong cloud composed of countless tiny drops but seemingly painted in an unchanging golden brown which rose, unbreakable, fixed, slender and swift, to mingle with the clouds in the sky. Unfortunately, a gust of wind was enough to scatter it obliquely on the ground; at times indeed a single disobedient jet swerved and, had they not kept a respectful distance, would have drenched to their skins the incautious crowd of gazers.

One of these little accidents, which occurred only

when the breeze freshened for a moment, was somewhat unpleasant. Mme d'Arpajon had been led to believe that the Duc de Guermantes, who in fact had not yet arrived, was with Mme de Surgis in one of the galleries of pink marble to which one ascended by the double colonnade, hollowed out of the wall, which rose from the brink of the fountain. Now, just as Mme d'Arpajon was making for one of these colonnades, a strong gust of warm air deflected the jet of water and inundated the fair lady so completely that, the water streaming down from her low neckline inside her dress, she was as thoroughly soaked as if she had been plunged into a bath. Whereupon, a few feet away, a rhythmical roar resounded, loud enough to be heard by a whole army, and at the same time periodically prolonged as though it were being addressed not to the army as a whole but to each unit in turn; it was the Grand Duke Vladimir, laughing whole-heartedly on seeing the immersion of Mme d'Arpajon, one of the funniest sights, as he was never tired of repeating afterwards, that he had ever seen in his life. Some charitable persons having suggested to the Muscovite that a word of sympathy from himself was perhaps called for and would give pleasure to the lady who, notwithstanding her forty years and more, mopping herself up with her scarf without appealing to anyone for help, was bravely extricating herself in spite of the water that was mischievously spilling over the edge of the basin, the Grand Duke, who had a kind heart, felt that he ought to comply, and before the last military tattoo of his laughter had altogether subsided, one heard a fresh roar, even more vociferous than the last. "Bravo, old girl!" he cried, clapping his hands as though at the theatre. Mme d'Arpajon was not at all pleased that her dexterity should be commended at the expense of her youth. And when someone remarked to her, in a voice drowned by the roar of the water, over which the princely thunder could nevertheless be heard: "I think His Imperial Highness said something to you," "No! It was to Mme de Souvré," was her reply.

I passed through the gardens and returned by the stair, upon which the absence of the Prince, who had vanished with Swann, swelled the crowd of guests round M. de Charlus, just as, when Louis XIV was not at Versailles, there was a more numerous attendance upon Monsieur, his brother. I was stopped on my way by the Baron, while behind me two ladies and a young man came up to greet him.

"It's nice to see you here," he said to me, holding out his hand. "Good evening, Madame de La Trémoïlle, good evening, my dear Herminie." But doubtless the memory of what he had said to me as to his own supreme position in the Hôtel Guermantes made him wish to appear to be drawing, from a circumstance which displeased him but which he had been unable to prevent, a satisfaction which his lordly insolence and hysterical glee immediately invested in a cloak of exaggerated sarcasm: "It's nice," he went on, "but above all it's extremely funny." And he broke into peals of laughter which appeared to be indicative at once of his amusement and of the inadequacy of human speech to express it. Certain of the guests, meanwhile, who knew both how difficult he was of access and how prone to offensive outbursts, had been drawn towards us by curiosity and now, with an almost indecent haste, took to their heels. "Come, now, don't be cross," he said to me, patting me gently on the shoulder, "you know I'm fond of you. Good evening, Antioche, good evening, Louis-René. Have you been to look at the fountain?" he asked me in a tone that was more affirmative than questioning. "Very pretty, is it not? Marvellous though it is, it could be better still, naturally, if certain things were removed, and then there would be nothing like it in France. But even as it stands, it's quite one of the best things. Bréauté will tell you that it was a mistake to put lamps round it, to try and make people forget that it was he who was responsible for that absurd idea. But on the whole he didn't manage to spoil it too much. It's far more difficult to disfigure a great work of art than to create one. Not that we hadn't a vague suspicion all along that Bréauté wasn't quite a match for Hubert Robert."

I drifted back into the stream of guests who were going into the house. "Have you seen my delicious cousin Oriane lately?" asked the Princess who had now deserted her post by the door and with whom I was making my way back to the rooms. "She's coming tonight. I saw her this afternoon," my hostess added, "and she promised she would. Incidentally, I gather you'll be dining with us both to meet the Queen of Italy at the embassy on Thursday. There'll be every imaginable royalty—it will be most alarming." They could not in any way alarm the Princesse de Guermantes, whose rooms swarmed with them and who would say "my little Coburgs" as she might have said "my little dogs." And so she said: "It will be most alarming," out of sheer silliness, a characteristic which, in society people, overrides even their vanity. With regard to her own genealogy, she knew less than a history graduate. As regards the people of her circle, she liked to show that she knew the nicknames with which they had been la-

belled. Having asked me whether I was dining the following week with the Marquise de la Pommelière, who was
often called "la Pomme," the Princess, having elicited a
negative reply, remained silent for some moments. Then,
without any other motive than a deliberate display of involuntary erudition, banality, and conformity to the prevailing spirit, she added: "She's quite an agreeable
woman, la Pomme!"

While the Princess was talking to me, it so happened
that the Duc and Duchesse de Guermantes made their
entrance. But I was unable to go at once to meet them,
for I was waylaid by the Turkish Ambassadress, who,
pointing to our hostess whom I had just left, exclaimed as
she seized me by the arm: "Ah! What a delightful woman
the Princess is! What a superior person! I feel sure that, if
I were a man," she went on, with a trace of oriental
servility and sensuality, "I would give my life for that heavenly creature." I replied that I did indeed find her charming, but that I knew her cousin the Duchess better. "But
there is no comparison," said the Ambassadress. "Oriane
is a charming society woman who gets her wit from
Mémé and Babal, whereas Marie-Gilbert is *somebody*."

I never much like to be told like this, without a
chance to reply, what I ought to think about people whom
I know. And there was no reason why the Turkish Ambassadress should be in any way better qualified than myself to judge the merits of the Duchesse de Guermantes.
On the other hand (and this also explained my irritation
with the Ambassadress), the defects of a mere acquaintance, and even of a friend, are to us real poisons, against
which we are fortunately immunised. But, without applying any standard of scientific comparison and talking of

anaphylaxis, we may say that, at the heart of our friendly or purely social relations, there lurks a hostility momentarily cured but sporadically recurrent. As a rule, we suffer little from these poisons so long as people are "natural." By saying "Babal" and "Mémé" to indicate people with whom she was not acquainted, the Turkish Ambassadress suspended the effects of the immunisation which normally made me find her tolerable. She irritated me, and this was all the more unfair inasmuch as she did not speak like this to make me think that she was an intimate friend of "Mémé," but owing to a too rapid education which made her name these noble lords in accordance with what she believed to be the custom of the country. She had crowded her course into a few months instead of working her way up gradually.

But on thinking it over, I found another reason for my disinclination to remain in the Ambassadress's company. It was not so very long since, at "Oriane's," this same diplomatic personage had said to me, with a purposeful and serious air, that she found the Princesse de Guermantes frankly antipathetic. I felt that I need not stop to consider this change of front: the invitation to the party this evening had brought it about. The Ambassadress was perfectly sincere in saying that the Princesse de Guermantes was a sublime creature. She had always thought so. But, having never before been invited to the Princess's house, she had felt herself bound to give this non-invitation the appearance of a deliberate abstention on principle. Now that she had been asked, and would presumably continue to be asked in the future, she could give free expression to her feelings. There is no need, in accounting for nine out of ten of the opinions that we hold about other people, to go so far as crossed love or exclusion from public office. Our judgment remains uncertain: the withholding or bestowal of an invitation determines it. At all events, the Turkish Ambassadress, as the Duchesse de Guermantes remarked while making a tour of inspection through the rooms with me, "looked well." She was, above all, extremely useful. The real stars of society are tired of appearing there. He who is curious to gaze at them must often migrate to another hemisphere, where they are more or less alone. But women like the Ottoman Ambassadress, a newcomer to society, are never weary of shining there, and, so to speak, everywhere at once. They are of value at entertainments of the sort known as receptions or routs, to which they would let themselves be dragged from their deathbeds rather than miss one. They are the supers upon whom a hostess can always count, determined never to miss a party. Hence foolish young men, unaware that they are false stars, take them for the queens of fashion, whereas it would require a formal lecture to explain to them by virtue of what reasons Mme Standish, who remains unknown to them, painting cushions far away from society, is at least as great a lady as the Duchesse de Doudeauville.

In the ordinary course of life, the eyes of the Duchesse de Guermantes were abstracted and slightly melancholy; she made them sparkle with a flame of wit only when she had to greet some friend or other, precisely as though the said friend had been some witty remark, some charming touch, some treat for delicate palates, the sampling of which has brought an expression of refined delight to the face of the connoisseur. But at big receptions, as she had too many greetings to bestow, she de-

cided that it would be tiring to have to switch off the
light after each. Just as a literary enthusiast, when he goes
to the theatre to see a new play by one of the masters of
the stage, testifies to his certainty that he is not going to
spend a dull evening by having, while he hands his hat
and coat to the attendant, his lip adjusted in readiness for
a sapient smile, his eye kindled for knowing approval;
similarly it was from the very moment of her arrival that
the Duchess lit up for the whole evening. And while she
was handing over her evening cloak, of a magnificent
Tiepolo red, exposing a huge collar of rubies round her
neck, having cast over her dress that final rapid, meticulous and exhaustive dressmaker's glance which is also that
of a woman of the world, Oriane made sure that her eyes
were sparkling no less brightly than her other jewels. In
vain did sundry "kind friends" such as M. de Jouville
fling themselves upon the Duke to keep him from entering: "But don't you know that poor Mama is at the point
of death? He has just been given the last sacraments." "I
know, I know," answered M. de Guermantes, thrusting
the tiresome fellow aside in order to enter the room. "The
viaticum has had an excellent effect," he added with a
smile of pleasure at the thought of the ball which he was
determined not to miss after the Prince's party. "We
didn't want people to know that we had come back," the
Duchess said to me, unaware of the fact that the Princess
had already disproved this statement by telling me that
she had seen her cousin for a moment and that she had
promised to come. The Duke, after a protracted stare
with which he proceeded to crush his wife for the space of
five minutes, observed: "I told Oriane about your misgivings." Now that she saw that they were unfounded, and

that she need take no action to dispel them, she pronounced them absurd, and went on chaffing me about
them. "The idea of supposing that you weren't invited!
One's always invited! Besides, there was me. Do you
think I couldn't have got you an invitation to my cousin's
house?" I must admit that subsequently she often did
things for me that were far more difficult; nevertheless, I
took care not to interpret her words in the sense that I
had been too modest. I was beginning to learn the exact
value of the language, spoken or mute, of aristocratic affability, an affability that is happy to shed balm upon the
sense of inferiority of those towards whom it is directed,
though not to the point of dispelling that inferiority, for
in that case it would no longer have any *raison d'être*.
"But you are our equal, if not our superior," the Guermantes seemed, in all their actions, to be saying; and they
said it in the nicest way imaginable, in order to be loved
and admired, but not to be believed; that one should discern the fictitious character of this affability was what
they called being well-bred; to suppose it to be genuine, a
sign of ill-breeding. Shortly after this, as it happened, I
was to receive a lesson which finally enlightened me, with
the most perfect accuracy, as to the extent and limits of
certain forms of aristocratic affability. It was at an afternoon party given by the Duchesse de Montmorency for
the Queen of England. There was a sort of royal procession to the buffet, at the head of which walked Her
Majesty on the arm of the Duc de Guermantes. I happened to arrive at that moment. With his free hand the
Duke conveyed to me, from a distance of nearly fifty
yards, countless signs of friendly welcome, which appeared to mean that I need not be afraid to approach, that

I should not be devoured alive instead of the sandwiches. But I, who was becoming word-perfect in the language of the court, instead of going even one step nearer, made a deep bow from where I was, without smiling, the sort of bow that I should have made to someone I scarcely knew, then proceeded in the opposite direction. Had I written a masterpiece, the Guermantes would have given me less credit for it than I earned by that bow. Not only did it not pass unperceived by the Duke, although he had that day to acknowledge the greetings of more than five hundred people; it also caught the eye of the Duchess, who, happening to meet my mother, told her of it, and, so far from suggesting that I had done wrong, that I ought to have gone up to him, said that her husband had been lost in admiration of my bow, that it would have been impossible for anyone to put more into it. They never ceased to find in that bow every possible merit, without however mentioning the one which had seemed the most precious of all, to wit that it had been tactful; nor did they cease to pay me compliments which I understood to be even less a reward for the past than a hint for the future, after the fashion of a hint delicately conveyed to his pupils by the head of an educational establishment: "Do not forget, my boys, that these prizes are intended not so much for you as for your parents, so that they may send you back next term." So it was that Mme de Marsantes, when someone from a different world entered her circle, would praise in his hearing those unobtrusive people "who are there when you want them and the rest of the time let you forget their existence," as one indirectly reminds a servant who smells that the practice of taking a bath is beneficial to the health.

While, before she had even left the entrance hall, I
was talking to Mme de Guermantes, I could hear a voice
of a sort which henceforth I was able to identify without
the least possibility of error. It was, in this particular instance, the voice of M. de Vaugoubert talking to M. de
Charlus. A skilled physician need not even make his patient unbutton his shirt, nor listen to his breathing—the
sound of his voice is enough. How often, in time to come,
was my ear to be caught in a drawing-room by the intonation or laughter of some man whose artificial voice, for
all that he was reproducing exactly the language of his
profession or the manners of his class, affecting a stern
aloofness or a coarse familiarity, was enough to indicate
"He is a Charlus" to my trained ear, like the note of a
tuning-fork! At that moment the entire staff of one of the
embassies went past, pausing to greet M. de Charlus. For
all that my discovery of the sort of malady in question
dated only from that afternoon (when I had surprised
M. de Charlus with Jupien) I should have had no need to
ask questions or to sound the chest before giving a diag-
nosis. But M. de Vaugoubert, when talking to M. de
Charlus, appeared uncertain. And yet he should have
known where he stood after the doubts of his adolescence.
The invert believes himself to be the only one of his kind
in the universe; it is only in later years that he imagines—
another exaggeration—that the unique exception is the
normal man. But, ambitious and timorous, M. de Vaugoubert had not for many years past surrendered himself
to what would to him have meant pleasure. The career of
diplomacy had had the same effect upon his life as taking
orders. Combined with his assiduous frequentation of the
School of Political Sciences, it had doomed him from his

twentieth year to the chastity of a Desert Father. And so, as each of our senses loses some of its strength and keenness, becomes atrophied when it is no longer exercised, M. de Vaugoubert, just as the civilised man is no longer capable of the feats of strength, of the acuteness of hearing of the cave-dweller, had lost that special perspicacity which was rarely lacking in M. de Charlus; and at official banquets, whether in Paris or abroad, the Minister Plenipotentiary was no longer capable of identifying those who, beneath the disguise of their uniform, were at heart his congeners. Certain names mentioned by M. de Charlus, indignant if he himself was cited for his inclinations, but always delighted to give away those of other people, caused M. de Vaugoubert an exquisite surprise. Not that, after all these years, he dreamed of taking advantage of any windfall. But these rapid revelations, similar to those which in Racine's tragedies inform Athalie and Abner that Joas is of the House of David, that Esther, "enthroned in the purple," has "Yid" parents, changing the aspect of the X——Legation, or of one or another department of the Ministry of Foreign Affairs, rendered those palaces as mysterious, in retrospect, as the Temple at Jerusalem or the throne-room at Susa. At the sight of the youthful staff of his embassy advancing in a body to shake hands with M. de Charlus, M. de Vaugoubert assumed the astonished air of Elise exclaiming, in *Esther*: "Great heavens! What a swarm of innocent beauties issuing from all sides presents itself to my gaze! How charming a modesty is depicted on their faces!" Then, athirst for more definite information, he glanced smilingly at M. de Charlus with a fatuously interrogative and concupiscent expression: "Why, of course they are," said M. de

Charlus with the learned air of a scholar speaking to an ignoramus. From that instant M. de Vaugoubert (greatly to the annoyance of M. de Charlus) could not tear his eyes away from these young secretaries whom the X——Ambassador to France, an old stager, had not chosen blindfold. M. de Vaugoubert remained silent; I could only see his eyes. But, being accustomed from my childhood to apply, even to what is voiceless, the language of the classics, I read into M. de Vaugoubert's eyes the lines in which Esther explains to Elise that Mordecai, in his zeal for his religion, has made it a rule that only those maidens who profess it shall be employed about the Queen's person. "And now his love for our nation has peopled this palace with daughters of Zion, young and tender flowers wafted by fate, transplanted like myself beneath a foreign sky. In a place set apart from profane eyes, he" (the worthy Ambassador) "devotes his skill and labour to shaping them."

At length M. de Vaugoubert spoke, otherwise than with his eyes. "Who knows," he said sadly, "whether in the country where I live the same thing does not exist also?" "It is probable," replied M. de Charlus, "starting with King Theodosius, though I don't know anything definite about him." "Oh, dear, no! not in the least!" "Then he has no right to look it so completely. Besides, he has all the little tricks. He has that 'my dear' manner, which I detest more than anything in the world. I should never dare to be seen walking in the street with him. Anyhow, you must know him for what he is, it's common knowledge." "You're entirely mistaken about him. In any case he's quite charming. On the day the agreement with France was signed, the King embraced me. I've never been so moved." "That was the moment to tell him what you wanted." "Oh, good heavens! What an idea! If he were even to suspect such a thing! But I have no fear in that direction." Words which I heard, for I was standing close by, and which made me recite to myself: "The King unto this day knows not who I am, and this secret keeps my tongue still enchained."

This dialogue, half mute, half spoken, had lasted only a few moments, and I had barely entered the first of the drawing-rooms with the Duchesse de Guermantes, when a little dark lady, extremely pretty, stopped her:

"I've been looking for you everywhere. D'Annunzio saw you from a box in the theatre, and he wrote the Princesse de T—— a letter in which he says that he never saw anything so lovely. He would give his life for ten minutes' conversation with you. In any case, even if you can't or won't, the letter is in my possession. You must fix a day to come and see me. There are some secrets which I cannot tell you here. I see you don't remember me," she added, turning to me; "I met you at the Princesse de Parme's" (where I had never been). "The Emperor of Russia is anxious for your father to be sent to Petersburg. If you could come in on Tuesday, Isvolski himself will be there, and he'll talk to you about it. I have a present for you, my dear," she went on, turning back to the Duchess, "which I should not dream of giving to any-one but you. The manuscripts of three of Ibsen's plays, which he sent to me by his old attendant. I shall keep one and give you the other two."

The Duc de Guermantes was not overpleased by these offers. Uncertain whether Ibsen or D'Annunzio were dead or alive, he could see in his mind's eye a tribe of authors and playwrights coming to call upon his wife and putting her in their works. People in society are too apt to think of a book as a sort of cube one side of which has been removed, so that the author can at once "put in" the people he meets. This is obviously rather underhand, and writers are a pretty low class. True, it's not a bad thing to meet them once in a way, for thanks to them, when one reads a book or an article, one "gets to know the inside story," one "sees people in their true colours." On the whole, though, the wisest thing is to stick to dead authors. M. de Guermantes considered "perfectly decent" only the gentleman who did the funeral notices in the *Gaulois*. He, at any rate, was content to include M. de Guermantes at the head of the list of people present "among others" at funerals at which the Duke had given his name. When he preferred that his name should not appear, instead of giving it, he sent a letter of condolence to the relatives of the deceased, assuring them of his deep and heartfelt sympathy. If, then, the family inserted an announcement in the paper: "Among the letters received, we may mention one from the Duc de Guermantes," etc., this was the fault not of the ink-slinger but of the son, brother, father of the deceased whom the Duke thereupon denounced as upstarts, and with whom he decided for the future to have no further dealings (what he called, not being very well up in the meaning of such expressions, "having a bone to pick"). At all events, the names of Ibsen and D'Annunzio, and his uncertainty as to their continued survival, brought a frown to the brow of the Duke, who was not yet far enough away from us to avoid hearing the various blandishments of Mme Timoléon d'Amoncourt. She was a charming woman, her wit, like her beauty, so entrancing that either of them by itself would have made her shine. But, born outside the world in which she now lived, having aspired at first merely to a literary salon, the friend successively—by no means the lover, her morals were above reproach—and exclusively of all the great writers, who gave her their manuscripts, wrote books for her, chance having once introduced her into the Faubourg Saint-Germain, these literary privileges served her well there. She was now in a position where she had no need to dispense other graces than those shed by her presence. But, accustomed in the past to worldly wisdom, social wiles, services to render, she persevered in these things even when they were no longer necessary. She had always a state secret to reveal to you, a potentate whom you must meet, a water-colour by a master to present to you. There was indeed in all these superfluous attractions a trace of falsehood, but they made her life a comedy that scintillated with complications, and it was true to say that she was responsible for the appointment of prefects and generals.

As she strolled by my side, the Duchesse de Guermantes allowed the azure light of her eyes to float in front of her, but vaguely, so as to avoid the people with whom she did not wish to enter into relations, whose presence she discerned from time to time like a menacing reef in the distance. We advanced between a double hedge of guests, who, conscious that they would never come to know "Oriane," were anxious at least to point her out, as a curiosity, to their wives: "Quick, Ursule, come and look at Madame de Guermantes talking to that young man." And one felt that in another moment they would be clambering upon the chairs for a better view, as at the military review on the 14th July or the Grand Prix at Longchamp.

Not that the Duchesse de Guermantes had a more aristocratic salon than her cousin. The former's was frequented
by people whom the latter would never have been willing
to invite, chiefly because of her husband. She would never
have been at home to Mme Alphonse de Rothschild, who,
an intimate friend of Mme de La Trémoïlle and of Mme
de Sagan, as was Oriane herself, was constantly to be seen
in the house of the last-named. It was the same with
Baron Hirsch, whom the Prince of Wales had brought to
her house but not to that of the Princess, who would not
have approved of him, and also with certain outstanding
Bonapartist or even Republican celebrities whom the
Duchess found interesting but whom the Prince, a convinced Royalist, would on principle not have allowed inside his house. His anti-semitism, being also founded on
principle, did not yield before any social distinction, however strongly accredited, and if he was at home to Swann,
whose friend he had been from time immemorial—being,
however, the only Guermantes who addressed him as
Swann and not as Charles—this was because, knowing
that Swann's grandmother, a Protestant married to a Jew,
had been the Duc de Berry's mistress, he endeavoured,
from time to time, to believe in the legend which made
out Swann's father to be that prince's natural son. On this
hypothesis, which incidentally was false, Swann, the son
of a Catholic father himself the son of a Bourbon by a
Catholic mother, was a Gentile to his fingertips.

"What, you don't know these splendours?" said the
Duchess, referring to the rooms through which we were
moving. But, having given its due meed of praise to her
cousin's "palace," she hastened to add that she infinitely
preferred her own "humble den." "This is an admirable

house to *visit*. But I should die of misery if I had to stay and sleep in rooms that have witnessed so many historic events. It would give me the feeling of having been left behind after closing-time, forgotten, in the Château of Blois, or Fontainebleau, or even the Louvre, with no antidote to my depression except to tell myself that I was in the room in which Monaldeschi was murdered. As a sedative, that is not good enough. Why, here comes Mme de Saint-Euverte. We've just been dining with her. As she is giving her great annual beanfeast tomorrow, I supposed she would be going straight to bed. But she can never miss a party. If this one had been in the country, she would have jumped on a delivery-van rather than not go to it."

As a matter of fact, Mme de Saint-Euverte had come this evening less for the pleasure of not missing another person's party than in order to ensure the success of her own, recruit the latest additions to her list, and, so to speak, hold an eleventh-hour review of the troops who were on the morrow to perform such brilliant manoeuvres at her garden-party. For in the course of the years the guests at the Saint-Euverte parties had almost entirely changed. The female celebrities of the Guermantes world, formerly so sparsely scattered, had—loaded with attentions by their hostess—begun gradually to bring their friends. At the same time, by a similarly gradual process, but in the opposite direction, Mme de Saint-Euverte had year by year reduced the number of persons unknown to the world of fashion. One after another had ceased to be seen. For some time the "batch" system was in operation, which enabled her, thanks to parties over which a veil of silence was drawn, to summon the unelected separately to entertain one another, which dispensed her from having to invite them with the best people. What cause had they for complaint? Were they not given (*panem et circenses*) light refreshments and a select musical programme? And so, in a kind of symmetry with the two exiled duchesses whom formerly, when the Saint-Euverte salon was only starting, one used to see holding up its shaky pediment like a pair of caryatids, in these later years one could distinguish, mingling with the fashionable throng, only two heterogeneous persons: old Mme de Cambremer and the architect's wife with a fine voice who often had to be asked to sing. But, no longer knowing anybody at Mme de Saint-Euverte's, bewailing their lost comrades, feeling out of place, they looked as though they might at any moment die of cold, like two swallows that have not migrated in time. And so, the following year, they were not invited. Mme de Franquetot made an appeal on behalf of her cousin, who was so fond of music. But as she could obtain for her no more explicit reply than the words: "Why, people can always come in and listen to music, if they like; there's nothing criminal about that!" Mme de Cambremer did not find the invitation sufficiently pressing, and abstained.

Such a transformation having been effected by Mme de Saint-Euverte, from a leper colony to a gathering of great ladies (the latest form, apparently ultra-smart, that it had assumed), it might seem odd that the person who on the following day was to give the most brilliant party of the season should need to appear overnight to address a final appeal to her troops. But the fact was that the pre-eminence of Mme de Saint-Euverte's salon existed only for those whose social life consists exclusively in reading the accounts of afternoon and evening parties in the *Gaulois* or the *Figaro*, without ever having been present at any of them. To these worldlings who see the world only through the newspapers, the enumeration of the British, Austrian, etc., ambassadresses, of the Duchesses d'Uzès, de La Trémoïlle, etc., etc., was sufficient to make them automatically imagine the Saint-Euverte salon to be the first in Paris, whereas it was among the last. Not that the reports were mendacious. The majority of the persons mentioned had indeed been present. But each of them had come in response to entreaties, civilities, favours, and with the sense of doing infinite honour to Mme de Saint-Euverte. Such salons, shunned rather than sought after, which are attended as a sort of official duty, deceive no one but the fair readers of the "Society" columns. They pass over a really fashionable party, the sort at which the hostess, who could have had all the duchesses in existence, every one of them athirst to be "numbered among the elect," has invited only two or three. And so these hostesses, who do not send a list of their guests to the papers, ignorant or contemptuous of the power that publicity has acquired today, are considered fashionable by the Queen of Spain but are overlooked by the crowd, because the former knows and the latter does not know who they are.

Mme de Saint-Euverte was not one of these women, and, like the busy bee she was, had come to gather up for the morrow everyone who had been invited. M. de Charlus was not among these, having always refused to go to her house. But he had quarrelled with so many people that Mme de Saint-Euverte might put this down to his peculiar nature.

Of course, if it had been only Oriane, Mme de Saint-
Euverte need not have put herself to the trouble, for the
invitation had been given by word of mouth, and moreover accepted with that charming and deceptive grace
which is practised to perfection by those Academicians
from whose doors the candidate emerges with a warm
glow, never doubting that he can count upon their support. But there were others as well. The Prince d'Agrigente—would he come? And Mme de Durfort? And so,
keeping a weather eye open, Mme de Saint-Euverte had
thought it expedient to appear on the scene in person; insinuating with some, imperative with others, to all alike
she hinted in veiled words at unimaginable attractions
which could never be seen anywhere again, and promised
each of them that they would find at her house the person
they most desired or the personage they most needed to
meet. And this sort of function with which she was invested on one day in the year—like certain public offices
in the ancient world—as the person who is to give on the
morrow the biggest garden-party of the season, conferred
upon her a momentary authority. Her lists were made up
and closed, so that while she wandered slowly through the
Princess's rooms dropping into one ear after another:
"You won't forget tomorrow," she had the ephemeral
glory of averting her eyes, while continuing to smile, if
she caught sight of some ugly duckling who was to
be avoided or some country squire for whom the bond
of a schoolboy friendship had secured admission to
"Gilbert's," and whose presence at her garden-party
would be no gain. She preferred not to speak to him so as
to be able to say later on: "I issued my invitations ver-
bally, and unfortunately I didn't meet you anywhere."

And so she, a mere Saint-Euverte, set to work with her gimlet eyes to pick and choose among the guests at the Princess's party. And she imagined herself, in so doing, to be every inch a Duchesse de Guermantes.

It must be said that the latter too did not enjoy to the extent that one might suppose the unrestricted use of her greetings and smiles. Sometimes, no doubt, when she withheld them, it was deliberately: "But the woman bores me to tears," she would say. "Am I expected to talk to her about the party for the next hour?" (A duchess of swarthy complexion went past, whose ugliness and stupidity, and certain irregularities of conduct, had exiled her not from society but from certain elegant circles. "Ah!" murmured Mme de Guermantes, with the sharp, unerring glance of the connoisseur who is shown a false jewel, "so they invite *that* here!" From the mere sight of this semi-tarnished lady, whose face was overburdened with moles from which black hairs sprouted, Mme de Guermantes gauged the mediocrity of this party. They had been brought up together, but she had severed all relations with the lady; and responded to her greeting only with the curtest little nod. "I cannot understand," she said to me as if to excuse herself, "how Marie-Gilbert can invite us with all these dregs. It looks as though there are people from every parish. Mélanie Pourtalès arranged things far better. She could have the Orthodox Synod and the Oratoire Protestants in her house if she liked, but at least she didn't invite us on those days.") But in many cases, it was from timidity, fear of a scene with her husband, who did not like her to entertain artists and such-like (Marie-Gilbert took a kindly interest in dozens of them: you had to take care not to be accosted by some illustrious German diva), from some misgivings, too, with regard to nationalist feeling, which, inasmuch as she was endowed like M. de Charlus with the wit of the Guermantes, she despised from the social point of view (people were now, for the greater glory of the General Staff, sending a plebeian general in to dinner before certain dukes), but to which nevertheless, as she knew that she was considered unsound in her views, she made large concessions, even dreading the prospect of having to shake hands with Swann in these anti-semitic surroundings. With regard to this, her mind was soon set at rest, for she learned that the Prince had refused to have Swann in the house and had had "a sort of an altercation" with him. There was no risk of her having to converse in public with "poor Charles," whom she preferred to cherish in private.

"And who in the world is that?" Mme de Guermantes exclaimed, on seeing a little lady with a slightly lost air, in a black dress so simple that you would have taken her for a pauper, make her a deep bow, as did also her husband. She did not recognise the lady and, in her insolent way, drew herself up as though offended and stared at her without responding: "Who is that person, Basin?" she asked with an air of astonishment, while M. de Guermantes, to atone for Oriane's impoliteness, bowed to the lady and shook hands with her husband. "Why, it's Mme de Chaussepierre, you were most impolite." "I've never heard of Chaussepierre." "Old mother Chanlivault's nephew." "I haven't the faintest idea what you're talking about. Who is the woman, and why does she bow to me?" "But you know perfectly well; she's Mme de Charleval's daughter, Henriette Montmorency." "Oh, but I knew her mother quite well. She was charming, extremely intelligent. What made her go and marry all these people I've never heard of? You say she calls herself Mme de Chaussepierre?" she asked, spelling out the name with a questioning look, as though she were afraid of getting it wrong. The Duke looked at her sternly. "It's not so ridiculous as you appear to think, to be called Chaussepierre! Old Chaussepierre was the brother of the aforesaid Chanlivault, of Mme de Sennecour and of the Vicomtesse du Merlerault. They're excellent people." "Oh, do stop," cried the Duchess, who, like a lion-tamer, never cared to give the impression of being intimidated by the devouring glare of the animal. "Basin, you are the joy of my life. I can't imagine where you unearthed those names, but I congratulate you on them. If I did not know Chaussepierre, I have at least read Balzac—you're not the only one—and I've even read Labiche. I can appreciate Chanlivault, I do not object to Charleval, but I must confess that du Merlerault is a masterpiece. However, I must admit that Chaussepierre is not bad either. You must have gone about collecting them, it's not possible. You mean to write a book," she added, turning to me, "you ought to make a note of Charleval and du Merlerault. You won't find anything better." "He'll find himself in the dock, and will go to prison; you're giving him very bad advice, Oriane." "I hope, for his own sake, that he has younger people than me at his disposal if he wishes to ask for bad advice, especially if he means to follow it. But if he means to do nothing worse than write a book!"

At some distance from us, a wonderful, proud young woman stood out delicately from the throng in a white dress, all diamonds and tulle. Mme de Guermantes watched her talking to a whole group of people fascinated by her grace.

"Your sister is the belle of the ball, as usual; she is charming tonight," she said, as she took a chair, to the Prince de Chimay who was passing.

Colonel de Froberville (the General of that name was his uncle) came and sat down beside us, as did M. de Bréauté, while M. de Vaugoubert, after hovering about us (by an excess of politeness which he maintained even when playing tennis, thus, by dint of asking leave of the eminent personages present before hitting the ball, invariably losing the game for his partner), returned to M. de Charlus (until that moment almost concealed by the huge skirt of the Comtesse Molé, whom he professed to admire above all other women), just as several members of the latest diplomatic mission to Paris chanced to be greeting the Baron. At the sight of a young secretary with a particularly intelligent look, M. de Vaugoubert fastened on M. de Charlus a smile in which a single question visibly shone. M. de Charlus would perhaps readily have compromised someone else, but he was exasperated to feel himself compromised by a smile on another person's lips which could have but one meaning. "I know absolutely nothing about the matter. I beg you to keep your curiosity to yourself. It leaves me more than cold. Besides, in this instance, you are making a mistake of the first order. I believe this young man to be absolutely the opposite." Here M. de Charlus, irritated at being thus given away by a fool, was not speaking the truth. Had the Baron been correct, the secretary would have been the exception to the rule in that embassy. It was in fact composed of widely different personalities, many of them extremely second-rate, so that, if one sought to discover what could have been the motive of the selection that had brought them together, the only one possible seemed to be inversion. By setting at the head of this little diplomatic Sodom an ambassador on the contrary enamoured of women with the comic exaggeration of a revue compère, who drilled his battalion of transvestites like clockwork, the authorities seemed to have been obeying the law of contrasts. In spite of what he had beneath his nose, he did not believe in inversion. He gave an immediate proof of this by marrying his sister to a chargé d'affaires whom he believed, quite mistakenly, to be a womaniser. After this he became rather a nuisance and was soon replaced by a new Excellency, who ensured the homogeneity of the party. Other embassies sought to rival this one, but could never dispute the prize (as in the *concours général*, where a certain *lycée* always heads the list), and more than ten years had to pass before, heterogeneous attachés having been introduced into this too perfect unit, another could at last wrest the disreputable palm from it and march out in front.

Reassured as regards her fear of having to talk to Swann, Mme de Guermantes now felt merely curious as to the subject of the conversation he had had with their host. "Do you know what it was about?" the Duke asked M. de Bréauté. "I did hear," the other replied, "that it was about a little play which the writer Bergotte produced at their house. It was a delightful show, I gather. But it seems the actor made himself up to look like Gilbert, whom, as it happens, Master Bergotte had intended to depict." "Oh, I should have loved to see Gilbert taken off," said the Duchess with a dreamy smile. "It was about this

little performance," M. de Bréauté went on, thrusting forward his rodent's jaw, "that Gilbert demanded an explanation from Swann, who merely replied what everyone
thought very witty: 'Why, not at all, it wasn't the least bit
like you, you are far funnier!' It appears, though," M. de
Bréauté continued, "that the little play was quite delightful. Mme Molé was there, and she was immensely
amused." "What, does Mme Molé go there?" said the
Duchess in astonishment. "Ah! that must be Mémé's doing. That's what always happens in the end to that sort of
house. One fine day everybody begins to flock to it, and
I, who have deliberately remained aloof on principle, find
myself left to mope alone in my corner." Already, since
M. de Bréauté's speech, the Duchesse de Guermantes
(with regard, if not to Swann's house, at least to the hypothesis of encountering him at any moment) had, as we
see, adopted a fresh point of view. "The explanation that
you have given us," said Colonel de Froberville to M. de
Bréauté, "is entirely unfounded. I have good reason to
know. The Prince purely and simply gave Swann a dressing-down and begged to instruct him, as our fathers used
to say, that he was not to show his face in the house
again, in view of the opinions he flaunts. And, to my
mind, my uncle Gilbert was right a thousand times over,
not only in giving Swann a piece of his mind—he ought
to have broken off relations with a professed Dreyfusard
six months ago."

Poor M. de Vaugoubert, from being a too dawdling
tennis-player having now become a mere inert tennis-ball
which is driven to and fro without compunction, found
himself projected towards the Duchesse de Guermantes,
to whom he made obeisance. He was none too well re-

ceived, Oriane living in the belief that all the diplomats—
or politicians—of her world were nincompoops.

M. de Froberville had inevitably benefited from the
preferential position that had of late been accorded to military men in the social world. Unfortunately, if the wife of
his bosom was a quite authentic relative of the Guermantes, she was also an extremely poor one, and, as he
himself had lost his fortune, they went scarcely anywhere,
and were the sort of people who were apt to be overlooked except on big occasions, when they had the good
fortune to bury or marry a relation. Then, they did really
enter into communion with high society, like those nomi-
nal Catholics who approach the altar rails only once a
year. Their material situation would indeed have been deplorable had not Mme de Saint-Euverte, faithful to her affection for the late General de Froberville, done
everything to help the household, providing frocks and
entertainments for the two girls. But the Colonel, though
generally considered a good fellow, was lacking in the
spirit of gratitude. He was envious of the splendours of a
benefactress who celebrated them herself without pause or
restraint. The annual garden-party was for him, his wife
and children a marvellous pleasure which they would not
have missed for all the gold in the world, but a pleasure
poisoned by the thought of the joy of self-satisfied pride
that Mme de Saint-Euverte derived from it. The accounts
of this garden-party in the newspapers, which, after giving
a detailed report, would add with Machiavellian guile:
"We shall come back to this brilliant gathering," the complementary details about the women's clothes, appearing
for several days in succession—all this was so painful to
the Frobervilles that although they were cut off from most

pleasures and knew that they could count upon the pleasure of this one afternoon, they were moved every year to
hope that bad weather would spoil the success of the
party, to consult the barometer and to anticipate with delight the threatenings of a storm that might ruin everything.

"I shall not discuss politics with you, Froberville,"
said M. de Guermantes, "but, so far as Swann is concerned, I can tell you frankly that his conduct towards
ourselves has been beyond words. Although he was originally introduced into society by ourselves and the Duc de
Chartres, they tell me now that he is openly Dreyfusard. I
should never have believed it of him, an epicure, a man of
practical judgment, a collector, a connoisseur of old books,
a member of the Jockey, a man who enjoys the respect of
all, who knows all the good addresses and used to send us
the best port you could wish to drink, a dilettante, a family man. Ah! I feel badly let down. I don't mind about
myself, it's generally agreed that I'm only an old fool
whose opinion counts for nothing, mere ragtag and bob-
tail, but if only for Oriane's sake, he ought not to have
done that, he should have openly disavowed the Jews and
the partisans of the accused.

"Yes, after the friendship my wife has always shown
him," went on the Duke, who evidently considered that to
denounce Dreyfus as guilty of high treason, whatever
opinion one might hold in one's heart of hearts as to his
guilt, constituted a sort of thank-offering for the manner
in which one had been received in the Faubourg Saint-
Germain, "he ought to have dissociated himself. For, you
can ask Oriane, she had a real friendship for him."

The Duchess, thinking that a quiet, ingenuous tone

would give a more dramatic and sincere value to her words, said in a schoolgirl voice, as though simply letting the truth fall from her lips, and merely allowing a slightly melancholy expression to becloud her eyes: "Yes, it's true, I have no reason to conceal the fact that I did feel a sincere affection for Charles!"

"There, you see, I don't have to make her say it. And after that, he carries his ingratitude to the point of being a Dreyfusard!"

"Talking of Dreyfusards," I said, "it appears that Prince Von is one."

"Ah, I'm glad you reminded me of him," exclaimed M. de Guermantes, "I was forgetting that he had asked me to dine with him on Monday. But whether he's a Dreyfusard or not is entirely immaterial to me, since he's a foreigner. I don't give two straws for his opinion. With a Frenchman it's another matter. It's true that Swann is a Jew. But, until today—forgive me, Froberville—I have always been foolish enough to believe that a Jew can be a Frenchman, I mean an honourable Jew, a man of the world. Now, Swann was that in every sense of the word. Well, now he forces me to admit that I was mistaken, since he has taken the side of this Dreyfus (who, guilty or not, never moved in his world, whom he wouldn't ever have met) against a society that had adopted him, had treated him as one of its own. There's no question about it, we were all of us prepared to vouch for Swann, I would have answered for his patriotism as for my own. And this is how he repays us! I must confess that I should never have expected such a thing from him. I thought better of him. He was a man of intelligence (in his own line, of course). I know that he had already been guilty of the aberration of that shameful marriage. And by the way, do you know someone who was really hurt by Swann's marriage? My wife. Oriane often has what I might call an affectation of insensibility. But at heart she feels things with extraordinary keenness." (Mme de Guermantes, delighted by this analysis of her character, listened to it with a modest air but did not utter a word, from a scrupulous reluctance to acquiesce in it but principally from fear of cutting it short. M. de Guermantes might have gone on talking for an hour on this subject and she would have sat as still, or even stiller, than if she had been listening to music.) "Well, I remember when she heard of Swann's marriage she was genuinely hurt. She felt that it was very bad on the part of someone to whom we had shown so much friendship. She was very fond of Swann; she was deeply grieved. Am I not right, Oriane?"

Mme de Guermantes felt that she ought to reply to so direct a challenge on a point of fact which would enable her unobtrusively to confirm the tribute which she felt had come to an end. In a shy and simple tone, and with an air all the more studied in that it sought to appear "heartfelt," she said with a meek reserve: "It's true, Basin is quite right."

"But still, that wasn't quite the same thing as this. After all, love is love, although, in my opinion, it ought to confine itself within certain limits. I could excuse a young fellow, a snotty-nosed youth, for letting himself be carried away by utopian ideas. But Swann, a man of intelligence, of proved refinement, a fine judge of pictures, an intimate friend of the Duc de Chartres, of Gilbert himself!"

The tone in which M. de Guermantes said this was, incidentally, quite inoffensive, without a trace of the vul-

garity which he too often showed. He spoke with a
slightly indignant melancholy, but his whole manner ex-
uded that gentle gravity which constitutes the broad and
unctuous charm of certain portraits by Rembrandt, that of
the Burgomaster Six, for example. One felt that for the
Duke there was no question of the immorality of Swann's
conduct with regard to the "Affair," so self-evident was it;
it caused him the grief of a father who sees one of his
sons, for whose education he has made the greatest sacrifices, deliberately ruin the magnificent position he has
created for him and dishonour a respected name by es-
capades which the principles or prejudices of his family
cannot allow. It is true that M. de Guermantes had not
displayed so profound and pained an astonishment when
he learned that Saint-Loup was a Dreyfusard. But, for one
thing, he regarded his nephew as a young man gone
astray, from whom nothing would be surprising until he
began to mend his ways, whereas Swann was what M. de
Guermantes called "a level-headed man, a man occupying
a position in the front rank." Moreover, and above all, a
considerable period of time had elapsed during which, if,
from the historical point of view, events had to some extent seemed to justify the Dreyfusard thesis, the anti-
Dreyfusard opposition had greatly increased in violence,
and from being purely political had become social. It was
now a question of militarism, of patriotism, and the waves
of anger that had been stirred up in society had had time
to gather the force which they never have at the beginning
of a storm. "Don't you see," M. de Guermantes went on,
"even from the point of view of his beloved Jews, since he
is absolutely determined to stand by them, Swann has
made a bloomer of incalculable significance. He has

proved that they're all secretly united and are somehow forced to give their support to anyone of their own race, even if they don't know him personally. It's a public menace. We've obviously been too easy-going, and the mistake Swann is making will create all the more stir since he was respected, not to say received, and was almost the only Jew that anyone knew. People will say: *Ab uno disce omnes.*" (Satisfaction at having hit at the right moment upon so apt a quotation alone brightened with a proud smile the melancholy countenance of the betrayed nobleman.)

I was longing to know exactly what had happened between the Prince and Swann, and to catch the latter, if he had not already gone home. "I don't mind telling you," the Duchess answered me when I spoke to her of this desire, "that I for my part am not over-anxious to see him, because it appears, from what I was told just now at Mme de Saint-Euverte's, that he wants me to make the acquaintance of his wife and daughter before he dies. God knows I'm terribly distressed that he should be ill, but in the first place I hope it isn't as serious as all that. And besides, it isn't a valid reason, because otherwise it would be really too easy. A writer with no talent would only have to say: 'Vote for me at the Academy because my wife is dying and I wish to give her this last happiness.' There would be no more entertaining if one was obliged to make friends with all the dying. My coachman might come to me with: 'My daughter is seriously ill, get me an invitation to the Princesse de Parme's.' I adore Charles, and I should hate having to refuse him, and so I prefer to avoid the risk of his asking me. I hope with all my heart that he isn't dying, as he says, but really, if it has to happen, it

wouldn't be the moment for me to make the acquaintance
of those two creatures who have deprived me of the most
agreeable of my friends for the last fifteen years, and
whom he would leave on my hands without my even being able to make use of their society to see him, since he
would be dead!"

Meanwhile M. de Bréauté had not ceased to brood
upon the refutation of his story by Colonel de Froberville.

"I don't question the accuracy of your version, my
dear fellow," he said, "but I had mine from a good
source. It was the Prince de La Tour d'Auvergne who
told me."

"I'm surprised that a learned man like yourself should
still say 'Prince de La Tour d'Auvergne,' " the Duc de
Guermantes broke in. "You know that he's nothing of the
kind. There is only one member of that family left: Oriane's uncle, the Duc de Bouillon."

"Mme de Villeparisis's brother?" I asked, remembering that she had been Mlle de Bouillon.

"Precisely. Oriane, Mme de Lambresac is saying
how-d'ye-do to you."

And indeed, one saw from time to time, forming and
fading like a shooting star, a faint smile directed by the
Duchesse de Lambresac at somebody whom she had
recognised. But this smile, instead of taking definite shape
in an active affirmation, in a language mute but clear, was
drowned almost immediately in a sort of ideal ecstasy
which expressed nothing, while her head drooped in a
gesture of blissful benediction, recalling that which a
slightly senile prelate bestows upon a crowd of communi-
cants. There was not the least trace of senility about Mme
de Lambresac. But I was already acquainted with this

particular type of old-fashioned distinction. At Combray
and in Paris, all my grandmother's friends were in the
habit of greeting one another at a social gathering with as
seraphic an air as if they had caught sight of someone of
their acquaintance in church, at the moment of the Elevation or during a funeral, and were offering him a languid
greeting which ended in prayer. At this point a remark
made by M. de Guermantes was to complete the comparison that I was making. "But you have seen the Duc de
Bouillon," he said to me. "He was just leaving my library
this afternoon as you came in, a short gentleman with
white hair." It was the man I had taken for a man of
business from Combray, and yet, now that I came to
think it over, I could see the resemblance to Mme de
Villeparisis. The similarity between the evanescent greetings of the Duchesse de Lambresac and those of my
grandmother's friends had begun to arouse my interest by
showing me how in all narrow and closed societies, be
they those of the minor gentry or of the great nobility, the
old manners persist, enabling us to recapture, like an ar-
chaeologist, something of the upbringing, and the ethos it
reflects, that prevailed in the days of the Vicomte d'Arlin-
court and Loiisa Puget. Better still now, the perfect conformity in appearance between a petty bourgeois from
Combray of his generation and the Duc de Bouillon reminded me of what had already struck me so forcibly
when I had seen Saint-Loup's maternal grandfather, the
Duc de La Rochefoucauld, in a daguerreotype in which
he was exactly similar, in dress, appearance and manner,
to my great-uncle—that social, and even individual, differences are merged when seen from a distance in the uni-
formity of an epoch. The truth is that similarity of dress

and also the reflexion of the spirit of the age in facial composition occupy so much more important a place in a person's make-up than his caste, which bulks large only in his own self-esteem and the imagination of other people, that in order to realise that a nobleman of the time of Louis-Philippe differs less from an ordinary citizen of the time of Louis-Philippe than from a nobleman of the time of Louis XV, it is not necessary to visit the galleries of the Louvre.

At that moment, a Bavarian musician with long hair, whom the Princesse de Guermantes had taken under her wing, bowed to Oriane. She responded with a nod, but the Duke, furious at seeing his wife greet a person whom he did not know, who looked rather weird, and, so far as M. de Guermantes understood, had an extremely bad reputation, turned upon his wife with a terrible and inquisitorial air, as much as to say: "Who in the world is that barbarian?" Poor Mme de Guermantes's position was already distinctly complicated, and if the musician had felt a little pity for this martyred wife, he would have made off as quickly as possible. But, whether from a desire not to submit to the humiliation that had just been inflicted on him in public, before the eyes of the Duke's oldest and most intimate friends, whose presence there had perhaps been responsible to some extent for his silent bow, and to show that it was on the best of grounds and not without knowing her already that he had greeted the Duchesse de Guermantes, or whether in obedience to an obscure but irresistible impulse to commit a gaffe which drove him— at a moment when he ought to have trusted to the spirit—to apply the whole letter of the law of etiquette, the musician came closer to Mme de Guermantes and

said to her: "Madame la Duchesse, I should like to have
the honour of being presented to the Duke." Mme de
Guermantes was miserable in the extreme. But after all,
even if she was a deceived wife, she was still Duchesse de
Guermantes and could not appear to have been stripped
of the right to introduce to her husband the people whom
she knew. "Basin," she said, "allow me to present to you
M. d'Herweck."

"I need not ask whether you are going to Mme de
Saint-Euverte's tomorrow," Colonel de Froberville said to
Mme de Guermantes, to dispel the painful impression
produced by M. d'Herweck's ill-timed request. "The
whole of Paris will be there."

Meanwhile, turning towards the indiscreet musician
with a single movement and as though he were carved out
of a solid block, the Duc de Guermantes, drawing himself
up, monumental, mute, wrathful, like Jupiter Tonans, remained thus motionless for some seconds, his eyes ablaze
with anger and astonishment, his crinkly hair seeming to
emerge from a crater. Then, as though carried away by an
impulse which alone enabled him to perform the act of
politeness that was demanded of him, and after appearing
by his aggressive demeanour to be calling the entire company to witness that he did not know the Bavarian musician, clasping his white-gloved hands behind his back, he
jerked his body forward and bestowed upon the musician
a bow so profound, instinct with such stupefaction and
rage, so abrupt, so violent, that the trembling artist recoiled, bowing as he went, in order not to receive a
formidable butt in the stomach.

"Well, the fact is I shan't be in Paris," the Duchess
answered Colonel de Froberville. "I must tell you (though

I ought to be ashamed to confess such a thing) that I have lived all these years without seeing the stained-glass windows at Montfort-l'Amaury. It's shocking, but there it is. And so, to make amends for my shameful ignorance, I decided that I would go and see them tomorrow."

M. de Bréauté smiled a subtle smile. For he was well aware that, if the Duchess had been able to live all these years without seeing the windows at Montfort-l'Amaury, this artistic excursion had not all of a sudden taken on the urgent character of an "emergency" operation and might without danger, after having been put off for more than twenty-five years, be retarded for twenty-four hours. The plan that the Duchess had formed was simply the Guermantes way of decreeing that the Saint-Euverte establishment was definitely not a socially respectable house, but a house to which you were invited so that your name might afterwards be flaunted in the account in the *Gaulois*, a house that would award the seal of supreme elegance to those, or at any rate to her (should there be but one), who would not be seen there. The delicate amusement of M. de Bréauté, coupled with the poetical pleasure which society people felt when they saw Mme de Guermantes do things which their own inferior position did not allow them to imitate but the mere sight of which brought to their lips the smile of the peasant tied to his glebe when he sees freer and more fortunate men pass by above his head—this delicate pleasure could in no way be compared with the concealed but frantic delight which M. de Froberville instantaneously experienced.

The efforts that this gentleman was making so that people should not hear his laughter had made him turn as red as a turkey-cock, in spite of which it was with a running interruption of hiccups of joy that he exclaimed in a pitying tone: "Oh! poor aunt Saint-Euverte, she'll make herself sick over it! No, the unhappy woman isn't to have her duchess! What a blow! It'll be the death of her!" He doubled up with laughter, and in his exhilaration could not help stamping his feet and rubbing his hands. Smiling out of one eye and one small corner of her lips at M. de Froberville, whose amiable intention she appreciated, though she found less tolerable the deadly boredom of his company, Mme de Guermantes finally decided to leave him.

"I say, I'm afraid I'm going to *have* to bid you good-night," she said to him as she rose with an air of melancholy resignation, and as though it grieved her. Beneath the magic spell of her blue eyes her gently musical voice made one think of the poetical lament of a fairy. "Basin wants me to go and talk to Marie for a while."

In reality, she was tired of listening to Froberville, who went on envying her her visit to Montfort-l'Amaury, when she knew quite well that he had never heard of the windows before in his life, and besides would not for anything in the world have missed going to the Saint-Euverte party. "Good-bye, I've barely said a word to you, but it's always like that at parties—we never really see each other, we never say the things we should like to; in fact it's the same everywhere in this life. Let's hope that when we are dead things will be better arranged. At any rate we shan't always be having to put on low-cut dresses. And yet one never knows. We may perhaps have to display our bones and worms on great occasions. Why not? Just look at old mother Rampillon—do you see any great difference between her and a skeleton in an open dress? It's true that she has every right to look like that, for she must be at least a hundred. She was already one of those sacred monsters before whom I refused to bow the knee when I made my first appearance in society. I thought she had been dead for years; which for that matter would be the only possible explanation for the spectacle she presents. It's most impressive and liturgical; quite *Campo Santo!*"

The Duchess had moved away from Froberville. He followed her: "Just one word in your ear." Slightly irritated, "Well, what is it now?" she said to him stiffly. And he, having been afraid lest at the last moment she might change her mind about Montfort-l'Amaury: "I didn't like to mention it for Mme de Saint-Euverte's sake, so as not to upset her, but since you don't intend to be there, I may tell you that I'm glad for your sake, because she has measles in the house!" "Oh, good gracious!" said Oriane, who had a horror of diseases. "But that wouldn't matter to me, I've had it already. You can't get it twice." "So the doctors say. I know people who've had it four times. Anyhow, you are warned." As for himself, the fictitious measles would have needed to attack him in reality and to chain him to his bed before he would have resigned himself to missing the Saint-Euverte party to which he had looked forward for so many months. He would have the pleasure of seeing so many smart people there, the still greater pleasure of remarking that certain things had gone wrong, and the supreme pleasure of being able for long afterwards to boast that he had mingled with the former and, exaggerating or inventing them, of deploring the latter.

I took advantage of the Duchess's moving to rise also in order to make my way to the smoking-room and find

out the truth about Swann. "Don't believe a word of what
Babal told us," she said to me. "Little Molé would never
poke her nose into a place like that. They tell us that to
entice us. Nobody ever goes to them and they are never
asked anywhere either. He admits it himself: 'We spend
the evenings alone by our own fireside.' As he always says
we, not like royalty, but to include his wife, I don't press
him. But I know all about it." We passed two young men
whose great and dissimilar beauty derived from the same
woman. They were the two sons of Mme de Surgis, the
latest mistress of the Duc de Guermantes. Both were re-
splendent with their mother's perfections, but each in a
different way. To one had passed, rippling through a virile body, the regal bearing of Mme de Surgis, and the
same glowing, rufous, pearly paleness flooded the marmo-
real cheeks of mother and son; but his brother had received the Grecian brow, the perfect nose, the statuesque
neck, the eyes of infinite depth; composed thus of separate
gifts, which the goddess had shared between them, their
twofold beauty offered one the abstract pleasure of thinking that the cause of that beauty was something outside
themselves; it was as though the principal attributes of
their mother had been incarnated in two different bodies;
this one was her stature and her complexion, the other her
gaze, as Mars and Venus were only the Strength and the
Beauty respectively of Jupiter. Full of respect though they
were for M. de Guermantes, of whom they said: "He is a
great friend of our parents," the elder nevertheless
thought that it would be wiser not to come up and greet
the Duchess, of whose hostility towards his mother he
was aware though without perhaps understanding the reason, and at the sight of us he slightly averted his head.

The younger, who imitated his brother in everything, because, being stupid and moreover short-sighted, he did not dare to have his own opinion, inclined his head at the same angle, and the pair slipped past us towards the cardroom, one behind the other, like a pair of allegorical figures.

Just as I reached this room, I was stopped by the Marquise de Citri, still beautiful though practically foaming at the mouth. Of decently noble birth, she had sought and made a brilliant match in marrying M. de Citri, whose great-grandmother had been an Aumale-Lorraine. But no sooner had she tasted this satisfaction than her natural cantankerousness had given her a horror of high society which did not absolutely preclude social life. Not only, at a party, did she deride everyone present, but her derision was so violent that mere laughter was not sufficiently acrid and developed into a guttural hiss. "Ah!" she said to me, pointing to the Duchesse de Guermantes who had now left my side and was already some way off, "what defeats me is that she can lead this sort of existence." Was this the remark of a frenzied saint, astonished that the Gentiles did not come of their own accord to perceive the Truth, or that of an anarchist athirst for carnage? In any case there could be no possible justification for this criticism. In the first place, the "existence led" by Mme de Guermantes differed very little (except in indignation) from that led by Mme de Citri. Mme de Citri was amazed to find the Duchess capable of that mortal sacrifice: attendance at one of Marie-Gilbert's parties. It must be said in this particular instance that Mme de Citri was genuinely fond of the Princess, who was indeed the kindest of women, and knew that by attending

her reception she was giving her great pleasure. Hence, in
order to come to the party, she had put off a dancer
whom she regarded as a genius and who was to have initiated her into the mysteries of Russian choreography. Another reason which to some extent stultified the
concentrated rage which Mme de Citri felt on seeing Oriane greet one or other of the guests was that the Duchess,
although at a far less advanced stage, showed the symptoms of the malady that was devouring Mme de Citri.
We have seen, moreover, that she had carried the germs
of it from her birth. In fact, being more intelligent than
Mme de Citri, Mme de Guermantes would have had
more justification than she for this nihilism (which was
more than merely social), but it is true that certain qualities help us to endure the defects of our neighbour more
than they make us suffer from them; and a man of great
talent will normally pay less attention to other people's
foolishness than would a fool. We have already described
at sufficient length the nature of the Duchess's wit to convince the reader that, if it had nothing in common with
high intelligence, it was at least wit, a wit adroit in making use (like a translator) of different grammatical forms.
Now nothing of this sort seemed to entitle Mme de Citri
to look down upon qualities so closely akin to her own.
She found everyone idiotic, but in her conversation, in her
letters, showed herself distinctly inferior to the people
whom she treated with such disdain. She had moreover
such a thirst for destruction that, when she had more or
less given up society, the pleasures that she then sought
were subjected, each in turn, to her terrible undermining
power. After she had given up parties for musical
evenings, she used to say: "You like listening to that sort

of thing, to music? Goodness me, it depends on the
mood. But how deadly it can be! Ah, Beethoven!—what a
bore! (*la barbe*)." With Wagner, then with Franck, with
Debussy, she did not even take the trouble to say the
word *barbe*, but merely drew her hand over her face with
a tonsorial gesture. Presently, everything became boring.
"Beautiful things are such a bore. Ah, pictures!—they're
enough to drive you mad. How right you are, it is such a
bore having to write letters!" Finally it was life itself that
she declared to be boring (*rasante*), leaving you to wonder
where she took her term of comparison.

I do not know whether it was the effect of what the
Duchesse de Guermantes, on the evening when I first
dined at her house, had said of this interior, but the card-
room or smoking-room, with its pictorial floor, its tripods,
its figures of gods and animals that gazed at you, the
sphinxes stretched out along the arms of the chairs, and
most of all the huge table of marble or enamelled mosaic,
covered with symbolical signs more or less imitated from
Etruscan and Egyptian art, gave me the impression of a
magician's cell. And, indeed, on a chair drawn up to the
glittering augural table, M. de Charlus in person, never
touching a card, oblivious of what was going on around
him, incapable of observing that I had entered the room,
seemed precisely a magician applying all the force of his
will and reason to drawing a horoscope. Not only were his
eyes starting from his head like the eyes of a Pythian
priestess on her tripod, but, so that nothing might distract
him from labours which required the cessation of the
most simple movements, he had (like a mathematician
who will do nothing else until he has solved his problem)
laid down beside him the cigar which he had previously

been holding between his lips but had no longer the necessary equanimity of mind to think of smoking. Seeing the
two crouching deities on the arms of the chair that stood
facing him, one might have thought that the Baron was
endeavouring to solve the riddle of the Sphinx, had it not
been rather that of a young and living Oedipus seated in
that very armchair where he had settled down to play.
Now, the figure to which M. de Charlus was applying all
his mental powers with such concentration, and which
was not in fact one of the sort that are commonly studied
more geometrico, was that which was proposed to him by
the lineaments of the young Comte de Surgis; it appeared,
so profound was M. de Charlus's absorption in front of it,
to be some rebus, some riddle, some algebraical problem,
of which he must try to penetrate the mystery or to work
out the formula. In front of him the sibylline signs and
the figures inscribed upon that Table of the Law seemed
the grimoire which would enable the old sorcerer to tell in
what direction the young man's destiny was shaping. Suddenly he became aware that I was watching him, raised
his head as though he were waking from a dream, smiled
at me and blushed. At that moment Mme de Surgis's
other son came up behind the one who was playing, to
look at his cards. When M. de Charlus had learned from
me that they were brothers, his face could not conceal the
admiration he felt for a family which could create masterpieces so splendid and so diverse. And what would have
added to the Baron's enthusiasm would have been the discovery that the two sons of Mme de Surgis-le-Duc were
sons not only of the same mother but of the same father.
The children of Jupiter are dissimilar, but that is because
he married first Metis, whose destiny it was to bring into

the world wise children, then Themis, and after her Eurynome, and Mnemosyne, and Leto, and only as a last resort Juno. But to a single father Mme de Surgis had borne these two sons who had each received beauty from her, but a different beauty.

At last I had the pleasure of seeing Swann come into this room, which was extremely large, so large that he did not at first catch sight of me. A pleasure mingled with sadness, a sadness which the other guests did not, perhaps, feel, their feeling consisting rather in that sort of fascination which is exercised by the strange and unexpected signs of an approaching death, a death that a man already has, in the popular saying, written on his face. And it was with an almost offensive amazement, in which there were elements of tactless curiosity, of cruelty, of relieved and at the same time anxious self-scrutiny (a blend of *suave mari magno* and *memento quia pulvis*, Robert would have said), that all eyes were fastened on that face the cheeks of which had been so eaten away, so whittled down, by illness, like a waning moon, that except at a certain angle, the angle doubtless from which Swann looked at himself, they stopped short like a flimsy piece of scenery to which only an optical illusion can add the appearance of depth. Whether because of the absence of those cheeks, no longer there to modify it, or because arteriosclerosis, which is also a form of intoxication, had reddened it as would drunkenness, or deformed it as would morphine, Swann's punchinello nose, absorbed for long years into an agreeable face, seemed now enormous, tumid, crimson, the nose of an old Hebrew rather than of a dilettante Valois. Perhaps, too, in these last days, the physical type that characterises his race was becoming more pronounced in him, at the same time as a sense of moral solidarity with the rest of the Jews, a solidarity which Swann seemed to have forgotten throughout his life, and which, one after another, his mortal illness, the Dreyfus case and the anti-semitic propaganda had reawakened. There are certain Jews, men of great refinement and social delicacy, in whom nevertheless there remain in reserve and in the wings, ready to enter their lives at a given moment, as in a play, a cad and a prophet. Swann had arrived at the age of the prophet. Certainly, with that face of his from which, under the influence of his disease, whole segments had vanished, as when a block of ice melts and whole slabs of it fall off, he had of course changed. But I could not help being struck by the much greater extent to which he had changed in relation to myself. Admirable and cultivated though he was, a man I was anything but bored to meet, I could not for the life of me understand how I had been able to invest him long ago with such mystery that his appearance in the Champs-Elysées in his silk-lined cape would make my heart beat to the point where I was ashamed to approach him, and that at the door of the flat where such a being dwelt I could not ring the bell without being overcome with boundless agitation and alarm. All this had vanished not only from his house but from his person, and the idea of talking to him might or might not be agreeable to me, but had no effect whatever upon my nervous system.

And furthermore, how he had changed since that very afternoon, when I had met him—after all, only a few hours earlier—in the Duc de Guermantes's study! Had he really had a scene with the Prince, which had deeply upset him? The supposition was not necessary. The slightest efforts that are demanded of a person who is very ill quickly become for him an excessive strain. He has only to be exposed, when already tired, to the heat of a crowded drawing-room, for his features to change dramatically and turn blue, as happens in a few hours with an overripe pear or milk that is about to turn. Besides this, Swann's hair had thinned in places, and, as Mme de Guermantes remarked, needed attention from the furrier, looked as if it had been camphorated, and camphorated badly. I was just crossing the room to speak to Swann when unfortunately a hand fell upon my shoulder.

"Hallo, old boy, I'm in Paris for forty-eight hours. I called at your house and they told me you were here, so that it's to you that my aunt is indebted for the honour of my company at her party." It was Saint-Loup. I told him how greatly I admired the house. "Yes, it's very much the historic monument. Personally I find it deadly. We mustn't go near my uncle Palamède, or we shall be caught. Now that Mme Molé has gone (she's the one who rules the roost just now) he's rather at a loose end. I gather it was quite a spectacle, he never let her out of his sight for a moment, and didn't leave her until he'd seen her into her carriage. I bear my uncle no ill will, only I do think it odd that my family council, which has always been so hard on me, should be composed of the very ones who have lived it up the most, beginning with the biggest roisterer of the lot, my uncle Charlus, who is my surrogate guardian, has had more women than Don Juan, and is still carrying on in spite of his age. There was talk at one time of having me made a ward of court. I bet when all those gay old dogs met to consider the question and had me up to preach to me and tell me I was breaking my mother's heart, they dared not look one another in the face for fear of laughing. If you examined the composition of the council, you'd think they had deliberately chosen the greatest skirt-chasers."

Leaving aside M. de Charlus, with regard to whom my friend's astonishment did not seem to me more justi-fied—though for different reasons, reasons which, more-over, were afterwards to undergo some modification in my mind—Robert was quite wrong to think it extraordinary that lessons in worldly wisdom should be given to a young man by people who have played the fool or are still doing so. Even if it is simply a question of atavism and family likeness, it is inevitable that the uncle who deliv-ers the lecture should have more or less the same failings as the nephew whom he has been deputed to scold. Nor is the uncle in the least hypocritical in so doing, deluded as he is by the faculty people have of believing, in every new set of circumstances, that "this is quite different," a fac-ulty which enables them to adopt artistic, political and other errors without perceiving that they are the same er-rors which they exposed, ten years ago, in another school of painting which they condemned, another political affair which they felt to deserve a loathing that they no longer feel, and espouse those errors without recognising them in a fresh disguise. Besides, even if the faults of the uncle are different from those of the nephew, heredity may none the less to a certain extent be responsible, for the effect does not always resemble the cause, as a copy resembles its original, and even if the uncle's faults are worse, he may easily believe them to be less serious.

When M. de Charlus had made indignant remon-strances to Robert, who in any case was unaware of his uncle's true inclinations at the time—and even if it had still been the time when the Baron used to denounce his own inclinations—he might perfectly well have been sincere in considering, from the point of view of a man of the world, that Robert was infinitely more culpable than himself. Had not Robert, at the time when his uncle had been deputed to make him listen to reason, come within an inch of getting himself ostracised by society? Had he not very nearly been blackballed at the Jockey? Had he not made himself a public laughing-stock by the vast sums that he threw away upon a woman of the lowest type, by his friendships with people—authors, actors, Jews—not one of whom moved in society, by his opinions, which were indistinguishable from those held by traitors, by the grief he was causing to all his family? How could this scandalous existence be compared with that of M. de Charlus who had managed, so far, not only to retain but to enhance still further his position as a Guermantes, being in society an absolutely privileged person, sought after, adulated in the most exclusive circles, and a man who, married to a Bourbon princess, a woman of eminence, had succeeded in making her happy, had shown a devotion to her memory more fervent, more scrupulous than is customary in society, and had thus been as good a husband as a son?

"But are you sure that M. de Charlus has had all those mistresses?" I asked, not, of course, with the diabolical intention of revealing to Robert the secret that I had discovered, but irritated, nevertheless, at hearing him maintain an erroneous theory with such smug assurance. He merely shrugged his shoulders in response to what he took for ingenuousness on my part. "Not that I blame

him in the least, I consider that he's perfectly right." And
he proceeded to outline to me a theory of conduct that
would have horrified him at Balbec (where he was not
content with branding seducers, death seeming to him the
only punishment adequate to their crime). Then, however,
he had still been in love and jealous. Now he even went
so far as to sing the praises of houses of assignation.
"They're the only places where you can find a shoe to fit
you, sheathe your weapon, as we say in the Army." He
no longer felt for places of that sort the disgust that had
inflamed him at Balbec when I made an allusion to them,
and hearing what he now said, I told him that Bloch had
introduced me to one, but Robert replied that the one
which Bloch frequented must be "pretty vile, a poor
man's paradise!—It all depends, though: where was it?" I
remained vague, for I had just remembered that it was
there that Rachel whom Robert had so passionately loved
used to give herself for a louis. "Anyhow, I can take you
to some far better ones, full of stunning women." Hearing
me express the desire that he should take me as soon as
possible to the ones he knew, which must indeed be far
superior to the house to which Bloch had introduced me,
he expressed sincere regret that he would be unable to do
so on this occasion as he was leaving Paris next day. "It
will have to be my next leave," he said. "You'll see, there
are young girls there, even," he added with an air of mystery. "There's a little Mademoiselle de . . . I think it's
d'Orgeville—I can let you have the exact name—who is
the daughter of quite tip-top people; her mother was by
way of being a La Croix-l'Evêque, and they're really out
of the top drawer—in fact they're more or less related, if
I'm not mistaken, to my aunt Oriane. Anyhow, you have

only to see the child to realise at once that she must be somebody's daughter" (I could detect, hovering for a moment over Robert's voice, the shadow of the Guermantes family genie, which passed like a cloud, but at a great height and without stopping). "She looks to me a marvellous proposition. The parents are always ill and can't look after her. Gad, the child must have some amusement, and I count upon you to provide it!" "Oh, when are you coming back?" "I don't know. If you don't absolutely insist upon duchesses" (duchess being for the aristocracy the only title that denotes a particularly brilliant rank, as the lower orders talk of "princesses"), "in a different class of goods there's Mme Putbus's chambermaid."

At this moment, Mme de Surgis entered the room in search of her sons. As soon as he saw her M. de Charlus went up to her with a friendliness by which the Marquise was all the more agreeably surprised in that an icy coldness was what she had expected from the Baron, who had always posed as Oriane's protector and alone of the family—the rest being too often inclined to indulgence towards the Duke's irregularities because of his wealth and from jealousy of the Duchess—kept his brother's mistresses ruthlessly at a distance. And so Mme de Surgis would have fully understood the motives for the attitude that she dreaded to find in the Baron, but never for a moment suspected those for the wholly different welcome that she did receive from him. He spoke to her with admiration of the portrait that Jacquet had painted of her years before. This admiration waxed indeed to an enthusiasm which, if it was partly calculating, with the object of preventing the Marquise from going away, of "engaging" her, as Robert used to say of enemy armies whose forces one wants to keep tied down at a particular point, was also perhaps sincere. For, if everyone was pleased to admire in her sons the regal bearing and the beautiful eyes of Mme de Surgis, the Baron could taste an inverse but no less keen pleasure in finding those charms combined in the mother, as in a portrait which does not in itself provoke desire, but feeds, with the aesthetic admiration that it does provoke, the desires that it awakens. These now gave in retrospect a voluptuous charm to Jacquet's portrait itself, and at that moment the Baron would gladly have purchased it to study therein the physiological pedigree of the two Surgis boys.

"You see, I wasn't exaggerating," Robert said in my ear. "Just look at my uncle's attentiveness to Mme de Surgis. Though I must say it does surprise me. If Oriane knew, she would be furious. Really, there are enough women in the world without his having to go and pounce on her," he went on. Like everybody who is not in love, he imagined that one chooses the person one loves after endless deliberation and on the strength of diverse qualities and advantages. Besides, while completely mistaken about his uncle, whom he supposed to be devoted to women, Robert, in his rancour, spoke too lightly of M. de Charlus. One is not always somebody's nephew with impunity. It is often through him that a hereditary habit is transmitted sooner or later. We might indeed arrange a whole gallery of portraits, named like the German comedy *Uncle and Nephew*, in which we should see the uncle watching jealously, albeit unconsciously, for his nephew to end by becoming like himself. I might even add that this gallery would be incomplete were we not to include in it uncles who are not blood relations, being the uncles only of their nephews' wives. For the Messieurs de Charlus of this world are so convinced that they themselves are the only good husbands, and what is more the only ones of whom a wife would not be jealous, that generally, out of affection for their niece, they make her marry another Charlus. Which tangles the skein of family likenesses. And, to affection for the niece is added at times affection for her betrothed as well. Such marriages are not uncommon, and are often what is called happy.

"What were we talking about? Oh yes, that big, fair girl, Mme Putbus's maid. She goes with women too, but I don't suppose you mind that. I tell you frankly, I've never seen such a gorgeous creature." "I imagine her as being rather Giorgionesque?" "Wildly Giorgionesque! Oh, if I only had a little time in Paris, what wonderful things there are to be done! And then one goes on to the next. Because love is all rot, you know, I've finished with all that."

I soon discovered, to my surprise, that he had equally finished with literature, whereas it was merely with regard to literary men that he had struck me as being disillusioned at our last meeting. ("They're practically all a pack of scoundrels," he had said to me, a remark that was to be explained by his justified resentment towards certain of Rachel's friends. For they had persuaded her that she would never have any talent if she allowed Robert, "scion of an alien race," to acquire an influence over her, and with her used to make fun of him, to his face, at the dinners he gave for them.) But in reality Robert's love of Letters was in no sense profound, did not spring from his true nature, was only a by-product of his love of Rachel, and had faded with the latter at the same time as his loathing for voluptuaries and his religious respect for the virtue of women.

"There's something rather strange about those two young men. Look at that curious passion for gambling, Marquise," said M. de Charlus, drawing Mme de Surgis's attention to her two sons, as though he were completely unaware of their identity. "They must be a pair of orientals, they have certain characteristic features, they're perhaps Turks," he went on, so as to give further support to his feigned innocence and at the same time to exhibit a vague antipathy, which, when in due course it gave place to affability, would prove that the latter was addressed to the young men solely in their capacity as sons of Mme de Surgis, having begun only when the Baron discovered who they were. Perhaps, too, M. de Charlus, whose insolence was a natural gift which he delighted in exercising, was taking advantage of the few moments in which he was supposed not to know the name of these two young men to have a little fun at Mme de Surgis's expense and to indulge in his habitual mockery, as Scapin takes advantage of his master's disguise to give him a sound drubbing.

"They are my sons," said Mme de Surgis, with a blush that would not have coloured her cheeks had she been shrewder without necessarily being more virtuous. She would then have understood that the air of absolute indifference or of sarcasm which M. de Charlus displayed towards a young man was no more sincere than the wholly superficial admiration which he showed for a woman expressed his true nature. The woman to whom he could go on indefinitely paying the prettiest compliments might well be jealous of the look which, while talking to her, he shot at a man whom he would pretend afterwards not to have noticed. For that look was different from the looks which M. de Charlus kept for women; a special look, springing from the depths, which even at a party could not help straying naïvely in the direction of young men, like the look in a tailor's eye which betrays his profession by immediately fastening upon your attire.

"Oh, how very odd!" replied M. de Charlus with some insolence, as though his mind had to make a long journey to arrive at a reality so different from what he had pretended to suppose. "But I don't know them," he added, fearing lest he might have gone a little too far in the expression of his antipathy and have thus paralysed the Marquise's intention of effecting an introduction. "Would you allow me to introduce them to you?" Mme de Surgis inquired timidly. "Why, good gracious, just as you please, I don't mind, but I'm perhaps not very entertaining company for such young people," M. de Charlus intoned with the air of chilly reluctance of someone allowing himself to be forced into an act of politeness.

"Arnulphe, Victurnien, come here at once," said Mme de Surgis. Victurnien rose purposefully. Arnulphe, though he could not see further than his brother, followed him meekly.

"It's the sons' turn, now," muttered Saint-Loup. "It's enough to make one die laughing. He tries to curry favour with everyone, down to the dog in the yard. It's all the funnier as my uncle detests pretty boys. And just look how seriously he's listening to them. If it was me who tried to introduce them to him, he'd send me away with a flea in my ear. Listen, I shall have to go and say how-d'ye-do to Oriane. I have so little time in Paris that I want to try and see all the people here that otherwise I ought to leave cards on."

"How well brought-up they seem, what charming manners," M. de Charlus was saying.

"Do you think so?" Mme de Surgis replied, highly delighted.

Swann, having caught sight of me, came over to Saint-Loup and myself. His Jewish gaiety was less subtle than his socialite witticisms: "Good evening," he said to us. "Heavens! all three of us together—people will think it's a meeting of the Syndicate. In another minute they'll be looking for the money-box!" He had not observed that M. de Beauserfeuil was just behind him and could hear what he said. The General could not help wincing. We heard the voice of M. de Charlus close beside us: "What, so you're called Victurnien, after the *Cabinet des Antiques*," the Baron was saying, to prolong his conversation with the two young men. "By Balzac, yes," replied the elder Surgis, who had never read a line of that novelist's work, but to whom his tutor had remarked, a few days earlier, upon the similarity of his Christian name and d'Esgrignon's. Mme de Surgis was delighted to see her son shine, and M. de Charlus in ecstasy at such a display of learning.

"It appears that Loubet[4] is entirely on our side, I have it from an absolutely trustworthy source," Swann informed Saint-Loup, but this time in a lower tone so as not to be overheard by the General. He had begun to find his wife's Republican connexions more interesting now that the Dreyfus case had become his chief preoccupation.

"I tell you this because I know that you are with us up to the hilt."

"Not quite to that extent; you're completely mistaken," Robert replied. "It's a bad business, and I'm sorry I ever got involved in it. It was no affair of mine. If it were to begin over again, I should keep well clear of it. I'm a soldier, and my first loyalty is to the Army. If you stay with M. Swann for a moment, I shall be back presently. I must go and talk to my aunt."

But I saw that it was with Mlle d'Ambresac that he went to talk, and was distressed by the thought that he had lied to me about the possibility of their engagement. My mind was set at rest when I learned that he had been introduced to her half an hour earlier by Mme de Marsantes, who was anxious for the marriage, the Ambresacs being extremely rich.

"At last," said M. de Charlus to Mme de Surgis. "I find a young man with some education, who has read a bit, who knows who Balzac is. And it gives me all the more pleasure to meet him where that sort of thing has become most rare, in the house of one of my peers, one of ourselves," he added, laying stress upon the words. It was all very well for the Guermantes to profess to regard all men as equal; on the great occasions when they found themselves among "well-born" people, especially if they were not quite so "well-born" as themselves, whom they were anxious and able to flatter, they did not hesitate to trot out old family memories. "At one time," the Baron went on, "the word aristocrat meant the best people, in intellect and in heart. Now, here is the first person I've come across in our world who has ever heard of Victurnien d'Esgrignon. No, I'm wrong in saying the first. There are also a Polignac and a Montesquiou," added M. de Charlus, who knew that this twofold association must inevitably thrill the Marquise. "However, in your sons' case it runs in the family: their maternal grandfather had a famous eighteenth-century collection. I will show you mine if you will give me the pleasure of coming to luncheon with me one day," he said to the young Victurnien. "I can show you an interesting edition of the *Cabinet des Antiques* with corrections in Balzac's own hand. I shall be charmed to bring the two Victurniens face to face."

I could not bring myself to leave Swann. He had arrived at that stage of exhaustion in which a sick man's body becomes a mere retort in which to study chemical reactions. His face was mottled with tiny spots of Prussian blue, which seemed not to belong to the world of living things, and emitted the sort of odour which, at school, after "experiments," makes it so unpleasant to have to remain in a "science" classroom. I asked him if it was true that he had had a long conversation with the Prince de Guermantes and if he would tell me what it had been about.

"Yes," he said, "but go for a moment first with M. de Charlus and Mme de Surgis. I'll wait for you here."

And indeed M. de Charlus, having suggested to Mme de Surgis that they should leave this room, which was too hot, and go and sit for a while in another, had invited not the two sons to accompany their mother, but myself. In this way he had made himself appear, after having successfully hooked them, to have lost all interest in the two

young men. He was moreover paying me an inexpensive
compliment, Mme de Surgis-le-Duc being socially in
rather bad odour.

Unfortunately, no sooner had we sat down in an alcove from which there was no way of escape than Mme
de Saint-Euverte, a favourite butt for the Baron's jibes,
came past. She, perhaps to mask or else openly to disre-
gard the ill will which she inspired in M. de Charlus, and
above all to show that she was on intimate terms with a
woman who was talking so familiarly to him, gave a disdainfully friendly greeting to the famous beauty, who acknowledged it while peeping out of the corner of her eye
at M. de Charlus with a mocking smile. But the alcove
was so narrow that Mme de Saint-Euverte, when she went
behind us to continue her canvass of her guests for the
morrow, found herself cornered and could not easily escape—a heaven-sent opportunity which M. de Charlus,
anxious to display his insolent wit before the mother of
the two young men, took good care not to let slip. A silly
question which I put to him without any malicious intent
gave him the cue for a triumphal tirade of which the
wretched Saint-Euverte, more or less immobilised behind
us, could not have missed a single word.

"Would you believe it, this impertinent young man,"
he said, indicating me to Mme de Surgis, "has just asked
me, without the slightest concern for the proper reticence
in regard to such needs, whether I was going to Mme de
Saint-Euverte's, in other words, I suppose, whether I was
suffering from diarrhoea. I should endeavour in any case
to relieve myself in some more comfortable place than the
house of a person who, if my memory serves me, was celebrating her centenary when I first began to move in soci-

ety, that is to say, not in her house. And yet who could be more interesting to listen to? What a host of historic memories, seen and lived through in the days of the First Empire and the Restoration, and intimate revelations, too, which certainly had nothing of the 'Saint' about them but must have been extremely 'vertes'[5] if one may judge by the friskiness still left in those venerable hams. What would prevent me from questioning her about those thrilling times is the sensitiveness of my olfactory organ. The proximity of the lady is enough. I suddenly say to myself: oh, good lord, someone has broken the lid of my cesspool, when it's simply the Marquise opening her mouth to emit some invitation. And you can imagine that if I had the misfortune to go to her house, the cesspool would expand into a formidable sewage-cart. She bears a mystic name, though, which has always made me think with jubilation, although she has long since passed the date of her jubilee, of that stupid line of so-called 'deliquescent' poetry: 'Ah, green, how green my soul was on that day . . .' But I require a cleaner sort of verdure. They tell me that the indefatigable old street-walker gives 'garden-parties.' Myself, I should describe them as 'invitations to explore the sewers.' Are you going to wallow there?" he asked Mme de Surgis, who now found herself in a quandary. Wishing to pretend for the Baron's benefit that she was not going, and knowing that she would give days of her life rather than miss the Saint-Euverte party, she got out of it by a compromise, that is to say by expressing uncertainty. This uncertainty took a form so clumsily amateurish and so miserably tacked together that M. de Charlus, not afraid of offending Mme de Surgis,

whom nevertheless he was anxious to please, began to
laugh to show her that "it didn't wash."

"I always admire people who make plans," she said.
"I often change mine at the last moment. There's a question of a summer frock which may alter everything. I shall
act upon the inspiration of the moment."

For my part, I was incensed at the abominable little
speech that M. de Charlus had just made. I would have
liked to shower blessings upon the giver of garden-parties.
Unfortunately, in the social as in the political world, the
victims are such cowards that one cannot for long remain
indignant with their executioners. Mme de Saint-Euverte,
who had succeeded in escaping from the alcove to which
we were barring the entry, brushed against the Baron in-
advertently as she passed him, and, by a reflex of snobbishness which wiped out all her anger, perhaps even in
the hope of securing an opening of a kind at which this
could not be the first attempt, exclaimed: "Oh! I beg your
pardon, Monsieur de Charlus, I hope I did not hurt you,"
as though she were kneeling before her lord and master.
The latter did not deign to reply otherwise than by a
broad ironical smile, and conceded only a "Good
evening," which, uttered as though he had noticed the
Marquise's presence only after she had greeted him, was
an additional insult. Finally, with an extreme obsequious-
ness which pained me for her sake, Mme de Saint-Euverte
came up to me and, drawing me aside, murmured in my
ear: "Tell me, what have I done to M. de Charlus? They
say that he doesn't consider me smart enough for him,"
she added, laughing heartily. I remained serious. For one
thing, I thought it stupid of her to appear to believe or to

wish other people to believe that nobody, really, was as smart as herself. For another thing, people who laugh so heartily at what they themselves have said, when it is not funny, dispense us accordingly, by taking upon themselves the responsibility for the mirth, from joining in it.

"Other people assure me that he is cross because I don't invite him. But he doesn't give me much encouragement. He seems to avoid me." (This expression struck me as inadequate.) "Try to find out, and come and tell me tomorrow. And if he feels remorseful and wishes to come too, bring him. Forgive and forget. Indeed, I should be quite glad to see him, because it would annoy Mme de Surgis. I give you a free hand. You have a remarkable flair for these matters and I don't wish to appear to be begging my guests to come. In any case, I count upon you absolutely."

It occurred to me that Swann must be getting tired of waiting for me. Moreover I did not wish to be too late in returning home because of Albertine, and, taking leave of Mme de Surgis and M. de Charlus, I went in search of my invalid in the card-room. I asked him whether what he had said to the Prince in their conversation in the garden was really what M. de Bréauté (whom I did not name) had reported to us, about a little play by Bergotte. He burst out laughing: "There's not a word of truth in it, not one, it's a complete fabrication and would have been an utterly stupid thing to say. It's really incredible, this spontaneous generation of falsehood. I won't ask who it was that told you, but it would be really interesting, in a field as limited as this, to work back from one person to another and find out how the story arose. Anyhow, what concern can it be of other people, what the Prince said to

me? People are very inquisitive. I've never been inquisitive, except when I was in love, and when I was jealous.
And a lot I ever learned! Are you jealous?" I told Swann
that I had never experienced jealousy, that I did not even
know what it was. "Well, you can count yourself lucky. A
little jealousy is not too unpleasant, for two reasons. In
the first place, it enables people who are not inquisitive to
take an interest in the lives of others, or of one other at
any rate. And then it makes one feel the pleasure of
possession, of getting into a carriage with a woman, of
not allowing her to go about by herself. But that's only in
the very first stages of the disease, or when the cure is almost complete. In between, it's the most agonising torment. However, I must confess that I haven't had much
experience even of the two pleasures I've mentioned—the
first because of my own nature, which is incapable of
sustained reflexion; the second because of circumstances,
because of the woman, I should say the women, of whom
I've been jealous. But that makes no difference. Even
when one is no longer attached to things, it's still something to have been attached to them; because it was
always for reasons which other people didn't grasp. The
memory of those feelings is something that's to be found
only in ourselves; we must go back into ourselves to look
at it. You mustn't laugh at this idealistic jargon, but
what I mean to say is that I've been very fond of life and
very fond of art. Well, now that I'm a little too weary to
live with other people, those old feelings, so personal and
individual, that I had in the past, seem to me—it's the
mania of all collectors—very precious. I open my heart
to myself like a sort of showcase, and examine one by
one all those love affairs of which the rest of the world

can have known nothing. And of this collection, to which I'm now even more attached than to my others, I say to myself, rather as Mazarin said of his books, but in fact without the least distress, that it will be very tiresome to have to leave it all. But, to come back to my conversation with the Prince, I shall tell one person only, and that person is going to be you."

My attention was distracted by the conversation that M. de Charlus, who had returned to the card-room, was carrying on endlessly nearby. "And are you a reader too? What do you do?" he asked Comte Arnulphe, who had never heard even the name of Balzac. But his short-sightedness, since it caused him to see everything very small, gave him the appearance of seeing great distances, so that—rare poetry in a statuesque Greek god—remote, mysterious stars seemed to be engraved upon his pupils.

"Suppose we took a turn in the garden," I said to Swann, while Comte Arnulphe, in a lisping voice which seemed to indicate that mentally at least his development was incomplete, replied to M. de Charlus with an artlessly obliging precision: "Oh, you know, mainly golf, tennis, football, running, and especially polo." Thus had Minerva, having subdivided herself, ceased in certain cities to be the goddess of wisdom, and had become partly incarnated in a purely sporting, horse-loving deity, Athene Hippia. And he went to St Moritz also to ski, for Pallas Tritogeneia frequents the high peaks and outruns swift horsemen. "Ah!" replied M. de Charlus with the transcendental smile of the intellectual who does not even take the trouble to conceal his derision, but, on the other hand, feels himself so superior to other people and so far de-

spises the intelligence of those who are least stupid that he
barely differentiates between them and the most stupid, as
long as the latter are attractive to him in some other way.
While talking to Arnulphe, M. de Charlus felt that by the
mere act of addressing him he was conferring upon him a
superiority which everyone else must recognise and envy.
"No," Swann replied, "I'm too tired to walk about. Let's
sit down somewhere in a corner, I cannot remain on my
feet any longer." This was true, and yet the act of beginning to talk had already restored to him a certain vivacity.
For it is a fact that in the most genuine exhaustion there
is, especially in highly-strung people, an element that depends on attention and is preserved only by an act of
memory. We feel suddenly weary as soon as we are afraid
of feeling weary, and, to throw off our fatigue, it suffices
us to forget about it. To be sure, Swann was far from being one of those indefatigable invalids who, entering a
room worn out and ready to drop, revive in conversation
like a flower in water and are able for hours on end to
draw from their own words a reserve of strength which
they do not, alas, communicate to their hearers, who appear more and more exhausted the more the talker comes
back to life. But Swann belonged to that stout Jewish
race, in whose vital energy, its resistance to death, its individual members seem to share. Stricken severally by
their own diseases, as it is stricken itself by persecution,
they continue indefinitely to struggle against terrible agonies which may be prolonged beyond every apparently
possible limit, when already one can see only a prophet's
beard surmounted by a huge nose which dilates to inhale
its last breath, before the hour strikes for the ritual

prayers and the punctual procession of distant relatives begins, advancing with mechanical movements as upon an Assyrian frieze.

We went to sit down, but, before moving away from the group formed by M. de Charlus with the two young Surgis and their mother, Swann could not resist fastening upon the lady's bosom the lingering, dilated, concupiscent gaze of a connoisseur. He even put up his monocle for a better view, and, while he talked to me, kept glancing in her direction.

"Here, word for word," he said to me when we were seated, "is my conversation with the Prince, and if you remember what I said to you just now, you will see why I choose you as my confidant. There is another reason as well, which you will learn one day. 'My dear Swann,' the Prince de Guermantes said to me, 'you must forgive me if I have appeared to be avoiding you for some time past.' (I had never even noticed it, having been ill and avoiding society myself.) 'In the first place, I had heard it said, and I fully expected, that in the unhappy affair which is splitting the country in two your views were diametrically opposed to mine. Now, it would have been extremely painful to me to hear you express these views in my presence. I was so sensitive on the matter that when the Princess, two years ago, heard her brother-in-law, the Grand Duke of Hesse, say that Dreyfus was innocent, she was not content with promptly challenging the assertion but refrained from repeating it to me in order not to upset me. At about the same time, the Crown Prince of Sweden came to Paris and, having probably heard someone say that the Empress Eugénie was a Dreyfusist, confused her with the Princess (a strange confusion, you will admit, between a woman of the rank of my wife and a Spaniard, a good deal less well-born than people make out, and married to a mere Bonaparte) and said to her: Princess, I am doubly glad to meet you, for I know that you hold the same view as myself of the Dreyfus case, which does not surprise me since Your Highness is Bavarian. Which drew down upon the Prince the answer: Sir, I am no longer anything but a French Princess, and I share the views of all my fellow-countrymen. Well, my dear Swann, about eighteen months ago, a conversation I had with General de Beauserfeuil made me suspect that, not an error, but grave illegalities, had been committed in the conduct of the trial.' "

We were interrupted (Swann did not want his story to be overheard) by the voice of M. de Charlus who (without, as it happened, paying us the slightest attention) came past escorting Mme de Surgis and stopped in the hope of detaining her for a moment longer, either on account of her sons or from that reluctance common to all the Guermantes to bring anything to an end, which kept them plunged in a sort of anxious inertia. Swann informed me in this connexion, a little later, of something that, for me, stripped the name Surgis-le-Duc of all the poetry that I had found in it. The Marquise de Surgis-le-Duc boasted a far higher social position, far grander connexions by marriage, than her cousin the Comte de Surgis, who had no money and lived on his estate in the country. But the suffix to her title, "le Duc," had not at all the origin which I attributed to it, and which had made me associate it in my imagination with Bourg-l'Abbé, Bois-le-Roi, etc. All that had happened was that a Comte de Surgis had married, under the Restoration, the daughter of an im-

mensely rich industrial magnate, M. Leduc, or Le Duc,
himself the son of a chemical manufacturer, the richest
man of his day and a peer of France. King Charles X had
created for the son born of this marriage the marquisate
of Surgis-le-Duc, a marquisate of Surgis existing already
in the family. The addition of the bourgeois surname had
not prevented this branch from allying itself, on the
strength of its enormous fortune, with the first families of
the realm. And the present Marquise de Surgis-le-Duc,
being extremely well-born, could have enjoyed a very
high position in society. A demon of perversity had
driven her, scorning the position ready-made for her, to
flee from the conjugal roof and live a life of open scandal.
Whereupon the society she had scorned at twenty, when
it was at her feet, had cruelly spurned her at thirty, when,
after ten years, nobody except a few faithful friends
greeted her any longer, and she had had to set to work to
reconquer laboriously, inch by inch, what she had possessed as a birthright (a round trip that isn't uncommon).

As for the great nobles, her kinsmen, whom she had
disowned in the past, and who in their turn had disowned
her, she found an excuse for the joy that she would feel in
gathering them again to her bosom in the memories of
childhood that she would be able to recall with them.
And in saying this, with the object of disguising her snobbery, she was perhaps being less untruthful than she supposed. "Basin is all my girlhood!" she said on the day on
which he came back to her. And indeed it was partly true.
But she had miscalculated when she chose him for her
lover. For all the women friends of the Duchesse de
Guermantes were to rally round her, and so Mme de Surgis must descend for the second time that slope up which

she had so laboriously toiled. "Well!" M. de Charlus was saying to her in an effort to prolong the conversation, "you must lay my tribute at the feet of the beautiful portrait. How is it? What has become of it?" "Why," replied Mme de Surgis, "you know I haven't got it now; my husband wasn't pleased with it." "Not pleased! With one of the greatest works of art of our time, equal to Nattier's Duchesse de Châteauroux, and, moreover, perpetuating no less majestic and heart-shattering a goddess. Oh, that little blue collar! I swear, Vermeer himself never painted a fabric more consummately—but we must not say it too loud or Swann will fall upon us to avenge his favourite painter, the Master of Delft." The Marquise, turning round, addressed a smile and held out her hand to Swann, who had risen to greet her. But almost without concealment, because his advanced years had deprived him either of the will, from indifference to the opinion of others, or the physical power, from the intensity of his desire and the weakening of the controls that help to disguise it, as soon as Swann, on taking the Marquise's hand, had seen her bosom at close range and from above, he plunged an attentive, serious, absorbed, almost anxious gaze into the depths of her corsage, and his nostrils, drugged by her perfume, quivered like the wings of a butterfly about to alight upon a half-glimpsed flower. Abruptly he shook off the intoxication that had seized him, and Mme de Surgis herself, although embarrassed, stifled a deep sigh, so contagious can desire prove at times. "The painter was offended," she said to M. de Charlus, "and took it back. I have heard that it is now at Diane de Saint-Euverte's." "I decline to believe," said the Baron, "that a great picture can have such bad taste."*

"He is talking to her about her portrait. I could talk to her about that portrait just as well as Charlus," said Swann, affecting a drawling, raffish tone as he followed the retreating couple with his eyes. "And I should certainly enjoy talking about it more than Charlus," he added.

I asked him whether the things that were said about M. de Charlus were true, in doing which I was lying twice over, for if I had no proof that anybody ever had said anything, I had on the other hand been perfectly aware since that afternoon that what I was hinting at was true. Swann shrugged his shoulders, as though I had suggested something quite absurd.

"It's quite true that he's a charming friend. But I need hardly add that his friendship is purely platonic. He is more sentimental than other men, that's all; on the other hand, as he never goes very far with women, that has given a sort of plausibility to the idiotic rumours to which you refer. Charlus is perhaps greatly attached to his men friends, but you may be quite certain that the attachment is only in his head and in his heart. However, now we may perhaps be left in peace for a moment. Well, the Prince de Guermantes went on to say: 'I don't mind telling you that this idea of a possible illegality in the conduct of the trial was extremely painful to me, because I have always, as you know, worshipped the Army. I discussed the matter again with the General, and, alas, there could be no room for doubt. I need hardly tell you that, all this time, the idea that an innocent man might be undergoing the most infamous punishment had never even crossed my mind. But tormented by this idea of illegality,

I began to study what I had always declined to read, and
then the possibility, this time not only of illegality but of
the prisoner's innocence, began to haunt me. I did not
feel that I could talk about it to the Princess. Heaven
knows that she has become just as French as myself.
From the day of our marriage, I took such pride in showing her our country in all its beauty, and what to me is its
greatest splendour, its Army, that it would have been too
painful for me to tell her of my suspicions, which involved, it is true, a few officers only. But I come of a
family of soldiers, and I was reluctant to believe that officers could be mistaken. I discussed the case again with
Beauserfeuil, and he admitted that there had been culpable intrigues, that the memorandum was possibly not in
Dreyfus's writing, but that an overwhelming proof of his
guilt did exist. This was the Henry document. And a few
days later we learned that it was a forgery. After that, un-
beknownst to the Princess, I began to read the *Siècle* and
the *Aurore* every day. Soon I had no more doubts, and I
couldn't sleep. I confided my distress to our friend, the
abbé Poiré, who, I was astonished to find, held the same
conviction, and I got him to say masses for Dreyfus, his
unfortunate wife and their children. Meanwhile, one
morning as I went into the Princess's room, I saw her
maid trying to hide something from me that she had in
her hand. I asked her, chaffingly, what it was, and she
blushed and refused to tell me. I had the greatest confidence in my wife, but this incident disturbed me considerably (and the Princess too, no doubt, who must have
heard about it from her maid), for my dear Marie barely
uttered a word to me that day at luncheon. I asked the

abbé Poiré that day whether he could say my mass for
Dreyfus the following morning . . .' And so much for
that!" exclaimed Swann, breaking off his narrative.

I looked up, and saw the Duc de Guermantes bearing
down upon us. "Forgive me for interrupting you, my
boys. Young man," he went on, addressing me, "I am instructed to give you a message from Oriane. Marie and
Gilbert have asked us to stay and have supper at their
table with only five or six other people: the Princess of
Hesse, Mme de Ligne, Mme de Tarente, Mme de
Chevreuse, the Duchesse d'Arenberg. Unfortunately, we
can't stay—we're going on to a little ball of sorts." I was
listening, but whenever we have something definite to do
at a given moment, we depute a certain person inside us
who is accustomed to that sort of duty to keep an eye on
the clock and warn us in time. This inner servant reminded me, as I had asked him to remind me a few hours
before, that Albertine, who at the moment was far from
my thoughts, was to come and see me immediately after
the theatre. And so I declined the invitation to supper.
This does not mean that I was not enjoying myself at the
Princesse de Guermantes's. The truth is that men can
have several sorts of pleasure. The true pleasure is the one
for which they abandon the other. But the latter, if it is
apparent, or rather if it alone is apparent, may put people
off the scent of the other, reassure or mislead the jealous,
create a false impression. And yet, all that is needed to
make us sacrifice it to the other is a little happiness or a
little suffering. Sometimes a third category of pleasures,
more serious, but more essential, does not yet exist for us,
its potential existence betraying itself only by arousing regrets and discouragement. And yet it is to these pleasures

that we shall devote ourselves in time to come. To give a very minor example, a soldier in time of peace will sacrifice social life to love, but, once war is declared (and without there being any need to introduce the idea of patriotic duty), will sacrifice love to the passion, stronger than love, for fighting. For all that Swann assured me that he was happy to tell me his story, I could feel that his conversation with me, because of the lateness of the hour, and because he was so ill, was one of those exertions for which those who know that they are killing themselves by sitting up late, by overdoing things, feel an angry regret when they return home, a regret similar to that felt at the wild extravagance of which they have again been guilty by the spendthrifts who will nevertheless be unable to restrain themselves from throwing money out of the window again tomorrow. Once we have reached a certain degree of enfeeblement, whether it is caused by age or by ill health, all pleasure taken at the expense of sleep outside our normal habits, every disturbance of routine, becomes a nuisance. The talker continues to talk, from politeness, from excitement, but he knows that the hour at which he might still have been able to go to sleep has already passed, and he knows also the reproaches that he will heap upon himself during the insomnia and fatigue that must ensue. Already, moreover, even the momentary pleasure has come to an end, body and brain are too far drained of their strength to welcome with any readiness what seems entertaining to one's interlocutor. They are like a house on the morning before a journey or removal, where visitors become a perfect plague, to be received sitting upon locked trunks, with our eyes on the clock.

"At last we're alone," he said. "I quite forget where I

was. Oh yes, I had just told you, hadn't I, that the Prince
asked the abbé Poiré if he could say his mass next day for
Dreyfus. 'No, the abbé informed me' ("I say *me*," Swann
explained to me, "because it's the Prince who is speaking,
you understand?"), 'for I have another mass that I've been
asked to say for him tomorrow as well.—What, I said to
him, is there another Catholic as well as myself who is
convinced of his innocence?—It appears so.—But this
other supporter's conviction must be more recent than
mine.—Maybe, but this other was asking me to say
masses when you still believed Dreyfus guilty.—Ah, I can
see that it's no one in our world.—On the contrary! —Really, there are Dreyfusists among us, are there? You in-
trigue me; I should like to unbosom myself to this rare
bird, if it is someone I know.—It is.—What is his
name?—The Princesse de Guermantes. While I was
afraid of offending my dear wife's nationalistic opinions,
her faith in France, she had been afraid of alarming my
religious opinions, my patriotic sentiments. But privately
she had been thinking as I did, though for longer than I
had. And what her maid had been hiding as she went into
her room, what she went out to buy for her every morning, was the *Aurore*. My dear Swann, from that moment I
thought of the pleasure that I should give you if I told
you how closely akin my views upon this matter were to
yours; forgive me for not having done so sooner. If you
bear in mind that I had never said a word to the Princess,
it will not surprise you to be told that thinking the same
as yourself must at that time have kept me further apart
from you than thinking differently. For it was an extremely painful topic for me to broach. The more I believe that an error, that crimes even, have been committed,

the more my heart bleeds for the Army. It had never occurred to me that opinions like mine could possibly cause
you similar pain, until I was told the other day that you
emphatically condemned the insults to the Army and the
fact that the Dreyfusists agreed to ally themselves with
those who insulted it. That settled it. I admit that it has
been most painful for me to confess to you what I think
of certain officers, few in number fortunately, but it is a
relief to me not to have to keep away from you any
longer, and above all a relief to make it clear to you that if
I had other feelings it was because I hadn't a shadow of
doubt as to the soundness of the verdict. As soon as my
doubts began, I could wish for only one thing, that the
mistake should be rectified.' I confess that I was deeply
moved by the Prince de Guermantes's words. If you knew
him as I do, if you could realise the distance he has had
to travel in order to reach his present position, you would
admire him as he deserves. Not that his opinion surprises
me, his is such an upright nature!"

Swann was forgetting that during the afternoon he
had on the contrary told me that people's opinions as to
the Dreyfus case were dictated by atavism. At the most
he had made an exception on behalf of intelligence, because in Saint-Loup it had managed to overcome atavism
and had made a Dreyfusard of him. Now he had just seen
that this victory had been of short duration and that
Saint-Loup had passed into the opposite camp. And so it
was to moral uprightness that he now assigned the role
which had previously devolved upon intelligence. In reality we always discover afterwards that our adversaries had
a reason for being on the side they espoused, which has
nothing to do with any element of right that there may be

on that side, and that those who think as we do do so because their intelligence, if their moral nature is too base to be invoked, or their uprightness, if their perception is weak, has compelled them to.

Swann now found equally intelligent anybody who was of his opinion, his old friend the Prince de Guermantes as well as my schoolfellow Bloch, whom previously he had avoided and whom he now invited to lunch. Swann interested Bloch greatly by telling him that the Prince de Guermantes was a Dreyfusard. "We must ask him to sign our appeal on behalf of Picquart; a name like his would have a tremendous effect." But Swann, blending with his ardent conviction as a Jew the diplomatic moderation of a man of the world, whose habits he had too thoroughly acquired to be able to shed them at this late hour, refused to allow Bloch to send the Prince a petition to sign, even on his own initiative. "He cannot do such a thing, we mustn't expect the impossible," Swann repeated. "There you have a charming man who has travelled thousands of miles to come over to our side. He can be very useful to us. If he were to sign your petition, he would simply be compromising himself with his own people, would be made to suffer on our account, might even repent of his confidences and do nothing more." Furthermore, Swann withheld his own name. He considered it too Hebraic not to create a bad effect. Besides, even if he approved of everything that concerned reconsideration, he did not wish to be mixed up in any way in the anti-militarist campaign. He wore, a thing he had never done previously, the decoration he had won as a young militiaman in '70, and added a codicil to his will asking that, contrary to its previous provisions, he might be buried with the military honours due to his rank as Chevalier of the Legion of Honour. A request which assembled round the church of Combray a whole squadron of those troopers over whose fate Françoise used to weep in days gone by, when she envisaged the prospect of war. In short, Swann refused to sign Bloch's petition, with the result that, if he passed in the eyes of many people as a fanatical Dreyfusard, my friend found him lukewarm, infected with nationalism, and jingoistic.

Swann left me without shaking hands so as not to be forced into a general leave-taking in this room where he had too many friends, but said to me: "You ought to come and see your friend Gilberte. She has really grown up now and altered, you wouldn't know her. She would be so pleased!" I no longer loved Gilberte. She was for me like a dead person for whom one has long mourned, and then forgetfulness has come, and if she were to be resuscitated would no longer fit into a life which has ceased to be fashioned for her. I no longer had any desire to see her, not even that desire to show her that I did not wish to see her which, every day, when I was in love with her, I vowed to myself that I would flaunt before her when I loved her no longer.

Hence, seeking now only to give myself in Gilberte's eyes the air of having longed with all my heart to meet her again and of having been prevented by circumstances of the kind called "beyond our control," which indeed only occur, with any consistency at least, when we do nothing to thwart them, so far from accepting Swann's invitation with reserve, I did not leave him until he had promised to explain in detail to his daughter the mischances that had prevented and would continue to prevent me from going to see her. "In any case I shall write to her as soon as I get home," I added. "But be sure to tell her it will be a threatening letter, for in a month or two I shall be quite free, and then let her tremble, for I shall be coming to your house as regularly as in the old days."

Before parting from Swann, I had a word with him about his health. "No, it's not as bad as all that," he told me. "Still, as I was saying, I'm pretty worn out, and I accept with resignation whatever may be in store for me. Only, I must say that it would be very irritating to die before the end of the Dreyfus case. Those scoundrels have more than one card up their sleeves. I have no doubt of their being defeated in the end, but still they're very powerful, they have supporters everywhere. Just as everything is going on splendidly, it all collapses. I should like to live long enough to see Dreyfus rehabilitated and Picquart a colonel."

When Swann had left, I returned to the big drawing-room to find the Princesse de Guermantes, with whom I did not then know that I was one day to be so intimate. Her passion for M. de Charlus did not reveal itself to me at first. I noticed only that the Baron, after a certain date, and without having taken to the Princesse de Guermantes one of those sudden dislikes so familiar with him, while continuing to feel for her just as strong if not a stronger affection perhaps than ever, appeared irritated and displeased whenever one mentioned her name to him. He never included it now in his list of people with whom he wished to dine.

It is true that before this time I had heard an extremely malicious man about town say that the Princess had completely changed, that she was in love with M. de

Charlus, but this slander had appeared to me absurd and
had made me angry. I had indeed remarked with astonishment that, when I was telling her something that concerned myself, if M. de Charlus's name cropped up in the
middle, the Princess's attention at once became screwed
up to a higher pitch, like that of a sick man who, hearing
us talk about ourselves and listening, in consequence, in a
listless and absent-minded fashion, suddenly realises that
a name we have mentioned is that of the disease from
which he is suffering, which at once interests and delights
him. Thus, if I said to her: "Actually, M. de Charlus was
telling me . . ." the Princess at once gathered up the
slackened reins of her attention. And having on one occasion said in her hearing that M. de Charlus had at that
time a warm regard for a certain person, I was astonished
to see in the Princess's eyes that momentary glint, like the
trace of a fissure in the pupils, which is due to a thought
that our words have unwittingly aroused in the mind of
the person to whom we are talking, a secret thought that
will not find expression in words but will rise from the
depths which we have stirred to the momentarily altered
surface of his gaze. But if my remark had moved the
Princess, I did not then suspect in what way.

At all events, shortly after this she began to talk to
me about M. de Charlus, and almost without circumlocu-
tion. If she made any allusion to the rumours which a few
people here and there were spreading about the Baron, it
was merely to reject them as absurd and infamous inventions. But on the other hand she said: "I feel that any
woman who fell in love with a man of such immense
worth as Palamède ought to be magnanimous enough and
devoted enough to accept him and understand him as a

whole, for what he is, to respect his freedom, humour his
whims, seek only to smooth out his difficulties and console him in his griefs." Now, by such words, vague as
they were, the Princesse de Guermantes gave away what
she was seeking to idealise, just as M. de Charlus himself
did at times. Have I not heard him, again and again, say
to people who until then had been uncertain whether or
not he was being slandered: "I, who have had so many
ups and downs in my life, who have known all manner of
people, thieves as well as kings, and indeed, I must confess, with a slight preference for the thieves, I who have
pursued beauty in all its forms," and so forth; and by
these words which he thought adroit, and by contradicting
rumours which no one knew of (or, from inclination, restraint or concern for verisimilitude, to make a conces-
sion to the truth that he was alone in regarding as
minimal), he removed the last doubts from the minds of
some of his hearers, and inspired others, who had not yet
begun to doubt him, with their first. For the most dangerous of all concealments is that of the crime itself in the
mind of the guilty party. His constant awareness of it prevents him from imagining how generally unknown it is,
how readily a complete lie would be accepted, and on the
other hand from realising at what degree of truth other
people will begin to detect an admission in words which
he believes to be innocent. In any case there was no real
need to try to hush it up, for there is no vice that does
not find ready tolerance in the best society, and one has
seen a country house turned upside down in order that
two sisters might sleep in adjoining rooms as soon as their
hostess learned that theirs was a more than sisterly affection. But what revealed to me all of a sudden the Prin-

cess's love was a particular incident on which I shall not
dwell here, for it forms part of quite another story, in
which M. de Charlus allowed a queen to die rather than
miss an appointment with the hairdresser who was to
singe his hair for the benefit of a bus conductor whom he
found prodigiously intimidating.* However, to finish with
the Princess's love, I shall say briefly what the trifle was
that opened my eyes. I was, on the day in question, alone
with her in her carriage. As we were passing a post office
she stopped the coachman. She had come out without a
footman. She half drew a letter from her muff and was
preparing to step down from the carriage to put it into the
box. I tried to stop her, she made a show of resistance,
and we both realised that our instinctive movements had
been, hers compromising, in appearing to be protecting a
secret, mine indiscreet, in thwarting that protection. She
was the first to recover. Suddenly turning very red, she
gave me the letter. I no longer dared not to take it, but, as
I slipped it into the box, I could not help seeing that it
was addressed to M. de Charlus.

To return to this first evening at the Princesse de
Guermantes's, I went to bid her good night, for her
cousins, who had promised to take me home, were in a
hurry to be gone. M. de Guermantes wished, however, to
say good-bye to his brother, Mme de Surgis having found
time to mention to the Duke as she left that M. de Charlus had been charming to her and to her sons. This great
kindness on his brother's part, the first moreover that he
had ever shown in that line, touched Basin deeply and
aroused in him old family feelings which were never dormant for long. As we were saying good-bye to the
Princess he insisted, without actually thanking M. de

Charlus, on expressing his fondness for him, either because he genuinely had difficulty in containing it or in order that the Baron might remember that actions of the
sort he had performed that evening did not escape the
eyes of a brother, just as, with the object of creating salu-
tary associations of memory for the future, we give a
lump of sugar to a dog that has done its trick. "Well, little brother!" said the Duke, stopping M. de Charlus and
taking him tenderly by the arm, "so we walk past our elders without so much as a word? I never see you now,
Mémé, and you can't think how I miss you. I was turning
over some old letters the other day and came upon some
from poor Mamma, which are all so full of tenderness for
you."

"Thank you, Basin," M. de Charlus replied in a
broken voice, for he could never speak of their mother
without emotion.

"You must let me fix up a cottage for you at Guermantes," the Duke went on.

"It's nice to see the two brothers so affectionate towards each other," the Princess said to Oriane.

"Yes, indeed! I don't suppose you could find many
brothers like them. I shall invite you with him," the
Duchess promised me. "You've not quarrelled with him?
. . . But what can they be talking about?" she added in
an anxious tone, for she could catch only an occasional
word of what they were saying. She had always felt a certain jealousy of the pleasure that M. de Guermantes
found in talking to his brother of a past from which he
was inclined to keep his wife shut out. She felt that, when
they were happily together like this and she, unable to restrain her impatient curiosity, came and joined them, her

arrival was not well received. But this evening, this habitual jealousy was reinforced by another. For if Mme de
Surgis had told M. de Guermantes how kind his brother
had been to her so that the Duke might thank his brother,
at the same time devoted female friends of the Guermantes couple had felt it their duty to warn the Duchess
that her husband's mistress had been seen in close conversation with his brother. And Mme de Guermantes was
tormented by this.

"Think of the fun we used to have at Guermantes
long ago," the Duke went on. "If you came down sometimes in summer we could take up our old life again. Do
you remember old Father Courveau: 'Why is Pascal disturbing? Because he is dis . . . dis . . .' " "Turbed," put
in M. de Charlus as though he were still responding to
his tutor. "'And why is Pascal disturbed?; because he is
dis . . . because he is dis . . .' " "Turbing." "'Very
good, you'll pass, you're certain to get a distinction, and
Madame la Duchesse will give you a Chinese dictionary.'
How it all comes back to me, Mémé, and the old Chinese
vase Hervey de Saint-Denis[6] brought back for you, I can
see it now. You used to threaten us that you would go
and spend your life in China, you were so enamoured of
the country; even then you used to love going for long
rambles. Ah, you were always an odd one, for I can hon-
estly say that you never had the same tastes as other people in anything . . ." But no sooner had he uttered these
words than the Duke turned scarlet, for he was aware of
his brother's reputation, if not of his actual habits. As he
never spoke to him about it, he was all the more embarrassed at having said something which might be taken to
refer to it, and still more at having shown his embarrass-

ment. After a moment's silence: "Who knows," he said, to cancel the effect of his previous words, "you were perhaps in love with a Chinese girl before loving so many white ones, and finding favour with them, if I am to judge by a certain lady to whom you have given great pleasure this evening by talking to her. She was delighted with you." The Duke had vowed to himself that he would not mention Mme de Surgis, but, in the confusion that the gaffe he had just made had wrought in his ideas, he had pounced on the one that was uppermost in his mind, which happened to be precisely the one that ought not to have appeared in the conversation, although it had started it. But M. de Charlus had observed his brother's blush. And, like guilty persons who do not wish to appear embarrassed that you should talk in their presence of the crime which they are supposed not to have committed, and feel obliged to prolong a dangerous conversation: "I am charmed to hear it," he replied, "but I should like to go back to what you were saying before, which struck me as being profoundly true. You were saying that I never had the same ideas as other people—how right you are!— and you said that I had unorthodox tastes." "No I didn't," protested M. de Guermantes, who, as a matter of fact, had not used those words, and may not have believed that their meaning was applicable to his brother. Besides, what right had he to bully him about idiosyncrasies which in any case were vague enough or secret enough to have in no way impaired the Baron's tremendous position in society? What was more, feeling that the resources of his brother's position were about to be placed at the service of his mistresses, the Duke told himself that this was well worth a little tolerance in exchange; had he at that moment known of some "unorthodox" relationship of his brother's, then in the hope of the support that the other might give him, a hope linked with pious remembrance of the old days, M. de Guermantes would have passed it over, shutting his eyes to it, and if need be lending a hand. "Come along, Basin; good night, Palamède," said the Duchess, who, devoured by rage and curiosity, could endure no more, "if you have made up your minds to spend the night here, we might just as well stay to supper. You've been keeping Marie and me standing for the last half-hour." The Duke parted from his brother after a meaningful hug, and the three of us began to descend the immense staircase of the Princess's house.

On either side of us, on the topmost steps, were scattered couples who were waiting for their carriages. Erect, isolated, flanked by her husband and myself, the Duchess kept to the left of the staircase, already wrapped in her Tiepolo cloak, her throat clasped in its band of rubies, devoured by the eyes of women and men alike, who sought to divine the secret of her beauty and elegance. Waiting for her carriage on the same step of the staircase as Mme de Guermantes, but at the opposite side of it, Mme de Gallardon, who had long abandoned all hope of ever receiving a visit from her cousin, turned her back so as not to appear to have seen her, and, what was more important, so as not to offer proof of the fact that the other did not greet her. Mme de Gallardon was in an extremely bad temper because some gentlemen in her company had taken it upon themselves to speak to her of Oriane: "I haven't the slightest desire to see her," she had replied to them, "I did notice her, as a matter of fact, just now, and she's beginning to show her age. It seems she can't get over it, Basin says so himself. And I can well understand it, because, since she hasn't any brains, is as nasty as can be, and has bad manners, she must know very well that, once her looks go, she'll have nothing left to fall back on."

I had put on my overcoat, for which M. de Guermantes, who dreaded chills, reproached me as we went down together, because of the heated atmosphere indoors. And the generation of noblemen who more or less passed through the hands of Mgr Dupanloup speak such bad French (except the Castellane brothers) that the Duke expressed what was in his mind thus: "It is better not to put on your coat before going out of doors, at least *as a general thesis.*" I can see all that departing crowd now; I can see, if I am not mistaken in placing him upon that staircase, a portrait detached from its frame, the Prince de Sagan, whose last appearance in society this must have been, paying his respects to the Duchess with so ample a sweep of his top hat in his white-gloved hand, harmonising with the gardenia in his buttonhole, that one was surprised that it was not a plumed felt hat of the *ancien régime*, several ancestral faces from which were exactly reproduced in the face of this noble lord. He stopped for only a short time in front of her, but his attitudes in that brief moment were sufficient to compose a complete tableau vivant and, as it were, a historical scene. Moreover, as he has since died, and as I never had more than a glimpse of him in his lifetime, he has become for me so much a character in history, social history at least, that I am sometimes astonished when I think that a woman and a man whom I know are his sister and nephew.

While we were going down the staircase, a woman who appeared to be about forty but was in fact older was climbing it with an air of lassitude that became her. This was the Princesse d'Orvillers, a natural daughter, it was said, of the Duke of Parma, whose pleasant voice rang with a vaguely Austrian accent. She advanced, tall and stooping, in a gown of white flowered silk, her exquisite bosom heaving with exhaustion beneath a harness of diamonds and sapphires. Tossing her head like a royal palfrey embarrassed by its halter of pearls, of an incalculable value but an inconvenient weight, she let fall here and there a soft and charming gaze, of an azure which, as it gradually began to fade, became more caressing still, and greeted most of the departing guests with a friendly nod. "A fine time to arrive, Paulette!" said the Duchess. "Yes, I am so sorry! But really it was a physical impossibility," replied the Princesse d'Orvillers, who had acquired this sort of expression from the Duchesse de Guermantes, but added to it her own natural sweetness and the air of sincerity conveyed by the force of a distantly Teutonic accent in so tender a voice. She appeared to be alluding to complications of life too elaborate to be related, and not merely to parties, although she had just come on from a succession of these. But it was not they that forced her to come so late. As the Prince de Guermantes had for many years forbidden his wife to receive Mme d'Orvillers, the latter, when the ban was lifted, contented herself with replying to the other's invitations, so as not to appear to be thirsting after them, by simply leaving cards. After two or three years of this method, she came in person, but very late, as though after the theatre. In this way she gave herself the appearance of attaching no importance to the party, nor to being seen at it, but simply of having come to pay the Prince and Princess a visit, for their own sakes,

because she liked them, at an hour when, the great majority of their guests having already gone, she would "have
them more to herself."

"Oriane has really sunk very low," muttered Mme de
Gallardon. "I cannot understand Basin's allowing her to
speak to Mme d'Orvillers. I'm sure M. de Gallardon
would never have allowed me." For my part, I had recognised in Mme d'Orvillers the woman who, outside the
Hôtel Guermantes, used to cast languishing glances at me,
turn round, stop and gaze into shop windows. Mme de
Guermantes introduced me. Mme d'Orvillers was charming, neither too friendly nor piqued. She gazed at me as at
everyone else with her soft eyes . . . But I was never
again, when I met her, to receive from her one of those
overtures with which she had seemed to be offering herself. There is a special kind of look, apparently of recognition, which a young man receives from certain women—
and from certain men—only until the day on which they
have made his acquaintance and have learned that he is
the friend of people with whom they too are intimate.

We were told that the carriage was at the door. Mme
de Guermantes gathered up her red skirt as though to go
downstairs and get into the carriage, but, seized perhaps
by remorse, or by the desire to give pleasure and above all
to profit by the brevity which the material obstacle to
prolonging it imposed upon so boring an action, looked at
Mme de Gallardon; then, as though she had only just
caught sight of her, acting upon a sudden inspiration, before going down she tripped across the whole width of the
step and, upon reaching her delighted cousin, held out her
hand. "Such a long time," said the Duchess, who then, so
as not to have to enlarge upon all the regrets and legiti-

mate excuses that this formula might be supposed to contain, turned with a look of alarm towards the Duke, who indeed, having gone down with me to the carriage, was storming with rage on seeing that his wife had gone over to Mme de Gallardon and was holding up the stream of carriages. "Oriane is really very beautiful still!" said Mme de Gallardon. "People amuse me when they say that we're on bad terms; we may (for reasons which we have no need to tell other people) go for years without seeing one another, but we have too many memories in common ever to be separated, and deep down she must know that she cares far more for me than for all sorts of people whom she sees every day and who are not of her blood." Mme de Gallardon was in fact like those scorned lovers who try desperately to make people believe that they are better loved than those whom their fair one cherishes. And (by the praises which, oblivious of how they contradicted what she had been saying shortly before, she now lavished on the Duchesse de Guermantes) she proved indirectly that the other was thoroughly conversant with the maxims that ought to guide in her career a great lady of fashion who, at the selfsame moment when her most marvellous gown is exciting envy along with admiration, must be able to cross the whole width of a staircase to disarm it. "Do at least take care not to wet your shoes" (a brief but heavy shower of rain had fallen), said the Duke, who was still furious at having been kept waiting.

On our homeward drive, in the confined space of the coupé, those red shoes were of necessity very close to mine, and Mme de Guermantes, fearing that she might actually have touched me, said to the Duke: "This young man is going to be obliged to say to me, like the person in

some cartoon or other: 'Madame, tell me at once that you
love me, but don't tread on my feet like that.' " My
thoughts, however, were far from Mme de Guermantes.
Ever since Saint-Loup had spoken to me of a young girl
of good family who frequented a house of ill-fame, and of
the Baroness Putbus's chambermaid, it was in these two
persons that had now become coalesced and embodied the
desires inspired in me day by day by countless beauties of
two classes, on the one hand the vulgar and magnificent,
the majestic lady's-maids of great houses, swollen with
pride and saying "we" in speaking of duchesses, and on
the other hand those girls of whom it was enough sometimes, without even having seen them go past in carriages
or on foot, to have read the names in the account of a ball
for me to fall in love with them and, having conscien-
tiously searched the social directory for the country
houses in which they spent the summer (as often as not
letting myself be led astray by a similarity of names), to
dream alternately of going to live amid the plains of the
West, the dunes of the North, the pine-woods of the
South. But in vain did I fuse together all the most
exquisite fleshly matter to compose, after the ideal outline
traced for me by Saint-Loup, the young girl of easy virtue
and Mme Putbus's maid, my two possessible beauties still
lacked what I should never know until I had seen them:
individual character. I was to wear myself out in vain trying to picture, during the months when my desires were
focused on young girls, what the one Saint-Loup had spoken of looked like, and who she was, and during the
months in which I would have preferred a lady's-maid,
the lineaments of Mme Putbus's. But what peace of mind,
after having been perpetually troubled by my restless de-

sires for so many fugitive creatures whose very names I
often did not know and who were in any case so hard to
find, harder still to get to know, impossible perhaps to
conquer, to have drawn from all that scattered, fugitive,
anonymous beauty two choice specimens duly labelled,
whom I was at least certain of being able to procure when
I wished! I kept putting off the hour for getting down to
this twofold pleasure, as I put off the hour for getting
down to work, but the certainty of having it whenever I
chose dispensed me almost from the necessity of taking it,
like those sleeping tablets which one has only to have
within hand's reach to be able to do without them and to
fall asleep. In the whole universe I now desired only two
women, of whose faces I could not, it is true, form any
picture, but whose names Saint-Loup had given me and
whose compliance he had guaranteed. So that if, by what
he had said this evening, he had set my imagination a
heavy task, he had at the same time procured an apprecia-
ble relaxation, a prolonged rest for my will.

"Well!" said the Duchess, "aside from your parties,
can I be of any use to you? Have you found a salon to
which you would like me to introduce you?" I replied that
I was afraid the only one that tempted me was hardly elegant enough for her. "Whose is that?" she asked in a
hoarse, menacing voice, scarcely opening her lips.
"Baroness Putbus." This time she pretended to be really
angry. "Ah, no, really! I believe you're trying to make a
fool of me. I don't even know how I come to have heard
the creature's name. But she is the dregs of society. It's as
though you were to ask me for an introduction to my
dressmaker. In fact worse, for my dressmaker is charming.
You must be a little bit cracked, my poor boy. In any

case, I beseech you to be polite to the people I've introduced you to, to leave cards on them, and go and see
them, and not talk to them about Baroness Putbus of
whom they have never heard." I asked whether Mme
d'Orvillers was not inclined to be flighty. "Oh, not in the
least, you're mixing her up with someone else. She's
rather strait-laced, if anything. Isn't she, Basin?" "Yes, in
any case I don't think there has ever been any talk about
her," said the Duke.

"You won't come with us to the ball?" he asked me.
"I can lend you a Venetian cloak and I know someone
who will be deucedly glad to see you there—Oriane for
one, that goes without saying—but the Princesse de
Parme. She never tires of singing your praises, and swears
by you. It's lucky for you—since she's a trifle mature—
that she is a model of virtue. Otherwise she would certainly have taken you on as a cicisbeo, as they used to say
in my young days, a sort of *cavaliere servente*."

I was interested not in the ball but in my rendezvous
with Albertine. And so I refused. The carriage had
stopped, the footman was shouting for the gate to be
opened, the horses pawed the ground until it was flung
apart and the carriage passed into the courtyard. "So
long," said the Duke. "I've sometimes regretted living so
close to Marie," the Duchess said to me, "because although I'm very fond of her, I'm not quite so fond of her
company. But I've never regretted it so much as tonight,
since it has allowed me so little of yours." "Come, Oriane, no speechmaking."

The Duchess would have liked me to come inside for
a minute. She laughed heartily, as did the Duke, when I
said that I could not because I was expecting a girl to call

at any moment. "You choose a funny time to receive visitors," she said to me.

"Come along, my sweet, there's no time to lose," said M. de Guermantes to his wife. "It's a quarter to twelve, and time we were dressed . . ." He came into collision, outside his front door which they were grimly guarding, with the two ladies with the walking-sticks, who had not been afraid to descend at dead of night from their mountain-top to prevent a scandal. "Basin, we felt we must warn you, in case you were seen at that ball: poor Amanien has just died, an hour ago." The Duke was momentarily dismayed. He saw the famous ball collapsing in ruins for him now that these accursed mountaineers had informed him of the death of M. d'Osmond. But he quickly recovered himself and flung at his cousins a retort which reflected, together with his determination not to forgo a pleasure, his incapacity to assimilate exactly the niceties of the French language: "He's dead! No, no, they're exaggerating, they're exaggerating!" And without giving a further thought to his two relatives who, armed with their alpenstocks, prepared to make their nocturnal ascent, he fired off a string of questions at his valet:

"Are you sure my helmet has come?" "Yes, Monsieur le Duc." "You're sure there's a hole in it I can breathe through? I don't want to be suffocated, damn it!" "Yes, Monsieur le Duc." "Oh, hell and damnation, everything's going wrong this evening. Oriane, I forgot to ask Babal whether the shoes with pointed toes were for you!" "But, my dear, the dresser from the Opéra-Comique is here, he will tell us. I don't see how they could go with your spurs." "Let's go and find the dresser," said the Duke. "Good-bye, my boy, I'd ask you to come in while we are trying on our costumes—it would amuse you. But we should only waste time talking, it's nearly midnight and we mustn't be late in getting there or we shall spoil the show."

I too was in a hurry to get away from M. and Mme de Guermantes as quickly as possible. *Phèdre* finished at about half past eleven. Albertine must have arrived by now. I went straight to Françoise: "Is Mlle Albertine here?" "No one has called."

Good God, did that mean that no one would call! I was in torment, Albertine's visit seeming to me now all the more desirable the less certain it had become.

Françoise was upset too, but for quite a different reason. She had just installed her daughter at the table for a succulent repast. But, on hearing me come in, and seeing that there was no time to whip away the dishes and put out needles and thread as though it were a work party and not a supper party: "She's just had a spoonful of soup, and I forced her to gnaw a bit of bone," Françoise explained to me, to reduce thus to nothing her daughter's supper, as though its copiousness were a crime. Even at lunch or dinner, if I committed the sin of going into the kitchen, Françoise would pretend that they had finished, and would even excuse herself by saying: "I just felt like a *scrap*," or "a *mouthful*." But I was speedily reassured on seeing the multitude of dishes that covered the table, which Françoise, surprised by my sudden entry, like a thief in the night which she was not, had not had time to whisk out of sight. Then she added: "Go along to your bed now, you've done enough work today" (for she wished to make it appear that her daughter not only cost us nothing and lived frugally, but was actually working herself to death in our service). "You're only cluttering up the kitchen and disturbing Monsieur, who is expecting a visitor. Go on, upstairs," she repeated, as though she were obliged to use her authority to send her daughter to bed when in fact she was only there for appearances's sake now that supper had been ruined, and if I had stayed five minutes longer would have withdrawn of her own accord. And turning to me, in that charming, popular and yet highly individual French that was hers, Françoise added: "Monsieur can see that her face is just cut in two with want of sleep." I remained, delighted not to have to talk to Françoise's daughter.

I have said that she came from a small village which was quite close to her mother's, and yet differed from it in the nature of the soil and its cultivation, in dialect, and above all in certain characteristics of the inhabitants. Thus the "butcheress" and Françoise's niece did not get on at all well together, but had this point in common, that when they went out on an errand, they would linger for hours at "the sister's" or "the cousin's," being themselves incapable of finishing a conversation, in the course of which the purpose with which they had set out faded so completely from their minds that, if we said to them on their return: "Well! will M. le Marquis de Norpois be at home at a quarter past six?" they did not even slap their foreheads and say: "Oh, I forgot all about it," but "Oh! I didn't understand that Monsieur wanted to know that, I thought I had just to go and bid him good-day." If they "lost their heads" in this way about something that had been said to them an hour earlier, it was on the other hand impossible to get out of their heads what they had once heard said by "the" sister or "the" cousin. Thus, if

the butcheress had heard it said that the English made
war on us in '70 at the same time as the Prussians (and I
explained to her until I was tired that this was not the
case), every three weeks the butcheress would repeat to
me in the course of conversation: "It's all because of that
war the English made on us in '70 with the Prussians."
"But I've told you a hundred times that you're wrong," I
would say, and she would then answer, implying that her
conviction was in no way shaken: "In any case, that's no
reason for wishing them any harm. Plenty of water has
flowed under the bridges since '70," and so forth. On another occasion, advocating a war with England which I
opposed, she said: "To be sure, it's always better not to
go to war; but when you must, it's best to do it at once.
As the sister was explaining just now, ever since that war
the English made on us in '70, the commercial treaties
have ruined us. After we've beaten them, we won't allow
one Englishman into France unless he pays three hundred
francs admission, as we have to pay now to land in England."

Such was, in addition to great decency and civility
and, when they were talking, an obstinate refusal to allow
any interruption, going back time and time again to the
point they had reached if one did interrupt them, thus
giving their talk the unshakeable solidity of a Bach fugue,
the character of the inhabitants of this tiny village which
did not boast five hundred, set among its chestnuts, its
willows, and its fields of potatoes and beetroot.

Françoise's daughter, on the other hand (regarding
herself as an up-to-date woman who had got out of the
old ruts), spoke Parisian slang and was well versed in all
the jokes of the day. Françoise having told her that I had

come from the house of a princess: "Oh, indeed! The Princess of Brazil, I suppose, where the nuts come from." Seeing that I was expecting a visitor, she pretended to believe that my name was Charles. I replied innocently that it was not, which enabled her to get in: "Oh, I thought it was! And I was just saying to myself, *Charles attend* (charlatan)." This was not in the best of taste. But I was less unmoved when, to console me for Albertine's delay, she said to me: "I expect you'll go on waiting till doomsday. She's never coming. Ah, these modern flappers!"

And so her speech differed from her mother's; but, what is more curious, her mother's speech was not the same as that of her grandmother, a native of Bailleau-le-Pin, which was so close to Françoise's village. And yet the dialects differed slightly, like the two landscapes, Françoise's mother's village, on a slope descending into a ravine, being overgrown with willows. And, miles away from either of them, there was a small area of France where the people spoke almost precisely the same dialect as in Méséglise. I made this discovery at the same time as I experienced its tediousness, for I once came upon Françoise deep in conversation with a neighbour's housemaid, who came from this village and spoke its dialect. They could more or less understand one another, I could not understand a word, and they knew this but nevertheless continued (excused, they felt, by the joy of being fellow-countrywomen although born so far apart) to converse in this strange tongue in front of me, like people who do not wish to be understood. These picturesque studies in linguistic geography and below-stairs comradeship were renewed weekly in the kitchen, without my deriving any pleasure from them.

Since, whenever the outer gate opened, the concierge pressed an electric button which lighted the stairs, and since all the occupants of the building had already come in, I left the kitchen immediately and went to sit down in the hall, keeping my eyes fastened on the point where the slightly too narrow curtain did not completely cover the glass panel of our front door, leaving visible a vertical strip of semi-darkness from the stairs. If, suddenly, this strip turned to a golden yellow, that would mean that Albertine had just entered the building and would be with me in a minute; nobody else could be coming at that time of night. And I sat there, unable to take my eyes from the strip which persisted in remaining dark; I bent my whole body forward to make certain of noticing any change; but, gaze as I might, the vertical black band, despite my impassioned longing, did not give me the intoxicating delight that I should have felt had I seen it changed by a stroke of sudden and significant magic to a luminous bar of gold. This was indeed a great fuss to make about Albertine, to whom I had not given three minutes' thought during the Guermantes reception! But, reviving the feelings of anxious expectancy I had had in the past over other girls, Gilberte especially when she was late in coming, the prospect of having to forgo a simple physical pleasure caused me an intense mental suffering.

I was obliged to go back to my room. Françoise followed me. She felt that, as I had come away from my party, there was no point in my keeping the rose that I had in my buttonhole, and approached to take it from me. Her action, by reminding me that Albertine might perhaps not come, and by obliging me also to confess that I wished to look smart for her benefit, caused me an irritation that was intensified by the fact that, in tugging myself free, I crushed the flower and Françoise said to me: "It would have been better to let me take it than to go and spoil it like that." Indeed, her slightest word exasperated me. When we are waiting, we suffer so keenly from the absence of the person for whom we are longing that we cannot endure the presence of anyone else.

Françoise having left the room, it occurred to me that if I was now so concerned about my appearance for Albertine's sake, it was a great pity that I had so often let her see me unshaved, with several days' growth of beard, on the evenings when I let her come round to renew our caresses. I felt that she was indifferent to me and was giving me the cold shoulder. To make my room look a little more attractive, in case Albertine should still come, and because it was one of the prettiest things that I possessed, for the first time in years I placed on the bedside table the turquoise-studded cover which Gilberte had had made for me to hold Bergotte's booklet and which for so long I had insisted on keeping by me while I slept, together with the agate marble. As much perhaps as Albertine herself, who still did not come, her presence at that moment in an "elsewhere" which she had evidently found more agreeable, and of which I knew nothing, gave me a painful feeling which, in spite of what I had said to Swann scarcely an hour before as to my incapacity for being jealous, might, if I had seen her at less protracted intervals, have changed into an anxious need to know where, and with whom, she was spending her time. I dared not send round to Albertine's house, as it was too late, but in the hope that, having supper perhaps with some other girls in a café, she might take it into her head to telephone me, I turned the switch and, restoring the connexion to my own room, cut it off between the post office and the porter's lodge to which it was generally switched at that hour. A receiver in the little passage on to which Françoise's room opened would have been simpler, less inconvenient, but useless. The advance of civilisation enables people to display unsuspected qualities or fresh defects which make them dearer or more insupportable to their friends. Thus Bell's invention had enabled Françoise to acquire an additional defect, which was that of refusing, however important, however urgent the occasion might be, to make use of the telephone. She would manage to disappear whenever anybody tried to teach her how to use it, as people disappear when it is time for them to be vaccinated. And so the telephone was installed in my bedroom, and, so that it might not disturb my parents, a whirring noise had been substituted for the bell. I did not move, for fear of not hearing it. So motionless did I remain that, for the first time for months, I noticed the tick of the clock. Françoise came in to tidy up the room. She chatted to me, but I hated her conversation, beneath the uniformly trivial continuity of which my feelings were changing from one minute to the next, passing from fear to anxiety, from anxiety to complete despair. Belying the vaguely cheerful words which I felt obliged to address to her, I could sense that my face was so wretched that I pretended to be suffering from rheumatism, to account for the discrepancy between my feigned indifference and that woebegone expression; then I was afraid that her talk, although carried on in a low voice (not on account of Albertine, for Françoise considered that all possibility of her coming was long past), might prevent me from hearing the saving call which now would never come. At length Françoise went off to bed; I dismissed her firmly but gently, so that the noise she made in leaving the room should not drown that of the telephone. And I settled down again to listen, to suffer; when we are waiting, from the ear which takes in sounds to the mind which dissects and analyses them, and from the mind to the heart to which it transmits its results, the double journey is so rapid that we cannot even perceive its duration, and imagine that we have been listening directly with our heart.

I was tortured by the incessant recurrence of my longing, ever more anxious and never gratified, for the sound of a call; having arrived at the culminating point of a tortuous ascent through the coils of my lonely anguish, from the depths of a populous, nocturnal Paris brought miraculously close to me, there beside my bookcase, I suddenly heard, mechanical and sublime, like the fluttering scarf or the shepherd's pipe in *Tristan*, the top-like whirr of the telephone. I sprang to the instrument; it was Albertine. "I'm not disturbing you, ringing you up at this hour?" "Not at all . . ." I said, restraining my joy, for her remark about the lateness of the hour was doubtless meant as an apology for coming round in a moment, so late, and not that she was not coming. "Are you coming round?" I asked in a tone of indifference. "Well . . . no, unless you absolutely must see me."

Part of me, which the other part sought to join, was in Albertine. It was essential that she should come, but I did not tell her so at first; now that we were in communication, I said to myself that I could always oblige her at the last moment either to come to me or to let me rush round to her. "Yes, I'm near home," she said, "and miles away from you. I hadn't read your note properly. I've just found it again and was afraid you might be waiting up for me." I felt sure she was lying, and now, in my fury, it was from a desire not so much to see her as to inconvenience her that I was determined to make her come. But I felt it better to refuse at first what in a few moments I should try to procure. But where was she? With the sound of her voice were blended other sounds: a cyclist's horn, a woman's voice singing, a brass band in the distance, rang out as distinctly as the beloved voice, as though to show me that it was indeed Albertine in her actual surroundings who was beside me at that moment, like a clod of earth together with which we have carried away all the grass that was growing from it. The same sounds that I heard were striking her ear also, and were distracting her attention: true-to-life details, extraneous to the subject, valueless in themselves, all the more necessary to our perception of the miracle for what it was; simple, charming features descriptive of some Parisian street, bitter, cruel features, too, of some unknown festivity which, after she had come away from *Phèdre*, had prevented Albertine from coming to me. "I must warn you first of all that it's not that I wanted you to come, because, at this time of night, it would be a frightful nuisance . . ." I said to her. "I'm dropping with sleep. And besides, well, there are endless complications. I'm bound to say that there was no possibility of your misunderstanding my letter. You answered that it was all right. Well then, if you hadn't understood, what did you mean by that?" "I said it was all right, only I couldn't quite remember what we had arranged. But I see you're cross with me, I'm sorry. I wish now I'd never gone to *Phèdre*. If I'd known there was going to be all this fuss about it . . ." she went on, as people invariably do when, being in the wrong over one thing, they pretend to believe that they are being blamed for another. "I'm not in the least annoyed about *Phèdre*, seeing it was I who asked you to go to it." "Then you *are* angry with me; it's a nuisance it's so late now, otherwise I should have come round, but I shall call to-morrow or the day after and make it up." "Oh, please don't, Albertine, I beg of you; after making me waste an entire evening, the least you can do is to leave me in peace for the next few days. I shan't be free for a fort-night or three weeks. Listen, if it worries you to think that we seem to be parting in anger—and perhaps you're right, after all—then I'd much prefer, all things con-sidered, since I've been waiting for you all this time and you're still out, that you should come at once. I'll have a cup of coffee to keep myself awake." "Couldn't you possi-bly put it off till tomorrow? Because the trouble is . . ." As I listened to these words of excuse, uttered as though she did not intend to come, I felt that, with the longing to see again the velvet-soft face which in the past, at Balbec, used to direct all my days towards the moment when, by the mauve September sea, I should be beside that roseate flower, a very different element was painfully endeavour-ing to combine. This terrible need of a person was some-thing I had learned to know at Combray in the case of my mother, to the point of wanting to die if she sent word to me by Françoise that she could not come upstairs. This effort on the part of the old feeling to combine and form a single element with the other, more recent, which had for its voluptuous object only the coloured surface, the flesh-pink bloom of a flower of the sea-shore, was one that of-

ten results simply in creating (in the chemical sense) a
new body, which may last only a few moments. That
evening, at any rate, and for long afterwards, the two elements remained apart. But already, from the last words
that had reached me over the telephone, I was beginning
to understand that Albertine's life was situated (not in a
physical sense, of course) at so great a distance from mine
that I should always have to make exhausting explorations
in order to seize hold of it, and moreover was organised
like a system of earthworks which, for greater security,
were of the kind that at a later period we learned to call
"camouflaged." Albertine, in fact, belonged, although at a
slightly higher social level, to that type of person to whom
the concierge promises your messenger that she will deliver your letter when she comes in—until the day when
you realise that it is precisely she, the person you have
met in a public place and to whom you have ventured to
write, who is the concierge, so she does indeed live—
though in the lodge only—at the address she has given
you (which moreover is a private brothel of which the
concierge is the madame). Or else she gives as her address
an apartment house, where she is known to accomplices
who will not reveal her secret to you, from which your
letters will be forwarded, but where she doesn't live,
where at the very most she has left some belongings.
Lives entrenched behind five or six lines of defence, so
that when you try to see this woman, or to find out about
her, you invariably aim too far to the right, or to the left,
or too far in front, or too far behind, and can remain in
total ignorance for months, even years. In the case of Albertine, I felt that I should never discover anything, that,
out of that tangled mass of details of fact and falsehood, I

should never unravel the truth: and that it would always
be so, unless I were to shut her up in prison (but prisoners escape) until the end. That evening, this conviction
gave me only a vague anxiety, in which however I could
detect a shuddering anticipation of prolonged suffering to
come.

"No," I replied, "I told you a moment ago that I
wouldn't be free for the next three weeks—tomorrow no
more than any other day." "Very well, in that case . . . I
shall come this very instant . . . It's a nuisance, because
I'm at a friend's house, and she . . ." I sensed that she
had not believed that I would accept her offer to come,
which therefore was not sincere, and I decided to force
her hand. "What do you suppose I care about your
friend? Either come or don't, it's for you to decide. I'm
not asking you to come, it was you who suggested it."
"Don't be angry. I'll jump into a cab now and I'll be with
you in ten minutes."

Thus, from that nocturnal Paris out of whose depths
the invisible message had already wafted into my very
room, delimiting the field of action of a faraway person,
what was now about to materialise, after this preliminary
annunciation, was the Albertine whom I had known long
ago beneath the sky of Balbec, when the waiters of the
Grand Hotel, as they laid the tables, were blinded by the
glow of the setting sun, when, the glass panels having
been drawn wide open, the faintest evening breeze passed
freely from the beach, where the last strolling couples still
lingered, into the vast dining-room in which the first diners had not yet taken their places, and when, in the mirror
placed behind the cashier's desk, there passed the red reflexion of the hull and, lingering long, the grey reflexion

of the smoke of the last steamer for Rivebelle. I had ceased to wonder what could have made Albertine late, and when Françoise came into my room to inform me: "Mademoiselle Albertine is here," if I answered without even turning my head: "What in the world makes Mademoiselle Albertine come at this time of night?" it was only out of dissimulation. But then, raising my eyes to look at Françoise, as though curious to hear her answer which must corroborate the apparent sincerity of my question, I perceived, with admiration and fury, that, capable of rivalling Berma herself in the art of endowing with speech inanimate garments and the lines of her face, Françoise had taught their parts to her bodice, her hair—the whitest threads of which had been brought to the surface, were displayed there like a birth-certificate—and her neck, bent with fatigue and obedience. They commiserated with her for having been dragged from her sleep and from her warm bed, in the middle of the night, at her age, obliged to bundle into her clothes in haste, at the risk of catching pneumonia. And so, afraid that I might have seemed to be apologising for Albertine's late arrival, I added: "Anyhow, I'm very glad she has come, it's all for the best," and I gave free vent to my profound joy. It did not long remain unclouded, when I had heard Françoise's reply. Without uttering a word of complaint, seeming indeed to be doing her best to stifle an irrepressible cough, and simply folding her shawl over her bosom as though she felt cold, she began by telling me everything that she had said to Albertine, having not forgotten to ask after her aunt's health. "I was just saying, Monsieur must have been afraid that Mademoiselle wasn't coming, because this is no time to pay visits, it's nearly morning. But she must have been in some place that she was having a good time because she never so much as said she was sorry she had kept Monsieur waiting, she answered me as saucy as you please: 'Better late than never!' " And Françoise added these words that pierced my heart: "When she said that she gave herself away. Perhaps she would really have liked to hide herself, but . . ."

I had little cause for astonishment. I have said that Françoise rarely brought back word, when she was sent on an errand, if not of what she herself had said, on which she readily enlarged, at any rate of the awaited answer. But if, exceptionally, she repeated to us the words that our friends had said, however brief, she generally contrived, thanks if need be to the expression, the tone that, she assured us, had accompanied them, to make them somehow wounding. At a pinch, she would admit to having received a snub (probably quite imaginary) from a tradesman to whom we had sent her, provided that, being addressed to her as our representative, who had spoken in our name, it might rebound on us. The only thing then would be to tell her that she had misunderstood the man, that she was suffering from persecution mania and that the shopkeepers were not in league against her. However, their sentiments affected me little. Those of Albertine were a different matter. And in repeating the sarcastic words: "Better late than never!" Françoise at once evoked for me the friends with whom Albertine had finished the evening, thus preferring their company to mine. "She's a comical sight, she has a little flat hat on, and with those big eyes of hers it does make her look funny, especially with her cloak which she did ought to have sent to the amender's, for it's all in holes. She makes me laugh,"

Françoise added, as though mocking Albertine. Though she rarely shared my impressions, she felt the need to communicate her own. I refused even to appear to understand that this laugh was indicative of scorn and derision, but, to give tit for tat, replied, although I had never seen the little hat to which she referred: "What you call a 'little flat hat' is simply ravishing . . ." "That's to say, it's just a bit of rubbish," said Françoise, giving expression, frankly this time, to her genuine contempt. Then (in a mild and leisurely tone so that my mendacious answer might appear to be the expression not of my anger but of the truth, though without wasting any time in order not to keep Albertine waiting) I addressed these cruel words to Françoise: "You are excellent," I said to her in a honeyed voice, "you are kind, you have endless qualities, but you have never learned a single thing since the day you first came to Paris, either about ladies' clothes or about how to pronounce words without making howlers." And this reproach was particularly stupid, for those French words which we are so proud of pronouncing accurately are themselves only "howlers" made by Gaulish lips which mispronounced Latin or Saxon, our language being merely a defective pronunciation of several others. The genius of language in its living state, the future and past of French, that is what ought to have interested me in Françoise's mistakes. Wasn't "amender" for "mender" just as curious as those animals that survive from remote ages, such as the whale or the giraffe, and show us the states through which animal life has passed?

"And," I went on, "since you haven't managed to learn in all these years, you never will. But don't let that distress you: it doesn't prevent you from being a very

good soul, and making spiced beef with jelly to perfection, and lots of other things as well. The hat that you
think so simple is copied from a hat belonging to the
Princesse de Guermantes which cost five hundred francs.
In fact I mean to give Mlle Albertine an even finer one
very soon."

I knew that what would annoy Françoise more than
anything was the thought of my spending money on people she disliked. She answered me in a few words which
were made almost unintelligible by a sudden attack of
breathlessness. When I discovered afterwards that she had
a weak heart, how remorseful I felt that I had never denied myself the fierce and sterile pleasure of thus answering her back! Françoise detested Albertine, moreover,
because, being poor, Albertine could not enhance what
Françoise regarded as my superior position. She smiled
benevolently whenever I was invited by Mme de
Villeparisis. On the other hand, she was indignant that
Albertine did not practise reciprocity. I found myself being obliged to invent fictitious presents from the latter, in
the existence of which Françoise never for an instant believed. This want of reciprocity shocked her most of all in
the matter of food. That Albertine should accept dinners
from Mamma, when we were not invited to Mme Bontemps's (who in any case spent half her time out of Paris,
her husband accepting "posts" as in the old days when he
had had enough of the Ministry), seemed to her an indelicacy on the part of my friend which she rebuked indirectly by repeating a saying current at Combray:

"Let's eat my bread."
"Ay, that's the stuff."

"Let's eat thy bread."

"I've had enough."

I pretended to be writing.

"Who were you writing to?" Albertine asked me as she entered the room.

"To a pretty little friend of mine, Gilberte Swann. Don't you know her?"

"No."

I decided not to question Albertine as to how she had spent the evening, feeling that I should only reproach her and that we should have no time left, seeing how late it was already, to be reconciled sufficiently to proceed to kisses and caresses. And so it was with these that I chose to begin from the first moment. Besides, if I was a little calmer, I was not feeling happy. The loss of all equanimity, of all sense of direction, that we feel when we are kept waiting, persists after the arrival of the person awaited, and, taking the place inside us of the calm spirit in which we had been picturing her coming as so great a pleasure, prevents us from deriving any from it. Albertine was in the room: my disordered nerves, continuing to flutter, were still awaiting her.

"Can I have a nice kiss, Albertine?"

"As many as you like," she said to me in her good-natured way. I had never seen her looking so pretty.

"Another one? You know it's a great, great pleasure to me."

"And a thousand times greater to me," she replied. "Oh, what a pretty book-cover you have there!"

"Take it, I give it to you as a keepsake."

"You really are nice . . ."

One would be cured for ever of romanticism if one could make up one's mind, in thinking of the woman one loves, to try to be the man one will be when one no longer loves her. Gilberte's book-cover and her agate marble must have derived their importance in the past from some purely inward state, since now they were to me a book-cover and a marble like any others.

I asked Albertine if she would like something to drink. "I seem to see oranges over there and water," she said. "That will be perfect." I was thus able to taste, together with her kisses, that refreshing coolness which had seemed to me to be superior to them at the Princesse de Guermantes's. And the orange squeezed into the water seemed to yield to me, as I drank, the secret life of its ripening growth, its beneficent action upon certain states of that human body which belongs to so different a kingdom, its powerlessness to make that body live but on the other hand the process of irrigation by which it was able to benefit it—countless mysteries unveiled by the fruit to my sensory perception, but not at all to my intelligence.

When Albertine had gone, I remembered that I had promised Swann that I would write to Gilberte, and courtesy, I felt, demanded that I should do so at once. It was without emotion, and as though finishing off a boring school essay, that I traced upon the envelope the name *Gilberte Swann* with which at one time I used to cover my exercise-books to give myself the illusion that I was corresponding with her. For if, in the past, it had been I who wrote that name, now the task had been deputed by Habit to one of the many secretaries whom she employs. He could write down Gilberte's name all the more calmly in that, placed with me only recently by Habit, having but recently entered my service, he had never known Gilberte, and knew only, without attaching any reality to the words, because he had heard me speak of her, that she was a girl with whom I had once been in love.

I could not accuse her of coldness. The person I now was in relation to her was the clearest possible proof of what she herself had been: the book-cover, the agate marble had simply become for me in relation to Albertine what they had been for Gilberte, what they would have been to anybody who had not suffused them with the glow of an internal flame. But now there was in me a new turmoil which in its turn distorted the real force of things and words. And when Albertine said to me, in a further outburst of gratitude: "I do love turquoises!" I answered her: "Don't let these die," entrusting to them as to some precious jewel the future of our friendship, which in fact was no more capable of inspiring a sentiment in Albertine than it had been of preserving the sentiment that had once bound me to Gilberte.

There occurred at about this time a phenomenon which deserves mention only because it recurs in every important period of history. At the very moment I was writing to Gilberte, M. de Guermantes, just home from his ball, still wearing his helmet, was thinking that next day he would be compelled to go into formal mourning, and decided to bring forward by a week the cure he was due to take at a spa. When he returned from it three weeks later (to anticipate for a moment, since I have only just finished my letter to Gilberte), those friends of his who had seen him, so indifferent at the start, turn into a fanatical anti-Dreyfusard, were left speechless with amazement when they heard him (as though the action of the cure had not been confined to his bladder) declare: "Oh, well, there'll be a fresh trial and he'll be acquitted. You can't sentence a fellow without any evidence against him. Did you ever see anyone so gaga as Froberville? An officer leading the French people to the slaughter (meaning war)! Strange times we live in." The fact was that, in the meantime, the Duke had met at the spa three charming ladies (an Italian princess and her two sisters-in-law). After hearing them make a few remarks about the books they were reading or a play that was being given at the Casino, the Duke had at once realised that he was dealing with women of superior intellect whom, as he expressed it, he "wasn't up to." He had been all the more delighted to be asked to play bridge by the princess. But, the moment he entered her sitting-room, as he began to say to her, in the fervour of his double-dyed anti-Dreyfusism: "Well, we don't hear very much about the famous Dreyfus re-trial," his stupefaction had been great when he heard the princess and her sisters-in-law say: "It's becoming more certain every day. They can't keep a man in prison who has done nothing." "Eh? Eh?" the Duke had gasped at first, as at the discovery of a fantastic nickname employed in his household to turn to ridicule a person whom he had always regarded as intelligent. But, after a few days, just as, from cowardice and the spirit of imitation, we shout "Hallo, Jojotte" without knowing why at a great artist whom we hear so addressed by the rest of the household, the Duke, still greatly embarrassed by the novelty of this attitude, began nevertheless to say: "After all, if there's no evidence against him." The three charming ladies considered that he was not progressing rapidly enough and bullied him a bit: "But really, nobody with a

grain of intelligence can ever have believed for a moment
that there was anything." Whenever any revelation came
out that was "damning" to Dreyfus, and the Duke, supposing that now he was going to convert the three charming ladies, came to inform them of it, they burst out
laughing and had no difficulty in proving to him, with
great dialectic subtlety, that his argument was worthless
and quite absurd. The Duke had returned to Paris a fanatical Dreyfusard. And of course we do not suggest that
the three charming ladies were not, in this instance, mes-
sengers of truth. But it is to be observed that, every ten
years or so, when we have left a man imbued with a genuine conviction, it so happens that an intelligent couple,
or simply a charming lady, comes into his life and after a
few months he is won over to the opposite camp. And in
this respect there are many countries that behave like the
sincere man, many countries which we have left full of
hatred for another race and which, six months later, have
changed their minds and reversed their alliances.

I ceased for some time to see Albertine, but continued, failing Mme de Guermantes who no longer spoke to
my imagination, to visit other fairies and their dwellings,
as inseparable from themselves as is the pearly or enamelled valve or the crenellated turret of its shell from the
mollusc that made it and shelters inside it. I should not
have been able to classify these ladies, the problem being
insignificant and impossible not only to resolve but to
pose. Before coming to the lady, one had to approach the
fairy mansion. Now as one of them was always at home
after lunch in the summer months, before I reached her
house I would be obliged to lower the hood of my cab, so
scorching were the sun's rays, the memory of which,

without my realising it, was to enter into my general impression. I supposed that I was merely being driven to the
Cours-la-Reine; in reality, before arriving at the gathering
which a man of wider experience might well have derided,
I would receive, as though on a journey through Italy, a
delicious, dazzled sensation from which the house was
never afterwards to be separated in my memory. What
was more, in view of the heat of the season and the hour,
the lady would have hermetically closed the shutters of
the vast rectangular saloons on the ground floor in which
she entertained. I would have difficulty at first in recognising my hostess and her guests, even the Duchesse de
Guermantes, who in her husky voice bade me come and
sit down next to her, in a Beauvais armchair illustrating
the Rape of Europa. Then I would begin to make out on
the walls the huge eighteenth-century tapestries represent-
ing vessels whose masts were hollyhocks in blossom, beneath which I sat as though in the palace not of the Seine
but of Neptune, by the brink of the river Oceanus, where
the Duchesse de Guermantes became a sort of goddess of
the waters. I should never get to the end of it if I began
to describe all the different types of drawing-room. This
example will suffice to show that I introduced into my social judgments poetical impressions which I never took
into account when I came to add up the sum, so that,
when I was calculating the merits of a drawing-room, my
total was never correct.

Certainly, these were by no means the only sources of
error, but I have no time left, before my departure for
Balbec (where to my sorrow I am going to make a second
stay which will also be my last), to start upon a series of
pictures of society which will find their place in due

course. Here I need only say that to this first erroneous
reason (my relatively frivolous existence which made people suppose that I was fond of society) for my letter to
Gilberte, and for that reconciliation with the Swann family to which it seemed to point, Odette might very well,
and with equal inaccuracy, have added a second. I have
suggested hitherto the different aspects that the social
world assumes in the eyes of a single person only by supposing that it does not change: if the selfsame woman
who the other day knew nobody now goes everywhere,
and another who occupied a commanding position is ostracised, one is inclined to see in these changes merely
those purely personal ups and downs which from time to
time bring about, in the same section of society, in consequence of speculations on the stock exchange, a resounding collapse or enrichment beyond the dreams of avarice.
But there is more to it than that. To a certain extent social manifestations (vastly less important than artistic
movements, political crises, the trend that leads public
taste towards the theatre of ideas, then towards Impressionist painting, then towards music that is German and
complicated, then music that is Russian and simple, or towards ideas of social service, ideas of justice, religious reaction, outbursts of patriotism) are nevertheless an echo of
them, distant, disjointed, uncertain, changeable, blurred.
So that even salons cannot be portrayed in a static immobility which has been conventionally employed up to this
point for the study of characters, though these too must
be carried along as it were in a quasi-historical momen-
tum. The thirst for novelty that leads men of the fashionable world who are more or less sincere in their eagerness
to keep abreast of intellectual developments to frequent

the circles in which they can follow them makes them prefer as a rule some hostess as yet undiscovered, who represents still in their first freshness the hopes of a superior culture so faded and tarnished in the women who for long years have wielded the social sceptre and who, having no secrets from these men, no longer appeal to their imagination. And every period finds itself personified thus in new women, in a new group of women, who, closely identified with whatever may be the latest object of curiosity, seem, in their new attire, to be at that moment making their first appearance, like an unknown species born of the last deluge, irresistible beauties of each new Consulate, each new Directory. But very often the new hostesses are simply, like certain statesmen who may be in office for the first time but have for the last forty years been knocking at every door without seeing any open, women who were not known in society but who nevertheless had been entertaining for years past, for want of anyone better, a few "chosen friends." To be sure, this is not always the case, and when, with the prodigious flowering of the Russian Ballet, revealing one after another Bakst, Nijinsky, Benois and the genius of Stravinsky, Princess Yourbeletieff, the youthful sponsor of all these new great men, appeared wearing on her head an immense, quivering aigrette that was new to the women of Paris and that they all sought to copy, it was widely supposed that this marvellous creature had been imported in their copious luggage, and as their most priceless treasure, by the Russian dancers; but when presently, by her side in her stage box at every performance of the "Russians," seated like a true fairy godmother, unknown until that moment to the aristocracy, we see Mme Verdurin, we shall be able to tell the society people who may well suppose her to have recently entered the country with Diaghileff's troupe, that this lady, too, had already existed in different periods and had passed through various avatars from which this one differed only in being the first to bring about at last, henceforth assured, and more and more swiftly on the march, the success so long awaited by the Mistress. In Mme Swann's case, it is true, the novelty she represented had not the same collective character. Her salon had crystallised round one man, a dying man, who had progressed almost overnight, at the moment when his talent was exhausted, from obscurity to a blaze of glory. The craze for Bergotte's works was unbounded. He spent the whole day, on show, at Mme Swann's, who would whisper to some influential man: "I shall say a word to him: he'll write an article for you." He was, in fact, in a condition to do so, and even to write a little play for Mme Swann. A stage nearer to death, he was not quite so ill as at the time when he used to come and inquire after my grandmother. This was because intense physical pain had enforced a regime on him. Illness is the most heeded of doctors: to kindness and wisdom we make promises only; pain we obey.

It is true that the Verdurins and their little clan were at this time of far more lively interest than the faintly nationalist, more markedly literary, and pre-eminently Bergottesque salon of Mme Swann. The little clan was in fact the active centre of a long political crisis which had reached its maximum of intensity: Dreyfusism. But society people were for the most part so violently against reconsideration that a Dreyfusian salon seemed to them as inconceivable a phenomenon as, at an earlier period, a

Communard salon. True, the Princesse de Caprarola, who had made Mme Verdurin's acquaintance over a big exhibition which she had organised, had been to pay her a long visit in the hope of seducing a few interesting specimens of the little clan and incorporating them in her own salon, a visit in the course of which the Princess (playing a poor man's Duchesse de Guermantes) had taken the opposing view to accepted opinion and declared that the people in her world were idiots, all of which Mme Verdurin had thought most courageous. But this courage did not subsequently take her to the point of daring, under the gimlet eyes of nationalist ladies, to bow to Mme Verdurin at the Balbec races. As for Mme Swann, on the other hand, the anti-Dreyfusards gave her credit for being "sound," which, in a woman married to a Jew, was doubly meritorious. Nevertheless, people who had never been to her house imagined her as visited only by a few obscure Jews and disciples of Bergotte. In this way women far better qualified than Mme Swann are placed on the lowest rung of the social ladder, whether on account of their origins, or because they do not care about dinner-parties and receptions, at which they are never seen (an absence erroneously assumed to be due to their not having been invited), or because they never speak of their social connexions but only of literature and art, or because people conceal the fact that they go to their houses, or they, to avoid impoliteness to yet other people, conceal the fact that they entertain them—in short for countless reasons which, added together, make of this or that woman, in certain people's eyes, the sort of woman whom one does not know. So it was with Odette. Mme d'Epinoy, when busy collecting some subscriptions for the "Patrie

française," having been obliged to go and see her, as she
would have gone to her dressmaker, convinced moreover
that she would find only a lot of faces that were not even
despised but completely unknown, stood rooted to the
ground when the door opened not upon the drawing-room
she imagined but upon a magic hall in which, as in the
transformation scene of a pantomime, she recognised in
the dazzling chorus, reclining upon divans, seated in arm-
chairs, addressing their hostess by her Christian name, the
highnesses, the duchesses whom she, the Princesse
d'Epinoy, had the greatest difficulty in enticing into her
own drawing-room, and to whom at that moment, beneath the benevolent gaze of Odette, the Marquis du Lau,
Comte Louis de Turenne, Prince Borghese, the Duc d'Es-
trées, carrying orangeade and petits fours, were acting as
cupbearers and pantlers. The Princesse d'Epinoy, as she
instinctively took people's social status to be inherent in
themselves, was obliged to disincarnate Mme Swann and
reincarnate her in a fashionable woman. Ignorance of the
real existence led by women who do not advertise it in the
newspapers draws a veil of mystery over certain situations, thereby contributing to the diversification of salons.
In Odette's case, at the start, a few men of the highest society, anxious to meet Bergotte, had gone to dine in pri-
vacy at her house. She had had the tact, recently acquired,
not to advertise their presence; they found when they
went there—a memory perhaps of the little nucleus,
whose traditions Odette had preserved in spite of the
schism—a place laid for them at table, and so forth.
Odette took them with Bergotte (whom these excursions,
incidentally, finished off) to interesting first nights. They
spoke of her to various women of their own world who

were capable of taking an interest in such novelty. These women were convinced that Odette, an intimate friend of Bergotte, had more or less collaborated in his works, and believed her to be a thousand times more intelligent than the most outstanding women of the Faubourg, for the same reason that made them pin all their political faith to certain staunch Republicans such as M. Doumer and M. Deschanel, whereas they visualised France on the brink of ruin were her destinies entrusted to the monarchists who were in the habit of dining with them, men like Charette or Doudeauville. This change in Odette's status had been achieved with a discretion on her part that made it more secure and more rapid but allowed no suspicion to filter through to the public, which is prone to refer to the social columns of the *Gaulois* for evidence as to the advance or decline of a salon, with the result that one day, at the dress rehearsal of a play by Bergotte given in one of the most fashionable theatres in aid of a charity, the really dramatic moment was when people saw coming in and sitting down beside Mme Swann in the centre box, which was that reserved for the author, Mme de Marsantes and the lady who, by the gradual self-effacement of the Duchesse de Guermantes (glutted with honours, and taking the easy way out), was on the way to becoming the lioness, the queen of the age: the Comtesse Molé. "We never even imagined that she had begun to climb," people said of Odette as they saw the Comtesse Molé enter the box, "and look, she has reached the top of the ladder."

So that Mme Swann might suppose that it was from snobbery that I was taking up again with her daughter.

Odette, notwithstanding her brilliant friends, listened with close attention to the play, as though she had come there solely to see it performed, just as in the past she used to walk across the Bois for her health, as a form of exercise. Men who in the past had been less assiduously attentive to her came to the edge of the box, disturbing the whole audience, to reach up to her hand and so approach the imposing circle that surrounded her. She, with a smile that was still one of friendliness rather than of irony, replied patiently to their questions, affecting greater calm than might have been expected, a calm that was perhaps sincere, this exhibition being only the belated revelation of a habitual and discreetly hidden intimacy. Behind these three ladies to whom every eye was drawn was Bergotte flanked by the Prince d'Agrigente, Comte Louis de Turenne, and the Marquis de Bréauté. And it is easy to understand that, to men who were received everywhere and could not expect any further distinction save one for original research, this demonstration of their merit which they considered they were making in succumbing to the allurements of a hostess with a reputation for profound intellectuality, in whose house they expected to meet all the fashionable dramatists and novelists of the day, was more exciting, more lively than those evenings at the Princesse de Guermantes's, which, without any change of programme or fresh attraction, had been going on year after year, all more or less like the one we have described at such length. In that exalted world, the world of the Guermantes, in which people were beginning to lose interest, the latest intellectual fashions were not embodied in entertainments fashioned in their image, as in those sketches that Bergotte used to write for Mme Swann, or those veritable Committees of Public Safety (had society been capable of taking an interest in the Dreyfus case) at which, in

Mme Verdurin's house, Picquart, Clemenceau, Zola, Reinach and Labori used to assemble.

Gilberte, too, helped to strengthen her mother's position, for an uncle of Swann's had just left her nearly eighty million francs, which meant that the Faubourg Saint-Germain was beginning to take notice of her. The reverse of the medal was that Swann (who, however, was dying) held Dreyfusard opinions, though even this did not injure his wife and was actually of service to her. It did not injure her because people said: "He is dotty, his mind has quite gone, nobody pays any attention to him, his wife is the only person who counts and she is charming." But Swann's Dreyfusism was positively useful to Odette. Left to herself, she might have been unable to resist making advances to fashionable women which would have been her undoing. Whereas on the evenings when she dragged her husband out to dine in the Faubourg Saint-Germain, Swann, sitting sullenly in his corner, would not hesitate, if he saw Odette seeking an introduction to some nationalist lady, to exclaim aloud: "Really, Odette, you must be mad. I beg you to keep quiet. It's abject of you to ask to be introduced to anti-semites. I forbid it." People in society whom everyone else runs after are not accustomed either to such pride or to such ill-breeding. For the first time they were seeing someone who thought himself "superior" to them. Swann's growlings were much talked about, and cards with turned-down corners rained upon Odette. When she came to call upon Mme d'Arpajon there was a lively stir of friendly curiosity. "You didn't mind my introducing her to you," said Mme d'Arpajon. "She's very nice. It was Marie de Marsantes who told me about her." "No, not at all, I hear she's

so wonderfully clever, and she is charming. I'd been longing to meet her; do tell me where she lives." Mme
d'Arpajon told Mme Swann that she had enjoyed herself
hugely at the latter's house the other evening, and had
joyfully forsaken Mme de Saint-Euverte for her. And it
was true, for to prefer Mme Swann was to show that one
was intelligent, like going to concerts instead of to tea-
parties. But when Mme de Saint-Euverte called on Mme
d'Arpajon at the same time as Odette, as Mme de Saint-
Euverte was a great snob and Mme d'Arpajon, albeit she
treated her without ceremony, valued her invitations, she
did not introduce Odette, so that Mme de Saint-Euverte
should not know who she was. The Marquise, imagining
that it must be some princess who seldom went out since
she had never seen her, prolonged her call, replying indirectly to what Odette was saying, but Mme d'Arpajon remained adamant. And when Mme de Saint-Euverte
admitted defeat and took her leave, "I didn't introduce
you," her hostess told Odette, "because people don't
much care about going to her house and she's always inviting one; you'd never have heard the last of her." "Oh,
that's all right," said Odette with a pang of regret. But she
retained the idea that people did not care to go to Mme
de Saint-Euverte's, which was to a certain extent true, and
concluded that she herself held a position in society vastly
superior to Mme de Saint-Euverte's, although that lady
had a very high position, and Odette, so far, none at all.

She was not aware of this, and although all Mme de
Guermantes's friends were friends also of Mme d'Arpajon, whenever the latter invited Mme Swann, she would
say with an air of compunction: "I'm going to Mme
d'Arpajon's, but—you'll think me dreadfully old-fash-

ioned, I know—it shocks me because of Mme de Guermantes" (whom, as it happened, she had never met). Elegant men thought that the fact that Mme Swann knew
hardly anyone in high society meant that she must be a
superior woman, probably a great musician, and that it
would be a sort of extra-social distinction, as for a duke to
be a Doctor of Science, to go to her house. Utterly insignificant society women were attracted towards Odette
for a diametrically opposite reason; hearing that she attended the Colonne concerts and professed herself a Wagnerian, they concluded from this that she must be "rather
a lark," and were greatly excited by the idea of getting to
know her. But, being themselves none too firmly established, they were afraid of compromising themselves in
public if they appeared to be on friendly terms with
Odette, and if they caught sight of her at a charity concert, would turn away their heads, deeming it impossible
to greet, under the very nose of Mme de Rochechouart, a
woman who was perfectly capable of having been to
Bayreuth, which was as good as saying that she would
stick at nothing.

Since everybody becomes different when a guest in
another's house—quite apart from the marvellous meta-
morphoses that were accomplished thus in the fairy
palaces—in Mme Swann's drawing-room M. de Bréauté,
suddenly enhanced by the absence of the people with
whom he was normally surrounded, by his air of self-satisfaction at finding himself there, just as if instead of going out to a party he had slipped on his spectacles to shut
himself up and read the *Revue des Deux Mondes*, by the
mystic rite that he appeared to be performing in coming
to see Odette, M. de Bréauté himself seemed a new man.

I would have given a great deal to see what transformations the Duchesse de Montmorency-Luxembourg would
have undergone in this new environment. But she was one
of the people who could never be induced to meet Odette.
Mme de Montmorency, a great deal kindlier about Oriane
than Oriane was about her, surprised me greatly by saying of Mme de Guermantes: "She knows some clever people, and everybody likes her. I believe that if she had had
a little more persistence she would have succeeded in
forming a salon. The fact is, she never bothered about it,
and she's quite right, she's very well off as she is, sought
after by everyone." If Mme de Guermantes did not have
a "salon," what in the world could a "salon" be? The stupefaction which these words induced in me was no greater
than that which I caused Mme de Guermantes when I
told her that I enjoyed going to Mme de Montmorency's.
Oriane thought her an old cretin. "I go there," she said,
"because I'm forced to, she's my aunt; but you! She
doesn't even know how to get agreeable people to come to
her house." Mme de Guermantes did not realise that
agreeable people left me cold, that when she spoke to me
of "the Arpajon salon" I saw a yellow butterfly, and of
"the Swann salon" (Mme Swann was at home in the winter months between 6 and 7) a black butterfly with its
wings powdered with snow. At a pinch this last salon,
which was not one at all, she considered, although out of
bounds for herself, permissible for me on account of the
"clever people" to be found there. But Mme de Luxembourg! Had I already "produced" something that had attracted attention, she would have concluded that an
element of snobbishness may be combined with talent.
But I put the finishing touch to her disillusionment; I

confessed to her that I did not go to Mme de Montmorency's (as she supposed) to "take notes" and "make a study." Mme de Guermantes was in this respect no more in error than the social novelists who analyse mercilessly from the outside the actions of a snob or supposed snob, but never place themselves inside his skin, at the moment when a whole social springtime is bursting into blossom in the imagination. I myself, when I sought to analyse the great pleasure that I found in going to Mme de Montmorency's, was somewhat taken aback. She occupied, in the Faubourg Saint-Germain, an old mansion ramifying into pavilions which were separated by small gardens. In the outer hall a statuette, said to be by Falconet, represented a spring which did indeed exude a perpetual moisture. A little further on the concierge, her eyes always red, either from grief or neurasthenia, a headache or a cold in the head, never answered your inquiry, waved her arm vaguely to indicate that the Duchess was at home, and let a drop or two trickle from her eyelids into a bowl filled with forget-me-nots. The pleasure that I felt on seeing the statuette, because it reminded me of a "little gardener" in plaster that stood in one of the Combray gardens, was nothing to that which was given me by the great staircase, damp and resonant, full of echoes, like the stairs in certain old-fashioned bathing establishments, the vases filled with cinerarias—blue against blue—in the ante-room, and most of all the tinkle of the bell, which was exactly that of the bell in Eulalie's room. This tinkle brought my enthusiasm to its peak, but seemed to me too humble a matter for me to be able to explain it to Mme de Montmorency, with the result that she invariably saw me in a state of rapture of which she never guessed the cause.

THE INTERMITTENCIES OF
THE HEART

My second arrival at Balbec was very different from the first. The manager had come in person to meet me at Pont-à-Couleuvre, reiterating how greatly he valued his titled patrons, which made me afraid that he had ennobled me until I realised that, in the obscurity of his grammatical memory, *titré* meant simply *attitré*, or accredited. In fact, the more new languages he learned the worse he spoke the others. He informed me that he had placed me at the very top of the hotel. "I hope," he said, "that you will not interpolate this as a want of discourtesy. I was worried about giving you a room of which you are unworthy, but I did it in connexion with the noise, because in that room you will not have anyone above your head to disturb your trepan" (tympan). "And do not worry, I shall have the windows closed, so that they don't bang. Upon that point, I am intolerable" (this last word expressing not his own thought, which was that he would always be found inexorable in that respect, but, quite possibly, the thoughts of his underlings). The rooms were, as it proved, those we had had before. They were no lower down, but I had risen in the manager's esteem. I could light a fire if I liked (for, on the doctors' orders, I had left Paris at Easter), but he was afraid there might be "fixtures" in the ceiling. "See that you always wait before alighting a fire until the preceding one is extenuated" (extinguished). "The important thing is to take care not to avoid setting fire to the chimney, especially as, to cheer things up a bit, I have put an old china pottage on the mantelpiece which might become damaged."

He informed me with great sorrow of the death of the president of the Cherbourg bar: "He was an old fogy," he said (probably meaning "foxy") and gave me to understand that his end had been hastened by the dissertations, otherwise the dissipations, of his life. "For some time past I noticed that after dinner he would take a catnip in the reading-room" (catnap, presumably). "The last times, he was so changed that if you hadn't known who it was, to look at him, he was barely recognisant" (presumably recognisable).

A happy compensation: the senior judge from Caen had just received his "carton" (cordon) as Commander of the Legion of Honour. "Surely enough, he has capacities, but seems they gave him it principally because of his general impotence." There was a mention of this decoration, as it happened, in the previous day's *Echo de Paris*, of which the manager had as yet read only "the first paraph," in which M. Caillaux's foreign policy was severely trounced. "I consider they're quite right," he said. "He is putting us too much under the thimble of Germany" (under the thumb). As the discussion of a subject of this sort with a hotel-keeper seemed to me boring, I ceased to listen. I thought of the visual images that had made me decide to return to Balbec. They were very different from those of the earlier time, for the vision in quest of which I had come was as dazzlingly clear as the former had been hazy; they were to prove no less disappointing. The images selected by memory are as arbitrary, as narrow, as elusive as those which the imagination had formed and reality has destroyed. There is no reason why, existing outside ourselves, a real place should conform to the pictures in our memory rather than those in our dreams. And besides, a fresh reality will perhaps make us forget, detest even, the desires on account of which we set out on our journey.

Those that had made me set out for Balbec sprang to some extent from my discovery that the Verdurins (whose invitations I had never taken up, and who would certainly be delighted to see me, if I went to call upon them in the country with apologies for never having been able to call upon them in Paris), knowing that several of the faithful would be spending the holidays on that part of the coast, and having, for that reason, taken for the whole season one of M. de Cambremer's houses (La Raspelière), had invited Mme Putbus to stay with them. The evening on which I learned this (in Paris) I lost my head completely and sent our young footman to find out whether that lady would be taking her chambermaid to Balbec with her. It was eleven o'clock at night. The porter was a long time opening the front door, and for a wonder did not send my messenger packing, did not call the police, merely gave him a dressing-down, but with it the information that I desired. He said that the head lady's-maid would indeed be accompanying her mistress, first of all to the waters in Germany, then to Biarritz, and at the end of the season to Mme Verdurin's. From that moment my mind had been set at rest, content to have this iron in the fire. I had been able to dispense with those pursuits in the streets, wherein I lacked that letter of introduction to the beauties I encountered which I should have to the "Giorgione" in the fact of my having dined that very evening with her mistress at the Verdurins'. Besides, she might perhaps form a still better opinion of me when she learned that I knew not merely the middle-class tenants of La Raspelière but

its owners, and above all Saint-Loup who, unable to com-
mend me to the chambermaid from a distance (since she
did not know him by name), had written an enthusiastic
letter about me to the Cambremers. He believed that,
quite apart from any service that they might be able to
render me, Mme de Cambremer, the Legrandin daughter-
in-law, would interest me by her conversation. "She is an
intelligent woman," he had assured me. "She won't say
anything definitive" (*definitive* having taken the place of
sublime with Robert, who, every five or six years, would
modify a few of his favourite expressions while preserving
the more important intact), "but she's a real personality,
she has character and intuition, and throws out quite per-
tinent remarks. From time to time she's maddening, she
dashes off nonsense to 'put on dog,' which is all the more
ridiculous as nobody could be less grand than the Cambremers, she's not always 'in the swim,' but, taking her all
round, she is one of the people it's most bearable to talk
to."

No sooner had Robert's letter of introduction reached
them than the Cambremers, whether from a snobbishness
that made them anxious to oblige Saint-Loup, even indirectly, or from gratitude for what he had done for one of
their nephews at Doncières, or (most probably) from
kindness of heart and traditions of hospitality, had written
long letters insisting that I should stay with them, or, if I
preferred to be more independent, offering to find me
lodgings. When Saint-Loup had pointed out that I should
be staying at the Grand Hotel at Balbec, they replied that
at least they would expect a call from me as soon as I arrived and, if I did not appear, would come without fail to
hunt me out and invite me to their garden-parties.

No doubt there was no essential connexion between Mme Putbus's maid and the country round Balbec; she would not be for me like the peasant girl whom, as I strayed alone along the Méséglise way, I had so often summoned up in vain with all the force of my desire. But I had long since given up trying to extract from a woman as it were the square root of her unknown quantity, the mystery of which a mere introduction was generally enough to dispel. At least at Balbec, where I had not been for so long, I should have the advantage, failing the necessary connexion between the place and this woman, that my sense of reality would not be destroyed by habit as in Paris, where, whether in my own home or in a bedroom that I already knew, pleasure indulged in with a woman could not give me for one instant, amid everyday surroundings, the illusion that it was opening the door for me to a new life. (For if habit is a second nature, it prevents us from knowing our first, whose cruelties it lacks as well as its enchantments.) But I might perhaps experience this illusion in a strange place, where one's sensibility is revived by a ray of sunshine, and where my ardour would be finally consummated by the chambermaid I desired. However, we shall see that circumstances conspired in such a way that not only did this woman fail to come to Balbec, but I dreaded nothing so much as the possibility of her coming, so that the principal object of my expedition was neither attained nor indeed pursued.

It was true that Mme Putbus was not to be at the Verdurins' so early in the season; but pleasures which we have chosen may be remote if their coming is assured and if, in the interval of waiting, we can devote ourselves to the idleness of seeking to attract while powerless to love.

Moreover, I was not going to Balbec in a frame of mind as little practical as on the first occasion; there is always less egoism in pure imagination than in recollection; and I knew that I was going to find myself in one of those very places where fair strangers must abound; a beach offers them in no less profusion than a ball-room, and I looked forward to strolling up and down outside the hotel, on the front, with the same sort of pleasure that Mme de Guermantes would have procured me if, instead of getting me invited to brilliant dinner-parties, she had given my name more often for their lists of partners to hostesses who gave dances. To make female acquaintances at Balbec would be as easy for me now as it had been difficult before, for I was now as well supplied with friends and resources there as I had been destitute of them on my first visit.

I was roused from my meditations by the voice of the manager, to whose political dissertations I had not been listening. Changing the subject, he told me of the judge's delight on hearing of my arrival, and said that he was coming to pay me a visit in my room that very evening. The thought of this visit so alarmed me (for I was beginning to feel tired) that I begged him to prevent it (which he promised to do) and, as a further precaution, to post members of his staff on guard, for the first night, on my landing. He did not seem overfond of his staff. "I am obliged to keep running after them all the time because they are lacking in inertia. If I was not there they would never stir. I shall post the lift-boy on sentry outside your door." I asked him if the boy had yet become "head page." "He is not old enough yet in the house," was the answer. "He has comrades more aged than he is. It would cause an outcry. We must act with granulation in everything. I quite admit that he strikes a good aptitude at the door of his lift. But he is still a trifle young for such positions. With others in the place of longer standing, it would make a contrast. He is a little wanting in seriousness, which is the primitive quality" (doubtless, the primordial, the most important quality). "He needs his leg screwed on a bit tighter" (my interlocutor meant to say his head). "Anyhow, he can leave it all to me. I know what I'm about. Before I won my stripes as manager of the Grand Hotel, I smelt powder under M. Paillard." I was impressed by this simile, and thanked the manager for having come in person as far as Pont-à-Couleuvre. "Oh, that's nothing! The loss of time has been quite infinite" (for infinitesimal). Meanwhile, we had arrived.

Upheaval of my entire being. On the first night, as I was suffering from cardiac fatigue, I bent down slowly and cautiously to take off my boots, trying to master my pain. But scarcely had I touched the topmost button than my chest swelled, filled with an unknown, a divine presence, I was shaken with sobs, tears streamed from my eyes. The being who had come to my rescue, saving me from barrenness of spirit, was the same who, years before, in a moment of identical distress and loneliness, in a moment when I had nothing left of myself, had come in and had restored me to myself, for that being was myself and something more than me (the container that is greater than the contained and was bringing it to me). I had just perceived, in my memory, stooping over my fatigue, the tender, preoccupied, disappointed face of my grandmother, as she had been on that first evening of our arrival, the face not of that grandmother whom I had been astonished and remorseful at having so little missed, and who had nothing in common with her save her name, but of my real grandmother, of whom, for the first time since the afternoon of her stroke in the Champs-Elysées, I now recaptured the living reality in a complete and involuntary recollection. This reality does not exist for us so long as it has not been re-created by our thought (otherwise men who have been engaged in a titanic struggle would all of them be great epic poets); and thus, in my wild desire to fling myself into her arms, it was only at that moment— more than a year after her burial, because of the anachronism which so often prevents the calendar of facts from corresponding to the calendar of feelings—that I became conscious that she was dead. I had often spoken about her since then, and thought of her also, but behind my words and thoughts, those of an ungrateful, selfish, cruel young man, there had never been anything that resembled my grandmother, because, in my frivolity, my love of pleasure, my familiarity with the spectacle of her ill health, I retained within me only in a potential state the memory of what she had been. No matter at what moment we consider it, our total soul has only a more or less fictitious value, in spite of the rich inventory of its assets, for now some, now others are unrealisable, whether they are real riches or those of the imagination—in my own case, for example, not only of the ancient name of Guermantes but those, immeasurably graver, of the true memory of my grandmother. For with the perturbations of memory are linked the intermittencies of the heart. It is, no doubt, the existence of our body, which we may compare to a vase enclosing our spiritual nature, that induces us to suppose that all our inner wealth, our past joys, all our sorrows, are perpetually in our possession. Perhaps it is equally inexact to suppose that they escape or return. In any case if they remain within us, for most of the time it is in an unknown region where they are of no use to us, and where even the most ordinary are crowded out by memories of a different kind, which preclude any simultaneous occurrence of them in our consciousness. But if the context of sensations in which they are preserved is recaptured, they acquire in turn the same power of expelling everything that is incompatible with them, of installing alone in us the self that originally lived them. Now, inasmuch as the self that I had just suddenly become once again had not existed since that evening long ago when my grandmother had undressed me after my arrival at Balbec, it was quite naturally, not at the end of the day that had just passed, of which that self knew nothing, but—as though Time were to consist of a series of different and parallel lines— without any solution of continuity, immediately after the first evening at Balbec long ago, that I clung to the minute in which my grandmother had stooped over me. The self that I then was, that had disappeared for so long, was once again so close to me that I seemed still to hear the words that had just been spoken, although they were now no more than a phantasm, as a man who is half awake thinks he can still make out, close by, the sound of his receding dream. I was now solely the person who had sought a refuge in his grandmother's arms, had sought to obliterate the traces of his sorrow by smothering her with kisses, that person whom I should have had as much difficulty in imagining when I was one or other of those that for some time past I had successively been as now I should have had in making the sterile effort to experience the desires and joys of one of those that for a time at least

I no longer was. I remembered how, an hour before the moment when my grandmother had stooped in her dressing-gown to unfasten my boots, as I wandered along the stiflingly hot street, past the pastry-cook's, I had felt that I could never, in my need to feel her arms round me, live through the hour that I had still to spend without her. And now that this same need had reawakened, I knew that I might wait hour after hour, that she would never again be by my side. I had only just discovered this because I had only just, on feeling her for the first time alive, real, making my heart swell to breaking-point, on finding her at last, learned that I had lost her for ever. Lost for ever; I could not understand, and I struggled to endure the anguish of this contradiction: on the one hand an existence, a tenderness, surviving in me as I had known them, that is to say created for me, a love which found in me so totally its complement, its goal, its constant lodestar, that the genius of great men, all the genius that might have existed from the beginning of the world, would have been less precious to my grandmother than a single one of my defects; and on the other hand, as soon as I had relived that bliss, as though it were present, feeling it shot through by the certainty, throbbing like a recurrent pain, of an annihilation that had effaced my image of that tenderness, had destroyed that existence, retrospectively abolished our mutual predestination, made of my grandmother, at the moment when I had found her again as in a mirror, a mere stranger whom chance had allowed to spend a few years with me, as she might have done with anyone else, but to whom, before and after those years, I was and would be nothing.

Instead of the pleasures that I had been experiencing

of late, the only pleasure that it would have been possible for me to enjoy at that moment would have been, by touching up the past, to diminish the sorrows and sufferings of my grandmother's life. But I did not remember her only in that dressing-gown, a garment so appropriate as to have become almost symbolic of the pains, unhealthy no doubt but comforting too, which she took for me; gradually I began to remember all the opportunities that I had seized, by letting her see my sufferings and exaggerating them if necessary, to cause her a grief which I imagined as being obliterated immediately by my kisses, as though my tenderness had been as capable as my happiness of making her happy; and, worse than that, I who could conceive of no other happiness now but that of finding happiness shed in my memory over the contours of that face, moulded and bowed by tenderness, had striven with such insensate frenzy to expunge from it even the smallest pleasures, as on the day when Saint-Loup had taken my grandmother's photograph and I, unable to conceal from her what I thought of the childish, almost ridiculous vanity with which she posed for him, with her wide-brimmed hat, in a flattering half light, had allowed myself to mutter a few impatient, wounding words, which, I had sensed from a contraction of her features, had struck home; it was I whose heart they were rending, now that the consolation of countless kisses was for ever impossible.

But never again would I be able to erase that tightening of her face, that anguish of her heart, or rather of mine; for as the dead exist only in us, it is ourselves that we strike without respite when we persist in recalling the blows that we have dealt them. I clung to this pain, cruel

as it was, with all my strength, for I realised that it was
the effect of the memory I had of my grandmother, the
proof that this memory was indeed present within me. I
felt that I did not really remember her except through
pain, and I longed for the nails that riveted her to my
consciousness to be driven yet deeper. I did not try to
mitigate my suffering, to embellish it, to pretend that my
grandmother was only somewhere else and momentarily
invisible, by addressing to her photograph (the one taken
by Saint-Loup, which I had with me) words and entreaties as to a person who is separated from us but, retaining his personality, knows us and remains bound to us
by an indissoluble harmony. Never did I do this, for I
was determined not merely to suffer, but to respect the
original form of my suffering as it had suddenly come
upon me unawares, and I wanted to continue to feel it,
following its own laws, whenever that contradiction of
survival and annihilation, so strangely intertwined within
me, returned. I did not know for certain whether one day
I would draw a little truth from this painful and for the
moment incomprehensible impression, but I knew that if
I ever could extract that little truth, it would only be from
this impression and from none other, an impression at
once so particular and so spontaneous, which had neither
been traced by my intelligence nor deflected or attenuated
by my pusillanimity, but which death itself, the sudden
revelation of death, striking like a thunderbolt, had carved
within me, along a supernatural and inhuman graph, in a
double and mysterious furrow. (As for that forgetfulness
of my grandmother in which I had been living until now,
I could not even think of clinging to it to find some truth;
since in itself it was nothing but a negation, a weakening

of the faculty of thought incapable of re-creating a real moment of life and obliged to substitute for it conventional and neutral images.) Perhaps, however, the instinct of self-preservation, the ingenuity of the mind in safeguarding us from pain, already beginning to lay the foundations of its necessary but baneful edifice on the still smoking ruins, I relished too keenly the sweet joy of recalling this or that opinion held by the beloved being, recalling them as though she had been able to hold them still, as though she existed, as though I continued to exist for her. But as soon as I had succeeded in falling asleep, at that more truthful hour when my eyes closed to the things of the outer world, the world of sleep (on whose frontier my intelligence and my will, momentarily paralysed, could no longer strive to rescue me from the cruelty of my real impressions) reflected, refracted the painful synthesis of survival and annihilation, in the organic and now translucent depths of the mysteriously lighted viscera. World of sleep—in which our inner consciousness, subordinated to the disturbances of our organs, accelerates the rhythm of the heart or the respiration, because the same dose of terror, sorrow or remorse acts with a strength magnified a hundredfold if thus injected into our veins: as soon as, to traverse the arteries of the subterranean city, we have embarked upon the dark current of our own blood as upon an inward Lethe meandering sixfold, tall solemn forms appear to us, approach and glide away, leaving us in tears. I sought in vain for my grandmother's form when I had entered beneath the sombre portals; yet I knew that she did exist still, if with a diminished life, as pale as that of memory; the darkness was increasing, and the wind; my father, who was to take me to her, had not yet arrived. Suddenly my breath failed me, I felt my heart turn to stone; I had just remembered that for weeks on end I had forgotten to write to my grandmother. What must she be thinking of me? "Oh God," I said to myself, "how wretched she must be in that little room which they have taken for her, as small as for an old servant, where she's all alone with the nurse they have put there to look after her, from which she cannot stir, for she's still slightly paralysed and has always refused to get up! She must think that I've forgotten her now that she's dead; how lonely she must be feeling, how deserted! Oh, I must hurry to see her, I mustn't lose a minute, I can't wait for my father to come—but where is it? How can I have forgotten the address? Will she know me again, I wonder? How can I have forgotten her all these months? It's so dark, I shan't be able to find her; the wind is holding me back; but look! there's my father walking ahead of me"; I call out to him: "Where is grandmother? Tell me her address. Is she all right? Are you quite sure she has everything she needs?" "Yes, yes," says my father, "you needn't worry. Her nurse is well trained. We send a very small sum from time to time, so she can get your grandmother the little she needs. She sometimes asks what's become of you. She was told you were going to write a book. She seemed pleased. She wiped away a tear." And then I seemed to remember that shortly after her death, my grandmother had said to me, sobbing, with a humble look, like an old servant who has been given notice, like a stranger: "You will let me see something of you occasionally, won't you; don't let too many years go by without visiting me. Remember that you were my grandson, once, and that grandmothers don't forget." And seeing again

that face of hers, so submissive, so sad, so gentle, I
wanted to run to her at once and say to her, as I ought to
have said to her then: "Why, grandmother, you can see
me as often as you like, I have only you in the world, I
shall never leave you any more." What tears my silence
must have made her shed through all those months in
which I have never been to the place where she is lying!
What can she have been saying to herself? And it is in a
voice choked with tears that I too say to my father:
"Quick, quick, her address, take me to her." But he says:
"Well . . . I don't know whether you will be able to see
her. Besides, you know, she's very frail now, very frail,
she's not at all herself, I'm afraid you would find it rather
painful. And I can't remember the exact number of the
avenue." "But tell me, you who know, it's not true that
the dead have ceased to exist. It can't possibly be true, in
spite of what they say, because grandmother still exists."
My father smiles sadly: "Oh, hardly at all, you know,
hardly at all. I think it would be better if you didn't go.
She has everything that she wants. They come and keep
the place tidy for her." "But is she often alone?" "Yes,
but that's better for her. It's better for her not to think, it
could only make her unhappy. Thinking often makes people unhappy. Besides, you know, she's quite faded now. I
shall leave a note of the exact address, so that you can go
there; but I don't see what good you can do, and I don't
suppose the nurse will allow you to see her." "But you
know quite well I shall always live close to her, stags,
stags, Francis Jammes, fork." But already I had retraced
the dark meanderings of the stream, had ascended to the
surface where the world of the living opens, so that if I
still repeated: "Francis Jammes, stags, stags," the se-

quence of these words no longer offered me the limpid
meaning and logic which they had expressed so naturally
for me only a moment before, and which I could not now
recall. I could not even understand why the word "Aias"
which my father had said to me just now had immediately
signified: "Take care you don't catch cold," without any
possibility of doubt.

I had forgotten to close the shutters, and so probably
the daylight had awakened me. But I could not bear to
have before my eyes those sea vistas on which my grandmother used to gaze for hours on end; the fresh image of
their heedless beauty was at once supplemented by the
thought that she could not see them; I should have liked
to stop my ears against their sound, for now the luminous
plenitude of the beach carved out an emptiness in my
heart; everything seemed to be saying to me, like those
paths and lawns of a public garden in which I had once
lost her, long ago, when I was still a little child: "We
haven't seen her," and beneath the roundness of the pale
vault of heaven I felt crushed as though beneath a huge
bluish bell enclosing an horizon from which my grandmother was excluded. So as not to see anything any more,
I turned towards the wall, but alas, what was now facing
me was that partition which used to serve us as a morning
messenger, that partition which, as responsive as a violin
in rendering every nuance of a feeling, reported so exactly
to my grandmother my fear at once of waking her and, if
she were already awake, of not being heard by her and so
of her not coming, then immediately, like a second instrument taking up the melody, informing me of her coming
and bidding me be calm. I dared not put out my hand to
that wall, any more than to a piano on which my grand-

mother had been playing and which still vibrated from her touch. I knew that I might knock now, even louder, that nothing would wake her any more, that I should hear no response, that my grandmother would never come again. And I asked nothing more of God, if a paradise exists, than to be able, there, to knock on that wall with the three little raps which my grandmother would recognise among a thousand, and to which she would give those answering knocks which meant: "Don't fuss, little mouse, I know you're impatient, but I'm just coming," and that he would let me stay with her throughout eternity, which would not be too long for the two of us.

The manager came in to ask whether I should like to come down. He had most carefully supervised, just in case, my "placement" in the dining-room. As he had seen no sign of me, he had been afraid that I might have had a recurrence of my spasms. He hoped that it might be only a little "sore throats" and assured me that he had heard it said that they could be soothed with what he called "calyptus."

He brought me a message from Albertine. She had not been due to come to Balbec that year but, having changed her plans, had been for the last three days not in Balbec itself but ten minutes away by train at a neighbouring watering-place. Fearing that I might be tired after the journey, she had stayed away the first evening, but sent word now to ask when I could see her. I inquired whether she had called in person, not because I wished to see her, but so that I might arrange not to see her. "Yes," replied the manager. "But she would like it to be as soon as possible, unless you have not some quite necessitous reasons. You see," he concluded, "that everybody here desires you in the end." But for my part, I wished to see nobody.

And yet the day before, on my arrival, I had been seized once again by the indolent charm of seaside existence. The same taciturn lift-boy, silent this time from respect and not from disdain, and glowing with pleasure, had set the lift in motion. As I rose upon the ascending column, I had travelled once again through what had formerly been for me the mystery of a strange hotel, in which when you arrive, a tourist without protection or prestige, each resident returning to his room, each young girl going down to dinner, each servant passing along the eerie perspective of a corridor, not to mention the young lady from America with her chaperon, gives you a look in which you can read nothing that you would have liked to. This time, on the contrary, I had felt the almost too soothing pleasure of passing up through a hotel that I knew, where I felt at home, where I had performed once again that operation which we must always start afresh, longer, more difficult than the turning inside out of an eyelid, and which consists in the imposition of our own familiar soul on the terrifying soul of our surroundings. Must I now, I had asked myself, little suspecting the sudden change of mood that was in store for me, go always to new hotels where I shall be dining for the first time, where Habit will not yet have killed upon each landing, outside each door, the terrible dragon that seemed to be watching over an enchanted existence, where I shall have to approach those unknown women whom grand hotels, casinos, watering-places seem to bring together to live a communal existence as though in vast polyparies?

I had found pleasure even in the thought that the te-

dious judge was so eager to see me; I could see, on the
first evening, the waves, the azure mountain ranges of the
sea, its glaciers and its cataracts, its elevation and its careless majesty, merely upon smelling for the first time after
so long an interval, as I washed my hands, that peculiar
odour of the over-scented soap of the Grand Hotel—
which, seeming to belong at once to the present moment
and to my past visit, floated between them like the real
charm of a particular form of existence in which one
comes home only to change one's tie. The sheets on my
bed, too fine, too light, too large, impossible to tuck in, to
keep in position, which billowed out from beneath the
blankets in shifting whorls, would have distressed me before. Now they merely cradled upon the awkward,
swelling fullness of their sails the glorious sunrise, big
with hopes, of my first morning. But that sun did not
have time to appear. That very night the terrible, divine
presence had returned to life. I asked the manager to leave
me, and to give orders that no one was to enter my room.
I told him that I should remain in bed and rejected his
offer to send to the chemist's for the excellent drug. He
was delighted by my refusal for he was afraid that other
visitors might be bothered by the smell of the "calyptus."
It earned me the compliment: "You are in the movement"
(he meant: "in the right"), and the warning: "Take care
you don't dirty yourself at the door, I've had the lock
'elucidated' with oil; if any of the servants dares to knock
at your door, he'll be beaten 'black and white.' And they
can mark my words, for I'm not a repeater" (this evidently meant that he did not say a thing twice). "But
wouldn't you care for a drop of old wine, just to set you
up; I have a pig's head of it downstairs" (presumably

hogshead). "I shan't bring it to you on a silver dish like the head of Jonathan, and I warn you that it is not Château-Lafite, but it is virtually equivocal" (equivalent). "And as it's quite light, they might fry you a little sole." I declined everything, but was surprised to hear the name of the fish pronounced like that of the first king of Israel, Saul, by a man who must have ordered so many in his life.

Despite the manager's promises, a little later I was brought a calling-card from the Marquise de Cambremer. Having come over to see me, the old lady had inquired whether I was there and when she heard that I had arrived only the day before and was unwell, had not insisted but (not without stopping, doubtless, at the chemist's or the haberdasher's, while the footman jumped down from the box and went in to pay a bill or to give an order) had driven back to Féterne in her old barouche upon eight springs drawn by a pair of horses. Not infrequently indeed was the rumble of the latter to be heard and its trappings admired in the streets of Balbec and of various other little places along the coast, between Balbec and Féterne. Not that these halts outside shops were the object of these excursions. It was on the contrary some tea-party or garden-party at the house of some squire or burgess, socially quite unworthy of the Marquise. But she, though completely overshadowing, by her birth and her wealth, the petty nobility of the district, was in her perfect goodness and simplicity of heart so afraid of disappointing anyone who had invited her that she would attend all the most insignificant social gatherings in the neighbourhood. Certainly, rather than travel such a distance to listen, in the stifling heat of a tiny drawing-room,

to a singer who generally had no voice and whom in her
capacity as the lady bountiful of the countryside and as a
renowned musician she would afterwards be compelled to
congratulate with exaggerated warmth, Mme de Cambremer would have preferred to go for a drive or to remain
in her marvellous gardens at Féterne, at the foot of which
the drowsy waters of a little bay float in to die amid the
flowers. But she knew that the probability of her coming
had been announced by the host, whether he was a noble
or a freeman of Maineville-la-Teinturière or of Chatton-
court-l'Orgueilleux. And if Mme de Cambremer had
driven out that afternoon without making a formal appearance at the party, one or other of the guests who had
come from one of the little places that lined the coast
might have seen or heard the Marquise's barouche, thus
depriving her of the excuse that she had not been able to
get away from Féterne. Moreover, for all that these hosts
had often seen Mme de Cambremer appear at concerts
given in houses which they considered were no place for
her, the slight depreciation which in their eyes the position of the too obliging Marquise suffered thereby vanished as soon as it was they who were entertaining her,
and it was with feverish anxiety that they would ask
themselves whether or not they were going to see her at
their little party. What an assuagement of the doubts and
fears of days if, after the first song had been sung by the
daughter of the house or by some amateur on holiday in
the neighbourhood, one of the guests announced (an infallible sign that the Marquise was coming to the party) that
he had seen the famous barouche and pair drawn up outside the watchmaker's or the chemist's! Thereupon Mme
de Cambremer (who indeed would arrive before long, fol-

lowed by her daughter-in-law and the guests who were staying with her at the moment and whom she had asked permission, joyfully granted, to bring) shone once more with undiminished lustre in the eyes of the host and hostess, for whom the hoped-for reward of her coming had perhaps been the determining if unavowed cause of the decision they had made a month earlier to burden themselves with the trouble and expense of an afternoon party. Seeing the Marquise present at their gathering, they remembered no longer her readiness to attend those given by their less qualified neighbours, but the antiquity of her family, the splendour of her house, the rudeness of her daughter-in-law, *née* Legrandin, who by her arrogance emphasised the slightly insipid good-nature of the dowager. Already they could see in their mind's eye, in the social column of the *Gaulois*, the paragraph which they would concoct themselves in the family circle, with all the doors shut and barred, about "the little corner of Brittany where they have a good time, the ultra-select party from which the guests could hardly tear themselves away, promising their charming host and hostess that they would soon pay them another visit." Day after day they would watch for the newspaper to arrive, worried that they had not yet seen any notice in it of their party, and afraid lest they should have had Mme de Cambremer for their other guests alone and not for the whole reading public. At length the blessed day would arrive: "The season is exceptionally brilliant this year at Balbec. Small afternoon concerts are the fashion . . ." Heaven be praised, Mme de Cambremer's name had been spelt correctly, and "mentioned at random" but at the head of the list. All that remained would be to appear annoyed at this journal-

istic indiscretion which might get them into difficulties
with people whom they had not been able to invite, and
to ask hypocritically in Mme de Cambremer's hearing
who could have been so treacherous as to send the notice,
upon which the Marquise, every inch the lady bountiful,
would say: "I can understand your being annoyed, but I
must say I'm only too delighted that people should know
I was at your party."

On the card that was brought me, Mme de Cambremer had scribbled the message that she was giving an afternoon party "the day after tomorrow." And indeed only
two days earlier, tired as I was of social life, it would have
been a real pleasure to me to taste it, transplanted amid
those gardens in which, thanks to the exposure of Féterne,
fig trees, palms, rose bushes grew out in the open and
stretched down to a sea often as blue and calm as the
Mediterranean, upon which the hosts' little yacht would
sail across, before the party began, to fetch the most important guests from the places on the other side of the
bay, would serve, with its awnings spread to shut out the
sun, as an open-air refreshment room after the party had
assembled, and would set sail again in the evening to take
back those whom it had brought. A charming luxury, but
so costly that it was partly to meet the expenditure that it
entailed that Mme de Cambremer had sought to increase
her income in various ways, notably by letting for the first
time one of her properties, very different from Féterne:
La Raspelière. Yes, two days earlier, how welcome such a
party, peopled with minor nobles all unknown to me, in a
new setting, would have been to me as a change from the
"high life" of Paris! But now pleasures had no longer any
meaning for me. And so I wrote to Mme de Cambremer

to decline, just as, an hour ago, I had sent Albertine away: grief had destroyed in me the possibility of desire as completely as a high fever takes away one's appetite. My mother was to arrive the following day. I felt that I was less unworthy to live in her company, that I should understand her better, now that a whole alien and degrading existence had given way to the resurgence of the heart-rending memories that encircled and ennobled my soul, like hers, with their crown of thorns. So I thought; but in reality there is a world of difference between real grief, like my mother's—which literally crushes the life out of one for years if not for ever, when one has lost the person one loves—and that other kind of grief, transitory when all is said, as mine was to be, which passes as quickly as it has been slow in coming, which we do not experience until long after the event because in order to feel it we need first to "understand" the event; grief such as so many people feel, from which the grief that was torturing me at this moment differed only in assuming the form of involuntary memory.

That I was one day to experience a grief as profound as that of my mother will be seen in the course of this narrative, but it was neither then nor thus that I imagined it. Nevertheless, like an actor who ought to have learned his part and to have been in his place long beforehand but, having arrived only at the last moment and having read over once only what he has to say, manages to improvise so skilfully when his cue comes that nobody notices his unpunctuality, my new-found grief enabled me, when my mother came, to talk to her as though it had existed always. She supposed merely that the sight of these places which I had visited with my grandmother (which was not at all the case) had revived it. For the first time then, and because I felt a sorrow which was as nothing compared with hers but which opened my eyes, I realised with horror what she must be suffering. For the first time I understood that the blank, tearless gaze (because of which Françoise had little pity for her) that she had worn since my grandmother's death was fixed on that incomprehensible contradiction between memory and non-existence. Moreover, since, though still in deep mourning, she was more "dressed up" in this new place, I was more struck by the transformation that had occurred in her. It is not enough to say that she had lost all her gaiety; fused, congealed into a sort of imploring image, she seemed to be afraid of affronting by too sudden a movement, by too loud a tone of voice, the sorrowful presence that never left her. But above all, as soon as I saw her enter in her crape overcoat, I realised—something that had escaped me in Paris—that it was no longer my mother that I had before my eyes, but my grandmother. As, in royal and ducal families, on the death of the head of the house his son takes his title and, from being Duc d'Orléans, Prince de Tarente or Prince des Laumes, becomes King of France, Duc de La Trémoïlle, Duc de Guermantes, so by an accession of a different order and more profound origin, the dead annex the living who become their replicas and successors, the continuators of their interrupted life. Perhaps the great sorrow that, in a daughter such as Mamma, follows the death of her mother simply breaks the chrysalis a little sooner, hastens the metamorphosis and the appearance of a being whom we carry within us and who, but for this crisis which annihilates time and space, would have emerged more gradually. Perhaps, in our regret for

her who is no more, there is a sort of auto-suggestion
which ends by bringing out in our features resemblances
which potentially we already bore, and above all a cessation of our most characteristically individual activity (in
my mother, her common sense and the mocking gaiety
that she inherited from her father), which, so long as the
beloved person was alive, we did not shrink from exercising, even at her expense, and which counterbalanced the
traits that we derived exclusively from her. Once she is
dead, we hesitate to be different, we begin to admire only
what she was, what we ourselves already were, only
blended with something else, and what in future we shall
be exclusively. It is in this sense (and not in that other
sense, so vague, so false, in which the phrase is generally
understood) that we may say that death is not in vain,
that the dead continue to act upon us. They act upon us
even more than the living because, true reality being dis-
coverable only by the mind, being the object of a mental
process, we acquire a true knowledge only of things that
we are obliged to re-create by thought, things that are
hidden from us in everyday life . . . Lastly, in this cult of
grief for our dead, we pay an idolatrous worship to the
things that they loved. My mother could not bear to be
parted, not only from my grandmother's bag, which had
become more precious than if it had been studded with
sapphires and diamonds, from her muff, from all those
garments which served to accentuate the physical resemblance between them, but even from the volumes of Mme
de Sévigné which my grandmother took with her everywhere, copies which my mother would not have exchanged even for the original manuscript of the *Letters*.
She had often teased my grandmother, who could never

write to her without quoting some phrase of Mme de
Sévigné or Mme de Beausergent. In each of the three letters that I received from Mamma before her arrival at
Balbec, she quoted Mme de Sévigné to me as though
those three letters had been written not by her to me but
by my grandmother to her. She must at once go out on to
the front to see that beach of which my grandmother had
spoken to her every day in her letters. I saw her from my
window, dressed in black, and carrying her mother's sunshade, advancing with timid, pious steps over the sands
which beloved feet had trodden before her, and she
looked as though she were going in search of a corpse
which the waves would cast up at her feet. So that she
should not have to dine alone, I had to join her downstairs. The judge and the president's widow asked to be
introduced to her. And everything that was in any way
connected with my grandmother was so precious to her
that she was deeply touched, and remembered ever afterwards with gratitude what the judge said to her, just as
she was hurt and indignant that on the contrary the president's wife had not a word to say in memory of the dead
woman. In reality, the judge cared no more about my
grandmother than the president's wife. The affecting
words of the one and the other's silence, for all that my
mother put so vast a distance between them, were but alternative ways of expressing that indifference which we
feel towards the dead. But I think that my mother found
most comfort in the words in which I unintentionally betrayed a little of my own anguish. It could not but make
Mamma happy (notwithstanding all her affection for myself), like everything else that guaranteed my grandmother
survival in people's hearts. Daily after this my mother

went down and sat on the beach, in order to do exactly
what her mother had done, and read her two favourite
books, the *Memoirs* of Mme de Beausergent and the *Letters* of Mme de Sévigné. She, like all the rest of us, could
not bear to hear the latter called the "witty Marquise" any
more than to hear La Fontaine called "le Bonhomme."
But when, in reading the *Letters*, she came upon the
words "my daughter," she seemed to be listening to her
mother's voice.

She had the misfortune, on one of these pilgrimages
during which she did not like to be disturbed, to meet on
the beach a lady from Combray, accompanied by her
daughters. Her name was, I think, Mme Poussin. But
among ourselves we always referred to her as "Just You
Wait," for it was by the perpetual repetition of this
phrase that she warned her daughters of the evils that
they were laying up for themselves, saying for instance if
one of them was rubbing her eyes: "Just you wait until
you go and get ophthalmia." She greeted my mother from
afar with long, lachrymose bows, a sign not of condolence
but of the nature of her social training. Had we not lost
my grandmother and had we only had reasons to be
happy, she would have done the same. Living in comparative retirement at Combray within the walls of her large
garden, she could never find anything soft enough for her
liking, and subjected words and even proper names to a
softening process. She felt "spoon" to be too hard a word
to apply to the piece of silverware which measured out
her syrups, and said, in consequence, "spune"; she would
have been afraid of offending the gentle bard of Télé-
maque by calling him bluntly Fénelon—as I myself did
with every reason to know, having as my dearest friend

the best, bravest, most intelligent of men, whom no one who knew him could forget: Bertrand de Fénelon—and invariably said "Fénélon," feeling that the acute accent added a certain softness. The far from soft son-in-law of this Mme Poussin, whose name I have forgotten, having been notary public at Combray, ran off with the funds, and relieved my uncle, in particular, of a considerable sum of money. But most of the inhabitants of Combray were on such friendly terms with the rest of the family that no coolness ensued and people were merely sorry for Mme Poussin. She never entertained, but whenever people passed by her railings they would stop to admire the shade of her admirable trees, without being able to make out anything else. She hardly gave us any trouble at Balbec, where I encountered her only once, at a moment when she was saying to a daughter who was biting her nails: "Just you wait till you get a good whitlow."

While Mamma sat reading on the beach I remained in my room by myself. I recalled the last weeks of my grandmother's life, and everything connected with them, the outer door of the flat which had been propped open when I went out with her for the last time. In contrast with all this the rest of the world seemed scarcely real and my anguish poisoned everything in it. Finally my mother insisted on my going out. But at every step, some forgotten view of the casino, of the street along which, while waiting for her that first evening, I had walked as far as the Duguay-Trouin monument, prevented me, like a wind against which it is hopeless to struggle, from going further; I lowered my eyes in order not to see. And after I had recovered my strength a little I turned back towards the hotel, the hotel in which I knew that it was henceforth impossible that, however long I might wait, I should find my grandmother as I had found her there before, on the evening of our arrival. As it was the first time that I had gone out of doors, a number of servants whom I had not yet seen gazed at me curiously. On the very threshold of the hotel a young page took off his cap to greet me and at once put it on again. I supposed that Aimé had, to borrow his own expression, "tipped him the wink" to treat me with respect. But I saw a moment later that, as someone else entered the hotel, he doffed it again. The fact of the matter was that this young man had no other occupation in life than to take off and put on his cap, and did it to perfection. Having realised that he was incapable of doing anything else but excelled in that, he practised it as many times a day as possible, thus winning a discreet but widespread regard from the hotel guests, coupled with great regard from the hall porter upon whom devolved the duty of engaging the boys and who, until this rare bird alighted, had never succeeded in finding anyone who wasn't sacked within a week, greatly to the astonishment of Aimé who used to say: "After all, in that job they've only got to be polite, which can't be so very difficult." The manager required in addition that they should have what he called a good "present," meaning thereby that they should stay there, or more likely having misremembered the word "presence." The appearance of the lawn behind the hotel had been altered by the creation of several flower-beds and by the removal not only of an exotic shrub but of the page who, at the time of my former visit, used to provide an external decoration with the supple stem of his figure and the curious colouring of his hair. He had gone off with a Polish countess who had taken

him as her secretary, following the example of his two elder brothers and their typist sister, snatched from the hotel by persons of different nationality and sex who had
been attracted by their charm. The only one remaining
was the youngest, whom nobody wanted because he
squinted. He was highly delighted when the Polish countess or the protectors of the other two brothers came on a
visit to the hotel at Balbec. For, although he envied his
brothers, he was fond of them and could in this way cultivate his family feelings for a few weeks in the year. Was
not the Abbess of Fontevrault, deserting her nuns for the
occasion, in the habit of going to partake of the hospitality
which Louis XIV offered to that other Mortemart, his
mistress, Madame de Montespan? The boy was still in his
first year at Balbec; he did not as yet know me, but having heard his comrades of longer standing supplement the
word "Monsieur" with my surname when they addressed
me, he copied them from the first with an air of self-satisfaction, either at showing his familiarity with a person
whom he supposed to be well-known, or at conforming
with a usage of which five minutes earlier he had been
unaware but which he felt it was imperative to observe. I
could well appreciate the charm that this great hotel
might have for certain persons. It was arranged like a theatre, and was filled to the flies with a numerous and animated cast. For all that the visitor was only a sort of
spectator, he was perpetually involved in the performance,
not simply as in one of those theatres where the actors
play a scene in the auditorium, but as though the life of
the spectator was going on amid the sumptuosities of the
stage. The tennis-player might come in wearing a white
flannel blazer, but the porter would have put on a blue

frock-coat with silver braid in order to hand him his letters. If this tennis-player did not choose to walk upstairs,
he was equally involved with the actors in having by his
side, to propel the lift, its attendant no less richly attired.
The corridors on each floor engulfed a flock of chamber-
maids and female couriers, fair visions against the sea, like
the frieze of the Panathenaea, to whose modest rooms
devotees of ancillary feminine beauty would penetrate by
cunning detours. Downstairs, it was the masculine element that predominated and that made this hotel, in view
of the extreme and idle youth of the servants, a sort of
Judaeo-Christian tragedy given bodily form and perpetually in performance. And so I could not help reciting to myself, when I saw them, not indeed the lines of Racine that
had come into my head at the Princesse de Guermantes's
while M. de Vaugoubert stood watching young embassy
secretaries greet M. de Charlus, but other lines of Racine,
taken this time not from *Esther* but from *Athalie*: for in the
doorway of the hall, what in the seventeenth century was
called the portico, "a flourishing race" of young pages clustered, especially at tea-time, like the young Israelites of
Racine's choruses. But I do not believe that a single one
of them could have given even the vague answer that Joas
finds to satisfy Athalie when she inquires of the infant
Prince: "What is your office, then?" for they had none.
At the most, if one had asked of any of them, like the old
Queen: "But all these people shut within this place, what
is it that they do?" he might have said: "I watch the
solemn order of these ceremonies—and bear my part."
Now and then one of the young supers would approach
some more important personage, then this young beauty
would rejoin the chorus, and, unless it was the moment

for a spell of contemplative relaxation, they would all in-
terweave their useless, respectful, decorative, daily movements. For, except on their "day off," "reared in seclusion
from the world" and never crossing the threshold, they
led the same ecclesiastical existence as the Levites in
Athalie, and as I gazed at that "young and faithful troop"
playing at the foot of the steps draped with sumptuous
carpets, I felt inclined to ask myself whether I was entering the Grand Hotel at Balbec or the Temple of Solomon.

I went straight up to my room. My thoughts kept
constantly turning to the last days of my grandmother's
illness, to her sufferings which I relived, intensifying them
with that element, still harder to bear than even the sufferings of others, which is added to them by our cruel
pity; when we believe we are merely re-creating the grief
and pain of a beloved person, our pity exaggerates them;
but perhaps it is our pity that speaks true, more than the
sufferers' own consciousness of their pain, they being
blind to that tragedy of their existence which pity sees
and deplores. But my pity would have transcended my
grandmother's sufferings in a new surge had I known then
what I did not know until long afterwards, that on the eve
of her death, in a moment of consciousness and after
making sure that I was not in the room, she had taken
Mamma's hand, and, after pressing her fevered lips to it,
had said: "Good-bye, my child, good-bye for ever." And
this may also perhaps have been the memory upon which
my mother never ceased to gaze so fixedly. Then sweeter
memories returned to me. She was my grandmother and I
was her grandson. Her facial expressions seemed written
in a language intended for me alone; she was everything
in my life, other people existed merely in relation to her,

to the opinion she would express to me about them. But no, our relations were too fleeting to have been anything but accidental. She no longer knew me, I should never see her again. We had not been created solely for one another; she was a stranger to me. This stranger was before my eyes at the moment in the photograph taken of her by Saint-Loup. Mamma, who had met Albertine, had insisted upon my seeing her because of the nice things she had said about my grandmother and myself. I had accordingly made an appointment with her. I told the manager that she was coming, and asked him to put her in the drawing-room to wait for me. He told me that he had known her for years, herself and her friends, long before they had attained "the age of purity," but that he was annoyed with them because of certain things they had said about the hotel. "They can't be very 'illegitimate' if they talk like that. Unless people have been slandering them." I had no difficulty in guessing that "purity" here meant "puberty." "Illegitimate" puzzled me more. Was it perhaps a confusion with "illiterate," which in that case was a further confusion with "literate"? As I waited until it was time to go down and meet Albertine, I kept my eyes fixed, as on a drawing which one ceases to see by dint of staring at it, upon the photograph that Saint-Loup had taken, and all of a sudden I thought once again: "It's grandmother, I am her grandson," as a man who has lost his memory remembers his name, as a sick man changes his personality. Françoise came in to tell me that Albertine was there, and, catching sight of the photograph: "Poor Madame, it's the very image of her, down to the beauty spot on her cheek; that day the Marquis took her picture, she was very poorly, she had been taken bad

twice. 'Whatever happens, Françoise,' she says to me, 'you mustn't let my grandson know.' And she hid it well, she was always cheerful in company. When she was by herself, though, I used to find that she seemed to be in rather monotonous spirits now and then. But she soon got over it. And then she says to me, she says: 'If anything happened to me, he ought to have a picture of me to keep. And I've never had a single one made.' So then she sent me along with a message to the Marquis, and he was never to let you know that it was she had asked him, but could he take her photograph. But when I came back and told her yes, she didn't want it any longer, because she was looking so poorly. 'It would be even worse,' she says to me, 'than no photograph at all.' But she was a clever one, she was, and in the end she got herself up so well in that big pulled-down hat that it didn't show at all when she was out of the sun. She was so pleased with her photograph, because at that time she didn't think she would ever leave Balbec alive. It was no use me saying to her: 'Madame, it's wrong to talk like that, I don't like to hear Madame talk like that,' she'd got it into her head. And, lord, there were plenty of days when she couldn't eat a thing. That was why she used to make Monsieur go and dine far out in the country with M. le Marquis. Then instead of going to table she'd pretend to be reading a book, and as soon as the Marquis's carriage had started, up she'd go to bed. Some days she wanted to send word to Madame to come down so's she could see her once more. And then she was afraid of alarming her, as she hadn't said anything to her about it. 'It will be better for her to stay with her husband, don't you see, Françoise.'"
Looking me in the face, Françoise asked me all of a sud-

den if I was "feeling queer." I said that I was not; and she
went on: "Here you are keeping me tied up chatting with
you, and perhaps your visitor's already here. I must go
down. She's not the sort of person to have here. Why, a
fast one like that, she may be gone again by now. She
doesn't like to be kept waiting. Oh, nowadays, Mademoiselle Albertine, she's somebody!" "You are quite wrong,
she's a very respectable person, too good for this place.
But go and tell her that I shan't be able to see her today."

What compassionate declamations I should have provoked from Françoise if she had seen me cry. I carefully
hid myself from her. Otherwise I should have had her
sympathy. But I gave her mine. We do not put ourselves
sufficiently in the place of these poor maidservants who
cannot bear to see us cry, as though crying hurt us; or
hurt them, perhaps, for Françoise used to say to me when
I was a child: "Don't cry like that, I don't like to see you
crying like that." We dislike high-sounding phrases, as-
severations, but we are wrong, for in that way we close
our hearts to the pathos of country folk, to the legend
which the poor serving woman, dismissed, unjustly perhaps, for theft, pale as death, grown suddenly more humble as if it were a crime merely to be accused, unfolds,
invoking her father's honesty, her mother's principles, her
grandmother's admonitions. It is true that those same servants who cannot bear our tears will have no hesitation in
letting us catch pneumonia because the maid downstairs
likes draughts and it would not be polite to her to shut
the windows. For it is necessary that even those who are
right, like Françoise, should be wrong also, so that Justice
may be made an impossible thing. Even the humble pleasures of servants provoke either the refusal or the ridicule

of their masters. For it is always a mere nothing, but foolishly sentimental, unhygienic. And so they are in a position to say: "I only ask for this one thing in the whole
year, and I'm not allowed it." And yet their masters
would allow them far more, provided it was not stupid
and dangerous for them—or for the masters themselves.
To be sure, the humility of the wretched maid, trembling,
ready to confess the crime that she has not committed,
saying "I shall leave tonight if you wish," is a thing that
nobody can resist. But we must learn also not to remain
unmoved, despite the solemn and threatening banality of
the things that she says, her maternal heritage and the
dignity of the family "kaleyard," at the sight of an old
cook draped in the honour of her life and of her ancestry,
wielding her broom like a sceptre, putting on a tragic act,
her voice broken with sobs, drawing herself up majestically. That afternoon, I remembered or imagined scenes
of this sort which I associated with our old servant, and
from then onwards, in spite of all the harm that she might
do to Albertine, I loved Françoise with an affection, intermittent it is true, but of the strongest kind, the kind that
is founded upon pity.

True, I suffered all day long as I sat gazing at my
grandmother's photograph. It tortured me. Not so acutely,
though, as the visit I received that evening from the manager. When I had spoken to him about my grandmother,
and he had reiterated his condolences, I heard him say
(for he enjoyed using the words that he pronounced
wrongly): "Like the day when Madame your grandmother
had that sincup, I wanted to tell you about it, because you
see, on account of the other guests it might have given the
place a bad name. She ought really to have left that

evening. But she begged me to say nothing about it and promised me that she wouldn't have another sincup, or the first time she had one, she would go. However, the floor waiter reported to me that she had had another. But, lord, you were old clients we wanted to please, and since nobody made any complaint . . ." And so my grandmother had had syncopes which she never mentioned to me. Perhaps at the very moment when I was being least kind to her, when she was obliged, in the midst of her pain, to make an effort to be good-humoured so as not to irritate me, and to appear well so as not to be turned out of the hotel. "Sincup" was a word which, so pronounced, I should never have imagined, which might perhaps, applied to other people, have struck me as ridiculous, but which in its strange tonal novelty, like that of an original discord, long retained the faculty of arousing in me the most painful sensations.

Next day I went, at Mamma's request, to lie down for a while on the beach, or rather among the dunes, where one is hidden by their folds, and where I knew that Albertine and her friends would not be able to find me. My drooping eyelids allowed but one kind of light to pass, entirely pink, the light of the inner walls of the eyes. Then they shut altogether. Whereupon my grandmother appeared to me, seated in an armchair. So feeble was she that she seemed to be less alive than other people. And yet I could hear her breathe; now and again she made a sign to show that she had understood what we were saying, my father and I. But in vain did I take her in my arms, I could not kindle a spark of affection in her eyes, a flush of colour in her cheeks. Absent from herself, she appeared not to love me, not to know me, perhaps not to see me. I could not interpret the secret of her indifference, of her dejection, of her silent displeasure. I drew my father aside. "You can see, all the same," I said to him, "there's no doubt about it, she understands everything perfectly. It's a perfect imitation of life. If only we could fetch your cousin, who maintains that the dead don't live! Why, she's been dead for more than a year and yet she's still alive. But why won't she give me a kiss?" "Look, her poor head is drooping again." "But she wants to go to the Champs-Elysées this afternoon." "It's madness!" "You really think it can do her any harm, that she can die any further? It isn't possible that she no longer loves me. I keep on hugging her, won't she ever smile at me again?" "What can you expect, the dead are the dead."

A few days later I was able to look with pleasure at the photograph that Saint-Loup had taken of her; it did not revive the memory of what Françoise had told me, because that memory had never left me and I was growing used to it. But by contrast with what I imagined to have been her grave and pain-racked state that day, the photograph, still profiting by the ruses which my grandmother had adopted, which succeeded in taking me in even after they had been disclosed to me, showed her looking so elegant, so carefree, beneath the hat which partly hid her face, that I saw her as less unhappy and in better health than I had supposed. And yet, her cheeks having without her knowing it an expression of their own, leaden, haggard, like the expression of an animal that senses it has been chosen and marked down, my grandmother had an air of being under sentence of death, an air involuntarily sombre, unconsciously tragic, which escaped me but prevented Mamma from ever looking at that photograph, that photograph which seemed to her a photograph not so much of her mother as of her mother's disease, of an insult inflicted by that disease on my grandmother's brutally buffeted face.

Then one day I decided to send word to Albertine that I would see her presently. This was because, on a morning of intense and premature heat, the myriad cries of children at play, of bathers disporting themselves, of newsvendors, had traced for me in lines of fire, in wheeling, interlacing flashes, the scorching beach which the little waves came up one by one to sprinkle with their coolness; then the symphony concert had begun, mingled with the lapping of the surf, through which the violins hummed like a swarm of bees that had strayed out over the sea. At once I had longed to hear Albertine's laughter and to see her friends again, those girls silhouetted against the waves who had remained in my memory the inseparable charm, the characteristic flora of Balbec; and I had decided to send a line via Françoise to Albertine, making an appointment for the following week, while the sea, gently rising, with the unfurling of each wave completely buried in layers of crystal the melody whose phrases appeared to be separated from one another like those angel lutanists which on the roof of an Italian cathedral rise between the pinnacles of blue porphyry and foaming jasper. But on the day on which Albertine came, the weather had turned dull and cold again, and moreover I had no opportunity of hearing her laugh; she was in a very bad mood. "Balbec is deadly dull this year," she said to me. "I don't mean to stay any longer than I can help. You know I've been here since Easter, that's more than a month. There's not a soul here. You can imagine what fun it is."

Notwithstanding the recent rain and a sky that changed every moment, after escorting Albertine as far as Epreville, for she was, to borrow her expression, "shuttling" between that little watering-place, where Mme Bontemps had her villa, and Incarville, where she had been taken "en pension" by Rosemonde's family, I went off by myself in the direction of the high road that Mme de Villeparisis's carriage used to take when we went for drives with my grandmother; pools of water, which the sun, now bright again, had not yet dried, made a regular quagmire of the ground, and I thought of my grandmother who could never walk a yard without covering herself in mud. But on reaching the road I found a dazzling spectacle. Where I had seen with my grandmother in the month of August only the green leaves and, so to speak, the disposition of the apple-trees, as far as the eye could reach they were in full bloom, unbelievably luxuriant, their feet in the mire beneath their ball-dresses, heedless of spoiling the most marvellous pink satin that was ever seen, which glittered in the sunlight; the distant horizon of the sea gave the trees the background of a Japanese print; if I raised my head to gaze at the sky through the flowers, which made its serene blue appear almost violent, they seemed to draw apart to reveal the immensity of their paradise. Beneath that azure a faint but cold breeze set the blushing bouquets gently trembling. Blue-tits came and perched upon the branches and fluttered among the indulgent flowers, as though it had been an amateur of exotic art and colours who had artificially created this living beauty. But it moved one to tears because, to whatever lengths it went in its effects of refined artifice, one felt that it was natural, that these apple-trees were there in the heart of the country, like peasants on one of the high roads of France. Then the rays of the sun gave place suddenly to those of the rain; they streaked the whole horizon, enclosing the line of apple-trees in their grey net. But these continued to hold aloft their pink and blossoming beauty, in the wind that had turned icy beneath the drenching rain: it was a day in spring.

Chapter Two

In my fear lest the pleasure I found in this solitary excursion might weaken my memory of my grandmother, I sought to revive it by thinking of some great sorrow that she had experienced; in response to my appeal, that sorrow tried to reconstruct itself in my heart, threw up vast pillars there; but my heart was doubtless too small for it, I had not the strength to bear so great a pain, my attention was distracted at the moment when it was approaching completion, and its arches collapsed before they had joined, as the waves crumble before reaching their pinnacle.

And yet, if only from my dreams when I was asleep, I might have learned that my grief for my grandmother's death was diminishing, for she appeared in them less crushed by the idea that I had formed of her non-existence. I saw her an invalid still, but on the road to recovery; I found her in better health. And if she made any allusion to what she had suffered, I stopped her mouth with my kisses and assured her that she was now permanently cured. I should have liked to call the sceptics to witness that death is indeed a malady from which one recovers. Only, I no longer found in my grandmother the rich spontaneity of old. Her words were no more than a feeble, docile response, almost a mere echo of mine; she was now no more than the reflexion of my own thoughts.

Although I was still incapable of feeling a renewal of physical desire, Albertine was beginning nevertheless to inspire in me a desire for happiness. Certain dreams of shared affection, always hovering within us, readily combine, by a sort of affinity, with the memory (provided that this has already become slightly vague) of a woman with whom we have taken our pleasure. This sentiment recalled to me aspects of Albertine's face more gentle, less gay, quite different from those that would have been evoked by physical desire; and as it was also less pressing than that desire, I would gladly have postponed its realisation until the following winter, without seeking to see Albertine again at Balbec before her departure. But, even in the midst of a grief that is still acute, physical desire will revive. From my bed, where I was made to spend hours every day resting, I longed for Albertine to come and resume our former amusements. Do we not see, in the very room in which they have lost a child, its parents soon come together again to give the little angel a baby brother? I tried to distract my mind from this desire by going to the window to look at that day's sea. As in the former year, the seas, from one day to another, were rarely the same. Nor indeed did they at all resemble those of that first year, whether because it was now spring with its storms, or because, even if I had come down at the same time of year as before, the different, more changeable weather might have discouraged from visiting this coast certain indolent, vaporous, fragile seas which on blazing summer days I had seen slumbering upon the beach, their bluish breasts faintly stirring with a soft palpitation or above all because my eyes, taught by Elstir to retain precisely those elements that once I had deliberately rejected, would now gaze for hours at what in the former year they had been incapable of seeing. The contrast that used then to strike me so forcibly, between the country drives that I took with Mme de Villeparisis and the fluid, inaccessible, mythological proximity of the eternal Ocean, no longer existed for me. And there were days now when, on the contrary, the sea itself seemed almost rural. On the days, few and far between, of really fine weather, the heat had traced upon the waters, as though across fields, a dusty white track at the end of which the pointed mast of a fishing-boat stood up like a village steeple. A tug, of which only the funnel was visible, smoked in the distance like a factory set apart, while alone against the horizon a convex patch of white, sketched there doubtless by a sail but seemingly solid and as it were calcareous, was reminiscent of the sunlit corner of some isolated building, a hospital or a school. And the clouds and the wind, on the days when these were added to the sun, completed, if not the error of judgment, at any rate the illusion of the first glance, the suggestion that it aroused in the imagination. For the alternation of sharply defined patches of colour like those produced in the country by the proximity of different crops, the rough, yellow, almost muddy irregularities of the marine surface, the banks, the slopes that hid from sight a vessel upon which a crew of nimble sailors seemed to be harvesting, all this on stormy days made the sea a thing as varied, as solid, as undulating, as populous, as civilised as the earth with its carriage roads over which I used to travel and was soon to be travelling again. And once, unable any longer to hold out against my desire, instead of going back to bed I put on my clothes and set off for Incarville to find Albertine. I would ask her to come with me to Douville, where I would pay calls on Mme de Cambremer at Féterne and on Mme

Verdurin at La Raspelière. Albertine would wait for me
meanwhile upon the beach and we would return together
after dark. I went to take the train on the little local railway, of which I had picked up from Albertine and her
friends all the nicknames current in the district, where it
was known as the *Twister* because of its numberless wind-
ings, the *Crawler* because the train never seemed to move,
the *Transatlantic* because of a horrible siren which it
sounded to clear people off the line, the *Decauville* and
the *Funi*, albeit there was nothing funicular about it but
because it climbed the cliff, and, though not strictly
speaking a Decauville, had a 60 centimetre gauge, the
B.A.G. because it ran between Balbec and Grattevast via
Angerville, the *Tram* and the *T.S.N.* because it was a
branch of the Tramways of Southern Normandy. I took
my seat in a compartment in which I was alone; it was a
day of glorious sunshine, and stiflingly hot; I drew down
the blue blind which shut off all but a single ray of sunlight. But immediately I saw my grandmother, as she had
appeared sitting in the train on our departure from Paris
for Balbec, when, in her distress at seeing me drink beer,
she had preferred not to look, to shut her eyes and pretend to be asleep. I, who in my childhood had been unable to endure her anguish when my grandfather took a
drop of brandy, had not only inflicted upon her the anguish of seeing me accept, at the invitation of another, a
drink which she regarded as harmful to me, but had
forced her to leave me free to swill it down to my heart's
content; worse still, by my bursts of anger, my fits of
breathlessness, I had forced her to help, to advise me to
do so, with a supreme resignation of which I saw now in
my memory the mute, despairing image, her eyes closed

to shut out the sight. So vivid a memory had, like the stroke of a magic wand, restored the mood that I had been gradually outgrowing for some time past; what could I have done with Albertine when my lips were wholly possessed by the desperate longing to kiss a dead woman? What could I have said to the Cambremers and the Verdurins when my heart was beating so violently because the pain that my grandmother had suffered was being constantly renewed in it? I could not remain in the compartment. As soon as the train stopped at Maineville-la-Teinturière, abandoning all my plans, I alighted. Maineville had of late acquired considerable importance and a reputation all its own, because a director of various casinos, a purveyor of pleasure, had set up just outside it, with a luxurious display of bad taste that could vie with that of any grand hotel, an establishment to which we shall return anon and which was, to put it bluntly, the first brothel for smart people that it had occurred to anyone to build upon the coast of France. It was the only one. True, every port has its own, but intended for sailors only, and for lovers of the picturesque who are amused to see, next door to the age-old parish church, the hardly less ancient, venerable and moss-grown bawd standing in front of her ill-famed door waiting for the return of the fishing fleet.

Hurrying past the glittering house of "pleasure," insolently erected there despite the protests which the heads of families had addressed in vain to the mayor, I reached the cliff and followed its winding paths in the direction of Balbec. I heard, without responding to it, the appeal of the hawthorns. Less opulent neighbours of the blossoming apple-trees, they found them rather heavy, without denying the fresh complexion of the rosy-petalled daughters of those wealthy brewers of cider. They knew that, though less well endowed, they were more sought after, and were more than attractive enough simply in their crumpled whiteness.*

On my return, the hotel porter handed me a black-bordered letter in which the Marquis and the Marquise de Gonneville, the Vicomte and the Vicomtesse d'Amfreville, the Comte and the Comtesse de Berneville, the Marquis and the Marquise de Graincourt, the Comte d'Amenoncourt, the Comtesse de Maineville, the Comte and the Comtesse de Franquetot, the Comtesse de Chaverny *née* d'Aigleville, begged to announce, and from which I understood at length why it had been sent to me when I caught sight of the names of the Marquise de Cambremer *née* du Mesnil La Guichard, the Marquis and the Marquise de Cambremer, and saw that the deceased, a cousin of the Cambremers, was named Eléonore-Euphrasie-Humbertine de Cambremer, Comtesse de Criquetot. In the whole expanse of this provincial family, the enumeration of which filled several closely printed lines, not a single commoner, and on the other hand not a single known title, but the entire muster-roll of the nobles of the region who made their names—those of all the interesting places in the neighbourhood—ring out with their joyous endings in *ville*, in *court*, or sometimes on a duller note (in *tot*). Garbed in the roof-tiles of their castle or in the roughcast of their parish church, their nodding heads barely reaching above the vault of the nave or hall, and then only to cap themselves with the Norman lantern or the timbers of the pepperpot turret, they gave the impression of having sounded the rallying call to all the charming villages straggling or scattered over a radius of fifty leagues, and to have paraded them in massed formation, without a single absentee or a single intruder, on the compact, rectangular chess-board of the aristocratic letter edged with black.

My mother had gone upstairs to her room, meditating this sentence from Mme de Sévigné: "I see none of the people who seek to distract me; in veiled words they seek to prevent me from thinking of you, and that offends me"—because the judge had told her that she ought to find some distraction. To me he whispered: "That's the Princesse de Parme!" My fears were dispelled when I saw that the woman whom the judge pointed out to me bore not the slightest resemblance to Her Royal Highness. But as she had engaged a room in which to spend the night after paying a visit to Mme de Luxembourg, the report of her coming had the effect upon many people of making them take each newcomer for the Princesse de Parme—and upon me of making me go and shut myself up in my attic.

I had no wish to remain there by myself. It was barely four o'clock. I asked Françoise to go and find Albertine, so that she might spend the evening with me.

It would be untrue, I think, to say that there were already symptoms of that painful and perpetual mistrust which Albertine was to inspire in me, not to mention the special character, emphatically Gomorrhan, which that mistrust was to assume. Certainly, even that afternoon—but not for the first time—I waited a little anxiously. Françoise, once she had started, stayed away so long that I began to despair. I had not lighted the lamp. The daylight had almost gone. The flag over the Casino flapped in the wind. And, feebler still in the silence of the beach over which the tide was rising, and like a voice expressing and intensifying the jarring emptiness of this restless, unnatural hour, a little barrel-organ that had stopped outside the hotel was playing Viennese waltzes. At length Françoise arrived, but unaccompanied. "I've been as quick as I could but she wouldn't come because she didn't think she was looking smart enough. If she was five minutes painting herself and powdering herself, she was a good hour by the clock. It'll be a regular scentshop in here. She's coming, she stayed behind to tidy herself at the mirror. I thought I should find her here." There was still a long time to wait before Albertine appeared. But the gaiety and the charm that she showed on this occasion dispelled my gloom. She informed me (contrary to what she had said the other day) that she would be staying for the whole season and asked me whether we could not arrange, as in the former year, to meet daily. I told her that at the moment I was too sad and that I would rather send for her from time to time at the last moment, as I did in Paris. "If ever you're feeling gloomy or if you're in the mood, don't hesitate," she told me, "just send for me and I shall come at once, and if you're not afraid of its creating a scandal in the hotel, I shall stay as long as you like." Françoise, in bringing her to me, had assumed the joyous air she wore whenever she had gone to some trouble on my behalf and had succeeded in giving me pleasure. But her joy had nothing to do with Albertine herself, and the very next day she was to greet me with these penetrating words: "Monsieur ought not to see that young lady. I know quite well the sort she is, she'll make you unhappy." As I escorted Albertine to the door I saw in the

lighted dining-room the Princesse de Parme. I merely
gave her a glance, taking care not to be seen. But I must
confess that I found a certain grandeur in the royal politeness which had made me smile at the Guermantes's. It is
a fundamental rule that sovereign princes are at home
wherever they are, and this rule is conventionally expressed in obsolete and useless customs such as that
which requires the host to carry his hat in his hand in his
own house to show that he is not in his own home but in
the Prince's. Now the Princesse de Parme may not have
formulated this idea to herself, but she was so imbued
with it that all her actions, spontaneously invented to suit
the circumstances, expressed it. When she rose from table
she handed a lavish tip to Aimé, as though he had been
there solely for her and she were rewarding, before leaving
a country house, a butler who had been detailed to wait
upon her. Nor did she stop at the tip, but with a gracious
smile bestowed on him a few friendly, flattering words,
with a store of which her mother had provided her. She
all but told him that, just as the hotel was perfectly managed, so Normandy was a garden of roses and that she
preferred France to any other country in the world. Another coin slipped from the Princess's fingers for the wine
waiter whom she had sent for and to whom she insisted
on expressing her satisfaction like a general after an inspection. The lift-boy had come up at that moment with
a message for her; he too received a word, a smile and a
tip, all this interspersed with simple, encouraging remarks
intended to prove to them that she was only one of themselves. As Aimé, the wine waiter, the lift-boy and the rest
felt that it would be impolite not to grin from ear to ear at
a person who smiled at them, she was presently sur-

rounded by a cluster of servants with whom she chatted benevolently; such ways being unfamiliar in smart hotels, the people who passed by, not knowing who she was, thought they were seeing a regular visitor to Balbec who because of her mean extraction or for professional reasons (she was perhaps the wife of an agent for champagne) was less different from the domestics than the really smart visitors. As for me, I thought of the palace at Parma, of the advice, partly religious, partly political, given to this Princess, who behaved towards the lower orders as though she had been obliged to conciliate them in order to reign over them one day; or indeed, as though she were already reigning.

I went upstairs to my room, but I was not alone there. I could hear someone mellifluously playing Schumann. No doubt it happens at times that people, even those whom we love best, become permeated with the gloom or irritation that emanates from us. There is however an inanimate object which is capable of a power of exasperation to which no human being will ever attain: to wit, a piano.

Albertine had made me take a note of the dates on which she would be going away for a few days to visit various friends, and had made me write down their addresses as well, in case I should want her on one of those evenings, for none of them lived very far away. This meant that in seeking her out, from one girlfriend to another, I found her more and more entwined in ropes of flowers. I must confess that many of her friends—I was not yet in love with her—gave me, at one watering-place or another, moments of pleasure. These obliging young playmates did not seem to me to be very many. But re-

cently I thought of them again, and their names came
back to me. I counted that, in that one season, a dozen
conferred on me their ephemeral favours. Another name
came back to me later, which made thirteen. I then had a
sort of childish fear of settling on that number. Alas, I realised that I had forgotten the first, Albertine who was no
more and who made the fourteenth.

To resume the thread of my narrative, I had written
down the names and addresses of the girls with whom I
should find her on the days when she was not to be at Incarville, but had decided that on those days I would
rather take the opportunity to call on Mme Verdurin. In
any case, our desires for different women vary in intensity. One evening we cannot bear to be deprived of one
who, after that, for the next month or two, will trouble us
scarcely at all. And then there are the laws of alternation—which it is not the place to study here—whereby,
after an over-exertion of the flesh, the woman whose image haunts our momentary senility is one to whom we
would barely give more than a kiss on the forehead. As
for Albertine, I saw her seldom, and only on the very in-
frequent evenings when I felt that I could not do without
her. If such a desire seized me when she was too far from
Balbec for Françoise to be able to go and fetch her, I used
to send the lift-boy to Epreville, to La Sogne, to Saint-
Frichoux, asking him to finish his work a little earlier
than usual. He would come into my room, but would
leave the door open, for although he was conscientious at
his "job" which was pretty hard, consisting in endless
cleanings from five o'clock in the morning, he could never
bring himself to make the effort to shut a door, and, if
one pointed out to him that it was open, would turn back

and, summoning up all his strength, give it a gentle push.
With the democratic pride that marked him, a pride to
which, in the liberal avocations, the members of a profession that is at all numerous never attain, barristers, doctors and men of letters speaking simply of a "brother"
barrister, doctor or man of letters, he, rightly employing a
term that is confined to close corporations like the
Academy, would say to me in speaking of a page who was
in charge of the lift on alternate days: "I'll see if I can get
my *colleague* to take my place." This pride did not prevent him from accepting remuneration for his errands,
with a view to increasing what he called his "salary," a
fact which had made Françoise take a dislike to him:
"Yes, the first time you see him you'd think butter
wouldn't melt in his mouth, but there's days when he's as
friendly as a prison gate. They're all money-grubbers."
This was the category in which she had so often included
Eulalie, and in which, alas (when I think of all the trouble
that it was eventually to bring), she already placed Albertine, because she saw me often asking Mamma for trinkets
and other little presents on behalf of my impecunious
friend, something which Françoise considered inexcusable
because Mme Bontemps had only a general help.

A moment later the lift-boy, having removed what I
should have called his livery and he called his tunic,
would appear wearing a straw hat, carrying a cane and
holding himself stiffly erect, for his mother had warned
him never to adopt a "working-class" or "messenger boy"
manner. Just as, thanks to books, all knowledge is open to
a working man, who ceases to be such when he has finished his work, so, thanks to a "boater" and a pair of
gloves, elegance became accessible to the lift-boy who,

having ceased for the evening to take the guests upstairs, imagined himself, like a young surgeon who has taken off his smock, or Sergeant Saint-Loup out of uniform, a typical young man about town. He was not for that matter lacking in ambition, or in talent either in manipulating his machine and not bringing you to a standstill between two floors. But his vocabulary was defective. I credited him with ambition because he said in speaking of the porter, who was his immediate superior, "my porter," in the same tone in which a man who owned what the lift-boy would have called a "private mansion" in Paris would have referred to his janitor. As for the lift-boy's vocabulary, it is curious that someone who heard people, fifty times a day, calling for the "lift," should never himself call it anything but a "liff." There were certain things about this lift-boy that were extremely irritating: whatever I might say to him he would interrupt with the phrase: "I should think so!" or "Of course!" which seemed either to imply that my remark was so obvious that anybody would have thought of it, or else to take all the credit for it to himself, as though it were he that was drawing my attention to the subject. "I should think so!" or "Of course!", exclaimed with the utmost emphasis, issued from his lips every other minute, in connexion with things he would never have dreamed of, a trick which irritated me so much that I immediately began to say the opposite to show him that he had no idea what he was talking about. But to my second assertion, although it was incompatible with the first, he would reply no less stoutly: "I should think so!" "Of course!" as though these words were inevitable. I found it difficult, also, to forgive him the trick of employing certain terms that were proper to his calling, and would therefore have sounded perfectly correct in their literal sense, in a figurative sense only, which gave them an air of feeble witticism—for instance the verb "to pedal." He never used it when he had gone anywhere on his bicycle. But if, on foot, he had hurried to arrive somewhere in time, then, to indicate that he had walked fast, he would exclaim: "I should say I didn't half pedal!" The lift-boy was on the small side, ill-made and rather ugly. This did not prevent him, whenever one spoke to him of some tall, slim, lithe young man, from saying: "Oh, yes, I know, a fellow who is just my height." And one day when I was expecting him to bring me a message, hearing somebody come upstairs, I had in my impatience opened the door of my room and caught sight of a page as handsome as Endymion, with incredibly perfect features, who was bringing a message to a lady whom I did not know. When the lift-boy returned, in telling him how impatiently I had waited for the message, I mentioned to him that I had thought I heard him come upstairs but that it had turned out to be a page from the Hôtel de Normandie. "Oh, yes, I know," he said, "they have only the one, a fellow about my build. He's so like me in face, too, that we could easily be mistaken for one another; anybody would think he was my brother." Lastly, he always wanted to appear to have understood you perfectly from the first second, which meant that as soon as you asked him to do anything he would say: "Yes, yes, yes, yes, I understand all that," with a precision and a tone of intelligence which for some time deceived me; but other people, as we get to know them, are like a metal dipped in an acid bath, and we see them gradually lose their qualities (and their defects too, at times). Before giving him my instructions, I saw that he had left the door open; I pointed this out to him, for I was afraid that people might hear us; he acceded to my request and returned, having reduced the gap. "Anything to oblige. But there's nobody on this floor except us two." Immediately I heard one, then a second, then a third person go by. This annoyed me partly because of the risk of my being overheard, but mainly because I could see that it did not in the least surprise him and was a perfectly normal coming and going. "Yes, that'll be the maid next door going for her things. Oh, that's of no importance, it's the wine waiter putting away his keys. No, no, it's nothing, you can say what you want, it's my colleague just going on duty." Then, as the reasons that all these people had for passing did not diminish my dislike of the thought that they might overhear me, at a formal order from me he went, not to shut the door, which was beyond the strength of this cyclist who longed for a "motor-bike," but to push it a little closer to. "Now we'll be nice and peaceful." So peaceful were we that an American lady burst in and withdrew with apologies for having mistaken the number of her room. "You are to bring this young lady back with you," I told him, after banging the door shut with all my might (which brought in another page to see whether a window had been left open). "You remember the name: Mlle Albertine Simonet. Anyhow it's on the envelope. You need only say to her that it's from me. She will be delighted to come," I added, to encourage him and preserve my own self-esteem. "I should think so!" "On the contrary, it isn't at all natural to suppose that she should be glad to come. It's very inconvenient getting here from Berneville." "Don't I know it!" "You will tell her to come with you." "Yes, yes,

yes, yes, I understand perfectly," he replied, in that shrewd and precise tone which had long ceased to make a "good impression" upon me because I knew that it was almost mechanical and covered with its apparent clearness a great deal of vagueness and stupidity. "When will you be back?" "Shan't take too long," said the lift-boy, who, carrying to extremes the grammatical rule that forbids the repetition of personal pronouns before co-ordinate verbs, omitted the pronoun altogether. "Should be able to go all right. Actually, leave was stopped this afternoon, because there was a dinner for twenty at lunch-time. And it was my turn off duty today. Should be all right if I go out a bit this evening, though. Take my bike with me. Get there in no time." And an hour later he reappeared and said: "Monsieur's had to wait, but the young lady's come with me. She's down below." "Oh, thanks very much; the porter won't be cross with me?" "Monsieur Paul? Doesn't even know where I've been. Even the head doorman didn't say a word." But once, after I had told him: "You absolutely must bring her back with you," he reported to me with a smile: "You know I couldn't find her. She's not there. Couldn't wait any longer because I was afraid of copping it like my colleague who was 'missed from the hotel" (for the lift-boy, who used the word "rejoin" of a profession which one joined for the first time—"I should like to rejoin the post office"—to make up for this, or to mitigate the calamity if his own career was at stake, or to insinuate it more suavely and treacherously if the victim was someone else, elided the prefix and said: "I know he's been 'missed"). It was not out of malice that he smiled, but out of sheer timidity. He thought that he was diminishing the magnitude of his offence by making a joke of it. In the same way, when he said to me: "*You know* I couldn't find her," this did not mean that he really thought that I knew it already. On the contrary, he was all too certain that I did not know it, and, what was more, was scared of the fact. And so he said "you know" to spare himself the torments he would have to go through in uttering the words that would bring me the knowledge. We ought never to lose our tempers with people who, when we find them at fault, begin to snigger. They do so not because they are laughing at us, but because they are afraid of our displeasure. Let us show all pity and tenderness to those who laugh. For all the world as though he were having a stroke, the lift-boy's anxiety had wrought in him not merely an apoplectic flush but an alteration in his speech, which had suddenly become familiar. He wound up by telling me that Albertine was not at Epreville, that she would not be coming back there before nine o'clock, and that if betimes (which meant, by chance) she came back earlier, my message would be given her and in any case she would be with me before one o'clock in the morning.

It was not on that evening, however, that my cruel mistrust began to take solid form. No, to reveal it here and now, although the incident did not occur until some weeks later, it arose out of a remark made by Cottard. On the day in question Albertine and her friends had wanted to drag me to the casino at Incarville where, to my ultimate good fortune, I would not have joined them (wanting to pay a visit to Mme Verdurin who had invited me several times), had I not been held up at Incarville itself by a train breakdown which required a considerable time to repair. As I strolled up and down waiting for the men to finish working at it, I found myself all of a sudden face to face with Dr Cottard, who had come to Incarville to see a patient. I almost hesitated to greet him as he had not answered any of my letters. But friendliness does not express itself in everyone in the same way. Not having been brought up to observe the same fixed rules of behaviour as society people, Cottard was full of good intentions of which one knew nothing and even denied the existence, until the day when he had an opportunity of displaying them. He apologised, had indeed received my letters, had reported my whereabouts to the Verdurins who were most anxious to see me and whom he urged me to go and see. He even proposed to take me there that very evening, for he was waiting for the little local train to take him back there for dinner. As I was uncertain and as he had still some time before his train (for the breakdown threatened to be a fairly long one), I made him come with me to the little casino, one of those that had struck me as being so gloomy on the evening of my first arrival, now filled with the tumult of the girls, who, in the absence of male partners, were dancing together. Andrée came sliding along the floor towards me; I was meaning to go off with Cottard in a moment to the Verdurins', when I finally declined his offer, seized by an irresistible desire to stay with Albertine. The fact was that I had just heard her laugh. And this laugh at once evoked the flesh-pink, fragrant surfaces with which it seemed to have just been in contact and of which it seemed to carry with it, pungent, sensual and revealing as the scent of geraniums, a few almost tangible and secretly provoking particles.

One of the girls, a stranger to me, sat down at the piano, and Andrée invited Albertine to waltz with her.

Happy in the thought that I was going to remain in this little casino with these girls, I remarked to Cottard how well they danced together. But he, taking the professional point of view of a doctor and with an ill-breeding which overlooked the fact that they were my friends, although he must have seen me greet them, replied: "Yes, but parents are very rash to allow their daughters to form such habits. I should certainly never let mine come here. Are they pretty, though? I can't make out their features. There now, look," he went on, pointing to Albertine and Andrée who were waltzing slowly, tightly clasped together, "I've left my glasses behind and I can't see very well, but they are certainly keenly roused. It's not sufficiently known that women derive most excitement through their breasts. And theirs, as you see, are touching completely." And indeed the contact between the breasts of Andrée and of Albertine had been constant. I do not know whether they heard or guessed Cottard's observation, but they drew slightly apart while continuing to waltz. At that moment Andrée said something to Albertine, who laughed with the same deep and penetrating laugh that I had heard before. But the unease it roused in me this time was nothing but painful; Albertine appeared to be conveying, to be making Andrée share, some secret and voluptuous thrill. It rang out like the first or the last chords of an alien celebration. I left the place with Cottard, absorbed in conversation with him, thinking only at odd moments of the scene I had just witnessed. Not that Cottard's conversation was interesting. It had indeed, at that moment, become rather sour, for we had just seen Dr du Boulbon go past without noticing us. He had come down to spend some time on the other side of the bay from Balbec, where he was greatly in demand. Now, albeit Cottard was in the habit of declaring that he did no professional work during the holidays, he had hoped to build up a select practice along the coast, an ambition which du Boulbon's presence there was likely to hinder. Certainly, the Balbec doctor could not stand in Cottard's way. He was merely a thoroughly conscientious doctor who knew everything, and to whom you could not mention the slightest itch without his immediately prescribing, in a complicated formula, the ointment, lotion or liniment that would put you right. As Marie Gineste used to say in her pretty parlance, he knew how to "charm" cuts and sores. But he was in no way eminent. True, he had caused Cottard some slight annoyance. The latter, now that he was anxious to exchange his chair for that of Therapeutics, had begun to specialise in toxic actions. These, a perilous innovation in medicine, give an excuse for changing the labels in the chemists' shops, where every preparation is declared to be in no way toxic, unlike its substitutes, and indeed to be disintoxicant. It is the fashionable cry; at the most there may survive below in illegible lettering, like the faint trace of an older fashion, the assurance that the preparation has been carefully antisepticised. Toxic actions serve also to reassure the patient, who learns with joy that his paralysis is merely a toxic disturbance. Now, a grand duke who had come for a few days to Balbec and whose eye was extremely swollen had sent for Cottard who, in return for a wad of hundred-franc notes (the Professor refused to see anyone for less), had put down the inflammation to a toxic condition and prescribed a disintoxicant treatment. As the swelling did not go down, the grand duke fell back upon the general practitioner of Bal-

bec, who in five minutes had removed a speck of dust.
The following day, the swelling had gone. A celebrated
specialist in nervous diseases was, however, a more dangerous rival. He was a rubicund, jovial man, at once because the constant society of nervous wrecks did not
prevent him from enjoying excellent health, and also in
order to reassure his patients by the hearty merriment of
his "Good morning" and "Good-bye," while quite ready
to lend the strength of his muscular arms to fastening
them in strait-jackets later on. Nevertheless, whenever you
spoke to him at a gathering, whether political or literary,
he would listen to you with benevolent attention, as
though he were saying: "What can I do for you?" without
at once giving an opinion, as though it were a medical
consultation. But anyhow he, whatever his talent might
be, was a specialist. And so the whole of Cottard's rage
was concentrated upon du Boulbon. But I soon took my
leave of the Verdurins' professor friend, and returned to
Balbec, after promising him that I would pay them a visit
before long.

The mischief that his remarks about Albertine and
Andrée had done me was extreme, but its worst effects
were not immediately felt by me, as happens with those
forms of poisoning which begin to act only after a certain
time.

Albertine, on the night the lift-boy had failed to find
her, did not appear, in spite of his assurances. There is no
doubt that a person's charms are a less frequent cause of
love than a remark such as: "No, this evening I shan't be
free." We barely notice this remark if we are with friends;
we remain gay all the evening, a certain image never enters our mind; during those hours it remains dipped in

the necessary solution; when we return home we find the plate developed and perfectly clear. We become aware that life is no longer the life which we would have surrendered for a trifle the day before, because, even if we continue not to fear death, we no longer dare think of a parting.

From, however, not one o'clock in the morning (the limit fixed by the lift-boy), but three o'clock, I no longer felt as in former times the distress of seeing the chance of her coming diminish. The certainty that she would not now come brought me a complete and refreshing calm; this night was simply a night like so many others during which I did not see her—such was the notion on which I based myself. And thenceforth the thought that I should see her next day or some other day, outlining itself upon the blank which I submissively accepted, became comforting. Sometimes, during these nights of waiting, our anguish is due to a drug which we have taken. The sufferer, misinterpreting his own symptoms, thinks that he is anxious about the woman who fails to appear. Love is engendered in these cases, as are certain nervous ailments, by the inaccurate interpretation of a painful discomfort. An interpretation which it is useless to correct, at any rate so far as love is concerned, it being a sentiment which (whatever its cause) is invariably erroneous.

Next day, when Albertine wrote to me that she had only just got back to Epreville, and so had not received my note in time, and would come, if she might, to see me that evening, behind the words of her letter, as behind those that she had said to me once over the telephone, I thought I could detect the presence of pleasures, of people, whom she had preferred to me. Once again, my

whole body was stirred by the painful longing to know
what she could have been doing, by the latent love which
we always carry within us; I almost thought for a moment
that it was going to bind me to Albertine, but it did no
more than shudder on the spot and its last echoes died
out without its getting under way.

I had failed, during my first visit to Balbec—and perhaps, for that matter, Andrée had failed equally—to understand Albertine's character. I had believed it was
through simple frivolity on her part that all our supplica-
tions didn't succeed in keeping her with us and making
her forgo a garden-party, a donkey-ride, a picnic. During
my second visit to Balbec, I began to suspect that this
frivolity was merely a semblance, the garden-party a mere
screen, if not an invention. There occurred in a variety of
forms a phenomenon of which the following is an example
(a phenomenon as seen by me, of course, from my side of
the glass, which was by no means transparent, and without my having any means of determining what reality
there was on the other side). Albertine was making the
most passionate protestations of affection. She looked at
the time because she had to go and call upon a lady who
was at home, it appeared, every afternoon at five o'clock,
at Infreville. Tormented by suspicion, and feeling at the
same time far from well, I asked Albertine, I implored her
to stay with me. It was impossible (and indeed she could
stay only five minutes longer) because it would anger the
lady who was rather inhospitable, susceptible and, said
Albertine, very boring. "But one can easily cut a social
call." "No, my aunt has always told me that one must
above all be polite." "But I've often seen you being impolite." "It's not the same thing, this lady would be angry

with me and would get me into trouble with my aunt. I'm
pretty well in her bad books already. She insists that I
should go and see her at least once." "But if she's at
home every day?" Here Albertine, feeling that she was
caught, changed her line of argument. "I know she's at
home every day. But today I've made arrangements to
meet some other girls there. It will be less boring that
way." "So then, Albertine, you prefer this lady and your
friends to me since, rather than miss paying a boring call,
you prefer to leave me here alone, sick and wretched?"
"That the visit will be boring is neither here nor there.
I'm going for their sake. I shall bring them home in my
trap. Otherwise they won't have any way of getting
back." I pointed out to Albertine that there were trains
from Infreville up to ten o'clock at night. "Quite true, but
don't you see, it's possible that we may be asked to stay
to dinner. She's very hospitable." "Very well then, you'll
refuse." "I should only make my aunt angry." "Besides,
you can dine with her and catch the ten o'clock train."
"It's cutting it rather fine." "Then I can never go and
dine in town and come back by train. But listen, Albertine, I'll tell you what we'll do. I feel that the fresh air
will do me good; since you can't give up your lady, I'll
come with you to Infreville. Don't be alarmed, I shan't go
as far as the Tour Elisabeth" (the lady's villa), "I shall see
neither the lady nor your friends." Albertine looked as
though she had received a violent blow. For a moment,
she was unable to speak. She explained that the sea
bathing was not doing her any good. "If you don't want
me to come with you?" "How can you say such a thing,
you know that there's nothing I enjoy more than going
out with you." A sudden change of tactics had occurred.

"Since we're going out together," she said to me, "why
not go in the other direction. We might dine together. It
would be so nice. After all, that side of Balbec is much
the prettier. I'm getting sick and tired of Infreville and all
those little cabbage-green places." "But your aunt's friend
will be annoyed if you don't go and see her." "Very well,
let her be." "No, it's wrong to annoy people." "But she
won't even notice that I'm not there, she has people every
day; I can go tomorrow, the next day, next week, the
week after, it's exactly the same." "And what about your
friends?" "Oh, they've ditched me often enough. It's my
turn now." "But from the direction you suggest there's no
train back after nine." "Well, what's the matter with that?
Nine will do perfectly. Besides, one should never worry
about how to get back. We can always find a cart, a bike
or, if the worst comes to the worst, we have legs." "'We
can always find.' Albertine, how you go on! Out Infreville
way, where the villages run into one another, well and
good. But the other way, it's a very different matter."
"That way too. I promise to bring you back safe and
sound." I sensed that Albertine was giving up for my sake
some plan arranged beforehand of which she refused to
tell me, and that there was someone else who would be as
unhappy as I was. Seeing that what she had intended to
do was out of the question, since I insisted upon accompanying her, she was giving it up altogether. She knew
that the loss was not irremediable. For, like all women
who have a number of irons in the fire, she could rely on
something that never fails: suspicion and jealousy. Of
course she did not seek to arouse them, quite the contrary. But lovers are so suspicious that they instantly scent
out falsehood. With the result that Albertine, being no

better than anyone else, knew from experience (without
for a moment imagining that she owed it to jealousy) that
she could always be sure of not losing the people she had
jilted for an evening. The unknown person whom she was
deserting for me would be hurt, would love her all the
more for that (though Albertine did not know that this
was the reason), and, so as not to prolong the agony,
would return to her of his own accord, as I should have
done. But I had no desire either to give pain to another,
or to tire myself, or to enter upon the terrible path of investigation, of multiform, unending vigilance. "No, Albertine, I don't want to spoil your pleasure. You can go to
your lady at Infreville, or rather the person for whom she
is a pseudonym, it's all the same to me. The real reason
why I'm not coming with you is that you don't want me
to, because the outing with me is not the one you wanted
—the proof of it is that you've contradicted yourself at
least five times without noticing it." Poor Albertine was
afraid that her contradictions, which she had not noticed,
had been more serious than they were. Not knowing exactly what fibs she had told me, "It's quite on the cards
that I did contradict myself," she said. "The sea air makes
me lose my head altogether. I'm always calling things by
the wrong names." And (what proved to me that she
would not, now, require many tender affirmations to
make me believe her) I felt a stab in my heart as I listened to this admission of what I had but faintly imagined. "Very well, that's settled, I'm off," she said in a
tragic tone, not without looking at the time to see whether
she was making herself late for the other person, now that
I had provided her with an excuse for not spending the
evening with myself. "It's too bad of you. I alter all my

plans to spend a nice evening with you, and it's you that
won't have it, and you accuse me of telling lies. I've never
known you to be so cruel. The sea shall be my tomb. I
shall never see you any more." At these words my heart
missed a beat, although I was certain that she would come
again next day, as she did. "I shall drown myself, I shall
throw myself into the sea." "Like Sappho." "There you
go, insulting me again. You suspect not only what I say
but what I do." "But, my lamb, I didn't mean anything, I
swear to you. You know Sappho flung herself into the
sea." "Yes, yes, you have no faith in me." She saw from
the clock that it was twenty minutes to the hour; she was
afraid of missing her appointment, and choosing the
shortest form of farewell (for which as it happened she
apologised on coming to see me again next day, the other
person presumably not being free then), she dashed from
the room, crying: "Good-bye for ever," in a heartbroken
tone. And perhaps she was heartbroken. For, knowing
what she was about at that moment better than I, at once
more severe and more indulgent towards herself than I
was towards her, she may after all have had a fear that I
might refuse to see her again after the way in which she
had left me. And I believe that she was attached to me, so
much so that the other person was more jealous than I
was.

Some days later, at Balbec, while we were in the ball-
room of the casino, there entered Bloch's sister and
cousin, who had both turned out extremely pretty, but
whom I refrained from greeting on account of my girl
friends, because the younger one, the cousin, was notoriously living with the actress whose acquaintance she had
made during my first visit. Andrée, at a whispered allu-

sion to this scandal, said to me: "Oh! about that sort of thing I'm like Albertine; there's nothing we both loathe so much as that sort of thing." As for Albertine, sitting down to talk to me on the sofa, she had turned her back on the disreputable pair. I had noticed, however, that, before she changed her position, at the moment when Mlle Bloch and her cousin appeared, a look of deep attentiveness had momentarily flitted across her eyes, a look that was wont to impart to the face of this mischievous girl a serious, indeed a solemn air, and left her pensive afterwards. But Albertine had at once turned back towards me a gaze which nevertheless remained strangely still and dreamy. Mlle Bloch and her cousin having finally left the room after laughing very loud and uttering the most unseemly cries, I asked Albertine whether the little fair one (the one who was the friend of the actress) was not the girl who had won the prize the day before in the procession of flowers. "I don't know," said Albertine, "is one of them fair? I must confess they don't interest me particularly, I never looked at them. Is one of them fair?" she asked her friends with a detached air of inquiry. When applied to people whom Albertine passed every day on the front, this ignorance seemed to me too extreme to be entirely genuine. "They didn't appear to be looking at us much either," I said to Albertine, perhaps (on the assumption, which I did not however consciously envisage, that Albertine loved her own sex) to free her from any regret by pointing out to her that she had not attracted the attention of these girls and that, generally speaking, it is not customary even for the most depraved of women to take an interest in girls whom they do not know. "They weren't looking at us?" Albertine replied without thinking. "Why, they did nothing else the whole time." "But you can't possibly tell," I said to her, "you had your back to them." "Well then, what about that?" she replied, pointing out to me, set in the wall in front of us, a large mirror which I had not noticed and upon which I now realised that my friend, while talking to me, had never ceased to fix her beautiful preoccupied eyes.

From the day when Cottard accompanied me into the little casino at Incarville, although I did not share the opinion that he had expressed, Albertine seemed to me to be different; the sight of her made me angry. I myself had changed, quite as much as she had changed in my eyes. I had ceased to wish her well; to her face, behind her back when there was a chance of my words being repeated to her, I spoke of her in the most wounding terms. There were, however, moments of respite. One day I learned that Albertine and Andrée had both accepted an invitation to Elstir's. Feeling certain that this was in order that they might, on the return journey, amuse themselves like schoolgirls on holiday by imitating the manners of fast young women, and in so doing find an unmaidenly pleasure the thought of which tormented me, without announcing my intention, to embarrass them and to deprive Albertine of the pleasure on which she was counting, I paid an unexpected call at Elstir's studio. But I found only Andrée there. Albertine had chosen another day when her aunt was to go there with her. Then I told myself that Cottard must have been mistaken; the favourable impression that I received from Andrée's presence there without her friend remained with me and made me feel more kindly disposed towards Albertine. But this feeling lasted no longer than the healthy moments of those deli-

cate people who are subject to intermittent recoveries, and
are prostrated again by the merest trifle. Albertine incited
Andrée to actions which, without going very far, were
perhaps not altogether innocent; pained by this suspicion,
I would finally succeed in banishing it. No sooner was I
cured of it than it revived under another form. I had just
seen Andrée, with one of those graceful gestures that
came naturally to her, lay her head lovingly on Albertine's
shoulder and kiss her on the neck, half shutting her eyes;
or else they had exchanged a glance; or a remark had been
made by somebody who had seen them going down together to bathe: little trifles such as habitually float in the
surrounding atmosphere where the majority of people ab-
sorb them all day long without injury to their health or
alteration of their mood, but which have a morbid effect
and breed fresh suffering in a nature predisposed to receive them. Sometimes even without my having seen Albertine, without anyone having spoken to me about her, I
would suddenly call to mind some memory of her with
Gisèle in a posture which had seemed to me innocent at
the time but was enough now to destroy the peace of
mind that I had managed to recover; I had no longer any
need to go and breathe dangerous germs outside—I had,
as Cottard would have said, supplied my own toxin. I
thought then of all that I had been told about Swann's
love for Odette, of the way in which Swann had been
tricked all his life. Indeed, when I come to think of it, the
hypothesis that made me gradually build up the whole of
Albertine's character and give a painful interpretation to
every moment of a life that I could not control in its entirety, was the memory, the rooted idea of Mme Swann's
character, as it had been described to me. These accounts

contributed towards the fact that, in the future, my imagination played with the idea that Albertine might, instead
of being the good girl that she was, have had the same
immorality, the same capacity for deceit as a former pros-
titute, and I thought of all the sufferings that would in
that case have been in store for me if I had happened to
love her.

One day, outside the Grand Hotel, where we were
gathered on the front, I had just been addressing Albertine in the harshest, most humiliating language, and Rosemonde was saying: "Ah, how you've changed towards
her; she used to be the only one who counted, it was she
who ruled the roost, and now she isn't even fit to be
thrown to the dogs." I was proceeding, in order to make
my attitude towards Albertine still more marked, to say
all the nicest possible things to Andrée, who, if she was
tainted with the same vice, seemed to me more excusable
since she was sickly and neurasthenic, when we saw Mme
de Cambremer's barouche, drawn by its two horses at a
jog-trot, coming into the side street at the corner of which
we were standing. The judge, who at that moment was
advancing towards us, sprang back upon recognising the
carriage, in order not to be seen in our company; then,
when he thought that the Marquise's eye might catch his,
bowed to her with an immense sweep of his hat. But the
carriage, instead of continuing along the Rue de la Mer as
might have been expected, disappeared through the gate
of the hotel. It was quite ten minutes later when the lift-
boy, out of breath, came to announce to me: "It's the
Marquise de Camembert who's come to see Monsieur.
I've been up to the room, I looked in the reading-room, I
couldn't find Monsieur anywhere. Luckily I thought of

looking on the beach." He had barely ended his speech when, followed by her daughter-in-law and by an extremely ceremonious gentleman, the Marquise advanced towards me, having probably come on from some tea-party in the neighbourhood, bowed down not so much by age as by the mass of costly trinkets with which she felt it more sociable and more befitting her rank to cover herself, in order to appear as "dressed up" as possible to the people whom she went to visit. It was in fact that "descent" of the Cambremers on the hotel which my grandmother had so greatly dreaded when she wanted us not to let Legrandin know that we might perhaps be going to Balbec. Then Mamma used to laugh at these fears inspired by an event which she considered impossible. And here it was actually happening, but by different channels and without Legrandin's having had any part in it. "Do you mind my staying here, if I shan't be in your way?" asked Albertine (in whose eyes there lingered, brought there by the cruel things I had just been saying to her, a few tears which I observed without seeming to see them, but not without rejoicing inwardly at the sight), "there's something I want to say to you." A hat with feathers, itself surmounted by a sapphire pin, was perched haphazardly on Mme de Cambremer's wig, like a badge the display of which was necessary but sufficient, its position immaterial, its elegance conventional and its stability superfluous. Notwithstanding the heat, the good lady had put on a jet-black cloak, like a bishop's vestment, over which hung an ermine stole the wearing of which seemed to depend not upon the temperature and season, but upon the nature of the ceremony. And on Mme de Cambremer's bosom a baronial crest, fastened to a chain, dangled like a pectoral cross. The gentleman was an eminent barrister from Paris, of noble family, who had come down to spend a few days with the Cambremers. He was one of those men whose consummate professional experience inclines them to look down upon their profession, and who say, for instance: "I know I plead well, so it no longer amuses me to plead," or: "I'm no longer interested in operating, because I know I operate well." Intelligent, "artistic," they see themselves in their maturity, richly endowed by success, shining with that "intelligence," that "artistic" nature which their professional brethren acknowledge in them and which confer upon them an approximation of taste and discernment. They develop a passion for the paintings not of a great artist, but of an artist who nevertheless is highly distinguished, and spend upon the purchase of his work the fat incomes that their career procures for them. Le Sidaner was the artist chosen by the Cambremers' friend, who incidentally was extremely agreeable. He talked well about books, but not about the books of the true masters, those who have mastered themselves. The only irritating defect that this amateur displayed was his constant use of certain ready-made expressions, such as "for the most part," which gave an air of importance and incompleteness to the matter of which he was speaking. Mme de Cambremer had taken advantage, she told me, of a party which some friends of hers had been giving that afternoon in the Balbec direction to come and call upon me, as she had promised Robert de Saint-Loup. "You know he's coming down to these parts quite soon for a few days. His uncle Charlus is staying near here with his sister-in-law, the Duchesse de Luxembourg, and M. de Saint-Loup means to take the opportunity of paying his aunt a visit and going to see his old regiment, where he is very popular, highly respected. We often have visits from officers who are never tired of singing his praises. How nice it would be if you and he would give us the pleasure of coming together to Féterne."

I presented Albertine and her friends. Mme de Cambremer introduced us all to her daughter-in-law. The latter, so frigid towards the petty nobility with whom her seclusion at Féterne forced her to associate, so reserved, so afraid of committing herself, held out her hand to me with a radiant smile, feeling secure and delighted at seeing a friend of Robert de Saint-Loup, whom he, possessing a sharper social intuition than he allowed himself to betray, had mentioned to her as being a great friend of the Guermantes. So, unlike her mother-in-law, the young Mme de Cambremer employed two vastly different forms of politeness. It was at the most the former kind, curt and insufferable, that she would have conceded me had I met her through her brother Legrandin. But for a friend of the Guermantes she had not smiles enough. The most convenient room in the hotel for entertaining visitors was the reading-room, that place once so terrible into which I now went a dozen times every day, emerging freely, my own master, like those mildly afflicted lunatics who have so long been inmates of an asylum that the superintendent trusts them with a latch-key. And so I offered to take Mme de Cambremer there. And as this room no longer filled me with shyness and no longer held any charm for me, since the faces of things change for us like the faces of people, it was without any trepidation that I made this suggestion. But she declined it, preferring to remain out of doors, and we sat down in the open air, on the terrace of the hotel. I found there and rescued a volume of Mme de Sévigné which Mamma had not had time to carry off in her precipitate flight, when she heard that visitors had called for me. No less than my grandmother, she dreaded these invasions of strangers, and, in her fear of being too late to escape if she let herself be cornered, would flee with a rapidity which always made my father and me laugh at her. Mme de Cambremer carried in her hand, together with the handle of a sunshade, a number of embroidered bags, a hold-all, a gold purse from which there dangled strings of garnets, and a lace handkerchief. I could not help thinking that it would be more convenient for her to deposit them on a chair; but I felt that it would be improper and useless to ask her to lay aside the ornaments of her pastoral round and her social ministry. We gazed at the calm sea upon which, here and there, a few gulls floated like white petals. Because of the level of mere "medium" to which social conversation reduces us, and also of our desire to please not by means of those qualities of which we are ourselves unaware but of those which we think likely to be appreciated by the people who are with us, I began instinctively to talk to Mme de Cambremer née Legrandin in the strain in which her brother might have talked. "They have," I said, referring to the gulls, "the immobility and whiteness of water-lilies." And indeed they did appear to be offering a lifeless object to the little waves which tossed them about, so much so that the waves, by contrast, seemed in their pursuit of them to be animated by a deliberate intention, to have become imbued with life. The dowager Marquise could not find words enough to do justice to the superb view of the sea that we had from Balbec, and envied me, since from La

Raspelière (where in fact she was not living that year), she had only such a distant glimpse of the waves. She had two remarkable habits, due at once to her exalted passion for the arts (especially for music) and to her want of teeth. Whenever she talked of aesthetic subjects her salivary glands—like those of certain animals when in rut—became so overcharged that the old lady's toothless mouth allowed to trickle from the corners of her faintly mustachioed lips a few drops of misplaced moisture. Immediately she drew it in again with a deep sigh, like a person recovering his breath. Secondly, if some overwhelming musical beauty was at issue, in her enthusiasm she would raise her arms and utter a few summary opinions, vigorously masticated and if necessary issuing from her nose. Now it had never occurred to me that the vulgar beach at Balbec could indeed offer a "seascape," and Mme de Cambremer's simple words changed my ideas in that respect. On the other hand, as I told her, I had always heard people praise the matchless view from La Raspelière, perched on the summit of the hill, where, in a great drawing-room with two fireplaces, one whole row of windows swept the gardens and, through the branches of the trees, the sea as far as Balbec and beyond, and another row the valley. "How nice of you to say so, and how well you put it: the sea through the branches. It's exquisite—reminiscent of . . . a painted fan." And I gathered, from a deep breath intended to catch the falling spittle and dry the moustaches, that the compliment was sincere. But the Marquise *née* Legrandin remained cold, to show her contempt not for my words but for those of her mother-in-law. Indeed she not only despised the latter's intellect but deplored her affability, being always afraid that people

might not form a sufficiently high idea of the Cambremers.

"And how charming the name is," said I. "One
would like to know the origin of all those names."

"That one I can tell you," the old lady answered
modestly. "It is a family place, it came from my grandmother Arrachepel, not an illustrious family, but good
and very old country stock."

"What! not illustrious!" her daughter-in-law tartly interrupted her. "A whole window in Bayeux cathedral is
filled with their arms, and the principal church at
Avranches has all their tombs. If these old names interest
you," she added, "you've come a year too late. We managed to appoint to the living at Criquetot, in spite of all
the difficulties about changing from one diocese to another, the parish priest of a place where I myself have
some land, a long way from here, Combray, where the
worthy cleric felt that he was becoming neurasthenic. Unfortunately, the sea air didn't agree with him at his age;
his neurasthenia grew worse and he has returned to Combray. But he amused himself while he was our neighbour
in going about looking up all the old charters, and he
compiled quite an interesting little pamphlet on the place-
names of the district. It has given him a fresh interest,
too, for it seems he is spending his last years in writing a
magnum opus about Combray and its surroundings. I
shall send you his pamphlet on the surroundings of
Féterne. It's a most painstaking piece of scholarship.
You'll find the most interesting things in it about our old
Raspelière, of which my mother-in-law speaks far too
modestly."

"In any case, this year," replied the dowager Mme de

Cambremer, "La Raspelière is no longer ours and doesn't belong to me. But I can see that you have a painter's instincts; I am sure you sketch, and I should so like to show you Féterne, which is far finer than La Raspelière."

For ever since the Cambremers had let this latter residence to the Verdurins, its commanding situation had at once ceased to appear to them as it had appeared for so many years past, that is to say to offer the advantage, without parallel in the neighbourhood, of looking out over both sea and valley, and had on the other hand, suddenly and retrospectively, presented the drawback that one had always to go up or down hill to get to or from it. In short, one might have supposed that if Mme de Cambremer had let it, it was not so much to add to her income as to spare her horses. And she proclaimed herself delighted at being able at last to have the sea always so close at hand, at Féterne, she who for so many years (forgetting the two months that she spent there) had seen it only from up above and as though at the end of a vista. "I'm discovering it at my age," she said, "and how I enjoy it! It does me a world of good. I would let La Raspelière for nothing so as to be obliged to live at Féterne."

"To return to more interesting topics," went on Legrandin's sister, who addressed the old Marquise as "Mother" but with the passing of the years had come to treat her with insolence, "you mentioned water-lilies: I suppose you know Claude Monet's pictures of them. What a genius! They interest me particularly because near Combray, that place where I told you I had some land . . ." But she preferred not to talk too much about Combray.

"Why, that must be the series that Elstir told us

about, the greatest living painter," exclaimed Albertine, who had said nothing so far.

"Ah! I can see that this young lady loves the arts," cried old Mme de Cambremer; and drawing a deep breath, she recaptured a trail of spittle.

"You will allow me to put Le Sidaner before him, Mademoiselle," said the barrister, smiling with the air of a connoisseur. And as he had appreciated, or seen others appreciating, years ago, certain "audacities" of Elstir's, he added: "Elstir was gifted, indeed he almost belonged to the avant-garde, but for some reason or other he never kept up, he has wasted his life."

Mme de Cambremer-Legrandin agreed with the barrister so far as Elstir was concerned, but, greatly to the chagrin of her guest, bracketed Monet with Le Sidaner. It would be untrue to say that she was a fool; she overflowed with a kind of intelligence that I had no use for. As the sun was beginning to set, the seagulls were now yellow, like the water-lilies on another canvas of that series by Monet. I said that I knew it, and (continuing to imitate the language of her brother, whom I had not yet ventured to name) added that it was a pity that she had not thought of coming a day earlier, for, at the same hour, there would have been a Poussin light for her to admire. Had some Norman squireen, unknown to the Guermantes, told her that she ought to have come a day earlier, Mme de Cambremer-Legrandin would doubtless have drawn herself up with an offended air. But I might have been far more familiar still, and she would have been all smiles and sweetness; I might in the warmth of that fine afternoon devour my fill of that rich honey cake which the young Mme de Cambremer so rarely was and

which took the place of the dish of pastries that it had not
occurred to me to offer my guests. But the name of
Poussin, without altering the amenity of the society lady,
aroused the protests of the connoisseur. On hearing that
name, she produced six times in almost continuous succession that little smack of the tongue against the lips
which serves to convey to a child who is misbehaving at
once a reproach for having begun and a warning not to
continue. "In heaven's name, after a painter like Monet,
who is quite simply a genius, don't go and mention an old
hack without a vestige of talent, like Poussin. I don't
mind telling you frankly that I find him the deadliest
bore. I mean to say, you can't really call that sort of thing
painting. Monet, Degas, Manet, yes, there are painters if
you like! It's a curious thing," she went on, fixing a
searching and ecstatic gaze upon a vague point in space
where she could see what was in her mind, "it's a curious
thing, I used at one time to prefer Manet. Nowadays I
still admire Manet, of course, but I believe I like Monet
even more. Ah, the cathedrals!" She was as scrupulous as
she was condescending in informing me of the development of her taste. And one felt that the phases through
which that taste had evolved were not, in her eyes, any
less important than the different manners of Monet himself. Not that I had any reason to feel flattered by her
confiding her enthusiasms to me, for even in the presence
of the most dim-witted provincial lady, she could not remain for five minutes without feeling the need to confess
them. When a noble lady of Avranches, who would have
been incapable of distinguishing between Mozart and
Wagner, said in the young Mme de Cambremer's hearing: "We saw nothing new of any interest while we were

in Paris. We went once to the Opéra-Comique, they were doing *Pelléas et Mélisande*, it's dreadful stuff," Mme de Cambremer not only boiled with rage but felt obliged to exclaim: "Not at all, it's a little gem," and to "argue the point." It was perhaps a Combray habit which she had picked up from my grandmother's sisters, who called it "fighting the good fight," and loved the dinner-parties at which they knew all through the week that they would have to defend their idols against the Philistines. Similarly, Mme de Cambremer-Legrandin enjoyed "getting worked up" and having "a good set-to" about art, as other people do about politics. She stood up for Debussy as she would have stood up for a woman friend whose conduct had been criticised. She must however have known very well that when she said: "Not at all, it's a little gem," she could not improvise, for the person whom she was putting in her place, the whole progression of artistic culture at the end of which they would have reached agreement without any need of discussion. "I must ask Le Sidaner what he thinks of Poussin," the barrister remarked to me. "He's a regular recluse, never opens his mouth, but I know how to winkle things out of him."

"Anyhow," Mme de Cambremer went on, "I have a horror of sunsets, they're so romantic, so operatic. That is why I can't abide my mother-in-law's house, with its tropical plants. You'll see, it's just like a public garden at Monte-Carlo. That's why I prefer your coast here. It's more sombre, more sincere. There's a little lane from which one doesn't see the sea. On rainy days, there's nothing but mud, it's a little world apart. It's just the same at Venice, I detest the Grand Canal and I don't know anything so touching as the little alleys. But it's all a question of atmosphere."

"But," I remarked to her, feeling that the only way to rehabilitate Poussin in her eyes was to inform her that he was once more in fashion, "M. Degas affirms that he knows nothing more beautiful than the Poussins at Chantilly."

"Really? I don't know the ones at Chantilly," said Mme de Cambremer, who had no wish to differ from Degas, "but I can speak about the ones in the Louvre, which are hideous."

"He admires them immensely too."

"I must look at them again. My memory of them is a bit hazy," she replied after a moment's silence, and as though the favourable opinion which she was certain to form of Poussin before very long would depend, not upon the information that I had just communicated to her, but upon the supplementary and this time definitive examination that she intended to make of the Poussins in the Louvre in order to be in a position to change her mind.

Contenting myself with what was a first step towards retraction, since, if she did not yet admire the Poussins, she was adjourning the matter for further consideration, in order not to keep her on the rack any longer I told her mother-in-law how much I had heard of the wonderful flowers at Féterne. In modest terms she spoke of the little presbytery garden that she had behind the house, into which in the mornings, by simply pushing open a door, she went in her dressing-gown to feed her peacocks, hunt for newlaid eggs, and gather the zinnias or roses which, on the sideboard, framing the creamed eggs or fried fish

in a border of flowers, reminded her of her garden paths.
"It's true, we have a great many roses," she told me, "our
rose garden is almost too near the house, there are days
when it makes my head ache. It's nicer on the terrace at
La Raspelière where the breeze wafts the scent of the
roses, but not so headily."

I turned to her daughter-in-law: "It's just like *Pelléas*," I said to her, to gratify her taste for the modern,
"that scent of roses wafted up to the terraces. It's so
strong in the score that, as I suffer from hay-fever and
rose-fever, it sets me sneezing every time I listen to that
scene."

"What a marvellous thing *Pelléas* is," cried the young
Mme de Cambremer, "I'm mad about it"; and, drawing
closer to me with the gestures of a wild woman seeking to
captivate me, picking out imaginary notes with her fingers, she began to hum something which I took to represent for her Pelléas's farewell, and continued with a
vehement insistency as though it were important that she
should at that moment remind me of that scene, or rather
should prove to me that she remembered it. "I think it's
even finer than *Parsifal*," she added, "because in *Parsifal*
the most beautiful things are surrounded with a sort of
halo of melodic phrases, outworn by the very fact of being
melodic."

"I know you are a great musician, Madame," I said to
the dowager. "I should so much like to hear you play."

Mme de Cambremer-Legrandin gazed at the sea so as
not to be drawn into the conversation. Being of the opinion that what her mother-in-law liked was not music at
all, she regarded the talent, bogus according to her, but in
reality of the very highest order, that the other was ac-

knowledged to possess as a technical accomplishment devoid of interest. It was true that Chopin's only surviving pupil declared, and with justice, that the Master's style of playing, his "feeling," had been transmitted, through herself, to Mme de Cambremer alone, but to play like Chopin was far from being a recommendation in the eyes of Legrandin's sister, who despised nobody so much as the Polish composer.

"Oh! they're flying away," exclaimed Albertine, pointing to the gulls which, casting aside for a moment their flowery incognito, were rising in a body towards the sun.

"Their giant wings from walking hinder them," quoted Mme de Cambremer, confusing the seagull with the albatross.

"I do love them; I saw some in Amsterdam," said Albertine. "They smell of the sea, they come and sniff the salt air even through the paving stones."

"Ah! so you've been in Holland. Do you know the Vermeers?" Mme de Cambremer-Legrandin asked imperiously, in the tone in which she would have said: "You know the Guermantes?"—for snobbishness in changing its object does not change its accent. Albertine replied in the negative, thinking that they were living people. But her mistake was not apparent.

"I should be delighted to play to you," the dowager Mme de Cambremer said to me. "But you know I only play things that no longer appeal to your generation. I was brought up in the worship of Chopin," she said in a lowered tone, for she was afraid of her daughter-in-law, and knew that to the latter, who considered that Chopin was not music, to talk of playing him well or badly was meaningless. She admitted that her mother-in-law had technique, played the notes to perfection. "Nothing will ever make me say that she is a musician," was Mme de Cambremer-Legrandin's conclusion. Because she considered herself "advanced," because (in matters of art only) "one could never be far enough to the Left," she maintained not merely that music progressed, but that it progressed along a single straight line, and that Debussy was in a sense a super-Wagner, slightly more advanced again than Wagner. She did not realise that if Debussy was not as independent of Wagner as she herself was to suppose in a few years' time, because an artist will after all make use of the weapons he has captured to free himself finally from one whom he has momentarily defeated, he nevertheless sought, when people were beginning to feel surfeited with works that were too complete, in which everything was expressed, to satisfy an opposite need. There were theories, of course, to bolster this reaction temporarily, like those theories which, in politics, come to the support of the laws against the religious orders, or of wars in the East (unnatural teaching, the Yellow Peril, etc., etc.). People said that an age of speed required rapidity in art, precisely as they might have said that the next war could not last longer than a fortnight, or that the coming of railways would kill the little places beloved of the coaches, which the motor-car was none the less to restore to favour. Composers were warned not to strain the attention of their audience, as though we had not at our disposal different degrees of attention, among which it rests precisely with the artist himself to arouse the highest. For those who yawn with boredom after ten lines of a mediocre article have journeyed year after year to

Bayreuth to listen to the *Ring*. In any case, the day was to
come when, for a time, Debussy would be pronounced as
flimsy as Massenet, and the agitations of Mélisande de-
graded to the level of Manon's. For theories and schools,
like microbes and corpuscles, devour one another and by
their strife ensure the continuity of life. But that time was
still to come.

     As on the Stock Exchange, when a rise occurs, a
whole group of securities profit by it, so a certain number
of despised artists benefited from the reaction, either because they did not deserve such scorn, or simply—which
enabled one to be original when one sang their praises—
because they had incurred it. And people even went so far
as to seek out, in an isolated past, men of independent
talent upon whose reputation the present movement
would not have seemed likely to have any influence, but
of whom one of the new masters was understood to have
spoken favourably. Often it was because a master, whoever he may be, however exclusive his school, judges in
the light of his own untutored instincts, gives credit to
talent wherever it is to be found, or rather not so much to
talent as to some agreeable inspiration which he has enjoyed in the past, which reminds him of a precious moment in his adolescence. At other times it was because
certain artists of an earlier generation have in some fragment of their work achieved something that resembles
what the master has gradually become aware that he himself wanted to do. Then he sees the old master as a sort of
precursor; he values in him, under a wholly different
form, an effort that is momentarily, partially fraternal.
There are bits of Turner in the work of Poussin, phrases
of Flaubert in Montesquieu. Sometimes, again, this ru-

moured predilection of a master was due to an error, starting heaven knows where and circulated among his followers. But in that case the name mentioned profited by the auspices under which it was introduced in the nick of time, for if there is some independence, some genuine taste expressed in the master's choice, artistic schools go only by theory. Thus it was that the spirit of the times, following its habitual course which advances by digression, inclining first in one direction, then in the other, had brought back into the limelight a number of works to which the need for justice or for renewal, or the taste of Debussy, or a whim of his, or some remark that he had perhaps never made, had added the works of Chopin. Commended by the most trusted judges, profiting by the admiration that was aroused by *Pelléas*, they had acquired a fresh lustre, and even those who had not heard them again were so anxious to admire them that they did so in spite of themselves, albeit preserving the illusion of free will. But Mme de Cambremer-Legrandin spent part of the year in the country. Even in Paris, being an invalid, she was often confined to her room. It is true that the drawbacks of this mode of existence were noticeable chiefly in her choice of expressions, which she supposed to be fashionable but which would have been more appropriate to the written language, a distinction that she did not perceive, for she derived them more from reading than from conversation. The latter is not so necessary for an exact knowledge of current opinion as of the latest expressions. However, this rehabilitation of the *Nocturnes* had not yet been announced by the critics. The news of it had been transmitted only by word of mouth among the "young." Mme de Cambremer-Legrandin remained unaware of it. I gave myself the pleasure of informing her, but by addressing my remark to her mother-in-law, as when, at billiards, in order to hit a ball one plays off the cushion, that Chopin, so far from being out of date, was Debussy's favourite composer. "Really, how amusing," said the daughter-in-law with a knowing smile as though it had been merely a deliberate paradox on the part of the composer of *Pelléas*. Nevertheless it was now quite certain that in future she would always listen to Chopin with respect and even pleasure. Hence my words, which had sounded the hour of deliverance for the dowager, produced on her face an expression of gratitude to myself and above all of joy. Her eyes shone like the eyes of Latude in the play entitled *Latude, or Thirty-five Years in Captivity*, and her bosom inhaled the sea air with that dilatation which Beethoven has depicted so well in *Fidelio*, at the point where his prisoners at last breathe again "this life-giving air." I thought that she was going to press her hirsute lips to my cheek. "What, you like Chopin? He likes Chopin, he likes Chopin," she cried in an impassioned nasal twang, as she might have said: "What, you know Mme de Franquetot too?", with this difference, that my relations with Mme de Franquetot would have been a matter of profound indifference to her, whereas my knowledge of Chopin plunged her into a sort of artistic delirium. Her salivary hyper-secretion no longer sufficed. Not having even attempted to understand the part played by Debussy in the rediscovery of Chopin, she felt only that my judgment of him was favourable. Her musical enthusiasm overpowered her. "Elodie! Elodie! He likes Chopin!" Her bosom rose and she beat the air with her arms. "Ah! I knew at once that you were a musician," she cried, "I can quite understand your liking his work, *hhartistic* as you are. It's so beautiful!" And her voice was as pebbly as if, to express her ardour for Chopin, she had imitated Demosthenes and filled her mouth with all the shingle on the beach. Then came the ebb-tide, reaching as far as her veil which she had not time to lift out of harm's way and which was drenched, and finally the Marquise wiped away with her embroidered handkerchief the tide-mark of foam in which the memory of Chopin had steeped her moustaches.

"Good heavens," Mme de Cambremer-Legrandin exclaimed to me, "I'm afraid my mother-in-law's cutting it rather fine: she's forgotten that we've got my uncle de Ch'nouville dining. And besides, Cancan doesn't like to be kept waiting." The name "Cancan" meant nothing to me, and I supposed that she might perhaps be referring to a dog. But as for the Ch'nouville relatives, the explanation was as follows. With the passage of time the young Marquise had outgrown the pleasure that she had once found in pronouncing their name in this manner. And yet it was the prospect of enjoying that pleasure that had decided her choice of a husband. In other social circles, when one referred to the Chenouville family, the custom was (whenever, that is to say, the particle was preceded by a word ending in a vowel, for in the opposite case you were obliged to lay stress upon the *de*, the tongue refusing to utter Madam' d'Ch'nonceaux) that it was the mute *e* of the particle that was sacrificed. One said: "Monsieur d'Chenouville." The Cambremer tradition was different, but no less imperious. It was the mute *e* of Chenouville that was suppressed. Whether the name was preceded by *mon cousin* or by *ma cousine*, it was always *de Ch'nouville*

and never *de Chenouville*. (Of the father of these Chenou-
villes they said "our uncle," for they were not sufficiently
"upper crust" at Féterne to pronounce the word "unk"
like the Guermantes, whose studied jargon, suppressing
consonants and naturalising foreign words, was as difficult
to understand as old French or a modern dialect.) Every
newcomer into the family circle at once received, in the
matter of the Ch'nouvilles, a lesson which Mlle Legrandin
had not required. When, paying a call one day, she had
heard a girl say: "my aunt d'Uzai," "my unk de Rouan,"
she had not at first recognised the illustrious names which
she was in the habit of pronouncing Uzès and Rohan; she
had felt the astonishment, embarrassment and shame of a
person who sees before him on the table a recently invented implement of which he does not know the proper
use and with which he dare not begin to eat. But during
that night and the next day she had rapturously repeated:
"my aunt d'Uzai," with that suppression of the final *s*
that had stupefied her the day before but which it now
seemed to her so vulgar not to know that, one of her
friends having spoken to her of a bust of the Duchesse
d'Uzès, Mlle Legrandin had answered her crossly and in a
haughty tone: "You might at least pronounce her name
properly: Mame d'Uzai." From that moment she had realised that, by virtue of the transmutation of solid bodies
into more and more subtle elements, the considerable and
so honourably acquired fortune that she had inherited
from her father, the finished education that she had received, her assiduous attendance at the Sorbonne, whether
at Caro's lectures or at Brunetière's, and at the Lamoureux concerts, all this was to vanish into thin air, to
find its ultimate sublimation in the pleasure of being able

one day to say: "my aunt d'Uzai." This did not exclude
the thought that she would continue to associate, at least
in the early days of her married life, not indeed with certain friends whom she liked and had resigned herself to
sacrificing, but with certain others whom she did not like
and to whom she looked forward to being able to say
(since that, after all, was why she was marrying): "I must
introduce you to my aunt d'Uzai," and, when she saw
that such an alliance was beyond her reach, "I must introduce you to my aunt de Ch'nouville," and "I shall ask
you to dinner with the Uzai." Her marriage to M. de
Cambremer had procured for Mlle Legrandin the opportunity to use the former of these sentences but not the latter, the circle in which her parents-in-law moved not
being that which she had supposed and of which she
continued to dream. Thus, after saying to me of Saint-
Loup (adopting for the purpose one of his expressions, for
if in talking to her I employed Legrandin's expressions,
she by an inverse suggestion answered me in Robert's dialect which she did not know had been borrowed from
Rachel), bringing her thumb and forefinger together and
half-shutting her eyes as though she were gazing at something infinitely delicate which she had succeeded in cap-
turing: "He has a charming quality of mind," she began
to extol him with such warmth that one might have supposed that she was in love with him (it had indeed been
alleged that, some time back, when he was at Doncières,
Robert had been her lover), in reality simply in order that
I might repeat her words to him, and ended up with:
"You're a great friend of the Duchesse de Guermantes.
I'm an invalid, I seldom go out, and I know that she

sticks to a close circle of chosen friends, which I do think so wise of her, and so I know her very slightly, but I know she is a really remarkable woman." Aware that Mme de Cambremer barely knew her, and anxious to put myself on a level with her, I glossed over the subject and answered the Marquise that the person whom I did know well was her brother, M. Legrandin. At the sound of his name she assumed the same evasive air as I had on the subject of Mme de Guermantes, but combined with it an expression of displeasure, for she imagined that I had said this with the object of humiliating not myself but her. Was she gnawed by despair at having been born a Legrandin? So at least her husband's sisters and sisters-in-law asserted, noble provincial ladies who knew nobody and nothing, and were jealous of Mme de Cambremer's intelligence, her education, her fortune, and the physical attractions that she had possessed before her illness. "She can think of nothing else, that's what's killing her," these spiteful provincial ladies would say whenever they spoke of Mme de Cambremer to no matter whom, but preferably to a commoner, either—if he was conceited and stupid—to enhance, by this affirmation of the shamefulness of the commoner's condition, the value of the affability that they were showing him, or—if he was shy and sensitive and applied the remark to himself—to give themselves the pleasure, while receiving him hospitably, of insulting him indirectly. But if these ladies thought that they were speaking the truth about their sister-in-law, they were mistaken. She suffered not at all from having been born Legrandin, for she had forgotten the fact altogether. She was offended by my reminding her of it, and remained silent as though she had failed to understand, not thinking it necessary to enlarge upon or even to confirm my statement.

"Our cousins are not the chief reason for our cutting short our visit," said the dowager Mme de Cambremer, who was probably more satiated than her daughter-in-law with the pleasure to be derived from saying "Ch'nouville." "But, so as not to bother you with too many people, Monsieur," she went on, indicating the barrister, "was reluctant to bring his wife and son to the hotel. They are waiting for us on the beach, and must be getting impatient." I asked for an exact description of them and hastened in search of them. The wife had a round face like certain flowers of the ranunculus family, and a large vegetal growth at the corner of her eye. And, the generations of mankind preserving their characteristics like a family of plants, just as on the blemished face of his mother, an identical growth, which might have helped towards the classification of a variety of the species, protruded below the eye of the son. The barrister was touched by my civility to his wife and son. He expressed an interest in the subject of my stay at Balbec. "You must find yourself a bit homesick, for the people here are for the most part foreigners." And he kept his eye on me as he spoke, for, not caring for foreigners, albeit he had many foreign clients, he wished to make sure that I was not hostile to his xenophobia, in which case he would have beaten a retreat, saying: "Of course, Mme X—— may be a charming woman. It's a question of principle." As at that time I had no definite opinion about foreigners, I showed no sign of disapproval, and he felt himself to be on safe ground. He went so far as to invite me to come

one day to his house in Paris to see his collection of Le
Sidaners, and to bring with me the Cambremers, with
whom he evidently supposed me to be on intimate terms.
"I shall invite you to meet Le Sidaner," he said to me,
confident that from that moment I would live only in ex-
pectation of that happy day. "You shall see what a delightful man he is. And his pictures will enchant you. Of
course, I can't compete with the great collectors, but I do
believe that I own the largest number of his favourite can-
vases. They will interest you all the more, coming from
Balbec, since they're marine subjects, for the most part at
least." The wife and son, blessed with a vegetal nature,
listened composedly. One felt that their house in Paris
was a sort of temple to Le Sidaner. Temples of this sort
are not without their uses. When the god has doubts
about himself, he can easily stop the cracks in his opinion
of himself with the irrefutable testimony of people who
have dedicated their lives to his work.

At a signal from her daughter-in-law, the dowager
Mme de Cambremer prepared to depart, and said to me:
"Since you won't come and stay at Féterne, won't you at
least come to luncheon, one day this week, tomorrow for
instance?" And in her benevolence, to make the invitation
irresistible, she added: "You will *find* the Comte de
Crisenoy," whom I had never lost, for the simple reason
that I did not know him. She was beginning to dazzle me
with yet further temptations, but stopped short; for the
judge, who, on returning to the hotel, had been told that
she was on the premises, had crept about searching for
her everywhere, then waited his opportunity, and pretending to have caught sight of her by chance, came up now
to pay her his respects. I gathered that Mme de Cambre-

mer did not mean to extend to him the invitation to lunch that she had just addressed to me. And yet he had known her far longer than I, having for years past been one of the regular guests at the afternoon parties at Féterne whom I used so to envy during my former visit to Balbec. But old acquaintance is not the only thing that counts in society. And hostesses are more inclined to reserve their luncheons for new acquaintances who still whet their curiosity, especially when they arrive preceded by a warm and glowing recommendation from a Saint-Loup. The dowager Mme de Cambremer calculated that the judge could not have heard what she was saying to me, but, to salve her conscience, spoke to him in the most friendly terms. In the sunlight on the horizon that flooded the golden coastline of Rivebelle, invisible as a rule, we could just make out, barely distinguishable from the luminous azure, rising from the water, rose-pink, silvery, faint, the little bells that were sounding the Angelus round about Féterne. "That is rather *Pelléas*, too," I suggested to Mme de Cambremer-Legrandin. "You know the scene I mean." "Of course I do" was what she said; but "I haven't the faintest idea" was the message proclaimed by her voice and features, which did not mould themselves to the shape of any recollection, and by her smile, which floated in the air, without support. The dowager could not get over her astonishment that the sound of bells should carry so far, and rose, reminded of the time: "But, as a rule," I said, "we never see that part of the coast from Balbec, nor hear it either. The weather must have changed and enlarged the horizon in more ways than one. Unless the bells have come to look for you, since I see that they are making you leave; to you they are a dinner bell." The judge, little interested in the bells, glanced furtively along the esplanade, on which he was sorry to see so few people that evening. "You are a true poet," the dowager Mme de Cambremer said to me. "One feels you are so responsive, so artistic. Do come, I shall play you some Chopin," she went on, raising her arms with an air of ecstasy and pronouncing the words in a raucous voice that seemed to be shifting pebbles. Then came the deglutition of saliva, and the old lady instinctively wiped the stubble of her toothbrush moustache with her handkerchief. The judge unwittingly did me a great favour by offering the Marquise his arm to escort her to her carriage, a certain blend of vulgarity, boldness and love of ostentation prompting him to a mode of conduct which other people would hesitate to adopt but which is by no means unwelcome in society. He was in any case, and had been for years past, far more in the habit of such conduct than myself. While blessing him I did not venture to emulate him, and walked by the side of Mme de Cambremer-Legrandin who insisted upon seeing the book that I had in my hand. The name of Mme de Sévigné drew a grimace from her; and using a word which she had read in certain journals, but which, used in speech, given a feminine form and applied to a seventeenth-century writer, had an odd effect, she asked me: "Do you really think she's 'talentuous'?" The dowager gave her footman the address of a pastry-cook where she had to call before taking the road, which was pink in the evening haze, with the humped cliffs stretching away into the bluish distance. She asked her old coachman whether one of the horses which was apt to catch cold had been kept warm enough, and whether the other's shoe were not hurting him. "I shall write to you and make a

definite arrangement," she murmured to me. "I heard you
talking about literature to my daughter-in-law. She's
adorable," she added, not that she really thought so, but
she had acquired the habit—and kept it up out of the
kindness of her heart—of saying so, in order that her son
might not appear to have married for money. "Besides,"
she added with a final enthusiastic mumble, "she's so
hartthhisttic!" With this she stepped into her carriage,
nodding her head, holding the crook of her sunshade
aloft, and set off through the streets of Balbec, overloaded
with the ornaments of her ministry, like an old bishop on
his confirmation rounds.

"She has asked you to lunch," the judge said to me
sternly when the carriage had passed out of sight and I
came indoors with the girls. "We're not on the best of
terms. She feels that I neglect her. Good heavens, I'm
easy enough to get on with. If anybody needs me, I'm always there to say: Present! But they tried to get their
hooks into me. And that," he went on with a shrewd
look, waving his finger like a man arguing some subtle
distinction, "that is a thing I will not allow. It's a threat
to the liberty of my holidays. I was obliged to say: Stop
there! You seem to be in her good books. When you
reach my age you will see that society is a paltry thing,
and you will be sorry you attached so much importance to
these trifles. Well, I'm going to take a turn before dinner.
Good-bye, children," he shouted back at us, as though he
were already fifty paces away.

When I had said good-bye to Rosemonde and Gisèle,
they saw with astonishment that Albertine was staying
behind instead of accompanying them. "Why, Albertine,
what are you doing, don't you know what time it is?"

"Go home," she replied in a tone of authority. "I want to talk to him," she added, pointing to me with a submissive air. Rosemonde and Gisèle stared at me, filled with a new and strange respect. I enjoyed the feeling that, for a moment at least, in the eyes even of Rosemonde and Gisèle, I was to Albertine something more important than the time to go home, or than her friends, and might indeed share solemn secrets with her into which it was impossible for them to be admitted. "Shan't we see you again this evening?" "I don't know, it will depend on this person. Anyhow, tomorrow." "Let's go up to my room," I said to her when her friends had gone. We took the lift; she remained silent in the lift-boy's presence. The habit of being obliged to resort to personal observation and deduction in order to find out the business of their masters, those strange beings who converse among themselves and do not speak to them, develops in "employees" (as the lift-boy styled servants) a greater power of divination than "employers" possess. Our organs become atrophied or grow stronger or more subtle according as our need of them increases or diminishes. Since railways came into existence, the necessity of not missing trains has taught us to take account of minutes, whereas among the ancient Romans, who not only had a more cursory acquaintance with astronomy but led less hurried lives, the notion not only of minutes but even of fixed hours barely existed. Hence the lift-boy had gathered, and meant to inform his "colleagues," that Albertine and I were preoccupied. But he talked to us without ceasing because he had no tact. And yet I discerned upon his face, in place of the customary expression of friendliness and joy at taking me up in his lift, an air of extraordinary dejection and anxiety.

Since I knew nothing of the cause of this, in an attempt to distract his thoughts—although I was more preoccupied with Albertine—I told him that the lady who had just left was called the Marquise de Cambremer and not de Camembert. On the floor which we were passing at that moment, I caught sight of a hideous chambermaid carrying a bolster, who greeted me with respect, hoping for a tip when I left. I should have liked to know if she was the one whom I had so ardently desired on the evening of my first arrival at Balbec, but I could never arrive at any certainty. The lift-boy swore to me with the sincerity of most false witnesses, but without shedding his woebegone expression, that it was indeed by the name of Camembert that the Marquise had told him to announce her. And as a matter of fact it was quite natural that he should have heard her say a name which he already knew. Besides, having only those very vague notions of nobility, and of the names with which titles are composed, which are shared by many people who are not lift-boys, the name Camembert had seemed to him all the more probable inasmuch as, that cheese being universally known, it was not in the least surprising that a marquisate should have been extracted from so glorious a renown, unless it were the marquisate that had bestowed its celebrity upon the cheese. Nevertheless, as he saw that I refused to admit that I might be mistaken, and as he knew that masters like to see their most futile whims obeyed and their most obvious lies accepted, he promised me like a good servant that in future he would say Cambremer. It is true that none of the shopkeepers in the town, none of the peasants in the district, where the name and persons of the Cambremers were perfectly familiar, could ever have made the lift-boy's mistake. But the staff of the "Grand Hotel of Balbec" were none of them natives. They came direct, together with all the equipment and stock, from Biarritz, Nice and Monte-Carlo, one division having been transferred to Deauville, another to Dinard and the third reserved for Balbec.

But the lift-boy's anxious gloom continued to grow. For him thus to forget to show his devotion to me by the customary smiles, some misfortune must have befallen him. Perhaps he had been "'missed." I made up my mind in that case to try to secure his reinstatement, the manager having promised to ratify all my wishes with regard to his staff. "You can always do just what you like, I rectify everything in advance." Suddenly, as I stepped out of the lift, I guessed the meaning of the lift-boy's air of stricken misery. Because of Albertine's presence I had not given him the five francs which I was in the habit of slipping into his hand when I went up. And the idiot, instead of realising that I did not wish to make a display of largesse in front of a third person, had begun to tremble, supposing that it was all finished once and for all, that I would never give him anything again. He imagined that I was "on the rocks" (as the Duc de Guermantes would have said), and the supposition inspired him with no pity for myself but with a terrible selfish disappointment. I told myself that I was less unreasonable than my mother thought when I had not dared, one day, not to give the extravagant but feverishly awaited sum that I had given the day before. But at the same time the meaning that I had until then, and without a shadow of doubt, ascribed to his habitual expression of joy, in which I had no hesitation in seeing a sign of devotion, seemed to me to have become less certain. Seeing him ready, in his despair, to fling himself down from the fifth floor of the hotel, I asked myself whether, if our respective social stations were to be altered, in consequence let us say of a revolution, instead of politely working his lift for me the lift-boy, having become a bourgeois, would not have flung me down the well, and whether there was not, in certain of the lower orders, more duplicity than in society, where, no doubt, people reserve their offensive remarks until we are out of earshot, but their attitude towards us would not be insulting if we were hard up.

One cannot however say that the lift-boy was the most commercially minded person in the Balbec hotel. From this point of view the staff might be divided into two categories: on the one hand, those who drew distinctions between the guests, and were more grateful for the modest tip of an old nobleman (who, moreover, was in a position to relieve them from 28 days of military service by saying a word for them to General de Beautreillis) than for the thoughtless liberalities of a flashy vulgarian who by his very extravagance revealed a lack of breeding which only to his face did they call generosity; on the other hand, those to whom nobility, intellect, fame, position, manners were non-existent, concealed under a cash valuation. For these there was but a single hierarchy, that of the money one has, or rather the money one gives. Perhaps even Aimé himself, although pretending, in view of the great number of hotels in which he had served, to a great knowledge of the world, belonged to this latter category. At the most he would give a social turn, showing that he knew who was who, to this sort of appreciation, as when he said of the Princesse de Luxembourg: "There's a pile of money among that lot?" (the question mark at the end being to ascertain the facts, or to check such information as he had already ascertained, before supplying a client with a "chef" for Paris, or promising him a table on the left, by the door, with a view of the sea, at Balbec). In spite of this, without being free from mercenary tendencies, he would not have displayed them with the fatuous despair of the lift-boy. And yet the latter's artlessness helped perhaps to simplify things. It is a convenient feature of a big hotel, or of a house such as Rachel used at one time to frequent, that, without any intermediary, at the sight of a hundred-franc note, still more a thousand-franc one, even though it is being given on that particular occasion to someone else, the hitherto stony face of a servant or a woman will light up with smiles and offers of service. Whereas in politics, or in the relations between lover and mistress, there are too many things interposed between money and docility—so many things indeed that the very people upon whose faces money finally evokes a smile are often incapable of following the internal process that links them together, and believe themselves to be, indeed are, more refined. Besides, it rids polite conversation of such speeches as: "There's only one thing left for me to do—you'll find me tomorrow in the mortuary." Hence one meets in polite society few novelists, or poets, few of all those sublime creatures who speak of the things that are not to be mentioned.

As soon as we were alone and had moved along the corridor, Albertine began: "What have you got against me?" Had my harsh treatment of her been more painful to myself? Hadn't it been merely an unconscious ruse on my part, with the object of bringing her round to that attitude of fear and supplication which would enable me to interrogate her, and perhaps to find out which of the two hypotheses that I had long since formed about her was the correct one? However that may be, when I heard her question I suddenly felt the joy of one who attains to a long-desired goal. Before answering her, I escorted her to the door of my room. Opening it, I scattered the roseate light that was flooding the room and turning the white muslin of the curtains drawn for the night to golden damask. I went across to the window; the gulls had settled again upon the waves; but this time they were pink. I drew Albertine's attention to them. "Don't change the subject," she said, "be frank with me." I lied. I told her that she must first listen to a confession, that of a great passion I had had for Andrée for some time past, and I made her this confession with a simplicity and frankness worthy of the stage, but seldom expressed in real life except in declaring a love which one does not feel. Reverting to the fiction I had employed with Gilberte before my first visit to Balbec, but varying it, I went so far (in order to make her more ready to believe me when I told her now that I did not love her) as to let fall the admission that at one time I had been on the point of falling in love with her, but that too long an interval had elapsed, that she was no more to me now than a good friend, and that, even if I wished, it would no longer be possible for me to feel a more ardent sentiment for her. As it happened, in thus underlining to Albertine these protestations of coldness towards her, I was merely—because of a particular circumstance and with a particular object in view—making more perceptible, accentuating more markedly, that binary rhythm which love adopts in all those who have too little confidence in themselves to believe that a woman can ever fall in love with them, and also that they themselves can genuinely fall in love with her. They know themselves well enough to have observed that in the presence of the most divergent types of woman they felt the same hopes, the same agonies, invented the same romances, uttered the same words, and to have realised therefore that their feelings, their actions, bear no close and necessary relation to the woman they love, but pass to one side of her, splash her, encircle her, like the incoming tide breaking against the rocks, and their sense of their own instability increases still further their misgivings that this woman, by whom they so long to be loved, does not love them. Why should chance have brought it about, when she is simply an accident placed in the path of our surging desires, that we should ourselves be the object of the desires that she feels? And so, while feeling the need to pour out to her all those sentiments, so different from the merely human sentiments that our neighbour inspires in us, those highly specialised sentiments which are those of lovers, after having taken a step forward, in avowing to the one we love our passion for her, our hopes, we are overcome at once by the fear of offending her, and ashamed too that the language we have used to her was not fashioned expressly for her, that it has served us already, will serve us again for others, that if she does not love us she cannot understand us, and that we have spoken in that case with the lack of taste and discretion of a pedant who addresses an ignorant audience in subtle phrases which are not for them; and this fear and shame provoke the counter-rhythm, the reflux, the need, if only by first drawing back, hotly denying the affection previously confessed, to resume the offensive and regain respect and domination; the double rhythm is perceptible in the various periods of a single love affair, in all the corresponding periods of similar love affairs, in all those people whose self-analysis outweighs their self-esteem. If it was however somewhat more forcefully accentuated than usual in this speech which I was now making to Albertine, this was simply to allow me to pass more rapidly and more vigorously to the opposite rhythm which would be measured by my tenderness.

As though it must be painful to Albertine to believe what I was saying to her as to the impossibility of my loving her again after so long an interval, I justified what I called an eccentricity in my nature by examples taken from people with whom I had, by their fault or my own, allowed the time for loving them to pass, and been unable, however keenly I might have desired it, to recapture it. I thus appeared at one and the same time to be apologising to her, as for a want of courtesy, for this inability to begin loving her again, and to be seeking to make her understand the psychological reasons for that incapacity as though they had been peculiar to myself. But by explaining myself in this fashion, by dwelling upon the case of Gilberte, in regard to whom the argument had indeed been strictly true which was becoming so far from true when applied to Albertine, I was merely rendering my assertions as plausible as I pretended to believe that they were not. Sensing that Albertine appreciated what she believed to be my "plain speaking" and recognised my deductions as clearly self-evident, I apologised for the former by telling her that I knew that the truth was always unpleasant and in this instance must seem to her incomprehensible. She thanked me, on the contrary, for my sincerity and added that so far from being puzzled she understood perfectly a state of mind so frequent and so natural.

This avowal to Albertine of an imaginary sentiment for Andrée, and, towards herself, of an indifference which, so that it might appear altogether sincere and without exaggeration, I assured her incidentally, as though out of scrupulous politeness, must not be taken too literally, enabled me at length, without any danger that Albertine might interpret it as love, to speak to her with a tenderness which I had so long denied myself and which seemed to me exquisite. I almost caressed my confidante; as I spoke to her of her friend whom I loved, tears came to my eyes. But, coming at last to the point, I said to her that she knew what love was, its susceptibilities, its sufferings, and that perhaps, as the old friend that she now was, she might feel it in her heart to put an end to the distress she was causing me, not directly, since it was not herself that I loved, if I might venture to repeat that without offending her, but indirectly by wounding me in my love for Andrée. I broke off to admire and point out to Albertine a great, solitary, speeding bird which, far out in front of us, lashing the air with the regular beat of its wings, flew at full speed over the beach, which was stained here and there with gleaming reflexions like little torn scraps of red paper, and crossed it from end to end without slackening its pace, without diverting its attention, without deviating from its path, like an envoy carrying far afield an urgent and vital message. "It at least goes straight to the point!" said Albertine reproachfully. "You say that because you don't know what I was going to tell you. But it's so difficult that I prefer to leave it; I'm certain to make you angry; and then all that will have happened will be this: I shall in no way be better off with the girl I really love and I shall have lost a good friend." "But I swear to you that I won't be angry." She looked so sweet, so wistfully docile, as though her whole happiness depended on me, that I could barely restrain myself from kissing—with almost the same kind of pleasure that I should have had in kissing my mother—this new face which no longer presented the lively, flushed mien of a cheeky and perverse kitten with its little pink tip-tilted nose, but seemed, in the plenitude of its prostrate sadness, to have melted, in broad, flattened and pendent planes, into pure goodness. Leaving aside my love as though it were a chronic mania that had no connexion with her, putting myself in her place, I was moved to pity at the sight of this sweet girl, accustomed to being treated in a friendly and loyal fashion, whom the good friend that she might have supposed me to be had been pursuing for weeks past with persecutions which had at last arrived at their culminating point. It was because I placed myself at a standpoint that was purely human, external to both of us, from which my jealous love had evaporated, that I felt for Albertine that profound pity, which would have been less profound if I had not loved her. However, in that rhythmical oscillation which leads from a declaration to a quarrel (the surest, the most effectively perilous way of forming by opposite and successive movements a knot which will not be loosened and which attaches us firmly to a person), in the midst of the movement of withdrawal which constitutes one of the two elements of the rhythm, of what use is it to analyse further the refluences of human pity, which, the opposite of love, though springing perhaps unconsciously from the same cause, in any case produce the same effects? When we count up afterwards the sum of all that we have done for a woman, we often discover that the actions prompted by the desire to show that we love her, to make her love us, to win her favours, bulk scarcely larger than those due to the human need to repair the wrongs that we do to the loved one, from a mere sense of moral duty, as though we did not love her. "But tell me, what on earth have I done?" Albertine asked me. There was a knock at the door; it was the lift-boy; Albertine's aunt, who was passing the hotel in a carriage, had stopped on the chance of finding her there and taking her home. Albertine sent word that she could not come down, that they were to begin dinner without her, that she could not say at what time she would return. "But won't your aunt be angry?" "Not at all! She'll understand perfectly well." In other words—at this moment at least, which perhaps would never recur—a conversation with me was in Albertine's eyes, because of the circumstances, a thing of such self-evident importance that it must be given precedence over everything, a thing to which, refer-ring no doubt instinctively to a family code, enumerating certain situations in which, when the career of M. Bon-temps was at stake, a journey had been made without thinking twice, my friend never doubted that her aunt would think it quite natural to see her sacrifice the din-ner-hour. Having relinquished for my benefit that remote hour which she spent without me, among her own people, Albertine was giving it to me; I might make what use of it I chose. I finally made bold to tell her what had been reported to me about her way of life, and said that

notwithstanding the profound disgust I felt for women
tainted with that vice, I had not given it a thought until I
had been told the name of her accomplice, and that she
could readily understand, loving Andrée as I did, the pain
that this had caused me. It would have been more astute
perhaps to say that other women had also been mentioned
but that they were of no interest to me. But the sudden
and terrible revelation that Cottard had made to me had
struck home, had lacerated me, just as it was, complete in
itself without any accretions. And just as, before that moment, it would never have occurred to me that Albertine
was enamoured of Andrée, or at any rate could find pleasure in caressing her, if Cottard had not drawn my attention to their posture as they waltzed together, so I had
been incapable of passing from that idea to the idea, so
different for me, that Albertine might have, with women
other than Andrée, relations which could not even be excused by affection. Albertine, even before swearing to me
that it was not true, expressed, like everyone upon learning that such things are being said about them, anger,
concern, and, with regard to the unknown slanderer, a
fierce curiosity to know who he was and a desire to be
confronted with him so as to be able to confound him.
But she assured me that she bore me, at least, no resentment. "If it had been true, I would have told you. But
Andrée and I both loathe that sort of thing. We haven't
reached our age without seeing women with cropped hair
who behave like men and do the things you mean, and
nothing revolts us more." Albertine merely gave me her
word, a categorical word unsupported by proof. But this
was precisely what was best calculated to calm me, jealousy belonging to that family of morbid doubts which are

eliminated by the vigour of an affirmation far more surely
than by its probability. It is moreover the property of love
to make us at once more distrustful and more credulous,
to make us suspect the loved one, more readily than we
should suspect anyone else, and be convinced more easily
by her denials. We must be in love before we can care
that all women are not virtuous, which is to say before we
can be aware of the fact, and we must be in love too before we can hope, that is to say assure ourselves, that
some are. It is human to seek out what hurts us and then
at once to seek to get rid of it. Statements that are capable
of so relieving us seem all too readily true: we are not inclined to cavil at a sedative that works. Besides, however
multiform the person we love may be, she can in any case
present to us two essential personalities according to
whether she appears to us as ours, or as turning her desires elsewhere. The first of these personalities possesses
the peculiar power which prevents us from believing in
the reality of the second, the secret remedy to heal the
sufferings that this latter has caused us. The beloved object is successively the malady and the remedy that sus-
pends and aggravates it. Doubtless I had long been
conditioned, by the powerful impression made on my
imagination and my faculty for emotion by the example of
Swann, to believe in the truth of what I feared rather than
of what I should have wished. Hence the comfort brought
me by Albertine's affirmations came near to being jeopardised for a moment because I remembered the story of
Odette. But I told myself that, if it was right to allow for
the worst, not only when, in order to understand Swann's
sufferings, I had tried to put myself in his place, but now
that it concerned myself, in seeking the truth as though it

concerned someone else I must nevertheless not, out of
cruelty to myself, like a soldier who chooses the post not
where he can be of most use but where he is most exposed, end up with the mistake of regarding one supposition as more true than the rest simply because it was the
most painful. Was there not a vast gulf between Albertine, a girl of good middle-class parentage, and Odette, a
whore sold by her mother in her childhood? There could
be no comparison of their respective credibility. Besides,
Albertine had in no sense the same interest in lying to me
that Odette had had in lying to Swann. And in any case
to him Odette had admitted what Albertine had just denied. I should therefore be guilty of an error of reasoning
as serious—though in the opposite sense—as that which
would have inclined me towards a certain assumption because it caused me less pain than any other, in not taking
into account these material differences in their situations,
and in reconstructing the real life of my beloved solely
from what I had been told about Odette's. I had before
me a new Albertine, of whom I had already, it was true,
caught more than one glimpse towards the end of my previous visit to Balbec, a frank, kind Albertine who, out of
affection for myself, had just forgiven me my suspicions
and tried to dispel them. She made me sit down by her
side on my bed. I thanked her for what she had said to
me, assuring her that our reconciliation was complete, and
that I would never be harsh to her again. I told her that
she ought nevertheless to go home to dinner. She asked
me whether I was not glad to have her with me. And
drawing my head towards her for a caress which she had
never given me before and which I owed perhaps to the
healing of our quarrel, she drew her tongue lightly over

my lips, which she attempted to force apart. At first I kept them tight shut. "What an old spoilsport you are!" she said to me.

I ought to have gone away that evening and never seen her again. I sensed there and then that in a love that is not shared—one might almost say in love, for there are people for whom there is no such thing as shared love— we can enjoy only that simulacrum of happiness which had been given to me at one of those unique moments in which a woman's good nature, or her caprice, or mere chance, respond to our desires, in perfect coincidence, with the same words, the same actions, as if we were really loved. The wiser course would have been to consider with curiosity, to appropriate with delight, that little particle of happiness failing which I should have died without ever suspecting what it could mean to hearts less difficult or more privileged; to pretend that it formed part of a vast and enduring happiness of which this fragment only was visible to me; and—lest the next day should give the lie to this fiction—not to attempt to ask for any fresh favour after this one, which had been due only to the artifice of an exceptional moment. I ought to have left Balbec, to have shut myself up in solitude, to have remained there in harmony with the last vibrations of the voice which I had contrived to render loving for an instant, and of which I should have asked nothing more than that it might never address another word to me; for fear lest, by an additional word which henceforth could not but be different, it might shatter with a discord the sensory silence in which, as though by the pressure of a pedal, there might long have survived in me the tonality of happiness.

Calmed by my confrontation with Albertine, I began

once again to live in closer intimacy with my mother. She loved to talk to me gently about the days when my grandmother had been younger. Fearing that I might reproach myself with the sorrows with which I had perhaps darkened the close of my grandmother's life, she preferred to turn back to the years when my first studies had given my grandmother a satisfaction which until now had always been kept from me. We talked of the old days at Combray. My mother reminded me that there at least I used to read, and that at Balbec I might well do the same, if I was not going to work. I replied that, to surround myself with memories of Combray and of the pretty coloured plates, I should like to re-read the *Arabian Nights*. As, long ago at Combray, when she gave me books for my birthday, so it was in secret, as a surprise for me, that my mother now sent for both Galland's version and that of Mardrus.[7] But, after casting her eye over the two translations, my mother would have preferred that I should stick to Galland's, albeit hesitating to influence me because of her respect for intellectual liberty, her dread of interfering with my intellectual life and the feeling that, being a woman, on the one hand she lacked, or so she thought, the necessary literary equipment, and on the other hand ought not to judge a young man's reading by what she herself found shocking. Happening upon certain of the tales, she had been revolted by the immorality of the subject and the coarseness of the expression. But above all, preserving like precious relics not only her mother's brooch, her sunshade, her cloak, her volume of Mme de Sévigné, but also her habits of thought and speech, invoking on every occasion the opinion that she would have expressed, my mother could have no doubt of the un-

favourable judgment which my grandmother would have
passed on Mardrus's version. She remembered that at
Combray, while I sat reading Augustin Thierry before
setting out for a walk along the Méséglise way, my grandmother, pleased with my reading and my walks, was indignant nevertheless at seeing the person whose name
remained enshrined in the hemistich "Then reignèd
Mérovée" called Merowig, and refused to say "Carolin-
gians" for the "Carlovingians" to which she remained
loyal. And then I told her what my grandmother had
thought of the Greek names which Bloch, following
Leconte de Lisle, used to give to Homer's gods, going so
far, in the simplest matters, as to make it a religious duty,
in which he supposed literary talent to consist, to adopt a
Greek system of spelling. Having occasion, for instance,
to mention in a letter that the wine which they drank at
his home was true nectar, he would write "nektar," with a
k, which enabled him to titter at the mention of Lamar-
tine. Now if an *Odyssey* from which the names of Ulysses
and Minerva were missing was no longer the *Odyssey* to
her, what would she have said upon seeing corrupted,
even on the cover, the title of her Arabian tales, upon no
longer finding, exactly transcribed as she had all her life
been in the habit of pronouncing them, the immortally familiar names of Scheherazade or Dinarzade, while, themselves debaptised (if one may use the expression of
Muslim tales), even the charming Caliph and the powerful Genies were barely recognisable, being renamed, he
the "Khalifa" and they the "Gennis." However, my
mother handed over both books to me, and I told her that
I would read them on the days when I felt too tired to go
out.

These days were not very frequent, however. We used to go out picnicking as before in a band, Albertine, her friends and myself, on the cliff or to the farm called Marie-Antoinette. But there were times when Albertine bestowed on me a great pleasure. She would say to me: "Today I want to be alone with you for a while; it will be nicer if we are just by ourselves." Then she would give out that she had things to do—not that she had to account for her movements—and so that the others, if they went out for a picnic all the same without us, should not be able to find us, we would steal away like a pair of lovers, all by ourselves to Bagatelle or the Cross of Heulan, while the band, who would never think of looking for us there and never went there, waited indefinitely at Marie-Antoinette in the hope of seeing us appear. I remember the hot weather that we had then, when from the foreheads of the farm labourers toiling in the sun drops of sweat would fall, vertical, regular, intermittent, like drops of water from a cistern, alternating with the fall of the ripe fruit dropping from the tree in the adjoining orchard; they have remained to this day, together with that mystery of a woman's secret, the most enduring element in every love that offers itself to me. For a woman who is mentioned to me and to whom ordinarily I would not give a moment's thought, I will upset all my week's engagements to make her acquaintance, if it is a week of similar weather, and if I am to meet her in some isolated farmhouse. Even if I am aware that this kind of weather, this kind of assignation, have nothing to do with her, they are still the bait which, however familiar, I allow myself to be tempted by, and which is sufficient to hook me. I know that in cold weather, in a town, I might perhaps have desired this woman, but without the accompaniment of romantic feelings, without falling in love; love is none the less strong as soon as, by force of circumstances, it has enchained me—it is simply more melancholy, as over the years our feelings for other people become, in proportion as we grow more aware of the ever smaller part they play in our lives and realise that the new love which we would like to be so enduring, cut short in the same moment as life itself, will be the last.

There were still few people at Balbec, few girls. Sometimes I would see one standing on the beach, one devoid of charm and yet whom various coincidences seemed to identify as a girl whom I had been in despair at not being able to approach when she emerged with her friends from the riding school or gymnasium. If it was the same one (and I took care not to mention the matter to Albertine), then the girl that I had thought so intoxicating did not exist. But I couldn't arrive at any certainty, for the faces of these girls did not fill a constant space, did not present a constant form upon the beach, contracted, dilated, transmogrified as they were by my own expectancy, the anxiousness of my desire, or by a sense of self-sufficient well-being, the different clothes they wore, the rapidity of their walk or their stillness. From close to, however, two or three of them seemed to me adorable. Whenever I saw one of these, I longed to take her to the Avenue des Tamaris, or among the sandhills, or better still on to the cliff. But although in desire, as opposed to indifference, there is already that element of audacity which a first step, if only unilateral, towards realisation entails, all the same, between my desire and the action that my asking to kiss her would have been, there was all the indefinite "vacancy" of hesitation and shyness. Then I went into the café-bar, and proceeded to drink, one after another, seven or eight glasses of port wine. At once, instead of the impassable gulf between my desire and action, the effect of the alcohol traced a line that joined them together. No longer was there any room for hesitation or fear. It seemed to me that the girl was about to fly into my arms. I went up to her, and there sprang to my lips of their own accord the words: "I should like to go for a walk with you. You wouldn't care to go along the cliff? We shan't be disturbed behind the little wood that keeps the wind off the wooden bungalow that is empty just now." All the difficulties of life were smoothed away, there were no longer any obstacles to the conjunction of our two bodies. No longer any obstacles for me, at least. For they had not been dissipated for her, who had not been drinking port wine. Had she done so, had the outer world lost some of its reality in her eyes, the long-cherished dream that would then have appeared to her to be suddenly realisable might have been not at all that of falling into my arms.

Not only were the girls few in number but, at this season which was not yet "the season," they stayed only a short time. There is one I remember with a russet skin, green eyes and a pair of ruddy cheeks, whose slight symmetrical face resembled the winged seeds of certain trees. I cannot say what breeze wafted her to Balbec or what other bore her away. So sudden was her removal that for some days afterwards I was haunted by a chagrin which I made bold to confess to Albertine when I realised that the girl had gone for ever.

I should add that several of them were girls whom I

either did not know at all or had not seen for years. Often I wrote to them before meeting them. If their answers allowed me to believe in the possibility of love, what joy! One cannot, at the outset of a friendship with a woman, even if that friendship is destined to come to nothing, bear to be parted from these first letters that we receive. We like to have them with us all the time, like a present of rare flowers, still fresh, at which one ceases to gaze only to breathe their scent. The sentence that one knows by heart is pleasant to read again, and in those that one has committed less accurately to memory one wants to verify the degree of affection in some expression. Did she write: "Your precious letter"? A slight marring of one's bliss, which must be ascribed either to one's having read too quickly, or to the illegible handwriting of one's correspondent; she did not put: "your precious letter" but "your previous letter." But the rest is so tender. Oh, that more such flowers may come tomorrow! Then that is no longer enough, one must place the written words side by side with the eyes, the voice. One makes a rendezvous, and—without her having altered, perhaps—whereas one expected, from the description received or one's personal memory, to meet a Fairy Queen, one finds Puss-in-Boots. One makes another rendezvous, nevertheless, for the following day, for it is, after all, *she*, and it was she that one desired. For these desires for a woman of whom one has dreamed do not make the beauty of this or that particular feature absolutely essential. These desires are only the desire for this or that person; vague as perfumes, as styrax was the desire of Prothyraia, saffron the ethereal desire, spices the desire of Hera, myrrh the perfume of the clouds, manna the desire of Nike, incense the perfume of the sea. But these perfumes that are sung in the Orphic hymns are far fewer in number than the deities they cherish. Myrrh is the perfume of the clouds, but also of Protogonos, Neptune, Nereus, Leto; incense is the perfume of the sea, but also of the fair Dike, of Themis, of Circe, of the Nine Muses, of Eos, of Mnemosyne, of the Day, of Dikaiosyne. As for styrax, manna and spices, it would be impossible to name all the deities that inspire them, so many are they. Amphietes has all the perfumes except incense, and Gaia rejects only beans and spices. So it was with these desires that I felt for different girls. Less numerous than the girls themselves, they changed into disappointments and regrets closely similar one to another. I never wished for myrrh. I reserved it for Jupien and for the Princesse de Guermantes, for it is the desire of Protogonos "of twofold sex, with the roar of a bull, of countless orgies, memorable, indescribable, descending joyously to the sacrifices of the Orgiophants."

But presently the season was in full swing; every day there was some new arrival, and for the sudden increase in the frequency of my outings, which took the place of the charmed perusal of the *Arabian Nights*, there was an unpleasurable reason which poisoned them all. The beach was now peopled with girls, and, since the idea suggested to me by Cottard, while not supplied with fresh suspicions, had rendered me sensitive and vulnerable in that quarter and careful not to let any suspicion take shape in my mind, as soon as a young woman arrived at Balbec I felt ill at ease and proposed to Albertine the most distant excursions so that she might not make the newcomer's acquaintance and if possible might not even set eyes on her. I dreaded naturally even more those women whose dubious ways were remarked or their bad reputation already known; I tried to persuade my beloved that this bad reputation had no foundation, was a slander, perhaps, without admitting it to myself, from a fear, as yet unconscious, that she might seek to make friends with the depraved woman or regret her inability to do so because of me, or might conclude from the number of examples that a vice so widespread could not be blameworthy. In denying it of every guilty woman, I was not far from contending that sapphism did not exist. Albertine adopted my incredulity as to the viciousness of this one or that: "No, I think it's just a pose, she wants to put on airs." But then I regretted almost that I had pleaded their innocence, for it offended me that Albertine, formerly so severe, could believe that this "pose" was a thing so pleasing, so advantageous, that a woman innocent of such tastes should seek to adopt it. I began to wish that no more women would come to Balbec; I trembled at the thought that, as it was about the time when Mme Putbus was due to arrive at the Verdurins', her maid, whose tastes Saint-Loup had not concealed from me, might take it into her head to come down to the beach, and, if it were a day on which I was not with Albertine, might seek to corrupt her. I went as far as to ask myself whether, as Cottard had made no secret of the fact that the Verdurins thought highly of me and, while not wishing to appear, as he put it, to be running after me, would give a great deal to have me come to their house, I might not, on the strength of promises to bring all the Guermantes in existence to call on them in Paris, induce Mme Verdurin on some pretext or other to inform Mme Putbus that it was impossible to keep her there any longer and make her leave the place at once.

Notwithstanding these thoughts, and as it was chiefly the presence of Andrée that disturbed me, the soothing effect that Albertine's words had had upon me to some extent persisted—I knew moreover that presently I should have less need of it, since Andrée would be leaving with Rosemonde and Gisèle just about the time when the crowd began to arrive and would be spending only a few weeks more with Albertine. During these weeks, moreover, Albertine seemed to plan everything that she did, everything that was said, with a view to destroying my suspicions if any remained, or to preventing their recurrence. She contrived never to be left alone with Andrée, and insisted, when we came back from an excursion, on my accompanying her to her door, and on my coming to fetch her when we were going anywhere. Andrée meanwhile took just as much trouble on her side, seemed to avoid meeting Albertine. And this apparent understanding between them was not the only indication that Albertine must have informed her friend of our conversation and have asked her to be so kind as to calm my absurd suspicions.

About this time there occurred at the Grand Hotel a scandal which was not calculated to alter the trend of my anxieties. Bloch's sister had for some time past been indulging, with a retired actress, in secret relations which presently ceased to suffice them. They felt that to be seen would add perversity to their pleasure, and chose to flaunt their dangerous embraces before the eyes of all the world. They began with caresses, which might, after all, be attributed to a friendly intimacy, in the card-room, round the baccarat-table. Then they grew bolder. And finally, one evening, in a corner of the big ballroom that was not even dark, on a sofa, they made no more attempt to conceal what they were doing than if they had been in bed. Two officers, who happened to be nearby with their wives, complained to the manager. It was thought for a moment that their protest would be effective. But they suffered from the disadvantage that, having come over for the evening from Netteholme, where they lived, they could not be of any use to the manager. Whereas, without her even knowing it, and whatever remarks the manager might make to her, there hovered over Mlle Bloch the protection of M. Nissim Bernard. I must explain why. M. Nissim Bernard practised the family virtues in the highest degree. Every year he rented a magnificent villa at Balbec for his nephew, and no invitation would have dissuaded him from going home to dine at his own table, which was really theirs. But he never lunched at home. Every day at noon he was at the Grand Hotel. The fact of the matter was that he was keeping, as other men keep a dancer from the *corps de ballet*, a fledgling waiter of much the same type as the pages of whom we have spoken, and who made us think of the young Israelites in *Esther* and *Athalie*. It is true that the forty years' difference in age between M. Nissim Bernard and the young waiter ought to have preserved the latter from a contact that could scarcely have been agreeable. But, as Racine so wisely observes in those same choruses:

> Great God, with what uncertain tread
> A budding virtue 'mid such perils goes!
> What stumbling-blocks do lie before a soul
> That seeks Thee and would fain be innocent.

For all that the young waiter had been brought up "in seclusion from the world" in the Temple-Palace of Balbec, he had not followed the advice of Joad:

> In riches and in gold put not thy trust.

He had perhaps justified himself by saying: "The wicked cover the earth." However that might be, and albeit M. Nissim Bernard had not expected so rapid a conquest, on the very first day,

> Whether in fear, or anxious to caress,
> He felt those childish arms about him thrown.

And by the second day, M. Nissim Bernard having taken the young waiter out,

> The dire assault his innocence destroyed.

From that moment the boy's life was altered. He might only carry bread and salt, as his superior bade him, but his whole face sang:

> From flowers to flowers, from joys to joys
> Let our desires now range.
> Uncertain is our sum of fleeting years,
> Let us then hasten to enjoy this life!
> Honours and high office are the prize
> Of blind and meek obedience.
> For sorry innocence
> Who would want to raise his voice?

Since that day, M. Nissim Bernard had never failed to come and occupy his seat at the lunch-table (as a man

might occupy his seat in the stalls who was keeping a
dancer, a dancer in this case of a distinct and special type
which still awaits its Degas). It was M. Nissim Bernard's
delight to follow round the restaurant, as far as the remote
vistas where beneath her palm the cashier sat enthroned,
the gyrations of the adolescent in zealous attendance—attendance on everyone, and less on M. Nissim Bernard
now that the latter was keeping him, whether because the
young altar-boy did not think it necessary to display the
same civility to a person by whom he supposed himself to
be sufficiently well loved, or because that love annoyed
him or he feared lest, if discovered, it might make him
lose other opportunities. But this very coldness pleased
M. Nissim Bernard, because of all that it concealed;
whether from Hebraic atavism or in profanation of its
Christian feeling, he took a singular pleasure in the
Racinian ceremony, were it Jewish or Catholic. Had it
been a real performance of *Esther* or *Athalie*, M. Bernard
would have regretted that the gulf of centuries must prevent him from making the acquaintance of the author,
Jean Racine, so that he might obtain for his protégé a
more substantial part. But as the luncheon ceremony came
from no author's pen, he contented himself with being on
good terms with the manager and with Aimé, so that
the "young Israelite" might be promoted to the coveted
post of under-waiter, or even put in charge of a row of tables. A post in the cellars had been offered him. But M.
Bernard made him decline it, for he would no longer have
been able to come every day to watch him race about the
green dining-room and to be waited upon by him like a
stranger. Now this pleasure was so keen that every year
M. Bernard returned to Balbec and had his lunch away

from home, habits in which M. Bloch saw, in the former a poetical fancy for the beautiful light and the sunsets of this coast favoured above all others, in the latter the inveterate eccentricity of an old bachelor.

As a matter of fact, this misapprehension on the part of M. Nissim Bernard's relatives, who never suspected the true reason for his annual return to Balbec, and for what the pedantic Mme Bloch called his gastronomic absenteeism, was a deeper truth, at one remove. For M. Nissim Bernard himself was unaware of the extent to which a love for the beach at Balbec and for the view over the sea which one enjoyed from the restaurant, together with eccentricity of habit, contributed to the fancy that he had for keeping, like a little dancing girl of another kind which still lacks a Degas, one of his equally nubile servers. And so M. Nissim Bernard maintained excellent relations with the director of this theatre which was the hotel at Balbec, and with the stage-manager and producer Aimé—whose roles in this whole affair were far from clear. One day they would all contrive to procure an important part for his protégé, perhaps a post as head waiter. In the meantime M. Nissim Bernard's pleasure, poetical and calmly contemplative as it might be, was somewhat reminiscent of those women-loving men who always know—Swann, for example, in the past—that if they go out in society they will meet their mistress. No sooner had M. Nissim Bernard taken his seat than he would see the object of his affections appear on the scene, bearing in his hands fruit or cigars upon a tray. And so every morning, after kissing his niece, inquiring about my friend Bloch's work, and feeding his horses with lumps of sugar from the palm of his outstretched hand, he would betray a feverish haste to

arrive in time for lunch at the Grand Hotel. Had the
house been on fire, had his niece had a stroke, he would
doubtless have started off just the same. So that he
dreaded like the plague a cold that would confine him to
his bed—for he was a hypochondriac—and would oblige
him to ask Aimé to send his young friend across to visit
him at home, between lunch and tea-time.

He loved moreover all the labyrinth of corridors, private offices, reception-rooms, cloakrooms, larders, galleries
which composed the hotel at Balbec. With a strain of oriental atavism he loved a seraglio, and when he went out
at night might be seen furtively exploring its purlieus.

While, venturing down to the basement and endeavouring at the same time to escape notice and to avoid a
scandal, M. Nissim Bernard, in his quest of the young
Levites, put one in mind of those lines in *La Juive*:

O God of our Fathers, come down to us again,
Our mysteries veil from the eyes of wicked men!

I on the contrary would go up to the room of two sisters
who had come to Balbec with an old foreign lady as her
maids. They were what the language of hotels called two
courrières, and that of Françoise, who imagined that a
courier was a person who was there to run errands (*faire
des courses*) two *coursières*. The hotels have remained,
more nobly, in the period when people sang: "*C'est un
courrier de cabinet.*"[8]

Difficult as it was for a guest to penetrate to the servants' quarters, and vice versa, I had very soon formed a
mutual bond of friendship, as strong as it was pure, with
these two young persons, Mlle Marie Gineste and Mme

Céleste Albaret. Born at the foot of the high mountains in the centre of France, on the banks of rivulets and torrents (the water flowed actually under the family home, turning a millwheel, and the house had often been devastated by floods), they seemed to embody the spirit of those waters. Marie Gineste was more regularly rapid and staccato, Céleste Albaret softer and more languishing, spread out like a lake, but with terrible boiling rages in which her fury suggested the peril of spates and whirlwinds that sweep everything before them. They often came in the morning to see me when I was still in bed. I have never known people so deliberately ignorant, who had learned absolutely nothing at school, and yet whose language was somehow so literary that, but for the almost wild natural- ness of their tone, one would have thought their speech affected. With a familiarity which I reproduce verbatim, notwithstanding the eulogies (which I set down here in praise not of myself but of the strange genius of Céleste) and the criticisms, equally unfounded but absolutely sin- cere, which her remarks seem to imply towards me, while I dipped croissants in my milk, Céleste would say to me: "Oh! little black devil with raven hair, oh deep-dyed mis- chief! I don't know what your mother was thinking of when she made you, you're just like a bird. Look, Marie, wouldn't you say he was preening his feathers, and the supple way he turns his head right round, he looks so light, you'd think he was just learning to fly. Ah! it's lucky for you that you were born into the ranks of the rich, otherwise what would have become of you, spendthrift that you are? Look at him throwing away his croissant because it touched the bed. There he goes, now, look, he's spilling his milk. Wait till I tie a napkin round you, because you'll never do it for yourself, I've never seen anyone so foolish and clumsy as you." I would then hear the more regular sound of the torrent of Marie Gineste furiously reprimanding her sister: "Will you hold your tongue, now, Céleste. Are you mad, talking to Monsieur like that?" Céleste merely smiled; and as I detested having a napkin tied round my neck: "No, Marie, look at him, bang, he's shot straight up on end like a snake. A proper snake, I tell you." She was full of zoological similes, for, according to her, it was impossible to tell when I slept, I fluttered about all night like a moth, and in the daytime I was as swift as the squirrels, "you know, Marie, which we used to see at home, so nimble that even with the eyes you can't follow them." "But, Céleste, you know he doesn't like having a napkin when he's eating." "It isn't that he doesn't like it, it's so that he can say nobody can make him do anything he doesn't want to. He's a grand gentleman and he wants to show that he is. You change the sheets ten times over if need be, but he still won't be satisfied. Yesterday's had served their time, but today they've only just been put on the bed and they have to be changed already. Oh, I was right when I said that he was never meant to be born among the poor. Look, his hair's standing on end, puffing out with rage like a bird's feathers. Poor *feather-pether!*" Here it was not only Marie who protested, but myself, for I did not feel in the least like a grand gentleman. But Céleste would never believe in the sincerity of my modesty and would cut me short: "Oh, what a bag of tricks! Oh, the soft talk, the deceitfulness! Ah, rogue among rogues, churl of churls! Ah, Molière!" (This was the only writer's name that she knew, but she applied it to me, meaning thereby a person who

was capable both of writing plays and of acting them.)
"Céleste!" came the imperious cry from Marie, who, not
knowing the name of Molière, was afraid that it might be
some fresh insult. Céleste continued to smile: "Then you
haven't seen the photograph of him in his drawer, when
he was little? He tried to make us believe that he was always dressed quite simply. And there, with his little cane,
he's all furs and lace, such as not even a prince ever wore.
But that's nothing compared with his tremendous majesty
and his even more profound kindness." "So you go rum-
maging in his drawers now, do you?" growled the torrent
Marie. To calm Marie's fears I asked her what she
thought of M. Nissim Bernard's behaviour . . . "Ah!
Monsieur, there are things I wouldn't have believed could
exist until I came here." And for once going one better
than Céleste with an even more profound observation, she
added: "Ah! You see, Monsieur, one can never tell what
there may be in a person's life." To change the subject, I
spoke to her of the life led by my father, who worked
night and day. "Ah! Monsieur, there are people who keep
nothing of their life for themselves, not one minute, not
one pleasure, the whole thing is a sacrifice for others, they
are lives that are *offered up* . . . Look, Céleste, simply the
way he puts his hand on the counterpane and picks up his
croissant, what distinction! He can do the most insignificant things, and you'd think that the whole nobility of
France, right to the Pyrenees, was stirring in each of his
movements."

Overwhelmed by this portrait that was so far from
lifelike, I remained silent; Céleste interpreted my silence
as a further instance of guile: "Ah! forehead that looks so
pure and hides so many things, nice, cool cheeks like the

inside of an almond, little hands all soft and satiny, nails like claws," and so forth. "There, Marie, look at him sipping his milk with a reverence that makes me want to say my prayers. What a serious air! Someone really ought to take a picture of him as he is just now. He's just like a child. Is it by drinking milk, like them, that you've kept that clear complexion? Ah, what youth! Ah, what lovely skin! You'll never grow old. You're lucky, you'll never need to raise your hand against anyone, for you have eyes that know how to impose their will. Look at him now, he's angry. He shoots up, straight as a gospel truth."

Françoise did not at all approve of those she called the two "wheedlers" coming to talk to me like this. The manager, who made his staff keep watch over everything that went on, even pointed out to me gravely that it was not proper for a customer to talk to servants. I, who found the "wheedlers" better company than any visitor in the hotel, merely laughed in his face, convinced that he would not understand my explanations. And the sisters returned. "Look, Marie, at his delicate features. Oh, perfect miniature, finer than the most precious you could see in a glass case, because he has movement, and words you could listen to for days and nights."

It was a miracle that a foreign lady could have brought them there, for, without knowing anything of history or geography, they heartily detested the English, the Germans, the Russians, the Italians, all foreign "vermin," and cared, with certain exceptions, for French people alone. Their faces had so far preserved the moisture of the malleable clay of their native river beds, that, as soon as one mentioned a foreigner who was staying in the hotel, in order to repeat what he had said Céleste and Marie at once took on his facial expression, their mouths became his mouth, their eyes his eyes—one would have liked to preserve these admirable comic masks. Céleste indeed, while pretending merely to be repeating what the manager or one of my friends had said, would insert in her little narrative, apparently quite unwittingly, fictitious remarks in which were maliciously portrayed all the defects of Bloch, the judge, and others. Under the form of a report on a simple errand which she had obligingly undertaken, she would provide an inimitable portrait. They never read anything, not even a newspaper. One day, however, they found a book lying on my bed. It was a volume of the admirable but obscure poems of Saint-Léger Léger.[9] Céleste read a few pages and said to me: "But are you quite sure that it's poetry? Mightn't it just be riddles?" Obviously, to a person who had learned in her childhood a single poem: "Here below the lilacs die," there was a lack of transition. I fancy that their obstinate refusal to learn anything was due in part to the unhealthy climate of their early home. They had nevertheless all the gifts of a poet with more modesty than poets generally show. For if Céleste had said something noteworthy and, unable to remember it correctly, I asked her to repeat it, she would assure me that she had forgotten. They will never read any books, but neither will they ever write any.

Françoise was considerably impressed when she learned that the two brothers of these humble women had married, one the niece of the Archbishop of Tours, the other a relative of the Bishop of Rodez. To the manager, this would have conveyed nothing. Céleste would sometimes reproach her husband with his failure to understand her, and I myself was astonished that he could put up

with her. For at certain moments, quivering, raging, destroying everything, she was detestable. It is said that the
salt liquid which is our blood is only an internal survival
of the primitive marine element. Similarly, I believe that
Céleste, not only in her bursts of fury, but also in her
hours of depression, preserved the rhythm of her native
streams. When she was exhausted, it was after their fashion; she had literally run dry. Nothing could then have
revitalised her. Then all of a sudden the circulation was
restored in her tall, slender, magnificent body. The water
flowed in the opaline transparence of her bluish skin. She
smiled in the sun and became bluer still. At such moments she was truly celestial.

In spite of the fact that Bloch's family had never suspected the reason why their uncle never lunched at home,
and had accepted it from the first as the idiosyncrasy of
an elderly bachelor, attributable perhaps to the demands
of a liaison with some actress, everything that concerned
M. Nissim Bernard was taboo to the manager of the Balbec hotel. And it was for this reason that, without even
referring to the uncle, he had finally not ventured to find
fault with the niece, albeit recommending her to be a little
more circumspect. Mlle Bloch and her friend, who for
some days had imagined themselves to have been excluded from the Casino and the Grand Hotel, seeing that
all was well, were delighted to show those respectable
family men who held aloof from them that they might
with impunity take the utmost liberties. No doubt they
did not go so far as to repeat the public exhibition which
had revolted everybody. But gradually they returned to
their old ways. And one evening as I came out of the
Casino, which was half in darkness, with Albertine and

Bloch whom we had met there, they came by, linked together, kissing each other incessantly, and, as they passed
us, crowed and chortled and uttered indecent cries. Bloch
lowered his eyes so as to seem not to have recognised his
sister, and I was tortured by the thought that this private
and horrifying language was addressed perhaps to Albertine.

Another incident focused my preoccupations even
more in the direction of Gomorrah. I had noticed on the
beach a handsome young woman, slender and pale, whose
eyes, round their centre, scattered rays so geometrically
luminous that one was reminded, on meeting her gaze, of
some constellation. I thought how much more beautiful
she was than Albertine, and how much wiser it would be
to give up the other. But the face of this beautiful young
woman had been scoured by the invisible plane of a thoroughly depraved life, of the constant acceptance of vulgar
expedients, so much so that her eyes, though nobler than
the rest of her face, could radiate nothing but appetites
and desires. On the following day, this young woman being seated a long way away from us in the Casino, I saw
that she never ceased to fasten upon Albertine the alternating and revolving beam of her gaze. It was as though
she were making signals to her with a lamp. It pained me
that Albertine should see that she was being so closely
observed, and I was afraid that these incessantly rekindled
glances might be the agreed signal for an amorous assignation next day. For all I knew, this assignation might not
be the first. The young woman with the flashing eyes
might have come another year to Balbec. It was perhaps
because Albertine had already yielded to her desires, or to
those of a friend, that this woman allowed herself to ad-

dress to her those flashing signals. If so, they were doing more than demand something for the present; they invoked a justification for it in pleasant hours in the past.

This assignation, in that case, must be not the first, but the sequel to adventures shared in past years. And indeed her glance did not say: "Will you?" As soon as the young woman had caught sight of Albertine, she had turned her head and beamed upon her glances charged with recollection, as though she were afraid and amazed that my beloved did not remember. Albertine, who could see her plainly, remained phlegmatically motionless, with the result that the other, with the same sort of discretion as a man who sees his old mistress with a new lover, ceased to look at her and paid no more attention to her than if she had not existed.

But a day or two later, I received proof of this young woman's tendencies, and also of the probability of her having known Albertine in the past. Often, in the hall of the Casino, when two girls were smitten with mutual desire, a sort of luminous phenomenon occurred, as it were a phosphorescent trail flashing from one to the other. It may be noted, incidentally, that it is by the aid of such materialisations, impalpable though they be, by these astral signs that set a whole section of the atmosphere ablaze, that Gomorrah, dispersed, tends in every town, in every village, to reunite its separated members, to rebuild the biblical city while everywhere the same efforts are being made, if only in view of an intermittent reconstruction, by the nostalgic, the hypocritical, sometimes the courageous exiles of Sodom.

Once I saw the unknown woman whom Albertine had appeared not to recognise, just at the moment when

Bloch's cousin was passing by. The young woman's eyes flashed, but it was quite evident that she did not know the Jewish girl. She beheld her for the first time, felt a desire, scarcely any doubt, but by no means the same certainty as in the case of Albertine, Albertine upon whose friendship she must so far have counted that, in the face of her coldness, she had felt the surprise of a foreigner familiar with Paris but not a resident, who, having returned to spend a few weeks there, finds the site of the little theatre where he was in the habit of spending pleasant evenings occupied now by a bank.

Bloch's cousin went and sat down at a table where she turned the pages of a magazine. Presently the young woman came and sat down beside her with an abstracted air. But under the table one could presently see their feet wriggling, then their legs and hands intertwined. Words followed, a conversation began, and the young woman's guileless husband, who had been looking everywhere for her, was astonished to find her making plans for that very evening with a girl whom he did not know. His wife introduced Bloch's cousin to him as a childhood friend, under an inaudible name, for she had forgotten to ask her what her name was. But the husband's presence made their intimacy advance a stage further, for they addressed each other as *tu*, having known each other at their convent, an incident at which they laughed heartily later on, as well as at the hoodwinked husband, with a gaiety which afforded them an excuse for further caresses.

As for Albertine, I cannot say that anywhere, whether at the Casino or on the beach, her behaviour with any girl was unduly free. I found in it indeed an excess of coldness and indifference which seemed to be more than good breeding, to be a ruse planned to avert suspicion. When questioned by some girl, she had a quick, icy, prim way of replying in a very loud voice: "Yes, I shall be at the tennis-court about five. I shall go for a bathe tomorrow morning about eight," and of at once turning away from the person to whom she had said this—all of which had a horrible appearance of being meant to put one off the scent, and either to make an assignation, or rather, the assignation having already been made in a whisper, to utter these perfectly harmless words aloud so as not to attract undue attention. And when later on I saw her mount her bicycle and scorch away into the distance, I could not help thinking that she was on her way to join the girl to whom she had barely spoken.

However, when some handsome young woman stepped out of a motor-car at the end of the beach, Albertine could not help turning round. And she would at once explain: "I was looking at the new flag they've put up over the bathing place. They might have spent a bit more on it! The old one was pretty moth-eaten, but I really think this one is mouldier still."

On one occasion Albertine was not content with cold indifference, and this made me all the more wretched. She knew that I was concerned about the possibility of her meeting a friend of her aunt, who had a "bad name" and came now and again to spend a few days with Mme Bontemps. Albertine had pleased me by telling me that she would not speak to her again. And when this woman came to Incarville Albertine would say: "By the way, you know she's here. Have they told you?" as though to show me that she was not seeing her in secret. One day, when she told me this, she added: "Yes, I ran into her on the beach, and knocked against her as I passed, on purpose, to be rude to her." When Albertine told me this, there came back to my mind a remark made by Mme Bontemps, to which I had never given a second thought, when she had said to Mme Swann in my presence how brazen her niece Albertine was, as though that were a merit, and how Albertine reminded the wife of some official or other that her father had been a kitchen-boy. But a thing said by the woman we love does not long retain its purity; it cankers, it putrefies. An evening or two later, I thought again of Albertine's remark, and it was no longer the ill-breeding of which she boasted—and which could only make me smile—that it seemed to me to signify; it was something else, to wit that Albertine, perhaps even without any precise object, to tease this woman's senses, or wantonly to remind her of former propositions, accepted perhaps in the past, had swiftly brushed against her, had thought that I had perhaps heard of this as it had been done in public, and had wished to forestall an unfavourable interpretation.

However, the jealousy that was caused me by the women whom Albertine perhaps loved was abruptly to cease.

Albertine and I were waiting at the Balbec station of the little local railway. We had driven there in the hotel omnibus, because it was raining. Not far away from us was M. Nissim Bernard, who had a black eye. He had recently forsaken the chorister from *Athalie* for the waiter at a much frequented farmhouse in the neighbourhood, known as the "Cherry Orchard." This rubicund youth, with his blunt features, appeared for all the world to have

a tomato instead of a head. A tomato exactly similar
served as head to his twin brother. To the detached ob-
server, the charm of these perfect resemblances between
twins is that nature, as if momentarily industrialised,
seems to be turning out identical products. Unfortunately
M. Nissim Bernard looked at it from another point of
view, and this resemblance was only external. Tomato
No. 2 showed a frenzied zeal in catering exclusively to the
pleasures of ladies; Tomato No. I was not averse to com-
plying with the tastes of certain gentlemen. Now on every
occasion when, stirred, as though by a reflex, by the
memory of pleasant hours spent with Tomato No. I,
M. Bernard presented himself at the Cherry Orchard, being short-sighted (not that one had to be short-sighted to
mistake them), the old Jewish gentleman, unwittingly
playing Amphitryon, would accost the twin brother with:
"Will you meet me somewhere this evening?" He at once
received a thorough "hiding." It might even be repeated
in the course of a single meal, when he continued with the
second brother a conversation he had begun with the first.
In the end this treatment, by association of ideas, so put
him off tomatoes, even of the edible variety, that whenever he heard a newcomer order that vegetable at a neighbouring table in the Grand Hotel, he would murmur to
him: "You must excuse me, Monsieur, for addressing you
without an introduction. But I heard you order tomatoes.
They are bad today. I tell you in your own interest, for it
makes no difference to me, I never touch them myself."
The stranger would thank this philanthropic and disinterested neighbour effusively, call back the waiter, and pretend to have changed his mind: "No, on second thoughts,
definitely no tomatoes." Aimé, who had seen it all before,

would laugh to himself, and think: "He's an old rascal, that Monsieur Bernard, he's gone and made another of them change his order." M. Bernard, as he waited for the already overdue train, showed no eagerness to speak to Albertine and myself, because of his black eye. We were even less eager to speak to him. It would however have been almost inevitable if, at that moment, a bicycle had not come swooping towards us; the lift-boy sprang from its saddle, out of breath. Mme Verdurin had telephoned shortly after we left the hotel, to know whether I would dine with her two days later; we shall presently see why. Then, having given me the message in detail, the lift-boy left us, explaining, as one of those democratic "employees" who affect independence with regard to the gentry and restore the principle of authority among themselves, "I must be off, because of my chiefs."

Albertine's friends had gone away for some time. I was anxious to provide her with distractions. Even supposing that she might have found some happiness in spending the afternoons with no company but my own, at Balbec, I knew that such happiness is never complete and that Albertine, being still at the age (which some people never outgrow) when one has not yet discovered that this imperfection resides in the person who experiences the happiness and not in the person who gives it, might have been tempted to trace the cause of her disappointment back to me. I preferred that she should impute it to circumstances which, arranged by myself, would not give us an opportunity of being alone together, while at the same time preventing her from remaining in the Casino and on the beach without me. And so I had asked her that day to come with me to Doncières, where I was going to meet

Saint-Loup. With the same object of keeping her occupied, I advised her to take up painting, in which she had had lessons in the past. While working she would not ask herself whether she was happy or unhappy. I would gladly have taken her also to dine now and again with the Verdurins and the Cambremers, who certainly would have been delighted to see any friend introduced by myself, but I must first make certain that Mme Putbus was not yet at La Raspelière. It was only by going there in person that I could make sure of this, and, as I knew beforehand that on the next day but one Albertine would be going on a visit with her aunt, I had seized this opportunity to send Mme Verdurin a telegram asking her whether I could visit her on Wednesday. If Mme Putbus was there, I would contrive to see her maid, ascertain whether there was any danger of her coming to Balbec, and if so find out when, so as to take Albertine out of reach on that day. The little local railway, making a loop which did not exist at the time when I had taken it with my grandmother, now extended to Doncières-la-Goupil, a big station at which important trains stopped, among them the express by which I had come down to visit Saint-Loup from Paris and thence returned. And, because of the bad weather, the omnibus from the Grand Hotel took Albertine and myself to the station of Balbec-Plage.

The little train had not yet arrived, but one could see the lazy, sluggish plume of smoke which it had left in its wake and which now, reduced to its own power of locomotion as a not very mobile cloud, was slowly mounting the green slope of the cliff of Criquetot. Finally the little train, which it had preceded by taking a vertical course, arrived in its turn, at a leisurely crawl. The passengers

who were waiting to board it stepped back to make way
for it, but without hurrying, knowing that they were dealing with a good-natured, almost human stroller, who,
guided like the bicycle of a beginner by the obliging signals of the station-master, under the capable supervision
of the engine-driver, was in no danger of running over
anybody, and would come to a halt at the proper place.

My telegram explained the Verdurins' telephone message and had been all the more opportune since Wednesday (the next day but one happened to be a Wednesday)
was the day set apart for big dinner-parties by Mme Verdurin, at La Raspelière as in Paris, a fact of which I was
unaware. Mme Verdurin did not give "dinners," but she
had "Wednesdays." These Wednesdays were works of
art. While fully conscious that they had not their match
anywhere, Mme Verdurin introduced shades of distinction
between them. "Last Wednesday wasn't as good as the
one before," she would say. "But I believe the next will
be one of the most successful I've ever given." Sometimes
she went so far as to admit: "This Wednesday wasn't
worthy of the others. But I have a big surprise for you
next week." In the closing weeks of the Paris season, before leaving for the country, the Mistress would announce
the approaching end of the Wednesdays. It gave her an
opportunity to spur on the faithful. "There are only three
more Wednesdays left," or "Only two more," she would
say, in the same tone as though the world were coming to
an end. "You aren't going to let us down next Wednesday, for the finale." But this finale was a sham, for she
would announce: "Officially, there will be no more
Wednesdays. Today was the last for this year. But I shall
be at home all the same on Wednesday. We'll celebrate

Wednesday by ourselves; I dare say these little private Wednesdays will be the nicest of all." At La Raspelière, the Wednesdays were of necessity restricted, and since, if they met a friend who was passing that way, they would invite him for any evening he chose, almost every day of the week became a Wednesday. "I don't remember all the guests, but I know there's Madame la Marquise de Camembert," the lift-boy had told me; his memory of our discussion of the name Cambremer had not succeeded in conclusively supplanting that of the old word, whose syllables, familiar and full of meaning, came to the young employee's rescue when he was flummoxed by this difficult name, and were immediately preferred and readopted by him, not from laziness or as an old and ineradicable usage, but because of the need for logic and clarity which they satisfied.

We hastened in search of an empty carriage in which I could hold Albertine in my arms throughout the journey. Having failed to find one, we got into a compartment in which there was already installed a lady with a massive face, old and ugly, and a masculine expression, very much in her Sunday best, who was reading the *Revue des Deux Mondes*. Notwithstanding her vulgarity, she was ladylike in her gestures, and I amused myself wondering to what social category she could belong; I at once concluded that she must be the manageress of some large brothel, a procuress on holiday. Her face and her manner proclaimed the fact aloud. Only, I had hitherto been unaware that such ladies read the *Revue des Deux Mondes*. Albertine drew my attention to her with a wink and a smile. The lady wore an air of extreme dignity; and as I, for my part, was inwardly aware that I was invited, two days hence, to

the house of the celebrated Mme Verdurin at the terminal
point of the little railway line, that at an intermediate station I was awaited by Robert de Saint-Loup, and that a
little further on I would have given great pleasure to Mme
de Cambremer by going to stay at Féterne, my eyes
sparkled with irony as I gazed at this self-important lady
who seemed to think that, because of her elaborate attire,
the feathers in her hat, her *Revue des Deux Mondes*, she
was a more considerable personage than myself. I hoped
that the lady would not remain in the train much longer
than M. Nissim Bernard, and that she would alight at
least at Toutainville, but no. The train stopped at Epreville, and she remained seated. Similarly at Montmartin-
sur-Mer, at Parville-la-Bingard, at Incarville, so that in
desperation, when the train had left Saint-Frichoux, which
was the last station before Doncières, I began to embrace
Albertine without bothering about the lady.

At Doncières, Saint-Loup had come to meet me at
the station, with the greatest difficulty, he told me, for, as
he was staying with his aunt, my telegram had only just
reached him and he could not, having been unable to
make any arrangements beforehand, spare me more than
an hour of his time. This hour seemed to me, alas, far too
long, for as soon as we had left the train Albertine devoted her attention exclusively to Saint-Loup. She did not
say a word to me, barely answered me if I addressed her,
repulsed me when I approached her. With Robert, on the
other hand, she laughed her provoking laugh, she talked
to him volubly, played with the dog he had brought with
him, and, while teasing the animal, deliberately rubbed
against its master. I remembered that, on the day when
Albertine had allowed me to kiss her for the first time, I

had smiled with inward gratitude towards the unknown seducer who had wrought so profound a change in her and had so simplified my task. I thought of him now with horror. Robert must have realised that I was not indifferent to Albertine, for he did not respond to her advances, which put her in a bad humour with myself; then he spoke to me as though I was alone, and this, when she noticed it, raised me again in her esteem. Robert asked me if I would like to try and find, among the friends with whom he used to take me to dine every evening at Doncières when I was staying there, those who were still in the garrison. And as he himself indulged in that sort of teasing affectation which he reproved in others, "What's the good of your having worked so hard to *charm* them if you don't want to see them again?" he asked. I declined his offer, for I did not wish to run the risk of being parted from Albertine, but also because now I was detached from them. From them, which is to say from myself. We passionately long for there to be another life in which we shall be similar to what we are here below. But we do not pause to reflect that, even without waiting for that other life, in this life, after a few years, we are unfaithful to what we once were, to what we wished to remain immortally. Even without supposing that death is to alter us more completely than the changes that occur in the course of our lives, if in that other life we were to encounter the self that we have been, we should turn away from ourselves as from those people with whom we were once on friendly terms but whom we have not seen for years— such as Saint-Loup's friends whom I used so much to enjoy meeting every evening at the Faisan Doré, and whose conversation would now have seemed to me merely a bor-

ing importunity. In this respect, and because I preferred
not to go there in search of what had given me pleasure in
the past, a stroll through Doncières might have seemed to
me a prefiguration of an arrival in paradise. We dream
much of paradise, or rather of a number of successive par-
adises, but each of them is, long before we die, a paradise
lost, in which we should feel ourselves lost too.

He left us at the station. "But you may have nearly
an hour to wait," he told me. "If you spend it here, you'll
probably see my uncle Charlus, who is catching the train
to Paris, ten minutes before yours. I've already said good-
bye to him, because I have to be back before his train
leaves. I didn't tell him about you, because I hadn't got
your telegram."

To the reproaches which I heaped upon her when
Saint-Loup had left us, Albertine replied that she had intended, by her coldness towards me, to dispel any idea
that he might have formed if, at the moment when the
train stopped, he had seen me leaning against her with my
arm round her waist. He had indeed noticed this attitude
(I had not caught sight of him, otherwise I should have
sat up decorously beside Albertine), and had had time to
murmur in my ear: "So *that's* one of those priggish little
girls you told me about, who wouldn't go near Mlle de
Stermaria because they thought her fast?" I had indeed
mentioned to Robert, and in all sincerity, when I went
down from Paris to visit him at Doncières, and when we
were talking about our time at Balbec, that there was
nothing to be done with Albertine, that she was virtue itself. And now that I had long since discovered for myself
that this was false, I was even more anxious that Robert
should believe it to be true. It would have been sufficient

for me to tell Robert that I was in love with Albertine. He was one of those people who are capable of denying themselves a pleasure to spare a friend sufferings which they would feel as though they were their own. "Yes, she's still rather childish. But you don't know anything against her?" I added anxiously. "Nothing, except that I saw you clinging together like a pair of lovers."

"Your attitude dispelled absolutely nothing," I told Albertine when Saint-Loup had left us. "Quite true," she said to me, "it was stupid of me, I hurt your feelings, I'm far more unhappy about it than you are. You'll see, I shall never be like that again; forgive me," she pleaded, holding out her hand with a sorrowful air. At that moment, from the waiting-room in which we were sitting, I saw M. de Charlus pass slowly by, followed at a respectful distance by a porter loaded with his baggage.

In Paris, where I encountered him only at evening receptions, immobile, strapped up in dress-clothes, maintained in a vertical posture by his proud erectness, his eagerness to be admired, his conversational verve, I had not realised how much he had aged. Now, in a light travelling suit which made him appear stouter, as he waddled along with his swaying paunch and almost symbolic behind, the cruel light of day decomposed, into paint on his lips, into face-powder fixed by cold cream on the tip of his nose, into mascara on his dyed moustache whose ebony hue contrasted with his grizzled hair, everything that in artificial light would have seemed the healthy complexion of a man who was still young.

While I stood talking to him, though briefly, because of his train, I kept my eye on Albertine's carriage to show her that I was coming. When I turned my head towards

M. de Charlus, he asked me to be so kind as to summon
a soldier, a relative of his, who was standing on the opposite platform, as though he were waiting to take our train,
but in the opposite direction, away from Balbec. "He is in
the regimental band," said M. de Charlus. "As you are so
fortunate as to be still young enough, and I unfortunately
am old enough for you to save me the trouble of going
across to him . . ." I felt obliged to go across to the soldier in question, and saw from the lyres embroidered on
his collar that he was a bandsman. But, just as I was
preparing to execute my commission, what was my surprise, and, I may say, my pleasure, on recognising Morel,
the son of my uncle's valet, who recalled to me so many
memories. They made me forget to convey M. de Charlus's message. "What, are you at Doncières?" "Yes, and
they've put me in the band attached to the artillery." But
he made this answer in a dry and haughty tone. He had
become an intense "poseur," and evidently the sight of
myself, reminding him of his father's profession, was displeasing to him. Suddenly I saw M. de Charlus bearing
down on us. My dilatoriness had evidently taxed his patience. "I should like to listen to a little music this
evening," he said to Morel without any preliminaries. "I
pay five hundred francs for the evening, which may perhaps be of interest to one of your friends, if you have any
in the band." Knowing as I did the insolence of M. de
Charlus, I was none the less astonished at his not even
bidding good-day to his young friend. He did not however give me time for reflexion. Holding out his hand to
me affectionately, "Good-bye, my dear fellow," he said,
implying that I might now leave them. I had in any case
left my dear Albertine too long alone. "D'you know," I

said to her as I climbed into the carriage, "the seaside life
and the life of travel make me realise that the theatre of
the world is stocked with fewer settings than actors, and
with fewer actors than situations." "What makes you say
that?" "Because M. de Charlus asked me just now to
fetch one of his friends, whom this instant, on the platform of this station, I have just discovered to be one of
my own." But as I uttered these words, I began to wonder
how the Baron could have bridged the social gulf to which
I had not given a thought. It occurred to me first of all
that it might be through Jupien, whose niece, as the
reader may remember, had seemed to become enamoured
of the violinist. However, what baffled me completely was
that, when due to leave for Paris in five minutes, the
Baron should have asked for a musical evening. But, visualising Jupien's niece again in my memory, I was beginning to think that "recognitions" might indeed express an
important part of life, if one knew how to penetrate to the
romantic core of things, when all of a sudden the truth
flashed across my mind and I realised that I had been absurdly ingenuous. M. de Charlus had never in his life set
eyes upon Morel, nor Morel upon M. de Charlus, who,
dazzled but also intimidated by a soldier even though he
carried no weapon but a lyre, in his agitation had called
upon me to bring him a person whom he never suspected
that I already knew. In any case, for Morel, the offer of
five hundred francs must have made up for the absence of
any previous relations, for I saw that they were going on
talking, oblivious of the fact that they were standing close
beside our train. And remembering the manner in which
M. de Charlus had come up to Morel and myself, I saw
at once the resemblance to certain of his relatives when

they picked up a woman in the street. The desired object
had merely changed sex. After a certain age, and even if
we develop in quite different ways, the more we become
ourselves, the more our family traits are accentuated. For
Nature, even while harmoniously fashioning the design of
its tapestry, breaks the monotony of the composition
thanks to the variety of the faces it catches. Besides, the
haughtiness with which M. de Charlus had eyed the violinist is relative, and depends upon the point of view one
adopts. It would have been recognised by three out of
four society people, who bowed to him, not by the prefect
of police who, a few years later, was to keep him under
surveillance.

"The Paris train has been signalled, sir," said the
porter who was carrying his suitcases. "But I'm not taking
the train; put them in the cloakroom, damn you!" said
M. de Charlus, giving twenty francs to the porter, who was
astonished by the change of plan and charmed by the tip.
This generosity at once attracted a flower-seller. "Take
these carnations, look, this lovely rose, kind gentleman, it
will bring you luck." M. de Charlus, exasperated, handed
her a couple of francs, in exchange for which the woman
gave him her blessing, and her flowers as well. "Good
God, why can't she leave us alone," said M. de Charlus,
addressing himself to Morel in an ironically querulous
tone, as though he were at the end of his tether and found
a certain comfort in appealing to him for support; "what
we have to say to each other is quite complicated enough
as it is." Perhaps, the porter not yet being out of earshot,
M. de Charlus did not care to have too numerous an audience; perhaps these incidental remarks enabled his lofty
timidity not to broach too directly the request for an

assignation. The musician, turning with a frank, imperious and determined air to the flower-seller, raised a hand
which repulsed her and indicated to her that her flowers
were not wanted and that she was to clear off at once.
M. de Charlus observed with ecstasy this authoritative,
virile gesture, wielded by the graceful hand for which it
ought still to have been too weighty, too massively brutal,
with a precocious firmness and suppleness which gave to
this still beardless adolescent the air of a young David capable of challenging Goliath. The Baron's admiration was
unconsciously blended with the sort of smile with which
we observe in a child an expression of gravity beyond his
years. "*There's* somebody I should like to have to accompany me on my travels and help me in my business. How
he would simplify my life," M. de Charlus said to himself.

The train for Paris started, without M. de Charlus.
Then Albertine and I took our seats in our own train,
without my discovering what had become of M. de Charlus and Morel. "We must never quarrel any more, I beg
your pardon again," Albertine said to me, alluding to the
Saint-Loup incident. "We must always be nice to each
other," she added tenderly. "As for your friend Saint-
Loup, if you think that I'm the least bit interested in him,
you're quite mistaken. All that I like about him is that he
seems so very fond of you." "He's a very good fellow," I
said, taking care not to attribute to Robert those imaginary excellences which I should not have failed to invent,
out of friendship for him, had I been with anybody but
Albertine. "He's an excellent creature, frank, devoted,
loyal, someone you can rely on in any circumstances." In
saying this I confined myself, restrained by my jealousy,

to speaking the truth about Saint-Loup, but what I said was indeed the truth. But it expressed itself in precisely the same terms as Mme de Villeparisis had used in speaking to me of him, when I did not yet know him, imagined him to be so different, so proud, and said to myself: "People think him kind because he's a blue-blooded nobleman." In the same way, when she had said to me: "He would be so pleased," I thought to myself, after seeing him outside the hotel preparing to take the reins, that his aunt's words had been mere social banality, intended to flatter me. And I had realised afterwards that she had spoken sincerely, thinking of the things that interested me, of my reading, and because she knew that that was what Saint-Loup liked, as it was later to happen to me to say sincerely to somebody who was writing a history of his ancestor La Rochefoucauld, the author of the *Maximes*, and wished to consult Robert about him: "He will be so pleased." It was simply that I had learned to know him. But, when I set eyes on him for the first time, I had not supposed that an intelligence akin to my own could be enveloped in so much outward elegance of dress and attitude. By his feathers I had judged him to be a bird of another species. It was Albertine now who, perhaps a little because Saint-Loup, out of kindness to myself, had been so cold to her, said to me what I had once thought: "Ah, he's as devoted as all that! I notice that people are invariably credited with all the virtues when they belong to the Faubourg Saint-Germain." And yet, the fact that Saint-Loup belonged to the Faubourg Saint-Germain was something I had never once thought of again in the course of all these years in which, stripping himself of his prestige, he had demonstrated his virtues to

me. Such a change of perspective in looking at other people, more striking already in friendship than in merely social relations, is all the more striking still in love, where
desire so enlarges the scale, so magnifies the proportions
of the slightest signs of coldness, that it had required far
less than Saint-Loup had shown at first sight for me to
believe myself disdained at first by Albertine, to imagine
her friends as fabulously inhuman creatures, and to as-
cribe Elstir's judgment, when he said to me of the little
band with exactly the same sentiment as Mme de
Villeparisis speaking of Saint-Loup: "They're good girls,"
simply to the indulgence people have for beauty and a
certain elegance. Yet was this not the verdict I would automatically have expressed when I heard Albertine say:
"In any case, whether he's devoted or not, I sincerely
hope I shall never see him again, since he's made us quarrel. We must never quarrel again. It isn't nice." Since she
had seemed to desire Saint-Loup, I felt more or less cured
for the time being of the idea that she cared for women,
assuming that the two things were irreconcilable. And,
looking at Albertine's mackintosh, in which she seemed to
have become another person, the tireless vagrant of rainy
days, and which, close-fitting, malleable and grey, seemed
at that moment not so much intended to protect her
clothes from the rain as to have been soaked by it and to
be clinging to her body as though to take the imprint of
her form for a sculptor, I tore off that tunic which jealously enwrapped a longed-for breast and, drawing Albertine towards me:

"But won't you, indolent traveller, rest your head
And dream your dreams upon my shoulder?"

I said, taking her head in my hands, and showing her the wide meadows, flooded and silent, which extended in the gathering dusk to a horizon closed by the parallel chains of distant blue hills.

Two days later, on the famous Wednesday, in that same little train which I had again taken at Balbec to go and dine at La Raspelière, I was extremely anxious not to miss Cottard at Graincourt-Saint-Vast, where a second telephone message from Mme Verdurin had told me that I should find him. He was to join my train and would tell me where we had to get out to pick up the carriages that would be sent from La Raspelière to the station. And so, as the little train stopped for only a moment at Graincourt, the first station after Doncières, I had posted myself in readiness at the open window for fear of not seeing Cottard or of his not seeing me. Vain fears! I had not realised to what an extent the little clan had moulded all its regular members after the same type, so that, as they stood waiting on the platform, being moreover in full evening dress, they were immediately recognisable by a certain air of assurance, elegance and familiarity, by a look in their eyes which seemed to sweep across the serried ranks of the common herd as across an empty space in which there was nothing to arrest their attention, watching for the arrival of some fellow-member who had taken the train at an earlier station, and sparkling in anticipation of the talk that was to come. This sign of election, with which the habit of dining together had marked the members of the little group, was not all that distinguished them when they were massed together in full strength, forming a more brilliant patch in the midst of the troop of

passengers—what Brichot called the *pecus*, the herd—
upon whose drab faces could be discerned no notion relating to the name Verdurin, no hope of ever dining at La
Raspelière. To be sure, these common travellers would
have been less interested than myself—notwithstanding
the fame that several of the faithful had achieved—had
anyone quoted in their hearing the names of these men
whom I was astonished to see continuing to dine out
when many of them had already been doing so, according
to the stories that I had heard, before my birth, at a period at once so distant and so vague that I was inclined to
exaggerate its remoteness. The contrast between the con-
tinuance not only of their existence, but of the fullness of
their powers, and the obliteration of so many friends
whom I had already seen vanish here or there, gave me
the same feeling that we experience when in the stop-
press column of the newspapers we read the very announcement that we least expected, for instance that of an
untimely death, which seems to us fortuitous because the
causes that have led up to it have remained outside our
knowledge. This is the feeling that death does not descend uniformly upon all men, but that a more advanced
wave of its tragic tide carries off a life situated at the same
level as others which the waves that follow will long continue to spare. We shall see later on that the diversity of
the forms of death that circulate invisibly is the cause of
the peculiar unexpectedness of obituary notices in the
newspapers. Then I saw that, with the passage of time,
not only do real talents that may coexist with the most
commonplace conversation reveal and impose themselves,
but furthermore that mediocre persons arrive at those exalted positions, attached in the imagination of our child-

hood to certain famous elders, when it never occurred to us that a certain number of years later, their disciples, now become masters, would be famous too, and would inspire the respect and awe that they themselves once felt. But if the names of the faithful were unknown to the *pecus*, their aspect still singled them out in its eyes. Even in the train, when the coincidence of what they had been doing during the day assembled them all together, and they had only one isolated companion to collect at a subsequent station, the carriage in which they were gathered, designated by the sculptor Ski's elbow, flagged by Cottard's *Temps*, stood out from a distance like a special saloon, and rallied at the appointed station the tardy comrade. The only one who, because of his semi-blindness, might have missed these welcoming signals was Brichot. But one of the party would always volunteer to keep a look-out for him, and, as soon as his straw hat, his green umbrella and blue spectacles had been spotted, he would be gently but hastily guided towards the chosen compartment. So that it was inconceivable that one of the faithful, without exciting the gravest suspicions of his being "on the spree," or even of his not having come by the train, should not pick up the others in the course of the journey. Sometimes the opposite process occurred: one of the faithful might have had to go some distance down the line during the afternoon and would be obliged in consequence to make part of the journey alone before being joined by the group; but even when thus isolated, alone of his kind, he did not fail as a rule to produce a certain effect. The Future towards which he was travelling marked him out to the person on the seat opposite, who would say to himself "He must be somebody," and with the dim perspicacity of the travellers of Emmaus would discern a vague halo round the trilby of Cottard or of the sculptor Ski, and would be only half-astonished when at the next station an elegant crowd, if it were their terminal point, greeted the faithful one at the carriage door and escorted him to one of the waiting vehicles, all of them receiving a deep bow from the factotum of Douville station, or, if it were an intermediate station, invaded the compartment. This was what now occurred, with some precipitation, for several had arrived late, just as the train which was already in the station was about to start, with the troupe which Cottard led at the double towards the carriage at the window of which he had seen me signalling. Brichot, who was among this group of the faithful, had become more faithful than ever in the course of these years which had diminished the assiduity of others. As his sight became steadily weaker, he had been obliged, even in Paris, to reduce more and more his work after dark. Besides, he was out of sympathy with the modern Sorbonne, where ideas of scientific exactitude, after the German model, were beginning to prevail over humanism. He now confined himself exclusively to his lectures and to his duties as an examiner; hence he had a great deal more time to devote to social pursuits, that is to say to evenings at the Verdurins', or to those that now and again were given for the Verdurins by one or other of the faithful, tremulous with emotion. It is true that on two occasions love had almost succeeded in achieving what his work could no longer do: in detaching Brichot from the little clan. But Mme Verdurin, who "kept a weather eye open," and moreover, having acquired the habit in the interests of her salon, had come to take a disinterested pleasure in this

sort of drama and execution, had brought about an irremediable breach between him and the dangerous person,
being skilled (as she put it) at "putting things in order"
and "stopping the rot." This she had found all the easier
in the case of one of the dangerous persons in that the latter was simply Brichot's laundress, and Mme Verdurin,
having free access to the fifth-floor rooms of the Professor, who was crimson with pride whenever she deigned to
climb his stairs, had only had to throw the wretched
woman out. "What!" the Mistress had said to Brichot, "a
woman like myself does you the honour of calling upon
you, and you entertain a creature like that?" Brichot had
never forgotten the service that Mme Verdurin had rendered him by preventing his old age from foundering in
the mire, and became more and more attached to her,
whereas, in contrast to this renewal of affection and possibly because of it, the Mistress was beginning to be tired
of this too docile follower of whose obedience she could
be certain in advance. But Brichot acquired from his intimacy with the Verdurins a glamour which set him apart
from all his colleagues at the Sorbonne. They were dazzled by the accounts that he gave them of dinner-parties
to which they would never be invited, by the mention
made of him in the reviews, or the portrait of him exhib-
ited in the Salon, by some writer or painter of repute
whose talent the occupants of the other chairs in the Faculty of Letters esteemed but whose attention they had no
prospect of attracting, and in particular by the elegance of
the mundane philosopher's attire, an elegance which they
had mistaken at first for slovenliness until their colleague
had benevolently explained to them that a top hat could
quite acceptably be placed on the floor when one was

paying a call and was not the right thing for dinners in the country, however smart, where it should be replaced by a trilby, which was perfectly all right with a dinner-jacket.

For the first few moments after the little group had swept into the carriage, I could not even speak to Cottard, for he was completely breathless, not so much from having run in order not to miss the train as from astonishment at having caught it at the last second. He felt more than the joy of success, almost the hilarity of a merry prank. "Ah! that was a good one!" he said when he had recovered himself. "A minute later! 'Pon my soul, that's what they call arriving in the nick of time!" he added with a wink, intended not so much to inquire whether the expression was apt, for he now overflowed with confidence, but to express his self-satisfaction. At length he was able to introduce me to the other members of the little clan. I was dismayed to see that they were almost all in the dress which in Paris is called a "smoking." I had forgotten that the Verdurins were beginning to make tentative moves in the direction of fashionable ways, moves which, slowed down by the Dreyfus case, accelerated by the "new" music, they in fact denied, and would continue to deny until they were complete, like those military objectives which a general does not announce until he has reached them, so as not to appear defeated if he fails. Society for its part was quite prepared to go half-way to meet them. At the moment it had reached the point of regarding them as people to whose house nobody in Society went but who were not in the least perturbed by the fact. The Verdurin salon was understood to be a Temple of Music. It was there, people affirmed, that Vinteuil had found inspiration and encouragement. And although Vinteuil's sonata remained wholly unappreciated and almost unknown, his name, referred to as that of the greatest contemporary composer, enjoyed an extraordinary prestige. Finally, certain young men of the Faubourg having decided that they ought to be as well educated as the middle classes, three of them had studied music and among these Vinteuil's sonata enjoyed an enormous vogue. They would speak of it, on returning to their homes, to the intelligent mothers who had encouraged them to improve their minds. And, taking an interest in their sons' studies, these mothers would gaze with a certain respect at Mme Verdurin in her front box at concerts, following the music from the score. So far, this latent social success of the Verdurins had expressed itself in two facts only. In the first place, Mme Verdurin would say of the Princesse de Caprarola: "Ah! she's intelligent, that one, she's a charming woman. What I cannot endure are the imbeciles, the people who bore me—they drive me mad." Which would have made anybody at all perspicacious realise that the Princesse de Caprarola, a woman who moved in the highest society, had called upon Mme Verdurin. She had even mentioned the Verdurins' name in the course of a visit of condolence which she had paid to Mme Swann after the death of her husband, and had asked whether she knew them. "What name did you say?" Odette had asked with sudden wistfulness. "Verdurin? Oh, yes, of course," she had continued glumly, "I don't know them, or rather, I know them without really knowing them, they're people I used to meet with friends years ago, they're quite nice." When the Princesse de Caprarola had gone, Odette regretted not having told the bare truth. But the immediate falsehood

was not the fruit of her calculations, but the revelation of
her fears and her desires. She denied not what it would
have been adroit to deny, but what she would have liked
not to be the case, even if her interlocutor was bound to
hear an hour later that it was indeed the case. A little
later she had recovered her self-assurance, and would even
anticipate questions by saying, so as not to appear to be
afraid of them: "Mme Verdurin, why, I used to know her
terribly well," with an affectation of humility, like a great
lady who tells you that she has taken the tram. "There
has been a great deal of talk about the Verdurins lately,"
Mme de Souvré would remark. Odette, with the smiling
disdain of a duchess, would reply: "Yes, I do seem to
have heard a lot about them lately. Every now and then
there are new people like that who arrive in society,"
without reflecting that she herself was among the newest.
"The Princesse de Caprarola has dined there," Mme de
Souvré would continue. "Ah!" Odette would reply, accentuating her smile, "that doesn't surprise me. That sort of
thing always begins with the Princesse de Caprarola, and
then someone else follows suit, like Comtesse Molé."
Odette, in saying this, appeared to be filled with a profound contempt for the two great ladies who made a habit
of "house-warming" in recently established salons. One
felt from her tone that the implication was that she,
Odette, like Mme de Souvré, was not the sort of person to
let herself in for that sort of thing.

After the admission that Mme Verdurin had made of
the Princesse de Caprarola's intelligence, the second indication that the Verdurins were conscious of their future
destiny was that (without, of course, their having formally
requested it) they were most anxious that people should

now come to dine with them in evening dress. M. Verdurin could now have been greeted without shame by his
nephew, the one who was "a wash-out."

Among those who entered my carriage at Graincourt
was Saniette, who long ago had been driven from the Verdurins' by his cousin Forcheville, but had since returned.
His faults, from the social point of view, had originally
been—notwithstanding his superior qualities—somewhat
similar to Cottard's: shyness, anxiety to please, fruitless
attempts to succeed in doing so. But if the course of life,
by making Cottard assume (if not at the Verdurins',
where, because of the influence that past associations exert
over us when we find ourselves in familiar surroundings,
he had remained more or less the same, at least in his
practice, in his hospital work, and at the Academy of
Medicine) an outer shell of coldness, disdain, gravity, that
became more and more pronounced as he trotted out his
puns to his indulgent students, had created a veritable
gulf between the old Cottard and the new, the same defects had on the contrary become more extreme in Saniette the more he sought to correct them. Conscious that
he was frequently boring, that people did not listen to
him, instead of then slackening his pace as Cottard would
have done, and forcing their attention by an air of authority, not only did he try to win forgiveness for the unduly
serious turn of his conversation by adopting a playful
tone, but he speeded up his delivery, rushed his remarks,
used abbreviations in order to appear less long-winded,
more familiar with the matters of which he spoke, and
succeeded only, by making them unintelligible, in appearing interminable. His self-assurance was not like that of
Cottard, who so petrified his patients that when other

people lauded his social affability they would reply: "He's a different man when he receives you in his consulting room, you with your face to the light, and he with his back to it, and those piercing eyes." It failed to make any effect, one felt that it cloaked an excessive shyness, that the merest trifle would be enough to dispel it. Saniette, whose friends had always told him that he was wanting in self-confidence, and who had indeed seen men whom he rightly considered greatly inferior to himself obtain with ease the successes that were denied to him, now never began a story without smiling at its drollery, fearing lest a serious air might make his hearers underestimate the value of his wares. Sometimes, taking on trust the humour which he himself appeared to see in what he was about to say, his audience would oblige him with a general silence. But the story would fall flat. A kind-hearted fellow-guest would sometimes give Saniette the private, almost secret encouragement of a smile of approbation, conveying it to him furtively, without attracting attention, as one slips a note into someone's hand. But nobody went so far as to assume the responsibility, to risk the public backing of an honest laugh. Long after the story was ended and had fallen flat, Saniette, crestfallen, would remain smiling to himself, as though relishing in it and for himself the delectation which he pretended to find adequate and which the others had not felt.

As for the sculptor Ski—so styled on account of the difficulty they found in pronouncing his Polish surname, and because he himself, since he had begun to move in a certain social sphere, affected not to wish to be associated with his perfectly respectable but slightly boring and very numerous relations—he had, at forty-five and distinctly

ugly, a sort of boyishness, a dreamy wistfulness which
was the result of his having been, until the age of ten, the
most ravishing child prodigy imaginable, the darling of all
the ladies. Mme Verdurin maintained that he was more of
an artist than Elstir. Any resemblance that there may
have been between them was, however, purely external. It
was sufficient to make Elstir, who had met Ski once, feel
for him the profound repulsion that is inspired in us not
so much by the people who are completely different from
us as by those who are less satisfactory versions of ourselves, in whom are displayed our less attractive qualities,
the faults of which we have cured ourselves, unpleasantly
reminding us of how we must have appeared to certain
other people before we became what we now are. But
Mme Verdurin thought that Ski had more temperament
than Elstir because there was no art in which he did not
have some aptitude, and she was convinced that he would
have developed that aptitude into talent if he had been
less indolent. This indolence seemed to the Mistress to be
actually an additional gift, being the opposite of hard
work which she regarded as the lot of people devoid of
genius. Ski would paint anything you asked, on cuff-links
or on lintels. He sang like a professional and played from
memory, giving the piano the effect of an orchestra, less
by his virtuosity than by his vamped basses which suggested the inability of the fingers to indicate that at a certain point the cornet entered, which in any case he would
imitate with his lips. Searching for words when he spoke
so as to convey an interesting impression, just as he
would pause before banging out a chord with the exclamation "Ping!" to bring out the brass, he was regarded as
being marvellously intelligent, but as a matter of fact his

ideas boiled down to two or three, extremely limited. Bored with his reputation for whimsicality, he had taken it into his head to show that he was a practical, down-to-earth person, whence a triumphant affectation of fake precision, of fake common sense, aggravated by his having no memory and a fund of information that was always inaccurate. The movements of his head, his neck and his limbs would have been graceful if he had still been nine years old, with golden curls, a wide lace collar and red leather bootees. Having arrived at Graincourt station in the company of Cottard and Brichot with time to spare, he and Cottard had left Brichot in the waiting-room and had gone for a stroll. When Cottard proposed to turn back, Ski had replied: "But there's no hurry. It isn't the local train today, it's the departmental train." Delighted by the effect that this refinement of accuracy produced upon Cottard, he added, with reference to himself: "Yes, because Ski loves the arts, because he models in clay, people think he's not practical. Nobody knows this line better than I do." Nevertheless, when they had turned back towards the station, Cottard, all of a sudden catching sight of the smoke of the approaching train, had let out a bellow and exclaimed: "We shall have to run like the wind." And they had in fact arrived with not a moment to spare, the distinction between local and departmental trains having never existed except in the mind of Ski.

"But isn't the Princess on the train?" came in ringing tones from Brichot, whose huge spectacles, glittering like the reflectors that throat specialists attach to their foreheads to see into their patients' larynxes, seemed to have taken their life from the Professor's eyes, and, possibly because of the effort he made to adjust his sight to them, seemed themselves to be looking, even at the most trivial moments, with sustained attention and extraordinary fixity. Brichot's malady, as it gradually deprived him of his sight, had revealed to him the beauties of that sense, just as, frequently, we have to make up our minds to part with some object, to make a present of it for instance, in order to study it, regret it, admire it.

"No, no, the Princess went over to Maineville with some of Mme Verdurin's guests who were taking the Paris train. It isn't beyond the bounds of possibility that Mme Verdurin, who had some business at Saint-Mars, may be with her! In that case, she'll be coming with us, and we shall all travel together, which will be delightful. We shall have to keep our eyes skinned at Maineville and see what we shall see! Ah, well, never mind—we certainly came very near to missing the bus. When I saw the train I was flabbergasted. That's what you call arriving at the psychological moment. What if we'd missed the train and Mme Verdurin had seen the carriages come back without us? You can just picture it," added the doctor, who had not yet recovered from his excitement. "I must say we really are having quite a jaunt. Eh, Brichot, what have you to say about our little escapade?" inquired the doctor with a note of pride.

"Upon my soul," replied Brichot, "why, yes, if you'd found the train gone, that would have taken the gilt off the trumpets, as Villemain, our late professor of eloquence, would have said."

But I, engrossed from the very first by these people whom I did not know, was suddenly reminded of what Cottard had said to me in the ballroom of the little casino, and, as though it were possible for an invisible link to join an organ to the images of one's memory, the image of Albertine pressing her breasts against Andrée's brought a terrible pain to my heart. This pain did not last: the idea of Albertine's having relations with women seemed no longer possible since the occasion, forty-eight hours earlier, when the advances she had made to Saint-Loup had excited in me a new jealousy which had made me forget the old. I was innocent enough to believe that one taste necessarily excludes another.

At Harambouville, as the train was full, a farm labourer in a blue smock who had only a third-class ticket got into our compartment. The doctor, feeling that the Princess could not be allowed to travel with such a person, called a porter, showed a card which described him as medical officer to one of the big railway companies, and obliged the station-master to eject the intruder. This incident so pained and alarmed Saniette's timid spirit that, as soon as he saw it beginning, fearing already lest, in view of the crowd of peasants on the platform, it should assume the proportions of a popular uprising, he pretended to be suffering from a stomach-ache, and to avoid being accused of any share in the responsibility for the doctor's violence, rushed down the corridor pretending to be looking for what Cottard called the "waters." Failing to find it, he stood and gazed at the scenery from the other end of the "twister."

"If this is your first appearance at Mme Verdurin's, Monsieur," Brichot said to me, anxious to show off his talents before a newcomer, "you will find that there is no place where one feels more the *douceur de vivre*, to quote one of the inventors of dilettantism, of pococurantism, of all sorts of 'isms' that are in fashion among our little snoblings—I refer to M. le Prince de Talleyrand." For, when he spoke of these great noblemen of the past, he felt that it was witty and added "period colour" to prefix their titles with "Monsieur," and said "M. le Duc de La Rochefoucauld," "M. le Cardinal de Retz," referring to these from time to time also as "That *struggle for life*r de Gondi," "that *Boulangist* de Marcillac." And he never failed, when referring to Montesquieu, to call him, with a smile, "Monsieur le Président Secondat de Montesquieu." An intelligent man of society would have been irritated by this pedantry, which reeked of the lecture-room. But in the perfect manners of the man of society there is a pedantry too, when speaking of a prince, which betrays a different caste, that in which one prefixes the name "William" with "the Emperor" and addresses a Royal Highness in the third person. "Ah, now, that is a man," Brichot continued, still referring to "Monsieur le Prince de Talleyrand," "to whom we take off our hats. He is an ancestor."

"It's a delightful circle," Cottard told me, "you'll find a little of everything, for Mme Verdurin is not exclusive—distinguished scholars like Brichot, the nobility, for example, Princess Sherbatoff, an aristocratic Russian lady, a friend of the Grand Duchess Eudoxie, who even sees her alone at hours when no one else is admitted."

As a matter of fact the Grand Duchess Eudoxie, not wishing Princess Sherbatoff, who for years past had been ostracised by everyone, to come to her house when there might be other people, allowed her to come only in the early morning, when Her Imperial Highness was not at home to any of those friends to whom it would have been as disagreeable to meet the Princess as it would have been

awkward for the Princess to meet them. Since, for the last
three years, as soon as she came away from the Grand
Duchess, like a manicurist, Mme Sherbatoff would go to
Mme Verdurin, who had just woken up, and stick to her
for the rest of the day, one might say that the Princess's
loyalty surpassed even that of Brichot, constant as he was
at those Wednesdays, both in Paris, where he had the
pleasure of fancying himself a sort of Chateaubriand at
l'Abbaye-aux-Bois,[10] and in the country, where he saw
himself becoming the equivalent of what the man whom
he always referred to (with the knowing sarcasm of the
man of letters) as "M. de Voltaire" must have been in the
salon of Mme du Châtelet.

Her want of friends had enabled Princess Sherbatoff
for some years past to display towards the Verdurins a fidelity which made her more than an ordinary member of
the "faithful," the classic example of the breed, the ideal
which Mme Verdurin had long thought unattainable and
which now, in her later years, she at length found incarnate in this new feminine recruit. However keenly the
Mistress might feel the pangs of jealousy, it was without
precedent for the most assiduous of her faithful not to
have "defected" at least once. The most stay-at-home
yielded to the temptation to travel; the most continent fell
from virtue; the most robust might catch influenza, the
idlest be caught for his month's soldiering, the most indifferent go to close the eyes of a dying mother. And it was
in vain that Mme Verdurin told them then, like the Roman Empress, that she was the sole general whom her legion must obey, or like Christ or the Kaiser, that he who
loved his father or mother more than her and was not
prepared to leave them and follow her was not worthy of

her, that instead of wilting in bed or letting themselves be
made fools of by whores they would do better to stay
with her, their sole remedy and sole delight. But destiny,
which is sometimes pleased to brighten the closing years
of a life that stretches beyond the normal span, had
brought Mme Verdurin in contact with the Princess
Sherbatoff. Estranged from her family, an exile from her
native land, knowing nobody but the Baroness Putbus and
the Grand Duchess Eudoxie, to whose houses, because
she herself had no desire to meet the friends of the former, and the latter no desire that her friends should meet
the Princess, she went only in the early morning hours
when Mme Verdurin was still asleep, never once, so far as
she could remember, having been confined to her bed
since she was twelve years old, when she had had the
measles, having on the 31st of December replied to Mme
Verdurin who, afraid of being left alone, had asked her
whether she would not "shake down" there for the night,
in spite of its being New Year's Eve: "Why, what is there
to prevent me, any day of the year? Besides, tomorrow is
a day when one stays at home with one's family, and you
are my family," living in a boarding-house and moving
from it whenever the Verdurins moved, accompanying
them on their holidays, the Princess had so completely ex-
emplified to Mme Verdurin the line of Vigny:

You alone did seem to me that which one always seeks,

that the Lady President of the little circle, anxious to
make sure of one of her "faithful" even after death, had
made her promise that whichever of them survived the
other should be buried by her side. In front of strangers—

among whom we must always reckon the one to whom we lie the most because he is the one whose contempt would be most painful to us: ourselves—Princess Sherbatoff took care to represent her only three friendships—with the Grand Duchess, the Verdurins, and the Baroness Putbus—as the only ones, not which cataclysms beyond her control had allowed to emerge from the destruction of all the rest, but which a free choice had made her elect in preference to any other, and to which a taste for solitude and simplicity had made her confine herself. "I see *nobody* else," she would say, underlining the inflexible character of what appeared to be rather a rule that one imposes upon oneself than a necessity to which one submits. She would add: "I visit only three houses," as a dramatist who fears that it may not run to a fourth announces that there will be only three performances of his play. Whether or not M. and Mme Verdurin gave credence to this fiction, they had helped the Princess to instil it into the minds of the faithful. And they in turn were persuaded both that the Princess, among the thousands of invitations that were available to her, had chosen the Verdurins' alone, and that the Verdurins, deaf to the overtures of the entire aristocracy, had consented to make but a single exception, in favour of a great lady of more intelligence than the rest of her kind, the Princess Sherbatoff.

The Princess was very rich; she engaged for every first night a large box on the ground floor, to which, with Mme Verdurin's assent, she invited the faithful and nobody else. People would point out to one another this pale and enigmatic person who had grown old without turning white, turning red, rather, like certain tough and shrivelled hedgerow fruits. They admired both her influence

and her humility, for, having always with her an Academician, Brichot, a famous scientist, Cottard, the leading
pianist of the day, and at a later date M. de Charlus, yet
she made a point of reserving the least prominent box in
the theatre, sat at the back, paid no attention to the rest of
the house, lived exclusively for the little group, who,
shortly before the end of the performance, would withdraw in the wake of this strange sovereign, who was not
without a certain shy, bewitching, faded beauty. But if
Mme Sherbatoff did not look at the audience, if she
stayed in the shadows, it was to try to forget that there
existed a living world which she passionately desired and
could not know; the coterie in a box was to her what is to
certain animals their almost corpselike immobility in the
presence of danger. Nevertheless the thirst for novelty and
for the curious which possesses society people made them
pay even more attention perhaps to this mysterious
stranger than to the celebrities in the front boxes to whom
everybody paid a visit. They imagined that she must be
different from the people they knew, that a marvellous intellect combined with a discerning bounty retained round
about her that little circle of eminent men. The Princess
was compelled, if you spoke to her about anyone, or introduced her to anyone, to feign an intense coldness, in
order to keep up the fiction of her loathing of society.
Nevertheless, with the support of Cottard or of Mme
Verdurin, several new recruits succeeded in getting to
know her and such was her excitement at making a fresh
acquaintance that she forgot the fable of her deliberate
isolation, and went to the wildest extremes to please the
newcomer. If he was something of a nonentity, the rest
would be astonished. "How strange that the Princess, who

refuses to know anyone, should make an exception of such an uninteresting person." But these fertilising acquaintances were rare, and the Princess lived narrowly confined in the midst of the faithful.

Cottard said far more often: "I shall see him on Wednesday at the Verdurins'," than: "I shall see him on Tuesday at the Academy." He also spoke of the Wednesdays as of an equally important and inescapable occupation. But Cottard was one of those people, little sought-after, who make it as imperious a duty to obey an invitation as if such invitations were orders, like a military or judicial summons. It required a very important call to make him "fail" the Verdurins on a Wednesday, the importance depending moreover rather upon the rank of the patient than upon the gravity of his complaint. For Cottard, excellent fellow as he was, would forgo the delights of a Wednesday not for a workman who had had a stroke, but for a minister's cold. Even then he would say to his wife: "Make my apologies to Mme Verdurin. Tell her that I shall be coming later on. His Excellency really might have chosen some other day to catch a cold." One Wednesday, their old cook having cut open a vein in her arm, Cottard, already in his dinner-jacket to go to the Verdurins', had shrugged his shoulders when his wife had timidly inquired whether he could not bandage the wound: "Of course I can't, Léontine," he had groaned, "can't you see I've got my white waistcoat on?" So as not to annoy her husband, Mme Cottard had sent posthaste for the house surgeon. The latter, to save time, had taken a cab, with the result that, his carriage entering the courtyard just as Cottard's was emerging to take him to the Verdurins', five minutes had been wasted in manoeuvring

backwards and forwards to let one another pass. Mme
Cottard was worried that the house surgeon should see his
chief in evening dress. Cottard sat cursing the delay, from
remorse perhaps, and started off in a villainous temper
which it took all the Wednesday's pleasures to dispel.

If one of Cottard's patients were to ask him: "Do you
ever see the Guermantes?" it was with the utmost sincerity that the Professor would reply: "Perhaps not actually
the Guermantes, I can't be certain. But I meet all those
people at the house of some friends of mine. You must, of
course, have heard of the Verdurins. They know everybody. Besides, they at least aren't grand people who've
come down in the world. They've got the goods, all right.
It's generally estimated that Mme Verdurin is worth
thirty-five million. Well, thirty-five million, that's quite a
figure. And so she doesn't go in for half-measures. You
mentioned the Duchesse de Guermantes. I'll tell you the
difference. Mme Verdurin is a great lady, the Duchesse
de Guermantes is probably a pauper. You see the distinction, of course? In any case, whether the Guermantes go
to Mme Verdurin's or not, she entertains all the very best
people, the d'Sherbatoffs, the d'Forchevilles, e tutti quanti,
people of the top flight, all the nobility of France and
Navarre, with whom you would see me conversing as man
to man. Of course, those sort of people are only too glad
to meet the princes of science," he would add, with a
smile of fatuous conceit, brought to his lips by his proud
satisfaction not so much that the expression formerly reserved for men like Potain and Charcot should now be
applicable to himself, as that he knew at last how to employ all these expressions that were sanctioned by usage,
and, after a long course of swotting, had learned them by

heart. And so, after mentioning to me Princess Sherbatoff as one of the people who went to Mme Verdurin's, Cottard added with a wink: "That gives you an idea of the style of the house, if you see what I mean?" He meant that it was the very height of fashion. Now, to entertain a Russian lady who knew nobody but the Grand Duchess Eudoxie meant very little. But Princess Sherbatoff might not have known even her, and it would in no way have diminished Cottard's estimate of the supreme elegance of the Verdurin salon or his joy at being invited there. The splendour with which the people whose houses we visit seem to us to be endowed is no more intrinsic than that of stage characters in dressing whom it is useless for a producer to spend hundreds and thousands of francs in purchasing authentic costumes and real jewels which will make no impression, when a great designer will procure a far more sumptuous impression by focusing a ray of light on a doublet of coarse cloth studded with glass spangles and on a paper cloak. A man may have spent his life among the great ones of the earth, who to him have been merely boring relatives or tedious acquaintances because a familiarity engendered in the cradle had stripped them of all glamour in his eyes. Yet on the other hand, such glamour need only, by some accident, have come to be attached to the most obscure people, for innumerable Cottards to be permanently dazzled by titled ladies whose drawing-rooms they imagined as the centres of aristocratic elegance, ladies who were not even what Mme de Villeparisis and her friends were (noble ladies fallen from grace, whom the aristocracy that had been brought up with them no longer visited); no, if the ladies whose friendship has been the pride of so many people were to be named in the memoirs of these people together with those whom they entertained, no one, Mme de Cambremer no more than Mme de Guermantes, would be able to identify them. But what of that! A Cottard has thus his baroness or his marquise, who is for him "the Baroness" or "the Marquise," as, in Marivaux, the baroness whose name is never mentioned and who for all one knows may never even have had one. A Cottard is all the more convinced that she epitomises the aristocracy—which has never heard of the lady—in that, the more dubious titles are, the more prominently coronets are displayed upon wine glasses, silver, note-paper and luggage. Many Cottards who have supposed that they were living in the heart of the Faubourg Saint-Germain have perhaps had their imaginations more beguiled by feudal dreams than the men who really have lived among princes, just as, for the small shopkeeper who sometimes goes on a Sunday to look at buildings of the "olden days," it is often those of which every stone is of our own, the vaults of which have been painted blue and sprinkled with golden stars by pupils of Viollet-le-Duc, that provide the most potent sensation of the Middle Ages.

"The Princess will be at Maineville," Cottard went on. "She will be coming with us. But I shan't introduce you to her at once. It will be better to leave that to Mme Verdurin. Unless I find a loophole. Then you can rely on me to take the bull by the horns."

"What were you saying?" asked Saniette, as he rejoined us, pretending to have been taking the air.

"I was quoting to this gentleman," said Brichot, "a saying, which you will remember, of the man who, to my mind, is the first of the *fins-de-siècle* (of the eighteenth century, that is), by name Charles-Maurice, Abbé de Périgord. He began by promising to be an excellent journalist. But he took a wrong turning, by which I mean that he became a minister! Such scandals happen in life. A far from scrupulous politician to boot, who, with all the lofty contempt of a thoroughbred nobleman, did not hesitate to play both ends against the middle when he felt like it, and remained left of centre until his dying day."

At Saint-Pierre-des-Ifs we were joined by a glorious girl who, unfortunately, was not a member of the little group. I could not take my eyes off her magnolia skin, her dark eyes, the bold and admirable composition of her forms. After a moment she wanted to open a window, for it was hot in the compartment, and not wishing to ask leave of everybody, as I alone was without an overcoat she said to me in a quick, cool, cheerful voice: "Do you mind a little fresh air, Monsieur?" I would have liked to say to her: "Come with us to the Verdurins'" or "Give me your name and address." I answered: "No, fresh air doesn't bother me, Mademoiselle." Whereupon, without stirring from her seat: "Your friends don't object to smoke?" and she lit a cigarette. At the third station she sprang from the train. Next day, I inquired of Albertine who she could be. For, stupidly thinking that people could have but one sort of love, in my jealousy of Albertine's attitude towards Robert, I was reassured so far as women were concerned. Albertine told me, I believe quite sincerely, that she did not know. "I should so like to see her again," I exclaimed. "Don't worry, one always sees people again," replied Albertine. In this particular instance she was wrong; I never saw again, and never identified, the handsome girl with

the cigarette. We shall see, moreover, why for a long time
I ceased to look for her. But I never forgot her. I find myself at times, when I think of her, seized by a wild longing. But these recurrences of desire oblige us to reflect
that if we wish to rediscover these girls with the same
pleasure we must also return to the year which has since
been followed by ten others in the course of which her
bloom has faded. We can sometimes find a person again,
but we cannot abolish time. And so on until the unforeseen day, gloomy as a winter night, when one no longer
seeks that girl, or any other, when to find her would actually scare one. For one no longer feels that one has attractions enough to please, or strength enough to love. Not,
of course, that one is in the strict sense of the word impo-
tent. And as for loving, one would love more than ever.
But one feels that it is too big an undertaking for the little
strength one has left. Eternal rest has already interposed
intervals during which one can neither go out nor even
speak. Setting one's foot on the right step is an achieve-
ment, like bringing off a somersault. To be seen in such a
state by a girl one loves, even if one has kept the features
and all the golden locks of one's youth! One can no longer
face the strain of keeping up with the young. Too bad if
carnal desire increases instead of languishing! One procures for it a woman whom one need make no effort to
please, who will share one's couch for one night only and
whom one will never see again.

"Still no news, I suppose, of the violinist," said Cottard. For the event of the day in the little clan was the de-
fection of Mme Verdurin's favourite violinist. The latter,
who was doing his military service near Doncières, came
three times a week to dine at La Raspelière, having a

midnight pass. But two days ago, for the first time, the
faithful had been unable to discover him on the train. It
was assumed that he had missed it. But in vain had Mme
Verdurin sent to meet the next train, and the next, and so
on until the last, the carriage had returned empty.

"He's certain to have been put in the glasshouse,"
Cottard went on, "there's no other explanation of his desertion. Oh yes, in the Army, you know, with those fellows, it only needs a crusty sergeant-major."

"It will be all the more mortifying for Mme Verdurin," said Brichot, "if he defects again this evening, because our kind hostess has invited to dinner for the first
time the neighbours from whom she rented La Raspelière,
the Marquis and Marquise de Cambremer."

"This evening, the Marquis and Marquise de Cambremer!" exclaimed Cottard. "But I knew absolutely nothing about it. Naturally, I knew like everybody else that
they would be coming one day, but I had no idea it was
to be so soon. By Jove!" he went on, turning to me,
"what did I tell you? The Princess Sherbatoff, the Marquis and Marquise de Cambremer." And, after repeating
these names, lulling himself with their melody: "You see
that we move in good company," he said to me. "No
doubt about it, for your first appearance you've really
struck lucky. It's going to be an exceptionally brilliant
roomful." And, turning to Brichot, he went on: "The
Mistress will be furious. It's time we got there to lend her
a hand."

Ever since Mme Verdurin had been at La Raspelière
she had pretended for the benefit of the faithful to be under the disagreeable obligation of inviting her landlords
for one evening. By so doing she would obtain better

terms next year, she explained, and was inviting them
merely out of self-interest. But she affected to regard with
such terror, to make such a bugbear of the idea of dining
with people who did not belong to the little group, that
she kept putting off the evil day. The prospect did indeed
alarm her slightly for the reasons which she professed, albeit exaggerating them, if at the same time it enchanted
her for reasons of snobbery which she preferred to keep to
herself. She was therefore partly sincere, for she believed
the little clan to be something so unique, one of those
perfect entities which it takes centuries to produce, that
she trembled at the thought of seeing these provincials,
ignorant of the *Ring* and the *Meistersinger*, introduced into
its midst, people who would be unable to play their part
in the concert of general conversation and were capable of
ruining one of those famous Wednesdays, masterpieces as
incomparably fragile as those Venetian glasses which one
false note is enough to shatter. "Besides, they're bound to
be absolutely *anti*, and jingoistic," M. Verdurin had said.
"Oh, as to that I don't really mind, we've heard quite
enough about that business," Mme Verdurin had replied,
for, though a sincere Dreyfusard, she would nevertheless
have been glad to discover a social counterpoise to the
preponderant Dreyfusism of her salon. For Dreyfusism
was triumphant politically but not socially. Labori,
Reinach, Picquart, Zola were still, to people in society,
more or less traitors, who could only keep them estranged
from the little nucleus. And so, after this incursion into
politics, Mme Verdurin was anxious to return to the
world of art. Besides, were not d'Indy and Debussy on
the "wrong" side in the Affair! "As far as the Affair goes,
we have only to put them beside Brichot," she said (the

Professor being the only one of the faithful who had sided with the General Staff, thus forfeiting a great deal of esteem in the eyes of Mme Verdurin). "There's no need to be eternally discussing the Dreyfus case. No, the fact of the matter is that the Cambremers bore me." As for the faithful, no less excited by their unavowed desire to meet the Cambremers than they were taken in by Mme Verdurin's affected reluctance to invite them, they returned, day after day, in conversation with her, to the base arguments which she herself produced in favour of the invitation, and tried to make them irresistible. "Make up your mind to it once and for all," Cottard repeated, "and you'll get a reduction of the rent, they'll pay the gardener, you'll have the use of the meadow. That will be well worth a boring evening. I'm thinking only of you," he added, though his heart had leapt once when, in Mme Verdurin's carriage, he had passed old Mme de Cambremer's on the road, and he felt humiliated in front of the railway employees when he found himself standing beside the Marquis at the station. For their part, the Cambremers, living much too far outside the social "swim" ever to suspect that certain ladies of fashion now spoke of Mme Verdurin with a certain respect, imagined that she was a person who could know none but Bohemians, was perhaps not even legally married, and so far as people of "birth" were concerned would never meet any but themselves. They had resigned themselves to the thought of dining with her only in order to be on good terms with a tenant who, they hoped, would return again for many seasons, especially since they had learned, during the previous month, that she had recently inherited all those millions. It was in silence and without any vulgar pleasantries that they pre-

pared themselves for the fatal day. The faithful had given
up hope of its ever coming, so often had Mme Verdurin
already fixed in their hearing a date that was invariably
postponed. These false alarms were intended not merely
to make a show of the boredom that she felt at the
thought of this dinner-party, but to keep in suspense
those members of the little group who were staying in the
neighbourhood and were sometimes inclined to default.
Not that the Mistress guessed that the "great day" was as
delightful a prospect to them as to herself, but in order
that, having persuaded them that this dinner-party was
for her the most terrible of chores, she might appeal to
their devotedness. "You're not going to leave me all alone
with those freaks! We must assemble in full force to stand
the boredom. Naturally we shan't be able to talk about
any of the things that interest us. It will be a Wednesday
spoiled, but what is one to do!"

"Actually," Brichot observed for my benefit, "I fancy
that Mme Verdurin, who is highly intelligent and takes
infinite pains in the elaboration of her Wednesdays, was
by no means anxious to entertain these squireens of ancient lineage but small wit. She could not bring herself to
invite the dowager Marquise, but has resigned herself to
having the son and daughter-in-law."

"Ah! we are to see the young Marquise de Cambremer?" said Cottard with a smile into which he felt called
upon to introduce a tinge of lecherous gallantry, although
he had no idea whether Mme de Cambremer was good-
looking or not. But the title of Marquise conjured up in
his mind images of glamour and dalliance.

"Ah! I know her," said Ski, who had met her once
when he was out for a drive with Mme Verdurin.

"Not in the biblical sense of the word, I trust," said the doctor, darting a sly glance through his eyeglass; this was one of his favourite pleasantries.

"She is intelligent," Ski informed me. "Naturally," he went on, seeing that I said nothing, and dwelling with a smile upon each word, "she is intelligent and at the same time she is not, she lacks education, she is frivolous, but she has an instinct for pretty things. She may say nothing, but she will never say anything silly. And besides, her colouring is charming. She would be fun to paint," he added, half shutting his eyes as though he saw her posing in front of him.

As my opinion of her was quite the opposite of what Ski was expressing with so many qualifications, I observed merely that she was the sister of a very distinguished engineer, M. Legrandin.

"There, you see, you are going to be introduced to a pretty woman," Brichot said to me, "and one never knows what may come of that. Cleopatra was not even a great lady, she was the little woman, the thoughtless, dreadful little woman of our Meilhac, and just think of the consequences, not only to that dupe Antony, but to the whole of the ancient world."

"I've already been introduced to Mme de Cambremer," I replied.

"Ah! In that case, you will find yourself on familiar ground."

"I shall be all the more delighted to meet her," I answered him, "because she has promised me a book by the former curé of Combray about the place-names of this region, and I shall be able to remind her of her promise. I'm interested in that priest, and also in etymologies."

"Don't put too much faith in the ones he gives,"
replied Brichot, "there's a copy of the book at La
Raspelière, which I've glanced through casually without
finding anything of any value; it's riddled with errors. Let
me give you an example. The word *bricq* is found in a
number of place-names in this neighbourhood. The worthy cleric had the distinctly eccentric idea that it comes
from *briga*, a height, a fortified place. He finds it already
in the Celtic tribes, Latobriges, Nemetobriges, and so
forth, and traces it down to such names as Briand, Brion,
and so forth. To confine ourselves to the region through
which we have the pleasure of travelling with you at this
moment, Bricquebosc, according to him, would mean the
wood on the height, Bricqueville the habitation on the
height, Bricquebec, where we shall be stopping presently
before coming to Maineville, the height by the stream.
Now it's not like that at all, since *bricq* is the old Norse
word which means simply a bridge. Just as *fleur*, which
Mme de Cambremer's protégé takes infinite pains to connect, in one place with the Scandinavian words *floi*, *flo*, in
another with the Irish words *ae* and *aer*, is on the contrary, beyond any doubt, the *fjord* of the Danes, and
means harbour. Similarly, the excellent priest thinks that
the station of Saint-Martin-le-Vêtu, which adjoins La
Raspelière, means Saint-Martin-le-Vieux (*vetus*). It is un-
questionable that the word *vieux* has played an important
part in the toponymy of this region. *Vieux* comes as a rule
from *vadum*, and means a ford, as at the place called les
Vieux. It is what the English call *ford* (Oxford, Hereford).
But, in this particular instance, Vêtu is derived not from
vetus, but from *vastatus*, a place that is devastated and
bare. You have, round about here, Sottevast, the *vast* of

Setold, Brillevast, the *vast* of Berold. I am all the more
certain of the curé's mistake in that Saint-Martin-le-Vêtu
was formerly called Saint-Martin-du-Gast and even Saint-
Martin-de-Terregate. Now the *v* and the *g* in these words
are the same letter. We say *dévaster*, but also *gâcher*.
Jachères and *gâtines*[11] (from the High German *wastinna*)
have the same meaning: Terregate is therefore *terra vas-
tata*. As for Saint-Mars, formerly (evil be to him who evil
thinks) Saint-Merd, it is Saint-Medardus, which appears
variously as Saint-Médard, Saint-Mard, Saint-Marc, Cinq-
Mars, and even Dammas. Nor must we forget that, quite
close to here, places bearing the name Mars simply attest
to a pagan origin (the god Mars) which has remained alive
in this country but which the holy man refuses to recognise. The high places dedicated to the gods are especially
frequent, such as the mount of Jupiter (Jeumont). Your
curé declines to admit this, and yet, on the other hand,
wherever Christianity has left traces, they escape him. He
has gone as far afield as Loctudy, a barbarian name, according to him, whereas it is *Locus sancti Tudeni*; nor, in
the name Sammercoles, has he divined *Sanctus Martialis*.
Your curé," Brichot continued, seeing that I was interested, "derives the terminations *hon, home, holm*, from the
word *holl* (*hullus*), a hill, whereas it comes from the Norse
holm, an island, with which you are familiar in Stockholm,
and which is so widespread throughout this region: la
Houlme, Engohomme, Tahoume, Robehomme, Néhomme,
Quettehou, and so forth."

These names reminded me of the day when Albertine
had wished to go to Amfreville-la-Bigot (from the name
of two successive lords of the manor, Brichot told me),
and had then suggested that we should dine together at

Robehomme. "Isn't Néhomme," I asked, "somewhere near Carquethuit and Clitourps?"

"Precisely; Néhomme is the *holm*, the island or peninsula of the famous Viscount Nigel, whose name has survived also in Néville. The Carquethuit and Clitourps that you mention provide Mme de Cambremer's protégé with an occasion for further errors. Of course he realises that *carque* is a church, the *Kirche* of the Germans. You will remember Querqueville, Carquebut, not to mention Dunkerque. For there we should do better to stop and consider the famous word *dun*, which to the Celts meant high ground. And that you will find over the whole of France. Your abbé was hypnotised by Duneville. But in the Eure-et-Loir he would have found Châteaudun, Dun-le-Roi in the Cher, Duneau in the Sarthe, Dun in the Ariège, Dune-les-Places in the Nièvre, and many others. This word *dun* leads him into a curious error with regard to Douville, where we shall be alighting, where we shall find Mme Verdurin's comfortable carriages awaiting us. Douville, in Latin *donvilla*, says he. And Douville does indeed lie at the foot of high hills. Your curé, who knows everything, feels all the same that he has made a blunder. And indeed he has found, in an old cartulary, the name *Domvilla*. Whereupon he retracts; Douville, according to him, is a fief belonging to the abbot, *domino abbati*, of Mont-Saint-Michel. He is delighted with the discovery, which is distinctly odd when one thinks of the scandalous life that, according to the capitulary of Saint-Clair-sur-Epte, was led at Mont-Saint-Michel, though no more extraordinary than to picture the King of Denmark as suzerain of all this coast, where he encouraged the worship of Odin far more than that of Christ. On the other hand, the supposition that the *n* has been changed to *m* doesn't shock me, and requires less alteration than the perfectly correct Lyon, which also is derived from *Dun (Lugdunum)*. But the fact is, the abbé is mistaken. Douville was never Donville, but Doville, *Eudonis villa*, the village of Eudes. Douville was formerly called Escalecliff, the steps up the cliff. About the year 1233, Eudes le Bouteiller, Lord of Escalecliff, set out for the Holy Land; on the eve of his departure he made over the church to the Abbey of Blanchelande. By an exchange of courtesies, the village took his name, whence we have Douville to-day. But I must add that toponymy, of which moreover I know little or nothing, is not an exact science; had we not this historical evidence, Douville might quite well come from Ouville, that is to say *les Eaux*, the Waters. The forms in *ai* (Aigues-Mortes) of *aqua* are constantly changed to *eu* or *ou*. Now there were, quite close to Douville, certain famous springs. You can imagine that the curé was only too glad to find Christian traces there, especially as this area seems to have been pretty hard to evangelise, since successive attempts were made by St Ursal, St Gofroi, St Barsanore, St Laurent of Brèvedent, who finally handed over the task to the monks of Beaubec. But as regards *tuit* the writer is mistaken; he sees it as a form of *toft*, a building, as in Cricquetot, Ectot, Yvetot, whereas it is the *thveit*, the assart or reclaimed land, as in Braquetuit, le Thuit, Regnetuit, and so forth. Similarly, if he recognises in Clitourps the Norman *thorp* which means village, he maintains that the first syllable of the word must come from *clivus*, a slope, whereas it comes from *cliff*, a precipice. But his biggest blunders are due not so much to his ignorance as to his prejudices. However good

a Frenchman one is, there is no need to fly in the face of
the evidence and take Saint-Laurent-en-Bray to be the famous Roman priest, when he is actually Saint Lawrence
O'Toole, Archbishop of Dublin. But even more than his
patriotic sentiments, your friend's religious bigotry leads
him into outrageous errors. Thus you have not far from
our hosts at La Raspelière two places called Montmartin,
Montmartin-sur-Mer and Montmartin-en-Graignes. In
the case of Graignes, the good curé is quite right, he has
recognised that Graignes, in Latin *grania*, in Greek *krene*,
means ponds, marshes; how many instances of Cresmays,
Croen, Grenneville, Lengronne, could one not cite? But
when he comes to Montmartin, your self-styled linguist
positively insists that these must be parishes dedicated to
St Martin. He bases his assertion on the fact that that
saint is the patron of the two villages, but does not realise
that he was only recognised as such subsequently; or
rather he is blinded by his hatred of paganism; he refuses
to see that we should say Mont-Saint-Martin as we say
Mont-Saint-Michel if it were a question of St Martin,
whereas the name Montmartin refers in a far more pagan
fashion to temples dedicated to the god Mars, temples of
which, it is true, no other vestige remains, but which the
undisputed existence in the neighbourhood of vast Roman
camps would render more probable even without the
name Montmartin, which removes all doubt. You see that
the little book which you will find at La Raspelière is far
from perfect."

I protested that at Combray the curé had often told
us about interesting etymologies.

"He was probably better on his own ground. The

move to Normandy must have made him lose his bearings."

"It didn't restore his health," I added, "for he came here with neurasthenia and went away again with rheumatism."

"Ah, his neurasthenia is to blame. He has lapsed from neurasthenia into philology, as my worthy master Poquelin would have said. Tell us, Cottard, do you suppose that neurasthenia can have a pernicious effect on philology, philology a soothing effect on neurasthenia, and the relief from neurasthenia lead to rheumatism?"

"Absolutely: rheumatism and neurasthenia are vicarious forms of neuro-arthritism. You may pass from one to the other by metastasis."

"The eminent professor," said Brichot, "expresses himself, God forgive me, in a French as highly infused with Latin and Greek as M. Purgon himself, of Molièresque memory! Help me, uncle, I mean our sainted Sarcey . . ."[12]

But he was prevented from finishing his sentence for Cottard had leapt from his seat with a wild shout: "The devil!" he exclaimed on regaining his power of articulate speech, "we've passed Maineville (d'you hear?) and Renneville too." He had just noticed that the train was stopping at Saint-Mars-le-Vieux, where most of the passengers alighted. "They can't have run through without stopping. We must have failed to notice while we were talking about the Cambremers. Listen to me, Ski, wait a moment, I'm going to tell you something good" (Cottard had taken a fancy to this expression, in common use in certain medical circles). "The Princess must be on the

train, she can't have seen us, and will have got into another compartment. Come along and find her. Let's hope
this won't land us in the soup!"

And he led us all off in search of Princess Sherbatoff.
He found her in the corner of an empty compartment,
reading the *Revue des Deux Mondes*. She had long ago,
from fear of rebuffs, acquired the habit of keeping her
place, or remaining in her corner, in life as in trains, and
of not offering her hand until the other person had
greeted her. She went on reading as the faithful trooped
into her carriage. I recognised her immediately; this
woman who might have forfeited her social position but
was nevertheless of exalted birth, who in any event was
the pearl of a salon such as the Verdurins', was the lady
whom, on the same train, I had put down two days earlier
as possibly the keeper of a brothel. Her social personality,
which had been so doubtful, became clear to me as soon
as I learned her name, just as when, after racking our
brains over a puzzle, we at length hit upon the word
which clears up all the obscurity, and which, in the case
of a person, is his name. To discover two days later who
the person is with whom one has travelled in a train is a
far more amusing surprise than to read in the next number of a magazine the clue to the problem set in the previous number. Big restaurants, casinos, local trains, are the
family portrait galleries of these social enigmas.

"Princess, we must have missed you at Maineville!
May we come and sit in your compartment?"

"Why, of course," said the Princess who, upon hearing Cottard address her, but only then, raised from her
magazine a pair of eyes which, like the eyes of M. de
Charlus, although gentler, saw perfectly well the people of

whose presence she pretended to be unaware. Cottard, reflecting that the fact of my having been invited to meet the Cambremers was a sufficient recommendation, decided, after a momentary hesitation, to introduce me to the Princess, who bowed with great courtesy but appeared to be hearing my name for the first time.

"Confound it!" cried the Doctor, "my wife has forgotten to have the buttons on my white waistcoat changed. Ah, women! They never remember anything. Don't you ever marry, my boy," he said to me. And as this was one of the pleasantries which he considered appropriate when he had nothing else to say, he peeped out of the corner of his eye at the Princess and the rest of the faithful, who, because he was a professor and an Academician, smiled back at him, admiring his good humour and lack of arrogance.

The Princess informed us that the young violinist had been found. He had been confined to bed the day before by a sick headache, but was coming that evening and bringing with him a friend of his father whom he had met at Doncières. She had learned this from Mme Verdurin with whom she had lunched that morning, she told us in a rapid voice, rolling her *r*s, with her Russian accent, softly at the back of her throat, as though they were not *r*s but *l*s. "Ah! you lunched with her this morning," Cottard said to the Princess, but his eyes were on me, for the object of this remark was to show me on what intimate terms the Princess was with the Mistress. "You really are one of the faithful!"

"Yes, I love this little gloup, so intelligent, so agleeable, so simple, not snobbish or spiteful, and clevel to their fingel-tips."

"Devil take it! I must have lost my ticket, I can't find it anywhere," cried Cottard, without being unduly alarmed. He knew that at Douville, where a couple of landaus would be awaiting us, the collector would let him pass without a ticket, and would only touch his cap the more deferentially in order to provide an explanation for his leniency, which was that he had of course recognised Cottard as one of the Verdurins' regular guests. "They won't shove me in the lock-up for that," the Doctor concluded.

"You were saying, Monsieur," I inquired of Brichot, "that there used to be some famous waters near here. How do we know that?"

"The name of the next station is one of a multitude of proofs. It is called Fervaches."

"I don't undelstand what he's talking about," mumbled the Princess, as though she were saying to me out of kindness: "He's rather a bore, isn't he?"

"Why, Princess, Fervaches means hot springs. *Fervidae aquae*. But to return to the young violinist," Brichot went on, "I was quite forgetting, Cottard, to tell you the great news. Had you heard that our poor friend Dechambre, who used to be Mme Verdurin's favourite pianist, has just died? It's dreadful."

"He was still quite young," replied Cottard, "but he must have had some trouble with his liver, there must have been something sadly wrong in that quarter, he'd been looking very queer indeed for a long time past."

"But he wasn't as young as all that," said Brichot. "In the days when Elstir and Swann used to come to Mme Verdurin's, Dechambre had already made himself a reputation in Paris, and, what is remarkable, without having

first received the baptism of success abroad. Ah! he was
no follower of the Gospel according to St Barnum, that
fellow."

"You must be mistaken, he couldn't have been going
to Mme Verdurin's at that time, he was still in the nurs-
ery."

"But, unless my old memory plays me false, I was
under the impression that Dechambre used to play Vinteuil's sonata for Swann when that clubman, being at odds
with the aristocracy, had still no idea that he was one day
to become the embourgeoised prince consort of our
sainted Odette."

"That's impossible. Vinteuil's sonata wasn't played at
Mme Verdurin's until long after Swann ceased to come
there," said the Doctor, for he was one of those people
who work very hard and think they remember a great
many things which they imagine to be useful, but forget
many others, a condition which enables them to go into
ecstasies over the memories of people who have nothing
else to do. "You're not doing justice to your learning, and
yet you aren't suffering from softening of the brain," he
added with a smile. Brichot agreed that he was mistaken.

The train stopped. We were at La Sogne. The name
stirred my curiosity. "How I should like to know what all
these names mean," I said to Cottard.

"Ask M. Brichot, he may know, perhaps."

"Why, La Sogne is la Cicogne, *Siconia*," replied Brichot, whom I was longing to interrogate about many other
names.

Forgetting her attachment to her "corner," Mme
Sherbatoff kindly offered to change places with me so that
I might talk more easily with Brichot, whom I wanted to

ask about other etymologies that interested me, and assured me that she did not mind in the least whether she travelled with her face to the engine, or her back to it, or standing, or anyhow. She remained on the defensive until she had discovered a newcomer's intentions, but as soon as she had realised that these were friendly, she would do everything in her power to oblige. At length the train stopped at the station of Douville-Féterne, which being more or less equidistant from the villages of Féterne and Douville, bore for this reason both their names. "Good grief!" exclaimed Dr Cottard when we came to the barrier where the tickets were collected, pretending to have only just discovered his loss, "I can't find my ticket, I must have lost it." But the collector, taking off his cap, assured him that it did not matter and smiled respectfully. The Princess (giving instructions to the coachman, as though she were a sort of lady-in-waiting to Mme Verdurin, who, because of the Cambremers, had not been able to come to the station, as, for that matter, she rarely did) took me, and also Brichot, with herself in one of the carriages. The Doctor, Saniette and Ski got into the other.

The driver, although quite young, was the Verdurins' head coachman, the only one who was strictly qualified for the post. He took them, in the day-time, on all their excursions, for he knew all the roads, and in the evening went down to meet the faithful and brought them back to the station later on. He was accompanied by extra helpers (whom he chose himself) if the necessity arose. He was an excellent fellow, sober and skilled, but with one of those melancholy faces on which a fixed stare indicates a person who will worry himself sick over the merest trifle and even harbour black thoughts. But at the moment he was quite happy, for he had managed to secure a place for his brother, another excellent young man, with the Verdurins. We began by driving through Douville. Grassy knolls ran down from the village to the sea, spreading out into broad pastures which were extraordinarily thick, lush and vivid in hue from saturation in moisture and salt. The islands and indentations of Rivebelle, much closer here than at Balbec, gave this part of the coast the appearance, novel to me, of a relief map. We passed several little bungalows, almost all of which were let to painters, turned into a track upon which some loose cattle, as frightened as were our horses, barred our way for ten minutes, and emerged upon the cliff road.

"But, by the immortal gods," Brichot suddenly asked, "to return to that poor Dechambre, do you suppose Mme Verdurin *knows*? Has anyone *told* her?"

Mme Verdurin, like most people who move in society, simply because she needed the society of other people, never thought of them again for a single day as soon as, being dead, they could no longer come to her Wednesdays, or her Saturdays, or drop in for dinner. And it could not be said of the little clan, akin in this respect to every other salon, that it was composed of more dead than living members, seeing that, as soon as you were dead, it was as though you had never existed. But, to avoid the tedium of having to talk about the deceased, and even suspend the dinners—an inconceivable thing for the Mistress—as a token of mourning, M. Verdurin used to pretend that the death of the faithful had such an effect on his wife that, in the interest of her health, the subject must never be mentioned to her. Moreover, and perhaps just because the death of other people seemed to him so conclusive and so vulgar an accident, the thought of his own death filled him with horror and he shunned any reflexion that might have any bearing on it. As for Brichot, since he was a good-natured man and completely taken in by what M. Verdurin said about his wife, he dreaded for her sake the distress that such a bereavement must cause her.

"Yes, she *knew the worst* this morning," said the Princess, "it was impossible to *keep it from her.*"

"Ye gods!" cried Brichot, "ah! it must have been a terrible blow, a friend of twenty-five years' standing. There was a man who was one of us."

"Of course, of course, but it can't be helped," said Cottard. "Such events are bound to be painful; but Mme Verdurin is a brave woman, she is even more cerebral than emotional."

"I don't altogether agree with the Doctor," said the Princess, whose rapid speech and garbled diction made her somehow appear at once sulky and mischievous. "Beneath a cold exterior, Mme Verdurin conceals treasures of sensibility. M. Verdurin told me that he had had great difficulty in preventing her from going to Paris for the funeral; he was obliged to let her think that it was all to be held in the country."

"The devil! She wanted to go to Paris, did she? Of course, I know that she has a heart, too much heart perhaps. Poor Dechambre! As Madame Verdurin remarked not two months ago: 'Compared with him, Planté, Paderewski, even Risler himself are nowhere!' Ah, he could say with better reason than that show-off Nero, who has managed to hoodwink even German scholarship: *Qualis artifex pereo!* But he at least, Dechambre, must

have died in the fulfilment of his vocation, in the odour of
Beethovenian devotion; and bravely, I have no doubt; he
had every right, that interpreter of German music, to pass
away while celebrating the *Missa Solemnis*. But at any rate
he was the man to greet the Reaper with a trill, for that
inspired performer would produce at times, from the
Parisianised Champagne ancestry of which he came, the
gallantry and swagger of a guardsman."

From the height we had now reached, the sea no
longer appeared, as it did from Balbec, like an undulating
range of hills, but on the contrary like the view, from a
mountain-peak or from a road winding round its flank, of
a blue-green glacier or a glittering plain situated at a
lower level. The ripples of eddies and currents seemed to
be fixed upon its surface, and to have traced there for ever
their concentric circles; the enamelled face of the sea, imperceptibly changing colour, assumed towards the head of
the bay, where an estuary opened, the blue whiteness of
milk in which little black boats that did not move seemed
entangled like flies. I felt that from nowhere could one
discover a vaster prospect. But at each turn in the road a
fresh expanse was added to it and when we arrived at the
Douville toll-house, the spur of the cliff which until then
had concealed from us half the bay receded, and all of a
sudden I saw upon my left a gulf as profound as that
which I had already had in front of me, but one that
changed the proportions of the other and doubled its
beauty. The air at this lofty point had a keenness and purity that intoxicated me. I adored the Verdurins; that they
should have sent a carriage for us seemed to me a touching act of kindness. I should have liked to kiss the
Princess. I told her that I had never seen anything so

beautiful. She professed that she too loved this spot more than any other. But I could see that to her as to the Verdurins the thing that really mattered was not to gaze at the view like tourists, but to partake of good meals there, to entertain people whom they liked, to write letters, to read books, in short to live in these surroundings, passively allowing the beauty of the scene to soak into them rather than making it the object of their conscious attention.

After the toll-house, where the carriage had stopped for a moment at such a height above the sea that, as from a mountain-top, the sight of the blue gulf beneath almost made one dizzy, I opened the window; the sound, distinctly caught, of each wave breaking in turn had something sublime in its softness and clarity. Was it not like an index of measurement which, upsetting all our ordinary impressions, shows us that vertical distances may be compared with horizontal ones, contrary to the idea that our mind generally forms of them; and that, though they bring the sky nearer to us in this way, they are not great; that they are indeed less great for a sound which traverses them, as did the sound of those little waves, because the medium through which it has to pass is purer? And in fact if one drew back only a couple of yards behind the toll-house, one could no longer distinguish that sound of waves which six hundred feet of cliff had not robbed of its delicate, minute and soft precision. I thought to myself that my grandmother would have listened to it with the delight that she felt in all manifestations of nature or art that combine simplicity with grandeur. My exaltation was now at its height and raised everything round about me accordingly. It melted my heart that the Verdurins should have sent to meet us at the station. I said as much to the Princess, who seemed to think that I was greatly exaggerating so simple an act of courtesy. I know that she admitted subsequently to Cottard that she found me remarkably enthusiastic; he replied that I was too emotional, that I needed sedatives and ought to take up knitting. I pointed out to the Princess every tree, every little house smothered in its mantle of roses, I made her admire everything, I would have liked to take her in my arms and press her to my heart. She told me that she could see that I had a gift for painting, that I ought to take up sketching, that she was surprised that nobody had told me before. And she confessed that the country was indeed picturesque. We drove through the little village of Englesqueville perched on its hill—*Engleberti villa*, Brichot informed us. "But are you quite sure that this evening's dinner party will take place in spite of Dechambre's death, Princess?" he went on, without stopping to think that the arrival at the station of the carriage in which we were sitting was in itself an answer to his question.

"Yes," said the Princess, "M. Veldulin insisted that it should not be put off, precisely in order to keep his wife from *thinking*. And besides, after never failing for all these years to entertain on Wednesdays, such a change in her habits would have been bound to upset her. Her nerves are velly bad just now. M. Verdurin was particularly pleased that you were coming to dine this evening, because he knew that it would be a great distraction for Mme Verdurin," the Princess said to me, forgetting her pretence of having never heard my name before. "I think that it will be as well not to say *anything* in front of Mme Verdurin," she added.

"Ah! I'm glad you warned me," Brichot artlessly replied. "I shall pass on your advice to Cottard."

The carriage stopped for a moment. It moved on again, but the sound that the wheels had been making in the village street had ceased. We had turned into the drive of La Raspelière, where M. Verdurin stood waiting for us on the steps. "I did well to put on a dinner-jacket," he said, observing with pleasure that the faithful had put on theirs, "since I have such smart gentlemen in my party." And as I apologised for not having changed: "Why, that's quite all right. We're all friends here. I should be delighted to offer you one of my own dinner-jackets, but it wouldn't fit you."

The handclasp full of emotion which, by way of condolence at the death of the pianist, Brichot gave our host as he entered the hall of La Raspelière elicited no response from the latter. I told him how greatly I admired the scenery. "Ah! I'm delighted, and you've seen nothing yet; we must take you round. Why not come and spend a week or two here? The air is excellent."

Brichot was afraid that his handclasp had not been understood. "Ah! poor Dechambre!" he said, but in an undertone, in case Mme Verdurin was within earshot.

"It's dreadful," replied M. Verdurin cheerfully.

"So young," Brichot pursued the point.

Annoyed at being detained over these futilities, M. Verdurin replied hurriedly and with a high-pitched moan, not of grief but of irritated impatience: "Ah well, there we are, it's no use crying over spilt milk, talking about him won't bring him back to life, will it?" And, his civility returning with his joviality: "Come along, my dear Brichot, get your things off quickly. We have a bouillabaisse which mustn't be kept waiting. But, in heaven's name, don't start talking about Dechambre to Mme Verdurin. You know that she always hides her feelings, but she's quite morbidly sensitive. No, but I swear to you, when she heard that Dechambre was dead, she almost wept," said M. Verdurin in a tone of profound irony. Hearing him, one might have concluded that it implied a form of insanity to regret the death of a friend of thirty years' standing, and at the same time one gathered that the perpetual union of M. Verdurin and his wife did not preclude constant censure and frequent irritation on his part. "If you mention it to her, she'll go and make herself ill again. It's deplorable, three weeks after her bronchitis. When that happens, it's I who have to nurse her. You can understand that I've had more than enough of it. Grieve for Dechambre's fate in your heart as much as you like. Think of him, but don't speak about him. I was very fond of Dechambre, but you cannot blame me for being fonder still of my wife. Here's Cottard, now, you can ask him." And indeed he knew that a family doctor can do many little services, such as prescribing that one must not give way to grief.

The docile Cottard had said to the Mistress: "Upset yourself like that, and tomorrow you'll give *me* a temperature of 102," as he might have said to the cook: "Tomorrow you'll give me sweetbread." Medicine, when it fails to cure, busies itself with changing the sense of verbs and pronouns.

M. Verdurin was glad to find that Saniette, notwithstanding the snubs that he had had to endure two days earlier, had not deserted the little nucleus. And indeed Mme Verdurin and her husband had acquired, in their idleness, cruel instincts for which the great occasions, occurring too rarely, no longer sufficed. They had succeeded in effecting a breach between Odette and Swann, and between Brichot and his mistress. They would try it again with others, that was understood. But the opportunity did not present itself every day. Whereas, thanks to his quivering sensibility, his timorous and easily panicked shyness, Saniette provided them with a whipping-boy for every day in the year. And so, for fear of his defecting, they took care always to invite him with friendly and persuasive words, such as the senior boys at school or the old soldiers in a regiment address to a greenhorn whom they are anxious to cajole so that they may get him into their clutches with the sole object of ragging and bullying him when he can no longer escape.

"Whatever you do," Cottard reminded Brichot, not having heard what M. Verdurin had been saying, "mum's the word in front of Mme Verdurin."

"Have no fear, O Cottard, you are dealing with a sage, as Theocritus says. Besides, M. Verdurin is right, what is the use of lamentations?" Brichot added, for, though capable of assimilating verbal forms and the ideas which they suggested to him, but lacking subtlety, he had discerned and admired in M. Verdurin's remarks the most courageous stoicism. "All the same, it's a great talent that has gone from the world."

"What, are you still talking about Dechambre?" said M. Verdurin, who had gone on ahead of us, and, seeing that we were not following him, turned back. "Listen," he said to Brichot, "don't let's exaggerate. The fact of his be-

ing dead is no excuse for making him out a genius, which
he was not. He played well, I admit, but the main thing
was that he was in the right surroundings here; transplanted, he ceased to exist. My wife was infatuated with
him and made his reputation. You know what she's like. I
will go further: in the interest of his own reputation he
died at the right moment, *à point*, as the lobsters, grilled
according to Pampille's incomparable recipe, are going to
be, I hope (unless you keep us standing here all night
with your jeremiads in this kasbah exposed to all the
winds of heaven). You don't seriously expect us all to die
of hunger because Dechambre is dead, when for the last
year he was obliged to practise scales before giving a concert, in order to recover for the moment, and for the moment only, the suppleness of his wrists. Besides, you're
going to hear this evening, or at any rate to meet, for the
rascal is too fond of deserting his art for the card-table after dinner, somebody who is a far greater artist than
Dechambre, a youngster whom my wife has discovered"
(as she had discovered Dechambre, and Paderewski, and
the rest), "called Morel. The beggar hasn't arrived yet. I
shall have to send a carriage down to meet the last train.
He's coming with an old friend of his family whom he
ran into, and who bores him to tears, but otherwise, so as
not to get into trouble with his father, he would have
been obliged to stay down at Doncières and keep him
company: the Baron de Charlus."

The faithful entered the drawing-room. M. Verdurin,
who had remained behind with me while I took off my
things, took my arm by way of a joke, as one's host does
at a dinner-party when there is no lady for one to take in.
"Did you have a pleasant journey?" "Yes, M. Brichot told

me things which interested me greatly," said I, thinking
of the etymologies, and because I had heard that the Verdurins greatly admired Brichot. "I'm surprised to hear
that he told you anything," said M. Verdurin, "he's such
a retiring man, and talks so little about the things he
knows." This compliment did not strike me as being very
apt. "He seems charming," I remarked. "Exquisite, delightful, not an ounce of pedantry, such a light, fantastic
touch, my wife adores him, and so do I!" replied M. Verdurin in an exaggerated tone, as though reciting a lesson.
Only then did I grasp that what he had said to me about
Brichot was ironical. And I wondered whether M. Verdurin, since those far-off days of which I had heard reports, had not shaken off his wife's tutelage.

The sculptor was greatly astonished to learn that the
Verdurins were willing to have M. de Charlus in their
house. Whereas in the Faubourg Saint-Germain, where
M. de Charlus was so well known, nobody ever referred
to his morals (of which the majority had no suspicion and
others remained doubtful, crediting him rather with intense but platonic friendships, with indiscretions, while
the enlightened few carefully concealed them, shrugging
their shoulders at any insinuation upon which some malicious Gallardon might venture), these morals, the nature
of which was known to only a handful of intimates, were
on the contrary denounced daily far from the circle in
which he moved, just as, at times, the sound of artillery
fire is audible only beyond an intervening zone of silence.
Moreover, in those professional and artistic circles where
he was regarded as the personification of inversion, his
high social position and his noble origin were completely
unknown, by a process analogous to that which, among

the people of Romania, has brought it about that the
name of Ronsard is known as that of a great nobleman,
while his poetical work is unknown there. Furthermore,
the Romanian estimate of Ronsard's nobility is founded
upon an error. Similarly, if in the world of painters and
actors M. de Charlus had such a bad reputation, this was
due to their confusing him with a Comte Leblois de
Charlus who was not even related to him (or, if so, the
connexion was extremely remote), and who had been arrested, possibly by mistake, in the course of a notorious
police raid. In short, all the stories related of our M. de
Charlus referred to the other. Many professionals swore
that they had had relations with M. de Charlus, and did
so in good faith, believing that the false M. de Charlus
was the true one, the false one possibly encouraging,
partly from an affectation of nobility, partly to conceal his
vice, a confusion which was for a long time prejudicial to
the real one (the Baron we know), and afterwards, when
he had begun to go down the hill, became a convenience,
for it enabled him likewise to say: "It isn't me." And in
the present instance it was not him to whom the rumours
referred. Finally, what added even more to the falseness
of the comments on a true fact (the Baron's taste) was the
fact that he had had an intimate but perfectly pure friendship with an author who, in the theatrical world, had for
some reason acquired a similar reputation which he in no
way deserved. When they were seen together at a first
night, people would say: "You see," just as it was supposed that the Duchesse de Guermantes had immoral relations with the Princesse de Parme—an indestructible
legend, for it would have been dispelled only by a proximity to those two noble ladies to which the people who

spread it would presumably never attain other than by
staring at them through their glasses in the theatre and
slandering them to the occupant of the next stall. From
M. de Charlus's morals, the sculptor concluded all the
more readily that the Baron's social position must be
equally low, since he had no information whatsoever
about the family to which M. de Charlus belonged, his title or his name. Just as Cottard imagined that everybody
knew that the title of doctor of medicine meant nothing
and the title of hospital consultant meant something, so
people in society are mistaken when they suppose that everybody has the same idea of the social importance of
their name as they themselves and the other people of
their circle.

The Prince d'Agrigente was regarded as a flashy foreigner by a club servant to whom he owed twenty-five
louis, and regained his importance only in the Faubourg
Saint-Germain where he had three sisters who were
duchesses, for it is not among humble people, in whose
eyes he is of small account, but among smart people, who
know who is who, that a nobleman can hope to make an
impression. M. de Charlus, indeed, was to learn in the
course of the evening that his host had only the most superficial notions about the most illustrious ducal families.

Convinced that the Verdurins were making a grave
mistake in allowing an individual of tarnished reputation
to be admitted to so "select" a household as theirs, the
sculptor felt it his duty to take the Mistress aside. "You
are entirely mistaken; besides, I never pay any attention to
such tales, and even if it were true, I may be allowed to
point out that it could hardly compromise *me!*" replied
Mme Verdurin angrily, for, Morel being the principal fea-

ture of the Wednesdays, she was particularly anxious not to give him any offence. As for Cottard, he could not express an opinion, for he had asked leave to go upstairs for a moment to "do a little job" in the *buen retiro* and afterwards, in M. Verdurin's bedroom, to write an extremely urgent letter for a patient.

An eminent publisher from Paris who had come to call, expecting to be invited to stay to dinner, withdrew with savage abruptness, realising that he was not smart enough for the little clan. He was a tall, stout man, very dark, with a studious and somewhat trenchant look about him. He reminded one of an ebony paper-knife.

Mme Verdurin, who, to welcome us in her immense drawing-room, in which displays of grasses, poppies, field-flowers, picked only that morning, alternated with a similar theme painted in monochrome two centuries earlier by an artist of exquisite taste, had risen for a moment from a game of cards which she was playing with an old friend, begged us to excuse her for a minute or two until she finished her game while continuing to talk to us. What I told her about my impressions was not entirely pleasing to her. For one thing I was shocked to observe that she and her husband came indoors every day long before the hour of those sunsets which were considered so fine when seen from that cliff, and finer still from the terrace of La Raspelière, and which I would have travelled miles to see. "Yes, it's incomparable," said Mme Verdurin carelessly, with a glance at the huge windows which gave the room a wall of glass. "Even though we have it in front of us all the time, we never grow tired of it," and she turned her attention back to her cards. But my very enthusiasm made me exacting. I complained of not being able to see from the drawing-room the rocks of Darnetal which Elstir had told me were quite lovely at that hour, when they reflected so many colours. "Ah! you can't see them from here, you'd have to go to the end of the gardens, to the 'view of the bay.' From the seat there, you can take in the whole panorama. But you can't go there by yourself, you'll lose your way. I can take you there, if you like," she added half-heartedly. "Come now, no," said her husband, "haven't you had enough of those rheumatic pains you had the other day? Do you want a new lot? He can come back and see the view of the bay another time." I did not insist, and realised that it was enough for the Verdurins to know that this sunset made its way into their drawing-room or dining-room, like a magnificent painting, like a priceless Japanese enamel, justifying the high rent they were paying for La Raspelière, furnished, without their having constantly to raise their eyes towards it; the important thing here for them was to live comfortably, to go for drives, to eat well, to talk, to entertain agreeable friends whom they provided with amusing games of billiards, good meals, merry tea-parties. I noticed, however, later on, how intelligently they had got to know the district, taking their guests for excursions as "novel" as the music to which they made them listen. The part which the flowers of La Raspelière, the paths along the edge of the sea, the old houses, the undiscovered churches, played in M. Verdurin's life was so great that those who saw him only in Paris and who themselves substituted urban luxuries for seaside and country life could barely understand the exalted idea that he himself had of his own life, or the importance that his pleasures gave him in his own eyes. This importance was further enhanced by the fact that the Verdurins were convinced that La Raspelière, which they hoped to purchase, was a property without its match in the world. This superiority which their self-esteem made them attribute to La Raspelière justified in their eyes my enthusiasm which, but for that, would have annoyed them slightly, because of the disappointments which it involved (like those which my first experience of Berma had once caused me) and which I frankly admitted to them.

"I hear the carriage coming back," the Mistress suddenly murmured. Let us here briefly remark that Mme Verdurin, quite apart from the inevitable changes due to increasing years, no longer resembled what she had been at the time when Swann and Odette used to listen to the little phrase in her house. Even when she heard it played, she was no longer obliged to assume the air of exhausted admiration which she used to assume then, for that had become her normal expression. Under the influence of the countless headaches which the music of Bach, Wagner, Vinteuil, Debussy had given her, Mme Verdurin's forehead had assumed enormous proportions, like limbs that become permanently deformed by rheumatism. Her temples, suggestive of a pair of burning, pain-stricken, milk-white spheres, in which Harmony endlessly revolved, flung back silvery locks on either side, and proclaimed, on the Mistress's behalf, without any need for her to say a word: "I know what is in store for me tonight." Her features no longer took the trouble to formulate, one after another, aesthetic impressions of undue violence, for they had themselves become as it were their permanent expression on a superbly ravaged face. This attitude of resignation to the ever-impending sufferings inflicted by the

Beautiful, and the courage required to make her dress for dinner when she had barely recovered from the effects of the last sonata, caused Mme Verdurin, even when listening to the most heartrending music, to preserve a disdainfully impassive countenance, and even to hide herself to swallow her two spoonfuls of aspirin.

"Why, yes, here they are!" M. Verdurin exclaimed with relief on seeing the door open to admit Morel followed by M. de Charlus. The latter, to whom dining with the Verdurins meant not so much going into society as going into a place of ill repute, was as apprehensive as a schoolboy entering a brothel for the first time and showing the utmost deference towards its mistress. Hence the Baron's habitual desire to appear virile and cold was overshadowed (when he appeared in the open doorway) by those traditional ideas of politeness which are awakened as soon as shyness destroys an artificial pose and falls back on the resources of the subconscious. When it is a Charlus, whether he be noble or plebeian, who is stirred by such a sentiment of instinctive and atavistic politeness to strangers, it is always the spirit of a relative of the female sex, attendant like a goddess, or incarnate as a double, that undertakes to introduce him into a strange drawing-room and to mould his attitude until he comes face to face with his hostess. Thus a young painter, brought up by a godly, Protestant, female cousin, will enter a room, his trembling head to one side, his eyes raised to the ceiling, his hands clutching an invisible muff, the remembered shape of which and its real and tutelary presence will help the frightened artist to cross without agoraphobia the yawning abyss between the hall and the inner drawing-room. Thus it was that the pious relative whose memory is guiding him today used to enter a room years ago, and with so plaintive an air that one wondered what calamity she had come to announce until from her first words one realised, as now in the case of the painter, that she had come to pay an after-dinner call. By virtue of the same law, which ordains that life, in the interests of the still unfulfilled act, shall bring into play, utilise, adulterate, in a perpetual prostitution, the most respectable, sometimes the most sacred, occasionally only the most innocent legacies of the past, and albeit in this instance it engendered a different aspect, a nephew of Mme Cottard, who distressed his family by his effeminate ways and the company he kept, would always make a joyous entry as though he had a surprise in store for you or were going to inform you that he had been left a fortune, radiant with a happiness which it would have been futile to ask him to explain, it being due to his unconscious heredity and his misplaced sex. He walked on tiptoe, was no doubt himself astonished that he was not holding a cardcase, offered you his hand with a simper as he had seen his aunt do, and his only anxious look was directed at the mirror in which he seemed to wish to verify, although he was bare-headed, whether, as Mme Cottard had once inquired of Swann, his hat was askew. As for M. de Charlus, whom the society in which he had lived furnished at this critical moment with different examples, with other arabesques of amiability, and especially with the maxim that one must in certain cases, for the benefit of people of humble rank, bring into play and make use of one's rarest graces, normally held in reserve, it was with a fluttering, mincing gait and the same sweep with which a skirt would have enlarged and impeded his waddling motion that he advanced upon Mme Verdurin with so flattered and honoured an air that one would have said that to be presented to her was for him a supreme favour. His face, bent slightly forward, on which satisfaction vied with decorum, was creased with tiny wrinkles of affability. One might have thought that it was Mme de Marsantes who was entering the room, so salient at that moment was the woman whom a mistake on the part of Nature had enshrined in the body of M. de Charlus. Of course the Baron had made every effort to conceal this mistake and to assume a masculine appearance. But no sooner had he succeeded than, having meanwhile retained the same tastes, he acquired from this habit of feeling like a woman a new feminine appearance, due not to heredity but to his own way of living. And as he had gradually come to regard even social questions from the feminine point of view, and that quite unconsciously, for it is not only by dint of lying to other people but also by lying to oneself that one ceases to be aware that one is lying, although he had called upon his body to manifest (at the moment of his entering the Verdurins' house) all the courtesy of a great nobleman, that body, which had so well grasped what M. de Charlus had ceased to understand, displayed, to such an extent that the Baron would have deserved the epithet *ladylike*, all the seductions of a great lady. Besides, can one entirely separate M. de Charlus's appearance from the fact that sons, who do not always take after their fathers, even without being inverts and even though seekers after women, may consummate upon their faces the profanation of their mothers? But let us not consider here a subject that deserves a chapter to itself: the Profanation of the Mother.

Although other reasons may have dictated this transformation of M. de Charlus, and purely physical ferments may have set his chemistry "working" and made his body gradually change into the category of women's bodies, nevertheless the change that we record here was of spiritual origin. By dint of imagining oneself to be ill one becomes ill, one grows thin, one is too weak to rise from one's bed, one suffers from nervous enteritis. By dint of thinking tenderly of men one becomes a woman, and an imaginary skirt hampers one's movements. The obsession, as in the other instance it can affect one's health, may in this instance alter one's sex.

Morel, who accompanied him, came up to greet me. From that first moment, owing to a twofold change that occurred in him, he made (and alas, I was not quick enough to take account of it!) a bad impression on me. And this is why. I have said that Morel, having risen above his father's menial status, was generally pleased to indulge in a contemptuous familiarity. He had spoken to me, on the day when he brought me the photographs, without once addressing me as Monsieur, treating me superciliously. What was my surprise at Mme Verdurin's to see him bow very low before me, and before me alone, and to hear, before he had even uttered a syllable to anyone else, words of infinite respect—words such as I thought could not possibly flow from his pen or fall from his lips—addressed to myself. I at once suspected that he had some favour to ask of me. Taking me aside a minute later: "Monsieur would be doing me a very great service," he said to me, going so far this time as to address me in the third person, "by keeping from Mme Verdurin and her guests the nature of the profession that my father

practised in his uncle's household. It would be best to say
that, in your family, he was the steward of estates so vast
as to put him almost on a level with your parents."
Morel's request annoyed me intensely, not because it
obliged me to magnify his father's position, which was a
matter of complete indifference to me, but by requiring
me to exaggerate the apparent wealth of my own, which I
felt to be absurd. But he appeared so wretched so pressing, that I could not refuse him. "No, before dinner," he
said in an imploring tone, "Monsieur can easily find some
excuse for taking Mme Verdurin aside." This was what I
in fact did, trying to enhance to the best of my ability the
glamour of Morel's father without unduly exaggerating
the "style," the "worldly goods" of my own family. It
went off very smoothly, despite the astonishment of Mme
Verdurin, who had had a nodding acquaintance with my
grandfather. And as she had no tact and hated family life
(that dissolvent of the little nucleus), after telling me that
she remembered seeing my great-grandfather long ago,
and speaking to me of him as of somebody who was more
or less an idiot who would have been incapable of understanding the little group and who, to use her expression,
"was not one of us," she said to me: "Families are such a
bore, one longs to get away from them"; and at once proceeded to tell me of a trait in my great-grandfather's character of which I was unaware, although I had suspected it
at home (I had never known him, but he was much spoken of), his remarkable stinginess (in contrast to the
somewhat lavish generosity of my great-uncle, the friend
of the lady in pink and Morel's father's employer): "The
fact that your grandparents had such a smart steward only
goes to show that there are people of all complexions in a

family. Your grandfather's father was so stingy that at the end of his life when he was almost gaga—between you and me, he was never anything very special, you make up for the lot of them—he could not bring himself to pay a penny for his ride on the omnibus. So that they were obliged to have him followed by somebody who paid his fare for him, and to let the old miser think that his friend M. de Persigny, the Cabinet Minister, had given him a permit to travel free on the omnibuses. But I'm delighted to hear that *our* Morel's father was so distinguished. I was under the impression that he had been a schoolmaster, but it doesn't matter, I must have misunderstood. In any case, it makes not the slightest difference, for I must tell you that here we appreciate only true worth, the personal contribution, what I call participation. Provided that a person is artistic, provided in a word that he is one of the confraternity, nothing else matters." The way in which Morel was one of the confraternity was—so far as I was able to discover—that he was sufficiently fond of both women and men to satisfy either sex with the fruits of his experience of the other—as we shall see later on. But what it is essential to note here is that as soon as I had given him my word that I would speak on his behalf to Mme Verdurin, as soon, especially, as I had actually done so without any possibility of subsequent retractation, Morel's "respect" for myself vanished as though by magic, the formal language of respect melted away, and indeed for some time he avoided me, contriving to appear to despise me, so that if Mme Verdurin wanted me to give him a message, to ask him to play something, he would continue to talk to one of the faithful, then move on to another, changing his seat if I approached him. The others were

obliged to tell him three or four times that I had spoken
to him, after which he would reply, with an air of constraint, briefly—unless we were by ourselves. Then he
was expansive and friendly, for there was a charming side
to him. I concluded all the same from this first evening
that his must be a vile nature, that he would not shrink
from any act of servility if the need arose, and was incapable of gratitude. In which he resembled the majority of
mankind. But inasmuch as I had inherited a strain of my
grandmother's nature, and enjoyed the diversity of other
people without expecting anything of them or resenting
anything that they did, I overlooked his baseness, rejoiced
in his gaiety when it was in evidence, and indeed in what
I believe to have been a genuine affection on his part
when, having run through the whole gamut of his false
ideas of human nature, he realised (in fits and starts, for
he had strange reversions to blind and primitive savagery)
that my gentleness with him was disinterested, that my
indulgence arose not from a want of perception but from
what he called kindness; and above all I was enraptured
by his art, through which, although it was little more than
an admirable virtuosity, and although he was not, in the
intellectual sense of the word, a real musician, I heard
again or for the first time so much beautiful music. Moreover a manager (M. de Charlus, in whom I had not suspected these talents, although Mme de Guermantes, who
had known him as a very different person in their
younger days, asserted that he had composed a sonata for
her, painted a fan, and so forth), a manager modest in regard to his true merits, extremely gifted, contrived to
place this virtuosity at the service of a versatile artistic
sense which increased it tenfold. Imagine a purely skilful

performer in the Russian ballet, trained, taught, developed
in all directions by M. Diaghilev.

I had just given Mme Verdurin the message with
which Morel had entrusted me and was talking to M. de
Charlus about Saint-Loup, when Cottard burst into the
room announcing, as though the house were on fire, that
the Cambremers had arrived. Mme Verdurin, not wishing
to appear, in front of newcomers such as M. de Charlus
(whom Cottard had not seen) and myself, to attach any
great importance to the arrival of the Cambremers, did
not move, made no response to the announcement of
these tidings, and merely said to the Doctor, fanning herself gracefully and adopting the tone of a marquise in the
Théâtre-Français: "The Baron has just been telling
us . . ." This was too much for Cottard. Less brightly
than he would have done in the old days, for learning and
high positions had slowed down his delivery, but nevertheless with the excitement which he recaptured at the
Verdurins', he exclaimed: "A Baron! What Baron?
Where's the Baron?" staring round the room with an astonishment that bordered on incredulity. With the affected indifference of a hostess when a servant has broken
a valuable glass in front of her guests, and with the artificial, high-pitched tone of a Conservatoire prize-winner
acting in a play by the younger Dumas, Mme Verdurin
replied, pointing with her fan to Morel's patron: "Why,
the Baron de Charlus, to whom let me introduce you . . .
M. le Professeur Cottard." Mme Verdurin was for that
matter by no means sorry to have an opportunity of playing the leading lady. M. de Charlus proffered two fingers
which the Professor clasped with the kindly smile of a
"prince of science." But he stopped short upon seeing the

Cambremers enter the room, while M. de Charlus led me into a corner to have a word with me, not without feeling my muscles, which is a German habit.

M. de Cambremer bore little resemblance to the old Marquise. As she was wont to remark tenderly, he took entirely "after his papa." To anyone who had only heard of him, or of letters written by him, brisk and suitably expressed, his personal appearance was startling. No doubt one grew accustomed to it. But his nose had chosen, in placing itself askew above his mouth, perhaps the only oblique line, among so many possible ones, that one would never have thought of tracing upon this face, and one that indicated a vulgar stupidity, aggravated still further by the proximity of a Norman complexion on cheeks that were like two red apples. It is possible that M. de Cambremer's eyes retained between their eyelids a trace of the sky of the Cotentin, so soft upon sunny days when the wayfarer amuses himself counting in their hundreds the shadows of the poplars drawn up by the roadside, but those eyelids, heavy, bleared and drooping, would have prevented the least flash of intelligence from escaping. And so, discouraged by the meagreness of that azure gaze, one returned to the big crooked nose. By a transposition of the senses, M. de Cambremer looked at you with his nose. This nose of his was not ugly; it was if anything too handsome, too bold, too proud of its own importance. Arched, polished, gleaming, brand-new, it was amply disposed to make up for the spiritual inadequacy of the eyes. Unfortunately, if the eyes are sometimes the organ through which our intelligence is revealed, the nose (whatever the intimate solidarity and the unsuspected repercussion of one feature on another), the nose is generally the organ in which stupidity is most readily displayed.

Although the propriety of the dark clothes which M. de Cambremer invariably wore, even in the morning, might well reassure those who were dazzled and exasperated by the insolent brightness of the seaside attire of people whom they did not know, it was none the less impossible to understand why the wife of the judge should have declared with an air of discernment and authority, as a person who knows far more than you about the high society of Alençon, that on seeing M. de Cambremer one immediately felt oneself, even before one knew who he was, in the presence of a man of supreme distinction, of a man of perfect breeding, a change from the sort of person one saw at Balbec, a man in short in whose company one could breathe freely. He was to her, asphyxiated by all those Balbec tourists who did not know her world, like a bottle of smelling salts. It seemed to me on the contrary that he was one of those people whom my grandmother would at once have set down as "very common," and since she had no conception of snobbishness, she would no doubt have been stupefied that he could have succeeded in winning the hand of Mlle Legrandin, who must surely be difficult to please, having a brother who was "so well-bred." At best one might have said of M. de Cambremer's plebeian ugliness that it was to some extent redolent of the soil and had a hint of something very anciently local; one was reminded, on examining his faulty features, which one would have liked to correct, of those names of little Norman towns as to the etymology of which my friend the curé was mistaken because the peasants, mispronouncing or having misunderstood the Latin

or Norman words that underlay them, have finally perpet-
uated in a barbarism to be found already in the cartularies, as Brichot would have said, a misinterpretation and a
faulty pronunciation. Life in these little old towns may,
for all that, be pleasant enough, and M. de Cambremer
must have had his good points, for if it was in a mother's
nature that the old Marquise should prefer her son to her
daughter-in-law, on the other hand she who had other
children, of whom two at least were not devoid of merit,
was often heard to declare that the Marquis was, in her
opinion, the best of the family. During the short time he
had spent in the Army, his messmates, finding Cambremer too long a name to pronounce, had given him the
nickname Cancan, implying a flow of gossip, which he
had done nothing to deserve. He knew how to brighten a
dinner-party to which he was invited by saying when the
fish (even if it were putrescent) or the entrée came in: "I
say, that looks a fine beast." And his wife, who had
adopted on entering the family everything that she supposed to form part of their ethos, put herself on the level
of her husband's friends and perhaps sought to please him
like a mistress and as though she had been involved in his
bachelor existence, by saying in a casual tone when she
spoke of him to officers: "You shall see Cancan presently.
Cancan has gone to Balbec, but he will be back this
evening." She was furious at having compromised herself
this evening by coming to the Verdurins' and had done so
only in response to the entreaties of her mother-in-law
and her husband, in the interests of a renewal of the lease.
But, being less well-brought-up than they, she made no
secret of the ulterior motive and for the last fortnight had
been making fun of this dinner-party to her women

friends. "You know we're going to dine with our tenants. That will be well worth an increased rent. As a matter of fact, I'm rather curious to see what they've done to our poor old Raspelière" (as though she had been born in the house, and would find there all her old family associations). "Our old keeper told me only yesterday that you wouldn't know the place. I can't bear to think of all that must be going on there. I'm sure we shall have to have the whole place disinfected before we move in again." She arrived haughty and morose, with the air of a great lady whose castle, owing to a state of war, is occupied by the enemy, but who nevertheless feels herself at home and makes a point of showing the conquerors that they are intruders. Mme de Cambremer could not see me at first for I was in a bay at the side of the room with M. de Charlus, who was telling me that he had heard from Morel that his father had been a "steward" in my family, and that he, Charlus, credited me with sufficient intelligence and magnanimity (a term common to himself and Swann) to forgo the shabby and ignoble pleasure which vulgar little idiots (I was warned) would not have failed, in my place, to give themselves by revealing to our hosts details which they might regard as demeaning. "The mere fact that I take an interest in him and extend my protection over him, gives him a pre-eminence and wipes out the past," the Baron concluded. As I listened to him and promised the silence which I would have kept even without the hope of being considered in return intelligent and magnanimous, I looked at Mme de Cambremer. And I had difficulty in recognising the melting, savoury morsel I had had beside me the other day at tea-time on the terrace at Balbec in the piece of Norman shortbread I now

saw, hard as rock, in which the faithful would in vain
have tried to insert their teeth. Irritated in advance by the
good nature which her husband had inherited from his
mother, and which would make him assume a flattered
expression when the faithful were presented to him, but
nevertheless anxious to perform her duty as a society
woman, when Brichot was introduced to her she wanted
to introduce him to her husband, as she had seen her
more fashionable friends do, but, rage or pride prevailing
over the desire to show her knowledge of the world, instead of saying, as she ought to have done, "Allow me to
present my husband," she said: "I present you to my husband," holding aloft thus the banner of the Cambremers,
but to no avail, for her husband bowed as low before Brichot as she had expected. But all Mme de Cambremer's
ill humour vanished in an instant when her eye fell on
M. de Charlus, whom she knew by sight. Never had she
succeeded in obtaining an introduction, even at the time
of her liaison with Swann. For as M. de Charlus always
sided with the woman—with his sister-in-law against
M. de Guermantes's mistresses, with Odette, at that time
still unmarried, but an old flame of Swann's, against the
new—he had, as a stern defender of morals and faithful
protector of homes, given Odette—and kept—the promise
that he would never allow himself to be introduced to
Mme de Cambremer. She had certainly never imagined
that it was at the Verdurins' that she was at length to
meet this unapproachable person. M. de Cambremer
knew that this was a great joy to her, so great that he
himself was moved by it and gave his wife a look that implied: "You're glad you decided to come, aren't you?" He
spoke in fact very little, knowing that he had married a

superior woman. "Unworthy as I am," he would say at
every moment, and readily quoted a fable of La Fontaine
and one of Florian which seemed to him to apply to his
ignorance and at the same time to enable him, beneath
the outward form of a disdainful flattery, to show the men
of science who were not members of the Jockey that one
might be a sportsman and yet have read fables. The unfortunate thing was that he knew only two. And so they
kept cropping up. Mme de Cambremer was no fool, but
she had a number of extremely irritating habits. With her,
the corruption of names had absolutely nothing to do with
aristocratic disdain. She was not the person to say, like the
Duchesse de Guermantes (whom the mere fact of her
birth ought to have preserved even more than Mme de
Cambremer from such an absurdity), with a pretence of
not remembering the unfashionable name (although it is
now that of one of the women whom it is most difficult to
approach) of Julien de Monchâteau: "a little Madame . . .
Pico della Mirandola." No, when Mme de Cambremer
said a name wrong it was out of kindness of heart, so as
not to appear to know some damaging fact, and when, out
of truthfulness, she admitted it, she tried to conceal it by
distorting it. If, for instance, she was defending a woman,
she would try to conceal, while determined not to lie to
the person who had asked her to tell the truth, the fact
that Madame So-and-so was at the moment the mistress
of M. Sylvain Lévy, and would say: "No . . . I know absolutely nothing about her, I believe that people used to
accuse her of having inspired a passion in a gentleman
whose name I don't know, something like Cahn, Kohn,
Kuhn; anyhow, I believe the gentleman has been dead for
years and that there was never anything between them."

This is an analogous—but inverse—process to that adopted by liars who, in falsifying what they have done when giving an account of it to a mistress or merely to a friend, imagine that their listener will not immediately see that the crucial phrase (as with Cahn, Kohn, Kuhn) is interpolated, is of a different texture from the rest of the conversation, is false-bottomed.

Mme Verdurin whispered in her husband's ear: "Shall I offer my arm to the Baron de Charlus? As you'll have Mme de Cambremer on your right, we might divide the honours." "No," said M. Verdurin, "since the other is higher in rank" (meaning that M. de Cambremer was a marquis), "M. de Charlus is, after all, his inferior." "Very well, I shall put him beside the Princess." And Mme Verdurin introduced Mme Sherbatoff to M. de Charlus; each of them bowed in silence, with an air of knowing all about the other and of promising a mutual secrecy. M. Verdurin introduced me to M. de Cambremer. Before he had even begun to speak to me in his loud and slightly stammering voice, his tall figure and high complexion displayed in their oscillation the martial hesitation of a commanding officer who tries to put you at your ease and says: "I have heard about you, I shall see what can be done; your punishment shall be remitted; we don't thirst for blood here; everything will be all right." Then, as he shook my hand: "I believe you know my mother," he said to me. The verb "believe" seemed to him appropriate to the discretion of a first meeting but not to imply any uncertainty, for he went on: "I have a note for you from her." M. de Cambremer was childishly happy to revisit a place where he had lived for so long. "I'm at home again," he said to Mme Verdurin, while his eyes marvelled at recognising the flowers painted on panels over the doors, and the marble busts on their high pedestals. He might, all the same, have felt somewhat at sea, for Mme Verdurin had brought with her a quantity of fine old things of her own. In this respect Mme Verdurin, while regarded by the Cambremers as having turned everything upside down, was not revolutionary but intelligently conservative, in a sense which they did not understand. They thus wrongly accused her of hating the old house and of degrading it by hanging plain cloth curtains instead of their rich plush, like an ignorant parish priest reproaching a diocesan architect for putting back in its place the old carved wood which the cleric had discarded and seen fit to replace with ornaments purchased in the Place Saint-Sulpice. Furthermore, a herb garden was beginning to take the place, in front of the house, of the flower-beds that were the pride not merely of the Cambremers but of their gardener. The latter, who regarded the Cambremers as his sole masters and groaned beneath the Verdurins' yoke, as though the place were momentarily occupied by an invading army of roughneck soldiery, went in secret to unburden his grievances to its dispossessed mistress, complained bitterly of the contempt with which his araucarias, begonias, sempervivum and double dahlias were treated, and that they should dare in so grand a place to grow such common plants as camomile and maidenhair fern. Mme Verdurin sensed this silent opposition and had made up her mind, if she took a long lease of La Raspelière or even bought the place, to make one of her conditions the dismissal of the gardener, by whom his old mistress, on the contrary, set great store. He had worked for her for nothing when times were bad, and he adored her; but by that odd partitioning of opinion which we find among the people, whereby the most profound moral scorn is embedded in the most passionate admiration, which in turn overlaps old and undying grudges, he used often to say of Mme de Cambremer, who, caught by the invasion of '70 in a house that she owned in the East of France, had been obliged to endure for a month the contact of the Germans: "What many people have against Madame la Marquise is that during the war she took the side of the Prussians and even had them to stay in her house. At any other time, I could understand it; but in wartime she shouldn't have done it. It's not right." So that at one and the same time he was faithful to her unto death, venerated her for her kindness, and firmly believed that she had been guilty of treason. Mme Verdurin was annoyed that M. de Cambremer should claim to recognise La Raspelière so well. "You must notice a good many changes, all the same," she replied. "For one thing there were those big bronze Barbedienne devils and some horrid little plush chairs which I packed off at once to the attic, though even that's too good a place for them." After this acerbic riposte to M. de Cambremer, she offered him her arm to go in to dinner. He hesitated for a moment, saying to himself: "I can't really go in before M. de Charlus." But assuming the other to be an old friend of the house, since he did not have the place of honour, he decided to take the arm that was offered him and told Mme Verdurin how proud he felt to be admitted into the cenacle (it was thus that he styled the little nucleus, not without a smile of self-congratulation at knowing the term). Cottard, who was seated next to M. de Charlus, beamed at him through his pince-nez, to make his acquaintance and to break the ice, with a series of winks far more insistent than they would have been in the old days, and not interrupted by fits of shyness. And these winning glances, enhanced by the smile that accompanied them, were no longer contained by the glass of his pince-nez but overflowed on all sides. The Baron, who was only too inclined to see people of his sort everywhere, had no doubt that Cottard was one of them and was making eyes at him. At once he turned on the Professor the cold shoulder of the invert, as contemptuous of those who are attracted by him as he is ardent in pursuit of those he finds attractive. Although everyone speaks mendaciously of the pleasure of being loved, which fate constantly withholds, it is undoubtedly a general law, the application of which is by no means confined to the Charluses of this world, that the person whom we do not love and who loves us seems to us insufferable. To such a person, to a woman of whom we say not that she loves us but that she clings to us, we prefer the society of any other, no matter who, with neither her charm, nor her looks, nor her brains. She will recover these, in our estimation, only when she has ceased to love us. In this sense, we might regard the invitation aroused in an invert by a man he finds repellent who pursues him as simply the transposition, in a comical form, of this universal rule. But in his case it is much stronger. Hence, whereas the normal man seeks to conceal the irritation he feels, the invert is implacable in making it clear to the man who provokes it, as he would certainly not bring it home to a woman, M. de Charlus for instance to the Princesse de Guermantes, whose passion for him he found irksome but flattering. But when they see another man display a particular predilection towards them, then,

whether because they fail to recognise that it is the same
as their own, or because it is a painful reminder that this
predilection, exalted by them as long as it is they themselves who feel it, is regarded as a vice, or from a desire
to rehabilitate themselves by making a scene in circumstances in which it costs them nothing, or from a fear of
being unmasked which suddenly overtakes them when desire no longer leads them blindfold from one imprudence
to another, or from rage at being subjected, by the equivocal attitude of another person, to the injury which by
their own attitude, if that other person attracted them,
they would not hesitate to inflict on him, men who do not
in the least mind following a young man for miles, never
taking their eyes off him in the theatre even if he is with
friends, thereby threatening to compromise him with
them, may be heard to say, if a man who does not attract
them merely looks at them, "Monsieur, what do you take
me for?" (simply because he takes them for what they are)
"I don't understand you, no, don't attempt to explain,
you are quite mistaken," may proceed at a pinch from
words to blows, and, to a person who knows the imprudent stranger, wax indignant: "What, you know this
loathsome creature. The way he looks at one! . . . A fine
way to behave!" M. de Charlus did not go quite so far as
this, but assumed the offended, glacial air adopted, when
one appears to suspect them of being of easy virtue, by
women who are not, and even more by women who are.
Furthermore, the invert brought face to face with an invert sees not merely an unpleasing image of himself
which, being purely inanimate, could at the worst only injure his self-esteem, but a second self, living, active in the
same field, capable therefore of injuring him in his loves.

And so it is from an instinct of self-preservation that he will speak ill of the possible rival, whether to people who are able to do the latter some injury (nor does Invert No. 1 mind being thought a liar when he thus denounces Invert No. 2 in front of people who may know all about his own case), or to the young man whom he has "picked up," who is perhaps about to be snatched away from him and whom it is important to persuade that the very things which it is to his advantage to do with the speaker would be the bane of his life if he allowed himself to do them with the other person. To M. de Charlus, who was thinking perhaps of the wholly imaginary dangers in which the presence of this Cottard whose smile he misinterpreted might involve Morel, an invert who did not attract him was not merely a caricature of himself but also an obvious rival. A tradesman practising an uncommon trade who on his arrival in the provincial town where he intends to settle for life discovers that in the same square, directly opposite, the same trade is being carried on by a competitor, is no more discomfited than a Charlus who goes down to a quiet country spot to make love unobserved and, on the day of his arrival, catches sight of the local squire or the barber, whose aspect and manner leave no room for doubt. The tradesman often develops a hatred for his competitor; this hatred degenerates at times into melancholy, and, if there is the slightest suggestion of tainted heredity, one has seen in small towns the tradesman begin to show signs of insanity which is cured only by his being persuaded to "sell up" and move elsewhere. The invert's rage is even more obsessive. He has realised that from the very first instant the squire and the barber have coveted his young companion. Even though he repeats to him a hundred times a day that the barber and the squire are scoundrels whose company would bring disgrace on him, he is obliged, like Harpagon, to watch over his treasure, and gets up in the night to make sure that it is not being stolen. And it is this, no doubt, even more than desire, or the convenience of habits shared in common, and almost as much as that experience of oneself which is the only true experience, that makes one invert detect another with a rapidity and certainty that are almost infallible. He may be mistaken for a moment, but a rapid divination brings him back to the truth. Hence M. de Charlus's error was brief. His divine discernment showed him after the first minute that Cottard was not of his kind, and that he need fear his advances neither for himself, which would merely have annoyed him, nor for Morel, which would have seemed to him a more serious matter. He recovered his calm, and as he was still beneath the influence of the transit of Venus Androgyne, from time to time he smiled a faint smile at the Verdurins without taking the trouble to open his mouth, merely uncreasing a corner of his lips, and for an instant kindled a coquettish light in his eyes, he so obsessed with virility, exactly as his sister-in-law the Duchesse de Guermantes might have done.

"Do you shoot much, Monsieur?" said Mme Verdurin contemptuously to M. de Cambremer.

"Has Ski told you of the near shave we had today?" Cottard inquired of the Mistress.

"I shoot mostly in the forest of Chantepie," replied M. de Cambremer.

"No, I've told her nothing," said Ski.

"Does it deserve its name?" Brichot asked M. de

Cambremer, after a glance at me from the corner of his eye, for he had promised me that he would introduce the topic of etymology, begging me at the same time to conceal from the Cambremers the scorn that he felt for the researches of the Combray priest.

"I'm afraid I must be very stupid, but I don't grasp your question," said M. de Cambremer.

"I mean: do many magpies sing in it?" replied Brichot.

Cottard meanwhile could not bear Mme Verdurin's not knowing that they had nearly missed the train.

"Out with it," Mme Cottard said to her husband encouragingly, "tell us about your odyssey."

"Well, it really is rather out of the ordinary," said the doctor, and repeated his narrative from the beginning. "When I saw that the train was in the station, I was dumbfounded. It was all Ski's fault. You're pretty eccentric with your information, my dear fellow! And there was Brichot waiting for us at the station!"

"I assumed," said the scholar, casting around him what he could still muster of a glance and smiling with his thin lips, "that if you had been detained at Graincourt, it would mean that you had encountered some peripatetic siren."

"Will you hold your tongue! What if my wife were to hear you?" said the Doctor. "This wife of mine, it is jealous."

"Ah! that Brichot," cried Ski, moved to traditional merriment by Brichot's spicy witticism, "he's always the same," although he had no reason to suppose that the worthy academic had ever been specially lecherous. And, to embellish these time-honoured words with the ritual gesture, he made as though he could not resist the desire to pinch Brichot's leg. "He never changes, the rascal," Ski went on, without stopping to think of the effect, at once sad and comic, that Brichot's semi-blindness gave to his words: "Always an eye for the ladies."

"You see," said M. de Cambremer, "what it is to meet a scholar. Here have I been shooting for fifteen years in the forest of Chantepie, and I've never even thought of what the name meant."

Mme de Cambremer cast a stern glance at her husband; she did not like him to humiliate himself thus before Brichot. She was even more displeased when, at every "ready-made" expression that Cancan employed, Cottard, who knew the ins and outs of them all, having himself laboriously acquired them, pointed out to the Marquis, who admitted his stupidity, that they meant nothing: "Why 'drink like a fish'? Do you suppose fish drink more than other creatures? You say: 'mind your p's and q's.' Why p's and q's in particular? Why 'easy as pie'? Why 'at sixes and sevens'? Why 'sow one's wild oats'?"

But at this, the defence of M. de Cambremer was taken up by Brichot, who explained the origin of each expression. Mme de Cambremer, however, was chiefly occupied in examining the changes the Verdurins had introduced at La Raspelière, so that she could criticise some and import others, or perhaps the same ones, to Féterne. "I wonder what that chandelier is that's hanging all askew. I hardly recognise my old Raspelière," she went on, with a familiarly aristocratic air, as she might have spoken of an old servant meaning not so much to indicate his age as to say that he had seen her in her cradle. And as she was a trifle bookish in her speech: "All the same," she added in an undertone, "I can't help feeling that if I were living in another person's house I should feel some compunction about altering everything like this."

"It's a pity you didn't come with them," said Mme Verdurin to M. de Charlus and Morel, hoping that M. de Charlus was now "enrolled" and would submit to the rule that they must all arrive by the same train. "You're sure that Chantepie means the singing magpie, Chochotte?" she went on, to show that, like the great hostess that she was, she could join in every conversation at once.

"Tell me something about this violinist," Mme de Cambremer said to me, "he interests me. I adore music, and it seems to me that I have heard of him before. Complete my education." She had heard that Morel had come with M. de Charlus and hoped, by getting the former to come to her house, to make friends with the latter. She added, however, so that I might not guess her reason for asking, "M. Brichot interests me too." For, although she was highly cultivated, just as certain persons who are prone to obesity eat hardly anything and take exercise all day long without ceasing to grow visibly fatter, so Mme de Cambremer might spend her time, especially at Féterne, delving into ever more recondite philosophy, ever more esoteric music, and yet she emerged from these studies only to hatch intrigues that would enable her to break with the middle-class friends of her girlhood and to form the connexions which she had originally supposed to be part of the social life of her "in-laws" and had since discovered to be far more exalted and remote. A philosopher who was not modern enough for her, Leibniz, has said that the way is long from the intellect to the heart. It was a journey that Mme de Cambremer had been no more capable of making than her brother. Abandoning the study of John Stuart Mill only for that of Lachelier, the less she believed in the reality of the external world, the more desperately she sought to establish herself in a good position in it before she died. In her passion for realism in art, no object seemed to her humble enough to serve as a model to painter or writer. A fashionable picture or novel would have made her sick; Tolstoy's moujiks, or Millet's peasants, were the extreme social boundary beyond which she did not allow the artist to pass. But to cross the boundary that limited her own social relations, to raise herself to an intimate acquaintance with duchesses, this was the goal of all her efforts, so ineffective had the spiritual treatment to which she subjected herself by the study of great masterpieces proved in overcoming the congenital and morbid snobbery that had developed in her. This snobbery had even succeeded in curing certain tendencies to avarice and adultery to which in her younger days she had been inclined, just as certain peculiar and permanent pathological conditions seem to render those who are subject to them immune to other maladies. I could not however refrain, as I listened to her, from admiring, though without deriving any pleasure therefrom, the refinement of her expressions. They were those that are employed in a given period by all the people of the same intellectual range, so that the refined expression provides at once, like the arc of a circle, the means to describe and limit the entire circumference. And so the effect of these expressions is that the people who employ them bore me immediately, because I feel that I already know them, but are generally regarded as superior persons, and have often been offered me as delightful and unappreciated dinner neighbours.

"You cannot fail to be aware, Madame, that many forest regions take their name from the animals that inhabit them. Next to the forest of Chantepie, you have the wood Chantereine."

"I don't know who the queen may be, but you're not very courteous to her," said M. de Cambremer.

"Take that, Chochotte," said Mme de Verdurin. "And otherwise, did you have a pleasant journey?"

"We encountered only vague specimens of humanity who thronged the train. But I must answer M. de Cambremer's question; *reine*, in this instance, is not the wife of a king, but a frog. It is the name that the frog has long retained in this district, as is shown by the station Renneville, which ought to be spelt Reineville."

"I say, that looks a fine beast," said M. de Cambremer to Mme Verdurin, pointing to a fish. (It was one of the compliments by means of which he considered that he paid his whack at a dinner-party, and gave an immediate return of hospitality. "There's no need to invite them back," he would often say, in speaking to his wife of one or other couple of their acquaintance: "They were delighted to have us. It was they who thanked me for coming.") "I may tell you, though, that I've been going to Renneville every day for years, and I've never seen any more frogs there than anywhere else. Madame de Cambremer brought over to these parts the curé of a parish where she owns a considerable property, who has very much the same turn of mind as yourself, it seems to me. He has written a book."

"I know, I've read it with immense interest," Brichot replied hypocritically.

The satisfaction that his pride received indirectly from this answer made M. de Cambremer laugh long and loud. "Ah, well, the author of, what shall I call it, this geography, this glossary, dwells at great length upon the name of a little place of which we were formerly, if I may say so, the lords, and which is called Pont-à-Couleuvre. Of course I am only an ignorant rustic compared with such a fountain of learning, but I have been to Pont-à-Couleuvre a thousand times if he's been there once, and devil take me if I ever saw one of those beastly snakes there—I say beastly in spite of the tribute the worthy La Fontaine pays them." (*The Man and the Snake* was one of his two fables.)

"You haven't seen any, and you saw straight," replied Brichot. "Undoubtedly, the writer you mention knows his subject through and through, he has written a remarkable book."

"He has indeed!" exclaimed Mme de Cambremer. "That book, there's no doubt about it, is a real work of scholarship."

"No doubt he consulted various cartularies (by which we mean the lists of benefices and cures of each diocese), which may have furnished him with the names of lay patrons and ecclesiastical collators. But there are other sources. One of the most learned of my friends has delved into them. He found that the place in question was named Pont-à-Quileuvre. This odd name encouraged him to carry his researches further, to a Latin text in which the bridge that your friend supposes to be infested with snakes is styled *Pons cui aperit*: a closed bridge that was opened only upon due payment."

"You were speaking of frogs. I, when I find myself among such learned folk, feel like the frog before the Areopagus" (this being his other fable), said Cancan who often indulged, with a hearty laugh, in this pleasantry thanks to which he imagined himself to be making at one and the same time, with a mixture of humility and aptness, a profession of ignorance and a display of learning.

Meanwhile Cottard, blocked on one side by M. de Charlus's silence, and driven to seek an outlet elsewhere, turned to me with one of those questions which impressed his patients when it hit the mark and showed them that he could put himself so to speak inside their bodies, and if on the other hand it missed the mark, enabled him to check certain theories, to widen his previous standpoints. "When you come to a relatively high altitude, such as this where we now are, do you find that the change increases your tendency to breathlessness?" he asked me with the certainty of either arousing admiration or enlarging his own knowledge.

M. de Cambremer heard the question and smiled. "I can't tell you how delighted I am to hear that you have fits of breathlessness," he flung at me across the table. He did not mean that it cheered him up, though in fact it did. For this worthy man could not hear any reference to another person's sufferings without a feeling of well-being and a spasm of hilarity which speedily gave place to the instinctive pity of a kind heart. But his words had another meaning which was indicated more precisely by the sentence that followed: "I'm delighted," he explained, "be-

cause my sister has them too." In short, he was delighted
in the same way as if he had heard me mention as one of
my friends a person who was constantly coming to their
house. "What a small world!" was the reflexion which he
formed mentally and which I saw written upon his smiling face when Cottard spoke to me of my attacks. And
these began to establish themselves, from the evening of
this dinner-party, as a sort of common acquaintance, after
whom M. de Cambremer never failed to inquire, if only
to hand on a report to his sister.

As I answered the questions with which his wife kept
plying me about Morel, my thoughts returned to a conversation I had had with my mother that afternoon.
Without attempting to dissuade me from going to the
Verdurins' if there was a chance of my enjoying myself
there, she had pointed out that it was a circle of which
my grandfather would not have approved, which would
have made him exclaim: "On guard!" Then she had gone
on to say: "By the way, Judge Toureuil and his wife told
me they had been to lunch with Mme Bontemps. They
asked me no questions. But I seemed to gather from what
was said that a marriage between you and Albertine
would be the joy of her aunt's life. I think the real reason
is that they are all extremely fond of you. At the same
time the style in which they imagine that you would be
able to keep her, the sort of connexions they more or less
know that we have—all that is not, I fancy, entirely irrele-
vant, although it may be a minor consideration. I
wouldn't have mentioned it to you myself, because I'm
not keen on it, but as I imagine they'll mention it to you,
I thought I'd get a word in first." "But you yourself, what
do you think of her?" I asked my mother. "Well, I'm not

the one who's going to marry her. You could certainly do a great deal better in terms of marriage. But I feel that your grandmother would not have liked me to influence you. As a matter of fact, I can't say what I think of Albertine; I don't think of her. All I can say to you is, like Madame de Sévigné: 'She has good qualities, or so I believe. But at this first stage I can praise her only by negatives. She is not this: she has not the Rennes accent. In time, I shall perhaps say: she is that.' And I shall always think well of her if she can make you happy." But by these very words which left it to me to decide my own happiness, my mother had plunged me into that state of doubt in which I had been plunged long ago when, my father having allowed me to go to *Phèdre* and, what was more, to take up writing as a career, I had suddenly felt myself burdened with too great a responsibility, the fear of distressing him, and that melancholy which we feel when we cease to obey orders which, from one day to another, keep the future hidden, and realise that we have at last begun to live in real earnest, as a grown-up person, the life, the only life that any of us has at his disposal.

Perhaps the best thing would be to wait a little longer, to begin by seeing Albertine as I had seen her in the past, so as to find out whether I really loved her. I might take her, as a diversion, to see the Verdurins, and this thought reminded me that I had come there myself that evening only to learn whether Mme Putbus was staying there or was expected. In any case, she was not dining with them.

"Speaking of your friend Saint-Loup," said Mme de Cambremer, using an expression which betrayed more consistency in her train of thought than her remarks might have led one to suppose, for if she spoke to me about music she was thinking about the Guermantes, "you know that everybody is talking about his marriage to the niece of the Princesse de Guermantes. Though I may say that, for my part, all that society gossip concerns me not one whit." I was seized by a fear that I might have spoken unfeelingly to Robert about the girl in question, a girl full of sham originality, whose mind was as mediocre as her temper was violent. Hardly ever do we hear anything that does not make us regret something we have said. I replied to Mme de Cambremer, truthfully as it happened, that I knew nothing about it, and that anyhow I thought that the girl seemed rather young to be engaged.

"That is perhaps why it's not yet official. Anyhow there's a lot of talk about it."

"I ought to warn you," Mme Verdurin observed drily to Mme de Cambremer, having heard her talking to me about Morel and supposing, when she had lowered her voice to speak of Saint-Loup's engagement, that Morel was still under discussion. "You needn't expect any light music here. In matters of art, you know, the faithful who come to my Wednesdays, my children as I call them, are all fearfully advanced," she added with an air of terrified pride. "I say to them sometimes: My dear people, you move too fast for your Mistress, and she's not exactly notorious for being afraid of daring innovations. Every year it goes a little further; I can see the day coming when they will have no more use for Wagner or d'Indy."

"But it's splendid to be advanced, one can never be advanced enough," said Mme de Cambremer, scrutinising every corner of the dining-room as she spoke, trying to identify the things that her mother-in-law had left there and those that Mme Verdurin had brought with her, and to catch the latter red-handed in an error of taste. At the same time she tried to get me to talk of the subject that interested her most, M. de Charlus. She thought it touching that he should offer his patronage to a violinist: "He seems intelligent."

"Yes, his mind is extremely active for a man of his age," I replied.

"Age? But he doesn't seem at all old, look, the hair is still young." (For, during the last three or four years, the word hair had been used with the article by one of those unknown persons who launch the literary fashions, and everybody at the same radius from the centre as Mme de Cambremer would say "the hair," not without an affected smile. At the present day, people still say "the hair," but from an excessive use of the article the pronoun will be born again.)[13] "What interests me most about M. de Charlus," she went on, "is that one can feel that he is naturally gifted. I may tell you that I attach little importance to knowledge. I'm not interested in what's learnt."

These words were not incompatible with Mme de Cambremer's own particular quality, which was precisely imitated and acquired. But it so happened that one of the things one was required to know at that moment was that knowledge is nothing, and is not worth a straw when compared with originality. Mme de Cambremer had learned, with everything else, that one ought not to learn anything. "That is why," she explained to me, "Brichot, who has an interesting side to him, for I'm not one to despise a certain lively erudition, interests me far less."

But Brichot, at that moment, was occupied with one

thing only: hearing people talk about music, he trembled
lest the subject should remind Mme Verdurin of the
death of Dechambre. He wanted to say something that
would avert that harrowing memory. M. de Cambremer
provided him with an opportunity with the question:
"You mean to say that wooded places always take their
names from animals?"

"Not so," replied Brichot, happy to display his learning before so many strangers, among whom, I had told
him, he would be certain to interest one at least. "We
have only to consider how often, even in the names of
people, a tree is preserved, like a fern in a seam of coal.
One of our eminent Senators is called M. de Saulces de
Freycinet, which means, if I'm not mistaken, a spot
planted with willow and ash, *salix et fraxinetum*; his
nephew M. de Selves combines more trees still, since he is
named de Selves, *sylva*."

Saniette was delighted to see the conversation take so
animated a turn. Since Brichot was talking all the time, he
himself could preserve a silence which would save him
from being the butt of M. and Mme Verdurin's wit. And
growing even more sensitive in his joy and relief, he had
been touched when he heard M. Verdurin, notwithstanding the formality of so grand a dinner-party, tell the butler to put a jug of water in front of him since he never
drank anything else. (The generals responsible for the
death of most soldiers insist upon their being well fed.)
Moreover, Mme Verdurin had actually smiled at him
once. Decidedly, they were kind people. He was not going
to be tortured any more.

At this moment the meal was interrupted by one of
the party whom I have forgotten to mention, an eminent

Norwegian philosopher who spoke French very well but very slowly, for the twofold reason that, in the first place, having learned the language only recently and not wishing to make mistakes (though he did make a few), he referred each word to a sort of mental dictionary, and secondly, being a metaphysician, he always thought of what he intended to say while he was saying it, which, even in a Frenchman, is a cause of slowness. For the rest, he was a delightful person, although similar in appearance to many other people, save in one respect. This man who was so slow in his diction (there was an interval of silence after every word) developed a startling rapidity in escaping from the room as soon as he had said good-bye. His haste made one suppose, the first time one saw it, that he was suffering from colic or some even more urgent need.

"My dear—colleague," he said to Brichot, after deliberating in his mind whether colleague was the correct term, "I have a sort of—desire to know whether there are other trees in the—nomenclature of your beautiful French—Latin—Norman tongue. Madame" (he meant Mme Verdurin, although he dared not look at her) "has told me that you know everything. Is not this precisely the moment?"

"No, it's the moment for eating," interrupted Mme Verdurin, who saw the dinner becoming interminable.

"Very well," the Scandinavian replied, bowing his head over his plate with a resigned and sorrowful smile. "But I must point out to Madame that if I have permitted myself this questionnaire—pardon me, this questation—it is because I have to return tomorrow to Paris to dine at the Tour d'Argent or at the Hôtel Meurice. My French—confrère—M. Boutroux is to address us there about cer-

tain séances of spiritualism—pardon me, certain spirituous
evocations—which he has verified."

"The Tour d'Argent is not nearly as good as they
make out," said Mme Verdurin sourly. "In fact, I've had
some disgusting dinners there."

"But am I mistaken, is not the food that one con-
sumes at Madame's table an example of the finest French
cookery?"

"Well, it's not positively bad," replied Mme Verdurin, mollified. "And if you come next Wednesday, it
will be better."

"But I am leaving on Monday for Algiers, and from
there I am going to the Cape. And when I am at the
Cape of Good Hope, I shall no longer be able to meet my
illustrious colleague—pardon me, I shall no longer be able
to meet my confrère."

And he set to work obediently, after offering these
retrospective apologies, to devour his food at a headlong
pace. But Brichot was only too delighted to be able to furnish other vegetable etymologies, and replied, so greatly
interesting the Norwegian that he again stopped eating,
but with a sign to the servants that they might remove his
full plate and go on to the next course.

"One of the Immortals," said Brichot, "is named
Houssaye, or a place planted with holly-trees; in the name
of a brilliant diplomat, d'Ormesson, you will find the elm,
the *ulmus* beloved of Virgil, which gave its name to the
town of Ulm; in the names of his colleagues, M. de la
Boulaye, the birch (*bouleau*), M. d'Aunay, the alder
(*aune*), M. de Bussière, the box-tree (*buis*), M. Albaret,
the sapwood (*aubier*)" (I made a mental note that I must
tell this to Céleste), "M. de Cholet, the cabbage (*chou*),

and the apple-tree (*pommier*) in the name of M. dela Pommeraye, whose lectures we used to attend, do you remember, Saniette, in the days when the worthy Porel had been sent to the furthest ends of the earth, as Proconsul in Odéonia?"

On hearing the name Saniette on Brichot's lips, M. Verdurin glanced at his wife and at Cottard with an ironical smile which disconcerted their timid guest.

"You said that Cholet was derived from *chou*," I remarked to Brichot. "Does the name of a station I passed before reaching Doncières, Saint-Frichoux, also come from *chou?*"

"No, Saint-Frichoux is *Sanctus Fructuosus*, as *Sanctus Ferreolus* gave rise to Saint-Fargeau, but that's not Norman in the least."

"He knows too much, he's boring us," the Princess gurgled softly.

"There are so many other names that interest me, but I can't ask you everything at once." And turning to Cottard, "Is Madame Putbus here?" I asked him.

"No, thank heaven," replied Mme Verdurin, who had overheard my question, "I've managed to divert her holiday plans towards Venice, so we are rid of her for this year."

"I shall myself be entitled presently to two trees," said M. de Charlus, "for I have more or less taken a little house between Saint-Martin-du-Chêne and Saint-Pierre-des-Ifs."

"But that's quite close to here. I hope you'll come over often with Charlie Morel. You have only to come to an arrangement with our little group about the trains, you're just a stone's throw from Doncières," said Mme

Verdurin, who hated people not coming by the same train and at the hours when she sent carriages to meet them. She knew how stiff the climb was to La Raspelière, even by the zigzag path behind Féterne which was half an hour longer; she was afraid that those of her guests who came on their own might not find carriages to take them, or even, having in reality stayed away, might plead the excuse that they had not found a carriage at Douville-Féterne, and had not felt strong enough to make so stiff a climb on foot. To this invitation M. de Charlus responded with a silent nod.

"I bet he's an awkward customer, he's got a very starchy look," the Doctor whispered to Ski, for, having remained very unassuming in spite of a surface-dressing of arrogance, he made no attempt to conceal the fact that Charlus was snubbing him. "He's obviously unaware that at all the fashionable spas, and even in Paris, in all the clinics, the physicians, who naturally regard me as the 'big boss,' make it a point of honour to introduce me to all the noblemen present, not that they need to be asked twice. It makes my stay at the spas quite enjoyable," he added lightly. "Indeed at Doncières the medical officer of the regiment, who is the doctor who attends the Colonel, invited me to lunch to meet him, saying that I was fully entitled to dine with the General. And that general is a Monsieur *de* something. I don't know whether his title-deeds are more or less ancient than those of this Baron."

"Don't you worry about him, his is a very humble coronet," replied Ski in an undertone, and he added something indistinct including a word of which I caught only the last syllable, -*ast*, being engaged in listening to what Brichot was saying to M. de Charlus.

"No, as to that, I'm sorry to have to tell you, you have probably one tree only, for if Saint-Martin-du-Chêne is obviously *Sanctus Martinus juxta quercum*, on the other hand the word *if* [yew] may be simply the root *ave, eve*, which means moist, as in Aveyron, Lodève, Yvette, and which you see survive in our kitchen sinks (*éviers*). It is the word *eau* which in Breton is represented by *ster*, Stermaria, Sterlaer, Sterbouest, Ster-en-Dreuchen."

I did not hear the rest, for whatever the pleasure I might feel on hearing again the name Stermaria, I could not help listening to Cottard, near whom I was seated, as he murmured to Ski: "Really! I didn't know that. So he's a gentleman who knows how to cope in life. He's one of the happy band, is he? And yet he hasn't got rings of fat round his eyes. I shall have to watch out for my feet under the table or he might take a fancy to me. But I'm not at all surprised. I'm used to seeing noblemen in the showers in their birthday suits, they're all more or less degenerates. I don't talk to them, because after all I'm in an official position and it might do me harm. But they know quite well who I am."

Saniette, who had been scared by Brichot's interpellation, was beginning to breathe again, like a man who is afraid of storms when he finds that the lightning has not been followed by any sound of thunder, when he heard M. Verdurin interrogate him, fastening upon him a stare which did not let go of the poor man until he had finished speaking, so as to disconcert him from the start and prevent him from recovering his composure. "But you never told us that you went to those matinées at the Odéon, Saniette?"

Trembling like a recruit before a bullying sergeant,

Saniette replied, making his reply as exiguous as possible, so that it might have a better chance of escaping the blow: "Only once, to the *Chercheuse*."

"What's that he says?" shouted M. Verdurin, with an air of disgust and fury combined, knitting his brows as though he needed all his concentration to grasp something unintelligible. "It's impossible to understand what you say. What have you got in your mouth?" inquired M. Verdurin, growing more and more furious, and alluding to Saniette's speech defect.

"Poor Saniette, I won't have him made unhappy," said Mme Verdurin in a tone of false pity, so as to leave no one in doubt as to her husband's rudeness.

"I was at the Ch . . . Che . . ."

"Che, che, do try to speak distinctly," said M. Verdurin, "I can't understand a word you say."

Almost without exception, the faithful burst out laughing, looking like a group of cannibals in whom the sight of a wounded white man has aroused the thirst for blood. For the instinct of imitation and absence of courage govern society and the mob alike. And we all of us laugh at a person whom we see being made fun of, though it does not prevent us from venerating him ten years later in a circle where he is admired. It is in the same fashion that the populace banishes or acclaims its kings.

"Come, now, it's not his fault," said Mme Verdurin.

"It's not mine either, people ought not to dine out if they can't speak properly."

"I was at the *Chercheuse d'Esprit* by Favart."

"What! It's the *Chercheuse d'Esprit* that you call the *Chercheuse*? Why, that's marvellous! I might have gone on

trying for a hundred years without guessing it," cried
M. Verdurin, who nevertheless would have decided immediately that you were not literary, were not artistic,
were not "one of us," if he had heard you quote the full
title of certain works. For instance, one was expected to
say the *Malade,* the *Bourgeois,* and anyone who added
imaginaire or *gentilhomme* would have shown that he did
not "belong," just as in a drawing-room a person proves
that he is not in society by saying "M. de Montesquiou-
Fezensac" instead of "M. de Montesquiou."

"But it isn't so extraordinary," said Saniette, breathless with emotion but smiling, although he was in no
smiling mood.

Mme Verdurin could not contain herself: "Oh yes it
is!" she exclaimed with a snigger. "You may be quite sure
that nobody would ever have guessed that you meant the
Chercheuse d'Esprit."

M. Verdurin went on in a gentler tone, addressing
both Saniette and Brichot: "It's not a bad play, actually,
the *Chercheuse d'Esprit.*"

Uttered in a serious tone, this simple remark, in
which no trace of malice was to be detected, did Saniette
as much good and aroused in him as much gratitude as a
compliment. He was unable to utter a single word and
preserved a happy silence. Brichot was more loquacious.
"It's true," he replied to M. Verdurin, "and if it could be
passed off as the work of some Sarmatian or Scandinavian
author, we might put it forward as a candidate for the vacant post of masterpiece. But, be it said without any disrespect to the shade of the gentle Favart, he had not the
Ibsenian temperament." (Immediately he blushed to the
roots of his hair, remembering the Norwegian philoso-

pher, who looked unhappy because he was trying in vain to discover what vegetable the *buis* might be that Brichot had cited a little earlier in connexion with the name Bussière.) "However, now that Porel's satrapy is filled by a functionary who is a Tolstoyan of rigorous observance, it may come to pass that we shall witness *Anna Karenina* or *Resurrection* beneath the Odéonian architrave."

"I know the portrait of Favart to which you allude," said M. de Charlus. "I have seen a very fine print of it at the Comtesse Molé's."

This name made a great impression upon Mme Verdurin. "Oh! so you go to Mme de Molé's!" she exclaimed. She supposed that people said "the Comtesse Molé," "Madame Molé," simply as an abbreviation, as she heard people say "the Rohans" or in contempt, as she herself said, "Madame La Trémoïlle." She had no doubt that the Comtesse Molé, who knew the Queen of Greece and the Princesse de Caprarola, must have as much right as anybody to the particle, and for once in a way had decided to bestow it upon so brilliant a personage, and one who had been extremely civil to herself. And so, to make it clear that she had spoken thus on purpose and did not grudge the Comtesse her "de," she went on: "But I had no idea that you knew Madame de Molé!" as though it was doubly extraordinary, both that M. de Charlus should know the lady and that Mme Verdurin should not know that he knew her. Now society, or at least the people to whom M. de Charlus gave that name, forms a relatively homogeneous and closed whole. And whereas it is understandable that in the disparate vastness of the middle classes a barrister should say to somebody who knows one of his schoolfriends: "But how in the world do you come to know him?", to be surprised at a Frenchman's knowing the meaning of the word *temple* or *forest* would be hardly more extraordinary than to wonder at the accidents that might have brought together M. de Charlus and the Comtesse Molé. Moreover, even if such an acquaintance had not followed quite naturally from the laws that govern society, even if it had been fortuitous, how could there be anything strange in the fact that Mme Verdurin did not know of it, since she was meeting M. de Charlus for the first time, and his relations with Mme Molé were far from being the only thing she did not know about him, for in fact she knew nothing.

"Who was in this *Chercheuse d'Esprit*, my good Saniette?" asked M. Verdurin. Although he felt that the storm had passed, the old archivist hesitated before answering.

"There you go," said Mme Verdurin, "you frighten him, you make fun of everything he says, and then you expect him to answer. Come along, tell us who was in it, and you shall have some galantine to take home," said Mme Verdurin, making a cruel allusion to the penury into which Saniette had plunged himself by trying to rescue the family of a friend.

"I can remember only that it was Mme Samary who played the Zerbina," said Saniette.

"The Zerbina? What in the world is that?" M. Verdurin shouted, as though the house were on fire.

"It's one of the stock types in the old repertory, see *Le Capitaine Fracasse*, as who should say the Braggart, the Pedant."

"Ah, the pedant, that's you. The Zerbina! No, really the man's cracked," exclaimed M. Verdurin. (Mme Verdurin looked at her guests and laughed as though to apol-

ogise for Saniette.) "The Zerbina, he imagines that everybody will know at once what it means. You're like M. de
Longepierre, the stupidest man I know, who said to us
quite familiarly the other day 'the Banat.' Nobody had
any idea what he meant. Finally we were informed that it
was a province of Serbia."

To put an end to Saniette's torture, which hurt me
more than it hurt him, I asked Brichot if he knew what
the word Balbec meant. "Balbec is probably a corruption
of Dalbec," he told me. "One would have to consult the
charters of the Kings of England, suzerains of Normandy,
for Balbec was a dependency of the barony of Dover, for
which reason it was often styled Balbec d'Outre-Mer, Bal-
bec-en-Terre. But the barony of Dover itself came under
the bishopric of Bayeux, and, notwithstanding the rights
that were temporarily enjoyed over the abbey by the
Templars, from the time of Louis d'Harcourt, Patriarch
of Jerusalem and Bishop of Bayeux, it was the bishops of
that diocese who appointed to the benefice of Balbec. So it
was explained to me by the incumbent of Douville, a
bald, eloquent, fanciful man and a devotee of the table,
who lives by the rule of Brillat-Savarin, and who ex-
pounded to me in somewhat sibylline terms a loose peda-
gogy, while he fed me upon some admirable fried
potatoes."

While Brichot smiled to show how witty it was to
juxtapose such disparate matters and to employ an ironically lofty diction in treating of commonplace things,
Saniette was trying to find a loophole for some witticism
which would raise him from the abyss into which he had
fallen. The witticism was what was known as a "more or
less," but it had changed its form, for there is an evolu-

tion in puns as in literary styles, an epidemic that disappears is replaced by another, and so forth. At one time the typical "more or less" was the "height of . . ." But this was out of date, no one used it any more, except for Cottard who might still say, on occasion, in the middle of a game of piquet: "Do you know what is the height of absentmindedness? It's to think that the Edict of [*l'édit de*] Nantes was an Englishwoman." These "heights" had been replaced by nicknames. In reality it was still the old "more or less," but, as the nickname was in fashion, people did not notice. Unfortunately for Saniette, when these "more or lesses" were not his own, and as a rule were unknown to the little nucleus, he produced them so timidly that, in spite of the laugh with which he followed them up to indicate their humorous nature, nobody saw the point. And if on the other hand the joke was his own, as he had generally hit upon it in conversation with one of the faithful, and the latter had repeated it, appropriating the authorship, the joke was in that case known, but not as being Saniette's. And so when he slipped in one of these it was recognised, but, because he was its author, he was accused of plagiarism.

"Thus," Brichot continued, "*bec*, in Norman, is a stream; there is the Abbey of Bec, Mobec, the stream from the marsh (*mor* or *mer* meant a marsh, as in Morville, or in Bricquemar, Alvimare, Cambremer), Bricquebec, the stream from the high ground, coming from *briga*, a fortified place, as in Bricqueville, Bricquebosc, le Bric, Briand, or from *brice*, bridge, which is the same as *Brücke* in German (Innsbruck), and as the English *bridge* which ends so many place-names (Cambridge, for instance). You have moreover in Normandy many other in-

stances of *bec*: Caudebec, Bolbec, le Robec, le Bec-Hel-
louin, Becquerel. It's the Norman form of the German
Bach, Offenbach, Anspach; Varaguebec, from the old
word *varaigne*, equivalent to *warren*, means protected
woods or ponds. As for *dal*," Brichot went on, "it is a
form of *Thal*, a valley: Darnetal, Rosendal, and indeed,
close to Louviers, Becdal. The river that has given its
name to Balbec is, by the way, charming. Seen from a
falaise (*Fels* in German, in fact not far from here, standing
on a height, you have the picturesque town of Falaise),
it runs close under the spires of the church, which is actually a long way from it, and seems to be reflecting
them."

"I can well believe it," said I, "it's an effect that Elstir is very fond of. I've seen several sketches of it in his
studio."

"Elstir! You know Tiche?" cried Mme Verdurin. "But
do you know that we used to be the closest friends.
Thank heaven, I never see him now. No, but ask Cottard
or Brichot, he used to have his place laid at my table, he
came every day. Now, there's a man of whom you can say
that it did him no good to leave our little nucleus. I shall
show you presently some flowers he painted for me; you'll
see the difference from the things he's doing now, which I
don't care for at all, not at all! Why, I got him to do a
portrait of Cottard, not to mention all the sketches he did
of me."

"And he gave the Professor purple hair," said Mme
Cottard, forgetting that at the time her husband had not
been even a Fellow of the College. "Would you say that
my husband had purple hair, Monsieur?"

"Never mind!" said Mme Verdurin, raising her chin

with an air of contempt for Mme Cottard and of admiration for the man of whom she was speaking, "it was the work of a bold colourist, a fine painter. Whereas," she added, turning again to me, "I don't know whether you call it painting, all those outlandish great compositions, those hideous contraptions he exhibits now that he has given up coming to me. I call it daubing, it's all so hackneyed, and besides, it lacks relief and personality. There are bits of everybody in it."

"He has revived the grace of the eighteenth century, but in a modern form," Saniette burst out, fortified and emboldened by my friendliness, "but I prefer Helleu."

"There's not the slightest connexion with Helleu," said Mme Verdurin.

"Yes, yes, it's hotted-up eighteenth century. He's a steam Watteau," and he began to laugh.[14]

"Old, old as the hills. I've had that served up to me for years," said M. Verdurin, to whom indeed Ski had once repeated the remark, but as his own invention. "It's unfortunate that when once in a way you say something quite amusing and make it intelligible, it isn't your own."

"I'm sorry about it," Mme Verdurin went on, "because he was really gifted, he has wasted a very remarkable painterly talent. Ah, if only he'd stayed with us! Why, he would have become the greatest landscape painter of our day. And it was a woman who dragged him down so low! Not that that surprises me, for he was an attractive enough man, but common. At bottom, he was a mediocrity. I may tell you that I felt it at once. Really, he never interested me. I was quite fond of him, that was all. For one thing, he was so dirty! Tell me now, do *you* like people who never wash?"

"What is this prettily coloured thing that we're eating?" asked Ski.

"It's called strawberry mousse," said Mme Verdurin.

"But it's ex-qui-site. You ought to open bottles of Château-Margaux, Château-Lafite, port wine."

"I can't tell you how he amuses me, he never drinks anything but water," said Mme Verdurin, seeking to cloak with her delight at this flight of fancy her alarm at the thought of such extravagance.

"But not to drink," Ski went on. "You shall fill all our glasses, and they will bring in marvellous peaches, huge nectarines; there, against the sunset, it will be as luscious as a beautiful Veronese."

"It would cost almost as much," M. Verdurin murmured.

"But take away those cheeses with their hideous colour," said Ski, trying to snatch the plate from in front of his host, who defended his gruyère with all his might.

"You can see why I don't miss Elstir," Mme Verdurin said to me, "this one is far more gifted. Elstir is simply hard work, the man who can't tear himself away from his painting when he feels like it. He's the good pupil, the exam fiend. Ski, now, only follows his own fancy. You'll see him light a cigarette in the middle of dinner."

"By the way, I can't think why you wouldn't invite his wife," said Cottard, "he would be with us still."

"Will you mind what you're saying, please. I don't open my doors to trollops, Monsieur le Professeur," said Mme Verdurin, who had, on the contrary, done everything in her power to make Elstir return, even with his wife. But before they were married she had tried to separate them, had told Elstir that the woman he loved was stupid, dirty, immoral, a thief. For once in a way she had failed to effect a breach. It was with the Verdurin salon that Elstir had broken; and he was glad of it, as converts bless the illness or misfortune that has caused them to withdraw from the world and has shown them the way of salvation.

"He really is magnificent, the Professor," she said. "Why not declare outright that I keep a disorderly house. Anyone would think you didn't know what Madame Elstir was. I'd sooner have the lowest streetwalker at my table! Oh no, I'm not stooping to that! But in any case it would have been stupid of me to overlook the wife when the husband no longer interests me—he's out of date, he can't even draw."

"It's extraordinary in a man of his intelligence," said Cottard.

"Oh, no!" replied Mme Verdurin, "even at the time when he had talent—for he did have talent, the wretch, and to spare—what was tiresome about him was that he hadn't a spark of intelligence."

In order to form this opinion, Mme Verdurin had not waited for their quarrel, or until she had ceased to care for his painting. The fact was that, even at the time when he formed part of the little group, it sometimes happened that Elstir would spend whole days in the company of some woman whom, rightly or wrongly, Mme Verdurin considered a goose, and this, in her opinion, was not the conduct of an intelligent man. "No," she observed judiciously, "I consider that his wife and he are made for one another. Heaven knows, there isn't a more boring creature on the face of the earth, and I should go mad if I had to spend a couple of hours with her. But people say that he finds her very intelligent. There's no use denying it, our Tiche was *extremely stupid*. I've seen him bowled over by women you can't conceive, amiable idiots we'd never have allowed into our little clan. Well, he used to write to them, and argue with them, he, Elstir! That doesn't prevent his having charming qualities, oh, charming, and deliciously absurd, naturally." For Mme Verdurin was convinced that men who are truly remarkable are capable of all sorts of follies. A false idea in which there is nevertheless a grain of truth. Certainly, people's "follies" are insupportable. But a want of balance which we discover only in course of time is the consequence of the entering into a human brain of refinements for which it is not normally adapted. So that the oddities of charming people exasperate us, but there are few if any charming people who are not, at the same time, odd. "There, I shall be able to show you his flowers now," she said to me, seeing that her husband was making signals to her to rise. And she took M. de Cambremer's arm again. M. Verdurin wanted to apologise for this to M. de Charlus, as soon as he had got rid of Mme de Cambremer, and to give him his reasons, chiefly for the pleasure of discussing these social distinctions with a man of title, momentarily the inferior of those who assigned to him the place to which they considered him entitled. But first of all he was anxious to make it clear to M. de Charlus that intellectually he esteemed him too highly to suppose that he could pay any attention to these trivialities.

"Forgive my mentioning these trifles," he began, "for I can well imagine how little importance you attach to them. Middle-class minds take them seriously, but the others, the artists, the people who are really *of our sort*, don't give a rap for them. Now, from the first words we exchanged, I realised that you were *one of us!*" M. de Charlus, who attached a very different meaning to this expression, gave a start. After the Doctor's oglings, his host's insulting frankness took his breath away. "Don't protest, my dear sir, you are *one of us*, it's as clear as daylight," M. Verdurin went on. "Mind you, I don't know whether you practise any of the arts, but that's not necessary. Nor is it always sufficient. Dechambre, who has just died, played exquisitely, with the most vigorous execution, but he wasn't *one of us*, you felt at once that he wasn't. Brichot isn't *one of us*. Morel is, my wife is, I can feel that you are . . ."

"What were you going to say to me?" interrupted M. de Charlus, who was beginning to feel reassured as to M. Verdurin's meaning, but preferred that he should not utter these equivocal remarks quite so loud.

"Only that we put you on the left," replied M. Verdurin.

M. de Charlus, with a tolerant, genial, insolent smile, replied: "Why, that's not of the slightest importance, *here!*" And he gave a little laugh that was all his own—a laugh that came down to him probably from some Bavarian or Lorraine grandmother, who herself had inherited it, in identical form, from an ancestress, so that it had tinkled now, unchanged, for a good many centuries in little old-fashioned European courts, and one could appreciate its precious quality, like that of certain old musical instruments that have become very rare. There are times when, to paint a complete portrait of someone, we should have to add a phonetic imitation to our verbal description, and our portrait of the figure that M. de Charlus presented is liable to remain incomplete in the absence of that little laugh, so delicate, so light, just as certain works of Bach are never accurately rendered because our orchestras lack those small, high trumpets, with a sound so entirely their own, for which the composer wrote this or that part.

"But," explained M. Verdurin, hurt, "we did it on purpose. I attach no importance whatever to titles of nobility," he went on, with that contemptuous smile which I have seen so many people I have known, unlike my grandmother and my mother, assume when they speak of something they do not possess to those who will thereby, they imagine, be prevented from using it to show their superiority over them. "But you see, since we happened to have M. de Cambremer here, and he's a marquis, while you're only a baron . . ."

"Pardon me," M. de Charlus haughtily replied to the astonished Verdurin, "I am also Duke of Brabant, Squire of Montargis, Prince of Oléron, of Carency, of Viareggio and of the Dunes. However, it's not of the slightest importance. Please don't distress yourself," he concluded, resuming his delicate smile which blossomed at these final words: "I could see at a glance that you were out of your depth."

Mme Verdurin came across to me to show me Elstir's flowers. If the act of going out to dinner, to which I had grown so indifferent, by taking the form, which entirely revivified it, of a journey along the coast followed by an ascent in a carriage to a point six hundred feet above the sea, had produced in me a sort of intoxication, this feeling had not been dispelled at La Raspelière. "Just look at this, now," said the Mistress, showing me some huge and splendid roses by Elstir, whose unctuous scarlet and frothy whiteness stood out, however, with almost too creamy a relief from the flower-stand on which they were arranged. "Do you suppose he would still have the touch to achieve that? Don't you call that striking? And what marvellous texture! One longs to finger it. I can't tell you what fun it was to watch him painting them. One could feel that he was interested in trying to get just that effect." And the Mistress's gaze rested musingly on this present from the artist which epitomised not merely his great talent but their long friendship which survived only in these mementoes of it that he had bequeathed to her; behind the flowers that long ago he had picked for her, she seemed to see the shapely hand that had painted them, in the course of a morning, in their freshness, so that, they on the table, it leaning against the back of a chair in the dining-room, had been able to meet face to face at the Mistress's lunch-party, the still-living roses and their almost lifelike portrait. "Almost" only, for Elstir was unable to look at a flower without first transplanting it to that inner garden in which we are obliged always to remain. He had shown in this water-colour the appearance of the roses which he had seen, and which, but for him, no one would ever have known; so that one might say that they were a new variety with which this painter, like a skilful horticulturist, had enriched the rose family. "From the day he left the little nucleus, he was finished. It seems my dinners made him waste his time, that I hindered the development of his *genius*," she said in a tone of irony. "As if the society of a woman like myself could fail to be beneficial to an artist!" she exclaimed with a burst of pride.

Close beside us, M. de Cambremer, who was already

seated, seeing that M. de Charlus was standing, made as though to rise and offer him his chair. This offer may have arisen, in the Marquis's mind, from nothing more than a vague wish to be polite. M. de Charlus preferred to attach to it the sense of a duty which the simple squire knew that he owed to a prince, and felt that he could not establish his right to this precedence better than by declining it. And so he exclaimed: "Good gracious me! Please! The idea!" The astutely vehement tone of this protest had in itself something typically "Guermantes" which became even more evident in the imperious, supererogatory and familiar gesture with which he brought both his hands down, as though to force him to remain seated, upon the shoulders of M. de Cambremer who had not risen: "Come, come, my dear fellow," the Baron insisted, "that would be the last straw! There's really no need! In these days we keep that for Princes of the Blood."

I made no more impression on the Cambremers than on Mme Verdurin by my enthusiasm for their house. For the beauties they pointed out to me left me cold, whilst I was carried away by confused reminiscences; at times I even confessed to them my disappointment at not finding something correspond to what its name had made me imagine. I enraged Mme de Cambremer by telling her that I had supposed the place to be more rustic. On the other hand I broke off in an ecstasy to sniff the fragrance of a breeze that crept in through the chink of the door. "I see you like draughts," they said to me. My praise of a piece of green lustre plugging a broken pane met with no greater success: "How frightful!" exclaimed the Marquise. The climax came when I said: "My greatest joy was when

I arrived. When I heard my footsteps echoing in the gallery, I felt I had walked into some village *mairie*, with a map of the district on the wall." This time, Mme de Cambremer resolutely turned her back on me.

"You didn't find the arrangement too bad?" her husband asked her with the same compassionate anxiety with which he would have inquired how his wife had stood some painful ceremony. "They have some fine things."

But since malice, when the hard and fast rules of a sure taste do not confine it within reasonable limits, finds fault with everything in the persons or in the houses of the people who have supplanted you, "Yes, but they are not in the right places," replied Mme de Cambremer. "Besides, are they really as fine as all that?"

"You noticed," said M. de Cambremer, with a melancholy that was tempered with a note of firmness, "there are some Jouy hangings that are worn away, some quite threadbare things in this drawing-room!"

"And that piece of stuff with its huge roses, like a peasant woman's quilt," said Mme de Cambremer, whose entirely spurious culture was confined exclusively to idealist philosophy, Impressionist painting and Debussy's music. And, so as not to criticise merely in the name of luxury but in that of taste: "And they've put up draught-curtains! Such bad form! But what do you expect? These people simply don't know, where could they possibly have learned? They must be retired tradespeople. It's really not bad for them."

"I thought the chandeliers good," said the Marquis, though it was not evident why he should make an exception of the chandeliers, in the same way as, inevitably, whenever anyone spoke of a church, whether it was the

Cathedral of Chartres, or of Rheims, or of Amiens, or the church at Balbec, what he would always make a point of mentioning as admirable would be: "the organ-case, the pulpit and the misericords."

"As for the garden, don't speak about it," said Mme de Cambremer. "It's sheer butchery. Those paths running all lopsided."

I took the opportunity while Mme Verdurin was serving coffee to go and glance over the letter which M. de Cambremer had brought me and in which his mother invited me to dinner. With that faint trace of ink, the handwriting revealed an individuality which in the future I should be able to recognise among a thousand, without any more need to have recourse to the hypothesis of special pens than to suppose that rare and mysteriously blended colours are necessary to enable a painter to express his original vision. Indeed a paralytic, stricken with agraphia after a stroke and reduced to looking at the script as at a drawing without being able to read it, would have gathered that the dowager Mme de Cambremer belonged to an old family in which the zealous cultivation of literature and the arts had brought a breath of fresh air to its aristocratic traditions. He would have guessed also the period in which the Marquise had learned simultaneously to write and to play Chopin's music. It was the time when well-bred people observed the rule of affability and what was called the rule of the three adjectives. Mme de Cambremer combined both rules. One laudatory adjective was not enough for her, she followed it (after a little dash) with a second, then (after another dash) with a third. But, what was peculiar to her was that, in defiance of the literary and social aim which she set herself, the sequence of the three epithets assumed in Mme de Cambremer's letters the aspect not of a progression but of a diminuendo. Mme de Cambremer told me, in this first letter, that she had seen Saint-Loup and had appreciated more than ever his "unique—rare—real" qualities, that he was coming to them again with one of his friends (the one who was in love with her daughter-in-law), and that if I cared to come, with or without them, to dine at Féterne she would be "delighted—happy—pleased." Perhaps it was because her desire to be amiable outran the fertility of her imagination and the riches of her vocabulary that the lady, while determined to utter three exclamations, was incapable of making the second and third anything more than feeble echoes of the first. Had there only been a fourth adjective, nothing would have remained of the initial amiability. Finally, with a certain refined simplicity which cannot have failed to produce a considerable impression upon her family and indeed her circle of acquaintance, Mme de Cambremer had acquired the habit of substituting for the word "sincere" (which might in time begin to ring false) the word "true." And to show that it was indeed by sincerity that she was impelled, she broke the conventional rule that would have placed the adjective "true" before its noun, and planted it boldly after. Her letters ended with: *"Croyez à mon amitié vraie"*; *"Croyez à ma sympathie vraie."* Unfortunately, this had become so stereotyped a formula that the affectation of frankness was more suggestive of a polite fiction than the time-honoured formulas to whose meaning one no longer gives a thought.

I was, however, hindered from reading her letter by the confused hubbub of conversation over which rang out the louder accents of M. de Charlus, who, still on the

same topic, was saying to M. de Cambremer: "You reminded me, when you offered me your chair, of a gentleman from whom I received a letter this morning
addressed 'To His Highness the Baron de Charlus,' and
beginning: 'Monseigneur.' "[15]

"To be sure, your correspondent was exaggerating a
bit," replied M. de Cambremer, giving way to a discreet
show of mirth.

M. de Charlus had provoked this, but he did not partake in it. "Well, if it comes to that, my dear fellow," he
said, "I may tell you that, heraldically speaking, he was
entirely in the right. I'm not making a personal issue of it,
you understand. I'm speaking of it as though it were
someone else. But one has to face the facts, history is history, there's nothing we can do about it and it's not for us
to rewrite it. I need not cite the case of the Emperor
William, who at Kiel invariably addressed me as 'Monseigneur.' I have heard it said that he gave the same title
to all the dukes of France, which is improper, but is perhaps simply a delicate attention aimed over our heads at
France herself."

"More delicate, perhaps, than sincere," said M. de
Cambremer.

"Ah! there I must differ from you. Mind you, speaking personally, a gentleman of the lowest rank such as
that Hohenzollern, a Protestant to boot, and one who has
usurped the throne of my cousin the King of Hanover,
can be no favourite of mine," added M. de Charlus, with
whom the annexation of Hanover seemed to rankle more
than that of Alsace-Lorraine. "But I believe the penchant
that the Emperor feels for us to be profoundly sincere.
Fools will tell you that he is a stage emperor. He is on the

contrary marvellously intelligent; it's true that he knows nothing about painting, and has forced Herr Tschudi to withdraw the Elstirs from the public galleries. But Louis XIV did not appreciate the Dutch masters, he had the same fondness for pomp and circumstance, and yet he was, when all is said, a great monarch. Besides, William II has armed his country from the military and naval point of view in a way that Louis XIV failed to do, and I hope that his reign will never know the reverses that darkened the closing days of him who is tritely styled the Sun King. The Republic committed a grave error, to my mind, in spurning the overtures of the Hohenzollern, or responding to them only in driblets. He is very well aware of it himself and says, with that gift of expression that is his: 'What I want is a handclasp, not a raised hat.' As a man, he is vile; he abandoned, betrayed, repudiated his best friends, in circumstances in which his silence was as deplorable as theirs was noble," continued M. de Charlus, who was irresistibly drawn by his own tendencies to the Eulenburg affair,[16] and remembered what one of the most highly placed of the accused had said to him: "How the Emperor must have relied upon our delicacy to have dared to allow such a trial! But he was not mistaken in trusting to our discretion. We would have gone to the scaffold with our lips sealed." "All that, however, has nothing to do with what I was trying to explain, which is that, in Germany, mediatised princes like ourselves are *Durchlaucht*, and in France our rank of Highness was publicly recognised. Saint-Simon claims that we acquired it improperly, in which he is entirely mistaken. The reason that he gives, namely that Louis XIV forbade us to style him the Most Christian King and ordered us to call him simply the King, proves merely that we held our title from him, and not that we did not have the rank of prince. Otherwise, it would have had to be withheld from the Duc de Lorraine and God knows how many others. Besides, several of our titles come from the House of Lorraine through Thérèse d'Espinoy, my great-grandmother, who was the daughter of the Squire de Commercy."

Observing that Morel was listening, M. de Charlus proceeded to develop the reasons for his claim. "I have pointed out to my brother that it is not in the third part of the Gotha, but in the second, not to say the first, that the account of our family ought to be included," he said, without stopping to think that Morel did not know what the "Gotha" was. "But that is his affair, he is the head of our house, and so long as he raises no objection and allows the matter to pass, I can only shut my eyes."

"I found M. Brichot most interesting," I said to Mme Verdurin as she joined me, and I slipped Mme de Cambremer's letter into my pocket.

"He has a cultured mind and is an excellent man," she replied coldly. "Of course what he lacks is originality and taste, and he has a fearsome memory. They used to say of the 'forebears' of the people we have here this evening, the émigrés, that they had forgotten nothing. But they had at least the excuse," she said, borrowing one of Swann's epigrams, "that they had learned nothing. Whereas Brichot knows everything, and hurls chunks of dictionary at our heads during dinner. I'm sure there's nothing you don't know now about the names of all the towns and villages."

While Mme Verdurin was speaking, it occurred to me

that I had intended to ask her something, but I could not remember what it was.

"I'm sure you are talking about Brichot," said Ski. "Eh, Chantepie, and Freycinet, he didn't spare you anything. I was watching you, little Mistress."

"Oh yes, I saw you, I nearly burst."

I could not say today what Mme Verdurin was wearing that evening. Perhaps even at the time I was no more able to, for I do not have an observant mind. But feeling that her dress was not unambitious, I said to her something polite and even admiring. She was like almost all women, who imagine that a compliment that is paid to them is a literal statement of the truth, a judgment impartially, irresistibly pronounced as though it referred to a work of art that has no connexion with a person. And so it was with an earnestness which made me blush for my own hypocrisy that she replied with the proud and artless question that is habitual in such circumstances: "Do you like it?"

"You're talking about Chantepie, I'm sure," said M. Verdurin as he came towards us.

I had been alone, as I thought of my strip of green lustre and of a scent of wood, in failing to notice that, while he enumerated these etymological derivations, Brichot had been provoking derision. And since the impressions that for me gave things their value were of the sort which other people either do not feel or unthinkingly reject as insignificant, and which consequently (had I managed to communicate them) would have been misunderstood or else scorned, they were entirely useless to me and had the additional drawback of making me appear stupid in the eyes of Mme Verdurin who saw that I had "swallowed" Brichot, as I had already appeared stupid to Mme de Guermantes because I had enjoyed myself at Mme d'Arpajon's. With Brichot, however, there was another reason. I was not one of the little clan. And in every clan, whether it be social, political, or literary, one contracts a perverse facility for discovering in a conversation, in an official speech, in a story, in a sonnet, everything that the plain reader would never have dreamed of finding there. How often have I found myself, after reading with a certain excitement a tale skilfully told by a fluent and slightly old-fashioned Academician, on the point of saying to Bloch or to Mme de Guermantes: "How charming this is!" when before I had opened my mouth they exclaimed, each in a different language: "If you want to be really amused, read a story by So-and-so. Human stupidity has never sunk to greater depths." Bloch's scorn derived mainly from the fact that certain effects of style, pleasing enough in themselves, were slightly faded; that of Mme de Guermantes from the notion that the story seemed to prove the direct opposite of what the author meant, for reasons of fact which she had the ingenuity to deduce but which would never have occurred to me. I was no less surprised to discover the irony that underlay the Verdurins' apparent friendliness for Brichot than to hear some days later, at Féterne, the Cambremers say to me, on hearing my enthusiastic praise of La Raspelière: "You can't be sincere, after what they've done to it." It is true that they admitted that the china was good. Like the shocking draught-curtains, it had escaped my notice. "Anyhow, when you go back to Balbec, you'll now know what Balbec means," said M. Verdurin sarcastically. It

was precisely the things Brichot had taught me that interested me. As for what was called his wit, it was exactly
the same as had at one time been so highly appreciated by
the little clan. He talked with the same irritating fluency,
but his words no longer struck a chord, having to overcome a hostile silence or disagreeable echoes; what had
changed was not what he said but the acoustics of the
room and the attitude of his audience. "Take care," Mme
Verdurin murmured, pointing to Brichot. The latter,
whose hearing remained keener than his vision, darted at
the Mistress a short-sighted and philosophical glance
which he hastily withdrew. If his outward eyes had deteri-
orated, those of his mind had on the contrary begun to
take a larger view of things. He saw how little was to be
expected of human affection, and had resigned himself to
the fact. Undoubtedly the discovery pained him. It may
happen that even the man who on one evening only, in a
circle where he is usually greeted with pleasure, realises
that the others have found him too frivolous or too
pedantic or too clumsy or too cavalier, or whatever it may
be, returns home miserable. Often it is a difference of
opinion, or of approach, that has made him appear to
other people absurd or old-fashioned. Often he is perfectly well aware that those others are inferior to himself.
He could easily dissect the sophistries with which he has
been tacitly condemned, and is tempted to pay a call, to
write a letter: on second thoughts, he does nothing, and
awaits the invitation for the following week. Sometimes,
too, these falls from grace, instead of ending with the
evening, last for months. Arising from the instability of
social judgments, they increase that instability further.
For the man who knows that Mme X despises him, feel-

ing that he is respected at Mme Y's, pronounces her far superior to the other and migrates to her salon. This, however, is not the proper place to describe those men, superior to the life of society but lacking the capacity to realise themselves outside it, glad to be invited, embittered at being underrated, discovering annually the defects of the hostess to whom they have been offering incense and the genius of the other whom they have never properly appreciated, ready to return to the old love when they have experienced the drawbacks to be found equally in the new, and when they have begun to forget those of the old. We may judge by such temporary falls from grace of the chagrin that Brichot felt at this one, which he knew to be final. He was not unaware that Mme Verdurin sometimes laughed at him publicly, even at his infirmities, and knowing how little was to be expected of human affection, he continued nevertheless to regard the Mistress as his best friend. But, from the blush that crept over the scholar's face, Mme Verdurin realised that he had heard her, and made up her mind to be kind to him for the rest of the evening. I could not help remarking to her that she had not been very kind to Saniette. "What! Not kind to him! Why, he adores us, you've no idea what we are to him. My husband is sometimes a little irritated by his stupidity, and you must admit with some reason, but when that happens why doesn't he hit back instead of cringing like a whipped dog? It's so unmanly. I can't bear it. That doesn't mean that I don't always try to calm my husband, because if he went too far, all that would happen would be that Saniette would stay away; and I don't want that because I may tell you that he hasn't a penny in the world, he needs his dinners. But after all, if he takes offence, he can stay away, it's nothing to do with me. When you rely on other people you should try not to be such an idiot."

"The Duchy of Aumale was in our family for years before passing to the House of France," M. de Charlus was explaining to M. de Cambremer in front of a flabbergasted Morel, for whose benefit the whole dissertation was intended, if it was not actually addressed to him. "We took precedence over all foreign princes; I could give you a hundred examples. The Princesse de Croy having attempted, at the burial of Monsieur, to fall on her knees after my great-great-grandmother, the latter reminded her sharply that she had no right to the hassock, made the officer on duty remove it, and reported the matter to the King, who ordered Mme de Croy to call upon Mme de Guermantes and offer her apologies. The Duc de Bourgogne having come to us with ushers with raised batons, we obtained the King's authority to have them lowered. I know it is not good form to speak of the merits of one's own family. But it is well known that our people were always to the fore in the hour of danger. Our battle-cry, after we abandoned that of the Dukes of Brabant, was *Passavant!* So that it is not unjust on the whole that this right to be everywhere the first, which we had established for so many centuries in war, should afterwards have been granted to us at Court. And, to be sure, it was always acknowledged there. I may give you a further instance, that of the Princess of Baden. As she had so far forgotten herself as to attempt to challenge the precedence of that same Duchesse de Guermantes of whom I was speaking just now, and had attempted to go in first to the King's presence by taking advantage of a momentary hesitation which my ancestress may perhaps have shown (although there was no reason for it), the King called out: 'Come in, cousin, come in; Mme de Baden knows very well what her duty is to you.' And it was as Duchesse de Guermantes that she held this rank, albeit she was of no mean family herself, since she was through her mother niece to the Queen of Poland, the Queen of Hungary, the Elector Palatine, the Prince of Savoy-Carignano and the Elector of Hanover, afterwards King of England."

"*Maecenas atavis edite regibus!*" said Brichot, addressing M. de Charlus, who acknowledged the compliment with a slight nod.

"What did you say?" Mme Verdurin asked Brichot, anxious to make amends to him for her earlier words.

"I was referring, Heaven forgive me, to a dandy who was the flower of the nobility" (Mme Verdurin winced) "about the time of Augustus" (Mme Verdurin, reassured by the remoteness in time of this nobility, assumed a more serene expression), "to a friend of Virgil and Horace who carried their sycophancy to the extent of proclaiming to his face his more than aristocratic, his royal descent. In a word, I was referring to Maecenas, a bookworm who was the friend of Horace, Virgil, Augustus. I am sure that M. de Charlus knows all about Maecenas."

With a gracious sidelong glance at Mme Verdurin, because he had heard her make a rendezvous with Morel for the day after next and was afraid that she might not invite him also, "I should say," said M. de Charlus, "that Maecenas was more or less the Verdurin of antiquity."

Mme Verdurin could not altogether suppress a smile of self-satisfaction. She went over to Morel. "He's nice, your father's friend," she said to him. "One can see that

he's an educated man, and well bred. He will get on well
in our little nucleus. Where does he live in Paris?"

Morel preserved a haughty silence and merely proposed a game of cards. Mme Verdurin demanded a little
violin music first. To the general astonishment, M. de
Charlus, who never spoke of his own considerable gifts,
accompanied, in the purest style, the closing passage (uneasy, tormented, Schumannesque, but, for all that, earlier
than Franck's sonata) of the sonata for piano and violin
by Fauré. I felt that he would provide Morel, marvellously endowed as to tone and virtuosity, with just those
qualities that he lacked, culture and style. But I thought
with curiosity of this combination in a single person of a
physical blemish and a spiritual gift. M. de Charlus was
not very different from his brother, the Duc de Guermantes. Indeed, a moment ago (though this was rare), he
had spoken as bad a French as his brother. He having reproached me (doubtless in order that I might speak in
glowing terms of Morel to Mme Verdurin) with never
coming to see him, and I having pleaded discretion, he
had replied: "But, since it is I who ask, there's no one but
me who could possibly take huff." This might have been
said by the Duc de Guermantes. M. de Charlus was only
a Guermantes when all was said. But it had sufficed that
nature should have upset the balance of his nervous system enough to make him prefer, to the woman that his
brother the Duke would have chosen, one of Virgil's
shepherds or Plato's disciples, and at once qualities unknown to the Duc de Guermantes and often combined
with this lack of equilibrium had made M. de Charlus an
exquisite pianist, an amateur painter who was not devoid
of taste, and an eloquent talker. Who would ever have de-

tected that the rapid, nervous, charming style with which
M. de Charlus played the Schumannesque passage of
Fauré's sonata had its equivalent—one dare not say its
cause—in elements entirely physical, in the Baron's nervous weaknesses? We shall explain later on what we mean
by nervous weaknesses, and why it is that a Greek of the
time of Socrates, a Roman of the time of Augustus, might
be what we know them to have been and yet remain absolutely normal, not men-women such as we see around us
today. Just as he had real artistic aptitudes which had
never come to fruition, so M. de Charlus, far more than
the Duke, had loved their mother and loved his own wife,
and indeed, years afterwards, if anyone spoke of them to
him, would shed tears, but superficial tears, like the perspiration of an over-stout man, whose forehead will glis-
ten with sweat at the slightest exertion. With this
difference, that to the latter one says: "How hot you are,"
whereas one pretends not to notice other people's tears.
One, that is to say, society; for simple people are as distressed by the sight of tears as if a sob were more serious
than a haemorrhage. Thanks to the habit of lying, his sorrow after the death of his wife did not debar M. de Charlus from a life which was not in conformity with it.
Indeed later on, he was ignominious enough to let it be
known that, during the funeral ceremony, he had found
an opportunity of asking the acolyte for his name and address. And it may have been true.

When the piece came to an end, I ventured to ask for
some Franck, which appeared to cause Mme de Cambremer such acute pain that I did not insist. "You can't admire that sort of thing," she said to me. Instead she asked
for Debussy's *Fêtes*, which made her exclaim: "Ah! how

sublime!" from the first note. But Morel discovered that he could remember only the opening bars, and in a spirit of mischief, without any intention to deceive, began a March by Meyerbeer. Unfortunately, as he left little interval and made no announcement, everybody supposed that he was still playing Debussy, and continued to exclaim "Sublime!" Morel, by revealing that the composer was that not of *Pelléas* but of *Robert le Diable*, created a certain chill. Mme de Cambremer had scarcely time to feel it for herself, for she had just discovered a volume of Scarlatti and had flung herself upon it with an hysterical shriek. "Oh! play this, look, this piece, it's divine," she cried. And yet, of this composer long despised but recently promoted to the highest honours, what she had selected in her feverish impatience was one of those infernal pieces which have so often kept us from sleeping, while a merciless pupil repeats them ad infinitum on the next floor. But Morel had had enough music, and as he insisted upon cards, M. de Charlus, to be able to join in, proposed a game of whist.

"He was telling the Boss just now that he's a prince," said Ski to Mme Verdurin, "but it's not true, they're quite a humble family of architects."

"I want to know what it was you were saying about Maecenas. It interests me, don't you know!" Mme Verdurin repeated to Brichot, with an affability that carried him off his feet. And so, in order to shine in the Mistress's eyes, and possibly in mine: "Why, to tell you the truth, Madame, Maecenas interests me chiefly because he is the earliest apostle of note of that oriental god who numbers more followers in France today than Brahma, than Christ himself, the all-powerful god, Dun Gifa

Hoot." Mme Verdurin was no longer content, on these occasions, with burying her head in her hands. She would descend with the suddenness of the insects called ephemerids upon Princess Sherbatoff; were the latter within reach the Mistress would cling to her shoulder, dig her nails into it, and hide her face against it for a few moments like a child playing hide and seek. Concealed by this protecting screen, she was understood to be laughing until she cried, but could as well have been thinking of nothing at all as the people who, while saying a longish prayer, take the wise precaution of burying their faces in their hands. Mme Verdurin imitated them when she listened to Beethoven quartets, in order at the same time to show that she regarded them as a prayer and not to let it be seen that she was asleep. "I speak quite seriously, Madame," said Brichot. "Too numerous, I consider, today are the persons who spend their time gazing at their navels as though they were the hub of the universe. As a matter of doctrine, I have no objection to offer to any Nirvana which will dissolve us in the great Whole (which, like Munich and Oxford, is considerably nearer to Paris than Asnières or Bois-Colombes), but it is unworthy either of a true Frenchman, or of a true European even, when the Japanese are possibly at the gates of our Byzantium, that socialised anti-militarists should be gravely discussing the cardinal virtues of free verse." Mme Verdurin felt that she might dispense with the Princess's mangled shoulder, and allowed her face to become once more visible, not without pretending to wipe her eyes and gasping two or three times for breath. But Brichot was determined that I should have my share in the entertainment, and having learned, from those oral examinations which he

conducted like nobody else, that the best way to flatter
the young is to lecture them, to make them feel important, to make them regard you as a reactionary: "I have
no wish to blaspheme against the Gods of Youth," he
said, with that furtive glance at myself which an orator
turns upon a member of his audience when he mentions
him by name, "I have no wish to be damned as a heretic
and renegade in the Mallarméan chapel in which our new
friend, like all the young men of his age, must have
served the esoteric mass, at least as an acolyte, and have
shown himself deliquescent or Rosicrucian. But really, we
have seen more than enough of these intellectuals wor-
shipping art with a capital A, who, when they can no
longer intoxicate themselves upon Zola, inject themselves
with Verlaine. Having become etheromaniacs out of
Baudelairean devotion, they would no longer be capable of
the virile effort which the country may one day or another
demand of them, anaesthetised as they are by the great literary neurosis in the heated, enervating atmosphere, heavy with
unwholesome vapours, of a symbolism of the opium den."

Incapable of feigning the slightest admiration for Brichot's inept and motley tirade, I turned to Ski and assured
him that he was entirely mistaken as to the family to
which M. de Charlus belonged; he replied that he was
certain of his facts, and added that I myself had said that
his real name was Gandin, Le Gandin. "I told you," was
my answer, "that Mme de Cambremer was the sister of
an engineer called M. Legrandin. I never said a word to
you about M. de Charlus. There is about as much connexion between him and Mme de Cambremer as between
the Great Condé and Racine."

"Ah! I thought there was," said Ski lightly, with no

more apology for his mistake than he had made a few hours earlier for the mistake that had nearly made his party miss the train.

"Do you intend to remain long on this coast?" Mme Verdurin asked M. de Charlus, in whom she foresaw an addition to the faithful and trembled lest he should be returning too soon to Paris.

"Goodness me, one never knows," replied M. de Charlus in a nasal drawl. "I should like to stay until the end of September."

"You are quite right," said Mme Verdurin; "that's when we get splendid storms at sea."

"To tell you the truth, that is not what would influence me. I have for some time past unduly neglected the Archangel Michael, my patron saint, and I should like to make amends to him by staying for his feast, on the 29th of September, at the Abbey on the Mount."

"You take an interest in all that sort of thing?" asked Mme Verdurin, who might perhaps have succeeded in hushing the voice of her outraged anti-clericalism had she not been afraid that so long an expedition might make the violinist and the Baron "defect" for forty-eight hours.

"You are perhaps afflicted with intermittent deafness," M. de Charlus replied insolently. "I have told you that Saint Michael is one of my glorious patrons." Then, smiling with a benevolent ecstasy, his eyes gazing into the distance, his voice reinforced by an exaltation which seemed now to be not merely aesthetic but religious: "It is so beautiful at the Offertory when Michael stands erect by the altar, in a white robe, swinging a golden censer heaped so high with perfumes that the fragrance of them mounts up to God."

"We might go there in a party," suggested Mme Verdurin, notwithstanding her horror of the clergy.

"At that moment, when the Offertory begins," went on M. de Charlus who, for other reasons but in the same manner as good speakers in Parliament, never replied to an interruption and would pretend not to have heard it, "it would be wonderful to see our young friend Palestrinising and even performing an aria by Bach. The worthy Abbot, too, would be wild with joy, and it is the greatest homage, at least the greatest public homage, that I can pay to my patron saint. What an edification for the faithful! We must mention it presently to the young Angelico of music, himself a warrior like Saint Michael."

Saniette, summoned to make a fourth, declared that he did not know how to play whist. And Cottard, seeing that there was not much time left before the train, embarked at once on a game of écarté with Morel. M. Verdurin was furious, and bore down with a terrible expression upon Saniette: "Is there nothing you know how to play?" he shouted, furious at being deprived of the opportunity for a game of whist, and delighted to have found one for insulting the ex-archivist. The latter, terrorstricken, did his best to look clever: "Yes, I can play the piano," he said. Cottard and Morel were seated face to face. "Your deal," said Cottard. "Suppose we go nearer to the card-table," M. de Charlus, worried by the sight of Morel in Cottard's company, suggested to M. de Cambremer. "It's quite as interesting as those questions of etiquette which in these days have ceased to count for very much. The only kings that we have left, in France at least, are the kings in packs of cards, who seem to me to be positively swarming in the hand of our young virtu-

oso," he added a moment later, from an admiration for
Morel which extended to his way of playing cards, to flatter him also, and finally to account for his suddenly leaning over the young violinist's shoulder. "I-ee trrump,"
said Cottard, putting on a vile foreign accent; his children
would burst out laughing, like his students and the house
surgeon, whenever the Master, even by the bedside of a
serious case, uttered one of his hackneyed witticisms with
the impassive expression of an epileptic. "I don't know
what to play," said Morel, seeking advice from M. de
Cambremer. "Just as you please, you're bound to lose,
whatever you play, it's all the same (*c'est égal*)." "Galli-
Marié?" said the Doctor with a benign and knowing
glance at M. de Cambremer. "She was what we call a true
diva, she was a dream, a Carmen such as we shall never
see again. She was wedded to the part. I used to enjoy too
listening to Ingalli-Marié."

The Marquis rose, and with that contemptuous vulgarity of well-born people who do not realise that they are
insulting their host by appearing uncertain whether they
ought to associate with his guests, and plead English
habits as an excuse for a disdainful expression, asked:
"Who is that gentleman playing cards? What does he do
for a living? What does he *sell*? I rather like to know who
I'm with, so as not to make friends with any Tom, Dick
or Harry. But I didn't catch his name when you did me
the honour of introducing me to him." If M. Verdurin, on
the strength of these last words, had indeed introduced
M. de Cambremer *to* his fellow-guests, the other would
have been greatly annoyed. But, knowing that it was the
opposite procedure that had been observed, he thought it
gracious to assume a genial and modest air, without risk

to himself. The pride that M. Verdurin took in his intimacy with Cottard had gone on increasing ever since the
Doctor had become an eminent professor. But it no longer
found expression in the same ingenuous form as of old.
Then, when Cottard was scarcely known to the public, if
you spoke to M. Verdurin of his wife's facial neuralgia,
"There is nothing to be done," he would say, with the
naïve complacency of people who assume that anyone
whom they know must be famous, and that everybody
knows the name of their daughter's singing-teacher. "If
she had an ordinary doctor, one might look for a second
opinion, but when that doctor is called Cottard" (a name
which he pronounced as though it were Bouchard or
Charcot) "one simply has to bow to the inevitable."
Adopting a reverse procedure, knowing that M. de Cambremer must certainly have heard of the famous Professor
Cottard, M. Verdurin assumed an artless air. "He's our
family doctor, a worthy soul whom we adore and who
would bend over backwards for our sakes; he's not a doctor, he's a friend. I don't suppose you have ever heard of
him or that his name would convey anything to you, but
in any case to us it's the name of a very good man, of a
very dear friend, Cottard." This name, murmured in a
modest tone, surprised M. de Cambremer who supposed
that his host was referring to someone else. "Cottard? You
don't mean Professor Cottard?" At that moment one
heard the voice of the said Professor who, at an awkward
point in the game, was saying as he looked at his cards:
"This is where Greek meets Greek." "Why, yes, to be
sure, he is a professor," said M. Verdurin. "What! Professor Cottard! You're sure you're not mistaken! You're certain it's the same man! The one who lives in the Rue du

Bac!" "Yes, his address is 43, Rue du Bac. You know
him?" "But everybody knows Professor Cottard. He's a
leading light. It's as though you asked me if I knew
Bouffe de Saint-Blaise or Courtois-Suffit. I could see
when I heard him speak that he was not an ordinary person. That's why I took the liberty of asking you." "Well
then, what shall I play, trumps?" asked Cottard. Then
abruptly, with a vulgarity which would have been irritating even in heroic circumstances, as when a soldier uses a
coarse expression to convey his contempt for death, but
became doubly stupid in the safe pastime of a game of
cards, Cottard, deciding to play a trump, assumed a sombre, death-defying air and flung down his card as though
it were his life, with the exclamation: "There it is, and be
damned to it!" It was not the right card to play, but he
had a consolation. In a deep armchair in the middle of the
room, Mme Cottard, yielding to the effect, which she always found irresistible, of a good dinner, had succumbed
after vain efforts to the vast if gentle slumbers that were
overpowering her. In vain did she sit up now and then,
and smile, either in self-mockery or from fear of leaving
unanswered some polite remark that might have been addressed to her, she sank back, in spite of herself, into the
clutches of the implacable and delicious malady. More
than the noise, what awakened her thus, for an instant
only, was the glance (which, in her wifely affection, she
could see even when her eyes were shut, and anticipated,
for the same scene occurred every evening and haunted
her dreams like the thought of the hour at which one will
have to rise), the glance with which the Professor drew
the attention of those present to his wife's slumbers. To
begin with, he merely looked at her and smiled, for if as a

doctor he disapproved of this habit of falling asleep after dinner (or at least gave this scientific reason for getting angry later on, though it is not certain whether it was a determining reason, so many and diverse were the views that he held on the subject), as an all-powerful and teasing husband he was delighted to be able to make fun of his wife, to half-waken her only at first, so that she might fall asleep again and he have the pleasure of waking her anew.

By this time, Mme Cottard was sound asleep. "Now then, Léontine, you're snoring," the Professor called to her. "I'm listening to Mme Swann, my dear," Mme Cottard replied faintly, and dropped back into her lethargy. "It's absolute madness," exclaimed Cottard, "she'll be telling us presently that she wasn't asleep. She's like the patients who come to a consultation and insist that they never sleep at all." "They imagine it, perhaps," said M. de Cambremer with a laugh. But the doctor enjoyed contradicting no less than teasing, and would on no account allow a layman to talk medicine to him. "One doesn't imagine that one can't sleep," he promulgated in a dogmatic tone. "Ah!" replied the Marquis with a respectful bow, such as Cottard at one time would have made. "It's easy to see," Cottard went on, "that you've never administered, as I have, as much as two grains of trional without succeeding in provoking somnolence." "Quite so, quite so," replied the Marquis, laughing with a superior air, "I've never taken trional, or any of those drugs which soon cease to have any effect but ruin your stomach. When a man has been out shooting all night, like me, in the forest of Chantepie, I can assure you he doesn't need any trional to make him sleep." "It's only fools who say

that," replied the Professor. "Trional frequently has a remarkable effect on the tonicity of the nerves. You mention trional, have you any idea what it is?" "Well . . .
I've heard people say that it's a drug to make one sleep."
"You're not answering my question," replied the Professor, who, thrice weekly, at the Faculty, sat on the board
of examiners. "I'm not asking you whether it makes you
sleep or not, but what it is. Can you tell me what percent-
age it contains of amyl and ethyl?" "No," replied M. de
Cambremer, abashed. "I prefer a good glass of old brandy
or even 345 Port." "Which are ten times as toxic," the
Professor interrupted. "As for trional," M. de Cambremer
ventured, "my wife goes in for all that sort of thing, you'd
better talk to her about it." "She probably knows as much
about it as you do. In any case, if your wife takes trional
to make her sleep, you can see that mine has no need of
it. Come along, Léontine, wake up, you'll get stiff. Did
you ever see me fall asleep after dinner? What will you be
like when you're sixty, if you fall asleep now like an old
woman? You'll get fat, you're arresting your circulation.
She doesn't even hear what I'm saying." "They're bad for
one's health, these little naps after dinner, aren't they,
Doctor?" said M. de Cambremer, seeking to rehabilitate
himself with Cottard. "After a heavy meal one ought to
take exercise." "Stuff and nonsense!" replied the Doctor.
"Identical quantities of food have been taken from the
stomach of a dog that has lain quiet and from the stomach of a dog that has been running about, and it's in the
former that digestion has been found to be more advanced." "Then it's sleep that interrupts the digestion."
"That depends whether you mean oesophagic digestion,
stomachic digestion or intestinal digestion. It's pointless

giving you explanations which you wouldn't understand since you've never studied medicine. Now then, Léontine, quick march, it's time we were going." This was not true, for the Doctor was merely going to continue his game, but he hoped thus to cut short in a more drastic fashion the slumbers of the deaf mute to whom he had been addressing without a word of response the most learned exhortations. Either because a determination to remain awake survived in Mme Cottard, even in her sleep, or because the armchair offered no support to her head, it was jerked mechanically from left to right and up and down in the empty air, like a lifeless object, and Mme Cottard, with her nodding poll, appeared now to be listening to music, now to be in her death-throes. Where her husband's increasingly vehement admonitions failed of their effect, her sense of her own stupidity proved successful: "My bath is nice and hot," she murmured. "But the feathers on the dictionary . . ." she exclaimed, sitting up. "Oh, good gracious, what a fool I am! Whatever have I been saying? I was thinking about my hat, and I'm sure I said something silly. In another minute I would have dozed off. It's that wretched fire." Everybody laughed, for there was no fire in the room.

"You're making fun of me," said Mme Cottard, herself laughing, and raising her hand to her forehead with the light touch of a hypnotist and the deftness of a woman putting her hair straight, to erase the last traces of sleep, "I must offer my humble apologies to dear Mme Verdurin and get the truth from her." But her smile at once grew mournful, for the Professor, who knew that his wife sought to please him and trembled lest she fail to do so, had shouted at her: "Look at yourself in the mirror.

You're as red as if you had an eruption of acne. You look just like an old peasant."

"You know, he's charming," said Mme Verdurin, "he has such a delightfully sardonic good nature. And then, he snatched my husband from the jaws of death when the whole medical profession had given him up. He spent three nights by his bedside, without ever lying down. And so for me, you know," she went on in a grave and almost menacing tone, raising her hand to the twin spheres, shrouded in white tresses, of her musical temples, and as though we had threatened to assault the Doctor, "Cottard is sacred! He could ask me for anything in the world! As it is, I don't call him Doctor Cottard, I call him Doctor God! And even in saying that I'm slandering him, for this God does everything in his power to remedy some of the disasters for which the other is responsible."

"Play a trump," M. de Charlus said to Morel with a delighted air.

"A trump, here goes," said the violinist.

"You ought to have declared your king first," said M. de Charlus, "you're not paying attention to the game, but how well you play!"

"I have the king," said Morel.

"He's a fine man," replied the Professor.

"What's that thing up there with the sticks?" asked Mme Verdurin, drawing M. de Cambremer's attention to a superb escutcheon carved over the mantelpiece. "Are they your *arms*?" she added with sarcastic scorn.

"No, they're not ours," replied M. de Cambremer. "We bear *barry of five, embattled counterembattled or and gules, as many trefoils countercharged.* No, those are the arms of the Arrachepels, who were not of our stock, but from whom we inherited the house, and nobody of our line has ever made any changes here." ("That's one in the eye for her," muttered Mme de Cambremer.) "The Arrachepels (formerly Pelvilains, we are told) bore *or five piles couped in base gules.* When they allied themselves with the Féterne family, their blazon changed, but remained *cantoned within twenty cross crosslets fitchee in base or, a dexter canton ermine.* My great-grandmother was a d'Arrachepel or de Rachepel, whichever you like, for both forms are found in the old charters," continued M. de Cambremer, blushing deeply, for only then did the idea for which his wife had given him credit occur to him, and he was afraid that Mme Verdurin might have applied to herself words which had in no way been aimed at her. "History relates that in the eleventh century the first Arrachepel, Macé, known as Pelvilain, showed a special aptitude, in siege warfare, in tearing up piles. Whence the nickname Arrachepel under which he was ennobled, and the piles which you see persisting through the centuries in their arms. These are the piles which, to render fortifications more impregnable, used to be driven, bedded, if you will pardon the expression, into the ground in front of them, and fastened together laterally. They are what you quite rightly called sticks, though they had nothing to do with the floating sticks of our good La Fontaine. For they were supposed to render a stronghold impregnable. Of course, with our modern artillery, they make one smile. But you must bear in mind that I'm speaking of the eleventh century."

"Yes, it's not exactly up-to-date," said Mme Verdurin, "but the little campanile has character."

"You have," said Cottard, "the luck of a fiddlededee," a word which he regularly repeated to avoid using Moliére's.[17] "Do you know why the king of diamonds was invalided out of the army?"

"I shouldn't mind being in his shoes," said Morel, who was bored with military service.

"Oh! how unpatriotic!" exclaimed M. de Charlus, who could not refrain from pinching the violinist's ear.

"You don't know why the king of diamonds was invalided out of the army?" Cottard pursued, determined to make his joke, "it's because he has only one eye."

"You're up against it, Doctor," said M. de Cambremer, to show Cottard that he knew who he was.

"This young man is astonishing," M. de Charlus interrupted naïvely, pointing to Morel. "He plays like a god."

This observation did not find favour with the Doctor, who replied: "Wait and see. He who laughs last laughs longest."

"Queen, ace," Morel announced triumphantly, for fortune was favouring him.

The Doctor bowed his head as though powerless to deny this good fortune, and admitted, spellbound: "That's beautiful."

"We're so pleased to have met M. de Charlus," said Mme de Cambremer to Mme Verdurin.

"Had you never met him before? He's rather nice, most unusual, very much *of a period*" (she would have found it difficult to say which), replied Mme Verdurin with the complacent smile of a connoisseur, a judge and a hostess.

Mme de Cambremer asked me if I was coming to Féterne with Saint-Loup. I could not suppress a cry of admiration when I saw the moon hanging like an orange lantern beneath the vault of oaks that led away from the house. "That's nothing," said Mme Verdurin. "Presently, when the moon has risen higher and the valley is lit up, it will be a thousand times more beautiful. That's something you haven't got at Féterne!" she added scornfully to Mme de Cambremer, who did not know how to answer, not wishing to disparage her property, especially in front of the tenants.

"Are you staying much longer in the neighbourhood, Madame?" M. de Cambremer asked Mme Cottard, an inquiry that might be interpreted as a vague intention to invite her, but which dispensed him for the moment from making any more precise commitment. "Oh, certainly, Monsieur, I regard this annual exodus as most important for the children. Say what you like, they need fresh air. I may be rather primitive on this point but I believe that no cure is as good for children as healthy air—even if someone should give me a mathematical proof to the contrary. Their little faces are already completely changed. The doctors wanted to send me to Vichy; but it's too stuffy there, and I can look after my stomach when those big boys of mine have grown a little bigger. Besides, the Professor, with all the examining he has to do, has always got his shoulder to the wheel, and the heat tires him dreadfully. I feel that a man needs a thorough rest after he has been on the go all the year like that. Whatever happens we shall stay another month at least."

"Ah! in that case we shall meet again."

"In any case I shall be obliged to stay here as my husband has to go on a visit to Savoy, and won't be finally settled here for another fortnight."

"I like the view of the valley even more than the sea

view," Mme Verdurin went on. "You're going to have a splendid night for your journey."

"We ought really to find out whether the carriages are ready, if you are absolutely determined to go back to Balbec tonight," M. Verdurin said to me, "for I see no necessity for it myself. We could drive you over tomorrow morning. It's certain to be fine. The roads are excellent."

I said that it was impossible. "But in any case it isn't time to go yet," the Mistress protested. "Leave them alone, they have heaps of time. A lot of good it will do them to arrive at the station with an hour to wait. They're far better off here. And you, my young Mozart," she said to Morel, not venturing to address M. de Charlus directly, "won't you stay the night? We have some nice rooms overlooking the sea."

"No, he can't," M. de Charlus replied on behalf of the absorbed card-player who had not heard. "He has a pass until midnight only. He must go back to bed like a good little boy, obedient and well-behaved," he added in a smug, affected, insistent voice, as though he found a sadistic pleasure in employing this chaste comparison and also in letting his voice dwell, in passing, upon something that concerned Morel, in touching him, if not with his hand, with words that seemed to be tactile.

From the sermon that Brichot had addressed to me, M. de Cambremer had concluded that I was a Dreyfusard. As he himself was as anti-Dreyfusard as possible, out of courtesy to a foe he began to sing me the praises of a Jewish colonel who had always been very decent to a cousin of the Chevregnys and had secured for him the promotion he deserved. "And my cousin's opinions were

the exact opposite," said M. de Cambremer. He omitted
to mention what those opinions were, but I sensed that
they were as antiquated and misshapen as his own face,
opinions which a few families in certain small towns must
long have entertained. "Well, you know, I call that really
fine!" was M. de Cambremer's conclusion. It is true that
he was hardly employing the word "fine" in the aesthetic
sense in which his wife or his mother would have applied
it to different works of art. M. de Cambremer often made
use of this term, when for instance he was congratulating
a delicate person who had put on a little weight. "What,
you've gained half a stone in two months? I say, that's really fine!"

Refreshments were set out on a table. Mme Verdurin
invited the gentlemen to go and choose whatever drink
they preferred. M. de Charlus went and drank his glass
and at once returned to a seat by the card-table from
which he did not stir. Mme Verdurin asked him: "Did
you have some of my orangeade?" Whereupon M. de
Charlus, with a gracious smile, in a crystalline tone which
he rarely adopted, and with endless simperings and wrig-
glings of the hips, replied: "No, I preferred its neighbour,
which is strawberry-juice, I think. It's delicious." It is curious that a certain category of secret impulses has as an
external consequence a way of speaking or gesticulating
which reveals them. If a man believes or disbelieves in the
Virgin Birth, or in the innocence of Dreyfus, or in a plu-
rality of worlds, and wishes to keep his opinion to himself, you will find nothing in his voice or in his gait that
will betray his thoughts. But on hearing M. de Charlus
say, in that shrill voice and with that smile and those gestures, "No, I preferred its neighbour, the strawberry-

juice," one could say: "Ah, he likes the stronger sex,"
with the same certainty as enables a judge to sentence a
criminal who has not confessed, or a doctor a patient suffering from general paralysis who himself is perhaps unaware of his malady but has made some mistake in
pronunciation from which it can be deduced that he will
be dead in three years. Perhaps the people who deduce,
from a man's way of saying: "No, I preferred its neighbour, the strawberry-juice," a love of the kind called unnatural, have no need of any such scientific knowledge.
But that is because here there is a more direct relation between the revealing sign and the secret. Without saying so
to oneself in so many words, one feels that it is a gentle,
smiling lady who is answering and who appears affected
because she is pretending to be a man and one is not accustomed to seeing men put on such airs. And it is perhaps more gracious to think that a certain number of
angelic women have long been included by mistake in the
masculine sex where, feeling exiled, ineffectually flapping
their wings towards men in whom they inspire a physical
repulsion, they know how to arrange a drawing-room, to
compose "interiors." M. de Charlus was not in the least
perturbed that Mme Verdurin should be standing, and remained ensconced in his armchair so as to be nearer to
Morel. "Don't you think it criminal," said Mme Verdurin
to the Baron, "that that creature who might be enchanting
us with his violin should be sitting there at a card-table.
When one can play the violin like that!" "He plays cards
well, he does everything well, he's so intelligent," said
M. de Charlus, keeping his eye on the game, so as to be
able to advise Morel. This was not his only reason, however, for not rising from his chair for Mme Verdurin.

With the singular amalgam that he had made of his social conceptions at once as a great nobleman and as an art-lover, instead of being courteous in the same way as a man of his world would have been, he invented as it were tableaux-vivants for himself after Saint-Simon; and at that moment he was amusing himself by impersonating the Maréchal d'Huxelles, who interested him from other aspects also, and of whom it is said that he was so arrogant as to remain seated, with an air of indolence, before all the most distinguished persons at Court.

"By the way, Charlus," said Mme Verdurin, who was beginning to grow familiar, "you don't know of any penniless old nobleman in your Faubourg who would come to me as porter?" "Why, yes . . . why, yes," replied M. de Charlus with a genial smile, "but I don't advise it." "Why not?" "I should be afraid for your sake that the more elegant visitors would go no further than the lodge." This was the first skirmish between them. Mme Verdurin barely noticed it. There were to be others, alas, in Paris. M. de Charlus remained glued to his chair. He could not, moreover, restrain a faint smile on seeing how his favourite maxims as to aristocratic prestige and bourgeois cowardice were confirmed by the so easily won submission of Mme Verdurin. The Mistress appeared not at all surprised by the Baron's posture, and if she left him it was only because she had been perturbed by seeing me taken up by M. de Cambremer. But first of all, she wished to clear up the mystery of M. de Charlus's relations with Comtesse Molé. "You told me that you knew Mme de Molé. Does that mean you go there?" she asked, giving to the words "go there" the sense of being received there, of having received permission from the lady to go and call on her. M. de Charlus replied with an inflexion of disdain, an affectation of precision and in a sing-song tone: "Yes, sometimes." This "sometimes" inspired doubts in Mme Verdurin, who asked: "Have you ever met the Duc de Guermantes there?" "Ah! that I don't remember." "Oh!" said Mme Verdurin, "you don't know the Duc de Guermantes?" "And how could I not know him?" replied M. de Charlus, his lips curving in a smile. This smile was ironical; but as the Baron was afraid of letting a gold tooth be seen, he checked it with a reverse movement of his lips, so that the resulting sinuosity was that of a smile of benevolence. "Why do you say: 'How could I not know him?'" "Because he is my brother," said M. de Charlus carelessly, leaving Mme Verdurin plunged in stupefaction and uncertain whether her guest was making fun of her, was a natural son, or a son by another marriage. The idea that the brother of the Duc de Guermantes might be called Baron de Charlus never entered her head. She bore down upon me. "I heard M. de Cambremer invite you to dinner just now. It has nothing to do with me, you understand. But for your own sake, I very much hope you won't go. For one thing, the place is infested with bores. Oh, if you like dining with provincial counts and marquises whom nobody knows, you'll have all you could wish." "I think I shall be obliged to go there once or twice. I'm not altogether free, however, for I have a young cousin whom I can't leave by herself" (I felt that this fictitious kinship made it easier for me to take Albertine about), "but in the case of the Cambremers, as I've already introduced her to them . . ." "You shall do just as you please. One thing I can tell you: it's extremely unhealthy; when you've caught pneumonia, or a nice little

chronic rheumatism, what good will that do you?" "But
isn't the place itself very pretty?" "Mmmmyesss . . . If
you like. Frankly, I must confess that I'd far sooner have
the view from here over this valley. In any case, I
wouldn't have taken the other house if they'd paid us because the sea air is fatal to M. Verdurin. If your cousin is
at all delicate . . . But you yourself are delicate, I believe
. . . you have fits of breathlessness. Very well! You shall
see. Go there once, and you won't sleep for a week after
it; but it's not my business." And regardless of the inconsistency with what had gone before, she went on: "If it
would amuse you to see the house, which is not bad,
pretty is too strong a word, still it's amusing with its old
moat and its old drawbridge, as I shall have to sacrifice
myself and dine there once, very well, come that day, I
shall try to bring all my little circle, then it will be quite
nice. The day after tomorrow we're going to Harambouville in the carriage. It's a magnificent drive, and the cider
is delicious. Come with us. You, Brichot, you shall come
too. And you too, Ski. It will make a party which, as a
matter of fact, my husband must have arranged already. I
don't know whom all he has invited. Monsieur de Charlus, are you one of them?"

The Baron, who had not heard the whole speech and
did not know that she was talking of an excursion to
Harambouville, gave a start. "A strange question," he
murmured in a sardonic tone that nettled Mme Verdurin.
"Anyhow," she said to me, "before you dine with the
Cambremers, why not bring your cousin here? Does she
like conversation, and intelligent people? Is she agreeable?
Yes, very well then. Bring her with you. The Cambremers aren't the only people in the world. I can understand

their being glad to invite her, they must find it difficult to
get anyone. Here she will have plenty of fresh air, and
lots of clever men. In any case, I'm counting on you not
to fail me next Wednesday. I heard you were having a
tea-party at Rivebelle with your cousin, and M. de Charlus, and I forget who else. You should arrange to bring
the whole lot on here, it would be nice if you all came in
a body. It's the easiest thing in the world to get here, and
the roads are charming; if you like I can send down for
you. I can't imagine what you find attractive in Rivebelle,
it's infested with mosquitoes. Perhaps you're thinking of
the reputation of the local pancakes. My cook makes them
far better. I'll give you some Norman pancakes, the real
article, and shortbread; just let me show you. Ah! if you
want the sort of filth they give you at Rivebelle, you
won't get it from me, I don't poison my guests, Monsieur,
and even if I wished to, my cook would refuse to make
such unspeakable muck and would give in his notice.
Those pancakes you get down there, you can't tell what
they're made of. I knew a poor girl who got peritonitis
from them, which carried her off in three days. She was
only seventeen. It was sad for her poor mother," added
Mme Verdurin with a mournful air beneath the spheres of
her temples charged with experience and suffering. "However, go and have tea at Rivebelle if you enjoy being
fleeced and flinging money out of the window. But one
thing I beg of you—it's a confidential mission I'm entrusting you with—on the stroke of six bring all your
party here, don't allow them to go straggling away by
themselves. You can bring whom you please. I wouldn't
say that to everybody. But I'm sure your friends are nice,
I can see at once that we understand one another. Apart

from the little nucleus, there are some very agreeable people coming next Wednesday, as it happens. You don't know little Mme de Longpont? She's charming, and so witty, not in the least snobbish, you'll find you'll like her immensely. And she's going to bring a whole troupe of friends too," Mme Verdurin added to show me that this was the right thing to do and encourage me by the other's example. "We shall see which of you has most influence and brings most people, Barbe de Longpont or you. And then I believe somebody's going to bring Bergotte," she added vaguely, this attendance of a celebrity being rendered far from likely by a paragraph which had appeared in the papers that morning to the effect that the great writer's health was causing grave anxiety. "Anyhow, you'll see that it will be one of my most successful Wednesdays. I don't want to have any boring women. You mustn't judge by this evening, which has been a complete failure. Don't try to be polite, you can't have been more bored than I was, I myself thought it was deadly. It won't always be like tonight, you know! I'm not thinking of the Cambremers, who are impossible, but I've known society people who were supposed to be agreeable, and compared with my little nucleus they didn't exist. I heard you say that you thought Swann clever. I must say, to my mind it's greatly exaggerated, but without even speaking of the character of the man, which I've always found fundamentally antipathetic, sly, underhand, I often had him to dinner on Wednesdays. Well, you can ask the others, even compared with Brichot, who is far from being a genius, who's a good secondary schoolmaster whom I got into the Institute all the same, Swann was simply nowhere. He was so dull!" And as I expressed a contrary opinion: "It's the truth. I don't want to say a word against him since he was your friend, indeed he was very fond of you, he spoke to me about you in the most charming way, but ask the others here if he ever said anything interesting at our dinners. That, after all, is the test. Well, I don't know why it was, but Swann, in my house, never seemed to come off, one got nothing out of him. And yet the little he had he picked up here." I assured her that he was highly intelligent. "No, you only thought that because you didn't know him as long as I did. Really, one got to the end of him very soon. I was always bored to death by him." (Translation: "He went to the La Trémoïlles and the Guermantes and knew that I didn't.") "And I can put up with anything except being bored. That I cannot stand!" Her horror of boredom was now the reason upon which Mme Verdurin relied to explain the composition of the little group. She did not yet entertain duchesses be-cause she was incapable of enduring boredom, just as she was incapable of going for a cruise because of sea-sick-ness. I thought to myself that what Mme Verdurin said was not entirely false, and, whereas the Guermantes would have declared Brichot to be the stupidest man they had ever met, I remained uncertain whether he was not in reality superior, if not to Swann himself, at least to the people endowed with the wit of the Guermantes who would have had the good taste to avoid and the delicacy to blush at his pedantic pleasantries; I asked myself the question as though the nature of intelligence might be to some extent clarified by the answer that I might give, and with the earnestness of a Christian influenced by Port-Royal when he considers the problem of Grace.

"You'll see," Mme Verdurin continued, "when one

has society people together with people of real intelligence, people of our set, that's where one has to see
them—the wittiest society man in the kingdom of the
blind is only one-eyed here. Besides, he paralyses the others, who don't feel at home any longer. So much so that
I'm inclined to wonder whether, instead of attempting
mixtures that spoil everything, I shan't start special
evenings confined to the bores so as to have the full benefit of my little nucleus. However: you're coming again
with your cousin. That's settled. Good. At any rate you'll
get something to eat here, the pair of you. Féterne is star-
vation corner. Oh, by the way, if you like rats, go there at
once, you'll get as many as you want. And they'll keep
you there as long as you're prepared to stay. Why, you'll
die of hunger. When I go there, I shall dine before I start.
To make it a bit gayer, you must come here first. We
shall have a good high tea, and supper when we get back.
Do you like apple-tarts? Yes, very well then, our chef
makes the best in the world. You see I was quite right
when I said you were made to live here. So come and
stay. There's far more room here than you'd think. I
don't mention it, so as not to let myself in for bores. You
might bring your cousin to stay. She would get a change
of air from Balbec. With the air here, I maintain that I
can cure incurables. My word, I've cured some, and not
only this time. For I've stayed near here before—a place I
discovered and got for a mere song, and which had a lot
more character than their Raspelière. I can show it to you
if we go for a drive together. But I admit that even here
the air is really invigorating. Still, I don't want to say too
much about it, or the whole of Paris would begin to take
a fancy to my little corner. That's always been my luck.

Anyhow, give your cousin my message. We'll put you in
two nice rooms looking over the valley. You ought to see
it in the morning, with the sun shining through the mist!
By the way, who is this Robert de Saint-Loup you were
speaking of?" she said anxiously, for she had heard that I
was to pay him a visit at Doncières, and was afraid that
he might make me defect. "Why not bring him here instead, if he's not a bore. I've heard of him from Morel; I
fancy he's one of his greatest friends," she added, lying in
her teeth, for Saint-Loup and Morel were not even aware
of one another's existence. But having heard that Saint-
Loup knew M. de Charlus, she supposed that it was
through the violinist, and wished to appear in the know.
"He's not taking up medicine, by any chance, or literature? You know, if you want any help about examinations, Cottard can do anything, and I make what use of
him I please. As for the Academy later on—for I suppose
he's not old enough yet—I have several votes in my
pocket. Your friend would find himself on friendly soil
here, and it might amuse him perhaps to see over the
house. Doncières isn't much fun. Anyhow, do just as you
please, whatever suits you best," she concluded, without
insisting, so as not to appear to be trying to know people
of noble birth, and because she always maintained that
the system by which she governed the faithful, to wit
despotism, was named liberty. "Why, what's the matter
with you," she said, at the sight of M. Verdurin who, gesticulating impatiently, was making for the wooden terrace
that ran along the side of the drawing-room above the
valley, like a man who is bursting with rage and needs
fresh air. "Has Saniette been irritating you again? But
since you know what an idiot he is, you must resign your-

self and not work yourself up into such a state . . . I hate
it when he gets like this," she said to me, "because it's
bad for him, it sends the blood to his head. But I must
say that one would need the patience of an angel at times
to put up with Saniette, and one must always remember
that it's an act of charity to have him in the house. For
my part I must admit that he's so gloriously silly that I
can't help enjoying him. I dare say you heard what he
said after dinner: 'I can't play whist, but I can play the
piano.' Isn't it superb? It's positively colossal, and incidentally quite untrue, for he's incapable of doing either.
But my husband, beneath his rough exterior, is very sensitive, very kind-hearted, and Saniette's self-centred way
of always thinking about the effect he's going to make
drives him crazy . . . Come, dear, calm down, you know
Cottard told you that it was bad for your liver. And I'm
the one who'll have to bear the brunt of it all. Tomorrow
Saniette will come back and have his little fit of hysterics.
Poor man, he's very ill. But still, that's no reason why he
should kill other people. And then, even at moments
when he's really suffering, when one would like to comfort him, his silliness hardens one's heart. He's really too
stupid. You ought to tell him quite politely that these
scenes make you both ill, and he'd better not come back,
and since that's what he's most afraid of, it will have a
calming effect on his nerves," Mme Verdurin concluded.

The sea was only just discernible from the windows
on the right. But those on the other side revealed the valley, now shrouded in a snowy cloak of moonlight. From
time to time one heard the voices of Morel and Cottard.
"Have you any trumps?" "Yes." "From what I saw, 'pon
my soul . . ." said M. de Cambremer to Morel, in an-

swer to his question, for he had seen that the Doctor's hand was full of trumps. "Here comes the lady of diamonds," said the Doctor. "Zat iss trump, you know? My trick. But there isn't a Sorbonne any longer," said the Doctor to M. de Cambremer, "there's only the University of Paris." M. de Cambremer confessed that he did not see the point of this remark. "I thought you were talking about the Sorbonne," continued the Doctor. "I understood you to say: Sorbonne my soul," he added, with a wink, to show that this was a pun. "Just wait a moment," he said, pointing to his opponent, "I have a Trafalgar in store for him." And the prospect must have been excellent for the Doctor, for in his joy his shoulders began to shake voluptuously with laughter, a motion which in his family, in the "genus" Cottard, was an almost zoological sign of satisfaction. In the previous generation the movement used to be accompanied by that of rubbing the hands together as though one were soaping them. Cottard himself had originally employed both forms of mimicry simultaneously, but one fine day, nobody ever knew by whose intervention, wifely or perhaps professional, the rubbing of the hands had disappeared. The Doctor, even at dominoes, when he forced his opponent into a corner and made him take the double six, which was to him the keenest of pleasures, contented himself with the shoulder-shake. And when—which was as seldom as possible—he went down to his native village for a few days and met his first cousin who was still at the hand-rubbing stage, he would say to Mme Cottard on his return: "I thought poor René very common." "Have you any little dears?" he said, turning to Morel. "No? Then I play this old David." "Then you have five, you've won!" "A splendid victory,

Doctor," said the Marquis. "A Pyrrhic victory," said Cottard, turning to face the Marquis and looking at him over his glasses to judge the effect of his remark. "If there's still time," he said to Morel, "I give you your revenge. It's my deal. Ah! no, here come the carriages, it will have to be Friday, and I shall show you a trick you don't see every day."

M. and Mme Verdurin accompanied us to the door. The Mistress was particularly affectionate to Saniette so as to make certain of his returning next time. "But you don't look to me as if you were properly wrapped up, my boy," said M. Verdurin, whose age allowed him to address me in this paternal tone. "It looks as though the weather has changed." These words filled me with joy, as though the dormant life, the resurgence of different combinations which they implied in nature, heralded other changes, occurring in my own life, and created fresh possibilities in it. Merely by opening the door on to the garden, before leaving, one felt that a different weather had, at that moment, taken possession of the scene; cooling breezes, one of the joys of summer, were rising in the fir plantation (where long ago Mme de Cambremer had dreamed of Chopin) and almost imperceptibly, in caressing coils, in fitful eddies, were beginning their gentle nocturnes. I declined the rug which, on subsequent evenings, I was to accept when Albertine was with me, more to preserve the secrecy of pleasure than to avoid the risk of cold. A vain search was made for the Norwegian philosopher. Had he been seized by a colic? Had he been afraid of missing the train? Had an aeroplane come to fetch him? Had he been carried aloft in an Assumption? In any case he had vanished without anyone's noticing his departure, like a god.

"You are unwise," M. de Cambremer said to me, "it's as
cold as charity." "Why charity?" the Doctor inquired.
"Beware of your spasms," the Marquis went on. "My sister never goes out at night. However, she is in a pretty
bad state at present. In any case you oughtn't to stand
about bare-headed, put your tile on at once." "They are
not *a frigore* spasms," said Cottard sententiously. "Ah,
well," M. de Cambremer bowed, "of course, if that's your
view . . ." "View halloo," said the Doctor, his eyes twin-
kling behind his glasses. M. de Cambremer laughed, but,
convinced that he was in the right, insisted: "All the
same," he said, "whenever my sister goes out after dark,
she has an attack." "It's no use quibbling," replied the
Doctor, oblivious of his own discourtesy. "However, I
don't practise medicine by the seaside, unless I'm called
in for a consultation. I'm here on holiday." He was perhaps even more on holiday than he would have liked. M.
de Cambremer having said to him as they got into the
carriage together: "We're fortunate in having quite close
to us (not on your side of the bay, on the opposite side,
but it's quite narrow at that point) another medical
celebrity, Dr du Boulbon," Cottard, who as a rule, from
"deontology," abstained from criticising his colleagues,
could not help exclaiming, as he had exclaimed to me on
the fatal day when we had visited the little casino: "But
he isn't a doctor. He practises a sort of literary medicine,
whimsical therapy, pure charlatanism. All the same, we're
on quite good terms. I'd take the boat and go over and
pay him a visit if I didn't have to go away." But, from the
air which Cottard assumed in speaking of du Boulbon to
M. de Cambremer, I felt that the boat which he would
gladly have taken to call upon him would have greatly re-

sembled that vessel which, in order to go and spoil the
waters discovered by another literary doctor, Virgil (who
took all their patients from them as well), the doctors of
Salerno had chartered, but which sank with them during
the crossing. "Good-bye, my dear Saniette. Don't forget
to come tomorrow, you know how fond of you my husband is. He enjoys your wit and intelligence; yes indeed,
you know quite well he does. He likes putting on a show
of brusqueness, but he can't do without you. It's always
the first thing he asks me: 'Is Saniette coming? I do so enjoy seeing him.' " "I never said anything of the sort," said
M. Verdurin to Saniette with a feigned frankness which
seemed perfectly to reconcile what the Mistress had just
said with the manner in which he treated Saniette. Then,
looking at his watch, doubtless so as not to prolong the
leave-taking in the damp night air, he warned the coach-
men not to lose any time, but to be careful when going
down the hill, and assured us that we should be in plenty
of time for our train. The latter was to set down the faithful, one at one station, another at a second, and so on,
ending with myself, for no one else was going as far as
Balbec, and beginning with the Cambremers, who, in order not to bring their horses all the way up to La
Raspelière at night took the train with us at Douville-
Féterne. For the station nearest to them was not this one,
which, being already at some distance from the village,
was further still from the château, but La Sogne. On arriving at the station of Douville-Féterne, M. de Cambremer made a point of "crossing the palm," as Françoise
used to say, of the Verdurins' coachman (the nice, sensitive coachman, with the melancholy thoughts), for M. de
Cambremer was generous, in that respect "taking after his

mamma." But, possibly because his "papa's side" inter-
vened at this point, in the process of giving he had
qualms about the possibility of an error—either on his
part, if, for instance, in the dark, he were to give a sou instead of a franc, or on the part of the recipient who might
not notice the size of the present that was being given
him. And so he drew attention to it: "It is a franc I'm
giving you, isn't it?" he said to the coachman, turning the
coin until it gleamed in the lamplight, and so that the
faithful might report his action to Mme Verdurin. "Isn't
it? Twenty sous is right, as it's only a short drive." He
and Mme de Cambremer left us at La Sogne. "I shall tell
my sister," he repeated to me once more, "about your
spasms. I'm sure she'll be interested." I understood that
he meant: "will be pleased." As for his wife, she employed, in saying good-bye to me, two abbreviations
which even in writing, used to shock me at that time in a
letter, although one has grown accustomed to them since,
but which, when spoken, seem to me still, even today, in-
sufferably pedantic in their deliberate carelessness, in their
studied familiarity: "Delighted to have met you," she said;
"greetings to Saint-Loup, if you see him." In making this
speech, Mme de Cambremer pronounced the name
"Saint-Loupe." I never discovered who had pronounced it
thus in her hearing, or what had led her to suppose that it
ought to be so pronounced. However that may be, for
some weeks afterwards she continued to say "Saint-
Loupe," and a man who had a great admiration for her
and echoed her in every way did the same. If other people
said "Saint-Lou," they would insist, would say emphatically "Saint-Loupe," either to teach the others a lesson indirectly, or to distinguish themselves from them. But no

doubt women of greater social prestige than Mme de Cambremer told her, or gave her indirectly to understand, that this was not the correct pronunciation, and that what she regarded as a sign of originality was a solecism which would make people think her little conversant with the usages of society, for shortly afterwards Mme de Cambremer was again saying "Saint-Lou," and her admirer similarly ceased to hold out, either because she had admonished him, or because he had noticed that she no longer sounded the final consonant and had said to himself that if a woman of such distinction, energy and ambition had yielded, it must have been on good grounds. The worst of her admirers was her husband. Mme de Cambremer loved to tease other people in a way that was often highly impertinent. As soon as she began to attack me, or anyone else, in this fashion, M. de Cambremer would start watching her victim with a laugh. As the Marquis had a squint—a blemish which gives an impression of intended wit to the mirth even of imbeciles—the effect of this laughter was to bring a segment of pupil into the otherwise complete whiteness of his eye. Thus does a sudden rift bring a patch of blue into an otherwise clouded sky. His monocle moreover protected, like the glass over a valuable picture, this delicate operation. As for the actual intention of his laughter, it was hard to say whether it was friendly: "Ah! you rascal, you're a lucky man and no mistake! You've won the favour of a woman with a very pretty wit." Or vicious: "Well then, I hope you'll learn your lesson when you've swallowed all those insults." Or obliging: "I'm here, you know. I take it with a laugh because it's all pure fun, but I shan't let you be ill-treated." Or cruelly conniving: "I don't need to add my little pinch of salt, but you can see I'm enjoying all the snubs she's handing out to you. I'm laughing myself silly, because I approve, and I'm her husband. So if you should take it into your head to answer back, you'd have me to deal with, young fellow. First of all I'd fetch you a couple of monumental clouts, and then we should go and cross swords in the forest of Chantepie."

Whatever the correct interpretation of the husband's merriment, the wife's whimsical banter soon came to an end. Whereupon M. de Cambremer ceased to laugh, the temporary pupil vanished, and as one had forgotten for a minute or two to expect an entirely white eyeball, it gave this ruddy Norman an air at once anaemic and ecstatic, as though the Marquis had just undergone an operation, or were imploring heaven, through his monocle, for a martyr's crown.

Chapter Three

I was dropping with sleep. I was taken up to my floor not by the lift-boy but by the squinting page, who to make conversation informed me that his sister was still with the gentleman who was so rich, and that once, when she had taken it into her head to return home instead of sticking to her business, her gentleman friend had paid a visit to the mother of the squinting page and of the other more fortunate children, who had very soon made the silly creature return to her protection. "You know, sir, she's a fine lady, my sister is. She plays the piano, she talks Spanish. And, you'd never believe it of the sister of the humble employee who's taking you up in the lift, but she denies herself nothing; Madame has a maid to herself, and she'll have her own carriage one day, I shouldn't wonder. She's very pretty, if you could see her, a bit too high and mighty, but well, you can understand that. She's full of fun. She never leaves a hotel without relieving herself first in a wardrobe or a drawer, just to leave a little keepsake with the chambermaid who'll have to clean up. Sometimes she does it in a cab, and after she's paid her fare, she'll hide behind a tree, and she doesn't half laugh when the cabby finds he's got to clean his cab after her. My father had another stroke of luck when he found my young brother this Indian prince he used to know long ago. It's not the same style of thing, of course. But it's a superb position. If it wasn't for the travelling, it would be a dream. I'm the only one still on the shelf. But you never know. We're a lucky family; perhaps one day I shall be President of the Republic. But I'm keeping you babbling" (I had not uttered a single word and was beginning to fall asleep as I listened to the flow of his). "Good night, sir. Oh! thank you, sir. If everybody had as kind a heart as you, there wouldn't be any poor people left. But, as my sister says, 'there must always be poor people so that now that I'm rich I can shit on them.' You'll pardon the expression. Good night, sir."

Perhaps every night we accept the risk of experiencing, while we are asleep, sufferings which we regard as null and void because they will be felt in the course of a sleep which we suppose to be unconscious. And indeed on these evenings when I came back late from La Raspelière I was very sleepy. But after the weather turned cold I could not get to sleep at once, for the fire lighted up the room as though there were a lamp burning in it. Only it was nothing more than a brief blaze, and—like a lamp too, or like the daylight when night falls—its too bright light was not long in fading; and I entered the realm of sleep, which is like a second dwelling into which we move for that one purpose. It has noises of its own and we are sometimes violently awakened by the sound of bells, perfectly heard by our ears, although nobody has rung. It has its servants, its special visitors who call to take us out, so that we are ready to get up when we are compelled to realise, by our almost immediate transmigration into the other dwelling, our waking one, that the room is empty, that nobody has called. The race that inhabits it, like that of our first human ancestors, is androgynous. A man in it appears a moment later in the form of a woman. Things in it show a tendency to turn into men,

men into friends and enemies. The time that elapses for the sleeper, during these spells of slumber, is absolutely different from the time in which the life of the waking man is passed. Sometimes its course is far more rapid—a quarter of an hour seems a day—at other times far longer—we think we have taken only a short nap, when we have slept through the day. Then, in the chariot of sleep, we descend into depths in which memory can no longer keep up with it, and on the brink of which the mind has been obliged to retrace its steps.

The horses of sleep, like those of the sun, move at so steady a pace, in an atmosphere in which there is no longer any resistance, that it requires some little meteorite extraneous to ourselves (hurled from the azure by what Unknown?) to strike our regular sleep (which otherwise would have no reason to stop, and would continue with a similar motion world without end) and to make it swing sharply round, return towards reality, travel without pause, traverse the regions bordering on life—whose sounds the sleeper will presently hear, still vague but already perceptible even if distorted—and come to earth suddenly at the point of awakening. Then from those profound slumbers we awake in a dawn, not knowing who we are, being nobody, newly born, ready for anything, the brain emptied of that past which was life until then. And perhaps it is more wonderful still when our landing at the waking-point is abrupt and the thoughts of our sleep, hidden by a cloak of oblivion, have no time to return to us gradually, before sleep ceases. Then, from the black storm through which we seem to have passed (but we do not even say *we*), we emerge prostrate, without a thought, a *we* that is void of content. What hammer-blow has the

person or thing that is lying there received to make it unconscious of everything, stupefied until the moment when
memory, flooding back, restores to it consciousness or
personality? However, for both these kinds of awakening,
we must avoid falling asleep, even into a deep sleep, under the law of habit. For everything that habit ensnares in
her nets, she watches closely; we must escape her, take
our sleep at a moment when we thought we were doing
something quite other than sleeping, take, in a word, a
sleep that does not dwell under the tutelage of foresight,
in the company, albeit latent, of reflexion.

At all events, in these awakenings which I have just
described, and which I experienced as a rule when I had
been dining overnight at La Raspelière, everything occurred as though by this process, and I can testify to it, I,
the strange human who, while he waits for death to re-
lease him, lives behind closed shutters, knows nothing of
the world, sits motionless as an owl, and like that bird can
only see things at all clearly in the darkness. Everything
occurs as though by this process, but perhaps only a wad
of cotton-wool has prevented the sleeper from taking in
the internal dialogue of memories and the incessant ver-
biage of sleep. For (and this may be equally manifest in
the other, vaster, more mysterious, more astral system) at
the moment of his entering the waking state, the sleeper
hears a voice inside him saying: "Will you come to this
dinner tonight, my dear friend, it would be so nice?" and
thinks: "Yes, how nice it would be, I shall go"; then,
growing wider awake, he suddenly remembers: "My
grandmother has only a few weeks to live, so the doctor
assures us." He rings, he weeps at the thought that it will
not be, as in the past, his grandmother, his dying grand-

mother, but an indifferent valet that will come in answer to his summons. Moreover, when sleep bore him so far away from the world inhabited by memory and thought, through an ether in which he was alone, more than alone, without even the companionship of self-perception, he was outside the range of time and its measurements. But now the valet is in the room, and he dares not ask him the time, for he does not know whether he has slept, for how many hours he has slept (he wonders whether it should not be how many days, with such a weary body, such a rested mind, such a homesick heart has he returned, as from a journey too distant not to have taken a long time).

One can of course maintain that there is but one time, for the futile reason that it is by looking at the clock that one established as being merely a quarter of an hour what one had supposed a day. But at the moment of establishing this, one is precisely a man awake, immersed in the time of waking men, having deserted the other time. Perhaps indeed more than another time: another life. We do not include the pleasures we enjoy in sleep in the inventory of the pleasures we have experienced in the course of our existence. To take only the most grossly sensual of them all, which of us, on waking, has not felt a certain irritation at having experienced in his sleep a pleasure which, if he is anxious not to tire himself, he is not, once he is awake, at liberty to repeat indefinitely during that day. It seems a positive waste. We have had pleasure in another life which is not ours. If we enter up in a budget the pains and pleasures of dreams (which generally vanish soon enough after our waking), it is not in the current account of our everyday life.

Two times, I have said; perhaps there is only one after all, not that the time of the waking man has any validity for the sleeper, but perhaps because the other life, the life in which he sleeps, is not—in its profounder aspect—included in the category of time. I came to this conclusion when, after those dinner-parties at La Raspelière, I used to sleep so thoroughly. For this reason: I was beginning to despair, on waking, when I found that, after I had rung the bell ten times, the valet did not appear. At the eleventh ring he came. It was only the first after all. The other ten had been mere adumbrations, in my sleep which still hung about me, of the ring that I had been meaning to give. My numbed hands had never even moved. Now, on those mornings (and it is this that makes me think that sleep is perhaps independent of the law of time) my effort to wake up consisted chiefly in an effort to bring the obscure, undefined mass of the sleep in which I had just been living into the framework of time. It is no easy task; sleep, which does not know whether we have slept for two hours or two days, cannot provide us with any point of reference. And if we do not find one outside, not being able to re-enter time, we fall asleep again, for five minutes which seem to us three hours.

I have always said—and have proved by experience—that the most powerful soporific is sleep itself. After having slept profoundly for two hours, having fought with so many giants, and formed so many lifelong friendships, it is far more difficult to awake than after taking several grammes of veronal. And so, reasoning from one thing to the other, I was surprised to hear from the Norwegian philosopher, who had it from M. Boutroux, "my eminent colleague—pardon me, confrère," what M. Bergson

thought of the peculiar effects upon the memory of soporific drugs. "Naturally," M. Bergson had said to
M. Boutroux, according to the Norwegian philosopher,
"soporifics taken from time to time in moderate doses
have no effect upon that solid memory of our everyday
life which is so firmly established within us. But there are
other forms of memory, loftier but also more unstable.
One of my colleagues lectures on ancient history. He tells
me that if, overnight, he has taken a sleeping pill, he has
great difficulty, during his lecture, in recalling the Greek
quotations that he requires. The doctor who recommended these tablets assured him that they had no effect
on the memory. 'That is perhaps because you do not have
to quote Greek,' the historian answered, not without a
note of sarcastic pride."

I cannot say whether this conversation between
M. Bergson and M. Boutroux is accurately reported. The
Norwegian philosopher, albeit so profound and so lucid,
so passionately attentive, may have misunderstood. Personally, my own experience has produced the opposite results. The moments of forgetfulness that come to us in
the morning after we have taken certain narcotics have a
resemblance that is only partial, though disturbing, to the
oblivion that reigns during a night of natural and deep
sleep. Now what I find myself forgetting in either case is
not some line of Baudelaire, which on the contrary keeps
sounding in my ear "like a dulcimer," nor some concept
of one of the philosophers above-named; it is—if I am
asleep—the actual reality of the ordinary things that surround me, my non-perception of which makes me an
idiot; it is—if I am awakened and go out after an artificial
slumber—not the system of Porphyry or Plotinus, which I

can discuss as fluently as on any other day, but the answer that I have promised to give to an invitation, the
memory of which has been replaced by a pure blank. The
lofty thought remains in its place; what the soporific has
put out of action is the power to act in little things, in everything that demands exertion in order to recapture at
the right moment, to grasp some memory of everyday life.
In spite of all that may be said about survival after the
destruction of the brain, I observe that each alteration of
the brain is a partial death. We possess all our memories,
but not the faculty of recalling them, said, echoing
M. Bergson, the eminent Norwegian philosopher whose
speech I have made no attempt to imitate in order not to
slow things down even more. But not the faculty of recalling them. What, then, is a memory which we do not recall? Or, indeed, let us go further. We do not recall our
memories of the last thirty years; but we are wholly
steeped in them; why then stop short at thirty years, why
not extend this previous life back to before our birth? If I
do not know a whole section of the memories that are behind me, if they are invisible to me, if I do not have the
faculty of calling them to me, how do I know whether in
that mass that is unknown to me there may not be some
that extend back much further than my human existence?
If I can have in me and round me so many memories
which I do not remember, this oblivion (a *de facto* oblivion, at least, since I have not the faculty of seeing anything) may extend over a life which I have lived in the
body of another man, even on another planet. A common
oblivion obliterates everything. But what, in that case, is
the meaning of that immortality of the soul the reality of
which the Norwegian philosopher affirmed? The being

that I shall be after death has no more reason to remember the man I have been since my birth than the latter to remember what I was before it.

The valet came in. I did not mention to him that I had rung several times, for I was beginning to realise that hitherto I had only dreamed that I was ringing. I was alarmed nevertheless by the thought that this dream had had the clarity of consciousness. By the same token, might consciousness have the unreality of a dream?

Instead I asked him who it was that had been ringing so often during the night. He told me: "Nobody," and could prove his statement, for the bell-board would have registered any ring. And yet I could hear the repeated, almost furious peals which were still echoing in my ears and were to remain perceptible for several days. It is, however, unusual for sleep thus to project into our waking life memories that do not perish with it. We can count these meteorites. If it is an idea that sleep has forged, it soon breaks up into tenuous, irrecoverable fragments. But, in this instance, sleep had fashioned sounds. More material and simpler, they lasted longer.

I was astonished to hear from the valet how relatively early it was. I felt none the less rested. It is light sleeps that have a long duration, because, being an intermediate state between waking and sleeping, preserving a somewhat faded but constant impression of the former, they require infinitely more time to make us feel rested than a deep sleep, which may be short. I felt entirely relaxed for another reason. If remembering that we have tired ourselves is enough to make us feel our tiredness, saying to oneself "I've rested" is enough to create rest. Now I had been dreaming that M. de Charlus was a hundred and ten

years old, and had just boxed the ears of his own mother,
Mme Verdurin, because she had paid five billion francs
for a bunch of violets; I was thus assured of having slept
profoundly, had dreamed back to front what had been in
my thoughts overnight and all the possibilities of life at
the moment; this was enough to make me feel entirely
rested.

I should greatly have astonished my mother, who
could not understand M. de Charlus's assiduity in visiting
the Verdurins, had I told her who (on the very day on
which Albertine's toque had been ordered, without a word
about it to her, in order that it might come as a surprise)
M. de Charlus had brought to dine in a private room at
the Grand Hotel, Balbec. His guest was none other than
the footman of a lady who was a cousin of the Cambremers. This footman was very smartly dressed, and, as he
crossed the hall with the Baron, "looked the man of fashion," as Saint-Loup would have said, in the eyes of the
visitors. Indeed, the young page-boys, the Levites who
were swarming down the temple steps at that moment because it was the time when they came on duty, paid no
attention to the two newcomers, one of whom, M. de
Charlus, kept his eyes lowered to show that he was paying
little if any to them. He appeared to be trying to carve his
way through their midst. "Thrive then, dear hope of a sacred nation," he said, recalling a passage from Racine, and
applying to it a wholly different meaning. "Pardon?"
asked the footman, who was not well up in the classics.
M. de Charlus made no reply, for he took a certain pride
in never answering questions and in walking straight
ahead as though there were no other visitors in the hotel
and no one else existed in the world except himself, Baron

de Charlus. But, having continued to quote the speech of Josabeth: "Come, then, my daughters," he felt a revulsion and did not, like her, add: "Bid them approach," for these young people had not yet reached the age at which sex is completely developed and which appealed to M. de Charlus.

Moreover, if he had written to Mme de Chevregny's footman, because he had had no doubt of his docility, he had expected someone more virile. On seeing him, he found him more effeminate than he would have liked. He told him that he had been expecting someone else, for he knew by sight another of Mme de Chevregny's footmen, whom he had noticed upon the box of her carriage. This was an extremely rustic type of peasant, the very opposite of the present footman, who, regarding his mincing ways as a mark of his superiority and never doubting that it was these man-of-fashion airs that had captivated M. de Charlus, could not even guess whom the Baron meant. "But there's nobody else except one you can't have had your eye on—he's hideous, just like a great peasant." And at the thought that it was perhaps this lout whom the Baron had seen, he felt wounded in his self-esteem. The Baron guessed this, and, widening his quest, "But I haven't made a vow to know only Mme de Chevregny's people," he said. "Surely there are plenty of fellows in one house or another here, or in Paris, since you're going back there soon, that you could introduce to me?" "Oh, no!" replied the footman, "I never associate with anyone of my own class. I only speak to them on duty. But there's one very nice person I could introduce you to." "Who?" asked the Baron. "The Prince de Guermantes." M. de Charlus was vexed at being offered only a man so advanced in

years, one moreover to whom he had no need to apply to
a footman for an introduction. And so he declined the offer curtly, and, refusing to be put off by the menial's social pretensions, began to explain to him again what he
wanted, the style, the type, a jockey, for instance, and so
on. Fearing lest the notary, who went past at that moment, might have heard him, he thought it cunning to
show that he was speaking of anything in the world rather
than what his hearer might suspect, and said with emphasis and in ringing tones, but as though he were simply
continuing his conversation: "Yes, in spite of my age, I
still retain a passion for collecting, a passion for pretty
things. I will do anything to secure an old bronze, an
early chandelier. I adore the Beautiful."

But to make clear to the footman the change of subject he had so rapidly executed, M. de Charlus laid such
stress upon each word, and furthermore, in order to be
heard by the notary, he shouted his words so loud, that
this charade would have been enough to betray what it
concealed to ears more alert than those of the legal gentleman. The latter suspected nothing, any more than did any
of the other residents in the hotel, all of whom saw a
fashionable foreigner in the footman so smartly attired.
On the other hand, if the men of the world were deceived
and took him for a distinguished American, no sooner did
he appear before the servants than he was spotted by
them, as one convict recognises another, indeed scented
afar off, as certain animals scent one another. The waiters
raised their eyebrows. Aimé cast a suspicious glance. The
wine waiter, shrugging his shoulders, uttered behind his
hand (because he thought it polite) a disobliging remark
which everybody heard.

And even our old Françoise, whose sight was failing and who arrived at the foot of the staircase at that moment on her way to dine in the guests' servants' hall, raised her head, recognised a servant where the hotel guests never suspected one—as the old nurse Euryclea recognises Ulysses long before the suitors seated at the banquet—and seeing M. de Charlus arm in arm with him, assumed an appalled expression, as though all of a sudden slanders which she had heard repeated and had not believed had acquired a distressing verisimilitude in her eyes. She never spoke to me, or to anyone else, of this incident, but it must have caused a considerable commotion in her brain, for afterwards, whenever in Paris she happened to see "Julien," to whom until then she had been so greatly attached, she still treated him with politeness, but with a politeness that had cooled and was always tempered with a strong dose of reserve. This same incident, however, led someone else to confide in me: this was Aimé. When I passed M. de Charlus, the latter, not having expected to meet me, raised his hand and called out "Good evening" with the indifference—outwardly, at least—of a great nobleman who thinks he can do anything he likes and considers it shrewder not to appear to be hiding anything. Aimé, who at that moment was watching him with a suspicious eye and saw that I greeted the companion of the person in whom he was certain that he detected a servant, asked me that same evening who he was.

For, for some time past, Aimé had shown a fondness for chatting, or rather, as he himself put it, doubtless in order to emphasise the (to him) philosophical character of these chats, "discussing" with me. And as I often said to him that it distressed me that he should have to stand beside the table while I ate instead of being able to sit down and share my meal, he declared that he had never seen a guest show such "sound reasoning." He was chatting at that moment to two waiters. They had greeted me, I did not know why; their faces were unfamiliar, although their conversation reverberated with echoes that were not entirely new to me. Aimé was scolding them both because of their matrimonial engagements, of which he disapproved. He appealed to me, and I said that I could not have any opinion on the matter since I did not know them. They reminded me of their names, and said that they had often waited upon me at Rivebelle. But one had let his moustache grow, the other had shaved his off and had had his head cropped; and for this reason, although it was the same head as before that rested upon the shoulders of each of them (and not a different head as in the faulty restorations of Notre-Dame), it had remained almost as invisible to me as those objects which escape the most minute search and are actually staring everybody in the face where nobody notices them, on the mantelpiece. As soon as I knew their names, I recognised exactly the uncertain music of their voices because I saw once more the old faces which determined it. "They want to get married and they haven't even learned English!" Aimé said to me, overlooking the fact that I was little versed in the ways of the hotel trade, and could not be aware that if one does not know foreign languages one cannot be certain of getting a job.

Assuming that Aimé would have no difficulty in finding out that the newcomer was M. de Charlus, and indeed convinced that he must remember him, having waited on him in the dining-room when the Baron had come to see

Mme de Villeparisis during my former visit to Balbec, I told him his name. Not only did Aimé not remember the Baron de Charlus, but the name appeared to make a profound impression on him. He told me that he would look next day in his room for a letter which I might perhaps be able to explain to him. I was all the more astonished because M. de Charlus, when he had wished to give me one of Bergotte's books at Balbec the first year, had specially asked for Aimé, whom he must have recognised later on in that Paris restaurant where I had had lunch with Saint-Loup and his mistress and where M. de Charlus had come to spy on us. It is true that Aimé had not been able to execute these commissions in person, being on the former occasion in bed, and on the latter engaged in serving. I had nevertheless grave doubts as to his sincerity when he claimed not to know M. de Charlus. For one thing, he must have been to the Baron's liking. Like all the floor waiters of the Balbec hotel, like several of the Prince de Guermantes's footmen, Aimé belonged to a race more ancient than that of the Prince, and therefore more noble. When one asked for a private room, one thought at first that one was alone. But presently, in the pantry, one caught sight of a sculptural waiter, of that ruddy Etruscan kind of which Aimé was the epitome, slightly aged by excessive consumption of champagne and seeing the inevitable hour for mineral water approach. Not all the guests asked them merely to wait upon them. The underlings, who were young, scrupulous, and in a hurry, having mistresses waiting for them outside, made off. Hence Aimé reproached them with not being serious. He had every right to do so. He himself was certainly serious. He had a wife and children, and was ambitious on their be-

half. And so he never repulsed the advances made to him
by a strange lady or gentleman, even if it meant his staying all night. For business must come first. He was so
much of the type that might attract M. de Charlus that I
suspected him of falsehood when he told me that he did
not know him. I was wrong. The page had been perfectly
truthful when he told the Baron that Aimé (who had
given him a dressing-down for it next day) had gone to
bed (or gone out), and on the other occasion was busy
serving. But imagination outreaches reality. And the page-
boy's embarrassment had probably aroused in M. de
Charlus doubts as to the sincerity of his excuses, doubts
that had wounded feelings on his part of which Aimé had
no suspicion. We have seen moreover that Saint-Loup
had prevented Aimé from going out to the carriage and
that M. de Charlus, who had managed somehow or other
to discover the head waiter's new address, had suffered a
further disappointment. Aimé, who had not noticed him,
felt an astonishment that may be imagined when, on the
evening of that very day on which I had had lunch with
Saint-Loup and his mistress, he received a letter sealed
with the Guermantes arms from which I shall quote a few
passages here as an example of unilateral insanity in an
intelligent man addressing a sensible idiot.

"Monsieur, I have been unsuccessful, notwithstanding
efforts that would astonish many who have sought in vain
to be received and greeted by me, in persuading you to
listen to certain explanations which you have not asked of
me but which I have felt it to be incumbent upon my
dignity and your own to offer you. I propose therefore to
write down here what it would have been simpler to say
to you in person. I make no secret of the fact that, the

first time I set eyes upon you at Balbec, I found your face frankly antipathetic." Here followed reflexions on the resemblance—remarked only on the following day—to a deceased friend to whom M. de Charlus had been deeply attached. "For a moment I had the idea that you might, without in any way encroaching upon the demands of your profession, come to see me and, by joining me in the card games with which his gaiety used to dispel my gloom, give me the illusion that he was not dead. Whatever the nature of the more or less fatuous suppositions which you probably formed, suppositions more within the mental range of a servant (who does not even deserve the name of servant since he has declined to serve) than the comprehension of so lofty a sentiment, you no doubt thought to give yourself an air of importance, ignoring who I was and what I was, by sending word to me, when I asked you to fetch me a book, that you were in bed; but it is a mistake to imagine that impolite behaviour ever adds to charm, a quality in which in any case you are entirely lacking. I should have ended matters there had I not by chance had occasion to speak to you the following day. Your resemblance to my poor friend was so pronounced, banishing even the intolerable protuberance of your too prominent chin, that I realised that it was the deceased who at that moment was lending you his own kindly expression so as to permit you to regain your hold over me and to prevent you from missing the unique opportunity that was being offered you. Indeed, although I have no wish, since there is no longer any object and it is unlikely that I shall meet you again in this life, to introduce coarse questions of material interest, I should have been only too glad to obey the prayer of my dead friend (for I believe in the Communion of Saints and in their desire to intervene in the destiny of the living), that I should treat you as I used to treat him, who had his carriage and his servants, and to whom it was quite natural that I should consecrate the greater part of my fortune since I loved him as a father loves his son. You have decided otherwise. To my request that you should fetch me a book you sent the reply that you were obliged to go out. And this morning when I sent to ask you to come to my carriage, you then, if I may so speak without blasphemy, denied me for the third time. You will forgive me for not enclosing in this envelope the lavish gratuity which I intended to give you at Balbec and to which it would be too painful for me to restrict myself in dealing with a person with whom I had thought for a moment of sharing all that I possess. At the very most you could spare me the trouble of coming to your restaurant to make a fourth futile overture to which my patience will not extend." (Here M. de Charlus gave his address, stated the hours at which he would be at home, etc.) "Farewell, Monsieur. Since I assume that, resembling so strongly the friend whom I have lost, you cannot be entirely stupid, otherwise physiognomy would be a false science, I am convinced that if, one day, you think of this incident again, it will not be without a feeling of some regret and remorse. For my part, believe me, I am quite sincere in saying that I retain no bitterness. I should have preferred that we should part with a less unpleasant memory than this third futile approach. It will soon be forgotten. We are like those vessels which you must often have seen at Balbec, which have crossed one another's paths for a moment; it might have been to the advantage of each of them to stop; but one of them has decided otherwise; presently they will no longer even see one another on the horizon, and their meeting is a thing out of mind; but before this final parting, each of them salutes the other, and so at this point, Monsieur, wishing you all good fortune, does the Baron de Charlus."

Aimé had not even read this letter to the end, being able to make nothing of it and suspecting a hoax. When I had explained to him who the Baron was, he appeared to be lost in thought and to be feeling the regret that M. de Charlus had anticipated. I would not be prepared to swear that he might not at that moment have written a letter of apology to a man who gave carriages to his friends. But in the interval M. de Charlus had made Morel's acquaintance. At most, his relations with Morel being possibly platonic, M. de Charlus occasionally sought to spend an evening in company such as that in which I had just met him in the hall. But he was no longer able to divert from Morel the violent feelings which, unfettered a few years earlier, had been only too ready to fasten themselves upon Aimé and had dictated the letter which had embarrassed me for its writer's sake when the head waiter showed me it. It was, because of the anti-social nature of M. de Charlus's love, a more striking example of the insensible, sweeping force of those currents of passion by which the lover, like a swimmer, is very soon carried out of sight of land. No doubt the love of a normal man may also, when the lover through the successive fabrications of his desires, regrets, disappointments, plans, constructs a whole novel about a woman whom he does not know, cause the two legs of the compass to gape at a fairly considerable angle. All the same, such an angle was singularly widened by

the character of a passion which is not generally shared
and by the difference in social position between M. de
Charlus and Aimé.

Every day I went out with Albertine. She had decided
to take up painting again and had chosen as the subject of
her first attempts the church of Saint-Jean-de-la-Haise
which nobody ever visited and very few had even heard
of, which was difficult to get directions to, impossible to
find without being guided, and laborious to reach in its
isolation, more than half an hour from Epreville station,
after one had long left behind one the last houses of the
village of Quetteholme. As to the name Epreville, I found
that the curé's book and Brichot's information were at
variance. According to one, Epreville was the ancient
Sprevilla; the other derived the name from Aprivilla. On
our first visit we took a little train in the opposite direction from Féterne, that is to say towards Grattevast. But
we were in the dog days and it had been a terrible strain
to leave immediately after lunch. I should have preferred
not to set out so early; the luminous and burning air provoked thoughts of indolence and cool retreats. It filled my
mother's room and mine, according to their exposure, at
varying temperatures, like rooms in a Turkish bath.
Mamma's bathroom, festooned by the sun with a dazzling, Moorish whiteness, appeared to be sunk at the bottom of a well, because of the four plastered walls on
which it looked out, while far above, in the square gap,
the sky, whose fleecy white waves could be seen gliding
past, one above the other, seemed (because of the longing that one felt) like a tank filled with blue water and reserved for ablutions, either built on a terrace or seen
upside down in a mirror fixed to the window. Notwith-

standing this scorching temperature, we had taken the one
o'clock train. But Albertine had been very hot in the carriage, hotter still in the long walk across country, and I
was afraid of her catching cold when afterwards she had
to sit still in that damp hollow where the sun's rays did
not penetrate. However, having realised as long ago as our
first visits to Elstir that she would appreciate not merely
luxury but even a certain degree of comfort of which her
want of money deprived her, I had made arrangements
with a Balbec livery stable for a carriage to be sent to
fetch us every day. To escape from the heat we took the
road through the forest of Chantepie. The invisibility of
the innumerable birds, some of them sea-birds, that con-
versed with one another from the trees on either side of
us, gave the same impression of repose as one has when
one shuts one's eyes. By Albertine's side, clasped in her
arms in the depths of the carriage, I listened to these
Oceanides. And when by chance I caught sight of one of
these musicians as he flitted from one leaf to the shelter of
another, there was so little apparent connexion between
him and his songs that I could not believe that I was seeing their cause in that tiny body, fluttering, humble, star-
tled and unseeing. The carriage could not take us all the
way to the church. I stopped it when we had passed
through Quetteholme and bade Albertine good-bye. For
she had alarmed me by saying to me of this church as of
other monuments and of certain pictures: "What a pleasure it would be to see it with you!" This pleasure was
one that I did not feel myself capable of giving her. I felt
it myself in front of beautiful things only if I was alone or
pretended to be alone and did not speak. But since she
had hoped to be able, thanks to me, to experience artistic

sensations that cannot be communicated thus, I thought it more prudent to say that I must leave her, that I would come back to fetch her at the end of the day, but that in the meantime I must go back with the carriage to pay a call on Mme Verdurin or on the Cambremers, or even spend an hour with Mamma at Balbec, but never further afield. To begin with, that is to say. For, Albertine having once said to me petulantly: "It's a bore that nature has arranged things so badly and put Saint-Jean-de-la-Haise in one direction, La Raspelière in another, so that you're imprisoned for the whole day in the spot you've chosen," as soon as the toque and veil had come I ordered, to my eventual undoing, a motor-car from Saint-Fargeau (*Sanctus Ferreolus*, according to the curé's book). Albertine, whom I had kept in ignorance and who had come to call for me, was surprised when she heard in front of the hotel the purr of the engine, delighted when she learned that this motor was for ourselves. I took her upstairs to my room for a moment. She jumped for joy. "Are we going to pay a call on the Verdurins?" "Yes, but you'd better not go dressed like that since you'll have your motor-car. Here, you'll look better in these." And I brought out the toque and veil which I had hidden. "They're for me? Oh! you are an angel," she cried, throwing her arms round my neck. Aimé, who met us on the stairs, proud of Albertine's smart attire and of our means of transport, for these vehicles were still comparatively rare at Balbec, could not resist the pleasure of coming downstairs behind us. Albertine, anxious to display herself in her new garments, asked me to have the hood raised; we could lower it later on when we wished to be more private. "Now then," said Aimé to the driver, with whom he was not acquainted and who had not stirred, "don't you (*tu*) hear, you're to raise the hood?" For Aimé, sophisticated as a result of hotel life, in which moreover he had won his way to exalted rank, was not as shy as the cab driver to whom Françoise was a "lady"; despite the absence of any formal introduction, plebeians whom he had never seen before he addressed as *tu*, though it was hard to say whether this was aristocratic disdain on his part or democratic fraternity. "I'm engaged," replied the chauffeur, who did not know me by sight. "I'm ordered for Mlle Simonet. I can't take this gentleman." Aimé burst out laughing: "Why, you great bumpkin," he said to the driver, whom he at once convinced, "this is Mlle Simonet, and Monsieur, who wants you to open the roof of your car, is the person who has engaged you." And since, although personally he had no great liking for Albertine, Aimé was for my sake proud of her get-up, he whispered to the chauffeur: "Don't get the chance of driving a princess like that every day, do you?" On this first occasion I was unable to go to La Raspelière alone as I did on other days, while Albertine painted; she wanted to come there with me. Although she realised that it would be possible to stop here and there on our way, she could not believe that we could start by going to Saint-Jean-de-la-Haise, that is to say in another direction, and then make an excursion which seemed to be reserved for a different day. She learned on the contrary from the driver that nothing could be easier than to go to Saint-Jean, which he could do in twenty minutes, and that we might stay there if we chose for hours, or go on much further, for from Quetteholme to La Raspelière would not take more than thirty-five minutes. We realised this as soon as the vehicle, starting off, covered in one bound twenty paces of an excellent horse. Distances are only the relation of space to time and vary with it. We express the difficulty that we have in getting to a place in a system of miles or kilometres which becomes false as soon as that difficulty decreases. Art is modified by it also, since a village which seemed to be in a different world from some other village becomes its neighbour in a landscape whose dimensions are altered. In any case, to learn that there may perhaps exist a universe in which two and two make five and a straight line is not the shortest distance between two points would have astonished Albertine far less than to hear the driver say that it was easy to go in a single afternoon to Saint-Jean and La Raspelière. Douville and Quetteholme, Saint-Mars-le-Vieux and Saint-Mars-le-Vêtu, Gourville and Balbec-le-Vieux, Tourville and Féterne, prisoners hitherto as hermetically confined in the cells of distinct days as long ago were Méséglise and Guermantes, upon which the same eyes could not gaze in the course of a single afternoon, delivered now by the giant with the seven-league boots, clustered around our tea-time with their towers and steeples and their old gardens which the neighbouring wood sprang back to reveal.

Coming to the foot of the cliff road, the car climbed effortlessly, with a continuous sound like that of a knife being ground, while the sea, falling away, widened beneath us. The old rustic houses of Montsurvent came rushing towards us, clasping to their bosoms vine or rose-bush; the firs of La Raspelière, more agitated than when the evening breeze was rising, ran in every direction to escape from us, and a new servant whom I had never seen before came to open the door for us on the terrace while the gardener's son, betraying a precocious bent, gazed intently at the engine. As it was not a Monday we did not know whether we should find Mme Verdurin, for except on that day, when she had guests, it was unsafe to call upon her without warning. No doubt she was "in principle" at home, but this expression, which Mme Swann employed at the time when she too was seeking to form her little clan and attract customers without herself moving (even though she often did not get her money's worth) and which she mistranslated into "on principle," meant no more than "as a general rule," that is to say with frequent exceptions. For not only did Mme Verdurin like going out, but she carried her duties as a hostess to extreme lengths, and when she had had people to lunch, immediately after the coffee, liqueurs and cigarettes (notwithstanding the first somnolent effects of heat and digestion in which they would have preferred to watch through the leafy boughs of the terrace the Jersey packet sailing across the enamelled sea), the programme included a series of excursions in the course of which her guests, forced into carriages, were conveyed willy-nilly to look at one or other of the beauty spots that abound in the neighbourhood of Douville. This second part of the entertainment was, as it happened (once the effort to get up and climb into a carriage had been made), no less satisfying than the other to the guests, already conditioned by the succulent dishes, the vintage wines or sparkling cider to be easily intoxicated by the purity of the breeze and the magnificence of the sights. Mme Verdurin used to show these to visitors rather as though they were annexes (more or less detached) of her property, which you could not help going to see if you came to lunch with her and which conversely you would never have known had you not been entertained by the Mistress. This claim to arrogate to herself the exclusive right over the local sights, as over Morel's and formerly Dechambre's playing, and to compel the landscapes to form part of the little clan, was not in fact as absurd as it appears at first sight. Mme Verdurin deplored not only the lack of taste which in her opinion the Cambremers showed in the furnishing of La Raspelière and the arrangement of the garden, but also the excursions they made, with or without their guests, in the surrounding countryside. Just as, according to her, La Raspelière was only beginning to become what it should always have been now that it was the asylum of the little clan, so she insisted that the Cambremers, perpetually exploring in their barouche, along the railway line, by the shore, the one ugly road in the district, had been living in the place all their lives but did not know it. There was a grain of truth in this assertion. From force of habit, lack of imagination, want of interest in a country which seemed hackneyed because it was so near, the Cambremers when they left their home went always to the same places and by the same roads. To be sure, they laughed heartily at the Verdurins' pretensions to teach them about their own countryside. But if they were driven into a corner they and even their coachman would have been incapable of taking us to the splendid, more or less secret places to which M. Verdurin brought us, now breaking through the fence of a private but deserted property into which other people would not have thought it possible to venture, now leaving the carriage to follow a path which was not wide enough for wheeled traffic, but in either case with the certain recompense of a marvellous view. It must also be said that the garden at La Raspelière was in

a sense a compendium of all the excursions to be made in
a radius of many miles—in the first place because of its
commanding position, overlooking on one side the valley,
on the other the sea, and also because, on one and the
same side, the seaward side for instance, clearings had
been made through the trees in such a way that from one
point you embraced one horizon, from another a different
one. There was at each of these vantage points a bench;
you went and sat down in turn upon the bench from
which there was the view of Balbec, or Parville, or Douville. Even to command a single direction, one bench
would have been placed more or less on the edge of the
cliff, another set back. From the latter you had a fore-
ground of verdure and a horizon which seemed already
the vastest imaginable, but which became infinitely larger
if, continuing along a little path, you went to the next
bench from which you embraced the whole amphitheatre
of the sea. There you could catch distinctly the sound of
the waves, which did not penetrate to the more secluded
parts of the garden, where the sea was still visible but no
longer audible. These resting-places were known by the
occupants of La Raspelière by the name of "views." And
indeed they assembled round the château the finest views
of the neighbouring villages, beaches or forests, seen
greatly diminished by distance, as Hadrian collected in his
villa reduced models of the most famous monuments of
different regions. The name that followed the word
"view" was not necessarily that of a place on the coast,
but often that of the opposite shore of the bay which you
could make out, standing out in a certain relief notwithstanding the extent of the panorama. Just as you took a
book from M. Verdurin's library to go and read for an

hour at the "view of Balbec," so if the sky was clear the liqueurs would be served at the "view of Rivebelle," on condition however that the wind was not too strong, for, in spite of the trees planted on either side, the air up there was keen.

To revert to the afternoon drives which Mme Verdurin used to organise, if on her return she found the cards of some social butterfly "on a visit to the coast," the Mistress would pretend to be overjoyed but was actually broken-hearted at having missed his visit and (albeit people at this date came only to "see the house" or to make the acquaintance for a day of a woman whose artistic salon was famous but outside the pale in Paris) would at once get M. Verdurin to invite him to dine on the following Wednesday. As the tourist was often obliged to leave before that day, or was afraid to be out late, Mme Verdurin had arranged that on Mondays she was always to be found at tea-time. These tea-parties were not at all large, and I had known more brilliant gatherings of the sort in Paris, at the Princesse de Guermantes's, at Mme de Galliffet's or Mme d'Arpajon's. But this was not Paris, and the charm of the setting enhanced, in my eyes, not merely the pleasantness of the occasion but the merits of the visitors. A meeting with some society person, which in Paris would have given me no pleasure but which at La Raspelière, whither he or she had come from a distance via Féterne or the forest of Chantepie, changed in character and importance, became an agreeable incident. Sometimes it was a person whom I knew quite well and would not have gone a yard to meet at the Swanns'. But his name had a different reverberation on this cliff, like the name of an actor one has constantly seen in the theatre

printed in a different colour on a poster for some special
gala performance, where his fame is suddenly heightened
by the unexpectedness of the context. As in the country
people behave without ceremony, the social celebrity often
took it upon himself to bring the friends with whom he
was staying, murmuring to Mme Verdurin by way of excuse that he could not leave them behind as he was living
in their house; to his hosts on the other hand he pretended to be offering as a sort of courtesy this diversion,
in a monotonous seaside life, of being taken to a centre of
wit and intellect, of visiting a magnificent mansion and of
having an excellent tea. This composed at once an assembly of several persons of semi-distinction; and if a little
slice of garden with a few trees, which would seem paltry
in the country, acquires an extraordinary charm in the
Avenue Gabriel or the Rue de Monceau, where only
multi-millionaires can afford such a luxury, conversely
noblemen who would be background figures at a Parisian
reception were shown to full advantage on a Monday afternoon at La Raspelière. No sooner did they sit down at
the table covered with a cloth embroidered in red, beneath
the painted panels, to partake of pancakes, Norman puff
pastry, trifles, boat-shaped tartlets filled with cherries like
coral beads, cabinet puddings, than these guests were subjected, by the proximity of the great bowl of azure upon
which the window opened and which you could not help
seeing at the same time as them, to a profound alteration,
a transmutation which changed them into something more
precious than before. What was more, even before you set
eyes on them, when you came on a Monday to Mme Verdurin's, people who in Paris would scarcely turn their
jaded heads to look at the string of elegant carriages sta-

tioned outside a great house, felt their hearts throb at the sight of the two or three shabby dog-carts drawn up in front of La Raspelière, beneath the tall firs. No doubt this was because the rustic setting was different, and social impressions thanks to this transposition regained a certain freshness. It was also because the broken-down carriage that one hired to pay a call upon Mme Verdurin conjured up a pleasant drive and a costly bargain struck with a coachman who had demanded "so much" for the whole day. But the slight stir of curiosity with regard to fresh arrivals whom it was still impossible to distinguish arose also from the fact that everyone wondered, "Who can this be?"—a question which it was difficult to answer, when one did not know who might have come down to spend a week with the Cambremers or elsewhere, but which people always enjoy putting to themselves in rustic, solitary environments where a meeting with a human being whom one has not seen for a long time, or an introduction to somebody one does not know, ceases to be the tedious affair that it is in the life of Paris, and forms a delicious break in the empty monotony of lives that are too isolated, in which even the arrival of the mail becomes a pleasure. And on the day on which we arrived by motor-car at La Raspelière, as it was not Monday, M. and Mme Verdurin must have been devoured by that craving to see people which attacks both men and women and inspires a longing to throw himself out of the window in the patient who has been shut up away from his family and friends in an isolation clinic. For the new and more swift-footed servant, who had already made himself familiar with these expressions, having replied that "if Madame hasn't gone out she must be at the view of Douville," and that he would go and look for her, came back immediately to tell us that she was coming to welcome us. We found her slightly dishevelled, for she had come from the flower-beds, the poultry-yard and the kitchen garden, where she had gone to feed her peacocks and hens, to look for eggs, to gather fruit and flowers to "make her table-runner," which would recall her garden path in miniature, but would confer on the table the distinction of making it support the burden of only such things as were useful and good to eat; for round those other presents from the garden—the pears, the whipped eggs—rose the tall stems of bugloss, carnations, roses and coreopsis, between which one saw, as between blossoming boundary posts, the ships out at sea moving slowly across the glazed windows. From the astonishment which M. and Mme Verdurin, interrupted while arranging their flowers to receive the visitors who had been announced, showed upon finding that these visitors were merely Albertine and myself, it was easy to see that the new servant, full of zeal but not yet familiar with my name, had repeated it wrongly and that Mme Verdurin, hearing the names of guests whom she did not know, had nevertheless bidden him let them in, in her need of seeing somebody, no matter whom. And the new servant stood contemplating this spectacle from the door in order to learn what part we played in the household. Then he made off at a loping run, for he had entered upon his duties only the day before. When Albertine had quite finished displaying her toque and veil to the Verdurins, she gave me a warning look to remind me that we had not too much time left for what we meant to do. Mme Verdurin begged us to stay to tea, but we refused, when all of a sudden a suggestion was mooted which would have made an end of all the pleasures that I had promised myself from my drive with Albertine: the Mistress, unable to face the thought of leaving us, or perhaps of letting slip a new diversion, decided to accompany us. Accustomed for years past to the experience that similar offers on her part were not well received, and being probably uncertain whether this offer would find favour with us, she concealed beneath an excessive assurance the timidity that she felt in making it to us and, without even appearing to suppose that there could be any doubt as to our answer, asked us no question but said to her husband, referring to Albertine and myself, as though she were conferring a favour on us: "I shall see them home myself." At the same time there hovered over her lips a smile that did not strictly belong to them, a smile which I had already seen on the faces of certain people when they said to Bergotte with a knowing air: "I've bought your book, it's not bad," one of those collective, universal smiles which, when they feel the need of them—as one makes use of railways and removal vans—individuals borrow, except a few who are extremely refined, like Swann or M. de Charlus, on whose lips I never saw that smile appear. From that moment my visit was ruined. I pretended not to have understood. A moment later it became evident that M. Verdurin was to be of the party. "But it will be too far for M. Verdurin," I objected. "Not at all," replied Mme Verdurin with a condescending, cheerful air, "he says it will amuse him immensely to go with you young people over a road he has travelled so many times; if necessary, he will sit beside the driver, that doesn't frighten him, and we shall come back quietly by the train like good spouses. Look at him, he's quite delighted." She seemed to be speaking of an aged and famous painter full of good nature, who, younger than the youngest, takes a delight in daubing pictures to amuse his grandchildren. What added to my gloom was that Albertine seemed not to share it and to find some amusement in the thought of dashing all over the countryside with the Verdurins. As for myself, the pleasure that I had been looking forward to enjoying with her was so imperious that I refused to allow the Mistress to spoil it; I made up lies which were justified by Mme Verdurin's irritating threats but which Albertine unfortunately contradicted. "But we have a call to make," I said. "What call?" asked Albertine. "I'll explain to you later, there's no getting out of it." "Very well, we can wait outside," said Mme Verdurin, resigned to anything. At the last minute my anguish at being deprived of a happiness for which I had so longed gave me the courage to be impolite. I refused point-blank, whispering in Mme Verdurin's ear that because of some trouble which had befallen Albertine and about which she wished to consult me, it was absolutely essential that I should be alone with her. The Mistress looked furious: "All right, we shan't come," she said to me in a voice trembling with rage. I felt her to be so angry that, so as to appear to be giving way a little: "But we might perhaps . . ." I began. "No," she replied, more furious than ever, "when I say no, I mean no." I supposed that I had irrevocably offended her, but she called us back at the door to urge us not to "let her down" on the following Wednesday, and not to come with that contraption, which was dangerous at night, but by the train with the little group, and she stopped the car, which was already moving downhill through the park, because the footman had forgotten to put in the back the slice of tart and the short-bread which she had had wrapped up for us. We set off again, escorted for a moment by the little houses that came running to meet us with their flowers. The face of the countryside seemed to us entirely changed, for in the topographical image that we form in our minds of separate places the notion of space is far from being the most important factor. We have said that the notion of time segregates them even further. It is not the only factor either. Certain places which we see always in isolation seem to us to have no common measure with the rest, to be almost outside the world, like those people whom we have known in exceptional periods of our life, in the army or during our childhood, and whom we do not connect with anything. During my first stay at Balbec there was a hill which Mme de Villeparisis liked to take us up because from it you saw only the sea and the woods, and which was called Beaumont. As the road that she took to approach it, and preferred to other routes because of its old trees, went uphill all the way, her carriage was obliged to go at a crawling pace and took a very long time. When we reached the top we used to get down, walk for a while, get back into the carriage, and return by the same road, without seeing a single village, a single country house. I knew that Beaumont was something very special, very remote, very high, but I had no idea of the direction in which it was to be found, having never taken the Beaumont road to go anywhere else; besides, it took a very long time to get there in a carriage. It was obviously in the same department (or in the same province) as Balbec, but was situated for me on another plane, enjoyed a special privilege of extraterritoriality. But the motor-car respects no mystery, and, having passed through Incarville, whose houses still danced before my eyes, as we were going down the by-road that leads to Parville (*Paterni villa*), catching sight of the sea from a natural terrace over which we were passing, I asked the name of the place, and before the chauffeur had time to reply recognised Beaumont, close by which I passed thus without knowing it whenever I took the little train, for it was within two minutes of Parville. Like an officer in my regiment who might have struck me as someone special, too kindly and unassuming to be a nobleman, or altogether too remote and mysterious to be merely a nobleman, and whom I then might have discovered to be the brother-in-law or the cousin of people with whom I often dined, so Beaumont, suddenly linked with places from which I supposed it to be so distinct, lost its mystery and took its place in the district, making me think with terror that Madame Bovary and the Sanseverina might perhaps have seemed to me to be like ordinary people, had I met them elsewhere than in the closed atmosphere of a novel. It may be thought that my love of enchanted journeys by train ought to have kept me from sharing Albertine's wonder at the motor-car which takes even an invalid wherever he wishes to go and prevents one from thinking—as I had done hitherto—of the actual site as the individual mark, the irreplaceable essence of irremovable beauties. And doubtless this site was not, for the motor-car, as it had formerly been for the railway train when I came from Paris to Balbec, a goal exempt from the contingencies of ordinary life, almost ideal at the moment of departure and remaining so at the moment of arrival in that great dwelling where nobody lives and which bears only the name of the town, the station, with its promise at last of accessibility to the place of which it is, as it were, the materialisation. No, the motor-car did not convey us thus by magic into a town which we saw at first as the collectivity summed up in its name, and with the illusions of a spectator in a theatre. It took us backstage into the streets, stopped to ask an inhabitant the way. But, as compensation for so homely a mode of progress, there are the gropings of the chauffeur himself, uncertain of his way and going back over his tracks; the "general post" of the perspective which sets a castle dancing about with a hill, a church and the sea, while one draws nearer to it however much it tries to huddle beneath its age-old foliage; those ever-narrowing circles described by the motor-car round a spellbound town which darts off in every direction to escape, and which finally it swoops straight down upon in the depths of the valley where it lies prone on the ground; so that this site, this unique point, which on the one hand the motor-car seems to have stripped of the mystery of express trains, on the other hand it gives us the impression of discovering, of pinpointing for ourselves as with a compass, and helps us to feel with a more lovingly exploring hand, with a more delicate precision, the true geometry, the beautiful proportions of the earth.

What unfortunately I did not know at that moment and did not learn until more than two years later was that one of the chauffeur's customers was M. de Charlus, and that Morel, instructed to pay him and keeping part of the money for himself (making the chauffeur triple and quintuple the mileage), had become very friendly with him (while pretending not to know him in front of other people) and made use of his car for long journeys. If I had known this at the time, and that the confidence which the Verdurins were presently to feel in this chauffeur came, unknown to them perhaps, from that source, many of the sorrows of my life in Paris in the following year, much of my trouble over Albertine, would have been avoided; but I had not the slightest suspicion of it. In themselves, M. de Charlus's excursions by motor-car with Morel were of no direct interest to me. They were confined as a rule to a lunch or dinner in some restaurant along the coast where M. de Charlus was taken for an old and penniless servant and Morel, whose duty it was to pay the bill, for a too kind-hearted gentleman. I report the conversation at one of these meals, which may give an idea of the others. It was in a restaurant of elongated shape at Saint-Mars-le-Vêtu.

"Can't you get them to remove this thing?" M. de Charlus asked Morel, as though appealing to an intermediary without having to address the staff directly. "This thing" was a vase containing three withered roses with which a well-meaning head waiter had seen fit to decorate the table.

"Yes . . ." said Morel, embarrassed. "Don't you like roses?"

"My request ought on the contrary to prove that I do like them, since there are no roses here" (Morel appeared surprised) "but as a matter of fact I do not care much for them. I am rather susceptible to names; and whenever a rose is at all beautiful, one learns that it is called Baronne de Rothschild or Maréchale Niel, which casts a chill. Do you like names? Have you found pretty titles for your little concert numbers?"

"There is one that's called *Poème triste*."

"That's hideous," replied M. de Charlus in a shrill voice that rang out like a slap in the face. "But I ordered champagne," he said to the head waiter, who had supposed he was obeying the order by placing by the diners two glasses of sparkling liquid.

"Yes, sir."

"Take away that filth, which has no connexion with the worst champagne in the world. It is the emetic known as *cup*, which consists, as a rule, of three rotten strawberries swimming in a mixture of vinegar and soda-water . . . Yes," he went on, turning again to Morel, "you don't seem to know what a title is. And even in the interpretation of the things you play best, you seem not to be aware of the mediumistic side."

"What's that you say?" asked Morel, who, not having understood one word of what the Baron had said, was afraid that he might be missing something of importance, such as an invitation to lunch. M. de Charlus not having deigned to consider "What's that you say?" as a question, Morel in consequence received no answer, and thought it best to change the subject and give the conversation a sensual turn.

"I say, look at the little blonde selling the flowers you don't like; I bet she's got a little girlfriend. And the old woman dining at the table at the end, too."

"But how do you know all that?" asked M. de Charlus, amazed at Morel's intuition.

"Oh! I can spot them in an instant. If we walked together through a crowd, you'd see that I never make a mistake." And anyone looking at Morel at that moment, with his girlish air enshrined in his masculine beauty, would have understood the obscure divination which marked him out to certain women no less than them to him. He was anxious to supplant Jupien, vaguely desirous of adding to his regular salary the income which, he supposed, the tailor derived from the Baron. "And with gigolos I'm surer still. I could save you from making mistakes. They'll be having the fair at Balbec soon. We'll find lots of things there. And in Paris too, you'll see, you'll have a fine time." But the inherited caution of a servant made him give a different turn to the sentence on which he had already embarked. So that M. de Charlus supposed that he was still referring to girls. "Do you know," said Morel, anxious to excite the Baron's senses in a fashion which he considered less compromising for himself (although it was actually more immoral), "what I'd like would be to find a girl who was absolutely pure, make her fall in love with me, and take her virginity."

M. de Charlus could not refrain from pinching Morel's ear affectionately, but added ingenuously: "What good would that do you? If you took her maidenhead, you would be obliged to marry her."

"Marry her?" cried Morel, feeling that the Baron must be tipsy, or else giving no thought to the sort of man, more scrupulous in reality than he supposed, to whom he was speaking. "Marry her? No fear! I'd promise, but once the little operation was performed, I'd ditch her that very evening."

M. de Charlus was in the habit, when a fiction was capable of causing him a momentary sensual pleasure, of giving it his support and then withdrawing it a few minutes later, when his pleasure was at an end. "Would you really do that?" he said to Morel with a laugh, squeezing him more tightly still.

"Wouldn't I half!" said Morel, seeing that he was not displeasing the Baron by continuing to expound to him what was indeed one of his desires.

"It's dangerous," said M. de Charlus.

"I should have my kit packed and ready, and buzz off without leaving an address."

"And what about me?" asked M. de Charlus.

"I should take you with me, of course," Morel made haste to add, never having thought of what would become of the Baron, who was the least of his worries. "I say, there's a kid I should love to try that game on, she's a little seamstress who keeps a shop in M. le Duc's house."

"Jupien's girl," the Baron exclaimed as the wine-waiter entered the room. "Oh! never," he added, whether because the presence of a third person had cooled him down, or because even in this sort of black mass in which he took pleasure in defiling the most sacred things, he could not bring himself to allow the mention of people to whom he was bound by ties of friendship. "Jupien is a good man, and the child is charming. It would be terrible to cause them distress."

Morel felt that he had gone too far and was silent, but his eyes continued to gaze into space at the girl for whose benefit he had once begged me to address him as "*cher maître*" and from whom he had ordered a waistcoat. An industrious worker, the child had not taken any holiday, but I learned afterwards that while the violinist was in the neighbourhood of Balbec she never ceased to think of his handsome face, ennobled by the fact that having seen Morel in my company she had taken him for a "gentleman."

"I never heard Chopin play," said the Baron, "and

yet I might have done so. I took lessons from Stamati, but
he forbade me to go and hear the Master of the Nocturnes at my aunt Chimay's."

"That was damned silly of him," exclaimed Morel.

"On the contrary," M. de Charlus retorted warmly,
in a shrill voice. "It was a proof of his intelligence. He
had realised that I was a 'natural' and that I would succumb to Chopin's influence. It's of no importance, since I
gave up music when I was quite young, and everything
else, for that matter. Besides, one can more or less imagine him," he added in a slow, nasal, drawling voice,
"there are still people who did hear him, who can give
you an idea. However, Chopin was only an excuse to
come back to the mediumistic aspect which you are ne-
glecting."

The reader will observe that, after an interpolation of
common parlance, M. de Charlus had suddenly become
once more as precious and haughty in his speech as he
normally was. The idea of Morel's "ditching" without
compunction a girl whom he had outraged had enabled
him to enjoy an abrupt and consummate pleasure. From
that moment his sensual appetites were satisfied for a time
and the sadist (a true medium, he) who had for a few moments taken the place of M. de Charlus had fled, handing
over to the real M. de Charlus, full of artistic refinement,
sensibility and kindness. "You were playing the other day
the piano transcription of the Fifteenth Quartet, which in
itself is absurd because nothing could be less pianistic. It
is meant for people whose ears are offended by the over-
taut strings of the glorious Deaf One. Whereas it is precisely that almost sour mysticism that is divine. In any
case you played it very badly and altered all the *tempi*.

You ought to play it as though you were composing it:
the young Morel, afflicted with a momentary deafness and
with a non-existent genius, stands motionless for an instant; then, seized by the divine frenzy, he plays, he com-
poses the opening bars; after which, exhausted by this
trance-like effort, he collapses, letting his pretty forelock
drop to please Mme Verdurin, and, moreover, giving
himself time to restore the prodigious quantity of grey
matter which he has drawn upon for the Pythian objecti-
vation; then, having regained his strength, seized by a
fresh and overmastering inspiration, he flings himself
upon the sublime, imperishable phrase which the virtuoso
of Berlin" (we suppose M. de Charlus to have meant
Mendelssohn) "was to imitate unceasingly. It is in this,
the only truly dynamic and transcendent fashion, that I
shall make you play in Paris."

When M. de Charlus gave him advice of this sort,
Morel was far more alarmed than when he saw the head
waiter remove his spurned roses and "cup," for he wondered anxiously what effect it would create at his classes.
But he was unable to dwell upon these reflexions, for
M. de Charlus said to him imperiously: "Ask the head
waiter if he has a Bon Chrétien."

"A good Christian, I don't understand."

"Can't you see we've reached the dessert. It's a pear.
You may be sure Mme de Cambremer has them in her
garden, for the Comtesse d'Escarbagnas, whose double
she is, had them. M. Thibaudier sends them to her and
she says: 'Here is a Bon Chrétien which is worth tasting.'"

"No, I didn't know."

"I can see that you know nothing. If you have never
even read Molière . . . Oh, well, since you are no more

capable of ordering food than of anything else, just ask for a pear which happens to be grown in this neighbourhood, the Louise-Bonne d'Avranches."

"The what?"

"Wait a minute, since you're so stupid, I shall ask him myself for others, which I prefer. Waiter, have you any Doyenné des Comices? Charlie, you must read the exquisite passage written about that pear by the Duchesse Emilie de Clermont-Tonnerre."

"No, sir, I haven't."

"Have you any Triomphe de Jodoigne?"

"No, sir."

"Any Virginie-Baltet? Or Passe-Colmar? No? Very well, since you've nothing, we may as well go. The Duchesse d'Angoulême is not in season yet. Come along, Charlie."

Unfortunately for M. de Charlus, his lack of common sense, and perhaps, too, the probable chastity of his relations with Morel, made him go out of his way at this period to shower upon the violinist strange bounties which the other was incapable of understanding, and to which his nature, impulsive in its own way, but mean and ungrateful, could respond only by an ever-increasing coldness or violence which plunged M. de Charlus—formerly so proud, now quite timid—into fits of genuine despair. We shall see how, in the smallest matters, Morel, who now fancied himself an infinitely more important M. de Charlus, completely misunderstood, by taking them literally, the Baron's arrogant teachings with regard to the aristocracy. Let us for the moment simply say, while Albertine waits for me at Saint-Jean-de-la-Haise, that if there was one thing which Morel set above the nobility (and this was in itself fairly noble, especially in a person whose pleasure was to pursue little girls—on the sly—with the chauffeur), it was his artistic reputation and what the others might think of him in the violin class. No doubt it was an ugly trait in his character that, because he felt M. de Charlus to be entirely devoted to him, he appeared to disown him, to make fun of him, in the same way as, once I had promised not to reveal the secret of his father's position with my great-uncle, he treated me with contempt. But on the other hand his name as that of a qualified artist, Morel, appeared to him superior to a "name." And when M. de Charlus, in his dreams of platonic affection, wanted to make him adopt one of his family titles, Morel stoutly refused.

When Albertine thought it more sensible to remain at Saint-Jean-de-la-Haise and paint, I would take the car, and it was not merely to Gourville and Féterne, but to Saint-Mars-le-Vieux and as far as Criquetot that I was able to penetrate before returning to fetch her. While pretending to be occupied with something else besides her, and to be obliged to forsake her for other pleasures, I thought only of her. As often as not I went no further than the great plain which overlooks Gourville, and as it resembles slightly the plain that begins above Combray, in the direction of Méséglise, even at a considerable distance from Albertine I had the joy of thinking that, even if my eyes could not reach her, the powerful, soft sea breeze that was flowing past me, carrying further than they, must sweep down, with nothing to arrest it, as far as Quetteholme, until it stirred the branches of the trees that bury Saint-Jean-de-la-Haise in their foliage, caressing my beloved's face, and thus create a double link between us in this retreat indefinitely enlarged but free of dangers, as in those games in which two children find themselves momentarily out of sight and earshot of one another, and yet while far apart remain together. I returned by those roads from which there is a view of the sea, and where in the past, before it appeared among the branches, I used to shut my eyes to reflect that what I was about to see was indeed the plaintive ancestress of the earth, pursuing, as in the days when no living creature yet existed, her insane and immemorial agitation. Now, these roads were simply the means of rejoining Albertine; when I recognised them, completely unchanged, knowing how far they would run in a straight line, where they would turn, I remembered that I had followed them while thinking of Mlle de Stermaria, and also that this impatience to be back with Albertine was the same feeling as I had had when I walked the streets along which Mme de Guermantes might pass; they assumed for me the profound monotony, the moral significance of a sort of ruled line that my character must follow. It was natural, and yet it was not without importance; they reminded me that it was my fate to pursue only phantoms, creatures whose reality existed to a great extent in my imagination; for there are people—and this had been my case since youth—for whom all the things that have a fixed value, assessable by others, fortune, success, high positions, do not count; what they must have is phantoms. They sacrifice all the rest, devote all their efforts, make everything else subservient to the pursuit of some phantom. But this soon fades away; then they run after another only to return later on to the first. It was not the first time that I had gone in quest of Albertine, the girl I had seen that first year silhouetted against the sea.

Other women, it is true, had been interposed between the Albertine whom I had first loved and the one whom I rarely left now; other women, notably the Duchesse de Guermantes. But, the reader will say, why torment yourself so much with regard to Gilberte, why take such trouble over Mme de Guermantes, if, having become the friend of the latter, it is with the sole result of thinking no more of her, but only of Albertine? Swann, before his death, might have answered the question, he who had been a connoisseur of phantoms. Of phantoms pursued, forgotten, sought anew, sometimes for a single meeting, in order to establish contact with an unreal life which at once faded away, these Balbec roads were full. When I reflected that their trees—pear-trees, apple-trees, tamarisks—would outlive me, I seemed to be receiving from them a silent counsel to set myself to work at last, before the hour of eternal rest had yet struck.

I got out of the car at Quetteholme, ran down the sunken lane, crossed the brook by a plank and found Albertine painting in front of the church, all pinnacles, thorny and red, blossoming like a rose bush. The tympanum alone was smooth; and the smiling surface of the stone was abloom with angels who continued, before the twentieth-century couple that we were, to celebrate, taper in hand, the ceremonies of the thirteenth. It was they that Albertine was endeavouring to portray on her prepared canvas, and, imitating Elstir, she painted in sweeping brush-strokes, trying to obey the noble rhythm which, the master had told her, made those angels so different from all others that he knew. Then she collected her things. Leaning upon one another we walked back up the sunken path, leaving the little church, as quiet as though it had never seen us, to listen to the perpetual murmur of the brook. Presently the car set off, taking us home by a different way. We passed Marcouville-l'Orgueilleuse. Over its church, half new, half restored, the setting sun spread its patina, as fine as that of the centuries. Through it the great bas-reliefs seemed to be visible only beneath a fluid layer, half liquid, half luminous; the Blessed Virgin, St Elizabeth, St Joachim still swam in the impalpable tide, almost detached, at the surface of the water or the sunlight. Rising up in a warm haze, the innumerable modern statues towered on their pillars half-way up the golden webs of sunset. In front of the church a tall cypress seemed to be standing in a sort of consecrated enclosure. We got out of the car to look, and strolled around for a while. No less than of her limbs, Albertine was directly conscious of her toque of leghorn straw and of the silken veil (which were for her no less a source of sensations of well-being), and derived from them, as we walked round the church, a different sort of impetus, expressed by a lethargic contentment in which I found a certain charm. This veil and toque were but a recent, adventitious part of her, but a part that was already dear to me, as I followed its trail with my eyes, past the cypress, in the evening air. She herself could not see it, but guessed that the effect was pleasing, for she smiled at me, harmonising the poise of her head with the headgear that rounded it off. "I don't like it, it's restored," she said to me, pointing to the church and remembering what Elstir had said to her about the priceless, inimitable beauty of old stone. Albertine could tell a restoration at a glance. One could not help but marvel at the sureness of the taste she had already acquired in architecture, as contrasted with the deplorable taste she still retained in music. I cared no more than Elstir for this church; it was with no pleasure to myself that its sunlit front had come and posed before my eyes, and I had got out of the car to examine it only to oblige Albertine. And yet I felt that the great impressionist had contradicted himself; why exalt this fetish of objective architectural value, and not take into account the transfiguration of the church by the sunset? "No, definitely not," said Albertine, "I don't like it. But I like its name *orgueilleuse*. But what I must remember to ask Brichot is why Saint-Mars is called *le Vêtu*. We shall be going there the next time, shan't we?" she said, gazing at me out of her black eyes over which her toque was pulled down like the little "polo" of old. Her veil floated behind her. I got back into the car with her, happy in the thought that we should be going next day to Saint-Mars, where, in this blazing weather when one could think only of the delights of bathing, the two ancient steeples, salmon-pink, with their diamond-shaped tiles, slightly inflected and as it were palpitating, looked like a pair of old, sharp-snouted fish, moss-grown and coated with scales, which without seeming to move were rising in a blue, transparent water. On leaving Marcouville, we took a short cut by turning off at a crossroads where there was a farm. Sometimes Albertine made the car stop there and asked me to go alone and get some Calvados or cider for her to drink in the car. Although I was assured that it was not effervescent it proceeded to drench us from head to foot. We sat pressed close together. The people of the farm could scarcely see Albertine in the closed car as I handed them back their bottles; and we would drive off again as though to continue that lovers' existence which they might sup-

pose us to lead, and in which this halt for refreshment
had been only an insignificant moment—a supposition
that would have appeared only too plausible if they had
seen us after Albertine had drunk her bottle of cider; for
she seemed then positively unable to endure the existence
of a gap between herself and me which as a rule did not
trouble her; beneath her linen skirt her legs were pressed
against mine, and she brought her face closer too, the
cheeks pallid now and warm, with a touch of red on the
cheekbones, and something ardent and faded about them
such as one sees in girls from the working-class suburbs.
At such moments, her voice changed almost as quickly as
her personality; she forsook her own to adopt another that
was hoarse, brazen, almost dissolute. Night began to fall.
What a delight to feel her leaning against me, with her
toque and her veil, reminding me that it is always thus,
seated side by side, that we find couples who are in love!
I was perhaps in love with Albertine, but I did not dare
to let her see my love, so that, if it existed in me, it could
only be like an abstract truth, of no value until it had
been tested by experience; as it was, it seemed to me unrealisable and outside the plane of life. As for my jealousy, it urged me to leave Albertine as little as possible,
although I knew that it would not be completely cured
until I had parted from her for ever. I could even feel it
in her presence, but would then take care that the circumstances which had aroused it should not be repeated.
Once, for example, on a fine morning, we went to lunch
at Rivebelle. The great glazed doors of the dining-room
and of the hall shaped like a corridor in which tea was
served stood open on the same level as the sun-gilt lawns
of which the vast restaurant seemed to form a part. The

waiter with the pink face and black hair that writhed like
flames was flying from end to end of that vast expanse
less swiftly than in the past, for he was no longer an assistant but was now in charge of a row of tables; nevertheless, because of his natural briskness, he was to be
glimpsed, now here now there—sometimes at a distance,
in the dining-room, sometimes nearby, but out of doors
serving customers who preferred to eat in the garden—
like successive statues of a young god running, some in
the interior, incidentally well-lighted, of a dwelling that
extended on to green lawns, others beneath the trees, in
the bright radiance of open-air life. For a moment he was
close by us. Albertine replied absent-mindedly to what I
had just said to her. She was gazing at him with rounded
eyes. For a minute or two I felt that one may be close to
the person one loves and yet not have her with one. They
had the appearance of being engaged in a mysterious private conversation, rendered mute by my presence, which
might have been the sequel to meetings in the past of
which I knew nothing, or merely to a glance that he had
given her—at which I was the *terzo incomodo* from whom
their secret must be kept. Even when, peremptorily called
away by his boss, he had finally left us, Albertine while
continuing her meal seemed to be regarding the restaurant
and its gardens merely as a lighted running-track, on
which the swift-foot god with the black hair appeared
here and there amid the varied scenery. For a moment I
wondered whether she was not about to rise up and follow
him, leaving me alone at my table. But in the days that
followed I began to forget for ever this painful impression,
for I had decided never to return to Rivebelle, and had
extracted a promise from Albertine, who assured me that

she had never been there before, that she would never go there again. And I denied that the nimble-footed waiter had had eyes only for her, so that she should not believe that my company had deprived her of a pleasure. It did happen now and again that I would revisit Rivebelle, but alone, and there to drink too much, as I had done in the past. As I drained a final glass I gazed at a rosette painted on the white wall, and focused on it the pleasure that I felt. It alone in the world had any existence for me; I pursued it, touched it and lost it by turns with my wavering glance, and felt indifferent to the future, contenting myself with my rosette like a butterfly circling about another, stationary butterfly with which it is about to end its life in an act of supreme consummation.

It would perhaps have been a peculiarly opportune moment for giving up a woman whom no very recent or very keen suffering obliged me to ask for the balm against a malady which those who have caused it possess. I was calmed by these very outings, which, even if I considered them at the time merely as a foretaste of a morrow which itself, notwithstanding the longing with which it filled me, would not be different from today, had the charm of having been torn from the places which Albertine had frequented hitherto and where I had not been with her, at her aunt's or with her girlfriends—the charm not of a positive joy but simply of the assuagement of an anxiety, and yet extremely potent. For at an interval of a few days, when my thoughts turned to the farm outside which we had sat drinking cider, or simply to the stroll we had taken round Saint-Mars-le-Vêtu, remembering that Albertine had been walking by my side in her toque, the sense of her presence added of a sudden so strong a healing virtue to the indifferent image of the modern church that at the moment when the sunlit façade came thus of its own accord to pose before me in memory, it was like a great soothing compress laid upon my heart. I would drop Albertine at Parville, but only to join her again in the evening and lie stretched out by her side, in the darkness, upon the beach. True, I did not see her every day, yet I could say to myself: "If she were to give an account of how she spent her time, her life, it would still be me who played the largest part in it"; and we spent together long hours on end which brought into my days so sweet an intoxication that even when, at Parville, she jumped from the car which I was to send to fetch her an hour later, I felt no more alone in it than if before leaving me she had strewn it with flowers. I could have dispensed with seeing her every day; I was happy when I left her, and I knew that the calming effect of that happiness might last for several days. But at that moment I would hear Albertine as she left me say to her aunt or to a girlfriend: "Tomorrow at eight-thirty, then. We mustn't be late, the others will be ready at a quarter past." The conversation of a woman one loves is like the ground above a dangerous subterranean stretch of water; one senses constantly beneath the words the presence, the penetrating chill of an invisible pool; one perceives here and there its treacherous seepage, but the water itself remains hidden. The moment I heard these words of Albertine's my calm was destroyed. I wanted to ask her to let me see her the following morning, so as to prevent her from going to this mysterious rendezvous at half past eight which had been mentioned in my presence only in veiled terms. She would no doubt have begun by obeying me, while regretting that she had to give up her plans; in time she would have discovered my permanent need to upset them; I should have become the person from whom one hides things. And yet it is probable that these gatherings from which I was excluded amounted to very little, and that it was perhaps from the fear that I might find one or other of the participants vulgar or boring that I was not invited to them. Unfortunately this life so closely involved with Albertine's had an effect not only upon myself; to me it brought calm; to my mother it caused anxieties, her confession of which destroyed my calm. Once, as I entered the hotel happy in my own mind, resolved to terminate some day or other an existence the end of which I imagined to depend upon my own volition, my mother said to me, hearing me send a message to the chauffeur to go and fetch Albertine: "How you do spend money!" (Françoise in her simple and expressive language used to say with greater force: "That's the way the money goes.") "Try," Mamma went on, "not to become like Charles de Sévigné, of whom his mother said: 'His hand is a crucible in which gold melts.' Besides, I do really think you've gone about with Albertine quite enough. I assure you you're overdoing it, even to her it may seem ridiculous. I was delighted that you'd found some sort of distraction, and I'm not asking you never to see her again, but simply that it should be possible to meet one of you without the other."

My life with Albertine, a life devoid of keen pleasures—that is to say of keen pleasures that I could feel— that life which I intended to change at any moment, choosing a moment of calm, became suddenly necessary to me once more when, by these words of Mamma's, it seemed to be threatened. I told my mother that her words would delay for perhaps two months the decision for which they asked, which otherwise I would have reached before the end of that week. In order not to sadden me, Mamma laughed at this instantaneous effect of her advice, and promised not to raise the subject again so as not to prevent the rebirth of my good intention. But, since my grandmother's death, whenever Mamma gave way to mirth, the incipient laugh would be cut short and would end in an almost heartbroken expression of sorrow, whether from remorse at having been able for an instant to forget, or else from the recrudescence which this brief moment of forgetfulness had brought to her painful obsession. But to the thoughts aroused in her by the memory of my grandmother, a memory that was rooted in my mother's mind, I felt that on this occasion there were added others relating to myself, to what my mother dreaded as the sequel of my intimacy with Albertine; an intimacy which she dared not, however, hinder in view of what I had just told her. But she did not appear convinced that I was not mistaken. She remembered all the years in which my grandmother and she had refrained from speaking to me about my work and the need for a healthier way of life which, I used to say, the agitation into which their exhortations threw me alone prevented me from beginning, and which, notwithstanding their obedient silence, I had failed to pursue.

After dinner the car would bring Albertine back; there was still a glimmer of daylight; the air was less warm, but after a scorching day we both dreamed of delicious coolness; then to our fevered eyes the narrow slip of moon would appear at first (as on the evening when I had gone to the Princesse de Guermantes's and Albertine had telephoned me) like the delicate rind, then like the cool section of a fruit which an invisible knife was beginning to peel in the sky. Sometimes it was I who would go to fetch my beloved, a little later in that case; she would be waiting for me under the arcade of the market at Maineville. At first I could not make her out; I would begin to fear that she might not be coming, that she had misunderstood me. Then I would see her, in her white blouse with blue spots, spring into the car by my side with the light bound of a young animal rather than a girl. And it was like a dog too that she would begin to caress me interminably. When night had completely fallen and, as the manager of the hotel remarked to me, the sky was all "studied" with stars, if we did not go for a drive in the forest with a bottle of champagne, then, heedless of the late strollers on the faintly lighted esplanade, who in any case could not have seen anything a yard away on the dark sand, we would stretch out in the shelter of the dunes; that same body whose suppleness contained all the feminine, marine and sportive grace of the girls whom I had seen that first time against the horizon of the waves, I held pressed against my own, beneath the same rug, by the edge of the motionless sea divided by a tremulous path of light; and we listened to it with the same untiring pleasure, whether it held back its breath, suspended for so long that one thought the reflux would never come, or whether at last it gasped out at our feet the long-awaited murmur. Finally I would take Albertine back to Parville. When we reached her house, we were obliged to break off our kisses for fear that someone might see us; not wishing to go to bed, she would return with me to Balbec, from whence I would take her back for the last time to Parville;

the chauffeurs of those early days of the motor-car were
people who went to bed at all hours. And indeed I would
return to Balbec only with the first dews of morning,
alone this time, but still surrounded with the presence of
my beloved, gorged with an inexhaustible provision of
kisses. On my table I would find a telegram or a postcard.
Albertine again! She had written them at Quetteholme
when I had gone off by myself in the car, to tell me that
she was thinking of me. I would re-read them as I got
into bed. Then, above the curtains, I would glimpse the
bright streak of the daylight and would say to myself that
we must be in love with one another after all, since we
had spent the night in one another's arms. When, next
morning, I caught sight of Albertine on the front, I was
so afraid of her telling me that she was not free that day,
and could not accede to my request that we should go out
together, that I would delay it for as long as possible. I
would be all the more uneasy since she had a cold, preoccupied air; people were passing whom she knew; doubtless she had made plans for the afternoon from which I
was excluded. I would gaze at her, I would gaze at that
rosy face of Albertine's, tantalising me with the enigma of
her intentions, the unknown decision which was to create
the happiness or misery of my afternoon. It was a whole
state of soul, a whole future existence that had assumed
before my eyes the allegorical and fateful form of a girl.
And when at last I made up my mind, when, with the
most indifferent air that I could muster, I asked: "Are we
going out together now, and again this evening?" and she
replied: "With the greatest pleasure," then the sudden re-
placement, in the rosy face, of my long uneasiness by a
delicious sense of ease would make even more precious to

me those forms to which I was perpetually indebted for the sense of well-being and relief that we feel after a storm has broken. I repeated to myself: "How sweet she is, what an adorable creature!" in an excitement less fertile than that caused by intoxication, scarcely more profound than that of friendship, but far superior to that of social life. We would cancel our order for the car only on the days when there was a dinner-party at the Verdurins' and on those when, Albertine not being free to go out with me, I took the opportunity to inform anybody who wished to see me that I should be remaining at Balbec. I gave Saint-Loup permission to come on these days, but on these days only. For on one occasion when he had arrived unexpectedly, I had preferred to forgo the pleasure of seeing Albertine rather than run the risk of his meeting her, than endanger the state of happy calm in which I had dwelt for some time and see my jealousy revive. And my mind had not been set at rest until after Saint-Loup had gone. Therefore he made it a rule, regretfully but scrupulously observed, never to come to Balbec unless summoned there by me. In the past, when I thought with longing of the hours that Mme de Guermantes spent in his company, how I had valued the privilege of seeing him! People never cease to change place in relation to ourselves. In the imperceptible but eternal march of the world, we regard them as motionless, in a moment of vision too brief for us to perceive the motion that is sweeping them on. But we have only to select in our memory two pictures taken of them at different moments, close enough together however for them not to have altered in themselves—perceptibly, that is to say—and the difference between the two pictures is a measure of the dis-

placement that they have undergone in relation to us.
Robert alarmed me dreadfully by speaking to me of the
Verdurins, for I was afraid that he might ask me to take
him there, which would have been enough, because of the
jealousy I should constantly feel, to spoil all the pleasure
that I found in going there with Albertine. But fortunately
he assured me that, on the contrary, the one thing he desired above all others was not to know them. "No," he
said to me, "I find that sort of clerical atmosphere maddening." I did not at first understand the application of
the adjective "clerical" to the Verdurins, but the sequel to
his remark clarified his meaning, betraying his concessions
to those fashions in words which one is often astonished
to see adopted by intelligent men. "I mean the sort of circles," he said, "where people form a tribe, a religious order, a chapel. You aren't going to tell me that they're not
a little sect; they're all honey to the people who belong,
no words bad enough for those who don't. The question
is not, as for Hamlet, to be or not to be, but to belong or
not to belong. You belong, my uncle Charlus belongs. But
I can't help it, I've never gone in for that sort of thing, it
isn't my fault."

I need hardly say that the rule I had imposed upon
Saint-Loup, never to come and see me unless I had expressly invited him, I promulgated no less strictly in the
case of the various persons with whom I had gradually
made friends at La Raspelière, Féterne, Montsurvent, and
elsewhere; and when I saw from the hotel the smoke of
the three o'clock train which, in the anfractuosity of the
cliffs of Parville, left a stationary plume which long remained clinging to the flank of the green slopes, I had no
doubts as to the identity of the visitor who was coming to

tea with me and was still, like a classical deity, concealed
from me beneath that little cloud. I am obliged to confess
that this person whose visit I had authorised in advance
was hardly ever Saniette, and I have often reproached myself for this omission. But Saniette's own consciousness of
being a bore (even more so, naturally, when he came to
pay a call than when he told a story) had the effect that,
although he was more learned, more intelligent and better
than most people, it seemed impossible to feel in his company, not only any pleasure, but anything save an almost
intolerable irritation which spoiled one's whole afternoon.
Probably, if Saniette had frankly admitted this boredom
which he was afraid of causing, one would not have
dreaded his visits. Boredom is one of the least of the evils
that we have to endure, and his boringness existed perhaps only in the imagination of other people, or had been
inoculated into him by some process of suggestion which
had taken hold on his agreeable modesty. But he was so
anxious not to let it be seen that he was not sought after
that he dared not propose himself. Certainly he was right
not to behave like the people who are so glad to be able to
raise their hats in a public place that, not having seen you
for years and catching sight of you in a box at the theatre
with smart people whom they do not know, they give you
a furtive but resounding good-evening on the pretext of
the pleasure and delight they have felt on seeing you, on
realising that you are going about again, that you are
looking well, etc. But Saniette went to the other extreme.
He might, at Mme Verdurin's or in the little train, have
told me that he would have great pleasure in coming to
see me at Balbec were he not afraid of disturbing me.
Such a suggestion would not have alarmed me. On the

contrary, he offered nothing, but, with a tortured expression on his face and a stare as indestructible as a fired enamel, into the composition of which, however, there entered, together with a passionate desire to see one—unless he found someone else who was more entertaining—the determination not to let this desire be manifest, would say to me with a casual air: "You don't happen to know what you will be doing in the next few days, because I shall probably be somewhere in the neighbourhood of Balbec? Not that it makes the slightest difference, I just thought I'd ask." This casual air deceived nobody, and the reverse signs whereby we express our feelings by their opposites are so clearly legible that one asks oneself how there can still be people who say, for instance: "I have so many invitations that I don't know which way to turn" to conceal the fact that they have been invited nowhere. But what was more, this casual air, probably on account of the dubious elements that had gone to form it, gave you, what the fear of boredom or a frank admission of the desire to see you would never have done, the sort of discomfort, of repulsion, which in the category of relations of simple social courtesy is the equivalent of what, in amatory relations, is provoked by the lover's disguised offer, to a lady who does not return his love, to see her next day, while protesting that he does not greatly care—or not even that offer but an attitude of sham coldness. There emanated at once from Saniette's person an indefinable aura which made you answer him in the tenderest of tones: "No, unfortunately, this week, I must explain to you . . ." And I allowed to call upon me instead people who were a long way his inferiors but whose eyes were not filled with melancholy or their mouths twisted with bitter regret as his were at the thought of all the visits which he longed, while saying nothing about them, to pay to various people. Unfortunately, Saniette rarely failed to meet in the "crawler" the guest who was coming to see me, if indeed the latter had not said to me at the Verdurins': "Don't forget I'm coming to see you on Thursday," the very day on which I had just told Saniette that I should not be at home. So that he came in the end to imagine life as filled with entertainments arranged behind his back, if not actually at his expense. On the other hand, as none of us is ever all of a piece, this most discreet of men was morbidly tactless and indiscreet. On the one occasion on which he happened to come and see me uninvited, a letter, I forget from whom, had been left lying on my table. After the first few minutes, I saw that he was paying only the vaguest attention to what I was saying. The letter, of whose provenance he knew absolutely nothing, fascinated him and at any moment I expected his glittering eyeballs to detach themselves from their sockets and fly to the letter, insignificant in itself, which his curiosity had magnetised. He was like a bird irresistibly drawn towards a snake. Finally he could restrain himself no longer. He began by altering its position, as though he were tidying up my room; then, this not sufficing him, he picked it up, turned it over, turned it back again, as though mechanically. Another form of his tactlessness was that once he had fastened himself on to you he could not tear himself away. As I was feeling unwell that day, I asked him to go back by the next train, in half an hour's time. He did not doubt that I was feeling unwell, but replied: "I shall stay for an hour and a quarter, and then I shall go." Since then I have regretted that I did not tell him to come and see me whenever I was free. Who knows? Possibly I might have exorcised his ill fate, and other people would have invited him for whom he would immediately have deserted me, so that my invitations would have had the twofold advantage of restoring him to happiness and ridding me of his company.

On the days following those on which I had been "at home," I naturally did not expect any visitors and the motor-car would come again to fetch Albertine and me. And when we returned, Aimé, on the lowest step of the hotel, could not help looking, with passionate, curious, greedy eyes, to see what tip I was giving the chauffeur. However tightly I enclosed my coin or note in my clenched fist, Aimé's gaze tore my fingers apart. He would turn his head away a moment later, for he was discreet and well-mannered, and indeed was himself content with relatively modest remuneration. But the money that another person received aroused in him an irrepressible curiosity and made his mouth water. During these brief moments, he had the attentive, feverish air of a boy reading a Jules Verne novel, or of a diner seated at a neighbouring table in a restaurant who, seeing the waiter carving you a pheasant to which he himself either cannot or will not treat himself, abandons for an instant his serious thoughts to fasten upon the bird eyes lit with a smile of love and longing.

Thus, day after day, these excursions in the motor-car followed one another. But once, as I was going up to my room, the lift-boy said to me: "That gentleman has been, he gave me a message for you." The lift-boy uttered these words in a hoarse croak, coughing and expectorating in my face. "I haven't half got a cold!" he went on, as though I were incapable of perceiving this for myself. "The doctor says it's whooping-cough," and he began once more to cough and expectorate over me. "Don't tire yourself trying to talk," I said to him with an air of kindly concern, which was feigned. I was afraid of catching the whooping-cough which, with my tendency to choking spasms, would have been a serious matter for me. But he made it a point of honour, like a virtuoso who refuses to go sick, to go on talking and spitting all the time. "No, it doesn't matter," he said ("Perhaps not to you," I thought, "but to me it does"). "Besides, I shall be returning to Paris soon" ("So much the better, provided he doesn't give it to me first"). "They say Paris is very superb," he went on. "It must be even more superb than here or Monte-Carlo, although some of the pages and some of the guests, in fact even head waiters who've been to Monte-Carlo for the season have often told me that Paris was not so superb as Monte-Carlo. Perhaps they were being stupid, you've got to have your wits about you to be a head waiter—taking all the orders, reserving tables, you need quite a brain. I've heard it said that it's even tougher than writing plays and books."

We had almost reached my landing when the lift-boy carried me down again to the ground floor because he found that the button was not working properly, and in a moment he had put it right. I told him that I would prefer to walk upstairs, by which I meant, without putting it in so many words, that I preferred not to catch whooping-cough. But with a cordial and contagious burst of coughing the boy thrust me back into the lift. "There's no danger now, I've fixed the button." Seeing that he was still talking incessantly, and preferring to learn the name of my visitor and the message that he had left rather than the comparative beauties of Balbec, Paris, and Monte-Carlo, I said to him (as one might say to a tenor who is wearying one with Benjamin Godard, "Won't you sing me some Debussy?") "But who is the person who called to see me?" "It's the gentleman you went out with yesterday. I'll go and fetch his card, it's with my porter." As, the day before, I had dropped Robert de Saint-Loup at Doncières station before going to meet Albertine, I supposed that the lift-boy was referring to him, but it was the chauffeur. And by describing him in the words: "The gentleman you went out with," he taught me at the same time that a working man is just as much a gentleman as a man about town. A lesson in the use of words only. For in point of fact I had never made any distinction between the classes. And if, on hearing a chauffeur called a gentleman, I had felt the same astonishment as Count X who had only held that rank for a week and who, when I said "the Countess looks tired," turned his head round to see who I was talking about, it was simply because I was unaccustomed to that particular usage; I had never made any distinction between working people, the middle classes and the nobility, and I should have been equally ready to make any of them my friends. With a certain preference for working people, and after them for the nobility, not because I liked them better but because I knew that one could expect greater courtesy from them towards working people than one finds among the middle classes, either because the nobility are less disdainful or else because they are naturally polite to anybody, as beautiful women are glad to bestow a smile which they know will be joyfully welcomed. I cannot however pretend that this habit that I had of putting people of humble station on a level with people in society, even if it was quite understood by the latter, was always entirely pleasing to my mother. Not that, humanly speaking, she made the slightest distinction between one person and another, and if Françoise was ever in sorrow or in pain she was comforted and tended by Mamma with the same devotion as her best friend. But my mother was too much my grandfather's daughter not to accept, in social matters, the rule of caste. People at Combray might have kind hearts and sensitive natures, might have adopted the noblest theories of human equality, yet my mother, when a footman showed signs of forgetting his place, began to say "you" and gradually slipped out of the habit of addressing me in the third person, was moved by these presumptions to the same wrath that breaks out in Saint-Simon's *Memoirs* whenever a nobleman who is not entitled to it seizes a pretext for assuming officially the style of "Highness," or for not paying dukes the deference he owes to them and is gradually beginning to lay aside. There was a "Combray spirit" so deep-rooted that it would take centuries of natural kindness (my mother's was boundless) and egalitarian conviction to succeed in dissolving it. I cannot swear that in my mother certain particles of this spirit had not remained insoluble. She would have been as reluctant to shake hands with a footman as she was ready to give him ten francs (which for that matter gave him far more pleasure). To her, whether she admitted it or not, masters were masters and servants were the people who fed in the kitchen. When she saw the driver of a motor-car dining with me in the restaurant, she was not altogether pleased, and said to me: "It seems to me you might have a more suitable friend than a mechanic," as she might have said, had it been a question of my marriage: "You might have found somebody better than that." This particular chauffeur (fortunately I never dreamed of inviting him to dinner) had come to tell me that the motor-car company which had sent him to Balbec for the season had ordered him to return to Paris on the following day. This excuse, especially as the chauffeur was charming and expressed himself so simply that one would always have taken anything he said for gospel, seemed to us to be most probably true. It was only half so. There was as a matter of fact no more work for him at Balbec. And in any case the company, being only half convinced of the veracity of the young evangelist, bowed over his wheel of consecration, was anxious that he should return to Paris as soon as possible. And indeed if the young apostle wrought a miracle in multiplying his mileage when he was calculating it for M. de Charlus, when, on the other hand, it was a matter of rendering his account to the company, he divided what he had earned by six. In consequence of which the company, coming to the conclusion either that nobody wanted a car now at Balbec, which, so late in the season, was not improbable, or that it was being robbed, decided that, upon either hypothesis, the best thing was to recall him to Paris, not that there was very much work for him there. What the chauffeur wished was to avoid, if possible, the dead season. I have said—though I was unaware of this at the time, and the knowledge of it would have saved me much unhappiness—that he was on very friendly terms with Morel, although they showed no sign even of knowing each other in front of other people. From the day on which he was recalled, without knowing as yet that he had a means of avoiding departure, we were obliged to content ourselves for our excursions with hiring a carriage, or sometimes, as an amusement for Albertine and because she was fond of riding, a pair of saddle-horses. The carriages were unsatisfactory. "What a rattle-trap," Albertine would say. I would, in any case, often have preferred to be alone in it. Without being ready to fix a date, I longed to put an end to this existence which I blamed for making me renounce not so much work as pleasure. It sometimes happened too, however, that the habits which bound me were suddenly abolished, generally when some former self, full of the desire to live an exhilarating life, momentarily took the place of my present self. I felt this longing to escape especially strongly one day when, having left Albertine at her aunt's, I had gone on horseback to call on the Verdurins and had taken an unfrequented path through the woods the beauty of which they had extolled to me. Hugging the contours of the cliff, it alternately climbed and then, hemmed in by dense woods on either side, dived into wild gorges. For a moment the barren rocks by which I was surrounded, and the sea that was visible through their jagged gaps, swam before my eyes like fragments of another universe: I had recognised the mountainous and marine landscape which Elstir had made the scene of those two admirable water-colours, "Poet meeting a Muse" and "Young Man meeting a Centaur," which I had seen at the Duchesse de Guermantes's. The memory of them transported the place in which I now found myself so far outside the world of today that I should not have been surprised if, like the young man of the prehistoric age that Elstir had painted, I had come upon a mythological personage in the course of my ride.

Suddenly, my horse reared; he had heard a strange sound; it was all I could do to hold him and remain in the saddle; then I raised my tear-filled eyes in the direction from which the sound seemed to come and saw, not two hundred feet above my head, against the sun, between two great wings of flashing metal which were bearing him aloft, a creature whose indistinct face appeared to me to resemble that of a man. I was as deeply moved as an ancient Greek on seeing for the first time a demi-god. I wept—for I had been ready to weep the moment I realised that the sound came from above my head (aeroplanes were still rare in those days), at the thought that what I was going to see for the first time was an aeroplane. Then, just as when in a newspaper one senses that one is coming to a moving passage, the mere sight of the machine was enough to make me burst into tears. Meanwhile the airman seemed to be uncertain of his course; I felt that there lay open before him—before me, had not habit made me a prisoner—all the routes in space, in life itself; he flew on, let himself glide for a few moments over the sea, then quickly making up his mind, seeming to yield to some attraction that was the reverse of gravity, as though returning to his native element, with a slight adjustment of his golden wings he headed straight up into the sky.

To return to the subject of the chauffeur, he demanded of Morel that the Verdurins should not merely replace their break by a motor-car (which, given their generosity towards the faithful, was comparatively easy), but, what was more difficult, replace their head coachman, the sensitive young man with the tendency to black thoughts, by himself, the chauffeur. This change was carried out in a few days by the following device. Morel had begun by seeing that the coachman was robbed of everything that he needed for harnessing up. One day it was the bit that was missing, another day the curb. At other times it was the cushion of his box-seat that had vanished, or his whip, his rug, the martingale, the sponge, the chamois-leather. He always managed to borrow what he required from a neighbour, but he was late in bringing round the carriage, which put him in M. Verdurin's bad books and plunged him into a state of melancholy and gloom. The chauffeur, who was in a hurry to take his place, told Morel that he would have to return to Paris. It was time to do something drastic. Morel persuaded M. Verdurin's servants that the young coachman had declared that he would lay an ambush for the lot of them, boasting that he could take on all six of them at once, and told them that they could not let this pass. He himself did not want to get involved, but he was warning them so that they might forestall the coachman. It was agreed that while M. and Mme Verdurin and their guests were out walking the servants should set about the young man in the stables. Although it merely provided the opportunity for what was to happen, I may mention the fact—because the people concerned interested me later on—that the Verdurins had a friend staying with them that day whom they had promised to take for a walk before his departure, which was fixed for that same evening.

What surprised me greatly when we started off for our walk was that Morel, who was coming with us and was to play his violin under the trees, said to me: "Listen, I have a sore arm, and I don't want to say anything about it to Mme Verdurin, but you might ask her to send for one of her footmen, Howsler for instance, to carry my things."

"I think someone else would be more suitable," I replied. "He will be wanted here for dinner."

A look of anger flitted across Morel's face. "No, I'm not going to entrust my violin to any Tom, Dick or Harry."

I realised later on his reason for this choice. Howsler was the beloved brother of the young coachman, and, if he had been left at home, might have gone to his rescue. During our walk, dropping his voice so that the elder Howsler should not overhear: "What a good fellow he is," said Morel. "So is his brother, for that matter. If he hadn't that fatal habit of drinking . . ."

"Did you say drinking?" said Mme Verdurin, turning pale at the idea of having a coachman who drank.

"You've never noticed it? I always say to myself it's a miracle that he's never had an accident while he's been driving you."

"Does he drive anyone else, then?"

"You can easily see how many spills he's had, his face today is a mass of bruises. I don't know how he's escaped being killed, he's broken his shafts."

"I haven't seen him today," said Mme Verdurin, trembling at the thought of what might have happened to her, "you appal me."

She tried to cut short the walk so as to return at once, but Morel chose an air by Bach with endless variations to keep her away from the house. As soon as we got back she went to the stable, saw the new shafts and Howsler streaming with blood. She was on the point of telling him without more ado that she did not require a coachman any longer, and of paying him his wages, but of his own accord, not wishing to accuse his fellow-servants, to whose animosity he attributed retrospectively the theft of all his saddlery, and seeing that further patience would only end in his being left for dead on the ground, he asked leave to go at once, which settled matters. The chauffeur began his duties next day and, later on, Mme Verdurin (who had been obliged to engage another) was so well satisfied with him that she recommended him to me warmly as a man of the utmost reliability. I, knowing nothing of all this, engaged him by the day in Paris. But I am anticipating events; I shall come to all this when I reach the story of Albertine. At the present moment we are at La Raspelière, where I have just come to dine for the first time with my beloved, and M. de Charlus with Morel, the alleged son of a "steward" who drew a fixed salary of thirty thousand francs annually, kept his own carriage, and had any number of subordinate officials, gardeners, bailiffs and farmers at his beck and call. But, since I have so far anticipated, I do not wish to leave the reader under the impression that Morel was entirely wicked. He was, rather, a mass of contradictions, capable on certain days of genuine kindness.

I was naturally greatly surprised to hear that the coachman had been dismissed, and even more surprised when I recognised his successor as the chauffeur who had been driving Albertine and myself in his car. But he poured out to me a complicated story, according to which he was supposed to have been summoned back to Paris, whence an order had come for him to go to the Verdurins, and I did not doubt his word for an instant. The coachman's dismissal was the cause of Morel's talking to

me for a few minutes, to express his regret at the departure of that worthy fellow. In fact, even apart from the
moments when I was alone and he literally bounded towards me beaming with joy, Morel, seeing that everybody
made much of me at La Raspelière and feeling that he
was deliberately cutting himself off from the society of a
person who was no danger to him, since he had made me
burn my boats and had removed all possibility of my
treating him patronisingly (something which in any case I
had never dreamed of doing), ceased to hold aloof from
me. I attributed his change of attitude to the influence of
M. de Charlus, which as a matter of fact did make him in
certain respects less blinkered, more artistic, but in others,
when he applied literally the grandiloquent, insincere, and
moreover transient formulas of his master, made him
stupider than ever. That M. de Charlus might have said
something to him was as a matter of fact the only thing
that occurred to me. How could I have guessed then what
I was told afterwards (and was never certain of its truth,
Andrée's assertions about anything that concerned Albertine, especially later on, having always seemed to me to be
highly dubious, for, as we have already seen, she did not
genuinely like her and was jealous of her), something
which in any event, even if it was true, was remarkably
well concealed from me by both of them: that Albertine
was on the best of terms with Morel? The new attitude
which, about the time of the coachman's dismissal, Morel
adopted with regard to myself, enabled me to revise my
opinion of him. I retained the ugly impression of his character which had been suggested by the servility which this
young man had shown me when he needed me, followed,
as soon as the favour had been done, by a scornful aloof-

ness which he took to the point of seeming not to notice me. To this one had to add the evidence of his venal relations with M. de Charlus, and also of his gratuitously brutish impulses, the non-gratification of which (when it occurred) or the complications that they involved, were the cause of his sorrows; but his character was not so uniformly vile and was full of contradictions. He resembled an old book of the Middle Ages, full of mistakes, of absurd traditions, of obscenities; he was extraordinarily composite. I had supposed at first that his art, in which he was really a past master, had endowed him with qualities that went beyond the virtuosity of the mere performer. Once, when I spoke of my wish to start work, "Work, and you will achieve fame," he said to me. "Who said that?" I inquired. "Fontanes, to Chateaubriand." He also knew certain love letters of Napoleon. Good, I thought to myself, he's well-read. But this remark, which he had read God knows where, was evidently the only one that he knew in the whole of ancient or modern literature, for he repeated it to me every evening. Another, which he quoted even more frequently to prevent me from breathing a word about him to anybody, was the following, which he considered equally literary, whereas it is more or less meaningless, or at any rate makes no kind of sense except perhaps to a mystery-loving servant: "Beware of the wary." In fact, if one went from this stupid maxim to Fontanes's remark to Chateaubriand, one would have covered a whole stretch, varied but less contradictory than it might seem, of Morel's character. This youth who, provided there was money to be made by it, would have done anything in the world, and without remorse—perhaps not without an odd sort of vexation, amounting to nervous agitation, to which however the name remorse could not for a moment be applied—who would, had it been to his advantage, have plunged whole families into misery or even into mourning, this youth who put money above everything else, not merely above kindness, but above the most natural feelings of common humanity, this same youth nevertheless put above money his diploma as first-prize winner at the Conservatoire and the risk of anything being said to his discredit in the flute or counterpoint class. Hence his most violent rages, his most sombre and unjustifiable fits of ill-temper arose from what he himself (generalising doubtless from certain particular cases in which he had met with malevolent people) called universal treachery. He flattered himself on eluding it by never speaking about anyone, by keeping his cards close to his chest, by distrusting everybody. (Alas for me, in view of what was to happen after my return to Paris, his distrust had not "held" in the case of the Balbec chauffeur, in whom he had doubtless recognised a peer, that is to say, contrary to his maxim, a wary person in the proper sense of the word, a wary person who remains obstinately silent in front of decent people and at once comes to an understanding with a blackguard.) It seemed to him—and he was not absolutely wrong—that his distrust would enable him always to save his bacon, to come through the most dangerous adventures unscathed, without anyone at the Conservatoire being able to suggest anything against him, let alone to prove it. He would work, become famous, would perhaps one day, with his respectability still intact, be examiner in the violin on the board of that great and glorious Conservatoire.

But it is perhaps crediting Morel's brain with too

much logic to attempt to disentangle all these contradictions. His nature was really like a sheet of paper that has been folded so often in every direction that it is impossible to straighten it out. He seemed to have quite lofty principles, and in a magnificent hand, marred by the most elementary mistakes in spelling, spent hours writing to his brother to point out that he had behaved badly to his sisters, that he was their elder, their natural support, and to his sisters that they had shown a want of respect for himself.

Presently, as summer came to an end, when one got out of the train at Douville, the sun, blurred by the prevailing mist, had ceased to be more than a red blotch in a sky that was uniformly mauve. To the great peace which descends at dusk over these lush, saline meadows, and which had tempted a large number of Parisians, painters mostly, to spend their holidays at Douville, was added a humidity which made them seek shelter early in their little bungalows. In several of these the lamp was already lit. Only a few cows remained out of doors gazing at the sea and lowing, while others, more interested in humanity, turned their attention towards our carriages. A single painter who had set up his easel on a slight eminence was striving to render that great calm, that hushed luminosity. Perhaps the cattle would serve him unconsciously and benevolently as models, for their contemplative air and their solitary presence, when the human beings had withdrawn, contributed in their own way to the powerful impression of repose that evening diffuses. And, a few weeks later, the transposition was no less agreeable when, as autumn advanced, the days became really short, and we were obliged to make our journey in the dark. If I had been out in the afternoon, I had to go back to change at the latest by five o'clock, when at this season the round, red sun had already sunk half-way down the slanting mirror which formerly I had detested, and, like Greek fire, was setting the sea alight in the glass fronts of all my book-cases. Some incantatory gesture having resuscitated, as I put on my dinner-jacket, the alert and frivolous self that was mine when I used to go with Saint-Loup to dine at Rivebelle and on the evening when I had thought to take Mlle de Stermaria to dine on the island in the Bois, I began unconsciously to hum the same tune as I had hummed then; and it was only when I realised this that by the song I recognised the sporadic singer, who indeed knew no other tune. The first time I had sung it, I was beginning to fall in love with Albertine, but I imagined that I would never get to know her. Later, in Paris, it was when I had ceased to love her and some days after I had enjoyed her for the first time. Now it was when I loved her again and was on the point of going out to dinner with her, to the great regret of the manager who believed that I would end up living at La Raspelière altogether and deserting his hotel, and assured me that he had heard that fever was prevalent in that neighbourhood, due to the marshes of the Bec and their "stagnered" water. I was delighted by the multiplicity in which I saw my life thus spread over three planes; and besides, when one becomes for an instant one's former self, that is to say different from what one has been for some time past, one's sensibility, being no longer dulled by habit, receives from the slightest stimulus vivid impressions which make everything that has preceded them fade into insignificance, impressions to which, because of their intensity, we attach ourselves with the momentary enthusiasm of a drunkard. It was already dark when we got into the omnibus or carriage which was to take us to the station to catch the little train. And in the hall the judge would say to us: "Ah! so you're off to La Raspelière! Good God, she has a nerve, your Mme Verdurin, making you travel an hour by train in the dark, simply to dine with her. And then having to set out again at ten o'clock at night with a wind blowing like the very devil. It's easy to see that you have nothing better to do," he added, rubbing his hands together. No doubt he spoke thus from annoyance at not having been invited, and also from the self-satisfaction felt by "busy" men—however idiotic their business—at "not having time" to do what you are doing.

It is of course justifiable for the man who draws up reports, adds up figures, answers business letters, follows the movements of the stock exchange, to feel an agreeable sense of superiority when he says to you with a sneer: "It's all very well for you; you having nothing better to do." But he would be no less contemptuous, would be even more so (for dining out is a thing that the busy man does also), were your recreation writing *Hamlet* or merely reading it. Wherein busy men show a lack of forethought. For the disinterested culture which seems to them a comic pastime of idle people when they find them engaged in it is, they ought to reflect, the same as that which, in their own profession, brings to the fore men who may not be better judges or administrators than themselves but before whose rapid advancement they bow their heads, saying: "It appears he's extremely well-read, a most distinguished individual." But above all the judge was oblivious of the

fact that what pleased me about these dinners at La
Raspelière was that, as he himself said quite rightly,
though as a criticism, they "represented a real journey," a
journey whose charm appeared to me all the more intense
in that it was not an end in itself and one did not look to
find pleasure in it—this being reserved for the gathering
for which we were bound and which could not fail to be
greatly modified by all the atmosphere that surrounded it.
Night would already have fallen now when I exchanged
the warmth of the hotel—the hotel that had become my
home—for the railway carriage into which I climbed with
Albertine, in which a glimmer of lamplight on the window showed, at certain halts of the wheezy little train,
that we had arrived at a station. So that there should be
no risk of Cottard's missing us, and not having heard the
name of the station being called, I would open the door,
but what burst into the carriage was not any of the faithful, but the wind, the rain and the cold. In the darkness I
could make out fields and hear the sea; we were in the
open country. Before we joined the little nucleus, Albertine would examine herself in a little mirror, extracted
from a gold vanity case which she carried about with her.
The fact was that on our first visit, Mme Verdurin having
taken her upstairs to her dressing-room so that she might
tidy up before dinner, I had felt, amid the profound calm
in which I had been living for some time, a slight stir of
uneasiness and jealousy at being obliged to part from Albertine at the foot of the stairs, and had become so anxious while I was alone in the drawing-room among the
little clan, wondering what she could be doing, that I had
telegraphed the next day, after finding out from M. de
Charlus what the correct thing was at the moment, to or-

der from Cartier's a vanity case which was the joy of Albertine's life and also of mine. It was for me a guarantee of peace of mind, and also of my mistress's solicitude. For she had evidently seen that I did not like her to be parted from me at Mme Verdurin's and arranged to do all the titivation necessary before dinner in the train.

Among Mme Verdurin's regular guests, and reckoned the most faithful of them all, M. de Charlus had now figured for some months. Regularly, thrice weekly, the passengers sitting in the waiting-rooms or standing on the platform at Doncières-Ouest used to see this stout gentleman go by, with his grey hair, his black moustaches, his lips reddened with a salve less noticeable at the end of the season than in summer when the daylight made it look more garish and the heat liquefied it. As he made his way towards the little train, he could not refrain (simply from force of habit, as a connoisseur, since he now had a sentiment which kept him chaste or at least, for most of the time, faithful) from casting a furtive glance, at once inquisitorial and timorous, at the labourers, the soldiers, the young men in tennis clothes, after which he immediately let his eyelids droop over his half-shut eyes with the unctuousness of an ecclesiastic engaged in telling his beads, and with the modesty of a bride vowed to the one love of her life or of a well-brought-up young girl. The faithful were all the more convinced that he had not seen them, since he got into a different compartment from theirs (as Princess Sherbatoff often did too), like a man who does not know whether you will be pleased or not to be seen with him and who leaves you the option of coming and joining him if you choose. This option had not been taken, at first, by the Doctor, who had advised us to leave him by himself in his compartment. Making a virtue of his natural hesitancy now that he occupied a great position in the medical world, it was with a smile, a toss of the head, and a glance over his pince-nez at Ski, that he said in a whisper, either from malice or in the hope of eliciting the views of his companions in a roundabout way: "You see, if I was on my own, a bachelor . . . but because of my wife I wonder whether I ought to allow him to travel with us after what you told me." "What's that you're saying?" asked Mme Cottard. "Nothing, it doesn't concern you, it's not meant for women to hear," the Doctor replied with a wink, and with a majestic self-satisfaction which steered a middle course between the impassive expression he maintained in front of his pupils and patients and the uneasiness that used in the past to accompany his shafts of wit at the Verdurins', and went on talking *sotto voce*. Mme Cottard picked up only the words "a member of the confraternity" and "*tapette*,"[18] and as in the Doctor's vocabulary the former expression denoted the Jewish race and the latter a wagging tongue, Mme Cottard concluded that M. de Charlus must be a garrulous Jew. She could not understand why they should cold-shoulder the Baron for that reason, and felt it her duty as the senior lady of the clan to insist that he should not be left alone; and so we proceeded in a body to M. de Charlus's compartment, led by Cottard who was still perplexed. From the corner in which he was reading a volume of Balzac, M. de Charlus observed this indecision; and yet he had not raised his eyes. But just as deaf-mutes detect, from a movement of air imperceptible to other people, that someone has approached behind them, so the Baron, to apprise him of people's coldness towards him, had a veritable sensory hyperacuity. This, as it habitually does in every sphere, had engendered in M. de Charlus imaginary sufferings. Like those neuropaths who, feeling a slight lowering of the temperature, and deducing therefrom that there must be a window open on the floor above, fly into a rage and start sneezing, M. de Charlus, if a person appeared preoccupied in his presence, concluded that somebody had repeated to that person a remark that he had made about him. But there was no need even for the other person to have an absent-minded, or a sombre, or a smiling air; he would invent them. On the other hand, cordiality easily concealed from him the slanders of which he had not heard. Having detected Cottard's initial hesitation, while he held out his hand to the rest of the faithful when they were at a convenient distance (greatly to their surprise, for they did not think that they had yet been observed by the reader's lowered eyes), for Cottard he contented himself with a forward inclination of his whole person which he at once sharply retracted, without taking in his own gloved hand the hand which the Doctor had held out to him.

"We felt we simply must come and keep you company, Monsieur," Mme Cottard said kindly to the Baron, "and not leave you alone like this in your little corner. It is a great pleasure to us."

"I am greatly honoured," the Baron intoned, bowing coldly.

"I was so pleased to hear that you have definitely chosen this neighbourhood to set up your taber . . ."

She was going to say "tabernacle" but it occurred to her that the word was Hebraic and discourteous to a Jew who might see some innuendo in it. And so she pulled herself up in order to choose another of the expressions that were familiar to her, that is to say a ceremonious expression: "to set up, I should say, your *penates.*" (It is true that these deities do not appertain to the Christian religion either, but to one which has been dead for so long that it no longer claims any devotees whose feelings one need be afraid of hurting.) "We, unfortunately, what with term beginning, and the Doctor's hospital duties, can never take up residence for very long in one place." And glancing down at a cardboard box: "You see too how we poor women are less fortunate than the sterner sex; even to go such a short distance as to our friends the Verdurins', we are obliged to take a whole heap of impedimenta."

I meanwhile was examining the Baron's volume of Balzac. It was not a paper-covered copy, picked up on a bookstall, like the volume of Bergotte which he had lent me at our first meeting. It was a book from his own library, and as such bore the device: "I belong to the Baron de Charlus," for which was substituted at times, to show the studious tastes of the Guermantes: *"In proeliis non semper,"* or yet another motto: *"Non sine labore."* But we shall see these presently replaced by others, in an attempt to please Morel.

Mme Cottard, after a moment or two, hit upon a subject which she felt to be of more personal interest to the Baron. "I don't know whether you agree with me, Monsieur," she said to him presently, "but I am very broad-minded, and in my opinion there is a great deal of good in all religions as long as people practise them sincerely. I am not one of the people who get hydrophobia at the sight of a . . . . Protestant."

"I was taught that mine is the true religion," replied M. de Charlus.

"He's a fanatic," thought Mme Cottard. "Swann, until towards the end, was more tolerant; it's true that he was a convert."

Now the Baron, on the contrary, was not only a Christian, as we know, but endued with a mediaeval piety. For him, as for sculptors of the thirteenth century, the Christian Church was, in the living sense of the word, peopled with a swarm of beings whom he believed to be entirely real: prophets, apostles, angels, holy personages of every sort, surrounding the incarnate Word, his mother and her spouse, the Eternal Father, all the martyrs and doctors of the Church, as they may be seen in high relief thronging the porches or lining the naves of cathedrals. Out of all these M. de Charlus had chosen as his patrons and intercessors the Archangels Michael, Gabriel and Raphael, with whom he discoursed regularly so that they might convey his prayers to the Eternal Father before whose throne they stand. And so Mme Cottars's mistake amused me greatly.

To leave the religious sphere, let us note that the Doctor, who had come to Paris with the meagre equipment of a peasant mother's advice, and had then been absorbed in the almost purely material studies to which those who seek to advance in a medical career are obliged to devote themselves for a great many years, had never cultivated his mind; he had acquired increasing authority but no experience; he took the word "honoured" in its literal sense and was at once flattered by it because he was vain, and distressed because he had a kind heart. "That poor de Charlus," he said to his wife that evening, "he

made me feel sorry for him when he said he was honoured to travel with us. One feels, poor devil, that he
knows nobody, that he has to humble himself."

But soon, without any need to be guided by the charitable Mme Cottard, the faithful had succeeded in overcoming the qualms which they had all more or less felt at
first on finding themselves in the company of M. de
Charlus. No doubt in his presence they were incessantly
reminded of Ski's revelations, and conscious of the sexual
abnormality embodied in their travelling companion. But
this abnormality itself had a sort of attraction for them. It
gave to the Baron's conversation, remarkable in itself but
in ways which they could scarcely appreciate, a savour
which, they felt, made the most interesting conversation,
even Brichot's, appear slightly insipid in comparison.
From the very outset, moreover, they had been pleased to
admit that he was intelligent. "Genius is sometimes akin
to madness," the Doctor declared, and when the Princess,
athirst for knowledge, questioned him further, said not
another word, this axiom being all that he knew about genius and in any case seeming to him less demonstrable
than everything relating to typhoid and arthritis. And as
he had become proud and remained ill-bred: "No questions, Princess, do not interrogate me, I'm at the seaside
for a rest. Besides, you wouldn't understand, you know
nothing about medicine." And the Princess apologised
and held her peace, deciding that Cottard was a charming
man and realising that celebrities were not always ap-
proachable. In this initial period, then, they had ended by
finding M. de Charlus intelligent in spite of his vice (or
what is generally so named). Now it was, quite unconsciously, because of that vice that they found him more

intelligent than others. The simplest maxims to which, adroitly provoked by the sculptor or the scholar, M. de Charlus gave utterance concerning love, jealousy, beauty, because of the strange, secret, refined and monstrous experience on which they were based, assumed for the faithful that charm of unfamiliarity with which a psychology analogous to that which our own dramatic literature has offered us from time immemorial is clothed in a Russian or Japanese play performed by native actors. They might still venture, when he was not listening, upon a malicious witticism at his expense. "Oh!" the sculptor would whisper, seeing a young railwayman with the sweeping eyelashes of a dancing girl at whom M. de Charlus could not help staring, "if the Baron begins making eyes at the conductor, we shall never get there, the train will start going backwards. Just look at the way he's staring at him: this isn't a puffer-train but a poofter-train." But when all was said, if M. de Charlus did not appear, they were almost disappointed to be travelling only with people who were just like everybody else, and not to have with them this painted, paunchy, tightly-buttoned personage, reminiscent of a box of exotic and dubious origin exhaling a curious odour of fruits the mere thought of tasting which would turn the stomach. From this point of view, the faithful of the masculine sex enjoyed a keener satisfaction in the short stage of the journey between Saint-Martin-du-Chêne, where M. de Charlus got in, and Doncières, the station at which Morel joined the party. For so long as the violinist was not there (and provided that the ladies and Albertine, keeping to themselves so as not to inhibit the conversation, were out of hearing), M. de Charlus made no attempt to appear to be avoiding certain subjects and did not hesitate to speak of "what it is customary to call immoral practices." Albertine could not hamper him, for she was always with the ladies, like a well-brought-up girl who does not wish her presence to restrict the freedom of grown-up conversation. And I was quite resigned to not having her by my side, on condition however that she remained in the same coach. For though I no longer felt any jealousy and scarcely any love for her, and never thought about what she might be doing on the days when I did not see her, on the other hand, when I was there, a mere partition which might at a pinch be concealing a betrayal was intolerable to me, and if she withdrew with the ladies to the next compartment, a moment later, unable to remain in my seat any longer, at the risk of offending whoever might be talking, Brichot, Cottard or Charlus, to whom I could not explain the reason for my flight, I would get up, leave them without ceremony, and, to make certain that nothing abnormal was happening, go next door. And until we came to Doncières M. de Charlus without any fear of shocking his audience, would speak sometimes in the plainest terms of practices which, he declared, for his own part he did not consider either good or bad. He did this from cunning, to show his broad-mindedness, convinced as he was that his own morals aroused no suspicion in the minds of the faithful. He was well aware that there did exist in the world several persons who were, to use an expression which became habitual with him later on, "in the know" about himself. But he imagined that these persons were not more than three or four, and that none of them was at that moment on the Normandy coast. This illusion may appear surprising in so shrewd and so suspicious a man. Even in the case of those whom he believed to be more or less informed, he deluded himself that it was in the vaguest way, and hoped, by telling them this or that fact about someone, to clear the person in question from all suspicion on the part of a listener who out of politeness pretended to accept his statements. Even in my case, while he was aware of what I knew or guessed about him, he imagined that my conviction, which he believed to be of far longer standing than it actually was, was quite general, and that it was sufficient for him to deny this or that detail to be believed, whereas on the contrary, if a knowledge of the whole always precedes a knowledge of the details, it makes investigation of the latter infinitely easier and, having destroyed his cloak of invisibility, no longer allows the dissembler to hide whatever he chooses. Certainly when M. de Charlus, invited to a dinner-party by one of the faithful or a friend of one of the faithful, adopted the most devious means to introduce Morel's name among ten others which he mentioned, he never imagined that for the reasons, always different, which he gave for the pleasure or convenience he would find that evening in being invited with him, his hosts, while appearing to believe him implicitly, would substitute a single and invariable reason, of which he supposed them to be ignorant, namely that he was in love with him. Similarly, Mme Verdurin, seeming always entirely to acknowledge the motives, half-artistic, half-humanitarian, which M. de Charlus gave her for the interest that he took in Morel, never ceased to thank the Baron warmly for his touching kindness, as she called it, towards the violinist. Yet how astonished M. de

Charlus would have been if, one day when Morel and he were delayed and had not come by the train, he had heard the Mistress say: "We're all here now except the young ladies"! The Baron would have been all the more amazed in that, scarcely stirring from La Raspelière, he played the part there of a family chaplain, a stage priest, and would sometimes (when Morel had 48 hours' leave) sleep there for two nights in succession. Mme Verdurin would then give them adjoining rooms, and, to put them at their ease, would say: "If you want to have a little music, don't worry about us. The walls are as thick as a fortress, you have nobody else on your floor, and my husband sleeps like a log." On such days M. de Charlus would relieve the Princess of the duty of going to meet newcomers at the station, apologising for Mme Verdurin's absence on the grounds of a state of health which he described so vividly that the guests entered the drawing-room with solemn faces and uttered cries of astonishment on finding the Mistress up and doing and dressed for the evening.

For M. de Charlus had for the moment become for Mme Verdurin the faithfullest of the faithful, a second Princess Sherbatoff. Of his position in society she was not nearly so certain as of that of the Princess, imagining that if the latter cared to see no one outside the little nucleus it was out of contempt for other people and preference for it. As this pretence was precisely the Verdurins' own, they treating as bores everyone to whose society they were not admitted, it is incredible that the Mistress can have believed the Princess to have an iron-willed loathing for everything fashionable. But she stuck to her guns and was convinced that in the case of the Princess too it was in all sincerity and from a love of things intellectual that she avoided the company of bores. The latter were, as it happened, diminishing in numbers from the Verdurins' point of view. Life by the seaside exempted an introduction from the consequences for the future which might have been feared in Paris. Brilliant men who had come down to Balbec without their wives (which made everything much easier) made overtures to La Raspelière and, from being bores, became delightful. This was the case with the Prince de Guermantes, whom the absence of his Princess would not, however, have decided to go as a "grass widower" to the Verdurins' had not the magnet of Dreyfusism been so powerful as to carry him at one stroke up the steep ascent to La Raspelière, unfortunately on a day when the Mistress was not at home. Mme Verdurin as it happened was not certain that he and M. de Charlus moved in the same world. The Baron had indeed said that the Duc de Guermantes was his brother, but this was perhaps the untruthful boast of an adventurer. However elegant he had shown himself to be, however amiable, however "faithful" to the Verdurins, the Mistress still almost hesitated to invite him to meet the Prince de Guermantes. She consulted Ski and Brichot: "The Baron and the Prince de Guermantes, will they be all right together?"

"Good gracious, Madame, as to one of the two I think I can safely say . . ."

"One of the two—what good is that to me?" Mme Verdurin had retorted crossly. "I asked you whether they would get on all right together."

"Ah! Madame, that sort of thing is very difficult to know."

Mme Verdurin had been impelled by no malice. She

was certain of the Baron's proclivities, but when she expressed herself in these terms she had not for a moment been thinking about them, but had merely wished to know whether she could invite the Prince and M. de Charlus on the same evening without their clashing. She had no malevolent intention when she employed these ready-made expressions which are popular in artistic "little clans." To make the most of M. de Guermantes, she proposed to take him in the afternoon, after her lunch-party, to a charity entertainment at which sailors from the neighbourhood would give a representation of a ship setting sail. But, not having time to attend to everything, she delegated her duties to the faithfullest of the faithful, the Baron. "You understand, I don't want them to hang about like mussels on a rock, they must keep coming and going, and we must see them clearing the decks or whatever it's called. Since you're always going down to the harbour at Balbec-Plage, you can easily arrange a dress rehearsal without tiring yourself. You must know far better than I do, M. de Charlus, how to get round young sailors . . . But we really are giving ourselves a lot of trouble for M. de Guermantes. Perhaps he's only one of those idiots from the Jockey Club. Oh! heavens, I'm running down the Jockey Club, and I seem to remember that you're one of them. Eh, Baron, you don't answer me, are you one of them? You don't want to come out with us? Look, here's a book that has just come which I think you'll find interesting. It's by Roujon. The title is attractive: *Among Men.*"

For my part, I was all the more pleased that M. de Charlus often took the place of Princess Sherbatoff inasmuch as I was thoroughly in her bad books, for a reason that was at once trivial and profound. One day when I was in the little train being as attentive as ever to Princess Sherbatoff, I saw Mme de Villeparisis get in. She had, I knew, come down to spend some weeks with the Princesse de Luxembourg, but, chained to the daily necessity of seeing Albertine, I had never replied to the repeated invitations of the Marquise and her royal hostess. I felt remorse at the sight of my grandmother's friend, and, purely from a sense of duty (without deserting Princess Sherbatoff), sat talking to her for some time. I was, as it happened, entirely unaware that Mme de Villeparisis knew perfectly well who my companion was but did not wish to acknowledge her. At the next station, Mme de Villeparisis left the train, and indeed I reproached myself for not having helped her on to the platform. I resumed my seat by the side of the Princess. But it was as though (a cataclysm frequent among people who are socially insecure and afraid that one may have heard something to their discredit and hence may despise them) the curtain had risen upon a new scene. Buried in her *Revue des Deux Mondes*, Mme Sherbatoff could scarcely bring herself to reply to my questions and finally told me that I was giving her a headache. I had not the faintest idea of the nature of my crime. When I bade the Princess good-bye, the customary smile did not light up her face, her chin drooped in a curt acknowledgement, she did not even offer me her hand, and she never spoke to me again. But she must have spoken—though I have no idea what she said—to the Verdurins; for as soon as I asked them whether I ought not to make some polite gesture to Princess Sherbatoff, they replied in chorus: "No! No! No! Absolutely not! She doesn't care for polite speeches."

They did not say this in order to cause bad blood between us, but she had succeeded in persuading them that she was unmoved by civilities, impervious to the vanities of this world. One needs to have seen the politician who is reckoned the most unbending, the most intransigent, the most unapproachable, now that he is in office; one needs to have seen him at the time of his eclipse, humbly soliciting, with a bright, ingratiating smile, the haughty greeting of some second-rate journalist; one needs to have seen the transformation of Cottard (whom his new patients regarded as a ramrod), and to know what disappointments in love, what rebuffs to snobbery were the basis of the apparent pride, the universally acknowledged anti-snobbery of Princess Sherbatoff, in order to grasp that the rule among the human race—a rule that naturally admits of exceptions—is that the reputedly hard are the weak whom nobody wanted, and that the strong, caring little whether they are wanted or not, have alone that gentleness which the vulgar herd mistakes for weakness.

Besides, I ought not to judge Princess Sherbatoff severely. Her case is so common! One day, at the funeral of a Guermantes, a distinguished man who was standing next to me drew my attention to a tall, slender individual with handsome features. "Of all the Guermantes," my neighbour informed me, "that one is the most strange and remarkable. He is the Duke's brother." I replied imprudently that he was mistaken, that the gentleman in question, who was in no way related to the Guermantes, was named Fournier-Sarlovèze. The distinguished man turned his back on me and has never even looked at me since.

An eminent musician, a member of the *Institut*, occupying a high official position, who was acquainted with

Ski, came to Harambouville, where he had a niece, and
appeared at one of the Verdurins' Wednesdays. M. de
Charlus was especially polite to him (at Morel's request),
principally in order that on his return to Paris the Academician would allow him to attend various private concerts, rehearsals and so forth at which the violinist would
be playing. The Academician, who was flattered, and was
moreover a charming man, promised to do so and kept his
promise. The Baron was deeply touched by all the kindness and courtesy which this important personage (who,
for his own part, was exclusively and passionately a lover
of women) showed him, all the facilities that he procured
for him to see Morel in those official premises from which
outsiders are excluded, all the opportunities which the celebrated artist secured for the young virtuoso to perform,
to get himself known, by naming him in preference to
others of equal talent for private recitals which were likely
to make a special stir. But M. de Charlus never suspected
that he owed the maestro all the more gratitude in that
the latter, doubly deserving, or alternatively guilty twice
over, was fully aware of the relations between the young
violinist and his noble patron. He abetted them, certainly
not out of any sympathy for them since he was incapable
of understanding any other love than the love of women,
which had inspired the whole of his music, but from
moral indifference, a kindness and readiness to oblige
characteristic of his profession, social affability, and snobbery. He had so little doubt as to the character of those
relations that, at his first dinner at La Raspelière, he had
inquired of Ski, speaking of M. de Charlus and Morel as
he might have spoken of a man and his mistress: "Have
they been long together?" But, too much the man of the

world to let the parties concerned see that he knew, prepared, should any gossip arise among Morel's fellow-stu-
dents, to rebuke them and to reassure Morel by saying to
him in a fatherly tone: "One hears that sort of thing
about everybody nowadays," he continued to overwhelm
the Baron with civilities which the latter thought charming, but quite natural, being incapable of suspecting the
eminent maestro of so much vice or of so much virtue.
For nobody was ever base enough to repeat to M. de
Charlus the things that were said behind his back, and the
jokes about Morel. And yet this simple situation is
enough to show that even that thing which is universally
decried, which no one would dream of defending—gossip—has itself, whether it is aimed at ourselves and thus
becomes especially disagreeable to us, or whether it tells
us something about a third person of which we were unaware, a certain psychological value. It prevents the mind
from falling asleep over the factitious view which it has of
what it imagines things to be and which is actually no
more than their outward appearance. It turns this appearance inside out with the magic dexterity of an idealist
philosopher and rapidly presents to our gaze an unsuspected corner of the reverse side of the fabric. Could
M. de Charlus ever have imagined these words spoken by
a certain tender relative: "How on earth can you suppose
that Mémé is in love with me? You forget that I'm a
woman!" And yet she was genuinely, deeply attached to
M. de Charlus. Why then need we be surprised that in
the case of the Verdurins, on whose affection and good-
will he had no reason to rely, the remarks which they
made behind his back (and they did not, as we shall see,
confine themselves to remarks) should have been so dif-

ferent from what he imagined them to be, that is to say no more than a reflexion of the remarks that he heard when he was present? These latter alone decorated with affectionate inscriptions the little ideal bower to which M. de Charlus retired at times to dream, when he introduced his imagination for a moment into the idea that the Verdurins had of him. Its atmosphere was so congenial, so cordial, the repose it offered so comforting, that when M. de Charlus, before going to sleep, had withdrawn to it for a momentary relaxation from his worries, he never emerged from it without a smile. But, for each one of us, a bower of this sort is double: opposite the one which we imagine to be unique, there is the other which is normally invisible to us, the real one, symmetrical with the one we know, but very different, whose decoration, in which we should recognise nothing of what we expected to see, would horrify us as though it were composed of the odious symbols of an unsuspected hostility. What a shock it would have been for M. de Charlus if he had found his way into one of these hostile bowers, thanks to some piece of scandal, as though by one of those service staircases where obscene graffiti are scribbled outside the back doors of flats by unpaid tradesmen or dismissed servants! But, just as we do not possess that sense of direction with which certain birds are endowed, so we lack the sense of our own visibility as we lack that of distances, imagining as quite close to us the interested attention of people who on the contrary never give us a thought, and not suspecting that we are at that same moment the sole preoccupation of others. Thus M. de Charlus lived in a fool's paradise like the fish that thinks that the water in which it is swimming extends beyond the glass wall of its aquar-

ium which mirrors it, while it does not see close beside it
in the shadow the amused stroller who is watching its gyrations, or the all-powerful keeper who, at the unforeseen
and fatal moment, postponed for the present in the case of
the Baron (for whom the keeper, in Paris, will be Mme
Verdurin), will extract it without compunction from the
environment in which it was happily living to fling it into
another. Moreover, the races of mankind, insofar as they
are no more than collections of individuals, may furnish
us with examples more extensive, but identical in each of
their parts, of this profound, obstinate and disconcerting
blindness. Up to the present, if it was responsible for the
fact that M. de Charlus addressed to the little clan remarks of a futile subtlety or of an audacity which made
his listeners smile to themselves, it had not yet caused
him, nor was it to cause him, at Balbec, any serious inconvenience. A trace of albumin, of sugar, of cardiac ar-
rhythmia, does not prevent life from continuing normally
for the man who is not even aware of it, while the physician alone sees in it a prophecy of catastrophes in store.
At present the Baron's predilection for Morel—whether
platonic or not—merely led him to say spontaneously in
Morel's absence that he thought him very good-looking,
assuming that this would be interpreted quite innocently,
and thereby acting like a clever man who, when summoned to testify before a court of law, will not be afraid
to enter into details which are apparently to his disadvantage but for that very reason are more natural and less
vulgar than the conventional protestations of a stage cul-
prit. With the same freedom, always between Saint-Martin-du-Chêne and Doncières-Ouest—or conversely on the
return journey—M. de Charlus would readily speak of

people who had, it appeared, very peculiar ways, and would even add: "But after all, although I say peculiar, I don't really know why, for there's nothing so very peculiar about it," to prove to himself how thoroughly at his ease he was with his audience. And so indeed he was, provided that it was he who retained the initiative and knew that the gallery was mute and smiling, disarmed by credulity or good manners.

When M. de Charlus was not speaking of his admiration for Morel's beauty as though it had no connexion with a proclivity known as a vice, he would discuss that vice, but as though he himself were in no way addicted to it. Sometimes indeed he did not hesitate to call it by its name. When after examining the fine binding of his volume of Balzac, I asked him which was his favourite novel in the *Comédie humaine*, he replied, his thoughts irresistibly attracted towards an obsession: "Impossible to choose between tiny miniatures like the *Curé de Tours* and the *Femme abandonnée*, or the great frescoes like the series of the *Illusions perdues*. What! you've never read *Les Illusions perdues*? It's so beautiful—the scene where Carlos Herrera asks the name of the château he is driving past, and it turns out to be Rastignac, the home of the young man he used to love; and then the abbé falling into a reverie which Swann once called, and very aptly, the *Tristesse d'Olympio* of pederasty. And the death of Lucien! I forget who the man of taste was who, when he was asked what event in his life had grieved him most, replied: 'The death of Lucien de Rubempré in *Splendeurs et Misères*.'"

"I know that Balzac is all the rage this year, as pessimism was last," Brichot interrupted. "But, at the risk of giving pain to hearts that are smitten with the Balzacian fever, without laying any claim, God forbid, to the role of policeman of letters, and drawing up a list of offences against the laws of grammar, I must confess that the copious improviser whose alarming lucubrations you appear to me singularly to overrate has always struck me as being an insufficiently meticulous scribe. I have read these *Illusions perdues* of which you speak, Baron, flagellating myself to attain to the fervour of an initiate, and I confess in all simplicity of heart that those serial instalments of sentimental balderdash, composed in double or triple Dutch—*Esther heureuse, Où mènent les mauvais chemins, À combien l'amour revient aux vieillards*—have always had the effect on me of the mysteries of Rocambole, exalted by an inexplicable preference to the precarious position of a masterpiece."

"You say that because you know nothing of life," said the Baron, doubly irritated, for he felt that Brichot would not understand either his aesthetic reasons or the other kind.

"I quite realise," replied Brichot, "that, to speak like Master François Rabelais, you mean that I am *moult sorbonagre, sorbonicole et sorboniforme*. And yet, just as much as any of our friends here, I like a book to give an impression of sincerity and real life, I am not one of those clerks . . ."

"The *quart d'heure de Rabelais*,"[19] Dr Cottard broke in, with an air no longer of uncertainty but of confidence in his own wit.

". . . who take a vow of literature following the rule of the Abbaye-aux-Bois under the obedience of M. le Vicomte de Chateaubriand, Grand Master of humbug, according to the strict rule of the humanists. M. le Vicomte de Chateaubriand . . ."

"Chateaubriand *aux pommes?*" put in Dr Cottard.

"He is the patron saint of the brotherhood," continued Brichot, ignoring the Doctor's joke, while the latter, alarmed by the scholar's phrase, glanced anxiously at M. de Charlus. Brichot had seemed wanting in tact to Cottard, whose pun meanwhile had brought a subtle smile to the lips of Princess Sherbatoff: "With the Professor, the mordant irony of the complete sceptic never forfeits its rights," she said kindly, to show that Cottard's "quip" had not passed unperceived by herself.

"The sage is of necessity sceptical," replied the Doctor. "What do I know? *Gnōthi seauton*, said Socrates. He was quite right, excess in anything is a mistake. But I am dumbfounded when I think that those words have sufficed to keep Socrates's name alive all this time. What does his philosophy amount to? Very little when all is said. When one thinks that Charcot and others have done work that is a thousand times more remarkable and is at least based on something, on the suppression of the pupillary reflex as a syndrome of general paralysis, and that they are almost forgotten. After all, Socrates was nothing out of the common. Those people had nothing better to do than spend all their time strolling about and splitting hairs. Like Jesus Christ: 'Love one another!' it's all very pretty."

"My dear," Mme Cottard implored.

"Naturally my wife protests, women are all neurotic."

"But, my dear Doctor, I'm not neurotic," murmured Mme Cottard.

"What, she's not neurotic! When her son is ill, she

develops all the symptoms of insomnia. Still, I quite admit that Socrates, and all the rest of them, are necessary for a superior culture, to acquire the talent of exposition. I always quote his *gnōthi seauton* to my students at the beginning of the course. Old Bouchard, when he heard of it, congratulated me."

"I am not an upholder of form for form's sake, any more than I am inclined to treasure millionaire rhymes in poetry," Brichot went on. "But all the same, the not very human *Comédie humaine* is all too egregiously the antithesis of those works in which the art exceeds the matter, as that holy terror Ovid says. And it is permissible to prefer a middle way, which leads to the presbytery of Meudon or the hermitage of Ferney, equidistant from the Vallée-aux-Loups, in which René arrogantly performed the duties of a merciless pontificate, and from Les Jardies, where Honoré de Balzac, harried by the bailiffs, never ceased voiding upon paper, like a zealous apostle of gibberish, to please a Polish lady."

"Chateaubriand is far more alive than you say, and Balzac is, after all, a great writer," replied M. de Charlus, still too much impregnated with Swann's tastes not to be irritated by Brichot, "and Balzac was acquainted even with those passions which the rest of the world ignores, or studies only to castigate them. Without referring again to the immortal *Illusions perdues*, stories like *Sarrazine, La Fille aux yeux d'or, Une passion dans le désert*, even the distinctly enigmatic *Fausse Maîtresse*, can be adduced in support of my argument. When I spoke of this 'extranatural' aspect of Balzac to Swann, he said to me: 'You are of the same opinion as Taine.' I never had the honour of knowing Monsieur Taine," M. de Charlus continued (with that irritating habit of inserting an otiose "Monsieur" to which people in society are addicted, as though they imagine that by styling a great writer "Monsieur" they are doing him an honour, perhaps keeping him at his proper distance, and making it quite clear that they do not know him personally), "I never knew Monsieur Taine, but I felt myself greatly honoured by being of the same opinion as he."

Nevertheless, in spite of these ridiculous social affectations, M. de Charlus was extremely intelligent, and it is probable that if some remote marriage had established a connexion between his family and that of Balzac, he would have felt (no less than Balzac himself, for that matter) a satisfaction on which he would yet have been unable to resist preening himself as on a praiseworthy sign of condescension.

Occasionally, at the station after Saint-Martin-du-Chêne, some young men would get into the train. M. de Charlus could not refrain from looking at them, but as he cut short and concealed the attention that he paid them, he gave the impression of hiding a secret that was even more personal than the real one; it was as though he knew them, and betrayed the knowledge in spite of himself, after having accepted the sacrifice, before turning again to us, like children who, in consequence of a quarrel between parents, have been forbidden to speak to certain of their schoolfellows, but who when they meet them cannot forbear to raise their heads before lowering them again beneath the menacing gaze of their tutor.

At the word borrowed from the Greek with which M. de Charlus, in speaking of Balzac, had followed his allusion to *Tristesse d'Olympio* in connexion with *Splen-*

deurs et Misères, Ski, Brichot and Cottard had glanced at one another with a smile perhaps not so much ironical as tinged with that satisfaction which people at a dinner-party would show who had succeeded in making Dreyfus talk about his own case, or the Empress Eugénie about her reign. They were hoping to press him a little further upon this subject, but we were already at Doncières, where Morel joined us. In his presence, M. de Charlus kept a careful guard over his conversation and, when Ski tried to bring it back to the love of Carlos Herrera for Lucien de Rubempré, the Baron assumed the vexed, mysterious, and finally (seeing that nobody was listening to him) severe and judicial air of a father who hears a man saying something indecent in front of his daughter. Ski having shown some determination to pursue the subject, M. de Charlus, his eyes starting out of his head, raised his voice and with a meaningful glance at Albertine—who in fact could not hear what we were saying, being engaged in conversation with Mme Cottard and Princess Sherbatoff—and the hint of a double meaning of someone who wishes to teach ill-bred people a lesson, said: "I think it's high time we began to talk of subjects that might interest this young lady." But I realised that, for him, the young lady was not Albertine but Morel, and he confirmed, later on, the accuracy of my interpretation by the expressions he employed when he begged that there might be no more such conversations in front of Morel. "You know," he said to me, speaking of the violinist, "he's not at all what you might suppose, he's a very decent boy who has always been very serious and well-behaved." One sensed from these words that M. de Charlus regarded sexual inversion as a danger as menac-

ing to young men as prostitution is to women, and that if
he employed the epithet "serious" of Morel it was in the
sense that it has when applied to a young shop-girl.

Then Brichot, to change the subject, asked me
whether I intended to remain much longer at Incarville.
Although I had pointed out to him more than once that I
was staying not at Incarville but at Balbec, he always repeated the mistake, for it was by the name of Incarville
or Balbec-Incarville that he referred to this section of the
coast. One often finds people speaking thus about the
same things as oneself by a slightly different name. A
certain lady of the Faubourg Saint-Germain used invariably to ask me, when she meant to refer to the Duchesse
de Guermantes, whether I had seen Zénaïde lately, or
Oriane-Zénaïde, so that at first I did not understand her.
Probably there had been a time when, some relative of
Mme de Guermantes being named Oriane, she herself, to
avoid confusion, had been known as Oriane-Zénaïde.
Perhaps, too, there had originally been a station only at
Incarville, from which one went on by carriage to Balbec.

"Why, what have you been talking about?" said Albertine, astonished at the solemn, paternal tone which
M. de Charlus had suddenly adopted.

"About Balzac," the Baron hastily replied, "and you
are wearing this evening the very same costume as the
Princesse de Cadignan, not the first, which she wears at
the dinner-party, but the second."

This coincidence was due to the fact that, in choosing Albertine's clothes, I drew my inspiration from the
taste that she had acquired thanks to Elstir, who had a
liking for the sort of sobriety that might have been called
British had it not been tempered with a softness that was

purely French. As a rule the clothes he preferred offered
to the eye a harmonious combination of grey tones, like
the dress of Diane de Cadignan. M. de Charlus was almost the only person capable of appreciating Albertine's
clothes at their true value; his eye detected at a glance
what constituted their rarity, their worth; he would never
have mistaken one material for another, and could always
recognise the maker. But he preferred—in women—a little more brightness and colour than Elstir would allow.
And so, that evening, Albertine glanced at me with a
half-smiling, half-apprehensive expression, wrinkling her
little pink cat's nose. Meeting over her skirt of grey crêpe
de chine, her jacket of grey cheviot did indeed give the
impression that she was dressed entirely in grey. But,
signing to me to help her, because her puffed sleeves
needed to be smoothed down or pulled up for her to get
into or out of her jacket, she took it off, and as these
sleeves were of a Scottish plaid in soft colours, pink, pale
blue, dull green, pigeon's breast, the effect was as though
in a grey sky a rainbow had suddenly appeared. And she
wondered whether this would find favour with M. de
Charlus.

"Ah!" he exclaimed in delight, "now we have a ray, a
prism of colour. I offer you my sincerest compliments."

"But it's this gentleman who has earned them," Albertine replied politely, pointing to myself, for she liked
to show off what she had received from me.

"It's only the women who don't know how to dress
that are afraid of colours," went on M. de Charlus. "One
can be brilliant without vulgarity and soft without being
dull. Besides, you have not the same reasons as Mme de
Cadignan for wishing to appear detached from life, for

that was the idea which she wished to instil into d'Arthez with her grey gown."

Albertine, who was interested in this mute language of clothes, questioned M. de Charlus about the Princesse de Cadignan. "Oh! it's such a delightful story," said the Baron in a dreamy tone. "I know the little garden in which Diane de Cadignan used to stroll with Mme d'Espard. It belongs to one of my cousins."

"All this talk about his cousin's garden," Brichot murmured to Cottard, "may, like his pedigree, be of some importance to this worthy Baron. But what interest can it have for us who are not privileged to walk in it, do not know the lady, and possess no titles of nobility?" For Brichot had no idea that one might be interested in a dress and in a garden as works of art, and that it was as though in the pages of Balzac that M. de Charlus saw Mme de Cadignan's garden paths in his mind's eye. The Baron went on: "But you know her," he said to me, speaking of this cousin, and flatteringly addressing himself to me as to a person who, exiled amid the little clan, was to him, if not a citizen of his world, at any rate a frequenter of it. "Anyhow you must have seen her at Mme de Villeparisis's."

"Is that the Marquise de Villeparisis who owns the château at Baucreux?" asked Brichot, captivated.

"Yes, do you know her?" inquired M. de Charlus dryly.

"No, not at all," replied Brichot, "but our colleague Norpois spends part of his holidays every year at Baucreux. I have had occasion to write to him there."

I told Morel, thinking to interest him, that M. de Norpois was a friend of my father. But not by the slightest flicker of his features did he show that he had heard me, so little did he think of my parents, so far short did they fall in his estimation of what my great-uncle had been, who had employed Morel's father as his valet, and who moreover, being fond of "cutting a dash," unlike the rest of the family, had left a golden memory among his servants.

"It appears that Mme de Villeparisis is a superior woman," Brichot went on, "but I have never been allowed to judge of that for myself, nor for that matter has any of my colleagues. For Norpois, who is the soul of courtesy and affability at the *Institut*, has never introduced any of us to the Marquise. I know of no one who has been received by her except our friend Thureau-Dangin, who had an old family connexion with her, and also Gaston Boissier, whom she was anxious to meet because of a study of his that particularly interested her. He dined with her once and came back quite enthralled by her charm. Mme Boissier, however, was not invited."

At the sound of these names, Morel melted into a smile. "Ah! Thureau-Dangin," he said to me with an air of interest as great as had been his indifference when he heard me speak of the Marquis de Norpois and my father. "Thureau-Dangin; why he and your uncle were as thick as thieves. Whenever a lady wanted a front seat for a reception at the Academy, your uncle would say: 'I shall write to Thureau-Dangin.' And of course he got it at once, because you can imagine that M. Thureau-Dangin would never have dared refuse your uncle anything, because he'd soon have got his own back. I'm amused to hear the name Boissier, too, because that was where your uncle ordered all the presents he used to give the ladies at

New Year. I know all about it, because I knew the person
he used to send for them." He did indeed know him, for
it was his father. Some of these affectionate allusions by
Morel to my uncle's memory were prompted by the fact
that we did not intend to remain permanently in the Hôtel Guermantes, where we had taken an apartment only
on account of my grandmother. From time to time there
would be talk of a possible move. Now, to understand the
advice that Charles Morel gave me in this connexion, the
reader must know that my great-uncle had lived, in his
day, at 40*bis* Boulevard Malesherbes. The consequence
was that, in the family, as we often went to visit my uncle Adolphe until the fatal day when I caused a breach
between my parents and him by telling them the story of
the lady in pink, instead of saying "at your uncle's" we
used to say "at 40*bis*." Some cousins of Mamma's used to
say to her in the most natural tone: "Ah! so we can't expect you on Sunday since you're dining at 40*bis*." If I
were going to call on some relations, I would be warned
to go first of all "to 40*bis*," in order that my uncle might
not be offended by my not having begun my round with
him. He was the owner of the house and was very particular as to the choice of his tenants, all of whom either
were or became his personal friends. Colonel the Baron
de Vatry used to look in every day and smoke a cigar
with him in the hope of making him consent to repairs.
The carriage entrance was always kept shut. If my uncle
caught sight of some washing or a rug hanging from one
of the window-sills he would storm in and have it removed in less time than the police would take to do so
nowadays. All the same, he did let part of the house, reserving for himself only two floors and the stables. In

spite of this, knowing that he was pleased when people praised the excellent upkeep of the house, we used always to extol the comfort of the "little mansion" as though my uncle had been its sole occupant, and he encouraged the pretence, without issuing the formal contradiction that might have been expected. The "little mansion" was certainly comfortable (my uncle having installed in it all the most recent inventions). But it was in no way out of the ordinary. Only my uncle, while referring with false modesty to "my little hovel," was convinced, or at any rate had instilled into his valet, the valet's wife, the coachman, the cook, the idea that there was no place in Paris to compare, for comfort, luxury, and general attractiveness, with the little mansion. Charles Morel had grown up in this belief. He had not outgrown it. And so, even on days when he was not talking to me, if in the train I mentioned the possibility of our moving, at once he would smile at me and say with a knowing wink: "Ah! What you want is something in the style of 40*bis*! That's a place that would suit you down to the ground! Your uncle knew what he was about. I'm quite sure that in the whole of Paris there's nothing to compare with 40*bis*."

The melancholy air which M. de Charlus had assumed in speaking of the Princesse de Cadignan left me in no doubt that the tale in question had not reminded him only of the little garden of a cousin to whom he was not particularly attached. He became lost in thought, and as though he were talking to himself: "*The Secrets of the Princesse de Cadignan!*" he exclaimed, "what a masterpiece! How profound, how heartrending the evil reputation of Diane, who is afraid that the man she loves may hear of it. What an eternal truth, and more universal

than it might appear! How far-reaching it is!" He uttered
these words with a sadness in which one nevertheless felt
that he found a certain charm. Certainly M. de Charlus,
unaware to what extent precisely his proclivities were or
were not known, had been trembling for some time past
at the thought that when he returned to Paris and was
seen there in Morel's company, the latter's family might
intervene and so his future happiness be jeopardised.
This eventuality had probably not appeared to him hitherto except as something profoundly disagreeable and
painful. But the Baron was an artist to his fingertips. And
now that he had suddenly begun to identify his own situation with that described by Balzac, he took refuge, as it
were, in the story, and for the calamity which was perhaps in store for him and which he certainly feared, he
had the consolation of finding in his own anxiety what
Swann and also Saint-Loup would have called something
"very Balzacian." This identification of himself with the
Princesse de Cadignan had been made easier for M. de
Charlus by virtue of the mental transposition which was
becoming habitual with him and of which he had already
given several examples. It sufficed, moreover, to make the
mere conversion of a woman, as the beloved object, into a
young man immediately set in motion around him the
whole sequence of social complications which develop
round a normal love affair. When, for some reason or
other, a change in the calendar or in time-tables is introduced once and for all, if we make the year begin a few
weeks later, or if we make midnight strike a quarter of an
hour earlier, since the days will still consist of twenty-
four hours and the months of thirty days, everything that
depends upon the measure of time will remain unaltered.

Everything can have been changed without causing any disturbance, since the ratio between the figures is still the same. So it is with lives which adopt "Central European time" or the Eastern calendar. It would even seem that the gratification a man derives from keeping an actress played a part in this liaison. When, after their first meeting, M. de Charlus had made inquiries as to Morel's background, he had of course learned that he was of humble extraction, but a *demi-mondaine* with whom we are in love does not forfeit our esteem because she is the child of poor parents. On the other hand, the well-known musicians to whom he had addressed his inquiries had answered him, not even from any personal motive, like the friends who, when introducing Swann to Odette, had described her to him as more difficult and more sought after than she actually was, but simply in the stereotyped manner of men in a prominent position overpraising a beginner: "Ah, yes, a great talent, a remarkable reputation considering that he's still young, highly esteemed by the experts, will go far." And, with the habit which people who are innocent of inversion have of speaking of masculine beauty: "Besides, he's charming to watch when he plays; he looks better than anyone at a concert, with his pretty hair and distinguished poses; he has an exquisite head, in fact he's the very picture of a violinist." And so M. de Charlus, in any case over-excited by Morel, who did not fail to let him know how many propositions had been addressed to him, was flattered to take him home with him, to make a little dovecot for him to which he would often return. For during the rest of the time he wished him to be free, since this was essential to his career, which M. de Charlus wanted him to continue, how-

ever much money he had to give him, either because of
the thoroughly "Guermantes" idea that a man must do
something, that talent is the sole criterion of merit, and
that nobility or money are simply the nought that multi-
plies a value, or because he was afraid lest, having nothing to do and remaining perpetually in his company, the
violinist might grow bored. Moreover he did not wish to
deprive himself of the pleasure which he felt, at certain
grand concerts, in saying to himself: "The person they
are applauding at this moment is coming home with me
tonight." Elegant people, when they are in love, and
whatever the nature of their love, exercise their vanity in
ways that can destroy the previous advantages in which
their vanity would have found satisfaction.

Morel, feeling that I bore him no malice, that I was
sincerely attached to M. de Charlus and that I was at the
same time absolutely indifferent physically to both of
them, ended by displaying the same warm feelings towards me as a courtesan who knows that you do not desire her and that her lover has in you a sincere friend
who will not try to turn him against her. Not only did he
speak to me exactly as Rachel, Saint-Loup's mistress, had
spoken to me long ago, but what was more, to judge by
what M. de Charlus reported to me, he said to him about
me in my absence the same things that Rachel used to
say about me to Robert. Indeed M. de Charlus said to
me: "He likes you very much," as Robert had said: "She
likes you very much." And like the nephew on behalf of
his mistress, so it was on Morel's behalf that the uncle
often invited me to come and dine with them. There
were, moreover, just as many storms between them as
there had been between Robert and Rachel. To be sure,

after Charlie (Morel) had left us, M. de Charlus never stopped singing his praises, repeating—something by which he felt flattered—that the violinist was so kind to him. But it was evident nevertheless that often Charlie, even in front of all the faithful, looked irritated instead of always appearing happy and submissive as the Baron would have wished. This irritation became so extreme in course of time, in consequence of the weakness which led M. de Charlus to forgive Morel his want of politeness, that the violinist made no attempt to conceal it, or even deliberately affected it. I have seen M. de Charlus, on entering a railway carriage in which Morel was sitting with some of his fellow-soldiers, greeted by the musician with a shrug of the shoulders, accompanied by a wink in the direction of his comrades. Or else he would pretend to be asleep, as though this intrusion bored him beyond words. Or he would begin to cough, and the others would laugh, derisively mimicking the affected speech of men like M. de Charlus, and draw Charlie into a corner from which he would eventually return, as though forced to do so, to sit by M. de Charlus, whose heart was pierced by all these cruelties. It is inconceivable how he can have put up with them; and these ever-varied forms of suffering posed the problem of happiness in fresh terms for M. de Charlus, compelled him not only to demand more, but to desire something else, the previous combination being vitiated by a hideous memory. And yet, painful as these scenes came to be, it must be acknowledged that in the early days the genius of the Frenchman of the people instinctively invested Morel with charming forms of simplicity, of apparent candour, even of an independent pride which seemed to be inspired by disinterestedness.

This was not the case, but the advantage of this attitude was all the more on Morel's side in that, whereas the person who is in love is continually forced to return to the charge, to go one better, it is on the other hand easy for the person who is not in love to proceed along a straight line, inflexible and dignified. It existed by virtue of the privilege of heredity in the face—so open—of this Morel whose heart was so tightly shut, that face endued with the neo-Hellenic grace which blooms in the basilicas of Champagne. Notwithstanding his affectation of pride, often when he caught sight of M. de Charlus at a moment when he was not expecting to see him, he would be embarrassed by the presence of the little clan, would blush and lower his eyes, to the delight of the Baron, who read a whole novel into it. It was simply a sign of irritation and shame. The former sometimes expressed itself openly; for, calm and severely proper as Morel's attitude generally was, it was not infrequently belied. At times, indeed, at something which the Baron said to him, Morel would burst out in the harshest tones with an insolent retort which shocked everybody. M. de Charlus would lower his head with a sorrowful air, would make no reply, and with that faculty which doting fathers possess of believing that the coldness and rudeness of their children has passed unnoticed, would continue undeterred to sing the violinist's praises. M. de Charlus was not always so submissive, but as a rule his attempts at rebellion proved abortive, principally because, having lived among society people, in calculating the reactions that he might provoke he made allowance for the baser instincts, whether congenital or acquired; whereas, instead of these, he encountered in Morel a plebeian tendency to momentary indifference. Unfortunately for M. de Charlus, he did not understand that, for Morel, everything else gave precedence when the Conservatoire and his good reputation at the Conservatoire (but this, which was to be a more serious matter, did not arise for the moment) were in question. Thus, for instance, people of the middle class will readily change their surnames out of vanity, and noblemen for personal advantage. To the young violinist, on the contrary, the name Morel was inseparably linked with his first prize for the violin, and so impossible to alter. M. de Charlus would have liked Morel to owe everything to him, including his name. Reflecting that Morel's Christian name was Charles, which resembled Charlus, and that the house where they usually met was called les Charmes, he sought to persuade Morel that, a pretty name that is agreeable to pronounce being half the battle in establishing an artistic reputation, the virtuoso ought without hesitation to take the name Charmel, a discreet allusion to the scene of their assignations. Morel shrugged his shoulders. As a conclusive argument, M. de Charlus was unfortunately inspired to add that he had a valet of that name. He succeeded only in arousing the furious indignation of the young man. "There was a time when my ancestors were proud of the title of chamberlain or butler to the King," said the Baron. "There was also a time," replied Morel haughtily, "when my ancestors cut off your ancestors' heads." M. de Charlus would have been greatly surprised had he been capable of realising that, having resigned himself, failing "Charmel," to adopting Morel and conferring on him one of the titles of the Guermantes family which were at his disposal—but which circumstances, as we shall see, did not permit him

to offer the violinist—he would have met with a refusal
on the latter's part on the grounds of the artistic reputation attached to the name Morel, and of the things that
would be said about him at his classes. So far above the
Faubourg Saint-Germain did he place the Rue Bergère
and its Conservatoire! M. de Charlus was obliged to content himself with having symbolical rings made for
Morel, bearing the antique device: PLVS VLTRA CAR'LVS.
Certainly, in the face of an adversary of a sort with which
he was unfamiliar, M. de Charlus ought to have changed
his tactics. But which of us is capable of that? Moreover,
if M. de Charlus made blunders, Morel was not guiltless
of them either. Far more than the actual circumstance
which brought about the rupture between them, what was
destined, temporarily at least (but the temporary turned
out to be permanent), to be his downfall with M. de
Charlus was that his nature included not only the baseness which made him obsequious in the face of harshness
and respond with insolence to kindness. Running parallel
with this innate baseness, there was in him a complicated
neurasthenia of ill breeding, which, springing up on every
occasion when he was in the wrong or was becoming a
nuisance, meant that at the very moment when he needed
all his niceness, all his gentleness, all his gaiety to disarm
the Baron, he became sombre and aggressive, tried to
provoke discussions on matters where he knew that the
other did not agree with him, and maintained his own
hostile attitude with a weakness of argument and a
peremptory violence which enhanced that weakness. For,
very soon running short of arguments, he invented fresh
ones as he went along, in which he displayed the full extent of his ignorance and stupidity. These were barely

noticeable when he was in a friendly mood and sought only to please. On the other hand, nothing else was visible in his black moods, when, from being inoffensive, they became odious. Whereupon M. de Charlus felt that he could endure no more and that his only hope lay in a brighter morrow, while Morel, forgetting that the Baron was keeping him in the lap of luxury, would give an ironical smile of condescending pity, and say: "I've never taken anything from anybody. Which means that there's nobody to whom I owe a single word of thanks."

In the meantime, as though he were dealing with a man of the world, M. de Charlus continued to give vent to his rage, whether genuine or feigned, but in either case ineffective. It was not always so, however. Thus one day (which in fact came after this initial period) when the Baron was returning with Charlie and myself from a lunch-party at the Verdurins' expecting to spend the rest of the afternoon and evening with the violinist at Doncières, the latter's dismissal of him, as soon as we left the train, with: "No, I've an engagement," caused M. de Charlus so keen a disappointment that, although he tried to put a brave face on it, I saw the tears trickling down and melting the make-up on his eyelashes as he stood dazed beside the carriage door. Such was his grief that, as Albertine and I intended to spend the rest of the day at Doncières, I whispered to her that I would prefer not to leave M. de Charlus by himself, as he seemed for some reason or other upset. The dear girl readily assented. I then asked M. de Charlus if he would like me to accompany him for a little. He also assented, but did not want to put my "cousin" to any trouble. I took a certain fond pleasure (doubtless for the last time, since I had made up

my mind to break with her) in saying to her gently, as
though she were my wife: "Go back home by yourself, I
shall see you this evening," and in hearing her, as a wife
might, give me permission to do as I thought fit and au-
thorise me, if M. de Charlus, of whom she was fond,
needed my company, to place myself at his disposal. We
proceeded, the Baron and I, he waddling obesely, his je-
suitical eyes downcast, and I following him, to a café
where we ordered some beer. I felt M. de Charlus's eyes
anxiously absorbed in some plan. Suddenly he called for
paper and ink, and began to write at an astonishing
speed. While he covered sheet after sheet, his eyes glittered with furious day-dreams.

When he had written eight pages: "May I ask you to
do me a great service?" he said to me. "You will excuse
my sealing this note. But I must. You will take a carriage,
a car if you can find one, to get there as quickly as possible. You are certain to find Morel in his quarters, where
he has gone to change. Poor boy, he tried to bluster a little when we parted, but you may be sure that his heart is
heavier than mine. You will give him this note, and, if he
asks you where you saw me, you will tell him that you
stopped at Doncières (which, for that matter, is the truth)
to see Robert, which is not quite the truth perhaps, but
that you met me with a person whom you do not know,
that I seemed to be extremely angry, that you thought
you heard something about sending seconds (I am in fact
fighting a duel tomorrow). Whatever you do, don't say
that I'm asking for him, don't make any effort to bring
him here, but if he wishes to come with you, don't prevent him from doing so. Go, my boy, it is for his own
good, you may be the means of averting a great tragedy.

While you are away, I shall write to my seconds. I have prevented you from spending the afternoon with your cousin. I hope that she will bear me no ill will for that, indeed I am sure of it. For hers is a noble soul, and I know that she is one of those rare persons who are capable of rising to the grandeur of an occasion. You must thank her on my behalf. I am personally indebted to her, and I am glad that it should be so."

I was extremely sorry for M. de Charlus; it seemed to me that Charlie might have prevented this duel, of which he was perhaps the cause, and I was revolted, if that were the case, that he should have gone off with such indifference, instead of staying to help his protector. My indignation was even greater when, on reaching the house in which Morel lodged, I recognised the voice of the violinist, who, feeling the need to give vent to his cheerfulness, was singing boisterously: "Some Sunday morning, when the slog is over!" If poor M. de Charlus, who wished me to believe, and doubtless himself believed, that Morel's heart was heavy, had heard him at that moment!

Charlie began to dance with joy when he caught sight of me. "Hallo, old boy! (excuse me addressing you like that; in this blasted military life one picks up bad habits), what a stroke of luck seeing you! I have nothing to do all evening. Do let's spend it together. We can stay here if you like, or take a boat if you prefer that, or we can have some music, it's all the same to me."

I told him that I was obliged to dine at Balbec, and he seemed anxious that I should invite him to dine there also, but I had no desire to do so.

"But if you're in such a hurry, why have you come here?"

"I've brought you a note from M. de Charlus."

At this name all his gaiety vanished; his face tensed.

"What! he can't leave me alone even here. I'm nothing but a slave. Old boy, be a sport. I'm not going to open his letter. Tell him you couldn't find me."

"Wouldn't it be better to open it? I suspect it's something serious."

"Not on your life. You've no idea what lies, what infernal tricks that old scoundrel gets up to. It's a dodge to make me go and see him. Well, I'm not going. I want to spend the evening in peace."

"But isn't there going to be a duel tomorrow?" I asked him, having assumed that he was in the know.

"A duel?" he repeated with an air of stupefaction, "I never heard a word about it. Anyhow, I don't give a damn—the dirty old beast can go and get himself done in if he likes. But wait a minute, this is interesting, I'd better look at his letter after all. You can tell him you left it here for me, in case I should come in."

While Morel was speaking, I looked with amazement at the beautiful books which M. de Charlus had given him and which littered his room. The violinist having refused to accept those labelled: "I belong to the Baron" etc., a device which he felt to be insulting to himself, as a mark of vassalage, the Baron, with the sentimental ingenuity in which his ill-starred love abounded, had substituted others, borrowed from his ancestors, but ordered from the binder according to the circumstances of a melancholy friendship. Sometimes they were terse and

confident, as *Spes mea* or *Exspectata non eludet*; sometimes merely resigned, as *J'attendrai*. Others were gallant:
Mesmes plaisir du mestre, or counselled chastity, such as
that borrowed from the family of Simiane, sprinkled with
azure towers and fleurs-de-lis, and given a fresh meaning:
Sustentant lilia turres. Others, finally, were despairing,
and made an appointment in heaven with him who had
spurned the donor upon earth: *Manet ultima coelo*; and
(finding the grapes which he had failed to reach too sour,
pretending not to have sought what he had not secured)
M. de Charlus said in yet another: *Non mortale quod opto*.
But I had no time to examine them all.

If M. de Charlus, in dashing this letter down upon
paper, had seemed to be carried away by the daemon that
was inspiring his flying pen, as soon as Morel had broken
the seal (a leopard between two roses gules, with the
motto: *Atavis et armis*) he began to read the letter as
feverishly as M. de Charlus had written it, and over those
pages covered at breakneck speed his eye ran no less
swiftly than the Baron's pen. "Good God!" he exclaimed,
"this is the last straw! But where am I to find him?
Heaven only knows where he is now." I suggested that if
he made haste he might still find him perhaps at a tavern
where he had ordered beer as a restorative. "I don't know
whether I shall be coming back," he said to his landlady,
and added to himself, "it will depend on how things turn
out." A few minutes later we reached the café. I noticed
M. de Charlus's expression at the moment when he
caught sight of me. It was as though, seeing that I had
not returned unaccompanied, he could breathe again, had
been restored to life. Being in a mood not to be deprived
of Morel's company that evening, he had pretended to

have been informed that two officers of the regiment had spoken ill of him in connexion with the violinist and that he was going to send his seconds to call upon them. Morel had foreseen the scandal—his life in the regiment made impossible—and had come at once. In doing which he had not been altogether wrong. For to make his lie more plausible, M. de Charlus had already written to two friends (one was Cottard) asking them to be his seconds. And if the violinist had not appeared, we may be certain that, mad as he was (and in order to change his sorrow into rage), M. de Charlus would have sent them with a challenge to some officer or other with whom it would have been a relief to him to fight. In the meantime M. de Charlus, remembering that he came of a race that was of purer blood than the House of France, told himself that it was really very good of him to make such a fuss about the son of a butler whose employer he would not have condescended to know. Furthermore, if he now enjoyed almost exclusively the society of riff-raff, the latter's profoundly ingrained habit of not replying to letters, of failing to keep appointments without warning you beforehand or apologising afterwards, caused him such agitation and distress when, as was often the case, his heart was involved, and the rest of the time such irritation, inconvenience and anger, that he would sometimes begin to miss the endless letters over the most trifling matters and the scrupulous punctuality of ambassadors and princes who, even if he was, alas, indifferent to their charms, gave him at any rate some sort of peace of mind. Accustomed to Morel's ways, and knowing how little hold he had over him, how incapable he was of insinuating himself into a life in which vulgar friendships conse-

crated by habit occupied too much space and time to
leave a spare hour for a forsaken, touchy, and vainly imploring nobleman, M. de Charlus was so convinced that
the musician would not come, was so afraid of having
lost him for ever by going too far, that he could barely
repress a cry of joy when he saw him appear. But, feeling
himself the victor, he was determined to dictate the terms
of peace and to extract from them such advantages as he
might.

"What are you doing here?" he said to him. "And
you?" he added, looking at me, "I told you, whatever you
did, not to bring him back with you."

"He didn't want to bring me," said Morel, turning
upon M. de Charlus, in the artlessness of his coquetry, a
conventionally mournful and languorously old-fashioned
gaze which he doubtless thought irresistible, and looking
as though he wanted to kiss the Baron and to burst into
tears. "It was I who insisted on coming in spite of him. I
come, in the name of our friendship, to implore you on
my bended knees not to commit this rash act."

M. de Charlus was wild with joy. The reaction was
almost too much for his nerves; he managed, however, to
control them.

"The friendship which you somewhat inopportunely
invoke," he replied curtly, "ought, on the contrary, to
make you give me your approval when I decide that I
cannot allow the impertinences of a fool to pass unheeded. Besides, even if I chose to yield to the entreaties
of an affection which I have known better inspired, I
should no longer be in a position to do so, since my letters to my seconds have been dispatched and I have no
doubt of their acceptance. You have always behaved to-

wards me like a young idiot and, instead of priding yourself, as you had every right to do, upon the predilection
which I had shown for you, instead of making known to
the rabble of sergeants or servants among whom the law
of military service compels you to live, what a source of
incomparable pride a friendship such as mine was to you,
you have sought to apologise for it, almost to make an idiotic merit of not being grateful enough. I know that in so
doing," he went on, in order not to let it appear how
deeply certain scenes had humiliated him, "you are guilty
merely of having let yourself be carried away by the jealousy of others. But how is it that at your age you are
childish enough (and ill-bred enough) not to have seen at
once that your election by myself and all the advantages
that must accrue from it were bound to excite jealousies,
that all your comrades, while inciting you to quarrel with
me, were plotting to take your place? I did not think it
advisable to warn you of the letters I have received in
that connexion from all those in whom you place most
trust. I scorn the overtures of those flunkeys as I scorn
their ineffectual mockery. The only person for whom I
care is yourself, since I am fond of you, but affection has
its limits and you ought to have guessed as much."

Harsh as the word flunkey might sound in the ears of
Morel, whose father had been one, but precisely because
his father had been one, the explanation of all social mis-
adventures by "jealousy," an explanation simplistic and
absurd but indestructible, which in a certain social class
never fails to "work" as infallibly as the old tricks of the
stage with a theatre audience or the threat of the clerical
peril in a parliamentary assembly, found credence with
him almost as strongly as with Françoise or with Mme de

Guermantes's servants, for whom jealousy was the sole cause of the misfortunes that beset humanity. He had no doubt that his comrades had tried to oust him from his position and was all the more wretched at the thought of this disastrous albeit imaginary duel.

"Oh, how dreadful," exclaimed Charlie. "I shall never be able to hold up my head again. But oughtn't they to see you before they go and call upon this officer?"

"I don't know. I imagine so. I've sent word to one of them that I shall be here all evening, and I shall give him his instructions."

"I hope that before he comes I can make you listen to reason. Allow me at least to stay with you," Morel pleaded tenderly.

It was all that M. de Charlus wanted. He did not however yield at once.

"You would do wrong to apply in this case the proverbial 'spare the rod and spoil the child,' for you were the child in question, and I do not intend to spare the rod, even after our quarrel, for those who have basely sought to do you injury. Until now, in response to their inquisitive insinuations, when they dared to ask me how a man like myself could associate with a gigolo of your sort, sprung from the gutter, I have answered only in the words of the motto of my La Rochefoucauld cousins: 'It is my pleasure.' I have indeed pointed out to you more than once that this pleasure was capable of becoming my chiefest pleasure, without there resulting from your arbitrary elevation any debasement of myself." And in an impulse of almost insane pride he exclaimed, raising his arms in the air: "*Tantus ab uno splendor!* To condescend is not to descend," he added in a calmer tone, after this delirious outburst of pride and joy. "I hope at least that my two adversaries, notwithstanding their inferior rank, are of a blood that I can shed without reproach. I have made certain discreet inquiries in that direction which have reassured me. If you retained a shred of gratitude towards me, you ought on the contrary to be proud to see that for your sake I am reviving the bellicose humour of my ancestors, saying like them, in the event of a fatal outcome, now that I have learned what a little rascal you are: 'Death to me is life.' "

And M. de Charlus said this sincerely, not only because of his love for Morel, but because a pugnacious instinct which he quaintly supposed to have come down to him from his ancestors filled him with such joy at the thought of fighting that he would now have regretted having to abandon this duel which he had originally concocted with the sole object of bringing Morel to heel. He had never engaged in any affair of the sort without at once preening himself on his valour and identifying himself with the illustrious Constable de Guermantes, whereas in the case of anyone else this same action of taking the field would appear to him to be of the utmost triviality.

"I am sure it will be a splendid sight," he said to us in all sincerity, dwelling upon each word. "To see Sarah Bernhardt in *L'Aiglon*, what is that but cack? Mounet-Sully in *Oedipus*, cack! At the most it assumes a certain pallid transfiguration when it is performed in the Arena of Nîmes. But what is it compared to that unimaginable spectacle, the lineal descendant of the Constable engaged in battle?" And at the mere thought of it M. de Charlus, unable to contain himself for joy, began to make passes in the air reminiscent of Molière, causing us to move our glasses prudently out of the way, and to fear that, when the swords crossed, not only the combatants but the doctor and seconds would at once be wounded. "What a tempting spectacle it would be for a painter. You who know Monsieur Elstir," he said to me, "you ought to bring him." I replied that he was not in the neighbourhood. M. de Charlus suggested that he might be summoned by telegraph. "Oh, I'm only saying it for his sake," he added in response to my silence. "It is always interesting for a master—and in my opinion he is one—to record such instances of ethnic reviviscence. And they occur perhaps once in a century."

But if M. de Charlus was enchanted at the thought of a duel which he had meant at first to be entirely fictitious, Morel was thinking with terror of the stories which, thanks to the stir that this duel would cause, might be peddled around from the regimental band all the way to the holy of holies in the Rue Bergère. Seeing in his mind's eye the "class" fully informed, he became more and more insistent with M. de Charlus, who continued to gesticulate before the intoxicating idea of a duel. He begged the Baron to allow him not to leave him until two days later, the supposed day of the duel, so that he might keep him within sight and try to make him listen to the voice of reason. So tender a proposal overcame M. de Charlus's final hesitations. He promised to try to find a way out, and to postpone his decision until the day. In this way, by not settling the matter at once, M. de Charlus knew that he could keep Charlie with him for at least two days, and take the opportunity of obtaining from him undertakings for the future in exchange for abandoning the duel, an exercise, he said, which in itself delighted him and which he would not forgo without regret. And in saying this he was quite sincere, for he had always enjoyed taking the field when it was a question of crossing swords or exchanging shots with an opponent.

Cottard arrived at length, although extremely late, for, delighted to act as second but even more terrified at the prospect, he had been obliged to halt at all the cafés or farms on the way, asking the occupants to be so kind as to show him the way to "No. 100" or "a certain place." As soon as he arrived, the Baron took him into another room, for he thought it more in keeping with the rules for Charlie and me not to be present at the interview, and he excelled in making the most ordinary room serve as a temporary throne-room or council chamber. When he was alone with Cottard he thanked him warmly, but informed him that it seemed probable that the remark which had been repeated to him had never really been made, and requested that in view of this the Doctor would be so good as to let the other second know that, barring possible complications, the incident might be regarded as closed. Now that the prospect of danger had receded, Cottard was disappointed. He was indeed tempted for a moment to give vent to anger, but he remembered that one of his masters, who had enjoyed the most successful medical career of his generation, having failed to enter the Academy at his first election by two votes only, had put a brave face on it and had gone and shaken hands with his successful rival. And so the Doctor refrained from an expression of indignation which could have made no difference, and, after murmuring, he the most timorous of men, that there were certain things

which one could not overlook, added that in this case it
was better so, that this solution delighted him. M. de
Charlus, desirous of showing his gratitude to the Doctor,
just as the Duke his brother might have straightened the
collar of my father's great-coat or rather as a duchess
might put her arm round the waist of a plebeian lady,
brought his chair close to the Doctor's, notwithstanding
the distaste which the latter inspired in him. And, not
only without any physical pleasure, but having first to
overcome a physical repulsion—as a Guermantes, not as
an invert—in taking leave of the Doctor he clasped his
hand and caressed it for a moment with the kindly affection of a master stroking his horse's nose and giving it a
lump of sugar. But Cottard, who had never allowed the
Baron to see that he had so much as heard the vaguest
rumours as to his morals, but nevertheless regarded him
in his heart of hearts as belonging to the category of "ab-
normals" (indeed, with his habitual inaccuracy in the
choice of terms, and in the most serious tone, he had said
of one of M. Verdurin's footmen: "Isn't he the Baron's
mistress?"), persons of whom he had little personal experience, imagined that this stroking of his hand was the
immediate prelude to an act of rape for the accomplishment of which, the duel being a mere pretext, he had
been enticed into a trap and led by the Baron into this
remote apartment where he was about to be forcibly outraged. Not daring to leave his chair, to which fear kept
him glued, he rolled his eyes in terror, as though he had
fallen into the hands of a savage who, for all he knew, fed
upon human flesh. At length M. de Charlus, releasing his
hand and anxious to be hospitable to the end, said:
"Won't you come and have one with us, as they say—

what in the old days used to be called a *mazagran* or a *gloria*, drinks that are no longer to be found except, as archaeological curiosities, in the plays of Labiche and the cafés of Doncières. A *gloria* would be distinctly appropriate to the place, eh? And also to the occasion, what?"

"I am President of the Anti-Alcohol League," replied Cottard. "Some country sawbones has only got to pass, and it will be said that I do not practise what I preach. *Os homini sublime dedit coelumque tueri*," he added, not that this had any bearing on the matter, but because his stock of Latin quotations was extremely limited, albeit sufficient to astound his pupils.

M. de Charlus shrugged his shoulders and led Cottard back to where we were, after exacting a promise of secrecy which was all the more important to him since, the motive for the abortive duel being purely imaginary, it must on no account reach the ears of the officer whom he had arbitrarily selected as his adversary. While the four of us sat drinking, Mme Cottard, who had been waiting for her husband outside, where M. de Charlus had seen her perfectly well but had made no effort to summon her, came in and greeted the Baron, who held out his hand to her as though to a housemaid, without rising from his chair, partly in the manner of a king receiving homage, partly as a snob who does not wish a distinctly inelegant woman to sit down at his table, partly as an egoist who enjoys being alone with his friends and does not wish to be bothered. So Mme Cottard remained standing while she talked to M. de Charlus and her husband. But, possibly because politeness, the knowledge of the "done" thing, is not the exclusive prerogative of the Guermantes, and may all of a sudden illuminate and

guide the dimmest brains, or else because, being constantly unfaithful to his wife, Cottard felt at odd moments, by way of compensation, the need to protect her
against anyone who showed disrespect to her, the Doctor
suddenly frowned, a thing I had never seen him do before, and, without consulting M. de Charlus, said in a
tone of authority: "Come, Léontine, don't stand about
like that, sit down." "But are you sure I'm not disturbing
you?" Mme Cottard inquired timidly of M. de Charlus,
who, surprised by the Doctor's tone, had made no observation. Whereupon, without giving him a second chance,
Cottard repeated with authority: "I told you to sit down."

Presently the party broke up, and then M. de Charlus said to Morel: "I conclude from this whole affair,
which has ended more happily than you deserved, that
you do not know how to behave and that, at the expiry of
your military service, I must take you back myself to
your father, like the Archangel Raphael sent by God to
the young Tobias." And the Baron smiled with an air of
magnanimity, and a joy which Morel, to whom the
prospect of being thus led home afforded no pleasure, did
not appear to share. In the exhilaration of comparing
himself to the Archangel, and Morel to the son of Tobit,
M. de Charlus no longer thought of the purpose of his
remark, which had been to explore the ground to see
whether, as he hoped, Morel would consent to come with
him to Paris. Intoxicated by his love, or by his self-love,
the Baron did not see or pretended not to see the violinist's wry grimace, for, leaving him by himself in the café,
he said to me with a proud smile: "Did you notice how,
when I compared him to the son of Tobit, he became
wild with joy? That was because, being extremely intelli-

gent, he at once understood that the Father with whom he was henceforth to live was not his father after the flesh, who must be some horrible mustachioed valet, but his spiritual father, that is to say Myself. What a triumph for him! How proudly he reared his head! What joy he felt at having understood me! I am sure that he will now repeat day after day: 'O God who didst give the blessed Archangel Raphael as *guide* to thy servant Tobias upon a long journey, grant to us, thy servants, that we may ever be protected by him and armed with his succour.' I did not even need," added the Baron, firmly convinced that he would one day sit before the throne of God, "to tell him that I was the heavenly messenger. He realised it for himself, and was struck dumb with joy!" And M. de Charlus (whom joy, on the contrary, did not deprive of speech), heedless of the passers-by who turned to stare at him, assuming that he must be a lunatic, cried out alone and at the top of his voice, raising his hands in the air: "Alleluia!"

This reconciliation gave but a temporary respite to M. de Charlus's torments. Often, when Morel had gone on manoeuvres too far away for M. de Charlus to be able to go and visit him or to send me to talk to him, he would write the Baron desperate and affectionate letters, in which he assured him that he would have to put an end to his life because, owing to a ghastly affair, he needed twenty-five thousand francs. He did not mention what this ghastly affair was, and had he done so, it would doubtless have been an invention. As far as the money was concerned, M. de Charlus would willingly have sent it had he not felt that it would make Charlie independent of him and free to receive the favours of someone else.

And so he refused, and his telegrams had the dry, cutting tone of his voice. When he was certain of their effect, he longed for Morel to fall out with him for ever, for, knowing very well that it was the contrary that would happen, he could not help dwelling upon all the drawbacks that would be revived with this inevitable liaison. But if no answer came from Morel, he lay awake all night, had not a moment's peace, so great is the number of the things of which we live in ignorance, and of the deep, inner realities that remain hidden from us. Then he would think up every conceivable supposition as to the enormity which had put Morel in need of twenty-five thousand francs, would give it every possible form, attach to it, one after another, a variety of proper names. I believe that at such moments M. de Charlus (in spite of the fact that his snobbishness, which was now diminishing, had already been overtaken if not outstripped by his increasing curiosity as to the ways of the people) must have recalled with a certain nostalgia the graceful, many-coloured whirl of the fashionable gatherings at which the most charming men and women sought his company only for the disinterested pleasure that it afforded them, where nobody would have dreamed of "doing him down," of inventing a "ghastly affair" because of which one is prepared to take one's life if one does not at once receive twenty-five thousand francs. I believe that then, and perhaps because he had after all remained more "Combray" at heart than myself, and had grafted a feudal dignity on to his Germanic arrogance, he must have felt that one cannot with impunity lose one's heart to a servant, that the people are by no means the same thing as society: in short he did not "trust the people" as I have always done.

The next station on the little railway, Maineville, reminds me of an incident in which Morel and M. de
Charlus were concerned. Before I speak of it, I ought to
mention that the halt of the train at Maineville (when one
was escorting to Balbec an elegant new arrival who, to
avoid giving trouble, preferred not to stay at La
Raspelière) was the occasion of scenes less painful than
that which I shall describe in a moment. The new arrival,
having his light luggage with him in the train, generally
found that the Grand Hotel was rather too far away, but,
as there was nothing before Balbec except small beach-
resorts with uncomfortable villas, had yielded to a preference for luxury and well-being and resigned himself to
the long journey when, as the train came to a standstill at
Maineville, he suddenly saw looming up in front of him
the Palace, which he could never have suspected of being
a house of ill fame. "Well, don't let us go any further,"
he would invariably say to Mme Cottard, a woman well-
known for her practical judgment and sound advice.
"There's the very thing I want. What's the point of going on to Balbec, where I certainly shan't find anything
better. I can tell at a glance that it has every modern
comfort, and I can perfectly well invite Mme Verdurin
there, for I intend, in return for her hospitality, to give a
few little parties in her honour. She won't have so far to
come as if I stay at Balbec. It seems to me the very place
for her, and for your wife, my dear Professor. There are
bound to be reception rooms, and we shall bring the
ladies there. Between you and me, I can't imagine why
Mme Verdurin didn't come and settle here instead of taking La Raspelière. It's far healthier than an old house like
La Raspelière, which is bound to be damp, and isn't

clean either; they have no hot water laid on, one can
never get a wash. Maineville strikes me as being far more
agreeable. Mme Verdurin could have played her role as
hostess here to perfection. However, tastes differ; anyhow
I intend to remain here. Mme Cottard, won't you come
along with me? We shall have to be quick, of course, for
the train will be starting again in a minute. You can pilot
me through this establishment, which you doubtless
know inside out, since you must often have visited it. It's
an ideal setting for you." The others would have the
greatest difficulty in making the unfortunate new arrival
hold his tongue, and still more in preventing him from
leaving the train, while he, with the obstinacy which often arises from a gaffe, would insist, would gather his
luggage together and refuse to listen to a word until they
had assured him that neither Mme Verdurin nor Mme
Cottard would ever come to call upon him there. "Anyhow, I'm going to take up residence there. Mme Verdurin can write to me if she wishes to see me."

The incident that concerns Morel was of a more
highly specialised order. There were others, but I confine
myself at present, as the little train halts and the porter
calls out "Doncières," "Grattevast," "Maineville" etc., to
noting down the particular memory that the watering-
place or garrison town recalls to me. I have already mentioned Maineville (*media villa*) and the importance that it
had acquired from that luxurious house of prostitution
which had recently been built there, not without arousing
futile protests from the local mothers. But before I proceed to say why Maineville is associated in my memory
with Morel and M. de Charlus, I must mention the disproportion (which I shall have occasion to examine more

thoroughly later on) between the importance that Morel
attached to keeping certain hours free, and the triviality
of the occupations to which he pretended to devote them,
this same disproportion recurring amid the explanations
of another sort which he gave to M. de Charlus. He who
played the disinterested artist for the Baron's benefit (and
might do so with impunity in view of the generosity of
his patron), when he wished to have the evening to himself in order to give a lesson, etc., never failed to add to
his excuse the following words, uttered with a smile of
cupidity: "Besides, there may be forty francs to be got
out of it. That's not to be sneezed at. You must let me
go, because as you see it's in my interest. Damn it all, I
haven't got a regular income like you, I have my way to
make in the world, it's a chance of earning a little
money." In professing his anxiety to give his lesson,
Morel was not altogether insincere. For one thing, it is
false to say that money has no colour. A new way of
earning it gives a fresh lustre to coins that are tarnished
with use. Had he really gone out to give a lesson, it is
probable that a couple of louis handed to him as he left
the house by a girl pupil would have produced a different
effect on him from a couple of louis coming from the
hand of M. de Charlus. Besides, for a couple of louis the
richest of men would travel miles, which become leagues
when one is the son of a valet. But frequently M. de
Charlus had his doubts as to the reality of the violin lesson, doubts which were increased by the fact that often
the musician would offer pretexts of another sort, entirely
disinterested from the material point of view, and at the
same time absurd. Thus Morel could not help presenting
a picture of his life, but one that was intentionally, and

unintentionally too, so obscured that only certain parts of it were distinguishable. For a whole month he placed himself at M. de Charlus's disposal on condition that he might keep his evenings free, for he was anxious to put in a regular attendance at a course of algebra. Come and see M. de Charlus after his classes? Oh, that was impossible; the classes sometimes went on very late. "Even after two o'clock in the morning?" the Baron asked. "Sometimes." "But you can learn algebra just as easily from a book." "More easily, for I don't get very much out of the lessons." "Well then! Besides, algebra can't be of any use to you." "I like it. It soothes my nerves." "It cannot be algebra that makes him ask for night leave," M. de Charlus said to himself. "Can he be working for the police?" In any case Morel, whatever objection might be made, reserved certain evening hours, whether for algebra or for the violin. On one occasion it was for neither, but for the Prince de Guermantes who, having come down for a few days to that part of the coast to pay the Princesse de Luxembourg a visit, met the musician without knowing who he was or being known to him either, and offered him fifty francs to spend the night with him in the brothel at Maineville; a twofold pleasure for Morel, in the remuneration received from M. de Guermantes and in the delight of being surrounded by women who would flaunt their tawny breasts uncovered. In some way or other M. de Charlus got wind of what had occurred and of the place appointed, but did not discover the name of the seducer. Mad with jealousy, and in the hope of identifying the latter, he telegraphed to Jupien, who arrived two days later, and when, early the following week, Morel announced that he would again be absent, the Baron asked Jupien if he would undertake to bribe the woman who kept the establishment to hide them in some place where they could witness what occurred. "That's all right. I'll see to it, dearie," Jupien assured the Baron. It is hard to imagine the extent to which this anxiety agitated the Baron's mind, and by the very fact of doing so had momentarily enriched it. Love can thus be responsible for veritable geological upheavals of the mind. In that of M. de Charlus, which a few days earlier had resembled a plain so uniform that as far as the eye could reach it would have been impossible to make out an idea rising above the level surface, there had suddenly sprung into being, hard as stone, a range of mountains, but mountains as elaborately carved as if some sculptor, instead of quarrying and carting away the marble, had chiselled it on the spot, in which there writhed in vast titanic groups Fury, Jealousy, Curiosity, Envy, Hatred, Suffering, Pride, Terror and Love.

Meanwhile the evening on which Morel was to be absent had come. Jupien's mission had proved successful. He and the Baron were to be there about eleven o'clock, and would be put in a place of concealment. When they were still three streets away from this luxurious house of prostitution (to which people came from all the fashionable resorts in the neighbourhood), M. de Charlus had begun to walk on tiptoe, to disguise his voice, to beg Jupien not to speak so loud, lest Morel should hear them from inside. But, on creeping stealthily into the entrance hall, the Baron, who was not accustomed to places of the sort, found himself, to his terror and amazement, in a gathering more clamorous than the Stock Exchange or a saleroom. It was in vain that he begged the maids who

gathered round him to moderate their voices; in any case
their voices were drowned by the stream of auctioneering
cries from an old "madame" in a very brown wig with
the grave, wrinkled face of a notary or a Spanish priest,
who kept shouting in a thunderous voice, ordering the
doors to be alternately opened and shut, like a policeman
regulating the flow of traffic: "Take this gentleman to
number 28, the Spanish room." "Let no more in." "Open
the door again, these gentlemen want Mademoiselle
Noémie. She's expecting them in the Persian parlour."
M. de Charlus was as terrified as a countryman who has
to cross the boulevards; while, to take a simile infinitely
less sacrilegious than the subject represented on the capi-
tals of the porch of the old church of Couliville, the
voices of the young maids repeated in a lower tone, unceasingly, the madame's orders, like the catechisms that
one hears schoolchildren chanting beneath the echoing
vaults of a country church. Alarmed though he was,
M. de Charlus, who in the street had trembled lest he
should be heard, convinced in his own mind that Morel
was at the window, was perhaps not so frightened after
all in the din of those huge staircases on which one realised that from the rooms nothing could be seen. Coming at last to the end of his calvary, he found Mlle
Noémie, who was to conceal him with Jupien but began
by shutting him up in a sumptuously furnished Persian
sitting-room from which he could see nothing at all. She
told him that Morel had asked for some orangeade, and
that as soon as he was served the two visitors would be
taken to a room with a transparent panel. In the meantime, as she was wanted, she promised them, like a fairy
godmother, that to help them to pass the time she was

going to send them a "clever little lady." For she herself
had to go. The clever little lady wore a Persian wrapper,
which she wanted to remove. M. de Charlus begged her
to do nothing of the sort, and she rang for champagne
which cost 40 francs a bottle. Morel, during this time,
was in fact with the Prince de Guermantes; he had, for
form's sake, pretended to go into the wrong room by
mistake, and had entered one in which there were two
women, who had made haste to leave the two gentlemen
undisturbed. M. de Charlus knew nothing of this, but
stormed with rage, tried to open the doors, and sent for
Mlle Noémie, who, hearing the clever little lady give
M. de Charlus certain information about Morel which
was not in accordance with what she herself had told
Jupien, banished her promptly and presently sent, as a
substitute for the clever little lady, a "dear little lady"
who also showed them nothing but told them how respectable the house was and called, like her predecessor,
for champagne. The Baron, foaming with rage, sent again
for Mlle Noémie, who said to them: "Yes, it is taking
rather long, the ladies are doing poses, he doesn't look as
if he wanted to do anything." Finally, yielding to the
promises and threats of the Baron, Mlle Noémie went
away with an air of irritation, assuring them that they
would not be kept waiting more than five minutes. The
five minutes stretched to an hour, after which Noémie
came and escorted an enraged Charlus and a disconsolate
Jupien on tiptoe to a door which stood ajar, telling them:
"You'll see splendidly from here. However, it's not very
interesting just at present. He's with three ladies, and
he's telling them about his army life." At length the
Baron was able to see through the cleft of the door and

also the reflexion in the mirrors beyond. But a mortal terror forced him to lean back against the wall. It was indeed Morel that he saw before him, but, as though the pagan mysteries and magic spells still existed, it was rather the shade of Morel, Morel embalmed, not even Morel restored to life like Lazarus, an apparition of Morel, a phantom of Morel, Morel "walking" or "called up" in this room (in which the walls and couches everywhere repeated the emblems of sorcery), that was visible a few feet away from him, in profile. Morel had, as happens to the dead, lost all his colour; among these women, with whom one might have expected him to be making merry, he remained livid, fixed in an artificial immobility; to drink the glass of champagne that stood before him, his listless arm tried in vain to reach out, and dropped back again. One had the impression of that ambiguous state implied by a religion which speaks of immortality but means thereby something that does not exclude extinction. The women were plying him with questions: "You see," Mlle Noémie whispered to the Baron, "they're talking to him about his army life. It's amusing, isn't it?"—here she laughed—"You're glad you came? He's calm, isn't he," she added, as though she were speaking of a dying man. The women's questions came thick and fast, but Morel, inanimate, had not the strength to answer them. Even the miracle of a whispered word did not occur. M. de Charlus hesitated for barely a moment before he grasped what had really happened, namely that—whether from clumsiness on Jupien's part when he had called to make the arrangements, or from the expansive power of secrets once confided which ensures that they are never kept, or from the natural indis-

cretion of these women, or from their fear of the police—
Morel had been told that two gentlemen had paid a large
sum to be allowed to spy on him, unseen hands had spir-
ited away the Prince de Guermantes, metamorphosed into
three women, and the unhappy Morel had been placed,
trembling, paralysed with fear, in such a position that if
M. de Charlus could scarcely see him, he, terrified,
speechless, not daring to lift his glass for fear of letting it
fall, had a perfect view of the Baron.

The story, as it happened, ended no more happily for
the Prince de Guermantes. When he had been sent away
so that M. de Charlus should not see him, furious at his
disappointment without suspecting who was responsible
for it, he had implored Morel, still without letting him
know who he was, to meet him the following night in
the tiny villa which he had taken and which, despite the
shortness of his projected stay in it, he had, obeying the
same quirkish habit which we have already observed in
Mme de Villeparisis, decorated with a number of family
keepsakes so that he might feel more at home. And so,
next day, Morel, constantly looking over his shoulder for
fear of being followed and spied upon by M. de Charlus,
had finally entered the villa, having failed to observe any
suspicious passer-by. He was shown into the sitting-room
by a valet, who told him that he would inform "Monsieur" (his master had warned him not to utter the word
"Prince" for fear of arousing suspicions). But when Morel
found himself alone, and went to the mirror to see that
his forelock was not disarranged, he felt as though he was
the victim of a hallucination. The photographs on the
mantelpiece (which the violinist recognised, for he had
seen them in M. de Charlus's room) of the Princesse de

Guermantes, the Duchesse de Luxembourg and Mme de Villeparisis, left him at first petrified with fright. At the same moment he caught sight of the photograph of M. de Charlus, which was placed a little behind the rest. The Baron seemed to be transfixing him with a strange, unblinking stare. Mad with terror, Morel, recovering from his preliminary stupor and no longer doubting that this was a trap into which M. de Charlus had led him in order to put his fidelity to the test, leapt down the steps of the villa four at a time and set off along the road as fast as his legs would carry him, and when the Prince (thinking he had put a casual acquaintance through the required period of waiting, not without wondering whether the whole thing was entirely prudent and whether the individual in question might not be dangerous) came into the sitting-room, he found nobody there. In vain did he and his valet, fearful of burglary, and armed with revolvers, search the whole house, which was not large, the basement, and every corner of the garden, the companion of whose presence he had been certain had completely vanished. He met him several times in the course of the week that followed. But on each occasion it was Morel, the dangerous customer, who turned tail and fled, as though the Prince were more dangerous still. Stubborn in his suspicions, Morel never outgrew them, and even in Paris the sight of the Prince de Guermantes was enough to make him take to his heels. Thus was M. de Charlus protected from an infidelity which filled him with despair, and avenged without ever realising that he had been, still less how.

But already my memories of what I was told about all this are giving place to others, for the T. S. N., resuming its slow crawl, continues to set down or take up passengers at the succeeding stations.

At Grattevast, where his sister lived and where he had been spending the afternoon, M. Pierre de Verjus, Comte de Crécy (who was called simply the Comte de Crécy), would occasionally appear—a gentleman without means but of extreme distinction, whom I had come to know through the Cambremers, although he was by no means intimate with them. As he was reduced to an extremely modest, almost a penurious existence, I felt that a cigar and a drink were things that gave him so much pleasure that I formed the habit, on the days when I could not see Albertine, of inviting him to Balbec. A man of great refinement who expressed himself beautifully, with snow-white hair and a pair of charming blue eyes, he generally spoke, unassumingly and very delicately, of the comforts of life in a country house, which he had evidently known from experience, and also of pedigrees. On my inquiring what was engraved on his ring, he told me with a modest smile: "It is a sprig of verjuice grapes." And he added with degustatory relish: "Our arms are a sprig of verjuice grapes—symbolic, since my name is Verjus—slipped and leaved vert." But I fancy that he would have been disappointed if at Balbec I had offered him nothing better to drink than verjuice. He liked the most expensive wines, doubtless because he was deprived of them, because of his profound knowledge of what he was deprived of, because he had a taste for them, perhaps also because he had an exorbitant thirst. And so when I invited him to dine at Balbec, he would order the meal with a refined skill but eat a little too much, and drink copiously, making the waiters warm the wines that needed warming and place those that needed cooling upon ice. Before dinner and after, he would give the right date or number for a port or an old brandy, as he would have given the date of the creation of a marquisate which was not generally known but with which he was no less familiar.

As I was in Aimé's eyes a favoured customer, he was delighted that I should give these special dinners and would shout to the waiters: "Quick, lay number 25 for me," as though the table were for his own use. And, as the language of head waiters is not quite the same as that of section heads, assistants, boys, and so forth, when the time came for me to ask for the bill he would say to the waiter who had served us, making a continuous, soothing gesture with the back of his hand, as though he were trying to calm a horse that was ready to take the bit in its teeth: "Don't overdo it" (in adding up the bill), "gently does it." Then, as the waiter withdrew with this guidance, Aimé, fearing lest his recommendations might not be carried out to the letter, would call him back: "Here, let me make it out." And as I told him not to bother: "It's one of my principles that we ought never, as the saying is, to sting a customer." As for the manager, since my guest was attired simply, always in the same clothes, which were rather threadbare (albeit nobody would so well have practised the art of dressing expensively, like one of Balzac's dandies, had he possessed the means), he confined himself, out of respect for me, to watching from a distance to see that everything was all right, and beckoning to someone to place a wedge under one leg of the table which was not steady. This is not to say that he was not qualified, though he concealed his beginnings as a scullion, to lend a hand like anyone else. It required some exceptional circumstance nevertheless to induce him one day to carve the turkeys himself. I was out, but I heard afterwards that he carved them with a sacerdotal majesty, surrounded, at a respectful distance from the service-table, by a ring of waiters who, endeavouring thereby not so much to learn the art as to curry favour with him, stood gaping in open-mouthed admiration. The manager, however, as he plunged his knife with solemn deliberation into the flanks of his victims, from which he no more de-flected his eyes, filled with a sense of his high function, than if he were expecting to read some augury therein, was totally oblivious of their presence. The hierophant was not even conscious of my absence. When he heard of it, he was distressed: "What, you didn't see me carving the turkeys myself?" I replied that having failed, so far, to see Rome, Venice, Siena, the Prado, the Dresden gallery, the Indies, Sarah in *Phèdre*, I had learned to re-sign myself, and that I would add his carving of turkeys to my list. The comparison with the dramatic art (Sarah in *Phèdre*) was the only one that he seemed to under-stand, for he had learned through me that on days of gala performances the elder Coquelin had accepted beginners' roles, even those of characters who had only a single line or none at all. "All the same, I'm sorry for your sake. When shall I be carving again? It will need some great event, it will need a war." (It needed the armistice, in fact.) From that day onwards, the calendar was changed, and time was reckoned thus: "That was the day after the day I carved the turkeys myself." "It was exactly a week after the manager carved the turkeys himself." And so this prosectomy furnished, like the Nativity of Christ or the Hegira, the starting point for a calendar different from the rest, but neither so extensively adopted nor so long observed.

The sadness of M. de Crécy's life was due, just as much as to his no longer keeping horses and a succulent table, to his mixing exclusively with people who were capable of supposing that Cambremers and Guermantes were one and the same thing. When he saw that I knew that Legrandin, who had now taken to calling himself Legrand de Méséglise, had no sort of right to that name, being moreover lit up by the wine that he was drinking, he burst into a sort of transport of joy. His sister would say to me with a knowing look: "My brother is never so happy as when he has a chance to talk to you." He felt indeed that he was alive now that he had discovered somebody who knew the unimportance of the Cambremers and the grandeur of the Guermantes, somebody for whom the social universe existed. So, after the burning of all the libraries on the face of the globe and the emergence of a race entirely unlettered, might an old Latin scholar recover his confidence in life if he heard somebody quoting a line of Horace. Hence, if he never left the train without saying to me: "When is our next little reunion?", it was not only with the avidity of a parasite but with the relish of a scholar, and because he regarded our Balbec agapes as an opportunity for talking about subjects which were precious to him and of which he was never able to talk to anyone else, and in that sense analogous to those dinners at which the Society of Bibliophiles assembles on certain specified dates round the particularly succulent board of the Union Club. He was extremely modest so far as his own family was concerned, and it was not from M. de Crécy himself that I learned that it was a very noble family and an authentic branch transplanted to France of the English family which bears the title of Crecy. When I learned that he was a real Crécy, I told him that one of Mme de Guermantes's nieces had married an American named Charles Crecy, and said that I did not suppose there was any connexion between them. "None," he said. "Any more than—not, of course, that my family is so distinguished—heaps of Americans who are called Montgomery, Berry, Chandos or Capel have with the families of Pembroke, Buckingham or Essex, or with the Duc de Berry." I thought more than once of telling him, as a joke, that I knew Mme Swann, who as a courtesan had been known at one time by the name Odette de Crécy; but although the Duc d'Alençon could not have been offended if one spoke to him of Emilienne d'Alençon, I did not feel that I was on sufficiently intimate terms with M. de Crécy to carry the joke so far. "He comes of a very great family," M. de Montsurvent said to me one day. "His patronymic is Saylor." And he went on to say that on the wall of his old castle above Incarville, which was now almost uninhabitable and which he, although born very rich, was now too impoverished to put in repair, was still to be read the old motto of the family. I thought this motto very fine, whether applied to the impatience of a predatory race ensconced in that eyrie from which its members must have swooped down in the past, or, at the present day, to its contemplation of its own decline, awaiting the approach of death in that towering, grim retreat. It is in this double sense indeed that this motto plays upon the name Saylor, in the words: "*Ne sçais l'heure.*"

At Hermenonville M. de Chevregny would sometimes get in, a gentleman whose name, Brichot told us,
signified like that of Mgr de Cabrières "a place where
goats assemble." He was related to the Cambremers, for
which reason, and from a false appreciation of elegance,
the latter often invited him to Féterne, but only when
they had no other guests to dazzle. Living all the year
round at Beausoleil, M. de Chevregny had remained
more provincial than they. And so when he went for a
few weeks to Paris, there was not a moment to waste if
he was to "see everything" in the time; so much so that
sometimes, a little dazed by the number of spectacles too
rapidly digested, when he was asked if he had seen a particular play he would find that he was no longer absolutely sure. But this uncertainty was rare, for he had that
detailed knowledge of Paris only to be found in people
who seldom go there. He advised me which of the "nov-
elties" I ought to see ("It's well worth your while"), regarding them however solely from the point of view of
the pleasant evening that they might help to spend, and
so completely ignoring the aesthetic point of view as
never to suspect that they might indeed occasionally constitute a "novelty" in the history of art. So it was that,
speaking of everything in the same tone, he told us: "We
went once to the Opéra-Comique, but the show there
isn't up to much. It's called *Pelléas et Mélisande*. It's trivial. Périer always acts well, but it's better to see him in
something else. At the Gymnase, on the other hand,
they're doing *La Châtelaine*. We went back to it twice;
don't miss it, whatever you do, it's well worth seeing; besides, it's played to perfection; there's Frévalles, Marie
Magnier, Baron fils"; and he went on to cite the names of

actors of whom I had never heard, and without prefixing Monsieur, Madame or Mademoiselle like the Duc de Guermantes, who used to speak in the same ceremoniously contemptuous tone of the "songs of Mademoiselle Yvette Guilbert" and the "experiments of Monsieur Charcot." This was not M. de Chevregny's way: he said "Cornaglia and Dehelly" as he might have said "Voltaire and Montesquieu." For in him, with regard to actors as to everything that was Parisian, the aristocrat's desire to show his disdain was overcome by the provincial's desire to appear on familiar terms with everyone.

Immediately after the first dinner-party that I had attended at La Raspelière with what was still called at Féterne "the young couple," although M. and Mme de Cambremer were no longer, by any means, in their first youth, the old Marquise had written me one of those letters which one can pick out by their handwriting from among a thousand. She said to me: "Bring your delicious—charming—nice cousin. It will be a delight, a pleasure," failing always to observe the sequence that the recipient of her letter would naturally have expected, and with such unerring dexterity that I finally changed my mind as to the nature of these diminuendos, decided that they were deliberate, and found in them the same depravity of taste—transposed into the social key—that drove Sainte-Beuve to upset all the normal relations between words, to alter any expression that was at all habitual. Two methods, taught probably by different masters, clashed in this epistolary style, the second making Mme de Cambremer redeem the monotony of her multiple adjectives by employing them in a descending scale, and avoiding an ending on the common chord. On the other hand, I was inclined to see in these inverse gradations, no longer a stylistic refinement, as when they were the hand-iwork of the dowager Marquise, but a stylistic awkward-ness whenever they were employed by the Marquis her son or by her lady cousins. For throughout the family, to quite a remote degree of kinship and in admiring imita-tion of Aunt Zélia, the rule of the three adjectives was held in great favour, as was a certain enthusiastic way of catching your breath when talking. An imitation that had passed into the blood, moreover; and whenever, in the family, a little girl from her earliest childhood took to stopping short while she was talking to swallow her saliva, her parents would say: "She takes after Aunt Zélia," would sense that as she grew older her upper lip would soon tend to be shadowed by a faint moustache, and would make up their minds to cultivate her in-evitable talent for music.

It was not long before the relations of the Cambre-mers with Mme Verdurin were less satisfactory than with myself, for different reasons. They felt they must invite her to dine. The "young" Marquise said to me contemp-tuously: "I don't see why we shouldn't invite that woman. In the country one meets anybody, it's of no great consequence." But being at heart considerably awed, they frequently consulted me as to how they should put into effect their desire to make a polite ges-ture. Since they had invited Albertine and myself to dine with some friends of Saint-Loup, smart people of the neighbourhood who owned the château of Gourville and represented a little more than the cream of Norman soci-ety, to which Mme Verdurin, while pretending to despise it, was partial, I advised the Cambremers to invite the

Mistress to meet them. But the lord and lady of Féterne, in their fear (so timorous were they) of offending their noble friends, or else (so ingenuous were they) of the possibility that M. and Mme Verdurin might be bored by people who were not intellectual, or yet again (since they were impregnated with a spirit of routine which experience had not fertilised) of mixing different kinds of people and committing a solecism, declared that it would not "work," that they "wouldn't hit it off together," and that it would be much better to keep Mme Verdurin (whom they would invite with all her little group) for another evening. For this coming evening—the smart one, to meet Saint-Loup's friends—they invited nobody from the little nucleus but Morel, in order that M. de Charlus might indirectly be informed of the brilliant people whom they had to their house, and also that the musician might help to entertain their guests, for he was to be asked to bring his violin. They threw in Cottard as well, because M. de Cambremer declared that he had some "go" about him and would "go down well" at a dinner-party; besides, it might turn out useful to be on friendly terms with a doctor if they should ever have anybody ill in the house. But they invited him by himself, so as not to "start anything with the wife." Mme Verdurin was outraged when she heard that two members of the little group had been invited without herself to dine "informally" at Féterne. She dictated to the Doctor, whose first impulse had been to accept, a stiff reply in which he said: "We are dining that evening with Mme Verdurin," a plural intended to teach the Cambremers a lesson and to show them that he was not detachable from Mme Cottard. As for Morel, Mme Verdurin had no need to draw up for him an impolite course of behaviour, for he adopted one of his own accord, for the following reason. If he preserved with regard to M. de Charlus, insofar as his pleasures were concerned, an independence which distressed the Baron, we have seen that the latter's influence had made itself felt more strongly in other areas, and that he had for instance enlarged the young virtuoso's knowledge of music and purified his style. But it was still, at this point in our story at least, only an influence. At the same time there was one domain where anything that M. de Charlus might say was blindly accepted and acted upon by Morel. Blindly and foolishly, for not only were M. de Charlus's instructions false, but, even had they been valid in the case of a nobleman, when applied literally by Morel they became grotesque. The domain in which Morel was becoming so credulous and obeyed his master with such docility was the social domain. The violinist, who before meeting M. de Charlus had had no notion of society, had taken literally the brief and arrogant sketch of it that the Baron had outlined for him: "There are a certain number of outstanding families," M. de Charlus had told him, "first and foremost the Guermantes, who claim fourteen alliances with the House of France, which is flattering to the House of France if anything, for it was to Aldonce de Guermantes and not to Louis the Fat, his younger half-brother, that the throne of France should have passed. Under Louis XIV, we 'draped' at the death of Monsieur, as having the same grandmother as the king. A long way below the Guermantes, one may however mention the La Trémoïlles, descended from the Kings of Naples and the Counts of Poitiers; the d'Uzès, not very old as a family but the oldest peers; the Luynes, of very recent origin but with the lustre of distinguished marriages; the Choiseuls, the Harcourts, the La Rochefoucaulds. Add to these the Noailles (notwithstanding the Comte de Toulouse), the Montesquious and the Castellanes, and, I think I am right in saying, those are all. As for all the little people who call themselves Marquis de Cambremerde or de Gotoblazes, there is no difference between them and the humblest rookie in your regiment. Whether you go and do wee-wee at the Countess Cack's or cack at the Baroness Wee-wee's, it's exactly the same, you will have compromised your reputation and have used a shitty rag instead of toilet paper. Which is unsavoury."

Morel had piously taken in this history lesson, which was perhaps a trifle cursory; he looked upon these matters as though he were himself a Guermantes and hoped that he might some day have an opportunity of meeting the false La Tour d'Auvergnes in order to let them see, by the contemptuous way he shook hands with them, that he did not take them very seriously. As for the Cambremers, here was his very chance to prove to them that they were no better than "the humblest in his regiment." He did not answer their invitation, and on the evening of the dinner declined at the last moment by telegram, as pleased with himself as if he had behaved like a Prince of the Blood. It must be added here that it is impossible to imagine the degree to which, in a more general sense, M. de Charlus could be intolerable, meddlesome and even—he who was so clever—stupid, in all the circumstances where the flaws in his character came into play. We may say indeed that these flaws are like an intermittent disease of the mind. Who has not observed the phe-

nomenon in women, and even in men, endowed with remarkable intelligence but afflicted with nervous irritability? When they are happy, calm, satisfied with their
surroundings, we marvel at their precious gifts; it is the
truth, literally, that speaks through their lips. A touch of
headache, the slightest prick to their self-esteem, is
enough to alter everything. The luminous intelligence,
become brusque, convulsive and shrunken, no longer reflects anything but an irritable, suspicious, teasing self,
doing everything possible to displease.

The anger of the Cambremers was extreme; and in
the meantime other incidents brought about a certain tension in their relations with the little clan. As we were returning, the Cottards, Charlus, Brichot, Morel and I,
from a dinner at La Raspelière one evening after the
Cambremers, who had been to lunch with friends at
Harambouville, had accompanied us for part of our outward journey, "Since you're so fond of Balzac, and can
find examples of him in the society of today," I had remarked to M. de Charlus, "you must feel that those
Cambremers come straight out of the Scènes de la vie de
province." But M. de Charlus, for all the world as though
he had been their friend and I had offended him by my
remark, at once cut me short: "You say that because the
wife is superior to the husband," he remarked drily. "Oh,
I wasn't suggesting that she was the Muse du département,
or Mme de Bargeton, although . . ." M. de Charlus
again interrupted me: "Say rather, Mme de Mortsauf."
The train stopped and Brichot got out. "Didn't you see
us making signs to you? You're incorrigible." "What do
you mean?" "Why, haven't you noticed that Brichot is
madly in love with Mme de Cambremer?" I could see

from the attitude of the Cottards and Charlie that there was not a shadow of doubt about this in the little nucleus. I thought that it must be malice on their part. "What, you didn't notice how distressed he became when you mentioned her," went on M. de Charlus, who liked to show that he had experience of women, and spoke of the sentiment they inspire as naturally as if it was what he himself habitually felt. But a certain equivocally paternal tone in addressing all young men—in spite of his exclusive affection for Morel—gave the lie to the womanising views which he expressed. "Oh! these children," he said in a shrill, mincing, sing-song voice, "one has to teach them everything, they're as innocent as newborn babes, they can't even tell when a man is in love with a woman. I was more fly than that at your age," he added, for he liked to use the expressions of the underworld, perhaps because they appealed to him, perhaps so as not to appear, by avoiding them, to admit that he consorted with people whose current vocabulary they were. A few days later, I was obliged to bow to the facts and acknowledge that Brichot was enamoured of the Marquise. Unfortunately he accepted several invitations to lunch with her. Mme Verdurin decided that it was time to put a stop to these proceedings. Quite apart from what she saw as the importance of such an intervention for the politics of the little nucleus, she had developed an ever-keener taste for remonstrations of this sort and the dramas to which they gave rise, a taste which idleness breeds just as much in the bourgeoisie as in the aristocracy. It was a day of great excitement at La Raspelière when Mme Verdurin was seen to disappear for a whole hour with Brichot, whom (it transpired) she proceeded to inform that Mme de Cambremer cared nothing for him, that he was the laughing-stock of her drawing-room, that he would be dishonouring his old age and compromising his situation in the academic world. She went so far as to refer in touching terms to the laundress with whom he lived in Paris, and to their little girl. She won the day; Brichot ceased to go to Féterne, but his grief was such that for two days it was thought that he would lose his sight altogether, and in any case his disease had taken a leap forward from which it never retreated. In the meantime, the Cambremers, who were furious with Morel, deliberately invited M. de Charlus on one occasion without him. Receiving no reply from the Baron, they began to fear that they had committed a gaffe, and, deciding that rancour was a bad counsellor, wrote somewhat belatedly to Morel, an ineptitude which made M. de Charlus smile by proving to him the extent of his power. "You shall answer for us both that I accept," he said to Morel. When the evening of the dinner came, the party assembled in the great drawing-room of Féterne. In reality, the Cambremers were giving this dinner for those fine flowers of fashion M. and Mme Féré. But they were so afraid of displeasing M. de Charlus that although she had got to know the Férés through M. de Chevregny, Mme de Cambremer went into a frenzy of alarm when, on the day of the dinner-party, she saw him arrive to pay a call on them at Féterne. She thought up every imaginable excuse for sending him back to Beausoleil as quickly as possible, not quickly enough, however, for him not to run into the Férés in the courtyard, who were as shocked to see him dismissed like this as he himself was ashamed. But, whatever happened, the Cambremers wished to spare M. de

Charlus the sight of M. de Chevregny, whom they
judged to be provincial because of certain little points
which can be overlooked within the family but have to be
taken into account in front of strangers, who are in fact
the last people in the world to notice them. But we do
not like to display to them relatives who have remained at
the stage which we ourselves have struggled to outgrow.
As for M. and Mme Féré, they were in the highest degree what is described as "out of the top drawer." In the
eyes of those who so defined them, no doubt the Guermantes, the Rohans and many others were also out of the
top drawer, but their name made it unnecessary to say so.
Since not everyone was aware of the exalted birth of
M. Féré's mother, or of Mme Féré's, or of the extraordinarily exclusive circle in which she and her husband
moved, when you mentioned their name you invariably
added by way of explanation that they were "out of the
very top drawer." Did their obscure name prompt them
to a sort of haughty reserve? The fact remains that the
Férés refused to know people on whom the La Trémoïlles
would not have forborne to call. It had needed the position of queen of her particular stretch of coast, which the
old Marquise de Cambremer held in the Manche, to
make the Férés consent to come to one of her afternoons
every year. The Cambremers had invited them to dinner
and were counting largely on the effect that M. de Charlus was going to make on them. It was discreetly announced that he was to be one of the party. It chanced
that Mme Féré did not know him. Mme de Cambremer,
on learning this, felt a keen satisfaction, and the smile of
a chemist who is about to bring into contact for the first
time two particularly important bodies hovered over her

lips. The door opened, and Mme de Cambremer almost fainted when she saw Morel enter the room alone. Like a private secretary conveying his minister's apologies, like a morganatic wife expressing the Prince's regret that he is unwell (as Mme de Clinchamp used to do on behalf of the Duc d'Aumale), Morel said in the airiest of tones: "The Baron can't come. He's not feeling very well, at least I think that's the reason . . . I haven't seen him this week," he added, these last words completing the despair of Mme de Cambremer, who had told M. and Mme Féré that Morel saw M. de Charlus at every hour of the day. The Cambremers pretended that the Baron's absence was a blessing in disguise, and, without letting Morel hear them, said to their other guests: "We can do very well without him, can't we, it will be all the more agreeable." But they were furious, suspected a plot hatched by Mme Verdurin, and, tit for tat, when she invited them again to La Raspelière, M. de Cambremer, unable to resist the pleasure of seeing his house again and of mingling with the little group, came, but came alone, saying that the Marquise was so sorry, but her doctor had ordered her to stay at home. The Cambremers hoped by this partial attendance at the same time to teach M. de Charlus a lesson and to show the Verdurins that they were not obliged to treat them with more than a limited politeness, as Princesses of the Blood used in the old days to show duchesses out, but only as far as the middle of the second chamber. After a few weeks, they were scarcely on speaking terms.

M. de Cambremer explained it to me as follows: "I must tell you that with M. de Charlus it was rather difficult. He is an extreme Dreyfusard . . ."

"Oh, no!"

"Yes he is . . . Anyhow his cousin the Prince de Guermantes is, and they've come in for a lot of abuse because of it. I have some relatives who are very particular about that sort of thing. I can't afford to mix with those people, I should alienate the whole of my family."

"Since the Prince de Guermantes is a Dreyfusard, that will make things all the easier," said Mme de Cambremer, "because Saint-Loup, who is said to be going to marry his niece, is one too. In fact it may well be the reason for the marriage."

"Come now, my dear," her husband replied, "you mustn't say that Saint-Loup, who's a great friend of ours, is a Dreyfusard. One oughtn't to make such allegations lightly. You'll make him highly popular in the Army!"

"He was once, but he isn't any longer," I explained to M. de Cambremer. "As for his marrying Mlle de Guermantes-Brassac, is there any truth in that?"

"People are talking of nothing else, but you should be in a position to know."

"But I tell you, he himself told me he was a Dreyfusard," said Mme de Cambremer, "—not that there isn't every excuse for him, the Guermantes are half German."

"As regards the Guermantes of the Rue de Varenne, you can say entirely," said Cancan, "but Saint-Loup is another kettle of fish; he may have any number of German relations, but his father insisted on maintaining his title as a French nobleman; he joined the colours in 1871 and was killed in the war in the most gallant fashion. Although I'm a stickler in these matters, it doesn't do to exaggerate either one way or the other. *In medio . . . virtus*, ah, I forget the exact words. It's a remark I've heard Dr

Cottard make. Now, there's a man who always has a word for it. You ought to have a *Petit Larousse* here."

To avoid having to give a verdict on the Latin quotation, and to get away from the subject of Saint-Loup, as to whom her husband seemed to think that she was wanting in tact, Mme de Cambremer fell back upon the Mistress, whose quarrel with them was even more in need of an explanation. "We were delighted to let La Raspelière to Mme Verdurin," said the Marquise. "The only trouble is that she appears to imagine that together with the house and everything else that she has managed to lay her hands on, the use of the meadow, the old hangings, all sorts of things which weren't in the lease at all, she should also be entitled to make friends with us. The two things are entirely distinct. Our mistake lay in not getting everything done quite simply through a lawyer or an agency. At Féterne it doesn't much matter, but I can just imagine the face my aunt de Ch'nouville would make if she saw old mother Verdurin come marching in on one of my days with her hair all over the place. As for M. de Charlus, of course he knows some very nice people, but he knows some very nasty people too." I asked who. Driven into a corner, Mme de Cambremer finally said: "People say that it was he who was keeping a certain Monsieur Moreau, Morille, Morue, I can't remember exactly. Nothing to do, of course, with Morel the violinist," she added, blushing. "When I realised that Mme Verdurin imagined that because she was our tenant in the Manche she would have the right to come and call upon me in Paris, I saw that it was time to cut the painter."

Notwithstanding this quarrel with the Mistress, the Cambremers were on quite good terms with the faithful, and would readily get into our compartment when they were travelling by the train. Just before we reached Douville, Albertine, taking out her mirror for the last time, would sometimes deem it necessary to change her gloves or to take off her hat for a moment, and, with the tortoiseshell comb which I had given her and which she wore in her hair, to smooth out the knots, to fluff up the curls, and if necessary to push up her chignon over the waves which descended in regular valleys to her nape. Once we were in the carriages which had come to meet us, we no longer had any idea where we were; the roads were not lighted; we could tell by the louder noise of the wheels that we were passing through a village, we thought we had arrived, we found ourselves once more in the open country, we heard bells in the distance, we forgot that we were in evening dress, and we had almost fallen asleep when, at the end of this long stretch of darkness which, what with the distance we had travelled and the hitches and delays inseparable from railway journeys, seemed to have carried us on to a late hour of the night and almost half-way back to Paris, suddenly, after the crunching of the carriage wheels over a finer gravel had revealed to us that we had turned into the drive, there burst forth, reintroducing us into a social existence, the dazzling lights of the drawing-room, then of the dining-room where we were suddenly taken aback by hearing eight o'clock strike when we imagined it was long past, while the endless dishes and vintage wines would circulate among the men in tails and the women with bare arms, at a dinner glittering with light like a real metropolitan dinner-party but surrounded, and thereby changed in character, by the strange and sombre double veil which, diverted from their primal solemnity, the nocturnal, rural, maritime hours of the journey there and back had woven for it. Soon indeed the return journey obliged us to leave the radiant and quickly forgotten splendour of the lighted drawing-room for the carriages, in which I arranged to be with Albertine so that she should not be alone with other people, and often for another reason as well, which was that we could both do many things in a dark carriage, in which the jolts of the downward drive would moreover give us an excuse, should a sudden ray of light fall upon us, for clinging to one another. When M. de Cambremer was still on visiting terms with the Verdurins, he would ask me: "You don't think this fog will bring on your spasms? My sister's were terribly bad this morning. Ah! you've been having them too," he said with satisfaction. "I shall tell her tonight. I know that as soon as I get home the first thing she'll ask will be whether you've had any lately." He spoke to me of my sufferings only to lead up to his sister's, and made me describe mine in detail simply that he might point out the difference between them and hers. But notwithstanding these differences, as he felt that his sister's spasms entitled him to speak with authority, he could not believe that what "succeeded" with hers was not indicated as a cure for mine, and it irritated him that I would not try these remedies, for if there is one thing more difficult than submitting oneself to a regime it is refraining from imposing it on other people. "Not that I need speak, a mere layman, when you are here before the Areopagus, at the fountainhead of wisdom. What does Professor Cottard think about them?"

I saw his wife once again, as a matter of fact, because

she had said that my "cousin" behaved rather weirdly, and I wished to know what she meant by this. She denied having said it, but at length admitted that she had been speaking of a person whom she thought she had seen with my cousin. She did not know the person's name and said finally that, if she was not mistaken, it was the wife of a banker, who was called Lina, Linette, Lisette, Lia, anyhow something like that. I felt that "wife of a banker" was inserted merely to put me off the scent. I wanted to ask Albertine whether it was true. But I preferred to give the impression of knowing rather than inquiring. Besides, Albertine would not have answered me at all, or would have answered me only with a "no" of which the "n" would have been too hesitant and the "o" too emphatic. Albertine never related facts that were damaging to her, but always other facts which could be explained only by the former, the truth being rather a current which flows from what people say to us, and which we pick up, invisible though it is, than the actual thing they have said. Thus, when I assured her that a woman whom she had known at Vichy was disreputable, she swore to me that this woman was not at all what I supposed and had never attempted to make her do anything improper. But she added, another day, when I was speaking of my curiosity as to people of that sort, that the Vichy lady had a friend too, whom she, Albertine, did not know, but whom the lady had *promised* to introduce to her." That she should have promised her this could only mean that Albertine wished it, or that the lady had known that by offering the introduction she would be giving her pleasure. But if I had pointed this out to Albertine, I should have given the impression that my revelations came exclusively from her;

I should have put a stop to them at once, never have learned anything more, and ceased to make myself feared. Besides, we were at Balbec, and the Vichy lady and her friend lived at Menton; the remoteness, the impossibility of the danger made short work of my suspicions.

Often, when M. de Cambremer hailed me from the station, I had just been taking advantage of the darkness with Albertine, not without some difficulty as she had struggled a little, fearing that it was not dark enough. "You know, I'm sure Cottard saw us; anyhow, if he didn't, he must have noticed your breathless voice, just when they were talking about your other kind of breathlessness," Albertine said to me when we arrived at Douville station where we took the little train home. But if this return journey, like the outward one, by giving me a certain impression of poetry, awakened in me the desire to travel, to lead a new life, and so made me want to abandon any intention of marrying Albertine, and even to break off our relations for good, it also, by the very fact of their contradictory nature, made this breach easier. For, on the homeward journey just as much as on the other, at every station we were joined in the train or greeted from the platform by people whom we knew; the furtive pleasures of the imagination were overshadowed by those other, continual pleasures of sociability which are so soothing, so soporific. Already, before the stations themselves, their names (which had so fired my imagination ever since the day I had first heard them, that first evening when I had travelled down to Balbec with my grandmother) had become humanised, had lost their strangeness since the evening when Brichot, at Albertine's request, had given us a more complete account of their etymology. I had been charmed by the "flower" that ended certain names, such as Fiquefleur, Honfleur, Flers, Barfleur, Harfleur, etc., and amused by the "beef" that comes at the end of Bricqueboeuf. But the flower vanished, and also the beef, when Brichot (and this he had told me on the first day in the train) informed us that *fleur* means a harbour (like *fiord*), and that *boeuf*, in Norman *budh*, means a hut. As he cited a number of examples, what had appeared to me a particular instance became general: Bricqueboeuf took its place by the side of Elbeuf, and even in a name that was at first sight as individual as the place itself, like the name Pennedepie, in which peculiarities too impenetrable for reason to elucidate seemed to me to have been blended from time immemorial in a word as coarse, flavoursome and hard as a certain Norman cheese, I was disappointed to find the Gallic *pen* which means mountain and is as recognisable in Penmarch as in the Apennines. Since, at each halt of the train, I felt that we should have friendly hands to shake if not visitors to receive in our carriage, I said to Albertine: "Hurry up and ask Brichot about the names you want to know. You mentioned to me Marcouville-l'Orgueilleuse."

"Yes, I love that *orgueil*, it's a proud village," said Albertine.

"You would find it prouder still," Brichot replied, "if instead of its French or even its low Latin form, as we find it in the cartulary of the Bishop of Bayeux, *Marcovilla superba*, you were to take the older form, more akin to the Norman, *Marculphivilla superba*, the village, the domain of Merculph. In almost all these names which end in *ville*, you might see still marshalled upon this

coast the ghosts of the rude Norman invaders. At Hermenonville, you had, standing at the carriage door, only
our excellent Doctor, who, obviously, has nothing of the
Norse chieftain about him. But, by shutting your eyes,
you might have seen the illustrious Herimund (*Her-
imundivilla*). Although, I can never understand why, people choose these roads, between Loigny and Balbec-Plage,
rather than the very picturesque roads that lead from
Loigny to old Balbec, Mme Verdurin has perhaps taken
you out that way in her carriage. If so, you have seen Incarville, or the village of Wiscar; and Tourville, before
you come to Mme Verdurin's, is the village of Turold.
Moreover, there were not only the Normans. It seems
that the Germans (*Alemanni*) came as far as here: Aumenancourt, *Alemanicurtis*—don't let us speak of it to that
young officer I see there; he would be capable of refusing
to visit his cousins there any more. There were also Sax-
ons, as is proved by the springs of Sissonne (the goal of
one of Mme Verdurin's favourite excursions, and rightly
so), just as in England you have Middlesex, Wessex. And
what is inexplicable, it seems that the Goths, *gueux* as
they were called, came as far as this, and even the Moors,
for Mortagne comes from *Mauretania*. Their traces still
remain at Gourville—*Gothorumvilla*. Some vestige of the
Latins subsists also, for instance Lagny (*Latiniacum*)."

"I should like to know the explanation of Thorpehomme," said M. de Charlus. "I understand *homme*," he
added, at which the sculptor and Cottard exchanged
meaning glances. "But *Thorpe?*"

"*Homme* does not in the least mean what you are naturally led to suppose, Baron," replied Brichot, glancing
mischievously at Cottard and the sculptor. "*Homme* has

nothing to do, in this instance, with the sex to which I am not indebted for my mother. *Homme* is *holm*, which means a small island, etc. As for *Thorpe*, or village, we find that in any number of words with which I have already bored our young friend. Thus in Thorpehomme there is not the name of a Norman chief, but words of the Norman language. You see how the whole of this country has been Germanised."

"I think that is an exaggeration," said M. de Charlus. "Yesterday I was at Orgeville."

"This time I give you back the man I took from you in Thorpehomme, Baron. Without wishing to be pedantic, a charter of Robert I gives us, for Orgeville, *Otgerivilla*, the domain of Otger. All these names are those of ancient lords. Octeville-la-Venelle is a corruption of l'Avenel. The Avenels were a family of repute in the Middle Ages. Bourguenolles, where Mme Verdurin took us the other day, used to be written Bourg de Môles, for that village belonged in the eleventh century to Baudoin de Môles, as also did La Chaise-Baudoin; but here we are at Doncières."

"Heavens, look at all these subalterns trying to get in," said M. de Charlus with feigned alarm. "I'm thinking of you, for it doesn't affect me, I'm getting out here."

"You hear, Doctor?" said Brichot. "The Baron is afraid of officers passing over his body. And yet it's quite appropriate for them to be here in strength, for Doncières is precisely the same as Saint-Cyr, *Dominus Cyriacus*. There are plenty of names of towns in which *Sanctus* and *Sancta* are replaced by *Dominus* and *Domina*. Besides, this peaceful military town sometimes has a spurious look of Saint-Cyr, of Versailles, and even of Fontainebleau."

During these homeward journeys (as on the outward ones) I used to tell Albertine to put on her things, for I knew very well that at Aumenancourt, Doncières, Epreville, Saint-Vast we should be receiving brief visits from friends. Nor did I find these disagreeable, whether it might be, at Hermenonville (the domain of Herimund) a visit from M. de Chevregny, seizing the opportunity, when he had come down to meet other guests, of asking me to come over to lunch next day at Beausoleil, or (at Doncières) the sudden irruption of one of Saint-Loup's charming friends, sent by him (if he himself was not free) to convey to me an invitation from Captain de Borodino, from the officers' mess at the Coq-Hardi, or from the sergeants' at the Faisan Doré. Saint-Loup often came in person, and during the whole of the time he was with us I contrived, without letting anyone notice, to keep Albertine a prisoner under my unnecessarily vigilant eye. On one occasion however my watch was interrupted. During a protracted stop, Bloch, after greeting us, was making off at once to join his father—who, having just succeeded to his uncle's fortune, and having leased a country house by the name of La Commanderie, thought it befitting a country gentleman always to go about in a post-chaise, with postilions in livery—and asked me to accompany him to the carriage. "But make haste, for these quadrupeds are impatient. Come, O beloved of the gods, thou wilt give pleasure to my father." But I could not bear to leave Albertine in the train with Saint-Loup; they might, while my back was turned, get into conversation, go into another compartment, smile at one another, touch one another; my eyes, glued to Albertine, could not detach themselves from her so long as Saint-Loup was there. Now I could see quite well that Bloch, who had asked me as a favour to go and pay my respects to his father, in the first place thought it very ungracious of me to refuse when there was nothing to prevent me from doing so, the porters having told us that the train would remain for at least a quarter of an hour in the station, and almost all the passengers, without whom it would not leave, having alighted; and, what was more, had not the least doubt that it was because quite clearly—my conduct on this occasion furnished him with a decisive proof of it—I was a snob. For he was not unaware of the names of the people in whose company I was. In fact M. de Charlus had said to me some time before this, without remembering or caring that the introduction had been made long ago: "But you must introduce your friend to me; your behaviour shows a lack of respect for myself," and had talked to Bloch, who had seemed to please him immensely, so much so that he had gratified him with an: "I hope to meet you again." "Then it's final—you won't walk a hundred yards to say how-d'ye-do to my father, who would be so pleased?" Bloch said to me. I was sorry to appear to be lacking in comradeship, and even more so for the reason for which Bloch supposed that I was lacking in it, and to feel that he imagined that I was not the same towards my middle-class friends when I was with people of "birth." From that day he ceased to show the same friendliness towards me, and, what pained me more, had no longer the same regard for my character. But, in order to disabuse him as to the motive which made me remain in the carriage, I should have had to tell him something—to wit, that I was jealous of Albertine—which would have distressed me even more than letting him suppose that I was stupidly worldly. So it is that in theory we find that we ought always to explain ourselves frankly, to avoid misunderstandings. But very often life arranges these in such a way that, in order to dispel them, in the rare circumstances in which it might be possible to do so, we must reveal either—which was not the case here—something that would annoy our friend even more than the imaginary wrong that he imputes to us, or a secret the disclosure of which—and this was my predicament—appears to us even worse than the misunderstanding. And moreover, even without my explaining to Bloch, since I could not, my reason for not accompanying him, if I had begged him not to be offended, I should only have increased his umbrage by showing him that I had observed it. There was nothing to be done but to bow before the decree of fate which had willed that Albertine's presence should prevent me from accompanying him, and that he should suppose that it was on the contrary the presence of important people—the only effect of which, had they been a hundred times more important, would have been to make me devote my attention exclusively to Bloch and reserve all my civility for him. In this way, accidentally and absurdly, a minor incident (in this case the juxtaposition of Albertine and Saint-Loup) has only to be interposed between two destinies whose lines have been converging towards one another, for them to deviate, stretch further and further apart, and never converge again. And there are friendships more precious than Bloch's for myself which have

been destroyed without the involuntary author of the offence having any opportunity to explain to the offended
party what would no doubt have healed the injury to his
self-esteem and called back his fugitive affection.

Friendships more precious than Bloch's would not,
for that matter, be saying very much. He had all the
faults that I most disliked, and it happened by chance
that my affection for Albertine made them altogether intolerable. Thus in that brief moment in which I was talking to him while keeping my eye on Robert, Bloch told
me that he had been to lunch at Mme Bontemps's and
that everybody had spoken about me in the most glowing
terms until the "decline of Helios." "Good," thought I,
"since Mme Bontemps regards Bloch as a genius, the enthusiastic approval that he will have expressed for me will
do more than anything that the others can have said, it
will get back to Albertine. Any day now she is bound to
learn—I'm surprised that her aunt has not repeated it to
her already—that I'm a 'superior person.'" "Yes," Bloch
went on, "everybody sang your praises. I alone preserved
a silence as profound as though, in place of the repast
(poor, as it happened) that was set before us, I had absorbed poppies, dear to the blessed brother of Thanatos
and Lethe, the divine Hypnos, who enwraps in pleasant
bonds the body and the tongue. It is not that I admire
you less than the band of ravening dogs with whom I had
been bidden to feed. But I admire you because I understand you, and they admire you without understanding
you. To tell the truth, I admire you too much to speak of
you thus in public. It would have seemed to me a profanation to praise aloud what I carry in the profoundest

depths of my heart. In vain did they question me about you, a sacred Pudor, daughter of Kronion, kept me mute."

I did not have the bad taste to appear annoyed, but this Pudor seemed to me akin—far more than to Kronion—to the reticence that prevents a critic who admires you from speaking of you because the secret temple in which you sit enthroned would be invaded by the mob of ignorant readers and journalists; to the reticence of the statesman who does not recommend you for a decoration because you would be lost in a crowd of people who are not your equals; to the reticence of the Academician who refrains from voting for you in order to spare you the shame of being the colleague of X—— who is devoid of talent; to the reticence, finally, more respectable and at the same time more criminal, of the sons who implore us not to write about their dead father who abounded in merit, in order to ensure silence and repose, to prevent us from maintaining the stir of life and the sound of glory round the deceased, who himself would prefer the echo of his name upon the lips of men to all the wreaths upon his tomb, however piously borne.

If Bloch, while grieving me by his inability to understand the reason that prevented me from going to greet his father, had exasperated me by confessing that he had depreciated me at Mme Bontemps's (I now understood why Albertine had never made any allusion to this lunch-party and remained silent when I spoke to her of Bloch's affection for myself), my young Jewish friend had produced upon M. de Charlus an impression that was quite the opposite of annoyance.

Of course, Bloch now believed not only that I was

incapable of depriving myself for a second of the company of smart people, but that, jealous of the advances
that they might make to him (M. de Charlus, for instance), I was trying to put a spoke in his wheel and to
prevent him from making friends with them; but for his
part the Baron regretted that he had not seen more of my
friend. As was his habit, he took care not to betray this
feeling. He began by asking me various questions about
Bloch, but in so casual a tone, with an interest that
seemed so feigned, that it was as though he was not listening to the answers. With an air of detachment, in a
chanting voice that expressed inattention more than indifference, and as though simply out of politeness to myself,
M. de Charlus asked: "He looks intelligent, he said he
wrote, has he any talent?" I told him that it had been
very kind of him to say that he hoped to see Bloch again.
The Baron gave not the slightest sign of having heard my
remark, and as I repeated it four times without eliciting a
reply, I began to wonder whether I had been the victim
of an acoustic mirage when I thought I heard M. de
Charlus utter those words. "He lives at Balbec?" crooned
the Baron in a tone so far from interrogatory that it is regrettable that the written language does not possess a sign
other than the question mark to end such apparently un-
questioning remarks. It is true that such a sign would be
of little use except to M. de Charlus. "No, they've taken
a place near here, La Commanderie." Having learned
what he wished to know, M. de Charlus pretended to despise Bloch. "How appalling," he exclaimed, his voice resuming all its clarion vigour. "All the places or properties
called La Commanderie were built or owned by the
Knights of the Order of Malta (of whom I am one), as

the places called Temple or Cavalerie were by the Templars. That I should live at La Commanderie would be the most natural thing in the world. But a Jew! However, I am not surprised; it comes from a curious instinct for sacrilege, peculiar to that race. As soon as a Jew has enough money to buy a place in the country he always chooses one that is called Priory, Abbey, Minster, Chantry. I had some business once with a Jewish official, and guess where he lived: at Pont-l'Evêque. When he fell into disfavour, he had himself transferred to Brittany, to Pont-l'Abbé. When they perform in Holy Week those indecent spectacles that are called 'the Passion,' half the audience are Jews, exulting in the thought that they are about to hang Christ a second time on the Cross, at least in effigy. At one of the Lamoureux concerts, I had a wealthy Jewish banker sitting next to me. They played the *Childhood of Christ* by Berlioz, and he was thoroughly dismayed. But he soon recovered his habitually blissful expression when he heard the Good Friday music. So your friend lives at the Commanderie, the wretch! What sadism! You must show me the way to it," he added, resuming his air of indifference, "so that I may go there one day and see how our former domains endure such a profanation. It is unfortunate, for he has good manners, and he seems cultivated. The next thing I shall hear will be that his address in Paris is Rue du Temple!"

M. de Charlus gave the impression, by these words, that he was seeking merely to find a fresh example in support of his theory; but in reality he was asking me a question with a dual purpose, the principal one being to find out Bloch's address.

"Yes indeed," put in Brichot, "the Rue du Temple

used to be called Rue de la Chevalerie-du-Temple. And in that connexion will you allow me to make a remark, Baron?"

"What? What is it?" said M. de Charlus tartly, the proffered remark preventing him from obtaining his information.

"No, it's nothing," replied Brichot in alarm. "It was in connexion with the etymology of Balbec, about which they were asking me. The Rue du Temple was formerly known as the Rue Barre-du-Bec, because the Abbey of Bec in Normandy had its Bar of Justice there in Paris."

M. de Charlus made no reply and looked as if he had not heard, which was one of his favourite forms of rudeness.

"Where does your friend live in Paris? As three streets out of four take their name from a church or an abbey, there seems every chance of further sacrilege there. One can't prevent Jews from living in the Boulevard de la Madeleine, the Faubourg Saint-Honoré or the Place Saint-Augustin. So long as they do not carry their perfidy a stage further, and pitch their tents in the Place du Parvis-Notre-Dame, Quai de l'Archevêché, Rue Chanoinesse or Rue de l'Ave-Maria, we must make allowance for their difficulties."

We could not enlighten M. de Charlus, not being aware of Bloch's address at the time. But I knew that his father's office was in the Rue des Blancs-Manteaux.

"Oh, isn't that the last word in perversity!" exclaimed M. de Charlus, appearing to find a profound satisfaction in his own cry of ironical indignation. "Rue des Blancs-Manteaux!" he repeated, dwelling with emphasis upon each syllable and laughing as he spoke. "What sac-

rilege! To think that these White Mantles polluted by
M. Bloch were those of the mendicant friars, styled Serfs
of the Blessed Virgin, whom Saint Louis established
there. And the street has always housed religious orders.
The profanation is all the more diabolical since within a
stone's throw of the Rue des Blancs-Manteaux there is a
street whose name escapes me, which is entirely conceded
to the Jews, with Hebrew characters over the shops, bak-
eries for unleavened bread, kosher butcheries—it's positively the Judengasse of Paris. That is where M. Bloch
ought to reside. Of course," he went on in a lofty,
grandiloquent tone suited to the discussion of aesthetic
matters, and giving, by an unconscious atavistic reflex,
the air of an old Louis XIII musketeer to his uptilted
face, "I take an interest in all that sort of thing only from
the point of view of art. Politics are not in my line, and I
cannot condemn wholesale, because Bloch belongs to it, a
nation that numbers Spinoza among its illustrious sons.
And I admire Rembrandt too much not to realise the
beauty that can be derived from frequenting the syna-
gogue. But after all a ghetto is all the finer the more homogeneous and complete it is. You may be sure,
moreover, so far are business instincts and avarice mingled in that race with sadism, that the proximity of the
Hebraic street in question, the convenience of having
close at hand the fleshpots of Israel, will have made your
friend choose the Rue des Blancs-Manteaux. How curious
it all is! It was there, by the way, that there lived a
strange Jew who boiled the Host, after which I think they
boiled him, which is stranger still since it seems to suggest that the body of a Jew can be equivalent to the Body
of Our Lord. Perhaps it might be possible to arrange for

your friend to take us to see the church of the White Mantles. Just think that it was there that they laid the body of Louis d'Orléans after his assassination by Jean sans Peur, which unfortunately did not rid us of the Orléans family. Personally, I have always been on the best of terms with my cousin the Duc de Chartres, but they are nevertheless a race of usurpers who caused the assassination of Louis XVI and the dethronement of Charles X and Henri V. Of course it runs in the family, since their ancestors include Monsieur, who was so styled doubtless because he was the most astounding old woman, and the Regent and the rest of them. What a family!"

This speech, anti-Jewish or pro-Hebrew—according to whether one pays attention to the overt meaning of its sentences or the intentions that they concealed—had been comically interrupted for me by a remark which Morel whispered to me, to the chagrin of M. de Charlus. Morel, who had not failed to notice the impression that Bloch had made, murmured his thanks in my ear for having "given him the push," adding cynically: "He wanted to stay, it's all jealousy, he'd like to take my place. Just like a Yid!"

"We might have taken advantage of this prolonged halt," M. de Charlus went on, "to ask your friend for some interpretations of ritual. Couldn't you fetch him back?" he pleaded desperately.

"No, it's impossible, he has gone away in a carriage, and besides, he's vexed with me."

"Thank you, thank you," Morel murmured.

"Your excuse is preposterous, one can always overtake a carriage, there is nothing to prevent your taking a car," replied M. de Charlus, in the tone of a man accustomed to carry everything before him. But observing my silence: "What is this more or less imaginary carriage?" he said to me insolently, and with a last ray of hope.

"It is an open post-chaise which must by this time have reached La Commanderie."

M. de Charlus bowed before the impossible and made a show of jocularity. "I can understand their recoiling from the idea of a new brougham. It might have swept them clean."

At last we were warned that the train was about to start, and Saint-Loup left us. But this was the only day on which by getting into our carriage he unwittingly caused me pain, when I momentarily thought of leaving him with Albertine in order to go with Bloch. On every other occasion his presence did not torment me. For of her own accord Albertine, to spare me any uneasiness, would on some pretext or other place herself in such a position that she could not even unintentionally brush against Robert, almost too far away even to shake hands with him; turning her eyes away from him, she would plunge, as soon as he appeared, into ostentatious and almost affected conversation with one of the other passengers, continuing this make-believe until Saint-Loup had gone. So that the visits which he paid us at Doncières, causing me no pain, no worry even, were in no way discordant from the rest, all of which I found pleasing because they brought me so to speak the homage and the hospitality of this land. Already, as the summer drew to a close, on our journeys from Balbec to Douville, when I saw in the distance the little resort of Saint-Pierre-des-Ifs where, for a moment in the evening, the crest of the cliffs glittered pink like the snow on a mountain at sunset, it no longer recalled to my mind—let alone the melancholy which its strange, sudden emergence had aroused in me on the first evening, when it filled me with such a longing to take the train back to Paris instead of going on to Balbec—the spectacle that in the morning, Elstir had told me, might be enjoyed from there, at the hour before sunrise, when all the colours of the rainbow are refracted from the rocks, and when he had so often wakened the little boy who had served him as model one year, to paint him, nude, upon the sands. The name Saint-Pierre-des-Ifs announced to me merely that there would presently appear a strange, witty, painted fifty-year-old with whom I should be able to talk about Chateaubriand and Balzac. And now, in the mists of evening, behind that cliff of Incarville which had filled my mind with so many dreams in the past, what I saw, as though its old sandstone wall had become transparent, was the comfortable house of an uncle of M. de Cambremer in which I knew that I should always find a warm welcome if I did not wish to dine at La Raspelière or return to Balbec. So that it was not merely the place-names of this district that had lost their initial mystery, but the places themselves. The names, already half-stripped of a mystery which etymology had replaced by reasoning, had now come down a stage further still. On our homeward journeys, at Hermenonville, at Incarville, at Harambouville, as the train came to a standstill, we could make out shadowy forms which we did not at first identify and which Brichot, who could see nothing at all, might perhaps have mistaken in the darkness for the ghosts of Herimund, Wiscar and Herimbald. But they came up to our carriage. It was merely M. de Cambremer, now completely estranged from the Verdurins, who had come to see off his own guests and who, on behalf of his wife and his mother, came to ask me whether I would not let him "snatch me away" to spend a few days at Féterne where I should be entertained successively by a lady of great musical talent who would sing me the whole of Gluck, and a famous chess-player with whom I could have some splendid games, which would not interfere with the fishing expeditions and yachting trips in the bay, or even with the Verdurin dinner-parties, for which the Marquis gave me his word of honour that he would "lend" me, sending me there and fetching me back again, for my greater convenience and also to make sure of my returning. "But I cannot believe that it's good for you to go so high up. I know my sister could never stand it. She would come back in a fine state! She's not at all well just now . . . Really, you had such a bad attack as that! Tomorrow you'll hardly be able to stand!" And he shook with laughter, not from malevolence but for the same reason which made him laugh whenever he saw a lame man hobbling along the street, or had to talk to a deaf person. "And before that? What, you hadn't had an attack for a fortnight? Do you know, that's simply marvellous. Really, you ought to come and stay at Féterne, you could talk to my sister about your attacks."

At Incarville it was the Marquis de Montpeyroux who, not having been able to go to Féterne, for he had been away shooting, had come "to meet the train" in top boots and with a pheasant's plume in his hat, to shake hands with the departing guests and at the same time with myself, bidding me expect, on the day of the week that would be most convenient to me, a visit from his son, whom he thanked me for inviting, adding that he would be very glad if I would make the boy read a little; or else M. de Crécy, come out to digest his dinner, he explained, smoking his pipe, accepting a cigar or indeed more than one, and saying to me: "Well, you haven't named a day for our next Lucullan evening. We have nothing to say to each other? Allow me to remind you that we left unsettled the question of the two Montgomery families. We really must settle it. I'm relying on you." Others had come simply to buy newspapers. And many others came and chatted with us who, I have often suspected, were to be found upon the platform of the station nearest to their little manor simply because they had nothing better to do than to converse for a moment with people of their acquaintance. They were a setting for social intercourse like any other, in fact, these halts of the little train, which itself appeared conscious of the role that had been allotted to it, had contracted a sort of human kindliness: patient, of a docile nature, it waited as long as one wished for the stragglers, and even after it had started, would stop to pick up those who signalled to it; they would then run after it panting, in which they resembled it, though they differed from it in that they were running to overtake it at full speed whereas it was merely exercising a wise deliberation. And so Hermenonville, Harambouville, Incarville no longer suggested to me even the rugged grandeurs of the Norman Conquest, not content with having entirely rid themselves of the unaccountable melancholy in which I had seen them steeped long ago in the moist evening air. Doncières! To me, even after I had come to know it and had awakened from my dream, how long there had survived in that name those pleasantly glacial streets, lighted windows, succulent fowls! Doncières! Now it was merely the station at which Morel joined the train, Egleville (*Aquilae villa*) the one at which Princess Sherbatoff generally awaited us, Maineville the station at which Albertine left the train on fine evenings, when, if she was not too tired, she felt inclined to enjoy a moment more of my company, having, if she took a footpath, little if any further to walk than if she had alighted at Parville (*Paterni villa*). Not only did I no longer feel the anxious dread of loneliness which had gripped my heart the first evening; I had no longer any need to fear its reawakening, nor to feel myself a homesick stranger in this land productive not only of chestnut-trees and tamarisks, but of friendships which from beginning to end of the route formed a long chain, interrupted like that of the blue hills, hidden here and there in the anfractuosity of the rock or behind the lime-trees of the avenue, but delegating at each stopping-place an amiable gentleman who came to punctuate my journey with a cordial handclasp, to prevent me from feeling its length, to offer if need be to continue it with me. Another would be at the next station, so that the whistle of the little train parted us from one friend only to enable us to meet others. Between the most isolated properties and the railway which skirted them almost at the pace of a person walking fairly fast, the distance was so slight that at the moment when, from the platform, outside the waiting-room, their owners hailed us, we might almost have imagined that they were doing so from their own doorstep, from their bedroom window, as though the little departmental line had been merely a provincial street and the isolated country house an urban mansion; and even at the few

stations where no "good evening" sounded, the silence
had a nourishing and calming plenitude, because I knew
that it was formed from the slumber of friends who had
gone to bed early in the neighbouring manor, where my
arrival would have been greeted with joy if I had been
obliged to arouse them to ask for some hospitable service.
Apart from the fact that habit so fills up our time that we
have not, after a few months, a free moment in a town
where on our first arrival the day offered us the absolute
disposal of all its twelve hours, if one of these had by any
chance fallen vacant it would no longer have occurred to
me to devote it to visiting some church for the sake of
which I had first come to Balbec, or even to compare a
scene painted by Elstir with the sketch that I had seen of
it in his studio, but rather to go and play one more game
of chess with M. Féré. It was indeed the corrupting
effect, as it was also the charm, of this country round
Balbec, to have become for me a land of familiar acquaintances; if its territorial distribution, its extensive cultivation, along the entire length of the coast, with different
forms of agriculture, gave of necessity to the visits which
I paid to these different friends the aspect of a journey,
they also reduced that journey to the agreeable proportions of a series of visits. The same place-names, so disturbing to me in the past that the mere *Country House
Directory*, when I leafed through the section devoted to
the Department of the Manche, caused me as much dis-
may as the railway time-table, had become so familiar to
me that even in that time-table itself I could have consulted the page headed *Balbec to Douville via Doncières*
with the same happy tranquillity as an address-book. In
this too social valley, along the flanks of which I felt that

there clung, whether visible or not, a numerous company of friends, the poetical cry of the evening was no longer that of the owl or the frog, but the "How goes it?" of M. de Criquetot or the "Khaire" of Brichot. Its atmosphere no longer aroused anguish, and, charged with purely human exhalations, was easily breathable, indeed almost too soothing. The benefit that I did at least derive from it was that of looking at things only from a practical point of view. The idea of marrying Albertine appeared to me to be madness.

Chapter Four

I was only waiting for an opportunity for a final rupture. And, one evening, as Mamma was setting out next day for Combray, where she was to attend the deathbed of one of her mother's sisters, leaving me behind so that I might continue to benefit, as my grandmother would have wished, from the sea air, I had announced to her that I had irrevocably decided not to marry Albertine and would very soon stop seeing her. I was glad to have been able, by these words, to gratify my mother's wishes on the eve of her departure. She had made no secret of the fact that she was indeed extremely gratified. I also had to have things out with Albertine. As I was on my way back with her from La Raspelière, the faithful having alighted, some at Saint-Mars-le-Vêtu, others at Saint-Pierre-des-Ifs, others again at Doncières, feeling particularly happy and detached from her, I had decided, now that there were only our two selves in the carriage, to broach the subject at last. Besides, the truth was that the member of the band of Balbec girls whom I loved, although she was absent at that moment, as were the rest of her friends, but was coming back there (I enjoyed being with them all, because each of them had for me, as on the day when I first saw them, something of the essence of all the rest, as though they belonged to a race apart), was Andrée. Since she was coming back again to Balbec in a few days' time, it was certain that she would at once pay me a visit, and then, in order to remain free, not to have to marry her if I did not

wish to do so, to be able to go to Venice, but at the same
time to have her entirely to myself in the meantime, the
plan that I would adopt would be that of not seeming at
all eager to come to her, and as soon as she arrived, when
we were talking together, I would say to her: "What a
pity I didn't see you a few weeks earlier. I should have
fallen in love with you; now my heart is bespoken. But
that makes no difference, we shall see one another frequently, for I am unhappy about my other love, and you
will help to console me." I smiled inwardly as I thought
of this conversation, for in this way I should give Andrée
the impression that I was not really in love with her;
hence she would not grow tired of me and I should take a
joyful and pleasant advantage of her affection. But all this
only made it all the more necessary that I should at last
speak seriously to Albertine, in order not to behave dis-
honourably, and, since I had decided to devote myself to
her friend, she herself must be given clearly to understand
that I was not in love with her. I must tell her so at once,
as Andrée might arrive any day. But as we were approaching Parville, I felt that we might not have time that
evening and that it was better to put off until next day
what was now irrevocably settled. I confined myself,
therefore, to discussing with her our dinner that evening
at the Verdurins'. As she was putting on her coat, the
train having just left Incarville, the last station before
Parville, she said to me: "Tomorrow then, more Verdurin.
You won't forget that you're coming to call for me." I
could not help answering rather tersely: "Yes, that is if I
don't 'defect,' because I'm beginning to find that sort of
life really stupid. In any case, if we do go, in order that
my time at La Raspelière may not be totally wasted, I

must remember to ask Mme Verdurin about something
that could interest me a great deal, provide me with a
subject for study, and give me pleasure as well, because
I've really had very little this year at Balbec."

"That's not very polite to me, but I forgive you, because I can see that you're overwrought. What is this
pleasure?"

"That Mme Verdurin should let me hear some things
by a musician whose work she knows very well. I know
one of his things myself, but it seems there are others and
I should like to know if the rest of his work is published,
if it's different from what I know."

"What musician?"

"My dear child, when I've told you that his name is
Vinteuil, will you be any the wiser?"

We may have revolved every possible idea in our
minds, and yet the truth has never occurred to us, and it
is from without, when we are least expecting it, that it
gives us its cruel stab and wounds us for ever.

"You can't think how you amuse me," replied Albertine, getting up, for the train was about to stop. "Not
only does it mean a great deal more to me than you suppose, but even without Mme Verdurin I can get you all
the information that you require. You remember my
telling you about a friend, older than me, who had been a
mother, a sister to me, with whom I spent the happiest
years of my life, at Trieste, and whom in fact I'm expecting to join in a few weeks at Cherbourg, where we shall
set out on a cruise together (it sounds a bit weird, but you
know how I love the sea)? Well, this friend (oh! not at all
the type of woman you might suppose!), isn't this extraordinary, is the best friend of your Vinteuil's daughter, and

I know Vinteuil's daughter almost as well as I know her. I always call them my two big sisters. I'm not sorry to show you that your little Albertine can be of use to you in this question of music, about which you say, and quite rightly, that I know nothing at all."

At the sound of these words, uttered as we were entering the station of Parville, so far from Combray and Montjouvain, so long after the death of Vinteuil, an image stirred in my heart, an image which I had kept in reserve for so many years that even if I had been able to guess, when I stored it up long ago, that it had a noxious power, I should have supposed that in the course of time it had entirely lost it; preserved alive in the depths of my being—like Orestes whose death the gods had prevented in order that, on the appointed day, he might return to his native land to avenge the murder of Agamemnon—as a punishment, as a retribution (who knows?) for my having allowed my grandmother to die; perhaps rising up suddenly from the dark depths in which it seemed for ever buried, and striking like an Avenger, in order to inaugurate for me a new and terrible and only too well-merited existence, perhaps also to make dazzlingly clear to my eyes the fatal consequences which evil actions eternally engender, not only for those who have committed them but for those who have done no more, or thought that they were doing no more, than look on at a curious and entertaining spectacle, as I, alas, had done on that afternoon long ago at Montjouvain, concealed behind a bush where (as when I had complacently listened to the account of Swann's love affairs) I had perilously allowed to open up within me the fatal and inevitably painful road of Knowledge. And at the same time, from my bitterest grief

I derived a feeling almost of pride, almost of joy, that of a man whom the shock he has just received has carried at a bound to a point to which no voluntary effort could have brought him. The notion of Albertine as the friend of Mlle Vinteuil and of Mlle Vinteuil's friend, a practising and professional Sapphist, was as momentous, compared to what I had imagined when I doubted her most, as are the telephones that soar over streets, cities, fields, seas, linking one country to another, compared to the little acousticon of the 1889 Exhibition which was barely expected to transmit sound from one end of a house to the other. It was a terrible *terra incognita* on which I had just landed, a new phase of undreamed-of sufferings that was opening before me. And yet this deluge of reality that engulfs us, however enormous it may be compared with our timid and microscopic suppositions, has always been foreshadowed by them. It was doubtless something akin to what I had just learned, something akin to Albertine's friendship with Mlle Vinteuil, something which my mind would never have been capable of inventing, that I had obscurely apprehended when I became so uneasy at the sight of Albertine and Andrée together. It is often simply from lack of creative imagination that we do not go far enough in suffering. And the most terrible reality brings us, at the same time as suffering, the joy of a great discovery, because it merely gives a new and clear form to what we have long been ruminating without suspecting it.

The train had stopped at Parville, and, as we were the only passengers in it, it was in a voice weakened by a sense of the futility of his task, by the force of habit which nevertheless made him perform it and inspired in him simultaneously exactitude and indolence, and even more by a longing for sleep, that the porter shouted: "Parville!" Albertine, who stood facing me, seeing that she had arrived at her destination, stepped across the compartment and opened the door. But this movement which she thus made to get off the train tore my heart unendurably, just as if, contrary to the position independent of my body which Albertine's seemed to be occupying a yard away from it, this separation in space, which an accurate draughtsman would have been obliged to indicate between us, was only apparent, and anyone who wished to make a fresh drawing of things as they really were would now have had to place Albertine, not at a certain distance from me, but inside me. She gave me such pain by her withdrawal that, reaching after her, I caught her desperately by the arm.

"Would it be physically possible," I asked her, "for you to come and spend the night at Balbec?"

"Physically, yes. But I'm dropping with sleep."

"You'd be doing me an enormous favour . . ."

"Very well, then, though I don't in the least understand. Why didn't you tell me sooner? I'll stay, though."

My mother was asleep when, after engaging a room for Albertine on a different floor, I entered my own. I sat down by the window, suppressing my sobs so that my mother, who was separated from me only by a thin partition, might not hear me. I had not even remembered to close the shutters, for at one moment, raising my eyes, I saw facing me in the sky that same faint glow as of a dying fire which one saw in the restaurant at Rivebelle in a study that Elstir had made of a sunset effect. I remembered the exaltation I had felt when, on the day of my first arrival at Balbec, I had seen from the railway this same image of an evening which preceded not the night but a new day. But no day now would be new to me any more, would arouse in me the desire for an unknown happiness; it would only prolong my sufferings, until the point when I should no longer have the strength to endure them. The truth of what Cottard had said to me in the casino at Incarville was now confirmed beyond a shadow of doubt. What I had long dreaded, had vaguely suspected of Albertine, what my instinct deduced from her whole personality and my reason controlled by my desire had gradually made me repudiate, was true! Behind Albertine I no longer saw the blue mountains of the sea, but the room at Montjouvain where she was falling into the arms of Mlle Vinteuil with that laugh in which she gave utterance as it were to the strange sound of her pleasure. For, with a girl as pretty as Albertine, was it possible that Mlle Vinteuil, having the desires she had, had not asked her to gratify them? And the proof that Albertine had not been shocked by the request, but had consented, was that they had not quarrelled, that indeed their intimacy had steadily increased. And that graceful movement with which Albertine had laid her chin upon Rosemonde's shoulder, gazed at her smilingly, and deposited a kiss upon her neck, that movement which had reminded me of Mlle Vinteuil but in interpreting which I had nevertheless hesitated to admit that an identical line traced by a gesture must of necessity be the result of an identical inclination, who knew whether Albertine might not quite simply have learned it from Mlle Vinteuil? Gradually, the lifeless sky took fire. I who until then had never awakened without a smile at the humblest things, the bowl of coffee, the sound of the rain, the roar of the wind, felt that the day which in a moment was about to dawn, and all the days to come, would no longer bring me the hope of an unknown happiness, but only the prolongation of my agony. I still clung to life; but I knew that I had nothing now but bitterness to expect from it. I ran to the lift, heedless of the hour, to ring for the lift-boy who acted as night watchman, and asked him to go to Albertine's room and to tell her that I had something of importance to say to her, if she could see me there. "Mademoiselle says she would rather come to you," was the answer he brought me. "She will be here in a moment." And presently, sure enough, in came Albertine in her dressing-gown.

"Albertine," I said to her in a low voice, warning her not to raise hers so as not to wake my mother, from whom we were separated only by that partition whose thinness, today a nuisance, because it confined us to whispers, resembled in the past, when it so clearly echoed my grandmother's intentions, a sort of musical diaphanousness, "I'm ashamed to have disturbed you. Listen to me. To make you understand, I must tell you something which you do not know. When I came here, I left a woman whom I was to have married, who was ready to sacrifice everything for me. She was to start on a journey this morning, and every day for the last week I have been wondering whether I should have the courage not to telegraph to her that I was coming back. I did have the courage, but it made me so wretched that I thought I would kill myself. That is why I asked you last night if you would come and sleep at Balbec. If I had to die, I should have liked to bid you farewell."

And I let the tears which my fiction rendered natural flow freely.

"My poor boy, if I had only known, I should have spent the night beside you," cried Albertine, the idea that I might perhaps marry this woman, and that her own chance of making a "good marriage" was thus vanishing, never even crossing her mind, so sincerely was she moved by a grief the cause of which I was able to conceal from her, but not its reality and strength. "As a matter of fact," she said to me, "last night, throughout the entire journey from La Raspelière, I could see that you were nervous and unhappy, and I was afraid there must be something wrong." In reality my grief had begun only at Parville, and my nervous irritability, which was very different but which fortunately Albertine identified with it, arose from the tedium of having to spend a few more days in her company. She added: "I shan't leave you any more, I'm going to spend all my time here." She was offering me, in fact—and she alone could offer it—the sole remedy for the poison that was consuming me, a remedy homogeneous with it indeed, for although one was sweet and the other bitter, both were alike derived from Albertine. At that moment Albertine—my sickness—ceasing to cause me to suffer, left me—she, Albertine the remedy—as weak as a convalescent. But I reflected that she would presently be leaving Balbec for Cherbourg, and from there going to Trieste. Her old habits would be reviving. What I wished above everything else was to prevent Albertine from taking the boat, to make an attempt to carry her off to Paris. It was true that from Paris, more easily even than from Balbec, she might, if she wished, go to Trieste, but in Paris we should see; perhaps I might ask Mme de Guermantes to exert her influence indirectly upon Mlle Vinteuil's friend so that she should not remain at Trieste, to make her accept a situation elsewhere, perhaps with the Prince de——— , whom I had met at Mme de Villeparisis's and, indeed, at Mme de Guermantes's. And he, even if Albertine wished to go to his house to see her friend, might, warned by Mme de Guermantes, prevent them from meeting. Of course I might have reminded myself that in Paris, if Albertine had those tastes, she would find many other people with whom to gratify them. But every impulse of jealousy is unique and bears the imprint of the creature—in this instance Mlle Vinteuil's friend—who has aroused it. It was Mlle Vinteuil's friend who remained my chief preoccupation. The mysterious passion with which I had once thought of Austria because it was the country from which Albertine came (her uncle had been a counsellor at the Embassy there), because I could study its geographical peculiarities, the race that inhabited it, its historic buildings, its scenery, in Albertine's smile and in her ways, as in an atlas or an album of photographs—this mysterious passion I still felt but, by an inversion of symbols, in the domain of horror. Yes, it was from there that Albertine came. It was there that, in every house, she could be sure of finding, if not Mlle Vinteuil's friend, others of her kind. The habits of her childhood would revive, they would be meeting in three months' time for Christmas, then for the New Year, dates which were already painful to me in themselves, owing to an unconscious memory of the misery that I had felt on those days when, long ago, they separated me, for the whole of the Christmas holidays, from Gilberte. After the long dinner-parties, after the midnight revels, when everybody was gay and animated, Albertine would adopt the same poses with her friends there that I had seen her adopt with An-

drée—albeit her friendship for Andrée might for all I
knew be innocent—the same, perhaps, that Mlle Vinteuil,
pursued by her friend, had revealed before my eyes at
Montjouvain. To Mlle Vinteuil, while her friend titillated
her desires before flinging herself upon her, I now gave
the inflamed face of Albertine, of an Albertine whom I
heard utter as she fled, then as she surrendered herself,
her strange, deep laugh. What, in comparison with the
anguish that I was now feeling, was the jealousy I had felt
on the day when Saint-Loup had met Albertine with me
at Doncières and she had flirted with him, or that I had
felt when I thought of the unknown initiator to whom I
was indebted for the first kisses that she had given me in
Paris, on the day when I was waiting for a letter from
Mlle de Stermaria? That other kind of jealousy, provoked
by Saint-Loup or by any young man, was nothing. I
should have had at the most in that case to fear a rival
over whom I should have tried to gain the upper hand.
But here the rival was not of the same kind as myself, had
different weapons; I could not compete on the same
ground, give Albertine the same pleasures, nor indeed
conceive of them exactly. In many moments of our life,
we would barter the whole of our future for a power that
in itself is insignificant. I would at one time have for-
sworn all the good things in life to get to know Mme
Blatin, because she was a friend of Mme Swann. Today,
in order that Albertine might not go to Trieste, I would
have endured every possible torment, and if that proved
insufficient, would have inflicted torments on her, would
have isolated her, kept her under lock and key, would
have taken from her the little money that she had so that
it should be physically impossible for her to make the

journey. Just as, long ago, when I was anxious to go to
Balbec, what had urged me to set off was the longing for
a Persian church, for a stormy sea at daybreak, so what
was now rending my heart as I thought that Albertine
might perhaps be going to Trieste, was that she would be
spending Christmas night there with Mlle Vinteuil's
friend: for the imagination, when it changes its nature and
turns into sensibility, does not thereby acquire control of
a larger number of simultaneous images. Had anyone told
me that she was not at that moment either at Cherbourg
or at Trieste, that there was no possibility of her seeing
Albertine, how I should have wept for joy! How my
whole life and its future would have been changed! And
yet I knew quite well that this localisation of my jealousy
was arbitrary, that if Albertine had these tastes, she could
gratify them with others. And perhaps even these same
girls, if they could have seen her elsewhere, would not
have tortured my heart so acutely. It was Trieste, it was
that unknown world in which I could feel that Albertine
took a delight, in which were her memories, her friendships, her childhood loves, that exhaled that hostile, inexplicable atmosphere, like the atmosphere that used to float
up to my bedroom at Combray, from the dining-room in
which I could hear, talking and laughing with strangers
amid the clatter of knives and forks, Mamma who would
not be coming upstairs to say good-night to me; like the
atmosphere that, for Swann, had filled the houses to
which Odette went at night in search of inconceivable
joys. It was no longer as of a delightful place where the
people were pensive, the sunsets golden, the church bells
melancholy, that I thought now of Trieste, but as of an
accursed city which I should have liked to see instanta-

neously burned down and eliminated from the real world.
That city was embedded in my heart as a fixed and permanent point. The thought of letting Albertine leave
presently for Cherbourg and Trieste filled me with horror;
as did even that of remaining at Balbec. For now that the
revelation of her intimacy with Mlle Vinteuil had become
almost a certainty, it seemed to me that at every moment
when Albertine was not with me (and there were whole
days on which, because of her aunt, I was unable to see
her), she was giving herself to Bloch's sister and cousin,
possibly to other girls as well. The thought that that very
evening she might see the Bloch girls drove me mad. And
so, when she told me that for the next few days she would
stay with me all the time, I replied: "But the fact is, I
want to go back to Paris. Won't you come with me? And
wouldn't you like to come and live with us for a while in
Paris?"

At all costs I must prevent her from being alone, for
some days at any rate, must keep her with me so as to be
certain that she could not meet Mlle Vinteuil's friend. In
reality it would mean her living alone with me, for my
mother, seizing the opportunity of a tour of inspection
which my father had to make, had taken it upon herself
as a duty, in obedience to my grandmother's wishes, to go
down to Combray and spend a few days there with one of
my grandmother's sisters. Mamma had no love for her
aunt because she had not been to my grandmother, so
loving to her, what a sister should be. Thus, when they
grow up, do children remember with resentment the people who have been unkind to them. But having become
my grandmother, Mamma was incapable of resentment;
her mother's life was to her like a pure and innocent

childhood from which she would draw those memories whose sweetness or bitterness regulated her actions with other people. Her aunt might have been able to provide Mamma with certain priceless details, but now she would have difficulty in obtaining them, the aunt being seriously ill (they spoke of cancer). Reproaching herself for not having gone sooner, because she wanted to keep my father company, she saw this as an additional reason for doing what her mother would have done, and, just as she went on the anniversary of the death of my grandmother's father, who had been such a bad parent, to lay upon his grave the flowers which my grandmother had been in the habit of taking there, so, to the side of the grave which was about to open, my mother wished to convey the soft words which her aunt had not come to offer to my grandmother. While she was at Combray, my mother would busy herself with certain alterations which my grandmother had always wished to have made, but only under her daughter's supervision. And so they had not yet been begun, Mamma not wishing, by leaving Paris before my father, to make him feel too keenly the burden of a grief in which he shared but which could not afflict him as it afflicted her.

"Ah! that wouldn't be possible just at present," Albertine replied. "Besides, why should you need to go back to Paris so soon, if the lady has gone?"

"Because I shall feel calmer in a place where I knew her than at Balbec, which she has never seen and which I've begun to loathe."

Did Albertine realise later on that this other woman had never existed, and that if, that night, I had really longed for death, it was because she had thoughtlessly re-

vealed to me that she had been on intimate terms with
Mlle Vinteuil's friend? It is possible. There are moments
when it appears to me probable. At any rate, that morning, she believed in the existence of this other woman.

"But you ought to marry this lady," she said to me,
"it would make you happy, my sweet, and I'm sure it
would make her happy as well."

I replied that the thought that I might make this
woman happy had almost made me decide to marry her;
when, not long since, I had inherited a fortune which
would enable me to provide my wife with ample luxury
and pleasures, I had been on the point of accepting the
sacrifice of the woman I loved. Intoxicated by the gratitude that I felt for Albertine's kindness, coming so soon
after the terrible blow she had dealt me, just as one would
think nothing of promising a fortune to the waiter who
pours one out a sixth glass of brandy, I told her that my
wife would have a motor-car and a yacht, that from that
point of view, since Albertine was so fond of motoring
and yachting, it was unfortunate that she was not the
woman I loved, that I should have been the perfect husband for her, but that we should see, we should no doubt
be able to meet on friendly terms. Nevertheless, since
even when we are drunk we refrain from hailing passers-
by for fear of blows, I was not guilty of the imprudence
(if such it was) that I should have committed in Gilberte's
time, of telling her that it was she, Albertine, whom I
loved.

"You see, I came very near to marrying her. But I
didn't dare do it, after all, for I wouldn't have wanted to
make a young woman live with anyone so sickly and trou-
blesome as myself."

"But you must be mad. Anybody would be delighted to live with you, just look how people run after you. They're always talking about you at Mme Verdurin's, and in high society too, I'm told. She can't have been at all nice to you, that lady, to make you lose confidence in yourself like that. I can see what she is, she's a wicked woman, I detest her. Ah, if I were in her shoes!"

"Not at all, she is very kind, far too kind. As for the Verdurins and all the rest, I don't care a hang. Apart from the woman I love, whom in any case I've given up, I care only for my little Albertine; she is the only person in the world who, by letting me see a great deal of her—that is, during the first few days," I added, in order not to alarm her and to be able to ask anything of her during those days, "—can bring me a little consolation."

I made only a vague allusion to the possibility of marriage, adding that it was quite impracticable since our characters were too different. Being, in spite of myself, still pursued in my jealousy by the memory of Saint-Loup's relations with "Rachel when from the Lord" and of Swann's with Odette, I was too inclined to believe that, once I was in love, I could not be loved in return, and that pecuniary interest alone could attach a woman to me. No doubt it was foolish to judge Albertine by Odette and Rachel. But it was not her that I was afraid of, it was myself; it was the feelings that I was capable of inspiring that my jealousy made me underestimate. And from this judgment, possibly erroneous, sprang no doubt many of the calamities that were to befall us.

"Then you decline my invitation to come to Paris?"

"My aunt wouldn't like me to leave just at present. Besides, even if I can come later on, wouldn't it look

rather odd, my descending on you like that? In Paris everybody will know that I'm not your cousin."

"Very well, then. We can say that we're more or less
engaged. It can't make any difference, since you know
that it isn't true."

Albertine's neck, which emerged in its entirety from
her nightdress, was strongly built, bronzed, grainy in texture. I kissed it as purely as if I had been kissing my
mother to calm a childish grief which I did not believe
that I would ever be able to eradicate from my heart. Albertine left me in order to go and dress. Already her devotion was beginning to falter; earlier she had told me
that she would not leave me for a second (and I felt sure
that her resolution would not last long, since I was afraid,
if we remained at Balbec, that that very evening, in my
absence, she might see the Bloch girls), whereas now she
had just told me that she wished to call at Maineville and
that she would come back and see me in the afternoon.
She had not gone home the evening before; there might
be letters there for her, and besides, her aunt might be
anxious about her. I had replied: "If that's all, we can
send the lift-boy to tell your aunt that you're here and to
pick up your letters." And, anxious to appear amenable
but annoyed at being tied down, she had frowned for a
moment and then, at once, very sweetly, had said: "All
right" and had sent the lift-boy. Albertine had not been
out of the room a moment before the boy came and
tapped gently on my door. I could not believe that, while
I was talking to Albertine, he had had time to go to
Maineville and back. He came now to tell me that Albertine had written a note to her aunt and that she could, if I
wished, come to Paris that very day. It was unfortunate

that she had given him this message orally, for already,
despite the early hour, the manager was about, and came
to me in a great state to ask me whether there was anything wrong, whether I was really leaving, whether I
could not stay just a few days longer, the wind that day
being rather "frightened" (frightful). I did not wish to explain to him that at all costs I wanted Albertine to be out
of Balbec before the hour at which the Bloch girls took
the air, especially since Andrée, who alone might have
protected her, was not there, and that Balbec was like one
of those places in which an invalid who can no longer
bear it is determined, even if he should die on the journey, not to spend another night. Moreover I should have
to struggle against similar entreaties, in the hotel first of
all, where the eyes of Marie Gineste and Céleste Albaret
were red. (Marie indeed was giving vent to the swift-flow-
ing tears of a mountain stream; Céleste, who was gentler,
urged her to be calm; but, Marie having murmured the
only line of poetry that she knew: "Here below the lilacs
die," Céleste could contain herself no longer, and a flood
of tears spilled over her lilac-hued face; I dare say they
had forgotten my existence by that evening.) Later, on the
little local railway, despite all my precautions against being seen, I met M. de Cambremer who turned pale at the
sight of my boxes, for he was counting upon me for the
day after tomorrow; he infuriated me by trying to persuade me that my breathless fits were caused by the
change in the weather, and that October would do them
all the good in the world, and asked me whether I could
not "postpone my departure by a sennight," an expression
the fatuity of which enraged me perhaps only because

what he was suggesting to me made me feel ill. And while he talked to me in the railway carriage, at each station I was afraid of seeing, more terrible than Herimbald or Guiscard, M. de Crécy imploring me to invite him, or, more dreadful still, Mme Verdurin bent upon inviting me. But this was not to happen for some hours. I had not got there yet. I had to face only the despairing entreaties of the manager. I ushered him out of the room, for I was afraid that, although he kept his voice low, he would end by disturbing Mamma. I remained alone in my room, that room with the too lofty ceiling in which I had been so wretched on my first arrival, in which I had thought with such longing of Mlle de Stermaria, had watched for the appearance of Albertine and her friends, like migratory birds alighting upon the beach, in which I had possessed her with such indifference after I had sent the lift-boy to fetch her, in which I had experienced my grandmother's kindness, then realised that she was dead; those shutters, beneath which shone the early morning light, I had opened the first time to look out upon the first ramparts of the sea (those shutters which Albertine made me close in case anybody should see us kissing). I became aware of my own transformations by contrasting them with the unchangingness of my surroundings. One grows accustomed to these as to people, and when, all of a sudden, one recalls the different meaning that they used to convey to one and then, after they had lost all meaning, the events, very different from those of today, which they enshrined, the diversity of the acts performed beneath the same ceiling, between the same glazed bookshelves, the change in one's heart and in one's life which that diversity implies,

seem to be increased still further by the unalterable per-
manence of the setting, reinforced by the unity of the
scene.

Two or three times it occurred to me, for a moment,
that the world in which this room and these bookshelves
were situated, and in which Albertine counted for so little,
was perhaps an intellectual world, which was the sole reality, and my grief something like what we feel when we
read a novel, a thing of which only a madman would
make a lasting and permanent grief that prolonged itself
through his life; that a tiny flicker of my will would suffice, perhaps, to attain to this real world, to re-enter it by
breaking through my grief as one breaks through a paper
hoop, and to think no more about what Albertine had
done than we think about the actions of the imaginary
heroine of a novel after we have finished reading it. For
that matter, the mistresses whom I have loved most passionately have never coincided with my love for them.
That love was genuine, since I subordinated everything
else to seeing them, keeping them for myself alone, and
would weep aloud if, one evening, I had waited for them
in vain. But it was more because they had the faculty of
arousing that love, of raising it to a paroxysm, than because they were its image. When I saw them, when I
heard their voices, I could find nothing in them which resembled my love and could account for it. And yet my
sole joy lay in seeing them, my sole anxiety in waiting for
them to come. It was as though a virtue that had no connexion with them had been artificially attached to them
by nature, and that this virtue, this quasi-electric power,
had the effect upon me of exciting my love, that is to say
of controlling all my actions and causing all my suffer-

ings. But from this, the beauty, or the intelligence, or the kindness of these women was entirely distinct. As by an electric current that gives us a shock, I have been shaken by my loves, I have lived them, I have felt them: never have I succeeded in seeing or thinking them. Indeed I am inclined to believe that in these relationships (I leave out of account the physical pleasure which is their habitual accompaniment but is not enough in itself to constitute them), beneath the outward appearance of the woman, it is to those invisible forces with which she is incidentally accompanied that we address ourselves as to obscure deities. It is they whose good will is necessary to us, with whom we seek to establish contact without finding any positive pleasure in it. The woman herself, during our assignation with her, does little more than put us in touch with these goddesses. We have, by way of oblation, promised jewels and travels, uttered incantations which mean that we adore and, at the same time, contrary incantations which mean that we are indifferent. We have used all our power to obtain a fresh assignation, but one that is accorded to us without constraint. Would we in fact go to so much trouble for the woman herself, if she were not complemented by these occult forces, considering that, once she has left us, we are unable to say how she was dressed and realise that we never even looked at her?

What a deceptive sense sight is! A human body, even a beloved one, as Albertine's was, seems to us, from a few yards, from a few inches away, remote from us. And similarly with the soul that inhabits it. But if something brings about a violent change in the position of that soul in relation to us, shows us that it is in love with others and not with us, then by the beating of our shattered heart we feel that it is not a few feet away from us but within us that the beloved creature was. Within us, in regions more or less superficial. But the words: "That friend is Mlle Vinteuil" had been the *Open sesame*, which I should have been incapable of discovering by myself, that had made Albertine penetrate to the depths of my lacerated heart. And I might search for a hundred years without discovering how to open the door that had closed behind her.

I had ceased for a moment to hear these words ringing in my ears while Albertine had been with me just now. While kissing her, as I used to kiss my mother at Combray, to calm my anguish, I believed almost in Albertine's innocence, or at least did not think continuously of the discovery that I had made of her vice. But now that I was alone the words rang out afresh like those noises inside the ear which one hears as soon as someone stops talking to one. Her vice now seemed to me to be beyond any doubt. The light of approaching sunrise, by modifying the appearance of the things around me, made me once again, as if for a moment I were shifting my position in relation to it, even more bitterly aware of my suffering. I had never seen the dawn of so beautiful or so sorrowful a morning. And thinking of all the indifferent landscapes which were about to be lit up and which, only yesterday, would have filled me simply with the desire to visit them, I could not repress a sob when, with a gesture of oblation mechanically performed and symbolising, in my eyes, the bloody sacrifice which I was about to have to make of all joy, every morning, until the end of my life, a solemn renewal, celebrated as each day dawned, of my daily grief and of the blood from my wound, the golden egg of the sun, as though propelled by the rupture of equilibrium brought about at the moment of coagulation by a change of density, barbed with tongues of flame as in a painting, burst through the curtain behind which one had sensed it quivering for a moment, ready to appear on the scene and to spring forward, and whose mysterious congealed purple it annihilated in a flood of light. I heard myself weeping. But at that moment, to my astonishment, the door opened and, with a throbbing heart, I seemed to see my grandmother standing before me, as in one of those apparitions that had already visited me, but only in my sleep. Was it all only a dream, then? Alas, I was wide awake. "You see a likeness to your poor grandmother," said Mamma, for it was she, speaking gently as though to calm my fear, acknowledging however the resemblance, with a beautiful smile of modest pride which had always been innocent of coquetry. Her dishevelled hair, whose grey tresses were not hidden and strayed about her troubled eyes, her ageing cheeks, my grandmother's own dressing-gown which she was wearing, all these had for a moment prevented me from recognising her and had made me uncertain whether I was still asleep or my grandmother had come back to life. For a long time past my mother had resembled my grandmother far more than the young and smiling Mamma of my childhood. But I had ceased to think of this resemblance. So it is, when one has been sitting reading for a long time, one's mind absorbed, not noticing how the time was passing, that suddenly one sees round about one the sun that shone yesterday at the same hour call up the same harmonies, the same effects of colour that precede a sunset. It was with a smile that my mother drew my attention to my error, for it was pleasing to her that she should bear so strong a resemblance to her mother.

"I came," she said, "because while I was asleep I thought I heard someone crying. It wakened me. But how is it that you aren't in bed? And your eyes are filled with tears. What's the matter?"

I took her head in my arms: "Mamma, listen, I'm afraid you'll think me very changeable. But first of all, yesterday I spoke to you not at all nicely about Albertine; what I said was unfair."

"But what difference can that make?" said my mother, and, catching sight of the rising sun, she smiled sadly as she thought of her own mother, and, so that I might not lose the benefit of a spectacle which my grandmother used to regret that I never watched, she pointed to the window. But beyond the beach of Balbec, the sea, the sunrise, which Mamma was pointing out to me, I saw, with a gesture of despair which did not escape her notice, the room at Montjouvain where Albertine, curled up like a great cat, with her mischievous pink nose, had taken the place of Mlle Vinteuil's friend and was saying amid peals of her voluptuous laughter: "Well, all the better if they do see us! What, I wouldn't dare to spit on that old monkey?" It was this scene that I saw, beyond the scene which was framed in the open window and which was no more than a dim veil drawn over the other, superimposed upon it like a reflexion. It seemed, indeed, itself almost unreal, like a painted view. Facing us, where the cliff of Parville jutted out, the little wood in which we had played "ferret" dipped the picture of its foliage down into the sea, beneath the still-golden varnish of the water, as at the hour when often, at the close of day, after I had gone there to rest in the shade with Albertine, we had risen as we saw the sun sink in the sky. In the confusion of the night mists which still hung in pink and blue tatters over the water littered with the pearly debris of the dawn, boats sailed by, smiling at the slanting light which gilded their sails and the points of their bowsprits as when they are homeward bound at evening: an imaginary scene, shivering and deserted, a pure evocation of the sunset which did not rest, as at evening, upon the sequence of the hours of the day which I was accustomed to see precede it, detached, interpolated, more insubstantial even than the horrible image of Montjouvain which it did not succeed in cancelling, covering, concealing—a poetical, vain image of memory and dreams.

"But come," my mother was saying, "you said nothing unpleasant about her, you told me that she bored you a little, that you were glad you had given up the idea of marrying her. That's no reason for you to cry like that. Remember that your Mamma is going away today and couldn't bear to leave her big pet in such a state. Especially, my poor child, as I haven't time to comfort you. Even if my things are packed, one never has any time on the morning of a journey."

"It's not that."

And then, calculating the future, weighing up my desires, realising that such an affection on Albertine's part for Mlle Vinteuil's friend, and one of such long standing, could not have been innocent, that Albertine had been initiated, and, as every one of her instinctive actions made plain to me, had moreover been born with a predisposition towards that vice which my anxiety had all too often sensed in her, in which she must never have ceased to indulge (in which she was indulging perhaps at that moment, taking advantage of an instant in which I was not present), I said to my mother, knowing the pain that I was causing her, which she did not reveal and which betrayed itself only by that air of serious preoccupation which she wore when she was comparing the gravity of making me unhappy or making me ill, that air which she had worn at Combray for the first time when she had resigned herself to spending the night in my room, that air which at this moment was extraordinarily like my grandmother's when she had allowed me to drink brandy, I said to my mother: "I know how unhappy I'm going to make you. First of all, instead of remaining here as you wished, I want to leave at the same time as you. But that too is nothing. I don't feel well here, I'd rather go home. But listen to me, don't be too distressed. This is it. I was deceiving myself, I deceived you in good faith yesterday, I've been thinking it over all night. I absolutely must—and let's settle the matter at once, because I'm quite clear about it now, because I won't change my mind again, because I couldn't live without it—I absolutely must marry Albertine."

NOTES · ADDENDA · SYNOPSIS

Notes

1 (p. 14) *Altesse*, like *majesté*, being feminine, takes the feminine pronoun.

2 (p. 21) *Les deux sexes mourront chacun de son côté*: from Alfred de Vigny's *La Colère de Samson*.

3 (p. 62) The reference is to Maurice Paléologue, French Ambassador in St Petersburg during the Great War.

4 (p. 132) Emile Loubet, President of the Republic from 1899 to 1906.

5 (p. 136) *Vert* = spicy, risqué.

6 (p. 159) Marquis d'Hervey de Saint-Denis: a distinguished French sinologist.

7 (p. 318 Of the two French versions of the *Arabian Nights*, Galland's *Les Mille et Une Nuits* (1704–17) is elegant, scholarly but heavily bowdlerised, and Mardrus's *Les Mille Nuits et Une Nuit* (1899–1904) coarser and unexpurgated.

8 (p. 331) A popular tune from Offenbach's *Les Brigands*. A *courrier de cabinet* is the equivalent of a King's or Queen's Messenger.

9 (p. 336) Better known under his pen-name Saint-John Perse.

10 (p. 373) Mme Récamier's property on the outskirts of Paris, where she held her salon.

11 (p. 389) *Jachères* = fallow land; *gâtines* = sterile marshland.

12 (p. 393) Francisque Sarcey: middlebrow drama critic noted for his avuncular style.

13 (p. 445) The French has *le cheveu* instead of the normal *les cheveux*.

14 (p. 459) Untranslatable pun. The French of course is *Watteau à vapeur, echoing bateau à vapeur* = steamer.

15 (p. 470) *Monseigneur* is the formula for addressing royalty.

16 (p. 471)   Philipp, Prince Eulenburg, a close friend and adviser of William II, was involved in a homosexual scandal in 1906.

17 (p. 494)   The French say *une veine de cocu* for "the luck of the devil."

18 (p. 594)   *Tapette* can mean both "chatterbox" and "nancy boy."

19 (p. 612)   Idiomatic expression meaning "the moment of reckoning."

Page 145. *The manuscript has a longer version of M. de Charlus's reply*:

"Good heavens, what a fate for that unfortunate canvas to be a prisoner in the house of such a person! To go there once by chance is in itself an error of taste; but to spend one's life there, especially if one is a thing of beauty, is so painful as to be quite unpardonable. There are certain forms of disgrace which it's a crime to resign oneself to . . . [As a good Catholic, I honour St Euverte: *crossed out*] and I can remember very well from the Lives of the Saints what this confessor's qualifications for canonisation were; and indeed, if you like, as a no less good pagan, I respect Diana and admire her crescent, especially when it is placed in your hair by Elstir. But as for the contradictory monster, or even the monster pure and simple, whom you call Diane de Saint-Euverte, I confess I do not take the desire for a union of the churches as far as that. The name recalls the time when altars used to be raised to St Apollo. It is a very distant time—a time from which the person you speak of must incidentally date, judging by her face, which has strangely survived exhumation. And yet, in spite of everything, she is a person with whom one has certain things in common; she has always manifested a singular love of beauty." This observation would have appeared incomprehensible to the Marquise if for some minutes past, having ceased to understand, she had not given up listening. The love of beauty which caused M. de Charlus to cherish, together with a great deal of social contempt, a more deep-rooted respect for Mme de Saint-Euverte, was deduced from the fact that she always had as footmen a numerous and carefully selected pack of irreproachably vigorous young men. "Yes, what a destiny for a beautiful work of art which was spoiled from the start by living face to face with you! There is something tragic about the fate of these captive paintings. Just think, if ever you pay a brief visit to that lady from the *Golden Legend*, with what despair the poor portrait, imprisoned in its blue and rose-pink tones, must be saying to you:

> How different are our fates! I must remain
> But you are free to go . . .

And yet both of you are flowers. Flowers, themselves too in bondage, have contrived in their captivity sublime stratagems for passing on their messages. I confess that I should not be surprised if, with similar intelligence, some day when the windows of the Burgundian saint's wife were left open, your portrait unfolded its canvas wings and flew off, thus solving the problem of aerial navigation before mankind, and making Elstir, in a second and more unexpected form, the successor of Leonardo da Vinci."

Page 157. *In place of this sentence the manuscript has a long passage which was not included in the original edition and which Proust here declares his explicit intention to return to later in the novel, though he did not have time to do so*:

People in society noticed the Princess's febrility, and her fear, though she was still very far from ageing, lest the state of nervous agitation in which she now lived might prevent her from keeping her young appearance. Indeed one evening, at a dinner party to which M. de Charlus was also invited and at which, for that reason, she arrived looking radiant but somehow strange, I realised that this strangeness arose from the fact that, thinking to improve her complexion and to look younger—and probably for the first time in her life—she was heavily made up. She exaggerated even further the eccentricity of dress which had always been a slight weakness of hers. She had only to hear M. de Charlus speak of a portrait to have its sitter's elaborate finery copied and to wear it herself. One day when, thus bedecked with an immense hat copied from a Gainsborough portrait (*it*

would be better to think of a painter whose hats were really extraor-
dinary), she was harping on the theme, which had now become a
familiar one with her, of how sad it must be to grow old, and
quoted in this connexion Mme Récamier's remark to the effect
that she would know she was no longer beautiful when the little
chimney-sweeps no longer turned to look at her in the street.
"Don't worry, my dear little Marie," replied the Duchesse de
Guermantes in a caressing voice, so that the affectionate gentleness of her tone should prevent her cousin from taking offence
at the irony of the words, "you've only to go on wearing hats
like the one you have on and you can be sure that they'll always
turn round."

This love of hers for M. de Charlus which was beginning
to be bruited abroad, combined with what was gradually becoming known about the latter's way of life, was almost as much of
a help to the anti-Dreyfusards as the Princess's Germanic origin.
When some wavering spirit pointed out in favour of Dreyfus's
innocence the fact that a nationalist and anti-semitic Christian
like the Prince de Guermantes had been converted to a belief in
it, people would reply: "But didn't he marry a German?" "Yes,
but . . ." "And isn't that German woman rather highly strung?
Isn't she infatuated with a man who has bizarre tastes?" And in
spite of the fact that the Prince's Dreyfusism had not been
prompted by his wife and had no connexion with the Baron's
sexual proclivities, the philosophical anti-Dreyfusard would conclude: "There, you see! The Prince de Guermantes may be
Dreyfusist in the best of good faith; but foreign influence may
have been brought to bear on him by occult means. That's the
most dangerous way. But let me give you a piece of advice.
Whenever you come across a Dreyfusard, just scratch a bit. Not
far underneath you'll find the ghetto, foreign blood, inversion or
Wagneromania." And cravenly the subject would be dropped,
for it had to be admitted that the Princess was a passionate
Wagnerian.

Whenever the Princess was expecting a visit from me, since
she knew that I often saw M. de Charlus, she would evidently
prepare in advance a certain number of questions which she
then put to me adroitly enough for me not to detect what lay

behind them and which must have been aimed at verifying whether such and such an assertion, such and such an excuse by M. de Charlus in connexion with a certain address or a certain evening, were true or not. Sometimes, throughout my entire visit, she would not ask me a single question, however insignificant it might have appeared, and would try to draw my attention to this. Then, having said good-bye to me, she would suddenly, on the doorstep, ask me five or six as though without premeditation. So it went on, until one evening she sent for me. I found her in a state of extraordinary agitation, scarcely able to hold back her tears. She asked if she could entrust me with a letter for M. de Charlus and begged me to deliver it to him at all costs. I hurried round to his house, where I found him in front of the mirror wiping a few specks of powder from his face. He/ perused the letter—the most desperate appeal, I later learned—and asked me to reply that it was physically impossible that evening, that he was ill. While he was talking to me, he plucked from a vase one after another a number of roses each of a different hue, tried them in his buttonhole, and looked in the mirror to see how they matched his complexion, without being able to decide on any of them. His valet came in to announce that the barber had arrived, and the Baron held out his hand to say good-bye to me. "But he's forgotten his curling tongs," said the valet. The Baron flew into a terrible rage; only the unsightly flush which threatened to ruin his complexion persuaded him to calm down a little, though he remained plunged in an even more bitter despair than before because not only would his hair be less wavy than it might have been but his face would be redder and his nose shiny with sweat. "He can go and get them," suggested the valet. "But I haven't the time," wailed the Baron in an ululation calculated to produce as terrifying an effect as the most violent rage while generating less heat in him who emitted it. "I haven't the time," he moaned. "I must leave in half an hour or I shall miss everything." "Would Monsieur le Baron like him to come in, then?" "I don't know, I can't do without a touch of the curling tongs. Tell him he's a brute, a scoundrel. Tell him . . ."

At this point I left and hurried back to the Princess. Her

breast heaving with emotion, she scribbled another message and asked me to go round to him again: "I'm taking advantage of your friendship, but if you only knew why . . ." I returned to M. de Charlus. Just before reaching his house, I saw him join Jupien beside a parked cab. The headlights of a passing car lit up for a moment the peaked cap and the face of a bus conductor. Then I could see him no longer, for the cab had been halted in a dark corner near the entrance to a completely unlit cul-de-sac. I turned into this cul-de-sac so that M. de Charlus should not see me.

"Give me a second before I get in," M. de Charlus said to Jupien. "My moustache isn't ruffled?"

"No, you look superb."

"You're kidding me."

"Don't use such expressions, they don't suit you. They're all right for the fellow you're going to see."

"Ah, so he's a bit loutish! I'm not averse to that. But tell me, what sort of man is he, not too skinny?"

I realised from all this that if M. de Charlus was failing to go to the help of a glorious princess who was wild with grief, it was not for the sake of a rendezvous with someone he loved, or even desired, but of an arranged introduction to someone he had never met before.

"No, he isn't skinny; in fact he's rather plump and fleshy. Don't worry, he's just your type, you'll see, you'll be very pleased with him, my little lambkin," Jupien added, employing a form of address which seemed as personally inappropriate, as ritual, as when the Russians call a passer-by "little father."

He got into the cab with M. de Charlus, and I might have heard no more had not the Baron, in his agitation, omitted to shut the window and moreover begun, without realising, in order to appear at his ease, to speak in the shrill, reverberating tone of voice which he assumed when he was putting on a social performance.

"I'm delighted to make your acquaintance, and I really must apologise for keeping you waiting in this nasty cab," he said, in order to fill the vacuum in his anxious mind with words, and oblivious of the fact that the nasty cab must on the contrary seem perfectly nice to a bus conductor. "I hope you will give me the pleasure of spending an evening, a comfortable evening with me. Are you never free except in the evenings?"

"Only on Sundays."

"Ah! you're free on Sunday afternoons? Excellent. That makes everything much simpler. Do you like music? Do you ever go to concerts?"

"Yes, I often goes."

"Ah! very good indeed. You see how nicely we're getting on already? I really am delighted to know you. We might go to a Colonne concert. I often have the use of my cousin de Guermantes's box, or my cousin Philippe de Coburg's" (he did not dare say the King of Bulgaria for fear of seeming to be "showing off," but although the bus conductor had no idea what the Baron was talking about and had never heard of the Coburgs, this princely name seemed already too showy to M. de Charlus, who in order not to give the impression of over-rating what he was offering, modestly proceeded to disparage it). "Yes, my cousin Philippe de Coburg—you don't know him?" and at once, as a rich man might say to a third-class traveller: "One's so much more comfortable than in first-class," he went on: "All the more reason for envying you, really, because he's a bit of a fool, poor fellow. Or rather, it's not so much that he's a fool, but he's irritating—all the Coburgs are. But in any case I envy you: that open-air life must be so agreeable, seeing so many different people, and in a charming spot, surrounded by trees—for I believe my friend Jupien told me that the terminus of your line was at La Muette. I've often wanted to live out there. There's nowhere more beautiful in the whole of Paris. So it's agreed, then: we'll go to a Colonne concert. We can have the box closed. Not that I shouldn't be extremely flattered to be seen with you, but we'd be more peaceful . . . Society is so boring, isn't it? Of course I don't mean my cousin Guermantes who is charming and so beautiful."

Just as shy scholars who are afraid of being accused of pedantry abbreviate an erudite allusion and only succeed in appearing more long-winded by becoming totally obscure, so the Baron, in seeking to belittle the splendour of the names he cited, made his discourse completely unintelligible to the bus conductor. The latter, failing to understand its terms, tried to interpret it according to its tone, and as the tone was that of someone who is apologising, he was beginning to fear that he might not receive the sum that Jupien had led him to expect.

"When you go to concerts on Sunday, do *you* go to the Colonne ones too?"

"Pardon?"

"What concert-hall do you go to on Sundays?" the Baron repeated, slightly irritated.

"Sometimes to Concordia, sometimes to the Apéritif Concert, or to the Concert Mayol. But I prefer to stretch me legs a bit. It ain't much fun having to stay sitting down all day long."

"I don't like Mayol. He has an effeminate manner that I find horribly unpleasant. On the whole I detest all men of that type."

Since Mayol was popular, the conductor understood what the Baron said, but was even more puzzled as to why he had wanted to see him, since it could not be for something he hated.

"We might go to a museum together," the Baron went on. "Have you ever been to a museum?"

"I only know the Louvre and the Waxworks Museum."

I returned to the Princess, bringing back her letter. In her disappointment, she burst out at me angrily, but apologised at once.

"You're going to hate me," she said. "I hardly dare ask you to go back a third time."

I stopped the cab a little before the cul-de-sac, and turned into it. The carriage was still there. M. de Charlus was saying to Jupien: "Well, the most sensible thing is for you to get out first with him, and see him on his way, and then rejoin me here . . . All right, then, I hope to see you again. How shall we arrange it?"

"Well, you could send me a message when you go out for a meal at noon," said the conductor.

If he used this expression, which applied less accurately to the life of M. de Charlus, who did not "go out for a meal at noon," than to that of omnibus employees and others, this was doubtless not from lack of intelligence but from contempt for local colour. In the tradition of the old masters, he treated the character of M. de Charlus as a Veronese or a Racine those of the husband at the marriage feast in Cana or Orestes, whom they depict as though this legendary Jew and this legendary Greek had belonged, the one to the luxury-loving patriciate of Venice, the other to the court of Louis XIV. M. de Charlus was content to overlook the inaccuracy, and replied: "No, it would be simpler if you would arrange it with Jupien. I'll speak to him about it. Good-night, it's been delightful," he added, unable to relinquish either his worldly courtesy or his aristocratic hauteur. Perhaps he was even more formally polite at such moments than he was in society; for when one steps outside one's habitual sphere, shyness renders one incapable of invention, and it is the memory of one's habits that one calls upon for practically everything; hence it is upon the actions whereby one hoped to emancipate oneself from one's habits that the latter are most forcibly brought to bear, almost in the manner of those toxic states which intensify when the toxin is withdrawn.

Jupien got out with the conductor.

"Well then, what did I tell you?"

"Ah, I wouldn't mind a few evenings like that! I quite like hearing someone chatting away like that, steady like, a chap who doesn't get worked up. He isn't a priest?"

"No, not at all."

"He looks like a photographer I went to one time to get my picture taken. It's not him?"

"No, not him either."

"Come off it," said the conductor, who thought that Jupien was trying to deceive him and feared, since M. de Charlus had remained rather vague about future assignations, that he might "stand him up," "come off it, you can't tell me it isn't the photographer. I recognised him all right. He lives at 3, Rue de l'Echelle, and he's got a little black dog called Love, I think—so you see I know."

"You're talking rubbish," said Jupien. "I don't say there isn't a photographer who has a little black dog, but I do say he's not the man I introduced you to."

"All right, all right, you can say what you like, but I'm sticking to my own opinion."

"You can stick to it as long as you like for all I care. I'll call round tomorrow about the rendezvous."

Jupien returned to the cab, but the Baron, restive, had already got out of it.

"He's nice, most agreeable and well-mannered. But what's his hair like? He isn't bald, I hope? I didn't dare ask him to take his cap off. I was as nervous as a kitten."

"What a big baby you are!"

"Anyway we can discuss it, but the next time I should prefer to see him performing his professional functions. For instance I could take the corner seat beside him in his tram. And if it was possible by doubling the price, I should even like to see him do some rather cruel things—for example, pretend not to see the old ladies signalling to the tram and then having to go home on foot."

"You vicious thing! But that, dearie, would not be very easy, because there's also the driver, you see. He wants to be well thought of at work."

As I emerged from the cul-de-sac, I remembered the evening at the Princesse de Guermantes's (the evening which I interrupted in the middle of describing it with this anticipatory digression, but to which I shall return) when M. de Charlus denied being in love with the Comtesse Molé, and I thought to myself that if we could read the thoughts of the people we know we would often be astonished to find that the biggest space in them was occupied by something quite other than what we suspected. I walked round to M. de Charlus's house. He had not yet returned. I left the letter. It was learned next day that the Princesse de Guermantes had poisoned herself by mistaking one medicine for another, an accident after which she was for several months at death's door and withdrew from society for several years. It sometimes happened to me also after that evening, on taking a bus, to pay my fare to the conductor whom Jupien had "introduced" to M. de Charlus in the cab. He was a big man, with an ugly, pimpled face and a short-sightedness that made him now wear what Françoise called "specicles." I could never look at him without thinking of the perturbation followed by amazement which the Princesse de Guermantes would have shown if I had had her with me and had said to her: "Wait a minute, I'm going to show you the person for whose sake M. de Charlus resisted your three appeals on the evening you poisoned yourself, the person responsible for all your misfortunes. You'll see him in a moment, he isn't far from here." Doubtless the Princess's heart would have beaten wildly in anticipation. And her curiosity would perhaps have been mixed with a secret admiration for a person who had been so attractive as to make M. de Charlus, as a rule so kind to her, deaf to her entreaties. How often, in her grief mingled with hatred and, in spite of everything, a certain fellow-feeling, must she not have attributed the most noble features to that person, whether she believed it to be a man or a woman! And then, on seeing this creature, ugly, pimpled, vulgar, with red-rimmed, myopic eyes, what a shock! Doubtless the cause of our sorrows, embodied in a human form beloved of another, is sometimes comprehensible to us; the Trojan elders, seeing Helen pass by, said to one another:

One single glance from her eclipses all our griefs.

But the opposite is perhaps more common, because (just as, conversely, admirable and beautiful wives are always being abandoned by their husbands) it often happens that people who are ugly in the eyes of almost everyone excite inexplicable passions; for what Leonardo said of painting can equally well be said of love, that it is *cosa mentale*, something in the mind. Moreover one cannot even say that the reaction of the Trojan elders is more or less common than the other (stupefaction on seeing the person who has caused our sorrows): for one has only to let a little time go by and the case of the Trojan elders almost always merges with the other; in other words there is only one case. Had the Trojan elders never seen Helen, and had she been fated to grow old and ugly, if one had said to them one day: "You're about to see the famous Helen," it is probable that, confronted with a dumpy, red-faced, misshapen old woman, they would have been no less stupefied than the Princesse de Guermantes would have been at the sight of the bus conductor.

Page 251. *In place of this paragraph, the manuscript gives the following long development:*

Moving away from the dazzling "house of pleasure" insolently erected there despite the protests fruitlessly addressed to the mayor by the local families, I made for the cliffs and followed the sinuous paths leading towards Balbec. And I remembered certain walks along these paths with my grandmother. I had had a brief meeting earlier with a local doctor whom I was never to see again and who had told me that my grandmother would die soon; he was one of those people, perhaps malevolent, perhaps mad, perhaps afflicted with a fear of death which they want to induce in others as well, who later remind one of those witch-like vagrants encountered on a roadside who hurl some baneful and plausible prophecy at you. It was the first time I had thought of the possibility of her death. I could neither confide my anguish to her nor bear it myself when she left me. And whenever we took some particularly beautiful path together, I told myself that one day she would no longer be there when I took that path, and the mere idea that she would die one day turned my happiness in being with her to such torment that what I longed to do more than anything else was to forestall her and to die myself then and there. Now it was these same paths or similar ones that I was taking, and already the anguish I had felt in the train was fading, and if I had met Rosemonde [Albertine] I would have asked her to come with me. Suddenly I was attracted by the scent of the hawthorns which, as at Combray in the month of May, array themselves alongside a hedge in their large white veils and decorate this green French countryside with the Catholic whiteness of their demure procession. I went nearer, but my eyes did not know at what adjustment to set their optical apparatus in order to see the flowers at the same time along the hedge and in myself. Belonging at one and the same time to many springtimes, the petals stood out against a sort of magical deep background which, in spite of the strong sunlight, was plunged in semi-darkness either because of the twilight of my indistinct memories or because of the nocturnal hour of the Month of Mary. And then, in the flower which opened up before me in the hedge and which seemed to be animated by the clumsy flickering of my blurred and double vision, the flower that rose from my memory revolved without being able to fit itself exactly on to the elusive living blossoms in the tremulous hesitancy of their petals.

The hawthorns brought out the heaviness of the blossom of an apple-tree sumptuously established opposite them, like those dowryless girls of good family who, while being friends of the daughters of a big cider-maker and acknowledging their fresh complexions and good appearance, know that they themselves have more chic in their crumpled white dresses. I did not have the heart to remain beside them, and yet I had been unable to resist stopping. But Bloch's sisters, whom I caught sight of without their seeing me, did not even turn their heads towards the hawthorns. The latter had made no sign to them, had said nothing to them; they were like those devout young girls who never miss a Month of Mary, during which they are not afraid to steal a glance at a young man with whom they will make an assignation in the countryside, and by whom they will even allow themselves to be kissed in the chapel when there is no one about, but would never dream—because it has been strictly forbidden—of speaking to or playing with children of another religion.

prepare for their fancy-dress ball in spite of the death of their cousin d'Osmond (169; cf. **III** 807).

Visit from Albertine. Françoise and her daughter (170). Linguistic geography (173). I await Albertine's arrival with growing anxiety (174). A telephone call from Albertine (177). "This terrible need of a person": my mother and Albertine (179). How Françoise announces Albertine (182); the latter's visit (186). Afterwards I write to Gilberte Swann, with none of the emotion of old (188). The Duc de Guermantes's conversion to Dreyfusism (189).

Social visiting before my second trip to Balbec. I continue to see other fairies and their dwellings (190). Changes in the social picture (191); the Verdurin salon (194) and the rise of Odette's salon, centred round Bergotte (196). Mme de Montmorency (202).

The Intermittencies of the Heart (204)

My second stay in Balbec. The hotel manager's malapropisms (204). Principal motive for coming to Balbec: the hope of meeting at the Verdurins' Mme de Putbus's maid (206) and other unknown beauties (209). Upheaval of my entire being (210): the living presence of my grandmother is restored to me (211; cf. **II** 335); at the same time I discover that I have lost her for ever (213). My dream, my awakening and my heart-rending memories (216–19). A message from Albertine: I have no desire to see her, or anyone (220). An invitation from Mme de Cambremer, which I decline (226). My grief, however, is less profound than my mother's (228). Her resemblance to my grandmother (229). Meeting with Mme Poussin (231). The new young page at the hotel (233) and the domestic staff from the chorus of *Athalie* (235). Françoise's revelations about the circumstances in which Saint-Loup's photograph of my grandmother had been taken (237; cf. **II** 500). Further revelations, from the manager: my grandmother's syncopes (241). Another dream about her (241). I suddenly decide to see Albertine (243). Apple-trees in blossom (244).

Chapter Two

Resumption of intimacy with Albertine, and first suspicions. My grief at the death of my grandmother wanes and Albertine begins to inspire me with a desire for happiness (246). Sudden return of my grief in the little train (250). Albertine's visit to Balbec (253). The Princesse de Parme (254). My links with Albertine's friends (255). The lift-boy goes to fetch her (256): his manners and his speech (258). Beginnings of my mistrust of Albertine (262): Cottard's remark while she is dancing with Andrée (264). Albertine fails to turn up one evening (267). Painful curiosity about her secret life (268). Her lies about her proposed visit to a lady in Infreville (268–71). In the casino at Balbec: the girls she sees in the mirror (273). The memory of Odette's character applied to Albertine (275).

Visit from Mme de Cambremer while I am on the esplanade with Albertine and her friends (277). Her paraphernalia (277). Her daughter-in-law's two forms of politeness (279). Etymological curiosities (282). Aesthetic prejudices and snobbery of the young Mme de Cambremer (284); evolution of artistic theories (290); her pronunciation of Chenouville (294). She has forgotten her Legrandin origins (297). The Cambremers' friend, a worshipper at the shrine of Le Sidaner (299).

Albertine comes up to my room (303). The lift-boy's anxious and despondent air (304); its cause: the absence of the customary tip (305). The hotel staff and money (306). My calculated protestations of coldness towards Albertine and love for Andrée (308). Albertine denies having had relations with Andrée (313–5). Reconciliation and caresses (316). Excursions with Albertine (320). Brief desires for other girls (321). Jealousy (324).

Scandal in the Grand Hotel provoked by Bloch's sister and an actress (326), hushed up through the good offices of M. Nissim Bernard (327). Why the latter likes the hotel (327). My friendship with two young "couriers" (331); their language (332–5). Renewed suspicions about Albertine's Gomorrhan proclivities (338): the unknown woman in the casino (338); suspect rudeness to a friend of her aunt's (342). M. Nissim Bernard and the tomatoes (343). I go to Doncières with Albertine (345). A fat, vulgar, pretentious lady on the train (347). Albertine and Saint-Loup (348–51). M. de Charlus appears on the platform at Doncières (351). His first meeting with Morel (352–5).

An evening with the Verdurins at La Raspelière. The little train (358) and its "habitués": Cottard, Ski, Brichot (358–60). Social development of the Verdurin salon (363). Saniette (366); Ski (367). Princess Sherbatoff (372). Cottard and the Verdurin "Wednesdays" (377). The handsome unknown girl with the cigarette (381). Mme Verdurin has invited the Cambremers, whose tenant she is (383). Remarks of the "faithful" about the Cambremers (386). Brichot's etymologies (388–93). I recognise Princess Sherbatoff as the fat lady in the train to Doncières (394; cf. 347). News of the death of Dechambre, formerly Mme Verdurin's favourite pianist (396). Mme Verdurin and the death of the faithful (399). Beauty of the countryside (401). Dechambre disowned (405) in the interests of Morel, who is coming with Charlus (407). The latter's sexual proclivities better known among the "faithful" than in the Faubourg Saint-Germain (408). The Verdurins' indifference to the beauties of nature (411).

Arrival of Morel and M. de Charlus (414); evidence of the latter's femininity (414). Morel's request to me (417); his rudeness once he has obtained satisfaction (420). Arrival of the Cambremers (421), he vulgarly ugly (422), she haughty and morose (425); introductions (426). Mme Verdurin and social etiquette (427). The Cambremers' garden (429). M. de Charlus's momentary mistake about Cottard (431). The name Chantepie (434). Combination of culture and snobbery in Mme de Cambremer (437). M. de Cambremer takes an interest in my fits of breathlessness (441). My mother and Albertine (442).

More etymology from Brichot (446). The Norwegian philosopher (447). M. Verdurin bullies Saniette (451). Conversation about Elstir (458). A letter from the dowager Marquise de Cambremer: the rule of the three adjectives (469). M. de Charlus's claim to the rank of Highness (470). The Verdurins' attitude to Brichot (472). M. de Charlus's historical anecdotes (477). Mme de Cambremer's musical snobbery (480). Brichot holds forth (482). M. de Charlus and the Archangel Michael (484). M. de Cambremer discovers the identity of Professor

Chapter Three

A COMPREHENSIVE MODERN LIBRARY
READING GROUP GUIDE FOR

In Search of Lost Time

VOLUMES I–VI

is available online at
www.modernlibrary.com/rgg

A NOTE ON THE TYPE

The principal text of this Modern Library edition
was composed in a digitized version of
Horley Old Style, a typeface issued by
the English type foundry Monotype in 1925.
It has such distinctive features
as lightly cupped serifs and an oblique horizontal bar
on the lowercase "e."

MODERN LIBRARY IS ONLINE AT
WWW.MODERNLIBRARY.COM

MODERN LIBRARY ONLINE IS YOUR GUIDE TO CLASSIC LITERATURE ON THE WEB

THE MODERN LIBRARY E-NEWSLETTER

Our free e-mail newsletter is sent to subscribers, and features sample chapters, interviews with and essays by our authors, upcoming books, special promotions, announcements, and news.

To subscribe to the Modern Library e-newsletter, send a blank e-mail to: sub_modernlibrary@info.randomhouse.com or visit www.modernlibrary.com

THE MODERN LIBRARY WEBSITE

Check out the Modern Library website at www.modernlibrary.com for:

- The Modern Library e-newsletter
- A list of our current and upcoming titles and series
- Reading Group Guides and exclusive author spotlights
- Special features with information on the classics and other paperback series
- Excerpts from new releases and other titles
- A list of our e-books and information on where to buy them
- The Modern Library Editorial Board's 100 Best Novels and 100 Best Nonfiction Books of the Twentieth Century written in the English language
- News and announcements

Questions? E-mail us at modernlibrary@randomhouse.com
For questions about examination or desk copies, please visit
the Random House Academic Resources site at
www.randomhouse.com/academic